HERETICAL FISHING

A COZY GUIDE TO ANNOYING THE CULTS, OUTSMARTING THE FISH, AND ALIENATING ONESELF

BOOK 1

HAYLOCK JOBSON

Published in 2024 by Podium Publishing

Cover design by Mary Cruz

ISBN: 978-1-0394-5310-4

www.podiumentertainment.com

To you, the reader.

To my followers on Royal Road, whose words of encouragement endlessly urged me on—especially those kind souls that have supported me on Patreon. Without all of you, none of this would have been possible.

May your wildest dreams come true, as have mine.

PROLOGUE

It was a perfect day for fishing—or so I'd read. I got out of my car and took in the old wooden pier before me. A barrage of sensations hit. The sounds of small waves crashing, the cool breeze ruffling my hair, the warm feel of the midmorning sun kissing my skin, and the distinctive smell of sea spray whipped up by the wind. I had brought everything I needed: a fishing rod with line; a tackle box containing a myriad of different hooks, sinkers, and swivels; pliers; several leaders; a handful of other tools; and finally, an ice-and-bait-filled cooler.

No, we call it an esky in Australia, not a cooler, I reminded myself, trying to undo years of integration training.

I felt eyes following me as I awkwardly wrestled all my fishing gear toward the pier. A pair of teenage girls had their phones out, thinking they were discreet in their recording.

I was hoping it would take a little longer than that for someone to recognize me . . .

As I fought with the armfuls of equipment, and seeing another person with all his fishing gear in a cart, I made a mental note to purchase one.

The jetty was packed with anglers—at least a hundred people spread out along its length. I'd heard it got busy when the seasonal fish were around, but it was still shocking to see just how many people were present.

I eventually picked a spot halfway down the jetty with a young father and son on one side, and an older man with salt-and-pepper hair and weathered skin on the other. The father and son immediately glanced at me, whispering to each other. I did my best to not let it bother me.

"Don't let other's negative actions change your own good intentions," my therapist's words sounded in my head.

The older gentleman on the other side of me stood and watched the ocean. I turned to him. "Hey mate, mind if I set up here?"

"Not at all," he responded without looking up from the sea.

I smiled at him, then slowly and meticulously rigged my line, not making a single mistake with any of the knots after having absorbed the information of countless tutorial videos.

I picked out a small hook, a light sinker, and thin, five-pound leader for the small, seasonal fish I was targeting. The hook I chose was barbless; I wanted a challenge. Through my life experience, I'd learned it was best to jump in the deep end if you truly desired to master something. The goal for today was not to catch a fish, but to become a better fisherman.

Though, it would be nice to catch a fish . . .

I tried to put the bait on my hook, but the sandworm bunched up and exposed the hook, not at all presenting the way it had on the videos I'd watched. I looked at it in confusion for a moment before a voice pulled me from my thoughts.

"It's because of your hook," the old fisherman said, pointing at the slipping bait. "May I?"

"Uh, yeah, sure." I held out the line for the man to take.

"Your typical hook has barbs on the back that help hold bait in place." The angler deftly grabbed the line. "If you use barbless hooks like you've got here, it makes better sport, but the bait can sometimes fall down. What I like to do is slip part of the bait over the eye of the hook. That way, it will hold in place and look more natural to the fish."

Calloused fingers grabbed the bait and slid it up and over the eye of the hook. He jiggled the line and the bait stayed in place.

"Thanks mate, I appreciate it."

The man smiled, crow's-feet bunching up in the corner of his eyes. "No worries, lad. Happy to help." He turned his attention back to his own rod.

Following the directions of the seventeen videos I watched specifically relating to casting, I sent out the line. Admittedly, the cast was terrible. I let go too late, and the end of the line flew down closer to the pier than I'd intended. I didn't let the embarrassment of the cast in front of so many onlookers linger—instead, I focused on the line. My index finger was held against it softly, waiting for the tug that I knew would come when a fish took the bait.

The first bite filled me with adrenaline when it came, and I tugged the rod up with a little too much enthusiasm. The hook pulled out of the fish's mouth before it could eat it, and I wound the line in to find both the bait and fish gone. The second bite similarly filled me with adrenaline, but I was a little more patient—I waited for the fish to take the bait for a full second before softly setting the hook, then I wound in the line.

Anticipation burned as I reeled the fish in, but before I could catch sight of it, it spat the hook. I once more wound the line in to find the bait gone and no fish. Undeterred, I quickly reapplied my bait and made to cast it out again but paused when I saw the crowd now arrayed behind me. There were at least twenty people now standing and staring at me.

The news corporations had been relentless in their reporting of me over the past couple months, and even the spectacle of me going for a fish seemed enough to draw in the vultures. More than half of the crowd had phones out and faced toward me, likely recording to show their friends or sell it to one of the bottom-feeding news companies. I was used to the attention by now but felt bad for the surrounding fishermen being subjected to the same attention by proxy.

I turned to apologize to the young father and child, but saw them both watching, not fishing; the child's hands were wrapped around a recording cell phone, not a fishing rod. I rolled my eyes and turned to the older man on my other side.

"Sorry about all the attention. I'm happy to move on if you'd rather some peace and—"

"There's nothing to apologize for, lad," the man's deep, raspy voice interrupted.

"You sure, mate? There's a bit of a crowd following me—it's no drama if you don't want them here."

"It's hardly your fault." He turned and looked at me with startlingly blue eyes set in a sun-tanned and wizened face. "I know who you are, but that don't matter none. If you came here to fish, we're all equal; we're judged only by our actions and our day's catch." He looked up to the sky, exposing his face to the warm rays of the sun as he breathed in deeply through his nostrils, a smile of bliss crinkling his features. "Besides, who cares what anyone else is doing? It's a perfect day for fishin'."

I couldn't help but smile at the wise words of the old man, and, I too, turned my attention away from the crowd of onlookers.

Baiting the hook as I'd been shown, I took a moment to appreciate the warm sun before casting out the line again. The third bite came before the sinker hit the ocean floor. I let the fish take the bait for a moment, then set the hook with a firm tug. I began winding, ensuring I kept the line tight as the fish tried to swim away. The wiggle of the fish's head on the line filled me with excitement.

I caught the first glimpse of my prize as the sun reflected off its silvery scales just before it broke the surface. I wound the line up more, and with an unpracticed motion, awkwardly flicked the fish over the railing and onto the jetty.

Knowing the fish to be toothless, I gripped it carefully by the mouth and rushed it toward my measuring mat. It came in at twenty-seven centimeters, well over the twenty-centimeter minimum size for the species. I quickly retrieved the spike from my tackle box and dispatched the fish humanely before throwing it into the esky.

Looking up, the crowd had grown even more. Something behind them caught my eye, and I swore under my breath at the news van pulling up.

Time to go.

I thanked the old fisherman for his help as I hurriedly put the lid on my esky.

"Don't mention it," he said as he gazed over the water. "I'll see ya 'round, lad."

I spared a parting glance for the old man before turning away, a content smile on my face as I made my way back down the jetty and toward my car. The crowd parted for me as I clattered along, esky in one hand, rod and tackle box awkwardly held in the other. Remembering something, I stopped in place. I put everything down and fumbled for my phone. Placing two wireless earphones in, I pressed play. The instructional video on how to properly fillet the fish I had caught quickly drowned out the sounds of the surrounding crowd. I'd already watched the video at least a dozen times, but I was nothing if not thorough. I was determined to eat the fish as fresh as possible, and I'd clean and fillet my prize the moment I got back to my penthouse. I pictured the video that went along with the audio in my mind's eye as the instructor with a thick North Queensland accent described where to slice with the filleting knife.

A second news van pulled up behind the other, and I smiled at the first reporter asking me questions as I swiftly walked past him. The second reporter all but sprinted out of his van, hand and microphone extended, mouth moving inaudibly as his words were drowned out by the North Queensland man instructing how to remove the pin bones from the fillet.

It was in that moment—steps hastened by excitement, reporters yelling questions I couldn't hear with at least two dozen cameras and cell phones pointed at me, and in front of almost a hundred witnesses—that I moved between the two news vans and walked directly into the path of an oncoming truck.

For his part, the truck driver had noticed neither the news vans nor the crowd. He was looking at his phone, a phone made by a company my father founded. He drove a truck imported by a subsidiary of that same company, hauling a load of seasonal fish—the same seasonal fish I'd been fishing for—to a supermarket my dad had helped establish as the leading grocer on five of Earth's continents.

Jerry lived a menial life. He relied upon podcasts and audiobooks to get him through his boring work days of hauling fish along the same monotonous route. He looked down at his phone as he fumbled to hit the play button, and the two comedians with a podcast animatedly resumed their conjecture about what the richest man on Earth was doing after ruining his father's legacy and walking away from it all.

As soon as I stepped out in front of it, I saw the oncoming truck and knew I had no time to do anything but think. I lamented my life choices, cursing the unfairness of the universe for taking me now that I had finally taken steps on the right path. A profound desire to start things over was the last thing that went through my mind. Well, *technically,* that thought was the second to last thing that went through my mind. The *very* last thing was the bull bar of a 2015 Isuzu N-Series truck, filled with fish and driven by a man about to discover firsthand what the richest man in the world was doing after walking away from everything.

In a world long since abandoned by the god that created it, something miraculous occurred. Sound returned to a place of silence as an ancient construct struggled to start, its components caked with layers of rust and arcane waste. The construct had lain dormant for centuries, the source required to power its magic having fled with the ascended being that created it. That it tried to start at all in its current condition would have been sure to cause quite a stir among the ascended if any of them had been present to witness such an event.

The grinding complaints of the construct receded as the movement of cogs scraped away rust, and its self-cleaning function whisked away any lingering arcane waste. It whirred to life and began its task.

The construct was a fairly common thing for gods to possess. It was quite simple, really. It would search for anything matching parameters set by its maker, and when finding a match, would harness part of its maker's power in order to harvest it, hence the colloquial name used by the beings bearing the power to create them: harvester.

Many harvesters looked for multiple matches, the effort and expense needed to create such constructs causing their inventors to direct them toward multiple purposes. This harvester, however, searched for a singular thing—souls.

Not just any souls, mind you. This harvester had exhaustive parameters that, if boiled down, came to two distinctive requirements: the targeted soul must possess both incredible willpower and must have recently gone through a monumental shift in the application of that will.

The latter requirement—that of requiring a shift or change in goal—is an aspect that would be lost on most of the ascended. Even if they learned of the parameters set by the creator of this construct, they would likely assume it was the neurotic act of a god gone mad, or a test performed by a god with too much time on their hands. The god that created this harvester was neither.

In fact, if another ascended learned exactly *which* god had created this construct, they would have likely noted the parameter down for experimentation themselves—after they fled for their life, of course.

It was ubiquitously known that willpower was the main metric by which one could judge the weight of a soul. What was not so commonly known, however, was what it signified when a strong-willed individual possessed the ability to shift the application of that will.

It had a multiplicative effect on a soul's willpower, something which the creator of this construct knew well. And so, when a truck destroyed the body of an individual meeting and far exceeding the parameters programmed into the construct, it churned into action, reaching desperately for the severed soul.

The harvester recognized the weight of this soul, and lacking the creator that powered it, the harvester drew from the very world itself. A perceptive denizen of the long-abandoned world might have noticed a slight dimming of the sun, that the wind had vanished for a moment, or that the waves on the churning ocean seemed to flatten almost imperceptibly.

All it took was a moment before the moving parts of the harvester wound back down into stillness, and the world returned to its normal state. A sound rang out in the room, a great *clunk* coming from within the construct as a pivotal component snapped in half. A small engine within the construct stirred, almost as if in afterthought. Lacking the power to generate all the materials the soul needed, the harvester chose the most useful, focusing the retreating vestiges of power toward the creation of a small sack.

If a construct could feel emotion, the harvester would have felt content. It had completed one last task—its final procedure, one of profound ambition. The last whisper of willpower left behind by its creator dissipated, and it powered down for the last time as it sent the soul spiraling down to the world below.

CHAPTER ONE

ARRIVAL

I opened my eyes with a start. I sat up, squinting against the bright light of the surrounding world. With perfect precision, the moment before the truck struck me replayed in my mind. Amazed to find myself alive, I waited for my vision to adjust to what was clearly the artificial lighting of a hospital.

I made to sit up, but instead of a hospital bed's sheets, I felt cool grass between my fingers. A soft breeze blew, raising goose bumps and causing the grass to tickle my exposed sections of skin. Rolling over and getting to my knees, I stared down with astonishment at the grass beneath my open hands. The sound of trees blowing in the wind drew my attention, and I looked up—my eyes finally adjusted to the luminous surroundings. I was in a clearing. Only patches of sunlight filtered down through the canopy of tall trees above. Another gust blew, and the branches far above swayed hypnotically. I looked down, seeing I was wearing three-quarter pants made of a simple beige fabric. A similar shirt covered my torso, with loose sleeves going just past the elbows. I wiggled my toes, and feeling resistance there, checked and confirmed that I wore shoes made of the same material, with a thin, artificially made sole sewn into them.

"Where . . . where am I?" My voice sounded hoarse and deep.

The smell of the earthy forest hit me, a stark contrast to the sea spray I'd been inhaling what felt like only a moment ago. I breathed deeply, enjoying the sensation of cool, damp air as it passed through my nostrils.

Is this the afterlife?

I had delved into the theories of Buddhism, Taoism, and a number of other religious and philosophical beliefs in my search for myself, but I'd never truly believed in rebirth—or an afterlife at all, for that matter.

An odd sensation pulsed in my mind, and I became aware of something attempting to make itself known. With no small amount of hesitation, I leaned into the feeling, my brain subconsciously knowing how to acknowledge it.

[Error: Insufficient power. Superfluous systems offline.]
Please select a name.

I stared at the prompt in my vision, becoming stuck at the situation I found myself in. I dismissed the messages in the same way I'd acknowledged them, and the words cleared from my field of view. I blinked at the surrounding forest, almost expecting it to melt before my eyes at any moment when this fever dream ended.

I've heard the brain releases a massive dose of DMT when we die—is that what this is? The final dream of my soul departing?

The same sensation as before pulsed, and too curious to not acknowledge it, I did so.

Please select a name.

A text cursor blinked in and out of existence after the simple sentence, seeming to demand a response. I thought to myself for only a moment, and following a whim, entered a name.

Error: Name "Fisher" is invalid. Cannot select the name of a profession.

A profession?

What seemed to be System text already made this seem game-like—the mention of a fishing profession only further cemented the idea into my psyche.

Have I been reborn into a game world?

I'd been rather fond of isekai and portal fantasy books in my previous life, so this entire sequence being the result of DMT flooding my gray matter was a distinct possibility. Still, something about this situation felt entirely too . . . *real.*

I cleared the message again, and once more basked in the physical sensations of my body. The cool, wet grass beneath my hands and legs; the frigid air and the smells it brought along with it; the breeze that kicked up and tickled my skin; and the kiss of warm sunlight, filtered down through the trees above—all served to ground me in the moment.

The cursed nemesis returned with a familiar pulse, shattering my mindfulness.

Please select a name.

The text cursor blinked at me with incessant continuity, entirely uncaring of the existential predicament I found myself in.

God, I need a coffee before I can adequately handle this.

That thought brought on another creative whim—thinking of the Nobel Prize recipient that discovered caffeine, a substance with which I was *very* much dependent, I entered a name.

Name "Fischer" has been accepted. Welcome to the Kallis Realm.

A sensation akin to euphoria radiated from somewhere within but was gone as soon as it had come. I felt different somehow—as if indulging the blinking cursor and providing a name had fundamentally changed an aspect of myself.

Assuming this wasn't a dream, and I had in fact been isekai'd—something I noted, with no small amount of amusement, was entirely possible given my fateful encounter with truck-kun—I waited for another message to populate. A quest, a hint—anything. Nothing came.

I stood, my body stiff and sluggish as if waking from a long sleep. I stretched my hands toward the sky, the extension of my muscles bringing an unbidden smile to my face. Even given the situation I found myself in, some aspects of the human experience were simply too pleasant to ignore. Bending over, I curled down toward my toes—there was something on the ground beside my feet.

I picked up a small leather pouch, noting its heavy weight and the metallic jingle of its contents. I undid the drawstring and peered inside. It was filled with gold coins—a total of twenty-five—that had an unfamiliar face printed on one side, and a scythe on the other. I bit a coin; it was made of genuine gold.

I cast my eyes around the clearing, looking for any other starting equipment if this was truly a game world. I found nothing.

All right. So I have starter clothes, the same body, and a bag of gold. No weapon, no abilities, and no means of defending myself. Well, except for two Brazilian jujitsu classes run at a corporate event, and a handful of Muay Thai lessons.

"Quake in fear, monsters of this world—the fist of death has arrived!" Shaking my head and laughing at myself, I picked a random direction and started walking.

CHAPTER TWO

DECISION

I marveled at the beauty of this world as I traveled. The weather was perfect, and I barely worked up a sweat walking beneath the leaf cover far above thick and plentiful trunks. I didn't recognize any of the trees, though historically I wasn't what you'd call the outdoors type. I knew of the trees local to Australia from my childhood—Eucalyptus, Paper Bark, Norfolk Pine, and Acacia, to name a few—but none were present.

In my passing, I noted a light-brown species covered in loose fibrous strands. I pulled a section of the bark off and separated it into strips before stuffing it atop the gold coins in my leather pouch. I thought to find a high point to survey the area but couldn't make out any mountains or raised area of land to look from. The thick canopy of leaves above only let the blinding sun peak through, and the trunks themselves were too thick to climb without risking injury. I noted the passage of the sun as I moved, and seeing it climb higher in the sky as the day progressed, knew that I'd woken in the morning.

The day grew hotter; my mouth grew dry, my stomach hungry. The burble of water crept into my auditory field, and after a quick search, I found a shallow creek. It had a bed of river stones and was clear of algae and other plant growth, telling me that the water flowed continuously, or at least had done so in recent times. I rejoiced, inferring dozens of possibilities.

I followed the creek downstream, scanning the rocks for something that was desperately needed. What I thought was two hours later, and as the sun descended from its peak in the sky above, I found what I was looking for. I took careful steps down the small bank of the creek and retrieved my prize.

It was a large rock. One side had a concave dip that was just deep enough to hold water. Thankfully, it wasn't made of the relatively porous rock that most of the river stones were composed of—porous rocks could hold bubbles of air, which had a nasty habit of turning stones into primitive grenades when the air inside expanded after being placed in a campfire.

As I lifted the rock, an involuntary grunt escaped me. It was going to be a pain to carry, but I didn't have much of a choice. I set it down on top of the bank and started looking for the last pieces of the puzzle.

A few minutes later, with a handful of dried sticks, twigs, and a branch in hand, I started constructing my project. I pulled out the fibrous bark first, separating it meticulously into thinner strips. The small twigs were the next thing I grabbed, and I made a small tepee-shaped structure out of them, ascending from thinnest to thickest. I carefully placed the thin strips of bark within, ensuring I left enough room for oxygen to circulate, then I notched the dead branch with a sharp rock gathered from the creek. Using another stick, whose base fit almost perfectly into the notch I'd cut, I rubbed the stick between my hands with rapid and repeated movement.

As a form of escapism, I'd watched plenty of videos on survival, and primitive fire creation was a basic of almost every single one. Unlike the videos, however, creating an ember proved to be exceedingly difficult. Whether it was the wood used or my lack of experience, I couldn't say, but as the minutes stretched on and my arms started aching, I dropped the stick and let out a sigh. I felt the notch of the thick branch; it was warm, but nowhere near hot enough to spark the beginning of a campfire.

I stood and stretched, then left in search of the components for another method. With the sharpened rock, I cut a long section of fibers from a living vine. I pulled it taut between my hands. It didn't snap.

Now I just need something to tie it to . . .

After another search, I found a stick I thought would suffice. I bent it, and seeing it didn't snap, nodded to myself. I secured the strand of plant fibers to each end of it and peered down at the bow I'd created.

"What was it called again . . . ?" I mused aloud. "A bow drill . . . ?"

With a smile, I sat down by the notched branch once more and looped the length of vine around the stick I'd spun by hand. I pulled the bow toward me; the fibers held to the stick, not spinning as the videos had depicted. I clenched my jaw, furrowed my brows, and pushed as hard as I could. The bow snapped, the wood unable to handle the pressure exerted. With another sigh, I discarded the broken tool over my shoulder, placed the stick between both palms again, and started spinning it.

The sun had long since started descending from its peak, and the formerly pleasant heat of the day was no longer enjoyable as I hunched over, breathing heavily. Sweat poured from me, pooling around my eyes and dripping from the tip of my nose as I spun the stick back and forth with dogged determination. My arms trembled with the exertion, and I closed my eyes, trying and failing to ignore my body's complaints. My lungs worked like bellows, and I breathed through my nose, keeping the movements steady as best I could.

An odd smell hit me, and I opened my eyes, blinking sweat away as I stared down at the source. The branch was smoking. I pulled the stick away, seeing the smallest hint of red in the notch. I stood on shaky legs and almost fell over. With great care, I tipped the coal onto the bed of tinder. Cupping my hands around it, I blew. The ember glowed brighter but didn't catch on the bark fibers.

Please don't gutter out . . .

With each blow, the coal went a brighter red but shrunk smaller.

Please . . .

Just as I thought it would disappear and I'd have to start all over again, it happened. A small flame sprouted, then the small flame grew to a large one within a single breath. I placed my other sticks atop it with shaking arms, adding more fuel to the fire. They were consumed, and before I knew it, the campfire had stabilized.

I sat down heavily, leaning my arms back as a grin spread across my face. "Thank *god.*"

A familiar pulse came, along with the subsequent message.

[Error: Insufficient power. Superfluous systems offline.]

I was too tired to care; I dismissed it. Sweat drenched my clothes, and I ambled over to the creek, collapsing into the shallows and relishing in the water's cool touch. I dunked my head under, washing the grime away.

My clothes hung on sticks as I squatted by the fire, naked as the day I was born. Though an exhaustion still lingered, the impromptu swim left me feeling invigorated and the day's heat—along with that of the fire—was once more pleasant on my skin.

After a small rest, I gathered and placed other non-porous rocks around the campfire, filled my concave prize with water, and set it on top of the other rocks. I was all too aware of the danger presented by microscopic organisms, and with the human ingenuity to ensure anything I ingested was safe, I'd resolved not to take any chances.

I've already carked it once today. If I die again, it's not gonna be from dysentery.

I watched from a safe distance as the water boiled, just in case any of the rocks held a bubble of air that would explode once heated. None of them did.

When the water was boiling, I removed the concave stone from the flames with my notched branch and another stick and watched it with great impatience as the water cooled.

When it was cool enough to drink, but still quite warm, I drank greedily of the purified water. Even with the heat it held, the liquid was gloriously thirst quenching as it made its way past my tongue and down my throat.

The enjoyment was somewhat diminished by a familiar pulse and subsequent message.

[Error: Insufficient power. Superfluous systems offline.]

Very cool, System. Thanks for sharing.

I repeated the boiling process once more before snuffing out the fire. Picking up my makeshift cooking pot and notched branch, I continued following the creek downstream.

Another hour or two later, the water ran into a large body of water, approximately twenty meters across, that was surrounded by what had been my next goal—a potential source of food. Bushes loaded with blackberries were scattered around the pond's banks.

While I knew the methods for testing edibility listed in the books I'd read weren't flawless, I would soon starve if I didn't find something to eat. The berries were plentiful enough to justify taking the time to test them.

I wasted no time in setting up another fire, and after purifying and drinking a batch of water for myself, I set another rock-full to boiling.

I picked one of the berries and rubbed it into my skin. After fifteen minutes, I had developed no irritation on the patch, so I placed a berry on a stick and submerged it in the now-boiling water. I placed the boiled berry under my tongue when it had cooled enough, and again, I didn't experience any irritation. What juices escaped the berry tasted sweet, and I fought the urge to swallow it.

Next, I chewed the berry. I let the pulped fruit sit in my mouth for another fifteen minutes, and again, experienced no irritation. So, I swallowed it. To be safe, I had to wait at least eight hours to see if I experienced any itching, nausea, or other adverse effects from the berry.

With the afternoon sun still high in the sky, I started building a small shelter atop a flat patch of grass. When the sun was just starting to set over the horizon, I surveyed my newly constructed abode. It looked like shit. It was just longer than I was, about a meter high and a meter across, in the shape of a triangular prism. Well, it was supposed to be that shape, but if I was being honest, it looked more like an abstract-art installation.

The frame was constructed of branches and sticks from the surrounding forest and was lashed together with strips of the same bark I'd used to make my fire starter. I'd found a patch of palm-like trees a short walk further downstream, then tried to weave their leaves together to make up the walls of the crude tent. The videos I'd watched had woven palm leaves in a way that, even if it were to rain, the liquid should roll down the side, hopefully leaving the interior—and more importantly, the person inside—dry. I held no such delusions that this thing would keep out a drop of water, let alone a tropical storm.

"Oh well," I said with a sigh. "It'll have to do."

Before the sun could set, I purified more water, drank it, then snuffed out the fire. As frustrating as it would be creating another one in the morning, drawing attention to myself and getting shanked by a fantasy creature in my sleep seemed like a worse eventuality.

As darkness crept through the forest, the weariness of the day set in. I was emotionally and physically exhausted but couldn't fall asleep yet—I had to stay awake and attentive for any adverse effects of the test berry.

I meditated, relying on the skill set I'd been developing in my previous life. When I reached a mindset I regarded as open and logical, I allowed my thoughts to come.

I died.

I'm in another world.

I'd harbored some doubts as to the reality of my situation earlier in the day, but after a full day of living, breathing, and experiencing my surroundings, I no longer had any such misgivings.

. . . *What the hell am I gonna do?*

The world seemed to have some sort of System, just as in the novels I enjoyed so much in the before. The issue was it was non-functional, or at least only partially so.

I recalled the messages I'd received when waking, as well as after drinking purified water for the first time.

It said something about having insufficient power and systems being offline. Have I arrived in a faulty world? Or one where the functional System, along with human life, has long since departed?

That thought hit me with a surprising amount of sadness.

I had just begun a journey of self-discovery and the seeking of genuine bonds when my life was snuffed out.

Most of my life had been misspent—fixated on the eventual inheritance of my father's business empire, smothered by the weight of expectation. To wake up in a new world, but one lacking any other humans to interact with . . . what a miserable irony that would be.

If that's the case, what's my course of action? Will I try to level up and seek power like the protagonists in every isekai story, despite a seemingly dysfunctional System and a lack of any other humans?

While I'd spent many nights in my previous life imagining such an escape, the reality of it hit different now that I was actually here. I'd never imagined myself the hero type in those fantasies, but more of an economic conqueror. I recalled envisioning an underdeveloped world, where my vast training of business and capitalism would allow me to build a world-spanning empire.

I snorted. That was before I tried heading such an empire, and given my recent experience, that idea now seemed tedious, repulsive.

I already did that on Earth and look where it got me. Sad and alone—king atop an empire of dirt.

The thing that had drawn my attention, and indeed, had seemed to pull me out of the misery created by my hubris, was fishing. Something as simple as fishing—one of the world's oldest professions—had been exhilarating, calming, and everything in between.

"What did that old bloke say on the jetty?" I mused aloud. "'It's a perfect day for fishing.'"

I recalled the zen-like meditation of the wind in my hair and the sun on my face as I waited for a nibble on the line. The adrenaline spike and subsequent contentment that came when I caught that single fish was a feeling more enticing than all the pride I'd previously felt from corporate domination.

Long into the night, I pondered. By the time I fell asleep, I'd completely forgotten to celebrate the fact that the berry hadn't made me sick. I had, however, reached a conclusion. There were many things I desired in this second life of mine, but I could reduce them to two key deliverables: genuine interactions with others and as much fishing as humanly possible.

CHAPTER THREE

DISCOVERY

I woke the next morning with a stiff neck and back. My body was accustomed to the best mattresses money could buy—not a bed of literal grass and dirt. To make matters worse, halfway through the night my mediocre attempt at a shelter had collapsed on me, and I'd woken in a panic, fighting off my fallen roof like it was an attacker in the night.

"Those leaves and sticks never stood a chance . . ." I said, shadowboxing the air in an attempt to cheer myself up. It didn't work.

My stomach complained, but it was the groan of hunger, not the result of poisoning by berry. With more than a little dread for the work to come, I began crafting another fire. It took little time to collect the materials, and with a deep breath, I started spinning my fire-starting stick in the notch of the thick branch. To my surprise, the movement felt more natural, and my sense of dread dissipated like dust in the wind. I lost myself to the movements, and after only fifteen minutes or so, a wisp of smoke rose from the branch.

My eyes going wide, I redoubled my effort, steadily twisting the stick back and forth between my palms. The smoke grew, and with a swift movement I lifted the branch and poured the ember into my pile of tinder. I knelt and blew on the small coal, and after three breaths the fire bloomed.

After purifying more water and gulping it down, I plucked another berry and ate it raw. The berry was so sweet on my fasted tongue that tears swelled in my eyes. It took all of my significant willpower to not rush the bushes and eat berries by the handful—I needed to wait another eight hours to ensure the single uncooked fruit didn't make me sick.

As I sat and stared at the water and lamented my lack of coffee, movement across and to my right caught my eye. Darting my eyes toward it, the lizard part of my brain expected an attack. Excitement replaced fear at the sight of a black fish swimming in the pond, slowly making its way along the outskirts in search of prey. My mind whirled with possibilities, and my mouth salivated at the thought of fish cooked over a fire.

Could I craft a makeshift spear? Or even a fishing rod?

Given I had eight hours to kill before I could deem the raw berries safe to eat, I welcomed the distraction and rushed headlong toward it.

I found a suitable stick to use as a rod; it was neither too dry nor too green and had just the right amount of give. I returned to the palms and split a long string from the center of a frond to act as a line. Then came the most difficult part.

For a hook, I carved and slowly worked at a stick using the sharp rock from the day before. It was long and tedious work, and by the time I finished, the sun was low in the sky. As the last sliver of wood was carved away, a familiar pulse tugged at my mind.

[Error: Insufficient power. Superfluous systems offline.]

I rolled my eyes. "What would I do without you, System?"

Eight hours had passed while I fixated on carving the wooden hook, and I all but skipped over to the berry bush and ate a single handful of the fruit. They were both sweet and a little tart; my mouth hungered for more the moment I'd swallowed the last one. I had to wait another eight hours, however, before I would know for certain that the berries were safe for me to eat. I boiled some water, rehydrated, then set to searching for bait.

I turned over rocks along the bank but found nothing of use. I searched for fallen logs or rocks to turn in the forest, but again, I found nothing of use. I'd found a single rock to turn, and expecting a fat worm to be hiding underneath, all I found was dirt.

Walking back to the pond, I radiated frustration from both my hunger and futile search. As I walked, feeling sorry for myself and dragging my feet in abject dejection, I noticed a section of bark on a tree with odd markings that seemed to be falling away. Raising an eyebrow, I walked to the bark and carefully peeled it away, revealing a giant grub. It looked almost exactly like a witchetty grub, just a little darker. About the size of my thumb, it sat there uselessly, lacking the ability to do anything but burrow through wood. I smiled at my savior but paused as I went to pick it up.

Grubs and bugs are extremely nutrient dense, right? Would I be better off just eating this thing . . . ?

I glanced at the grub again, narrowing my eyes at the way its pincers worked at the air. Its weird little legs undulated ineffectually as they tried to find purchase. "Nope. Fuck that noise. You're bait, my unfortunate friend."

I picked the grub up carefully and ran back to the pond as the light slowly leeched out of the sky. I picked up my rod and slid the insect over the hook while silently apologizing to the ugly little thing. Then I cast my line out into the pond. With my feet in the cool water, and my eyes watching the tip of the line for any movement, a sense of ease radiated through me.

With the sun going down, I knew dusk was a good time to catch certain types of fish. Something about dawn and dusk made them grow hungry, and I wondered if the black fish I'd seen would—*oh shit, a bite!*

The line went taut, the fish on the other end of the line feeling much bigger than the one I'd seen before. The rod almost slipped from my hands, and before I could even attempt to pull the fish out, the line snapped.

I took a step back, almost falling over as the force pulling at me disappeared. I glared at the limply hanging strip of palm frond I'd used as a line, a sense of disappointment spreading as I saw it snapped off above where the hook had been secured.

Another message hit me.

[Error: Insufficient power. Superfluous systems offline.]

My eye twitched. *Is this thing just messing with me now?*

I breathed out a great sigh and walked back to the embers of my fire. Setting the rod down, I allowed myself a moment to think about my life choices. I'd spent most of the day carving that hook, and the monster living in this pond had taken all of that work away in less than a second. I barked a laugh and shook my head with a smile.

"All right. You win this round, fishy."

Despite losing a day's work, I'd also gone through two rounds of testing the berries, and I still felt fine after eating the handful of the black treasures growing on the surrounding bushes.

Before the sun set, I was determined to fix the shelter to, at the very least, not be an OHSA incident waiting to happen. Using the same material I used to start fires as a binding had clearly been a mistake, and after crafting the fishing line—which, admittedly, had also been a mistake—I had an idea.

I collected more of the fronds, then carefully pulled strips of fiber from the part connecting the leaves. I used these to bind the sticks together, and as I shook the frame, it was much more rigid than the previous night.

Rather than trying to weave the leaves together to make a patchwork roof, I lashed them to the sticks. The final product was time intensive, and much less aesthetically pleasing than the videos I'd watched, but was a vast improvement on yesterday's attempt.

As I tied the final frond into place, the System said g'day once more.

[Error: Insufficient power. Superfluous systems offline.]

"Yeah, yeah, I know," I said, rolling my eyes.

I stoked the fire again, and as more water purified, I used the last rays of the setting sun to weave a crude sling with which to carry my prized water-purifying vessel.

As I sat inside my shelter that evening—which hopefully wouldn't attack me in the middle of the night—I thought of my plans going forward. I could spend the next day carving another hook and attempting to conquer the monster of the pond, but I had a different plan. Assuming my stomach remained all right in the coming hours, I'd have a stable source of food. I would eat a bunch of the berries, store some more, and follow the creek further downstream. If I didn't find more of the bushes, I'd return and pick them all before taking off again. I had to leave for one very important reason: people.

All humans need access to drinkable water, and if I were to follow the creek all the way downstream, that would be my best chance of coming across civilization. The worst-case scenario, in my mind, was that I'd eventually find the ocean—a source of infinite fish and more abundant food than the forest could offer.

I was still awake when I thought it had been eight hours since last eating a handful of berries, but to be safe, I decided it best to wait until the morning before eating more. Without realizing it, I drifted off to sleep.

As the water boiled in my makeshift pot the following morning, I picked and ate berries to my heart's content. I made sure not to eat too many, all too wary that overindulging could make me sick with the sugar content. I stuffed as many as would fit atop the gold in the leather pouch, noting well how the bushes looked in my mind. Eating a lookalike berry could prove fatal, after all. With a sense of accomplishment and my hunger satiated, I followed the creek.

Small birds flitted through the trees above my head as I traveled, their morning songs soft and peaceful. The damp morning air caused goose bumps to sprout on my skin, but as I continued moving, my body warmed and the cool air became a source of reprieve.

It didn't take me long to find the first berry bush. It was growing just to the side of the stream and contained another few dozen berries among its green leaves. I examined the bush carefully, making sure that it was exactly the same as the ones surrounding the pond. Nodding to myself, I continued walking downstream.

If they're also growing here, there's a good chance they'll be throughout the entire forest . . .

I was correct in that assumption, and I spent the next few days following the stream and nibbling on the sweet offerings of the forest. I had to stop a few times a day to purify more water, and the last few hours of daylight each day were spent creating a small makeshift shelter to sleep in.

By the third day of travel, I'd become so deft at crafting the small huts that it took less than an hour, judging by the sun's shifting and fading light. Creating embers by hand had been steadily getting easier also, but it was still a pain to get going each time.

As I tied down the last palm leaf of my fourth shelter, the System spoke up.

[Error: Insufficient power. Superfluous systems offline.]

The messages were starting to bother me less, and I dismissed this one without a reaction, instead crawling into my shelter and falling asleep within minutes.

The sun was directly above the next day when I noticed something odd. In the forest ahead, there seemed to be a path clear of any trees. With bubbling anticipation I tried and failed to keep at bay, I power walked toward the anomaly. Anticipation became hope, and hope became joy. I had found a *road.*

The road wasn't paved; it was made only of dirt. The creek crossed paths with the road, and weathered sleepers made of dark wood formed an old-yet-sturdy bridge from bank to bank. The road didn't look like it had seen too much traffic recently, with patches of grass growing toward the middle of the trail, but the trees of the forest had yet to reclaim any space.

Which means it's been maintained—or in the very least, used—over the last five to ten years.

My joy swelled. I hadn't realized just how much I'd been hoping and praying to find other humans in this world. I told myself I'd be fine living a life of solitude if I didn't end up crossing paths with humanity—my palpable, almost physical relief at that moment told a different story.

As I looked both ways down the road, there was an important decision to make.

Which way do I go?

I looked at the creek for guidance, and seeing that it seemed to travel to the left of where I'd come, then ran adjacent to the road, my decision was made for me. I couldn't hold back a smile as I strode with renewed vigor down the road and along the creek.

As the sun set that night, I basked in the warmth of my campfire and the burn of physical exertion in my legs. The anticipation of what was to come was an unstoppable force, despite my best efforts. I knew there was a distinct possibility I wouldn't find anyone at the end of this road; I didn't know the past events that had occurred in this game-like world, and whatever broke the System may have also had a grievous effect on human life.

Another possibility was that I did find humanity at the end of the road, but they were hostile. That trees were cleared to make a road spoke of at least *some* advancement within their society, but it still wasn't impossible that I found myself on the pointy end of a tribal warrior's spear.

Still, the possibility of human interaction—the friendly kind, not the stabby-stabby kind—made my cheeks turn up into a broad smile, and I felt almost nervous at the idea of striking up conversation with strangers.

What do I say to them to seem like a regular person? Will they even speak English? I wonder what they're like . . .

With these thoughts and countless others on my mind, I drifted off to sleep in a camp beside the road.

The sun wasn't high enough to banish the cool air of the morning yet and was only just cresting the horizon when something beautiful grabbed my attention. The road had climbed a hill, and as I reached the peak, I could see what had to be the ocean poking up over the distant tree line. The shore was visible from my vantage point, and light-yellow sand arced out into dual headlands that formed a cove, at least a kilometer from end to end. To the right, and outside of the protected cove, a broad river mouth fed into the ocean. Further right, the land turned mountainous after another stretch of flat beach on the other side of the river.

Two things made my hopes soar. First, the saltwater of the sea, the freshwater of the river, and the brackish water of the two mixing meant one thing: an abundance and variety of aquatic life. Second, and most important, there were dozens of houses built on the shore, some of which had smoke billowing from their stone chimneys. To the left of the buildings, farmland stretched as far as the eye could see, crops of different kinds sprawling over the area. There were *people!*

CHAPTER FOUR

WELCOME

I tried to calm my racing heart as I walked along the road, passing cultivated fields on the way to the small village. I reached out to touch a stalk of what I knew to be sugarcane—the crop was prevalent in the coastal plains of my hometown on the east coast of Australia.

Apart from a few patches of wheat, corn, and something unrecognizable, the sugarcane was the only thing being grown. There were acres of it, stretching far to either side of the village's border.

The settlement itself had no visible wall or threshold, only a perimeter of dirt separating the houses from the crops, showing this was a peaceful area. I'd suspected so already, given that I wasn't eaten by wolves out in the forest, but it was still nice to know I didn't have to worry about goblin raids, monster attacks, or some other, equally tropey fantasy-world shenanigans.

Perhaps the smart plan would be to hang back and observe the town for a while, to watch the townspeople move and interact before seamlessly integrating myself among them. This thought came, and it passed. Through my relatively short yet experience-packed life, I'd learned to trust my instincts when they spoke up. There was something unquantifiable about the hunches fed to you by the universe. Whether the result of divine intervention, subconscious calculation, or something else, the result remained the same; intuition was ignored at one's own peril.

If my goal was to form bonds and connections—which it was—my instincts told me to be my authentic self from the very start. While skulking may give me more information, it would undoubtedly alter my later interactions, and may even lead to suspicion and derision if caught doing so.

With the contentment of doing the right thing, and a purpose-filled stride, I entered the street between two rows of houses. Both my contentment and stride were abruptly halted as I found the blunt side of a scythe's blade held to my throat. My eyes went wide, and I stared in shock at the wiry man across from me that held the impromptu weapon. Gray hair, countless wrinkles, a salt-and-pepper beard, and deeply tanned skin atop a farmer's frame blocked my passage through the street.

"Can I help you, lad?" the man asked, voice firm and as weathered as its speaker.

"I'm—uh—looking for people?" I found my words failing me. I'd never been physically threatened before—ever.

The man narrowed his eyes, pressing the blunted end of the scythe into my neck. "And what people would that be, *lad?*"

"There you are, Dad!" a feminine voice called. "Where have you—Dad! What are you doing?"

The stranger lowered the scythe but kept his eyes pinned on me. A young woman of mid-twenties to early-thirties stepped into view from between two houses. She grimaced at me in obvious apology.

"By Freya's bouncing bosom, I'm so sorry!" She put her hand on the scythe and lowered it further from my chest. "He didn't hurt you, did he?"

"N-no. I'm fine, really . . ." My voice still stammered, but this time for an entirely different reason—the girl was stunning.

She had sun-kissed skin, with small freckles covering her face and shoulders, and light-blonde hair that was partially tied up. Her blue eyes seemed to broadcast her intent, like windows into her soul—she appeared kind, honest, and caring. Maybe it was because I hadn't seen people in some time, or maybe it was the fact she'd saved me from the beach-bum grim reaper, but something about her drew me in.

"How many times have I told you, Dad? There's nothing to worry about here! It's a peaceful town! That's why we moved here, *remember?*"

"I caught this young feller just skulking about, all shady-like!" The man's voice was petulant as he defended himself against his daughter—a far cry from the gravelly determination it held earlier.

The woman turned to me, giving me a weak smile. "I'm so sorry. I'm Maria, and this is my dad, Roger."

"Oh, uh, nice to meet you. I'm Fischer."

The man squinted as a suspicious *hmmm* escaped his throat. "What kinda dumb name is *Fisher?*"

"Dad!"

I laughed and spelled out my name for the duo.

"Hmmm. Still a dumb name. Your parents cousins or somethin'?"

Maria shook her head and looked between me and her father, lost for words. I just laughed, unaffected by the old-timer's transparency. I'd dealt with plenty of blunt people in my previous life, and even I had to admit, Fischer *was* an odd name compared to Maria and Roger.

I thought I was in a fantasy world—where were the names like Zorian, Wei Shi Lindon, and Carl? Okay, maybe not that last one . . .

"I'm from a long way away." I gave them my most disarming smile. "You'll have to excuse my name—and any other idiosyncrasies, for that matter."

"We are, too! Aren't we, Dad?" Maria nudged her father, jumping at the chance to bowl through the fact her progenitor had held me at scythe-point just a minute ago. "Tell Fischer where you came from."

Roger nodded, taking the bait. "Well, I grew up on the coastal town of Yerba. It's far west of the capital, and back then there weren't a lot of jobs going around. Before I knew it, I found myself in the Imperial Army . . ."

Maria guided us through the streets as her father regaled us with a rather storied military career, the chance encounter that introduced him to his wife—Maria's mother, Sharon—the subsequent retirement from the Imperial Army, and the seeking of a coastal town to relax and raise a family. As his story wound ever on, Maria pointed out landmarks in what she called their small village.

"That's the mill—we only have the one, so it gets quite busy around wheat and corn harvesting time."

The squat building was made of rock and mortar, roughly four times the size of the surrounding houses, with a giant wooden windmill extending above.

"That there is one of the sugarcane refineries—we have plenty of those. Because cane grows so well here, a single refinery wouldn't be enough."

The refinery was made of the same material as the mill, but instead of a wooden windmill, four metal stacks reached into the sky, presumably attached to metal contraptions similar to those used to refine sugarcane on Earth.

"This bakery," Maria said, pointing to a small shopfront with a tanned woman behind the counter, "is the best bakery in the village. Forget what any of the fat cats to the north say—this is the best, bar none."

"Good morning, Maria!" the lady behind the counter called.

Maria gave her a beatific smile. "Morning, Sue!"

With the morning sun rising in the sky, people began leaving their homes and heading about their business for the day—except the bakers, whose work had long since begun, and whose chimneys had already been spewing smoke when I first laid eyes on the village.

The people I saw leaving their homes appeared fit, tanned, and focused; they were the epitome of working-class folk. All gave me odd looks, either my appearance or unfamiliarity making me somewhat of a spectacle.

"Now, that was when the war really took a turn for the worse . . ." Roger walked ahead of us, well and truly lost in his recounting of his second tour of duty. I wanted to listen in order to glean as much information as possible, but I found myself unable to tear my attention away from the buildings and people of the strange new world I had arrived in.

The buildings were crude, made of large stones and cement that held everything in place. The people seemed to have an almost alien look about them, like some sort of ethnicity I'd never seen before on Earth. I'd assumed it to be a feature of Maria and Roger, but as I took in more people, it became obvious they all possessed an almost Fae-like quality. There was still variance from person to person, especially regarding skin color, but as a whole, they shared many physical similarities.

"So . . ." Maria said, skull-dragging me from my thoughts. "What brings you all the way out here to Tropica Village?"

I'd considered what to say when—and *if*—I found people, and I'd prepared several lines of answer depending on the situation. Confronted with the reality of it, though, these carefully prepared plans were torn apart like sugarcane before a thresher. Following an instinct, I stated the truth instead. "I want to find a place to settle down, and I want to fish."

This statement made Maria purse her lips and almost imperceptibly raise an eyebrow. Roger was much less subtle. Having somehow heard my statement through his own monologue, he spun and faced us. "You dropped on your head or something, lad? Fishing is a fanciful hobby of the ancients—not a productive way to live your life."

"Dad! Fischer's just arrived here. Can you not chase him away already?"

Roger shook his head and scrunched his face, seeming disgusted. "If he's a fisherman, he's deadweight. I'm going to the field. I've wasted enough time on this fool already."

Without any further comment, Roger strode off and disappeared around a corner. Maria immediately apologized. "I'm sorry. The older he gets, the less his filter seems to work."

I laughed at the departed man and shook my head. "Don't worry about it. Other people's opinions won't change what I'm about."

Maria paused for a moment and wrung her hands as she clearly thought about what to say. I smiled, able to read her body language as if she were a book.

"You can say whatever you're thinking, Maria."

She jolted, then flushed and averted her eyes. "I . . . uh . . . I don't want to offend—"

"You won't offend me. As I said, I know what I'm about. What did you want to say?"

"Well, the thing is . . ." She paused as she gathered her courage. ". . . fishing kind of *is* frowned upon, and it'll be hard to sustain yourself and integrate into this village if you intend on fishing."

I cocked my head, genuine confusion hitting me. *How is a village in such a prime place for fishing not filled with anglers?* "I thought, given that this is a coastal town, fishing would be an integral part of the village's economy. Is that not the case?"

It was Maria's turn to show confusion—it oozed from her countenance. "Where have you come from that fishing is *ever* an integral part of anything?"

"A long, *long* way away."

"Well . . ." She looked at me with keen eyes. "Here, and everywhere else I've ever heard of, fishing hasn't been done since the gods left. Living off the land is the proper way to be, and living from the water is a waste of precious time. If you intend to fish, I hope you're prepared for the weird looks. I also hope you either intend to work a proper job, or have a large amount of coin to burn through . . ."

"No 'proper job' for me, I'm afraid." I smiled at her, glad that she was so forthcoming, but also not swayed by the warnings. "I intend to fish, and only to fish."

She stared at me with a weighing gaze. I'd felt many such looks fall upon me in my previous life, but it was both surprising, and a little scary, to feel such a heavy stare come from such a young woman. She sighed. "Well, I can see you won't be swayed. Do you intend to buy land?"

I beamed a smile at her acceptance. "I do."

"Come with me. I have to get to our field, but I can take a few minutes to introduce you to the village lord."

Lord? Does that mean the people of this village belong to a fiefdom? Or even a kingdom? I have to get that information . . .

As we traveled, the layout and condition of the streets changed. The roads grew wider and cleaner, and the houses were larger, made of more organized stone and mortar. Some even expressed some artistic flair with the layout and construction of the materials.

If where we'd been previously was the working district, this is the upper-crust part of town.

Maria led me to a building that was more akin to a cathedral than a house. It was three stories tall—another floor higher than any other structure I'd seen, including the refinery and mill. Made of stone all the same color of gray, with large sheets of glass interspersed on the higher floors, it presented a front of opulence compared to the rest of Tropica Village.

Maria knocked on the door, and after an extended stretch of time, it flew open.

CHAPTER FIVE

ACQUISITION

George, the lord of Tropica Village, was on only his fifth sugar-crusted pastry of the day when some cretin had the audacity to knock on his front door, interrupting the succulent and delicious-tasting treat. This assignment alone was already enough of a slight to his family's good name, but having to interact directly with the rabble was a daily insult.

"They dare disturb me, when I've not even finished my second breakfast?" he said.

His wife, Geraldine, rolled her eyes and made a noise of contempt around her mouthful of pastry.

The things I do for these peasants . . .

He grunted in frustration as he wrestled with his silk dressing gown, the damn thing seeming to have shrunken again.

I'll have to talk to that miserly seamstress about her materials.

He trudged down the stairs while sucking remnants of granular sugar from his fingers. Unleashing his fury on the door, he flung it open with wild abandon, casting his displeasure over the two people on his doorstep. One was a female field worker, who would have been a beautiful sight, if not for her sun-tainted skin and starved-looking form. The other was a man in his thirties he hadn't seen before. He didn't have the tanned skin of the other peasants, but he had the similarly malnourished body that all the working class did.

"Yes? What have you disturbed my morning for?" George asked, using his shrillest and therefore most-authoritarian voice.

"U-uh, this is Fischer," the plain woman said. "He's just arrived, and he wants to buy some land." She turned to the other peasant. "Fischer, this is George, the lord of Tropica. I have to get to work. I'll leave you to it." She fled, walking with haste back to the peasant side of town.

Fischer turned to him. "A pleasure to meet you, lord."

At least he has the good sense to show the proper respect, George thought, deciding to bestow upon him the gift of not rolling his eyes at the insolence of interrupting his third-favorite meal of the day. "Oh, is that so . . . Fischer, was it? And what sort of land do you desire?"

"Coastal. As close to, if not directly on the beach."

George was unable to stop himself from narrowing his eyes in confusion. "What would anyone want with a coastal strip of land?"

Fischer smiled plainly. "For fishing, mate. I want a plot of land to call my own, and I want to be as close to the water as possible."

George rubbed his eyes and let out a sigh. *Great. A madman has found his way to our shores.*

Employing his vast intellect, George devised a way to chase this madman away, and hopefully send him scurrying whence he came. "Unfortunately, my dear man, it isn't possible to break up the coastal land—crown laws, you understand?"

Fischer nodded, accepting the words of his betters as fact. "Of course. How big a property are we talking?"

"The stretch from the last field on the south side of Tropica, all the way up to and including the southern mountain range, is available. It is worth quite a sum, however . . ." George shook his head in feigned sadness. "Fifteen gold pieces, I regret to say. It may be out of your reach . . ."

George knew that if someone were to buy the sandy, useless stretch of land, that it'd be worth three, maybe four gold coins at most. What good would land that could hardly grow any of the staple commodities of the kingdom be, after all?

A smile lingered on Fischer's face, but his eyes narrowed slightly, the expression disconcerting and unreadable to George. "Fifteen? That seems a little steep, George. It's sandy land, after all, which isn't great for growing any of the crops I've seen. How far inland does the land stretch?"

George snorted, letting some of his disdain for the madman show. "All the way back to the village's boundary line—just over a kilometer." *What does he know of land prices? He couldn't afford a coffee, let alone the useless sand he wants.*

George's frustration with the intrusion growing, he looked Fischer up and down, his eyes lingering on the basic clothes. "Do you even have any gold, *sir?*"

Fischer kept his unsettling gaze on George as he reached into his bag with slow ease, grabbing something. He held it out. George stuck his hand out petulantly, half expecting this *Fischer* to drop a shell or other similarly useless trinket into his hand. When he saw what Fischer dropped onto his open palm, his eyes almost flew from their sockets. It wasn't just a gold coin. It was a coin of the ancients, a relic that, back in the city he'd grown up in, would fetch anywhere from fifty to sixty regular gold pieces—each enough to buy half this godforsaken village.

George looked back up at Fischer—the man had a vicious gleam in his eye. Before, George had seen Fischer's happiness as that of a peasant pleased to be interacting with his betters—now, all George could see was the predatory gleam of a hawk who'd cornered a mouse.

He put the coinless fist behind his back to hide the tremble he felt coming on; his other hand started to sweat beneath the treasure he'd just been handed so casually.

"Er—uh—no. I-I think I may have been hasty in my previous assessment." George let out a laugh that sounded forced to his own ears. "For a man such as yourself, a single coin should suffice. The land is as good as yours." He tried to smile, but he felt his eyes displaying his panic. Fischer's eyes flinched almost imperceptibly, and George felt the gaze bore right through him.

"A single coin?"

"Y-yes, Fischer! This will more than cover it! I-I'm sorry for the mix-up, it was an honest mistake . . ."

Fischer stared at him, the lack of emotion and predatory gleam pinning George down. Each moment Fischer remained silent made the pressure increase tenfold. "All right, then." He shot George a wink. "Don't go spending that coin all at once."

George nodded and swallowed, his throat scratchy and uncomfortable.

Fischer spoke again, freeing George from the building silence. "Is there a form I need to fill out?"

"I'll—uh—I'll handle the formalities and paperwork, and I'll come find you with them later. Good day, er—sir!" He bowed, slowly but firmly closing the door behind him. The moment it was closed, he collapsed against it, sliding down the wooden surface as sweat poured from his rotund body. *Who sent this man? Has the capital grown wise of the coins I've been skimming from the taxes sent their way?*

The coin was clearly a message. Who else, if not a representative of the capital themselves, could hold their composure while handling such a vast sum of wealth? That leather pouch of his may have held even more of the artifacts. Worse, George had lied to the man, telling a crown agent that the land couldn't be broken up. *He told me not to spend the coin—a direct warning.* Horror dawned as he realized he'd *kept* it. *Why didn't I hand it back? In my panic, I let a capital representative overpay . . . did he embroil me on purpose? What devious plan have I stepped headfirst into?* George's thoughts were troubled, his body numb, as he walked upstairs.

"George?" Geraldine asked as he walked back into their dining room. "What's wrong? You're white as a ghost . . ."

Unable to respond, he sat heavily in his chair and shoved a sugary pastry into his mouth. It tasted bland and dry.

A calm contentment blanketed my thoughts as I walked toward what had to be the south of the village—it was the undeveloped stretch of land, after all. It also made sense with Roger, the addled man from earlier, claiming this village to be on the eastern coast.

I couldn't believe what had just transpired. Just like that, I'd been granted so much land. I'd happily have given everything—up to and including the clothes on my back—if it meant I could have even an acre of beachfront property. Instead, I'd been given hectares—*hundreds* of hectares—of land. Land that was entirely mine—all for a *single* coin.

I was a little annoyed that I'd slipped so easily back into my CEO training, and I might have been better off just paying the demanded price. Negotiating was a hard habit to break; I'd have to do my best not to let it overtake my time here, lest I get dragged back into a life I found empty and wanting.

It felt wrong leaving without a contract, too, maybe I should go back and—I shook my head, realizing I was already slipping back into old habits. *Let it go, Fischer.* My therapist's voice once more sprung forth, unbidden. *"Show others trust, and they'll trust you in return . . ."*

I forced my focus toward the information I'd managed to extract. There *was* an overarching governing body—a monarchy, if George's use of the term "crown laws" meant anything. I wanted to get more information out of the village's lord, but that door was, quite literally, closed on me. I didn't want to force the issue and draw attention to myself. *Another time . . .*

As I continued my path southward, I smiled at the people I passed, not letting their odd looks and stares bother me. Even if I were the type of person to be caught off guard by such things, I was entirely too ecstatic to care.

I'd been shocked to see the state of the lord that opened the door. After seeing the rest of the village people, I had just assumed everyone would be lean from hard work—tanned from days spent in the sun. The lord of the town proved to be the exception. The man was, well, large. *Really* large. His skin was pasty, too, telling me he rarely—if ever—saw time in the sun.

I suppose that explains Maria calling the people to the north of the village fat cats.

George was the picture of noble entitlement from the stories, and he'd led with the expected, holier-than-thou attitude, but that quickly disappeared when I paid up. *George likely gave me an extortive quote, explaining the nervousness, but why did a single coin addle him . . . ? Was even the single coin an overpayment?*

This thought made a twinge of frustration bubble up inside me, but I quickly stamped it out. Who cares if he tried to fleece me and I overpaid? I still held twenty-four of the coins, and more importantly, I owned my own beach, river, and mountains!

Before I even realized, I was stepping out from between the houses of the town and between two fields of sugarcane. I stopped mid-step and turned to take in my surroundings. The air was fresh and carried the smell of salt. The sun was climbing ever higher, and now that there were no awnings protecting my skin from its rays, its touch was warm and pleasant.

A tear of happiness swelled in my eye, and the emotion of the moment overwhelmed me. I'd finally started to figure out life on Earth when I was robbed of that newfound path by truck-kun. Then, through a bizarre series of events triggered by divine intervention, pure happenstance, or some other, equally confusing interdimensional fuckery, I was reborn into this world and now possessed everything I could need. *Well, everything other than a house and a fishing rod . . . but I have all the tools and money I need to make that happen.* With that thought, I continued walking between the sugarcane and toward my property.

Before long, the fields of cane opened up into a flat stretch. Some weeds grew in the sandy soil, but it was mostly bare, which was the only reason the land hadn't been developed, I guessed. What would be the bane of others was a boon for me. If it had been anything other than sandy soil this side of the village, it would have been developed into farmland and crops. The fact that it wasn't worth farming meant that I was able to buy it. I bent down and spread my arms wide, hugging the ground. "I love you, sand."

"Er, you okay?"

I jumped at the voice, scrambling to my feet. There was a man in one of the fields I'd just passed. He looked to be about the same age as me, wore a large straw hat, a set of basic clothes, and carried a hoe slung over his shoulder.

"Uh, yeah, don't mind me." I laughed awkwardly. "I'm Fischer. I just bought this land."

"Oh, you did?" The man strode forward, hand extended. "I'm Barry. Most of the fields this side of Tropica are mine, so I guess we'll be neighbors. Nice to meet you, Fischer!"

"The pleasure's all mine, mate."

We clasped hands. He had strength that belied his size, the wiry muscles in his arm evidently hardened by years of slinging hoes.

"There's a lot of fields this side of the village," I said. "It's impressive that one man owns them all."

It was Barry's turn to laugh awkwardly, and he rubbed the back of his head with his free hand. "It's not as impressive as it might seem. My family and I run it, and the land was much cheaper on account of how sandy it is." Barry shrugged. "But we've worked out how to grow in the sandier stuff, it just takes a little more work. Let me know if you need help working it out—I'd be happy to give you some knowledge in exchange for a little work in our fields."

"Thanks, Barry. I'll keep that in mind, but I don't actually plan on doing any farming."

"No problem, you—*wait, what?*" Barry raised an eyebrow. "You don't plan on farming? What do you plan on doing, then?"

I smiled in delight. "Fishing!"

Barry cocked his head, then he laughed. He *really* laughed. He doubled over, leaning on his hoe for support, all the while I just smiled at him. "Thank you, Fischer," Barry said as he wiped tears from his eyes. "I needed that. Seriously, though, what are you planning on doing with the land? Livestock?"

"Oh, I'm as serious as a Queensland summer. I'll just be fishing, if I can help it."

Barry's face went through a series of emotions as he realized I was telling the truth. It settled somewhere between confused and troubled. "Well, the offer is there if you change your mind and want to learn about farming in sandy soil, all right? You take care, Fischer."

"Thanks, Barry. You too."

I spun and strode further into my land, not at all discouraged by the odd interaction. I'd have to work out why everyone was so averse to fishing. It seemed to be something to do with "the gods leaving" and "the ancients," whatever the hell that meant.

It was all a problem for another day because I had some land to explore—*my* land.

CHAPTER SIX

HOME

While the land I owned seemed to be barren farmland, it was anything but empty of life. Small weeds, grasses, and bushes grew sporadically, with small wren-like birds flying between them and making pretty sounds as they snatched up insects. I was tempted to walk directly down to the beach and make my way along it, but I had a better view of my lands from between the shoreline and the forest, and there was yet plenty of time in the day.

There were a few spindly trees that looked half dead—the kind that even a cyclone had no chance of uprooting—growing from the sandy soil around me as I walked. Other than those few, there were no trees until the forest a few hundred meters to the west.

George said that my land stretched back a kilometer—meaning vast swaths of that forest are mine. I smiled in delight. It didn't take me long to walk all the way to the river mouth, excited as I was.

As I arrived, I saw the familiar bushes bearing blackberries that had been my fuel and savior in the forest. In all likelihood, the same creek that had wet my thirst flowed down and into the very river before me. I took a moment to thank the land for everything it provided so far—if not for the berries, and especially the water, I may never have made it to Tropica.

There would be no shortage of wood for construction or fire, as along the banks of the river entire trees and branches lay felled, washed up by flooding in the recent past. I peeled the bark off one such tree, seeing the wood firm and unrotten beneath. There were also some of the spindly trees still thriving in their spots on the bank, their great roots reaching deep enough that they weren't washed away by raised water levels.

I walked over to one of the berry bushes and bent down, taking my time to inspect and make sure it was the exact same plant I knew to be safe. Satisfied, I indulged in the sweet berries.

I walked down to the water and cocked my head to the side as I stared at the river in confusion. I'd expected the waters to be muddy and brown, as most rivers are, but it was almost crystal clear. The floor of the river was covered with small stones, and it was shallower than initially expected, but still too deep to cross by foot.

Scooping up some of the water, and having started a small campfire, I started the purification process. As it boiled, I contemplated my options.

If I was being honest with myself, I felt paralyzed by choice. There was so much I wanted to do, all of which would take me in drastically different directions. As much as I wanted to get cracking on my fishing destiny, there were some things I had to sort out first. Water and food were still taken care of, if a little crudely, but I'd be able to develop something more long-term later.

I slapped my face, forcing myself to make a decision and end the paralysis. I would find somewhere flat to establish a shelter in the short-term, and a home in the long-term. The best thing to do would be to find a high vantage point and to look out over the land. I turned to the headland, which was only one hundred meters from my current position. The rock formation there was easily thirty meters tall, and twice that in length. *A perfect position to scout the area from.*

As I walked toward the stones, a wind rushing in from the coast buffeted me. I wasn't sure if it was the excitement of the day, but I felt stronger—my legs were filled with energy, like I could go on forever. It was as though my body had somehow grown more resilient; as if something powered my stride. The gale-force wind would have threatened to knock me over on Earth, but I now strode through it with ease.

When I got to the rocks, I looked for a place to climb, but found something even more interesting. There was a cavernous gap between the colossal boulders, shielded from the coastal winds by the natural stone formation. The space was flat and stood at least five meters above sea level. I knelt down and ran my hand through the earth. It was soft and pliable, meaning I could install the most vital things for any home, fantasy world or not—*plumbing.* With that, I knew I'd found the place to construct my temporary shelter, and eventually, my home.

I walked around the space, picturing how I'd one day lay out the permanent build. Four bedrooms—enough for friends to stay over, and maybe even a family one day; two bathrooms, both with a shower, toilets, and all the necessary plumbing required; a large kitchen with every pot and pan one could desire; and an even larger entertaining area outside, kitted with accompanying barbecue, a sink big enough to scale and fillet fish, and a large wooden deck for entertaining. Bending down, I put my hand against the cool earth where I pictured the entrance of the house would go.

There was a tug at my hip. Shooting to my feet, I spun, suspecting that someone had grabbed the leather pouch, but no one was there. I put my hand in the pouch and found it empty; the remaining coins that should be there were gone. My head spun, and the world itself seemed to shake. My legs failed me, and as the ground rushed up to meet me, I blacked out.

I woke to a blinding light blasting into my eyes. Blinking, I tried to look around, but the light was overwhelming to my addled mind. Something firm and cold was beneath me, and I felt it with my hands as I gingerly got to my feet. My vision cleared, and I seemed to be inside of some sort of building. It was made of light textured wood, with a great glass window that let in the blinding sunlight. *What . . . what happened? Was it a dream, after all?*

I turned from the sun, deciding to explore the building I now found myself in. I fumbled to a door, and grabbing the metal handle, I opened it. Stepping through the doorway, my eyes cleared in the reduced light. I saw something that both confused and amazed me.

A bed sat before me. It was made of sturdy lacquered wood, covered in plush bedding, sheets, and pillows, and adorned by a beautifully carved headboard. It wasn't just any bed, but the bed I'd been picturing in my head as the one I would furnish my forever home with. Where I'd pictured an en suite, there was a door.

I opened it to find a shower, sink, giant bathtub, and blessedly, a toilet. Absentmindedly, I walked over and flushed the toilet. It worked, and the water drained away, replaced with more of the clear liquid. I checked the sink and shower, both of which ran clear. The water in the sink smelled fine, and with no small amount of trepidation, I tasted some—it was fresh and clean. I knew there was a slight chance it contained hazardous microbes, but because there were other humans close by should I fall ill, or because my senses still hadn't completely returned, I chose to risk it.

As I walked out of the bedroom and back into the room I'd awoken in, the view took my breath away. My eyes had adjusted, and through a great glass window, the setting sun reflected off the waters of the river. The familiar headland, the same river mouth, and the far-off mountains were all there.

I checked the rest of the house quickly, all but running as I confirmed all the details I'd pictured. Three spare bedrooms, a communal bath, shower, a toilet, and a large kitchen with an attached dining area. The bathroom and kitchen were both less ostentatious than I'd pictured, which I supposed was because of some sort of limitation by the System, or because I didn't have any more currency to offer.

The difference in the kitchen was most notable, as it lacked an oven or stove of any kind. It was still lavish and looked more at home in a restaurant than a house. The entire thing was covered in stainless steel, with pots, pans, and utensils of every shape and size littered throughout, all organized meticulously on shelves and hooks.

There was a dining area attached with a large hardwood table within that was big enough to accommodate all ten of the seats tucked into it.

I stepped past the table toward double doors that led outside. I held my breath as I opened them, hoping against hope that what I'd pictured outside had made it into the build—but it wasn't meant to be. My pride, my joy, my ray of hope in the dark night was most definitely not there—there was no barbecue.

I found myself on a large wooden deck. It would be the perfect place for a barbecue, I reflected, protected from the wind as it was, but I guessed I'd just have to go about crafting my own in good time. "Cooking by campfire it is, then—if I catch any fish, that is." I laughed to myself as I realized I was complaining at not receiving a barbecue, when a house had just appeared from thin air.

Walking on the deck around to the front of the house, the view was stunning. The sun still played off the water, and the fading light cast an ethereal tint over the land. It was untouched by civilization; the view from my home showed none of the town, hidden as it was by the rock formation. All I saw was a river, ocean, sand, vegetation, mountains, and a beautiful sky painted pink by fading sunlight.

A wind picked up, and the air was cool as the warmth of the day fled alongside the sun. The breeze swirled around me, most of its force robbed by the relative shelter the house occupied. The moving air tickled the back of my neck as I watched the last vestige of sunlight disappear over the mountains to the west.

There was a small table with four chairs beside the front door, and I sat in one of them, not knowing what else to do. Remembering what happened earlier, I felt for the pouch at my side. It was still there, but as I'd suspected, was empty of the gold coins.

This world, this System . . . it had taken all twenty-four of my coins and had built me a home. As if to taunt me, I received an infuriatingly familiar prompt.

[Error: Insufficient power. Superfluous systems offline.]

"Well, I guess that means I won't have to make a shelter for the night . . ."

On the bank of the river just before my new home, there was a large swath of the berry-laden bushes, filled to the brim with the sugary snacks. They seemed to call to me, so I grabbed my stone bowl and went.

I inspected them, and sure enough, they were safe. I ate some, only now realizing just how hungry I'd become. Collecting some more for later in the bowl, I turned to look at my house. From down on the riverbank, it looked almost . . . quaint. The visible surface peeking from between sheets of rock hid the depth and size of the dwelling.

Is buildings springing up from nowhere a normal feature of this world? I somehow doubted it, given the materials and rather crude method with which the houses of the village were constructed. What would the villagers think if they came over and saw a house, where the day before there'd been nothing? *They'd probably burn me alive, like so many witches before me.*

A smile crept onto my face. This world was strange, confusing, and alien, but oh so exciting. I had no local currency, but I had access to food, water, shelter, and endless possibilities.

I stood up on shaky legs. As it turned out, trading a handful of gold for an instant-build house was rather exhausting. I ambled back to the master bedroom, and as soon as my head hit the pillow, I was out.

CHAPTER SEVEN

THE CULT OF CARCINIZATION

The next morning, I set off toward the village for two reasons. First and foremost, I didn't want anyone to discover the house, especially only a day after it constructed itself out of nothing. The longer I could stall, the more feasible it would be that I built it up over time. Second, I wanted more information.

As much as I wanted to throw myself into fishing—and fixate on it entirely—there would be no point if a lack of preparation caused my untimely death by whatever this world did to witches, practitioners of the dark arts, and other such evildoers.

The first person I ran into was Barry, who was also up in the predawn light. The farmer was all smiles, and it put my somewhat troubled mind at ease. Beside Barry stood a young boy of perhaps seven years old. He stood tall for someone his age, seeming to radiate the surety that comes from a young man standing beside his father.

"Good morning, Fischer," Barry said, wiping sweat from his brow.

"Morning, mate." I gestured at the young man. "This one yours?"

Barry smiled in delight, answering the question before he even spoke. "Aye, this is my son, Paul. Say hello, lad."

"H-Hello," Paul said, the previous confidence falling apart at having to talk to a stranger.

"Nice to meet you, mate. I was wondering how your dad managed all these fields, but seeing those brawny arms of yours, now I know!"

Paul smiled and puffed out his chest, and his father laughed. "It's your first morning here, isn't it, Fischer?" Barry asked.

"It is. Why's that?"

"Well, it's a tradition in our family to watch the sunrise from the beach. Would you care to join us?"

While that sounded amazing, I didn't want to miss the lord coming to find me for fear the man would seek me out and discover the house.

"I'd love to, mate, but George might come looking for me about the deed to my land, and I don't want to miss him."

"You talk funny," Paul said, looking at me with squinted eyes.

I laughed, unable to hold my mirth in.

Barry slapped his son lightly on the back of the head, giving him a glare. "Now, that's no way to talk to a neighbor, Paul. You say sorry to mister Fischer."

"No, no, it's fine." I smiled down at Paul. "I do talk funny, but it's normal where I come from, and just Fischer is fine. We're neighbors, after all."

Paul nodded, accepting the statement for fact, as only kids can.

"Well," Barry said, "what if Paul waits here to keep an eye out for that wandering lord of ours?"

"Dad! I want to see the sunrise, too!"

"None of that, lad." He shot a stern look at his son. "That can be your apology for your tongue running faster than your brain." Barry turned to me. "Would that be all right?"

"I don't want to impose . . ."

"Nonsense!" Barry waved the concern away. "Paul here has seen countless sunrises, and he'll see countless yet. It's your first morning in Tropica, and it feels right that you see it."

Seeing Paul's growing disappointment, I bent down so we were eye level. "Are you sure you can handle this, Paul?" Presented with a challenge, he straightened himself as I continued. "I don't even want to think what would happen if he were to walk onto my land and somehow lose the paperwork." I winced. "Maybe I should do it myself, or find an adult to keep an eye out for him . . ."

Paul's eyes widened then narrowed in resolve. "I can do it!"

"You're sure? I don't mind having to get someone a little older . . ."

"He won't get by me! I promise!"

"All right." I put a hand on his shoulder. "I trust you, mate. Make sure George doesn't get past you and onto my land."

Barry smiled at me as he led us down to the water. "That was expertly done. My boy would sooner eat shellfish than admit he wasn't capable of completing a task."

I grinned at him. "I have no doubt he'll rise to the challenge—he looked like a hawk when we left him."

Barry laughed. "Aye, that he did. I've never seen him so attentive. Do you have kids?"

"No, but I understand how to motivate people."

"No kidding. I might have to steal that tactic when it comes to planting season. Paul loves harvesting and tending to the fields, but something about planting makes his head wander elsewhere."

We arrived on the beach before the sun rose above the ocean, the light of its approach painting the sky directly east. Barry sat down, and I joined him. The air was cool, the wind not as harsh as it was the previous day. We sat in silence, both content to take in the beautiful scene playing out before us. The sunrise truly was stunning, and I could see why their family made a tradition of watching it each morning. *I think I'll have to make it a tradition of my own . . .*

Movement to our left caught my attention, and I lazily looked over to see something truly astounding. "Barry . . ."

"Yes, Fischer?"

"What the fuck is that?"

Barry turned his head, looking at where I was pointing.

There were five men on the beach near us. They walked on hunched legs, their bums almost on the sand, with their hands held beside their heads, snapping open and closed. They were crab walking into the surf.

"Oh, that?" Barry asked. "That's the Cult of Carcinization—don't mind them, they're harmless."

While I wasn't worried they would bring me harm, I was concerned for their mental health and general well-being.

"Is there a reason they're walking like crabs into the waves?"

The first of the men reached the sea, continuing his awkward shuffle into deeper waters.

"Their cult deifies crabs," Barry said, as if it was the most reasonable statement of all time. "They believe all paths of evolution eventually lead to crabs—a process called carcinization, hence the name."

I had . . . so many questions. "I suspected I'd find a church of some kind in the village, but you seem quite chill about the fact there's a cult right beside us, crab walking into the deep blue."

Two of the men clacked at each other with their hand-claws. Barry raised an eyebrow—at me, not the crab people. "Where do you come from that a *church* would be reasonable, but a cult wouldn't?"

"Very, *very* far away."

"Look, Fischer . . ." Barry composed his thoughts for a long moment before continuing. "I think I'm a good judge of character, and you seem like the honest sort to me, but all this talk of churches and fishing won't make you any friends around here."

I looked out to sea as I considered what to say back to the man. The sun was four of its own widths above the horizon, and I let the peace of the scene guide my thoughts. *How much can I trust this man? I obviously can't tell him I'm an inter-planet traveler, but just how much do I reveal . . . ?*

Just as with Barry, I thought myself an excellent judge of character—and Barry had plenty of character to spare. *The truth, then . . . just a little decorated.*

I let my honest emotions leak out, and gave Barry a half smile, half-wince. "I find myself out of my depths here, mate. I'm from so far away, it may as well be another world."

Barry nodded. "I guessed as much just from your pattern of speech, let alone your love of fishing and acceptance of churches."

"Would you mind giving me the rundown on why fishing is seen as such a bad thing here? I met a woman named Maria when I arrived yesterday and gathered it's something to do with the gods leaving?"

"Around these parts, and every other place I've ever heard of, living from the water is shunned." Barry looked confused. "I know you said it may as well be another planet, but it's hard to imagine a place that doesn't know of the gods' betrayal . . ."

I gave him a sheepish laugh. "Hard to believe as it is, that's where I come from. What was the gods' betrayal?"

Barry's eyes moved over the calm sea. "The gods of water set about the events that led to all the gods abandoning this world. As such, only a fool would rely upon the spoils of their domain."

"That would certainly explain everyone's reaction to me fishing . . ."

"Aye. Fishing is eating from the sea, not living from the land as is proper—it's heresy."

Never mind the pop-up house—am I going to get burned at the stake if I go fishing? "What would you villagers do to someone committing such heresy?"

"Do?" Barry cocked his head. "What do you mean?"

"You know . . . like punishment-wise. Am I going to lose a finger or my head for going fishing?"

Barry's eyes went wide, then he laughed. It wasn't a polite laugh—he roared his delight, so loud that even the crab men stopped their clacking momentarily, shooting us aggrieved glances. "No—no, Fischer. Not that. There is no punishment, it's just . . . people will treat you different, you understand?"

Oh, good. I smiled my delight back at him, genuine relief flooding me at the news that my new-world plans weren't halted. "Thanks for the warning, mate. I'm not too worried about how I'm seen, so that shouldn't be an issue."

Barry shook his head, but still smiled. "You're truly going to fish?"

"Yup!"

"Ah well, at least you've been warned what you're getting yourself into."

"What about the cult and church thing?" I asked. "Where I'm from, the societal view is flipped—churches are recognized places of worship, whereas cults are looked down upon."

He shook his head in exasperation. "I never want to go wherever you're from, Fischer—they got it all backward."

I grinned. "I wouldn't worry about that—I don't see you ever getting the opportunity. So, what's the difference between a cult and a church here?"

"Well, churches are blasphemous for a simple reason—there are no gods left to worship. They all ascended and won't be returning. A cult is normal, because they're worshipping the eventual rise of another human or creature to godhood.

"Every cult is hoping to one day become a church when their chosen creature becomes a spirit beast, or their human counterpart ascends—but until then, to call yourself a church would be a lie. Take the Cult of Carcinization, for example."

He pointed at the five men, who were now neck-deep in the calm water, only their heads and imitations of pincers visible. One clacked at another, who shuffled to the side to avoid the violence. "Their doctrine is that a crab will ascend and become a spirit beast. That we will all become crabs one day through carcinization, which means that to them, we are all holy beings just waiting to happen." He shrugged. "As I said, completely harmless."

At the mention of spirit beasts, all the novels on cultivation I'd read came rushing to mind. *So I've arrived in post-ascension Xianxia land? Neat.*

"I get it," I said. "So a church is inherently a lie, and therefore blasphemy, unless a spirit beast or ascended human emerges?"

"Just so."

"Are there many cults?"

"Probably more than there are grains of sand beneath your feet. They're not all as benevolent as the carcinization folk over there, so I'm glad Tropica only has two."

"Two?" I raised an eyebrow. "What's the other one?"

"The Cult of the Leviathan. They're an odd bunch and a real chore to be around, but also relatively harmless. Unlike the Cult of Carcinization, they deify lobsters. Their doctrine is that lobsters don't die of old age—they only die when they get too old to molt. Their plan is to help a lobster molt until it gets so old that it naturally becomes a spirit beast."

As he spoke, my smile grew wider and wider, and it was my turn to laugh uncontrollably. Barry laughed along with me, thinking I was laughing at the absurdity of the plan. Don't get me wrong, it was a ridiculous plan, but I was mostly laughing that 'the lorb' had managed to become the basis for an actual cult in post-ascension Xianxia land.

It took me a good while to regain my composure. *I love this place.*

CHAPTER EIGHT

THE CULT OF THE LEVIATHAN

It was a normal day at the Cult of the Leviathan's Tropica branch. Sebastian, who was the leader of this particular branch, was tending to the lobster crickets. The building he'd acquired with the funds he brought from the capital was a far cry from what he was used to, but as long as he had space to tend to his precious lobsters, he was happy.

"Do you need a hand with the baby lobsters, sir?" Gary, his idiotic follower, asked.

Sebastian felt the joy at his task drain from his face. "For the last time, Gary, they're crickets. Baby lobsters are called *crickets.*"

"Right. Sorry, sir."

Sebastian still couldn't believe that Gary was the only follower he could find in this middle-of-nowhere village. *I guess any help is better than no help.*

"Huh," Gary's stupid voice said. "What's going on with this blinking thing?"

Sebastian sighed as he looked up from his precious little crickets. "What blinking thing, Gary?"

"The thing in this bag over here—it's blinking red."

A spark of hope welled within Sebastian, and he rushed to his travel bag. When in the capital, he'd spent a large sum on an ancient artifact—an act that had resulted in his expulsion to this backwater village. The artifact was something that detected cultivation in beings and was supposed to light up when close to them. The leader of the capital branch had called it an overpriced paperweight, but that the light was now blinking proved Sebastian's genius.

He reached into his bag with barely contained glee. His eyes went wide as he pulled out the artifact; the light was indeed blinking.

He was going to usher this cult into a church; one of his precious crickets was going to grow into the great Leviathan of story. He would prove them all wrong, his genius was unparalleled, he—the glee on his face was replaced by confusion, then anger.

"Uh, sir?" Gary asked. "What's wrong?"

"Not good, Gary. *Very* not good."

"What isn't, sir?"

Sebastian held up the artifact for Gary to see. There were two sides to the artifact, one with the simple drawing of a human, the other with depictions of a cat, dog, and fish. The side that was blinking was the one with a human.

"Uh, what does that mean, sir?"

Sebastian snarled. "It means it isn't one of our precious lobsters that is taking steps toward ascension. We have someone in Tropica that needs to be taken care of."

In the capital city of Gormona, Trent, the first in line to the throne, who was considered by anyone other than his mother to be the human equivalent of a stubbed toe, was hiding.

Like hell I'll be attending something as stupid as decorum training. He was up to his fourth tutor on the subject, each of them being just as useless as the last. *My family pays them so much, and for what? I haven't learned a thing!*

Rather than be subjected to today's lesson, he had found a tucked-away room to hide in. That it was a royal decree to stay out of the artifact-filled room was perfect; no one would look for him in here.

He snickered to himself as he crawled further and further into the pile of ancient junk. "*Stay out of the artifact room,*" he whispered aloud in a mocking tone. "*It's just a room of scrap metal.*"

Reaching a hidden pocket in the giant collection of uselessness, he stood and stretched. He was between four different constructs, all of which were lifeless. "Just as they always have and always will be," he said, making sure to keep his voice down—it wouldn't do to have one of those cultivator freaks hear him and rat him out.

One of the artifacts had a glass screen, and the light from the gap above let him see his own reflection. It warped his head, making his generally displeasing appearance even more pronounced. Insecurity flaring, and feeling insulted by the inanimate object, he slapped it. "Shut up, idiot. You're ugly."

The screen lit up, and Trent's already too-large-for-his-head eyes went wider. There were words printed on the screen.

New milestone! Fischer has learned bushcraft!
New milestone! Fischer has learned construction!
New milestone! Fischer has learned fishing!

"What in Poseidon's puckered butthole . . ."

Having witnessed the sunrise, Barry and I walked back toward where we'd left his son, Paul. I smiled at the man. "Thanks for the hospitality, mate. The knowledge too. That sunrise was glorious."

Barry smiled back. "No need for thanks. That's what neighbors do."

Before we could find Paul, he found us. The boy came sprinting down from the sugarcane fields. "Mister Fischer! Mister Fischer! I found George!"

"Uh, thanks mate . . . where is he, though?"

"He's right . . ." Paul spun, appearing just as confused as I was. "He was right behind—"

The sweaty, morbidly obese form of the village lord came bursting from between two rows of sugarcane. "Wait just a second, you little shi—ah, Fischer, there you are."

The lord had a paper tray in one hand, a document flapping in the other. He placed the document atop the tray, using his free hand to retrieve a handkerchief and pat his sweaty brow. "I . . . I came . . . I came to bring your papers." He leaned the handkerchief-filled hand on his knee, trying to catch his breath.

"Cheers, George. You didn't have to bring them all the way out here, I was just coming to see you."

"Non . . . nonsense. I was more than happy to bring them."

I walked over, happily accepting the papers and glancing down at them. *Oh, good, they're not in English and I can't read whatever language this is—that's fun.*

"These . . . these are for you," George said, still struggling to recover from his brief exercise. He offered the tray out, which I gladly accepted—to give the man a chance to breathe, if nothing else. "They're . . . they're from . . . Lena's Café . . . the best . . . patisserie . . . in the village."

I noticed Barry's eyes go wide at the store's name. *High-end stuff, huh?*

"You uh, you all right, mate?" I asked the heaving lord.

"Just need to . . . catch my . . . breath." He half sat, half collapsed to the ground, resting his head on his arms as he took deep breaths.

Shrugging, I held the tray out to Barry and Paul. "Hungry, boys?"

Both their eyes went wide, and Paul looked like he was about to start drooling.

"Are you sure?" Barry asked, eyes still locked on the fifteen treats on the tray.

"Very," I said with a laugh. "Help yourselves."

They both grabbed one of the sugar-coated pastries, which looked like stuffed donuts. Paul bit into his first, and something like jam but a bit runnier dripped down the side of the pastry. The boy licked the escaping filling with fervor before it could drip to the ground.

Lobster cults, beachfront property, and now jam-filled donuts? This is my kind of village!

I waited to see Barry's reaction to eating his donut before I grabbed one myself, and the look on the hardened farmer's face was everything I could have hoped for. If there weren't others present, I was sure he would have cried tears of joy.

I bit into one, and the filling exploded into my mouth. I wasn't sure if the pastry was actually that good, or if it was because I'd been subsisting on purified water and berries for the last few days, but it was worthy of the reactions Paul and Barry had given.

"What's the red filling, George?" I asked after swallowing. "I've never tasted anything like it." It was like a mix between strawberry and passionfruit; sweet with just the right amount of tang.

"It's jam made from passiona husks."

"*Passiona?*" Barry almost yelled. "Paul! Thank Fischer and George!"

"Th-thank you!"

"I give thanks to both of you." Barry dipped his head.

"None of that, mate." I gave him a genuine smile. "That's what neighbors do, right? Happy to share."

George was just getting to his feet, brushing his considerable behind free of the sandy dirt he sat in.

"You want one, George?"

"Oh, I-I've had a tray already. Thank you, though."

"No, thank you for bringing them!" I turned to Paul and Barry. "You boys want another?"

"We couldn't possibly—"

"Yes!" Paul yelled.

They both glared at each other, giving me another genuine laugh for the day.

"Please, I insist." I shook the tray at them. "There's too many for just me—I might have to throw them out if you don't help me . . ."

They both came forward to get another—Barry sheepishly, Paul with enthusiasm that bordered on violence.

"I think I'll be getting on my way," George said. "It was a pleasure seeing you all."

He dipped his head to me, Barry, and Paul, then turned and headed for the town.

George's face contorted as he withdrew from the fields. He found a spot in the shade to rest and collect his thoughts. *There is no way someone of Fischer's station would be willingly consorting with peasant farmers—he was sending me a message: he's willing to win over the villagers, and I am replaceable.*

Just as egregious was the handing out of passiona-filled pastries to people of such a lowly station—right in front of him, no less. His mouth still watered at the treats he'd handed over. *As if I would ever turn down a fifth breakfast. He was testing me; gauging my greed in the face of offered pastries.*

It was a ghastly test to perform on someone—what kind of devious individual would play games with sweets? It showed just how far Fischer was willing to go.

George wiped the sweat from his brow with his already sodden cloth. *What in Triton's throbbing conch am I going to do? Fischer is on the offensive, and he's already ten steps ahead of me . . .*

"So what's the big deal with passiona husk?" I asked. "It's tasty, sure, but not good enough to make you treat me like a lord."

Barry winced at his past actions. "It's the price, Fischer. A single one of those pastries is worth two weeks of what we earn farming—the husk alone is worth a week and a half."

I looked at the tray of treats, frowned, and looked back up at Barry. "How are they worth so much? They're just donuts."

"The bushes are controlled and exceedingly expensive—they're engineered so they don't grow seeds, and you can only buy plants directly from the distributor."

Oh, good—there's a fantasy-world Monsanto. I couldn't help but shake my head in dismay.

"Could I ask you a favor, Barry?"

"Anything, Fischer."

"Would you check over this for me?" I held out the documents George gave me. "I don't know the local laws and customs, so I was hoping you could give it a once-over and check everything's up to scratch."

Barry cocked his head to the side as my sentence stretched on.

Guess I might need to tone down the vernacular . . .

"You . . . you want me to make sure it's legally binding?" he asked.

"Yeah, that's the one."

"Of course." Barry took the document. "Is it all right if I check it tonight? There's a lot of work to do in the fields yet today."

"Yeah, mate. No worries. Could I ask one more thing?"

He looked back to his fields, clearly feeling the need to get the day's work started. "What do you need?"

I gave him a disarming grin. "Just some directions."

CHAPTER NINE

CURRENCY

I arrived at my first destination with a broad smile and my tray of pastries in hand. I stepped into the clothing store, looking at the basic garments hanging on the walls. A kind-looking woman was behind the counter, and she gestured at the tray I was carrying.

"Sorry, dear, but there's no food allowed in the store."

"No worries!" I stepped up and displayed the ten remaining pastries. "I got a fresh tray of passiona-stuffed pastries from Lena's Café just now, and while I admit you *can* eat them, these aren't food—they're currency."

The woman was giving me an odd look, but at the mention of passiona and Lena's Café, barely contained greed quickly replaced her suspicion.

"Oh. *Oh.* C-currency is always welcome." She licked her lips absentmindedly. "What are you looking for, dear?"

I set the tray down on the counter. "I'm looking for a few sets of clothes and a roll or two of string or line—something thin, strong, and abrasion resistant."

"I think I may have just the thing for the line—one moment."

She all but ran out the door behind the counter, returning a moment later with a crate. She set it down on the counter. It was filled with rolls of different-sized string and plastic line. I felt my eyes light up. I'd been hoping this world had plastic-based lines akin to fishing line from my world but was willing to settle for fabric string if that was all they had. The crate before me was a treasure trove, and with the pastries George gifted me, I had the keys to the castle.

I sorted through them, picking out two rolls—a one-millimeter-thick roll, and another two-millimeter thick one.

"Y-you can have both for a quarter pastry."

I raised an eyebrow. "Do you have extra rolls, or are these the only ones?"

A man came from the door behind the counter. Judging by the bow and deference he showed me, the woman told him of the treats I was using as coin.

"Welcome to our store!" the man said. "I'm Steven, and this is my wife, Ruby."

I smiled at both of them. "Nice to meet you—I'm Fischer."

"We only have one of each roll," Ruby said, "but we can buy more when the merchant comes at the end of the month."

"Won't you need them before then?"

"Well, yes, but I'm sure we can make do without . . ."

I looked down at the rolls of line—both of which had what must be hundreds of meters of line. I shook my head. Before I could speak, the man intervened, misreading my intentions.

"An eighth! We only need an eighth for both rolls of line!"

Damn, this passiona stuff is serious business, huh?

I shook my head again with a smile. "I don't want to leave you without the tools for your craft, and I don't need that much." I rubbed my chin in thought. "Tell you what, I'll trade two whole pastries for half of both these lines, some small lengths of different colored string, and a few sets of clothes to—"

"*Deal!*" they both yelled, extending their hands. I laughed and shook both.

The man darted to my side of the counter, a measuring tape appearing from nowhere as he rushed me.

Ruby's eyes sparkled. "What kind of clothes do you need, dear? Formal wear? Pajamas? Active wear?"

I tossed my head back and forth in thought. *I didn't think that far ahead—I was just going to ask for three sets of regular clothes to wear while fishing . . . maybe I do need some variety, though . . .*

I started rattling off my thoughts as the man measured me. "I might go with two sets of the plain clothes I've seen the farmers wearing, and a set of more formal attire—nothing too ostentatious, but something a little more suited for going out, if that makes sense?"

"Of course, dear," Ruby said with a smile. "For what you've offered, we can do a lot better than that, though."

"Much better," Steven agreed as he measured my waist.

Ruby tapped the counter in thought. "How does a formal set, four work sets, and a set of silk pajamas sound?"

"Make it two sets of pajamas," Steven said, measuring my shoulders. "We can't have such an esteemed customer left wanting!"

"That sounds perfect." I stood a little straighter at Steven's prompting. "Don't worry about measurements for the work gear, whatever you have available should suit."

Ruby waved the comment away. "Nonsense. It won't take us long to have it all ready, so long as you're happy to come back later today?"

"That's no problem at all, Ruby. I'd be happy to come back and see both your friendly faces again."

She shot a humor-filled glance at her husband. "You'd better watch yourself, Steven—this one's generous *and* charming."

Her husband shared a smile with me as he let out an exaggerated sigh. "Yes, dear."

I arrived at my second destination with ease, Barry's instructions proving thorough. I walked into the furniture store, a bag containing my prized lines in one hand, my tray of eight pastries in the other. A bored man greeted me, but after explaining my purpose, he became just as energetic as the previous store owners.

"Hooks? I have all manner of hooks! One moment!"

He returned from the back with a tray separated into compartments, all of which were filled with hooks of different sizes you could hammer into a wall and hang things from.

"Think I could have a bunch of each size?" I asked.

His eyes danced as he looked between my tray and his. "For one of those pastries, you can have every damned hook we have!"

"How about half of each size?" I looked around the store and pointed at a section where curtain rods of all different lengths and widths leaned against a wall. "And a few of those rods?"

His hand extended, and I shook it happily.

"Is it all right if I come back for the rods? I have a few more stops."

"Of course! Come back whenever you want to pick them up!"

I held the tray out, and he tenderly picked up a pastry. As I walked out of the store, a moan of ecstasy escaped the man behind me.

My next stop was a tool store, and I cast a discerning eye at the layout of the wares as I walked toward the counter and the older gentleman behind it.

"G'day, mate. I'm new in town and was looking for a few things to get set up—name's Fischer, by the way."

He nodded at me, his long mustache bobbing with the movement. "Welcome to Tropica, Fischer. We haven't had a new farmer come in a while." He gave me a wide smile and spread his arms, gesturing at the stocked shelves. "I'm Thomas, and if you need anything to get your farming started, my store is the place to be. What do you need?"

I saw no point in correcting him, so I rattled off what I was looking for. "I need flint, pliers, a bucket, scissors, a file, a hammer, a large nail, a box with separated compartments, and a cart." I held out the tray. "One problem, though. I don't have any coin, and was hoping you'd accept some of these as payment."

Thomas's eyes filled with a now-familiar need as he saw what was inside. "I'm sure we can come to some sort of arrangement, Fischer."

He started walking around the store, collecting what I'd requested. As he moved, I couldn't help but analyze the organization of the shelves, a lifetime of learning dedicated to incremental improvements and profit margins coming out all too easily.

The layout makes sense from an organizational point of view, but having everything too easy for the customer to find means they don't look throughout the entire store and don't have much of a chance to make impulsive purchases. The average purchaser might experience a bit of frustration, but it's worth it in the long run for the increased sales.

"That's quite a bit of gear you need," Thomas said, but I barely heard him. "I think three of the pastries should be enough to cover it . . ."

I frowned and shook my head in annoyance as I realized I was acting on thoughts of my old world. *I didn't come here to build a business empire—I already know that to be an empty endeavor. I need to keep my thoughts on my intended goals.*

Thomas couldn't believe his luck. His wife had been pressuring him to try some of the more expensive eateries on the north side, but the expense was too much for the frugal man to even consider. Then, in walks a man bearing a taste of the most prestigious patisserie in the entire village, and he was willing to *trade.*

How much do I try to get out of him? The fact he's willing to trade them at all tells me he doesn't know their true worth. Five would be too much—even one *of them would more than cover what he's asking for . . .*

"That's quite a bit of gear you need," he said, keeping his face neutral as he picked out the requested items in his perfectly organized store. "I think three of the pastries should be enough to cover it . . ."

Thomas looked up to gauge the farmer's response, and Fischer's face contorted in anger. *Glaucus's swarthy pits, he does know what they're worth.* He felt his skin prickle as he realized he may have ruined this fortuitous opportunity.

I let my annoyance slide away. *There's no point chastising myself—I just have to remember not to let my business impulses take over.* The merchant was speaking, and I hadn't been listening.

"Sorry, Thomas, what did you say?"

"U-uh, does one pastry sound like a fair deal?"

I thought the tools would be more expensive than that . . .

"You're sure that's enough to cover it?"

"Y-yes, of course!"

Thomas ran—literally *ran* around the store as he collected the rest of the items. I smiled as I watched the man sprinting around his domain, a whirlwind of tools and efficiency.

"Is there a Mrs. Thomas?" I asked.

"Y-yes, Fischer. There is!"

"All right. Take two, then. Call it a tip for your energetic service."

A look somewhere between confusion and awe filled Thomas's face as he arrived back at the counter with everything packed in the requested cart.

"Y-you're sure?"

I laughed.

"I am, mate—take one for yourself, and one for the missus."

Thomas shook my hand as tears—genuine *tears*—welled in his eyes. "Thank you, Fischer. She'll truly appreciate it, as do I. Come back whenever you want—I'm in your debt."

"I'll be sure to come back if I've forgotten anything." I held out the tray for Thomas, and he took the pastries with great care, placing them on the counter and staring at them as if he couldn't believe they were real. "Until next time, mate."

I made my way to the blacksmith, tray in one hand, my new cart in the other.

"Just offcuts?" the behemoth of a blacksmith asked.

"Yep! The thinnest metal offcuts you have lying around, and do you have any soap?"

He strode with purpose toward a shelf at the back, turning his head in passing toward who I assumed was his apprentice. "Duncan! Thin metal offcuts!"

"Aye, Fergus!"

The similar-sized apprentice had overheard our conversation so far, and his muscular form lumbered around the forge, picking up scraps and throwing them into a bucket he held.

Less than a minute later, Fergus placed the biggest tub of soap I'd ever seen on the counter, and Duncan presented his bucket of metal offcuts. I extended my hand and the blacksmith wrapped it in two meaty paws as he shook my arm with vigor.

"What's your name, lad?" Fergus asked.

"Fischer. Nice to meet you, mate. Fergus, right?"

"Come back anytime, Fischer," his deep voice rumbled as he nodded at my question. "It's been a pleasure doing business."

"Cheers, Fergus! The pleasure is all mine."

Watching the bear of a man gingerly pick up a pastry and split it in half with great care was a sight to behold. He passed one-half to Duncan, who licked the passiona jam timidly, then stuffed the whole thing into his mouth. His eyes went wide as saucers as he chewed the baked treat. Following his apprentice's lead, Fergus did the same. Their noises of joy and laughter were music to my ears as I carted my spoils back toward the furniture store.

After picking up the rods and balancing them atop the rest of my loot, I took a moment to rest in the shade, intending to eat one of the pastries. Before I could even pick it up, someone slammed into my side.

"Out of my way, peasant!"

CHAPTER TEN

THE FIRST ACT OF CREATION

I looked down at the man that had bounced off me ineffectually. He was tangled in his own robe, arms and legs lashing out as he tried to get to his feet.

Did he just try to knock me down . . . ?

The man stood, finally free of the tangle of cloth and limbs, glaring his hatred at me. I looked at the robe he wore, seeing the likeness of a lobster embroidered on the left side of his chest.

Ah, one of the cult blokes Barry warned me about.

I held out the tray of food. "Fancy a pastry, mate? You're not yourself when you're hungry."

His face twisted in a snarl. "Watch where you're going, peasant!"

Damn, this fella must be starving.

"Righto, mate. I think if you checked the instant replay, you'd find me standing still and you walking into me and falling over, making a proper dickhead of yourself."

"Fischer!"

I turned to see Maria walking toward me, her disgruntled father right behind her. "I felt bad leaving you so soon after you arrived in town." She gave me an apologetic smile. "How did it go with the property?"

"All sorted!" I smiled in return. "I'm now the proud owner of all the undeveloped land south of town."

"All of it?" She cocked her head. "That's a lot of land . . ."

Roger let out a condescending *hmmm* as he squinted at me. "Bad farming land, that."

A weak hand pulled my shoulder from behind—well, it tried to. I slowly spun to look at my lobster-robed assailant, raising an eyebrow at the man who'd only succeeded in pulling himself off balance.

His eyes went wide. "Y-you'll pay for this!" He turned and dashed away.

I was more entertained than annoyed as I watched him shooting me furtive, over-the-shoulder glances in his retreat.

Bloody cultists, man . . .

"What did you do to get Sebastian so worked up?" Maria watched the fleeing man with amusement. "He's a bit of a dick, but I've never seen him *that* worked up . . ."

I shrugged. "Couldn't tell ya. I was just trying to have a snack when he came out of nowhere and ran into me."

Remembering what Roger said, I turned to him. "You're right, mate. My land *is* terrible land for farming." I gave him a wink. "Fantastic fishing land, though!"

The older man's scowl deepened, and before he could call me heretical, foolish, or some combination of both, I held out my tray to him and his daughter.

"Pastry?"

"Oooooh, yes please," Maria said, grabbing one without a second thought.

"No." Roger crossed his arms. "I don't break bread with heretical fools."

There it is.

Maria bit into it, her eyebrows coming together in confusion before shooting up in surprise. She slowly chewed, savoring every moment. She swallowed with a rapturous expression. "Is . . . is this . . ."

"Passiona-jam pastries from Lena's—courtesy of our village lord."

Roger's eyes went wide, and I could see a war of conflicting emotions being waged upon his face.

"Take one," I said with a laugh, jiggling the tray at him. "Call it a gift for telling me your war stories yesterday. I'm not even having one, so you wouldn't be breaking bread with this *heretical fool*."

"I guess I could accept *one* . . ."

He snatched the pastry like it might bite him. As he slowly sunk his teeth into it, I witnessed the war on his face come to an abrupt end; nothing could stand before the overwhelming power of baked goods.

"Thank you, Fischer . . ." Maria was staring down at the rest of her pastry with awe-filled eyes. "I don't know if I can ever repay this kindness."

"You're welcome. The look on both your faces is payment enough."

She turned to her father, who was taking small bites and looking everywhere but at me.

"Dad?"

He looked at her, then at me, feigning ignorance.

She glowered at him. "*Dad* . . ."

He gave in. "Thank you, Fischer," he mumbled. "I guess you're not so bad for a—"

She tapped him on the nose, cutting him off. "Just a thank you is enough." She rolled her eyes and turned to me. "Really, thank you. We'd never be able to afford anything this lavish." She punctuated her statement by taking a bite, and when the passiona hit her tongue, her eyes rolled into the back of her head with exaggerated delight.

"You're *both* very welcome." I shot Roger another wink, which brought on a scowl, but it quickly disappeared when Maria threatened to smack him.

I chuckled at the pair. "What are you two doing, anyway? I thought you'd be out in your fields."

"Well," she said around a mouthful before swallowing. "We were going to get lunch, but you sorted that out for us. Should we get back to the fields, Dad?"

"Aye, I feel refreshed. Let's get back out there and finish up early."

I waved goodbye and set off home.

* * *

Sweat poured from Sebastian's body as he turned a corner and leaned his back against the cool stone wall. *I found him.*

He hadn't been sure after running into the man; maybe he was just a particularly strong peasant. After hearing he'd arrived in the village yesterday, and after trying to turn his shoulder, though, Sebastian was positive.

He's the cultivator that my device has been detecting. What is he doing here? Why has a man of such power been allowed to leave the confines of the royal palace?

Sebastian had spent weeks walking around the capital with that device—none of the cultivators present had set it off.

He scoffed. *As if any of those fools could actually be called cultivators. This man, though, this 'Fischer' . . . the device had picked up his presence, meaning he was taking steps toward the stairs of ascension. If he isn't at the base of the stairwell already . . .*

He clenched his fists as resolve steeled itself in his mind.

I have to find out more about this man, and if necessary, will need to snuff him out—there can be no ascension other than that of the great Leviathan.

I searched the rows of sugarcane on the border of my property for my quarry, but it was my quarry that found me.

"Hey, Fischer!" Paul yelled, running up to me with youthful exuberance.

"G'day, Paul! I was just looking for you!"

The boy smiled up at me. "You were?"

I grinned back then got down to a knee and gave him a conspiratorial glance. "I have a mission for you."

His eyes danced, and he leaned in closer. "What . . . what is it?"

"Well, your dad said you own the surrounding farmland with your family, right?"

"Right. Me, my parents, my auntie, cousins, and grandparents—we all farm it together. Why? Do you need me to keep an eye out for something?"

I laughed as the boy leaned in further, physically drawn by the prospect of a secret mission.

"Nothing so secretive, mate." I held out my final two pastries. "I was hoping you could share this with your family."

"Really? They'd love that! Are you sure it's okay?"

"I'm sure, mate. Your mission is for all of them to have a taste."

"Thanks, mister Fischer!" The boy took the tray and disappeared into the rows of cane without a second glance.

There were two reasons for giving away my last pastries. The first was that it couldn't hurt to ingratiate myself to the people sharing a border with my domain. The second and most important, was that it brought me joy to share the scarce taste with people who'd likely never experienced it before.

I tasted literally everything money could buy in my previous life. The donuts are nice, sure, but I've tasted more Michelin-starred food than I can even recall. Let the farmers experience something new.

A grin spread across my face as I trudged back home, my cart and equipment in tow.

Besides . . . I'll be eating flame-grilled fish before the day is through.

Sitting on my front deck, I took three of the smallest hooks out. With my file in hand, I shaved off the nail end—there was a lip between the nail and the hook section that would lay flat against the wall when hammered into it, which I left on. I sharpened the hook ends carefully, taking my time to ensure a sharp point. Next, I cut small lengths of the different colored strings, making them just a little longer than the length of the hooks.

Sorting through the different metal offcuts I'd procured from the blacksmith, I picked three of the smallest ones, using the hammer to bend a lip at the base, then fold a ninety-degree angle lengthwise.

With the hammer and single large nail, I pounded a small hole in the lip I'd created in the metal's base, just small enough for the hook to slip through.

When I pushed the thin bits of metal over the hooks, they ran halfway from the base toward the tips. I took the colorful cuts of string, tying them in place so they held the metal sleeves against the base of the hooks. The threads of string protruded past the sharpened tips, hiding them.

I ran a single line of leader from one of the smaller poles and tied a rock to the end to act as a sinker. Then, I made three drop rigs of thinner fishing line running from the main one, all of which had my makeshift hooks on the end.

I held up my fantasy-world version of a sabiki rig, smiling at my creation. I'd decided my first course of action was to create simple jigs and see what baitfish were present along the shores of the ocean and river. The small, multicolored strings would entice fish to have a bite, and the strips of metal would act as a mirror for the sunlight, imitating the reflective scales of their prey.

A pulse grabbed my attention, and I rolled my eyes, knowing what would come next.

[Error: Insufficient power. Superfluous systems offline.]

Yeah, cheers System—I'll keep that in mind. I shook my head at the annoying prompt as I headed for the shore.

A cool breeze tickled my skin as I found a good place to cast my line. I walked along the rock of the headland—my headland—as I looked for a spot I thought would hold fish.

There was a calm patch right on the edge, a sheer drop of the rock's surface leading into an aqua-colored pool that faded into the deep blue of the ocean. With no small amount of anticipation, I cast my line.

The rock I'd attached slowly sank to the bottom, and I felt the soft thud of it hitting the sandy floor. One breath. Two breaths. Three breaths, and I felt the tug of a fish on the line. I pulled it up slowly, remembering the lesson I'd learned on the jetty in a previous life. I flung the sinker onto the rocks and smiled down with glee.

All three hooks had a small fish attached, about the length of my palm. I dipped my bucket into the ocean, filling it halfway with water before putting it on a flat section of rock. I placed the three fish inside, taking care to not get spiked by any of their fins.

[Error: Insufficient power. Superfluous systems offline.]
[Error: Insufficient power. Superfluous systems offline.]

"Oh my god!" I said aloud. "Can you just let me have a moment? These are the first fish I've caught here!"

I looked down at the three fish swimming in the bucket. They resembled sardines, but a little fatter. They were a silvery blue from above as they swam around in the salty water. I looked closer at one, and I felt something tug at me. My eyes lost focus.

Juvenile Shore Fish
Common
Found along the ocean shores of the Kallis Realm, this fish is a staple source of both food and bait.

My vision refocused as I dismissed the words.

"What the fuck?"

CHAPTER ELEVEN

AWAKENING

I stared down at the bucket of fish, reeling from the sensation of having the System show me something actually useful. *Why had it only let me do that with the juvenile shore fish?* I'd looked at plenty of things since arriving in this world, but something about the fish I'd caught had drawn me in. It felt natural, not at all jarring or forced.

This . . . this is fucking awesome!

I cast my line in the same spot again, and after another few breaths, reeled in another two fish. I felt the same sensation as before when I focused on the fish.

Juvenile Shore Fish

Common

Found along the ocean shores of the Kallis Realm, this fish is a staple source of both food and bait.

My eyes cleared, and I laughed in delight. I moved to the left, further toward the beach. When the stone of the headland ended and the sand of the shore was between my toes, I cast my line out again. I waited longer this time, but sure enough, the familiar tug came. I pulled in another juvenile shore fish, adding it to my bucket with a sense of joy.

I cast out again, and when I pulled in the line after another tug, I noticed movement in the water. Something large trailed the two fish on my hooks, and I leaned in with interest, trying to make out what it was. As it walked almost onto the shore, I saw a crab the size of my head. Seizing the opportunity, I pulled the fish in slowly, luring the crab closer to me.

With shaking hands and building anxiety, I pounced. I grabbed the crab by the back swimmers, making sure its no-doubt massive claws couldn't get a hold of me. Its legs scrambled as I pulled it from the water, my rod discarded and forgotten behind me as I held the crustacean high.

Crab and lobster had always been some of my favorite foods, and my mouth watered at the thought of crab for dinner—but then I noticed something disconcerting. The crab had no claws, its sockets empty where they'd once been.

"Oh, you poor thing . . ."

It had clearly been in the wars, having lost both its claws to a predator or another crab. There was a large scar where one of its eyestalks should be, and the carapace had healed over long ago.

I immediately felt guilty for having ambushed the thing. No wonder it had walked so close to the shore—it would be next to impossible to hunt without its claws, and the fish I dragged past it must have been too tempting a meal to pass up.

I walked over to my discarded line, throwing one of the fish into my bucket, and putting the other on the ground. I removed a nail from the pouch at my hip, humanely dispatching the fish with a single movement.

I walked back to the water, the crab in one hand, the dead fish in the other. I lowered both into the softly lapping water, placing the fish right in front of the crab and taking slow steps backward from it.

The crab didn't run. It froze on the spot, likely trying to play dead or pretend to be a rock. After only a moment, it shuffled up the fish I'd left there, using two forelegs to hold it in place as it started eating.

"Sorry, mate," I whispered, not wanting to spook the thing. "No use kicking you while you're down. You go have some babies and fill the waters with tasty crabs!"

The crab didn't respond, but the System was as chatty as ever.

[Error: Insufficient power. Superfluous systems offline.]

I rolled my eyes but then felt the crab drawing my attention.

Rock Crab
Uncommon
Found along the ocean shores of the Kallis Realm, this crab is prized for its sweet flesh and subtle taste.

Sweet flesh and subtle taste, you say? I felt my mouth water again. *If I find a healthy one, I'm gonna find out firsthand. Maybe I need to craft some crab pots eventually . . .*

I worked my way back along the shore, splashing some fresh oxygenated water in my bucket of fish. I caught three more of the juvenile shore fish before walking toward the banks of the river.

The river's waters were deep at the mouth, and I looked for a suitable spot to cast my line. The tide was heading out, flooding fresh water out into the bay before me. I found a place protected from the fast-flowing water by two outcroppings of rock. I cast the line out, and I waited with bated breath. I'd already caught so many fish today, but the thought of catching a new species in the brackish water where the ocean and river met filled me with excitement.

Tug.

Tug. Tug.

I pulled the line up, once more swinging my makeshift sinker onto the shore. There were two fish on my line, both new species.

One was a small black-and-white striped thing that had large barbs protruding from each fin.

Widow's Vengeance
Rare
Found in the brackish waters of the Kallis Realm, the poison of this fish is harvested for use in alchemical creations of an odious nature.

Yeah, that's a no from me. Fuck that noise. I grabbed the pliers from my pouch, carefully grabbing the fish by its lip and jiggling it off the hook. I carefully lobbed it as far from me as possible, and it hit the water with a splash.

I glanced down at the second fish, which looked similar to a tilapia. I took care to inspect it before touching, despite its harmless appearance.

Juvenile Cichlid
Common
Found in the fresh and brackish waters of the Kallis Realm, this fish is a staple source of both food and bait.

I picked the fish up, once more careful to not get spiked by any of its fins. I lowered it back into the water, feeling a sense of relaxation wash over me as it swam into the depths and out of sight. I only had a single bucket and didn't want to subject the freshwater fish to the salinity content of the water the shore fish were swimming in.

My stomach rumbled, and I realized how hungry I'd become after over an hour of fishing in the sun.

Surely one more cast couldn't hurt . . .

I picked up my rod, casting one more time before I went and crafted a fire. My sinker hit the surface of the water with a small splash. The running water of the river seemed to have stilled, meaning the tide was turning.

Tug.

Tug. Tug. Tug.

I pulled the line up, and as I was just about to swing it into the air, something heavy struck. The hit almost pulled the rod from my fingers, and my feet scrambled as I tried to steady myself. I tensed my core, and with a heavy swing, pulled whatever had hit my line clear of the water.

Two of the juvenile cichlids were on the highest of my two drop rigs, and on the third, a medium-sized eel thrashed and wound its long body over itself in an attempt to escape. I lowered it down to the rocks with care, doing my best to not hurt my catch. I bent down and inspected the wriggling eel.

Common Eel
Common
Found in the brackish waters of the Kallis Realm, this eel's flesh has high oil content and a strong scent, making it unpalatable food but excellent bait.

Damn, the System called it common twice. Did my boy dirty . . .

I released the two juvenile cichlids, and with the still-flopping eel attached to my rod in one hand, my bucket of juvenile shore fish in the other, I set off back to my house.

I held my hands over the flames of my campfire, relishing in the warmth it provided and the primal sense of satisfaction that flooded me.

"Thank god for that flint—I was getting seriously sick of starting fires by hand."

My brows furrowed in thought. *Wait . . . should I say thank the gods? This isn't Earth, after all . . .* I shook my head at myself. *Who cares? I have* fish!

My feast of gutted shore fish lay on a grill I'd retrieved from the kitchen, propped atop two large pots that held it far enough above the open flames to cook the fish without burning them.

After dispatching the eel, I'd wrapped it in a tea towel from the kitchen, then dipped it in the river. The water evaporating from the cloth would keep the eel inside cool, stopping it from spoiling prematurely.

The smell of the fish cooking was tantalizing, and I watched with growing impatience as the flesh curled above the heat of my campfire. I picked one up with my hands, juggling the piping-hot fish and blowing to cool it down. I pulled a section of meat off and the skin easily peeled away. Breathing around the hot mouthful, I chewed. The flavor exploded in my mouth, the small fibers of the fish making it seem to melt. The sense of accomplishment and the knowledge I'd caught the fish lent itself to the subtle flavor, making it possibly the most satisfying meal I'd ever experienced. All the expensive and exotic food I had in my previous life didn't compare; I'd *earned* this.

I ate the rest of the fish. The small bones I had to pick around did not impede the experience, rather slowing the process down, making me appreciate each bite all the more.

With the sun setting, I put the pots and grill aside before stoking my fire with more driftwood. I set off back toward town to collect my new clothes.

The crab ate every last bit of the fish it had found, even the bones and scales meticulously pulled into its mandible and pulped by the teeth in its stomach. As it digested the nutrients, a small light flashed from its body. A pop sounded, and it changed, two somethings extending from its body. Its single eyestalk looked at the two somethings with very un-crab-like curiosity. It moved the regrown claws with intention, testing the powerful muscles inside with an unfamiliar emotion. Words came to its newly formed consciousness, and it tasted them, chewing them just as it had the baitfish earlier.

Baitfish? Yes. Small fish. Tasty Fish.

Its entire body cocked to the side in thought, and it blew contemplative bubbles.

Human caught. Lifted. Let go. He gave fish . . . ?

It blew more bubbles, entirely overwhelmed by experiencing emotions of . . . *gratitude?*

A blur and a flash of silver.

Danger.

A predatory mouth filled with teeth and a carapace-crushing jaw darted for it, drawn in by the flash and pop it had emitted, intent on partaking of the crab's flesh. It held its claws out in a defensive stance it knew to be ineffectual; the fish was too large, its jaw too strong—the crab stood no chance before this predator.

Awareness. Fear. Danger. Run.

The crab had nowhere to hide; it sat in the unprotected waters of the shore.

Cannot hide—must fight.

The fish was on it within a second of the flash of silver, and the crab instinctively clacked its claws together, trying to fend off its doom. As the claws came together, they clamped on part of the fish, and sharp somethings shot out from each pincer. The eyestalk pondered the clouds of blood spreading from the dead attacker, one of the sharp somethings having split its head in two, the other severing the tail of its large assailant cleanly off.

Relief. Crab is safe.

No, not crab—I am safe. I am . . . strong?

It shrugged, a decidedly unfamiliar gesture, and grabbed the fish in both claws. The crab took a moment to blow bubbles of contentment as it looked at the giant source of food in its grasp. It recalled the time before awareness. Hunger. Fear. Pain. More hunger. It took a bite of the large fish, delighting in the crunch of its bones and the savory tang of its flesh as it continued to think.

I will not be hungry now. I eat.

The prey had become the predator.

No more fear—no more pain.

It took another bite, rather content with the situation.

CHAPTER TWELVE

GUARD CRAB

The sun was setting over the western mountains as I returned from town with a large bag of brand new clothes. I saw no one I recognized in my travels, the only people still out and about hurriedly finishing their last tasks for the day. I was glad I didn't have to stop and talk to anyone; I had an important task to return to.

I threw the clothes inside, put some more wood on the smoldering coals, and gathered the necessary equipment by the fire. I sharpened a large hook, not the largest, but that was understandable—the largest one I had could hold up curtain rods and looked large enough to hook a whale. I lost myself in filing the tip down, feeling a sense of urgency with the fading light, but knowing that rushing would only cause me to make a mistake.

When the tip was needle sharp, I filed off the nail end, putting it aside in my makeshift tackle box for use later. I got one of the larger rods, tied the thick line to it, and made another drop rig at the end. I tied a large rock in place, something that would hold its position well in the strong current of the river. I cut a slab off the eel, wet the tea towel with more water, and set off to the river, rod in hand, eel in the other, and the waning sunlight at my back. I slipped the eel slab onto the hook, pushing the top of the flesh over the jutting section of the hook, just as the fisherman had shown me in my past life with the worm.

Without a reel or flexible rod, I would have to throw the hook and sinker by hand, and I whirled it round and round with increasing velocity. Taking a deep breath of the salty dusk air, I smiled and released my line, sending the weight of the rock far out into the river.

The tide was coming in, and I aimed my cast toward the incoming water. The rock hit the water with a sizable splash and drifted further into the river as the weight of the water carried it.

With a soft thud and the line going taut, I knew it had reached the bottom. I watched the drift of the line, worried that the current would be too strong and sweep my bait into the shallows; it held fast, taking root on the river mouth's floor.

The eastern sky opposite the setting sun was a beautiful pink and blue, and my face settled into a wide smile as I waited patiently for a bite. Gulls and pelicans flew overhead, their wings spread wide as they rode the invisible currents of air.

"What a stunning place I've found myself in," I said aloud, my voice contending with the soft crashing of waves and calls of the birds above.

The sun continued to set, and just as it was nearing the point where it would be too dark to fish safely from the rocks, I felt a bite. It was an exploratory nibble, and I set my hands as I prepared for the fish at the other end of my line to take the bait.

Bump.

Bump.

Bump. Bump.

I waited, frozen in position, ready to strike.

Did it take the bait? I might have to—

The rod almost slipped from my fingers as the fish ate the hook and took off swimming. I leaned back, adrenaline spiking as I held onto the rod with all my might. It threatened to pull me off balance, but I bent my legs, leaning with the powerful tugs of its head as it tried to swim away.

It swam into the river mouth, and I ran with it, walking back from the rocky shore to keep the line taut.

"It's fucking *huge!*" I yelled, unable to keep a laugh from bubbling up after my words.

It swam back out of the river, making a mad dash for the ocean. I let it take some distance, walking with it to where the sand met the rocks. As I reached the rocks, I held fast, all too aware of the danger presented by the slick rocks now that I couldn't properly see. With my line drawn in the sand, and my feet planted in place, the fish pulled with all its might, and I stood still with all of mine.

The line snapped, and I fell on my ass with a loud *oof.* I lay in the cold sand, staring at the sky, and I roared with laughter. The fish had escaped, but I had done everything in my power, and it had defeated me. The curtain rods I was using as a fishing rod weren't ideal, and neither was my lack of a reel. It would have been a miracle had I landed a fish that size on such a primitive rod. That there were fish that large just waiting to be caught only filled me with more determination.

The thrill of the hunt had set in, and now it was just a matter of time. I smiled and watched the stars appearing in the sky.

I'll come back for you, ya big fishy bastard.

I collected the line and was surprised to find the rock still attached to the end. When I brought it by the light of the fire, I could see it had snapped off just above where the hook was attached. The line was frayed and damaged, and I suspected it had worn through where it touched the metal lip on the hook that was supposed to be a wall hanger.

Still quite full from the fish earlier, I gathered a handful of the berries from the bushes by the river, sitting in a chair by the fire as I ate them. I buried the tea towel-covered eel in the sand before going to bed, hoping that was enough to hide it from any would-be scavengers—if not, I'd just have to catch another.

The next day, I woke before the dawn. I stretched before getting out of bed, sorely missing my morning coffee and resolving to ask Barry about coffee or tea when I went and got my land documents from him.

I stepped out my front door, intending to go down to the river and wash my face, but froze mid-yawn at what I saw. Something had dug up my eel. The tea towel lay in the sand, discarded by the thief.

Well, I should have seen that coming.

Two clacks drew my attention, and I looked beside the campfire where they'd come from. A crab sat there, one claw raised in greeting and . . . waving? It waved again. Unsure if I was dreaming, I walked closer and saw a familiar scar on the crab's head. It was the crab from yesterday, the one I'd put back and given a fish to, but it now had two full claws—one of which was holding on to the last quarter of my eel.

Is that the same crab? There's no way it could have regrown its claws overnight . . . right?

I looked closer, and it was definitely the same one. The scar was identical. It waved again, more insistent after my lack of communication.

I stared my confusion at the crab, then waved back. "Uh, good morning?"

It nodded—actually nodded—and took another bite of my eel.

"You're the crab from yesterday, right?"

Another nod, and another bite.

"How did you grow your claws back?"

It hesitated, appearing to think, then it shrugged and took another bite.

I laughed. "What is up with this world?"

I sat down beside the crab, and it paused before offering me a bite of the eel.

"No thanks, little buddy. Would you mind saving me a bit, though? I was going to use it as bait."

It snipped the quarter that was left in half with a single *clack,* and I raised an eyebrow at the force that shot through the eel and hit the ground, sending sand flying.

Okay . . . if the sapience wasn't a dead giveaway, the aura attack just confirmed this isn't a normal crab.

"Do you have a name?"

It shook its carapace.

"Do you want a name?"

It paused, then blew bubbles in the affirmative. I don't know how I knew what the bubbles meant, but the cute little orbs blowing from its mouth definitely meant yes.

"Hmmm," I said as I stared at the scars on the crustacean who was helping itself to my bait. "You've definitely seen some battle, so something with a little edge to it. But you're also pretty cute, so your name needs to have some 'aww' factor."

The crab nodded in agreement.

I snapped my fingers. "Sergeant Snips!"

The crab—Sergeant Snips—nodded vigorously, blowing happy bubbles and snapping both their claws in delight.

"All right, Sergeant Snips it is. Are you gonna be staying around here, Snips? I technically own all this land, but I'm sure you've been here longer than me. You're more than welcome to hang out."

More happy bubbles.

I've always wanted a pet—I was expecting a dog or a cat, but hey, an aura-shooting sapient crab is pretty neat. Good defense, too.

"Wait, are you a girl, Snips? I'm picking up feminine vibes."

Affirmative bubbles.

"All right, good to know! I've gotta meet someone in town, Snips. You need anything?"

She shook her carapace, grabbed her portion of eel in one claw, and slowly retreated to the waters of the river—all the while waving her free claw at me.

I watched my new guard crab go, giving her a wave as she disappeared beneath the surface.

"Well, can't say I saw that one coming."

I walked over and picked up the section of eel left for me. The cut was clean, as if sliced by a laser cutter.

"Jesus. I'm glad we're on good terms—that's some serious slicing power."

I wrapped the eel in the tea towel, reburied it, and took off toward Barry's fields.

Barry was just heading to Fischer's place when the man found him.

"Fischer! Good morning! My family extended their thanks for the pastry yesterday—that was very kind."

"G'day, mate!" he said in his strange tongue. "No worries—happy to share. How'd the papers look, by the way? All ridgy-didge?"

Barry smiled at him, assuming he was asking if the paperwork was legally binding. "Aye, the papers all check out. The crown recognizes you as the owner of your land."

"Good stuff!" He took the papers, putting them away without looking them over. "Hey, Barry, do you have a moment to talk?"

Barry felt a spike of worry but nodded. He hadn't been suspicious of Fischer in the least—just the opposite, in fact. His wife, however, had expressed some concerns the previous evening.

"Who is this strange man, Barry? He comes from nowhere, speaks in a strange way, and showers us with gifts? What is he trying to get out of us?" she had asked.

"You right, mate?" Fischer asked, shaking Barry from his memories.

"Yeah, sorry." Barry gave him a strained smile. "Still waking up. What did you want to ask?"

Fischer sighed, and Barry's anxiety grew. "Here's the thing mate, I have a really odd question."

Was my wife right? Is he going to request something impossible now that he's ingratiated himself with us?

"Have you ever heard of anyone, uh . . ." Fischer scrunched his face, looking like the words pained him. "Have you ever heard of anyone getting strange messages from a System? Something about insufficient power, or the ability to inspect items?"

Barry felt his eyes go wide and his mouth drop open. "Fischer . . . have you experienced this?"

Seeing Barry's reaction, Fischer winced. "Would you believe me if I said no? Based on your reaction, I'm thinking it's not a good thing . . ."

"Do not tell anyone this, Fischer. No one. Not Paul, not my wife, not your own mother. This stays between us, understand?"

Fischer raised an eyebrow. "Uh, yeah, I mean I took a risk asking you because I trust you—I'm not going around yelling it from the rooftops, mate. What's the big deal, though?"

Barry shook his head with a sad smile. "Anyone receiving those messages is whisked off to the capital and confined. We've had people from this village taken, never to be seen again. The royals do something to those that show the spark of potential."

"The spark of potential? Jesus, mate, that's a lot. Thanks for letting me know."

Barry let out a weary sigh. "It's fine, Fischer. I'm sorry if I scared you, it just brought up some old memories better forgotten."

Fischer put a hand on his shoulder. "I'm the one that's sorry, mate. Someone you knew?"

"My wife's brother. We all owned our land together, and everything was going well until his spark awoke . . ." Barry trailed off in remembrance.

The speed at which they'd come, the superhuman power of the "cultivators," and their cold, lifeless eyes—each detail was unforgettable.

"Shit, I really am sorry, mate," Fischer said, breaking Barry from his thoughts. "Do you know what happened to him?"

"Nothing. We don't even know if he's dead or alive. The last few years have been hard on all of us, especially his wife."

"Well, if you need a hand, you know where to find me. I'm probably a useless farmer, but if you need a chinwag, I've got plenty of shores to fish from."

"Uh . . . chinwag?"

"Yeah, mate. A yarn. A chat. Same thing."

Barry laughed at Fischer's odd manner of speaking. "I'll keep that in mind."

"One more thing, Barry."

"Yes, Fischer?"

"Do you get many sapient, aura-blade shooting crabs around these parts, or is it just me?"

CHAPTER THIRTEEN

SAPIENT, AURA-BLADE SHOOTING CRAB

"Sergeant *Sniiiiiiiips!*" Fischer yelled, his hands held to his mouth as he projected his voice. Barry's morning so far had been a roller coaster of emotions. He'd started the morning with a wariness of his new neighbor fueled by his wife's suspicions, swiftly had that replaced by a desire to help the man when he revealed his spark, then just as quickly realized that Fischer had a disease of the mind.

"I swear she was just here," the madman said as he walked along the coast of his shoreline.

Maybe everyone would be better off if I let someone know about his spark of potential . . .

"I really should get back to my family, Fischer. I missed the sunrise, and they'll be getting worried—"

"There you are, you little scamp!" Fischer walked down to the water, leaning in. "I see your little peeper hiding there, Snips. I brought a friend to see you."

A small stream of bubbles floated to the surface in front of Fischer, and Barry leaned in to see what was causing it.

"Don't be like that, Snips," Fischer said with a laugh. "He's a trustworthy bloke, there's no need to be nervous."

Barry walked down beside Fischer, tentatively peering where the bubbles had risen. A single eye broke the surface of the water, gazing intently at him. Barry took an involuntary step back as he made out the body of a large crab beneath the eye.

"Sergeant Snips!" Fischer admonished with a tone you'd use on a petulant child. "It's rude to stare at guests, at least come out and say hello. He won't bite."

Barry felt his jaw drop open as the crab—Sergeant Snips—slowly walked out onto the beach. Sergeant Snips clacked her claws at him, streaming bubbles from the mouth.

"Snips says hello."

"H-hello?" Barry turned to Fischer. "You . . . you understand it?"

"Yeah—wait, you don't?"

"No, Fischer. Not in the slightest." Barry stared down at the being, implications running rampant through his mind. "This crab has taken a step—"

It snapped its claws loudly and cut him off, blowing a slew of bubbles.

Fischer cocked his head. "She wants to be called by her name, not 'it' or 'crab,' I think."

"O-of course. Sorry. I think *Sergeant Snips* has taken a step on the path of ascension."

"Yeah, I gathered as much. Is that a common thing?"

"Not at all." Barry stared down at the being with unconcealed wonder. "The Cult of Carcinization would lose their minds over this . . ."

"I probably don't need to say this," Fischer said, "but this stays between us, yeah? I don't want her subjected to any experimentation or culty bullshit."

A sharp *clack* sounded, and sand sprayed against Barry's legs. He looked down, seeing a medium-sized hole in the sand before him.

"Snips!" Fischer put his hands on his hips and stared down at her. "We don't threaten friends!"

Sergeant Snips dipped her head, blowing a slow stream of bubbles.

Fischer turned to Barry. "She says she's sorry."

"Uh, that's okay . . . and no, I won't say anything—this can stay between us."

Fischer nodded sharply, as did Sergeant Snips. "I know, but I appreciate you confirming it anyway." Fischer looked out at the sea and the sun rising above it. "She deserves a peaceful life just as much as the rest of us."

"I—I'm not sure you understand how monumental this is, Fischer." Barry shook his head minutely, unbelieving of what he was seeing. "For a creature to take even this small step . . . I didn't even know it was possible following the gods' betrayal."

Fischer smiled at him. "Yeah, I kinda picked up on that, but there's no use stressing about it—she's here, and she's friendly, that's all that really matters. She's gonna be staying on my—well, our land—for the foreseeable future."

How is he so calm about this? Does he truly comprehend the meaning of this crab's existence?

"Anyway, thanks for your discretion, Barry—and the info." Fischer gave him a genuine smile. "I don't want to worry your family by keeping you here too long, so if you've gotta get back, that's all good."

"Y-you're welcome, Fischer. I'd better be getting back to them." He turned, but paused, turning back to the being behind him. "It was nice meeting you, Sergeant Snips."

She nodded and blew some bubbles.

"She said it was nice meeting you too . . . I think."

Barry retreated as fast as possible without showing his urgency. He couldn't help but let his gaze linger on the crab waving goodbye with a raised pincer as he left.

What in Odin's good eye have I gotten myself into?

"I think that went pretty well," I said to Sergeant Snips as she waved goodbye to Barry. She bubbled her agreement.

I had taken Barry's measure, and deeming him trustworthy, had asked him about the odd System notifications and my ability to inspect fish. It was a gamble letting the farmer know of Sergeant Snips's existence, but I figured if he already held my fate in his hands by knowing of the "spark of potential" I possessed, whatever that was, knowing of my violently capable pet crab would only further dissuade him from telling anyone.

I bent down and rubbed the top of Sergeant Snips's carapace. "Just make sure you stay hidden from anyone else, all right? It wouldn't do to have the whole village learning about you."

She leaned into my petting, clearly enjoying the sensation.

"Are you up to anything, Snips? I have something to search for in the forest, and I think your sharp little digits might help."

She nodded and blew happy bubbles, gesturing with both claws toward the trees.

"All right! Let's get searching!"

I found the sound of Sergeant Snips's scuttling legs comforting as we made our way across the sands and into the forest. Her single eye never stopped roaming, and she seemed to enjoy the beauty of the day as much as I did.

"I'm looking for a plant or tree with long, straight, flexible limbs. Have you seen anything like that?"

She paused, taking a few moments to think before blowing unsure bubbles.

"You only recently gained the power you have, right? You seemed like a regular ol' uncommon rock crab when I gave you that fish yesterday . . ."

She nodded vigorously, happy that I understood her predicament.

"No worries, Snips! We'll just have to search for it together. I don't actually know if we can find what I'm looking for, but it's a beautiful morning for a stroll, isn't it?"

She clacked her claws and blew bubbles of agreement.

We walked along the riverbank, taking in the sights of the forest. The trees were mostly the same as the ones I'd already noted in this world, but I did see a few different species: one with a deep amber trunk, and another with an almost blue sheen to it. I stored their location in my mind, keen as I was on checking them out later.

When we reached what I thought was the border of my territory, we made a right angle and walked north. There was no reason to not check outside the bounds of my property, but I hadn't yet explored the forest that was mine.

A buzzing caught my attention, and I followed the noise, hoping it meant what I thought it did. My search was rewarded when we came upon a tree with a hollow in the trunk, the gap filled with honeycomb and a stream of bees flying in and out of the hive.

Sergeant Snips stared up at the anomaly, cocking her head back and forth in a decidedly adorable manner.

"They're called bees, Snips," I said with a laugh. "They make something called honey—humans love it, but I'm not sure if the sweet taste will agree with you."

She blew bubbles of interest, her beady eye watching the coming and going of the insects with great curiosity.

"They're actually quite similar to you, Snips. They have an exoskeleton just like your carapace, a segmented body, and jointed appendages."

This only amplified the curiosity, and her claws slowly opened and closed as she stared at them.

She really is intelligent. It must be an incredibly alien experience to suddenly gain sapience.

I smiled as I realized it wasn't so dissimilar to my situation—we were both exploring a strange new world.

I bent down and scratched the top of her body. "Let's keep going, Snips. The bees will be here if you want to come back and watch them, and I promise to give you a taste of their honey one day."

She nodded, her eye still glancing back at the stream of arriving and departing insects as we walked further north. Only a few hundred meters later, we came upon just what I'd been looking for.

"That's it!" I ran toward the large thicket sprouting skyward before us. "I can't believe we actually found it, Snips!"

She clacked excitedly, feeding off my enthusiasm.

I'd been looking for something similar to bamboo—a long, flexible, and strong basis for a fishing rod. Instead, I'd found the real thing. The patch of bamboo before us had shoots of every size, and I marveled at the larger ones with stems as wide as my arm and over seven meters tall.

"Imagine the rod I could craft with that sucker, Snips!"

Though I doubted she knew what I was talking about, she still bubbled her excitement back at me.

"All right," I said. "Could you snip this one, this one, and that one, and . . ." I indicated seven of the bamboo shoots, settling on the lucky number.

I can always come back for more later.

She scuttled over and cut the ones I'd shown, the wooden fibers standing no chance against her empowered claws. With six different rods over my shoulder, and one that Sergeant Snips insisted on carrying held in one of her claws, we set off back toward home.

My defense crab waved her goodbye as she slipped beneath the surface of the river. Waving back, I shook my head at what life had become. "This world is something else . . ."

Walking around the side of my house, I set most of the rods on the back deck to dry out. I wasn't actually sure if they'd function better when fresh or dried, but I intended to find out. I took two of the fresh rods with me as I walked around to my chairs. Collecting the makeshift tackle box and my smaller rod I'd used to catch fish yesterday, I got to work. I cut the line from the curtain rod, retying it to the tip of the bamboo one. I tested the strength of it, bending it back and forth with no small amount of force. It held, and I knew it would be more than enough to handle the smaller fish.

Maybe not for the eel, though . . .

It was still a crude construction, but I had plans to bring it closer to the technological level of rods on Earth. As with all things, though, it would take time.

"For now," I said, "I think I'll catch a late breakfast."

* * *

Sebastian glanced over his shoulder as he made his way through the northern streets of Tropica. He'd abandoned his cult garb for this mission; a plain brown cloak with a hood hiding his features draped his form as he neared the destination. He turned a corner, sighting the opulent house.

He stepped through the side gate of the property, handling the metal latch with care to not make too much noise. He walked along the house and around the back, coming to a room that was clearly a later addition to the building. Its construction was crude when compared to the house it clung to, its stone-and-mortar build more akin to the structures the peasants of the village used for their dwellings.

He knocked on the wooden door with the designated rhythm. *Tap-taptaptap-tap.*

"Come in," a soft voice said.

Sebastian opened the door slowly, and a sickly sweet smell rushed out to greet him. The inside of the room was dim; his eyes needed a moment to adjust. When they did, he saw all manner of dried plants hanging from the walls, different vials and distilling equipment atop drawers at the back of the room, and a single hunched figure swirling the contents of a cauldron atop a workbench before him.

"What brings you to the Cult of the Alchemist, Leviathan child?"

Sebastian felt the grimace cross his face but made no effort to hide it. It had surprised him when his contact back in the capital informed him of the alchemy cult's presence in Tropica, but he had no issue making use of the misguided fool across from him.

"I require a tincture, Alchemist *child.*" He spat the last word, throwing the insult right back at him. "Something of deadly potency."

"Deadly?" The alchemist raised his head, revealing a face filled with wrinkles and bearing a wicked grin. "Such things can be arranged . . . for the right recompense."

"Name your price, *alchemist.*" Again, he spat the last word, unwilling to suppress his disdain. "I have as little desire to spend time in each other's presence as you do."

The man chuckled in response, the noise sounding wet and wrong. "No need for such insults, child. I no more hate you than I hate the flies that buzz around my concoctions. We all have our place in this world—after all, do you not have a use for me?"

Sebastian slammed two silver coins on the bench in front of him—a substantial sum—wanting this interaction to be over as soon as possible. "I need a single dose for a single man."

The alchemist eyed the coins before lazily reaching out and grasping them. "And what has this man done to deserve such an end?" He slid the coins into his pocket. "While what you request will deliver a finality, it is not a kind way to go."

Sebastian snarled. "It is the concern of the Cult of the Leviathan."

The hooded figure looked at Sebastian for a long moment. He turned, opened a drawer, and grabbed something with serpentine sluggishness. At the same pace, he slid the small vial over to Sebastian. Sebastian snatched it and strode out the door without another word.

Neither the touch of the cool breeze nor the smell of fresh air registered as he strode back toward his headquarters, consumed as his thoughts were.

For his heresy, Fischer deserves a torturous death.

CHAPTER FOURTEEN

COFFEE

I sat in the shade of my porch, delighting in the meal of fish I'd just indulged in. *A perfect late breakfast, if I do say so myself.*

I felt tired, my brain sluggish, but my synapses fired enough for a moment of clarity to strike.

"Shit! I forgot to ask Barry about caffeine!" No wonder I was so tired. What is a morning without coffee—or at the very least, a hot cup of tea?

"How ya doing, Barry?" The man was so focused on his farm work he jumped at my words. "Woah, sorry mate. Didn't mean to spook you."

Barry's face was white, his eyes daunted. "O-oh, sorry, Fischer. My head was elsewhere. I'm doing good. How are you?"

Sheesh, I'll have to make some noise before I say g'day next time. He looks like he's seen a ghost.

"Yeah, I'm good Barry. I had another question for you."

Barry swallowed. "What is it?"

"Do you guys have coffee around here? Or tea?"

The farmer visibly relaxed. "Tea is plentiful, and there's a coffee shop on the north side of the village, but it's a little expensive . . ."

I rolled my eyes. "Same situation as the passiona husk? Is it genetically modified to not reproduce?"

"No, actually." He leaned on his hoe. "But it *is* heavily regulated. Coffee is one of our kingdom's main exports, and after genetic engineering led to poisonings or some such scandal, the kingdom cracked down and made it illegal to grow unless you have a permit."

I made to laugh at Barry's joke, but at seeing his serious demeanor, quickly pressed my lips together in a frown. "You're serious about it poisoning people?"

"Yes. It killed quite a few noble sons if the rumors are to be believed, but I don't really know all the details as truth."

I rubbed my chin. *Could be an elaborate hoax, set up to commoditize coffee and drive up the price . . .*

I sighed, fearing the information I was about to request. "The beans are super expensive, aren't they?"

Barry nodded with a grimace. "The merchant that comes once a month sells the beans for an extortive price unless you have an agreement with the crown. I don't know the details, but I've seen the noble lady with a coffee shop on the north side of Tropica buy them for cheaper than our food supplies."

I shook my head in dismay. "Tea is good, but nothing beats a good coffee. I'll see what I can do."

Barry raised an eyebrow. "You'll see what you can do? What do you mean?"

"You let me take care of that, mate." I shot him a wink. "See ya later, Barry."

"Uh, yeah, bye Fischer . . ."

I strode toward the village. If not for the kingdom's monopolization of beans, coffee would be easily accessible to everyone. All you needed was ground beans and water—not even hot water. One of my favorite types of coffee from my previous life was cold brew, and I'd often made it for myself at home, finding the brewing method relaxing, meditative.

No coffee for the common folk? How can I stand by and allow such oppression of the working class?

George's thoughts had been a mess since Fischer's arrival, and he was taking solace in his first lunch of the day, allowing the contrast of sweet and savory pastries to whisk his troubled mind to a place of comfort. A loud knock came from his front door, and a spike of dread sheared through his peace like a knife through freshly toasted buns.

"Want me to get it, love?" His wife waddled over and massaged his shoulders. He leaned into the soft touch of her well-fed form.

"Not at all." He kissed her hand. "It is a man's job to deal with the rabble—you enjoy first lunch, dear."

He walked down his stairs with care, holding the railings with butter-slick hands. Pausing before the door, he took a moment to catch his breath before opening the portal. When it swung open, the dread he'd been fighting off slammed into him.

"G'day George. How are ya, mate?"

"F-Fischer, hello." He wiped the sweat from his brow. "I'm well, and you?"

"Good, thanks! I had a suggestion for you, though."

A suggestion? What plans has he put in place since I last saw him . . . ?

"Er—of course, Fischer. What was it?"

"I came to ask about coffee."

"Uh . . . coffee?"

"Right. Coffee. I know that a noble lady purchases coffee for a reasonable price." Fischer leaned in. "Is there any way I can get that same discount for some beans?"

George felt his considerable jowls quiver. *He dares test my loyalty to the crown? The audacity!* "Unfortunately," he said, with deliberate pronunciation, "the decreased rate is only available to those that purchase a coffee machine from the capital. Lena has such a machine, which is why she can purchase the beans at a decreased price."

Fischer's eyebrow twitched in annoyance, confirming George's suspicions. *He was trying to trip me up! Oh, Fischer, my intellect is too vast for you to comprehend. You think I'd fall prey to such an obvious trap?*

"Of course," Fischer said. "The coffee machines are quite expensive, aren't they?"

With his victory over the crown agent, some of George's anxiety was washed away by the crushing weight of his superiority. "Naturally. The cheap beans are an incentive to buy one of the marvels created by the capital."

"Well, I assume as the lord of the village, you take a percentage of income as tax, right?"

George's perceived sense of superiority dissolved and sweat sprouted from his forehead again.

"Y-yes . . ." *So he is here for the taxes. I knew he had nefarious intentions. Oh, Fischer, you devious man, you scoundrel of the worst degree—*

"Well," Fischer said, interrupting his panic. "If the farmers were more productive, that would increase the yield of the village, right?"

What games does he play? What layered scheme is unfolding before me?

"It would mean that, yes," George said tentatively. "What is your suggestion?"

"Coffee."

"*. . . coffee?*"

"Right." Fischer nodded. "Coffee would improve the work output of the villagers, but from what I can tell, there's only a single shop that sells it on the north side of town, and it's too expensive for the common folk."

"W-well, yes, of course. It is an expensive drink for the upper crust—"

"That's no good, mate." Fischer shook his head. "Where I come from, it's an affordable commodity, and I think you'd see a significant improvement of the village's monetary output if it was accessible to all."

George paled, and he dabbed his forehead with a handkerchief. "It-it's not so simple—the cost of purchasing a coffee machine alone . . ."

"Think of it as an investment. You could even use some of the gold I gave you, right?"

After giving me explicit instructions not to spend the coin? What trap is he attempting to land me in?

"Anyway," Fischer said in his always demanding tone, "it's only a suggestion. If you were to pay the cost of a machine for one of the existing stores in town, namely Sue's bakery, she should be able to afford the beans and could pass on the savings to the rest of the villagers. It'd improve morale, output, and overall, the wealth of the village."

"What—what of the cost? It is no small thing."

Fischer waved the question away. "You could just use a bit of the funds already taken as tax and use it to generate even more income. What do you think?"

The statement was all the confirmation George needed that the capital agent before him knew of the gold he'd been skimming from the taxes.

"Y-you're right, Fischer." He plastered a smile on his face, trying to hide his distress. "That's a fantastic idea. I can—I *will* make the arrangements immediately."

George slammed the door, his significant weight leaning against it as he slid down to the floor. His head was swimming, and if he stood any longer, he may just faint. He lay down, staring at the ceiling as he tried to calm his breathing.

By the prosperous womb of Ceto, how will I extract myself from this mess?

* * *

Poor George, I thought as I walked back to Sue's bakery. *How did a man with such debilitating social anxiety end up the lord of a village? The bloke can't even talk to me without breaking into a sweat and becoming a stammering mess.*

The thought was fleeting, and I felt a broad smile spread over my face. The negotiations were successful, and it was only a matter of time before coffee was a mainstay for the south siders of Tropica.

"Good news, Sue!" I said as I approached her shopfront. "George agreed, and the equipment is being organized!"

Sue's motherly smile froze in place, and her eyebrows formed a vertical line between them.

"You're . . . you're serious?"

"Yep! All you'll have to do is offer the coffee at the agreed price of one copper." I winked at her. "I assume my coffee and snack deal is still good?"

"Of course! You can have all the free food and coffee you can handle if you're serious. You are serious, *right?* Don't mess with me, Fischer."

"I'm serious," I said with a laugh. "Mind if I grab a pastry now?" I pointed at a baked good that looked like a croissant. "That one there is calling to me."

"You can have every single one of them!"

"Just one will do. Thank you, though."

With a practiced motion, she swept the treat into a paper bag and handed it to me.

I contemplated everything I'd done and learned this morning as I sat in the shade with my delightful little pastry. First and foremost was that George responds to pressure. The monetary gain didn't seem to sway him at all, but with just a little leaning on my part, he'd caved and agreed. While my coffee goals were initially selfish, I really did want it to be accessible to everyone—it seemed like a travesty for the beans to be too expensive for the average person.

I'll have to keep that in mind going forward if I see ways I can improve the lives of the citizens of Tropica. I may be here for fishing, but that doesn't mean I won't step in when I can improve the lives of those around me. If nothing else, it would make people like me more—which I sorely need, given my heretical ways.

I took a bite of the fantasy croissant, raising an eyebrow at the flaky, buttery insides. *Damn—that's good.*

Another notable thing I'd learned came from Sue—she patiently explained the currency system, something I'd managed to avoid so far with my use of whole gold pieces and pastry bargaining chips.

There were copper, iron, silver, and gold pieces, converting up at a ten-to-one ratio. My use of one gold to purchase my land meant that I'd paid the equivalent of one thousand one-copper coffees—an absolute steal if you asked me, even if George had hustled me on the price.

Speaking of money, I had a terrible truth to confront: as much as I'd wanted to avoid doing anything other than fishing, I needed coin. Selling fish seemed unfeasible for the time being, considering it was heresy to live off the sea. I'd have to compromise if I wanted to do all the cool things I had planned for my fishing endeavors and property both.

Getting to my feet, I put the last bit of croissant in my mouth. I walked around the corner to thank Sue but stepped right into an ambush.

"There he is!" Sue said, pointing at me. "Go ask him about it!"

Maria, Roger, and Fergus, the blacksmith, turned their heads to me.

Fergus was the first to reach me, taking powerful strides. "Is it true?" he demanded.

"Er, is what true, mate?"

"The coffee! You're really giving Sue a coffee machine?"

"Uh, I mean technically George is, but yeah, she's getting a coffee machine."

The behemoth of a man laughed and clapped my shoulders. "I could kiss you, Fischer!" His eyes danced, and I thought he might actually kiss me for a moment. "I had coffee once as a gift when I finished my apprenticeship—I've never forgotten the taste or feeling but haven't been able to justify the cost of buying it!"

"You're starting to make me suspicious, Fischer," Maria said in a joking tone as she walked over. "You've done nothing but good since you arrived—what's the catch?"

"No catch," I said with a laugh. "Can't a guy just do good by his neighbors?"

Roger's scowl said *No, you can't,* but he remained silent.

"First the passiona pastries, now this?" Despite his size, Fergus was the personification of an excited child. "I don't think I can ever repay you . . ."

"About that, Fergus—I was about to come see you after thanking Sue for the lovely meal I just had."

"Oh, what about?"

Unbidden, my oldest nemesis returned.

[Error: Insufficient power. Superfluous systems offline.]

I wiped the sweat from my brow as I dismissed the unwelcome harassment.

"Are you sure you've never worked bellows before, Fischer?"

I stopped pumping, looking over at Fergus. Both he and Duncan, his apprentice, gaped at me with odd expressions.

"Yeah, why's that?"

"Because you're working that thing like a seasoned pro," Duncan said, still staring.

I glanced down at the pump and the forge it was attached to, not seeing the big deal. Sure, it was physical work, but it seemed straightforward enough for me. I'd expected it to be hotter too, but the heat radiating from the forge was almost cleansing.

"I'm just pumping." I shrugged. "You two are doing the actual work."

Fergus shook his head with a smile. "Maybe so, but thanks to you we'll finish today way ahead of schedule, even after making the cages you requested. You're sure that's all you want?"

I nodded. "That's all I need for now, mate. I wouldn't say no if you let me trade time on the bellows for more smithing in the future, though."

He roared a laugh. "I'd be a madman to turn that down with the speed we're getting things done!"

"Well, let's get back to it then." I resumed pumping the bellows. "I think you fellas deserve an early finish."

A few hours later, I was walking out of the smithy with seven cages piled atop each other.

"Er, you're sure you're all right with those, Fischer?"

"Yup! Cheers boys!" I called over my shoulder.

I hope Sergeant Snips is around when I get home—I have a need for those sharp clackers of hers.

Fergus watched Fischer go, his face frowning in confusion.

"Is he really human?" Duncan asked from beside him.

"He's certainly stronger than he looks. He was like a demon on the bellows."

"I hope he comes back every day—it was nice just being able to craft and not worry about keeping the forge lit." Duncan cocked his head as he stared after the departing man. "That's at least a hundred kilograms of metal he's carrying, right?"

"Closer to two hundred, I'd wager."

"Well, definitely not human, but he's a nice demon, at least."

Fergus bellowed a laugh. "Aye, that he is."

CHAPTER FIFTEEN

FARMING

"There you are!" I said with a laugh.

Sergeant Snips clacked her claws in delight as she emerged from the river.

"Do you have a moment to spare, Snips? I have a need for those clickety-clackers of yours."

She held out her claws, looked at them, then looked back at me and blew questioning bubbles.

"Oh, yeah, sorry. Your claws—I have need of your claws."

She nodded vigorously, urging me on with said clackers.

"All right! With me, Sergeant!"

I strode off toward the forest, my ever-reliable guard crab following. I looked about the trees as I tried to spot some pole-worthy trunks. Finding a suitably small and straight tree, I pointed at its base. "Reckon you could cut this down for me?"

Sergeant Snips obliged, unleashing a blast with both claws that sliced most of the way through the trunk. The tree fell, and she scuttled out of its path.

"Damn, Snips! That's some serious firepower!"

She blew happy bubbles as her single eye glanced between me and the fallen sapling.

"Would you be a dear and trim the top and branches off?"

A few cuts later, and I had a ten-foot-tall pole that was between four and five inches in diameter. I bent to pick it up and test its heft. I lifted it with ease.

Is this new body ridiculously strong or is this tree just super light—I can probably carry all four poles with ease.

I thought back to the objects I had Fergus and Duncan build and their reactions to me carrying my newly acquired cages back home.

Guess it's probably the body . . .

I shook the thought away. Strength was nice, and I was happy to make use of it, but there was no need to overthink it.

"All right, Snips, we need three more like this one. See any suitable trees?"

She scuttled off further into the forest in search of saplings, blowing gleeful bubbles all the way. I shook my head with a smile as I trailed her.

I set the four poles down on the sand. "Thanks for the help, Snips!"

Her carapace dipped below the water of the beach, her claws still visible as they franticly waved goodbye.

"All right," I said to myself. "Now to find a good spot . . ."

I could have asked my friendly crab to have a look for me, but if I was being honest, I was excited to go for a swim. I owned a beachfront property and hadn't even been for a single dip in the ocean—a crime against my Australian heritage.

Stripping down to my jocks—that the tailors Steven and Ruby had thankfully had the foresight to provide—I slowly walked out into the softly lapping waves. The water was the good kind of cold, enough to jolt the nervous system and wake me up, but not so freezing as to be uncomfortable.

I got up to my waist in the ocean, took a deep breath, and plunged my head under. I sat there for a long moment, holding my breath as the cool water surrounded me. The peace of the sea washed over me, and a content smile made its way to my face unbidden.

I swam out, floating on my back, the midafternoon sun warming the top of my body just as the cool ocean caressed my back. I lost track of time, allowing the moment of mindfulness to linger.

All right, that's enough relaxation.

I flipped over to my front, and casting my eyes over the ocean floor, I began my search. The entirety of the bay should be suitable for my purposes, but I was intent on finding the perfect spot that wouldn't impede my fishing and would keep my cages in the ideal tidal zone.

It didn't take me long. I picked a spot fifty meters northeast from the last bit of rock protruding from the headland. It was high tide, and I could still touch the sand while keeping my head above water, meaning the cages would stay submerged most of the time while still getting enough much-needed oxygen.

I swam back to the shore, tied my poles together with a length of line, and swam back out with them. I untied the first one and got to work, planting it firmly in the sand. I thought it would be quite challenging, but with my strength, I was easily able to lift myself atop the pole and twist it back and forth to root it firmly in the sand.

When the first one was buried a full five feet into the sandy flat, I gave it a good pull, and finding it holding steadfast, nodded to myself. I repeated the action for the other three poles, and when the final one was planted, I lifted myself atop it, inspecting my handwork. The four poles were placed in a line with just over six feet between each, their rigid forms visible to me through the clear waters of the bay.

As I was securing wire between the poles and attaching the first cage, a stream of bubbles floated up beside me, announcing the arrival of Sergeant Snips. She crawled up one of the poles, perching atop it and looking at my construction with intent curiosity.

I laughed at her expression and the way she cocked her body back and forth. I gave her a good rub on the top of her shell. "You'll just have to wait and see, Snips."

Her lone eyestalk was glued to me as I went about securing the six cages between the poles. The thick wire the blacksmiths had given me was perfect and would probably last years in the salty water. With a final twist, it was finished.

I turned to Sergeant Snips. "We just need one more thing—want to help me gather it?"

She blew so many bubbles that I had no idea what she was trying to say, but the enthusiastic bobbing of her head told me it was a definite yes.

"All right," I said with a laugh. "Meet me over at the rocks of the headland."

She emerged way before me, scuttling back and forth on the shore with impatience. When I'd almost reached the shore, she raced to the rocks, staring back at me and almost vibrating with anticipation. I jogged over and picked up my hammer and file, not wanting to keep my anxious guard crab waiting.

"See these?" I asked, bending down and pointing at the rocks.

She peered where I'd shown, cocking her head in confusion. I took the file, held the tip of it to the rocks, and with a swift smack of the hammer, peeled away the top shell I'd dislodged. Sergeant Snips leaned in so close that her eye almost touched the meat of the oyster.

"Try it," I urged.

She tentatively picked it up between her claws, seemed to smell it, and took a testing bite. Her body went rigid, and in the next second the entire thing was gone, sucked into her open mouth with glee.

I barked a laugh at the reaction, and before I could do anything, she lowered her claw to another of the shellfish and snipped it open. Well, she tried to snip it open, but all she succeeded in doing was showering us in shell, rock, and a fine mist of executed oyster.

"Er, maybe try a little softer, Snips." I wiped the liquefied mollusk from my face. "Want me to open another?"

She shook her body, and with a much more controlled clack of the claws, another oyster's lid flew away. She swept the salty flesh into her mouth faster than the eye could see.

"Make sure you don't eat all of these suckers, all right? I want some too, and we need some for the cages I just made."

She nodded at the former, then cocked her head when I said some were for the cages, once more lost in confusion.

I cracked one open for myself, savoring the unique flavor as I chewed and swallowed.

[Error: Insufficient power. Superfluous systems offline.]

I was having a nice time with my friend, System . . . I shook my head as I dismissed the prompt. "Want me to show you what I'm doing with them?"

She nodded vigorously, her inquisitive nature kicking in.

Using my large nail, I slowly chipped away at the oysters I intended to farm. I was deliberate and exacting, careful to dislodge each shell without damaging the lid or base of the oysters' now-mobile homes. When I had twenty-four of them in a pile, I started slipping them in my pouch.

"Back to the cages, Snips!"

Once more, she beat me there by a mile, swaying back and forth atop one of the poles with little patience as I swam over.

"These things are tasty, right, Snips?" I asked when I reached the first cage.

She nodded and blew bubbles of ascent.

"They're called oysters, and food isn't the reason I'm putting them in these cages—at least not the *entire* reason."

Her body tilted in thought—ever the attentive student.

I opened the roof of the cage, sliding four oysters inside. "These things can grow something called pearls. Everyone else in this town is a heretic and thinks eating fish or anything else from the sea is unthinkable."

She blew bubbles of dismay, and I nodded.

"I couldn't agree more, Snips. That means I can't make money from selling fish, but the pearls these have a chance to produce means in the future, I might be able to secure a reliable source of income."

She looked between the caged oysters and me, blowing curious bubbles that I took to mean "How?"

I slid a cut of wire around the top of the cage and twisted, securing it in place. "They reproduce by making larvae that float through the ocean and attach themselves to surfaces. I think just putting the cages here might have been enough to cultivate them, but by placing oysters directly in the cage, we ensure that the larvae are as close as possible when the oysters spit them out."

She paused, digesting the information, then nodded, blowing bubbles of comprehension.

"Clever girl, Snips. I'm not sure how long they'll take to grow—I don't actually know that much about their life cycle. But, with luck, we'll be able to harvest pearls from them soon."

I looked up at the fading light, the beauty of the sunset demanding my attention as it colored the western sky. A claw tapped me on the shoulder, drawing my attention. I turned to Snips, raising an eyebrow. She gave me a wave of the claws, a dip of the carapace, and jumped off the pole, sinking into the ocean and out of sight.

"Bye, Snips!" I yelled.

Shaking my head in amusement at my pal, I set about filling the rest of the cages.

I dug up a rather stinky bit of eel, leaning my head as far away from it as possible. Using a stick, I stabbed the bait, then carefully lowered it into the final bit of smithing Fergus and Duncan had done for me. I folded a bit of wire over the bait, securing it to the bottom of the crab pot.

Maybe I should have warned Snips about this. Ah well, she'll recognize the eel as the one she cut for me . . . probably . . .

I tied a length of line to the crab pot and set off toward the coast. I walked it out into the sea from the sandy beach, not trusting the relatively thin line to hold up against the sharp rocks. I tied the end of the line to a large stone, and with the excitement of the unknown, I walked back to the house, trying to put the crab pot out of mind, lest I check it every ten minutes and catch absolutely nothing. I felt a smile come across my face. It had been a long, productive day, and I'd taken steps to improve both my life and that of the villagers.

Guess I'll cook some fish and call it a night—oh, alongside some fresh oysters, of course!

Trent, the first in line to the throne and bane of all serving staff, opened the door to his hideout and slipped inside. He'd escaped the feast by pretending to go to the bathroom—only after filling his stomach with hunks of meat and countless sweets, of course.

He closed the door behind him with a soft *click* and started making his way into the veritable sea of ancient relics. A tiredness stole over him as he crawled further into the mess, and he relished the nap he was about to have while the rest of the royal family were downstairs doing useless things, like conversing and networking.

He found a familiar pocket and took a moment to check if the working relic still held power. He'd been surprised that it still showed information from the time of the ancients, listing the advancements of some long dead or ascended person named 'Fischer.'

He stretched as he got to his feet, and with practiced precision, gave the relic in question a good, hard slap.

That's what you get for insulting me, idiot. You will rue the day you looked down on Trent, the magnificent inherit—His thoughts cut off as the screen came to life, and another line of text had joined the other two.

New milestone! Fischer has learned blacksmithing!

His eyes became saucers, and his already drooping mouth opened even further. *What in Poseidon's salted taint is going on . . . ?*

CHAPTER SIXTEEN

THE NOOSE

It was a fitful sleep with the excitement of a set trap waiting to be checked, and I woke to the light of the already risen sun creeping through my open bedroom door. Anticipation rising, I sprung from my bed and ran out onto the sands. A wet *thwap* sounded, and I paused on the spot, turning toward the noise.

George stood to the right of me, eyes wide as he stared between me and my home, shoes covered in the topping of what looked to be a cake.

"Morning, George!" I gave him a broad grin. "How ya doing?"

George's face went white, and he stammered, "G-good morning, Fischer. I brought you coffee and a treat . . ." He looked down, only just now realizing that he was wearing a portion of the aforementioned treat, the rest having exploded across the sand.

I cared little for the cake, but my eyes locked onto the clay mug in his trembling hand.

"S-sorry, Fischer! I—"

"Mate! You shouldn't have!" I walked over and held my hand out for the mug, mouth watering. "You really brought me a coffee?"

He seemed to recover slightly. "Y-yes! I wanted to tell you that the coffee machine you requested should be here within the week, and I've organized a coffee for you from Lena's Café each morning until it arrives."

"Every day?" I took the cup. "Mate, you've outdone yourself."

I took a tentative sip, and the familiar taste of freshly brewed coffee consumed my senses. It was bitter, the roast a little darker than my usual tastes, but it would pair perfectly with something sweet. I closed my eyes and breathed in, moving my tongue to let the flavors circulate. "George, mate, I could kiss you right now."

He let out a strained laugh. "I'm glad you're happy. Sorry about the mess . . ." He looked down at the splattered remains of his other offering. "I-I was just so shocked to see your home . . ."

"Oh, this thing?" I looked at the visible face of my house. "Just a little something I knocked up over the last few days. You like it?"

"Y-yes! It is magnificent . . ."

"Glad to hear, mate! It's nowhere near as opulent as yours, but it suits me just fine."

His eyes were vacant as he stared at the abode.

After a long moment, I waved a hand in front of him. "You feeling all right, mate?"

He blinked rapidly, his eyes refocusing on me. "Ye—yes! Of course! I'd better get going, there's a lot to do back in the village!" He turned and strode slowly away in the direction of Tropica.

Poor bloke. I guess the house would be shocking, but his social anxiety seems debilitating.

"Thanks again, George!" I called after him, taking another big mouthful of my gloriously caffeinated beverage.

George couldn't feel his legs and barely recognized that he was moving at all.

This is worse than I thought . . .

Like the unwavering arrow of Apollo, seeing the house Fischer occupied had driven a shaft of despair into his heart. It appeared in only a few days—had Fischer built it before he even arrived? What resources must the man possess for him to deliver such expensive materials unseen, then erect it unnoticed?

He had woken that morning full of intent—he'd barely slept following the previous day's interaction with Fischer, and in the early hours of the morning, had decided to not let the machinations of the capital agent affect him. He'd meant to show a facade of calm surety when presenting the expensive food and drink. Seeing the house had dissolved that intention like granular sugar in a hot beverage.

It was made to resemble the ancient houses of old, and only the richest of nobles in the capital of Gormona could afford the materials required to make such an approximation.

Does he intend to use his home as the village's new base of power after ousting me?

Worse, a defensive wall of rock surrounded it.

He hasn't built a home but established a fortress from which to torment me.

He didn't even notice when his surroundings turned from sand and sugarcane to homes and streets, troubled as his thoughts were.

Did he antagonize me intentionally to draw me in? He was pleased for me to stumble upon his domain, smiling at me as I cast my eyes over it. Oh, Fischer, you devious man—I am but a puppet dancing on your strings . . .

I called and called for Sergeant Snips, wanting to give her a taste of the cake strewn over the sands, but she never came.

Guess she's gone off somewhere . . .

I felt a bare moment of worry, but it vanished when I remembered the capabilities of my defensive crab—she'd be able to fend for herself and would return when finished with whatever she was doing. I sipped the last bit of coffee, relishing the flavor and sensation of vigor already coursing through me.

Fueled by dopamine and excitement, I jogged to the trap waiting for me. I picked up the rock, happy to see the line still tied firmly to it. The line felt tight, and as I started pulling it in, it was heavy.

Is there something in the crab pot, or am I just imagining it?

Hand over hand, pull after pull, the suspense was agonizing, almost too much for me to handle. I finally caught sight of the crab pot, and anticipation bubbled over as I caught sight of light-yellow masses on the backside of my trap. I grabbed the metal handle on the close side and reefed it out of the water. Two crabs sat in the back corners, the same color as sand, and with a more streamlined shape than that of Sergeant Snips.

Sand Crab

Common

Found along the ocean shores, this crustacean is a staple of the Kallis Realm's coastal denizens.

So, less prized in flavor than rock crabs, but more common?

[Error: Insufficient power. Superfluous systems offline.]

"Can I just have a goddamn moment to myself, System?" I yelled. "That shit is getting tedious!"

I felt something in response, like a switch presented in response to my complaint. With a push, I mentally flicked it. Nothing seemed to change, but I had a feeling I'd just turned off the annoying notifications. I hoped that was the case.

Guess I'll have to wait and see . . .

Returning my attention to the cornered crabs, I opened the pot, carefully reaching behind the larger of the crabs with my hand. It backed further into the corner, and I easily grabbed its paddle-shaped back swimmers.

I inspected the bottom, seeing it had a pointed abdomen. I repeated the same for the other, seeing a broader, flatter abdomen. If they were anything like the crabs of Earth, which I strongly suspected they were, the pointed carapace underneath meant it was male, and the crab with a flatter one was female.

I carefully set down the female, watching intently as she swiftly swam into the depths and out of sight. Females were a source of reproduction, and although the rarity was listed as common, it still felt wrong eating a breeder.

I held up the male, which was the bigger of them. "Not your lucky day, mate."

I tied both pincers against its body with a length of line, removing the threat of getting a snipped finger. I left the pot there, with the line tied around the rock I'd used as an anchor, and set off home with the male.

I filled a large pot with fresh water from the river, placed the crab inside, and left it in my kitchen with a lid atop. I didn't want to cause the thing any undue distress, so left it in the insulated air of my house. With that thought lingering, and making a possible bad call, I cut the line that held its limbs close.

"Your time is almost done, crab," I said to it. "The least I can do is let you move about."

It tried to get me with one of its pincers—fair play—but I was too quick. With a few goals in mind, I made my way toward Tropica.

* * *

"You're sure this is a good idea, sir?" Gary asked.

Sebastian's eye twitched at his idiotic follower's insubordination. "Yes, I'm sure, Gary—now move out of the way."

"Y-yes, sir. Sorry, sir." He shuffled aside, leaving the path clear.

Sebastian left the house that functioned as the Cult of the Leviathan's Tropica branch. The purse at his side was a comforting weight, and his lip twinged up in annoyance at having to waste more of the Cult's funds.

Not a waste, he reminded himself. *A necessary cost to rid the world of the upstart that's disrupting my plans.*

He made his way toward the north side of the village, face firm and stride true. He wore his lobster regalia this time; there was no need to hide his comings and goings.

The wait for the café was long, and the bulbous bodies of minor nobles blocked his path. Their sizes brought him great disgust, but not for their attractiveness—their forms were the pinnacle of beauty standards. Sebastian's grievance was with how much it cost to sustain such a look. He had more than enough coin to cultivate such a body, but his purpose lay with the guidance of blessed lobsters toward divinity.

These people are heretics—they have no desire to truly serve the potential gods. Disgusting wastes of space, one and all.

The line dwindled, one enlarged person at a time, and he eventually reached the counter. The woman behind the counter, who he knew to be named Lena, looked down her nose at him.

"Yes?" Her voice was dismissive and petulant, a far cry from the deference and cheer she'd given everyone before him.

"One coffee, please," Sebastian said, trying his best to smile at the mountain of a woman.

"You may not be able to afford it, priest." She sniffed at him. "Five iron coins."

He breathed in slowly, trying to keep control of his features. "I heard the people before me paying only three irons, madam."

She shrugged a single shoulder, not bothering with both. "That was for people of note, who I know will come back with their mugs, or pay to replace a broken one. For you . . . if you bring it back tomorrow, I'll happily charge you three."

"And will I get the two irons back if I return it?"

"No," she said with a caustic smile. "It's a non-refundable deposit. You'll be charged three irons from then on—assuming those skinny hands of yours don't slip and smash one of them."

Sebastian couldn't control the half sneer that sprouted, but quickly smiled to replace it. "Of course, madam."

He reached into his pouch, counted out five irons, and held them out for her. She tapped on the counter, and he placed them there. She pulled out a cloth, grabbed the coins with them, and threw them into a jar as if they would bite.

"Won't be a moment, *sir.*" The last word was mocking, and as she turned away, Sebastian bared his teeth at her back.

Push me, vile wench, and you'll be next.

A minute later, she put the coffee-filled mug on the far side of the bench away from the line, then smiled brightly at the next person to order.

"Two coffees and thirty-four passiona pastries, Geraldine?"

"You know me so well, Lena—George and I just can't get enough!"

Sebastian tuned them out as he headed back south with Fischer's coffee, ignoring the scorn-laden glances of the people that lined up behind him.

A necessary cost, he reminded himself. *The cultivator might suspect if the first gift of coffee was poisoned, but if I make a habit of it, the noose will slide around his neck with ease.*

"Fischer!" a voice called as I walked through the village.

I turned, seeing the man in a lobster robe that had previously threatened me.

Sebastian, Maria had said . . .

"Hey, Sebastian. You in a better mood today?"

He rubbed the back of his head, giving me a smile vacant of joy. "I wanted to say sorry for my behavior the other day. I've brought you a coffee in apology."

I raised an eyebrow but accepted the drink. "Thanks!"

I downed the coffee in a single swig, handing him back the cup. "We all have bad days, so don't worry about it."

I clapped him on the shoulder by way of goodbye, and kept on walking, keen as I was to go about my errands.

Sebastian seethed as he made his way back to his precious lobsters.

I could have just poisoned the idiot then! He didn't even question it, didn't even bother tasting the thing that I'd spent so much damn coin on! It's going to cost me another three irons, and for what?

He sighed, and a malicious smile made its way out as he realized something.

That just means the next cup will deliver his doom. Enjoy the coffee, fool, for the next one will be your last.

He cackled as he went, ignoring the looks of passing villagers.

CHAPTER SEVENTEEN

A PRODUCTIVE DAY

Y*ou know, maybe that lobster bloke ain't all that bad,* I thought as I power walked through Tropica Village. People I'd never met before were smiling and waving at me, which was a welcome change from the usual suspicion and derision I faced. *Guess they've heard about the coffee machine coming in hot . . .*

Before I even realized it, I reached Steven and Ruby's . . . *tailors? Tailorors?* Whatever, I reached the clothes shop. The second coffee was kicking in, and in retrospect, it may not have been the best idea to subject this new body to who knew how many shots of coffee for the first time.

Ah well, it's gonna be a productive day, baby! I paused. *Did I just call myself baby in the third person? Definitely too much coffee . . .*

"Hello, Fischer!" Steven greeted, skull-dragging me out of my questionable introspection.

"G'day, mate! How are ya?"

"I'm great, thanks! Is it true you're buying Sue a coffee machine?"

"Not me, George is, but you're goddamn right she's getting a coffee machine, Steven! The people need it!"

He gave me a funny look. "Are you all right, Fischer?"

"Yeah, why mate?"

"You seem a little off? And your hands are shaking."

I looked down. "Huh. They are, aren't they? How 'bout that? Anyway, I need a hat, Steven. What you got for me?"

"Oh, right. What did you have in mind?"

"Straw hat, wide brim, red band around it."

If you're gonna wear a straw hat anyway, you may as well look like the future king of the pirates while doing it.

"Hmmm, we've got a few different types of straw hats, but we don't have any spare red fabric at the moment . . ." He looked around the store. "I could steal some from one of those red shirts if you don't mind waiting—"

"Forget it." I waved the half-formed suggestion away. "It's probably an intellectual property infringement waiting to happen. Let's just go with a plain straw hat—I do want the wide brim, though. Real wide."

"O-okay. One moment . . ."

He walked out back, returning with two boxes stacked atop each other. "We've got two different types of straw hats in. Which one would you . . . *Fischer?*"

"Yeah, Steven?"

"You sure you're all right?"

I realized I was bouncing on my heels at an erratic pace. I stopped. "Yeah, sorry, I think I had one too many coffees, but they were free, so what was I gonna say, no? I'm only human, Steven."

"Ah, I get it now," he said with a laugh. "You should see Ruby when she has an extra pot of tea in the morning. So, you wouldn't recommend having two when Sue's machine gets here?"

"What? Oh, no, I'd absolutely recommend it." I leaned over the boxes. "Now let's have a look at these hats . . ."

I walked out of the clothes shop with a spanking new hat, which Steven had refused payment for, saying something about the coffee machine, or the passiona pastries? Honestly, I forget. I was thinking about like five other things at the time.

I jogged to Thomas's tool store, stopping by Sue's for my complimentary baked good.

"Fischer!" He gave me a broad smile, his glorious mustache lending it even more joy. "Back for more tools, lad? What do you need?"

"Thomas! How are ya, mate? Your mustache is looking on point, by the way!"

He cocked his head. "Thank . . . you?"

"No worries, mate, I'm just calling it how I see it. I'm looking for an axe. You got anything?"

"Of course! What's it for?"

"Trees. Lots of trees."

"That I can do!" He walked around the counter, stepping to the back left of the store. He picked out the biggest axe on the wall, holding it out to me. "On the house, Fischer. It's the least I can do after the pastries and coffee machine!"

"Oh, thanks mate, I appreciate it!"

"How did you get George to agree to that, anyway?"

He held out the axe, and I took it. It felt light in my hands, but then again, everything seemed light to this new body of mine.

"Honestly, mate, I just asked him. I feel bad for the bloke—he seems super anxious."

"Anxious?" Thomas raised an eyebrow and gave a wry smile. "I've heard our village lord called a lot of things, but I've never heard it said that he's anxious . . ."

"Yeah, mate." I nodded—rather emphatically, by my estimation. "Debilitating social anxiety, poor thing. Oh, do you know what the go is with logging trees? Like, do I need to do it on my land, or is it chill if I just go willy-nilly chopping them down past my property line?"

Thomas cocked his head. "Er—you want to know if you can log trees in the forest?"

"Yeah, that's the one."

"What's it for?"

"Big fuckin' fence, mate. Maybe a stable or something down the line? You know, I haven't really thought about it that much, but definitely a fence."

"Aye, that's no issue. As long as you're not selling and it's for use on your land, crown laws permit logging. You can't log within five hundred meters of a settlement, but if you do it past the land you bought, that's well within your rights."

I beamed a smile. "Thanks so much, Thomas—and cheers for the axe! Bye!"

"You're welcome!" he yelled at my already leaving back. "Bye, Fischer!"

I took off running back home—axe in hand, and a smile on my face.

I thought I'd miss the use of Sergeant Snips's violently capable claws, but as it turned out, my concern was entirely misplaced. Like a caffeinated chainsaw, I made my way through countless trees in the forest beyond my property line with reckless abandon. A single swing was enough to cut halfway through saplings, fully grown trees being felled by a few more swings.

In my haste, I'd forgotten to get any nails to hold a fence in place, but I shrugged that off, deciding today would be a day for logging. I was selective with the trees chosen, not wanting to have a negative impact on the ecosystem—well, *too much* of a negative impact. I was removing trees, but I needed a fence, and that was that.

I was chopping down a single species with a light-brown trunk. I didn't know what they were, but the wood was sturdy. They were the most prevalent trees in the forest by far, and I had no doubt they'd repropagate given time.

I came across another of the light-blue trees I'd seen on my bamboo-searching excursion with Snips, and I thought to fell one, but as I swung the axe over my shoulder, a feeling of wrongness flooded me. Whether it was because they seemed rare, or because the universe was giving me a sign, I decided to follow my gut and leave the tree standing.

By the time the afternoon came around, I had a meter-high stack of the light-brown trunks on the sands of my land; next to it sat a similarly sized stack of saplings that would serve as the posts.

The exercise was both a means of getting shit done and working out the caffeine coursing through my veins. I let out a content sigh as I took in the results of my labor.

That's probably enough for now. I might need more, but I'd rather have too little than too many. I can always go chop more, after all, but I can't replant a severed trunk.

"Ho, Fischer!" a familiar voice called from behind me.

I turned, giving Barry a smile. "How ya going, mate?"

"I'm good." He gave me a concern-filled glance. "Are you well?"

"Uh, yeah mate. Why?"

"I had a few people come looking for me . . . they expressed their concern, saying they saw you running through town with an axe and a manic look about you."

"Oh," I said with a laugh, fanning my face with my new straw hat. "Yeah, don't mind that—I was gifted two cups of coffee this morning, and got a little excited about the prospect of building a fence."

His brow furrowed as he stared at the piles of wood now sitting on what was essentially my lawn. "You . . . chopped all this by yourself? Since this morning?"

"Yeah, mate. Caffeine is a helluva drug. While you're here . . . can I interest you in some dinner?"

He narrowed his eyes at me. "Is it from the sea?"

" . . . maybe."

"I'll keep you company, but I don't think I'll partake if it's all the same to you."

"No worries! Your company is more than welcome. Let's get a fire going."

We walked toward the headland, and as we rounded the corner, I caught sight of my home.

"Fancy a tour of my humble abode, mate?"

Barry's jaw dropped, and he looked between me and the house with disbelief. "When did you . . ."

"Over the last couple days. Come on, I'll show ya."

We walked through the house, and Barry showed an enjoyable amount of awe and confusion.

The cat was out of the bag with George finding out about it, and I'd trusted Barry so far with enough information to bring me down. It was only a matter of time until more people found out, so I saw no harm in letting my friendly neighbor know.

"Where . . . where does the water come from, and where does it go?" he asked, flushing the toilet at my prompting.

"Not too sure, to be honest."

"It's like something from the stories, Fischer." He turned a tap on, held his hand under the cool water, and turned it back off. "It's like magic."

"It's called plumbing," I said with a laugh, "and it's common where I'm from."

When we got to the kitchen, I gestured at my lack of a stove. "Haven't found time to sort out somewhere to cook, so I've just been using a campfire." I picked up the pot with a crab inside, opening the lid and showing Barry. "This is dinner if you change your mind."

The crab held its claws up in protest, promising a swift pinch for anyone daring enough to approach.

"Er—no, Fischer . . . thank you, though."

I shrugged, walking out of the house with the pot and nodding for Barry to follow. "No worries, offers open if you change your mind!"

I set to starting the fire, and Barry sat in contemplative silence.

"How did you do all this, Fischer?"

"Do what, mate?"

"This." He gestured vaguely at the house, the metal pot, and the surrounding area. "It's only been days . . . I've never seen anything of the like."

"You have to allow a man a bit of mystery, mate." I gave him a smile, unable to contain the elation his confused face brought me. "Besides, I'd say Sergeant Snips is a bit more amazing than that, wouldn't you?"

He nodded, giving a deep sigh as the corners of his mouth turned up. "You're a stalk of wheat, filled with unhusked grains of mystery."

"That's quite philosophical, mate, but you're not wrong. Thanks for accepting me and not pushing too hard on the details—I like you, Barry, and I'm glad we're neighbors."

He grinned at me. "I have a feeling things are going to just get more confusing with you around, but I'm glad you moved in—you're a source of constant amazement."

"Glad to hear it, mate. You, uh, might want to turn away for a moment if you're a bit squeamish."

With two swift movements, I grabbed the crab and put it on a block of wood with one hand, then dispatched it with the knife in the other before it realized I had even removed it from the pot. I emptied the river water on the sand, put the crab back in the pot, and stood up.

"Back in a moment, mate—need to clean this and get some seawater."

As the pot boiled, we sat in companionable silence, both lost in the flames of the fire. After twenty or so minutes, I checked my dinner. The shell was a bright pink; it was ready. I took the crab out with a pair of tongs, setting it on the wooden board to cool.

A welcomed clacking drew my attention, and Sergeant Snips emerged from the river, claws held high, a stream of excited bubbles streaming from her cute little head.

CHAPTER EIGHTEEN

WILDLIFE

"Snips!" I ran to meet my friend, giving her a good scratch on the carapace. "I was worried about you! Where did you get off to?" Her eyestalk twitched between me and Barry, blowing bubbles of . . . hesitation? Questioning?

"He's all right, Snips. No need to keep secrets from Barry."

She nodded firmly, then scuttled back into the river.

What is she up to . . . ?

She returned a moment later, and behind her a line of fellow rock crabs emerged.

I raised an eyebrow, not sure what was going on, but she seemed to have recruited more of her kind. There were five of them in total, and they formed an orderly line across the sand next to Snips.

Snips went to the first one, gesturing emphatically at the sand with one of her powerful claws. Its eyes looked at her, and for a moment nothing happened, then she gave it a light smack on the head, and two stones shot out of its mouth. I bent down to look at them—not just stones, they were *pearls!*

She repeated the same gesture with the other crabs, and a total of eight pearls lay on the sand, each as big as my pinky nail, glittering in the late afternoon sun. I picked them up, an unbelieving smile spreading across my face.

"Snips! You beautiful little scamp! Where did you find so many?"

She bubbled in delight, puffing her body up and swaying with joy. She turned and made a shooing gesture, and the five rock crabs scuttled off into the river.

I picked up the pearls, walking back toward Barry. "You're just in time for dinner, Snips! You deserve a reward for this!" She scuttled beside me, preening the entire way.

"Have you seen these before, Barry?" I held out the naturally formed stones, and his eyebrows shot up.

"No . . . what are they? They look almost like gems . . ."

"Technically, they're stones, but they can form naturally in oysters." I petted Sergeant Snips with my other hand. "This little scallywag gathered them with her crabby friends."

"I wonder what they're worth," he said. "I could see them being used in some pretty high-end stuff, Fischer. It's a shame they're from the sea."

"Er—maybe you can keep that tidbit to yourself, mate. I don't want to go devaluing them."

He nodded, giving me a conspiratorial look. "Not a problem, especially if you intend on selling them to the people on the north side of Tropica . . ."

I barked a laugh. "But of course! Who else could afford such prestigious gems, definitely gathered from the ground, and not the mouths of shellfish?"

We grinned at each other, and I started running plans in my head for how to market and sell the stones.

I know I didn't want to engage in any business, but these could allow me the freedom to fish to my heart's content!

When the cooked crab had sufficiently cooled, I snapped off a leg, holding it to Snips. "I didn't think you'd have any reservations about eating sand crab, but just making sure that's not an—"

She snatched the leg, shoving it into her mouth. A crunching ground out as she chewed it—shell and all—and she blew a stream of joyous bubbles when she finished devouring the first bite.

Well, that moral dilemma is settled . . .

I pulled a claw off, cracking it between my fingers and sliding the meat out with ease. The smell was intoxicating, and I took a moment to thank the crab for the gift of its flesh before placing it in my mouth. The flesh was sweet and salty, the flavor of it a perfect harmony. I moaned in delight, unable to contain the noise.

"That actually smells quite good . . ." Barry said.

"Why don't you try just a bit?" I raised an eyebrow. "It's not as if you lived from the sea—I did all the catching and cooking, after all, and if you don't eat it, Snips and I are going to."

Sergeant Snips blew agreeing bubbles as she helped herself to another leg.

"Maybe I'll try a bite . . ."

I pounced on his weakness, pulled the other front claw off, snapped it open and held out what my home state affectionately calls a Queensland lollipop. I held out the claw, chunk of meat extended, and he timidly grabbed it. Before he could question it any further, he shoved the morsel into his mouth. His face started with obvious trepidation, but was quickly overwhelmed by the objectively delicious taste, changing into an expression of contentment as he chewed and swallowed it.

"I—I gotta get back to the family." Barry got to his feet, giving the Sergeant and I a curt nod. "Thanks for the hospitality."

"Cheers for the company, mate! Take care!"

"Bye Fischer, farewell Sergeant Snips." He retreated toward his farmland with a purposeful gait.

I raised an eyebrow at Snips, to which she shrugged adorably. "What the hell do you reckon that was about?"

Barry had to leave. He knew if he had stayed any longer, he wouldn't have been able to turn down any more of the heretical food. He'd been unable to stop himself upon smelling it, but after tasting it . . . an entirely different desire had overcome him.

The flesh was sweet, covered in a layer of the savory water it was boiled in. The aroma promised a unique experience, and the flavor of it far surpassed that which was expected.

His need for more warred with his upbringing, the pressure of societal standards battling with his want for more. His thoughts were a jumbled disarray of back-and-forth arguments—even now, he wanted to turn, to run back and have just one more bite.

Fischer would allow me, wouldn't he? He was more than willing to share . . . He shook his head, deciding it was best to return to his family and forget the lingering urges. He picked up the pace, jogging home across the sand flats.

If he were more in control of himself, Barry may have noticed the strength flooding through his muscles, the essence of a single claw suffusing his very being. His strides were long, and nary a single drop of sweat formed as he began sprinting, trying and failing to outrun his yearning.

It was a picturesque sunrise on the shore of my property. The sun was high, a sea of clouds above me painted pink and standing out among their pale-blue backdrop. Fish were swimming through the sky, and I watched in delight as they danced and flew in great, circling arcs.

A fish slapped me in the face, and I recoiled. Another fish hit my other cheek, appearing from nowhere.

Huh?

I tried to stumble back, but my legs wouldn't move. Something hit my chin, popping and making a sense of disorientation overwhelm my peace.

Bubbles? W-what . . . ?

My eyes flew wide to see a crab's face taking up my entire field of view. I shuffled back, realizing I was in my bed, the predawn light leaching into my bedroom through the open door.

Sergeant Snips made an irate noise and spewed a torrent of bubbles, following my retreat and slapping both my cheeks with her claws one at a time.

"W-woah, Snips," I said, wiping bubbles of anger from my chin. "I'm awake. What's wrong?"

She scuttled off the bed, running to my open door and gesturing for me to follow. I trailed her, stretching and rubbing my eyes as I tried to gain comprehension.

She led me outside, and when we got there, I could hear a rhythmic tapping, like a hammer on a nail somewhere in the distance. Snips ran ahead of me ten meters at a time, stopping every time she got too far and waving me on wildly with her claws. The stream of bubbles had never stopped.

Man, something has really set her off . . .

The sound grew louder, the rhythmic tapping pausing at times before resuming their incessant march.

We got to the headland, and as she rounded it ahead of me, the spew of bubbles tripled and she used her entire body, along with her claws, to gesture emphatically at whatever was creating the ruckus.

I finally reached the Sergeant, the percussive noises tapping ever louder. I laid eyes on another creature, and my freshly woken mind struggled to make sense of what I was seeing. There was an otter on the jutting stone of the headland, bashing a rock into a bed of oysters. The lid of a mollusk flew away, and with a deft movement, the creature bent and sucked it into their mouth.

"*What the fuck . . . ?*"

The otter heard me, and shot its head toward us, the rock held high in two cute paws. We looked at each other for a long moment, no one moving or making a sound. Then, with its eyes still locked on me, the otter swung the rock down on an oyster.

This blatant disregard for our presence was enough to send Sergeant Snips into a frenzy, and she scuttled angrily toward the interloper, making a C'Thulian hiss. The otter retreated, diving into the sea with its rock as Snips clacked her claws and shot attacks through the now empty air. The guard crab leaped in after it, and I had a moment of serene quiet as they both disappeared beneath the waves.

A cool breeze tickled my skin, and I breathed deep of the sea spray it dragged along with it. I looked out at the water lapping the rocks, reflecting the light of the sun that threatened to breach the horizon.

The otter emerged on the rocks, twenty meters from where it was before, and gave me a sidelong glance as it resumed smashing a different section of oysters. It ate one, started hitting the next, and a rabid crab emerged behind it. Sergeant Snips blew bubbles of fury as she scuttled at it, the clacking of claws replacing the chorus of rock against shellfish. The otter dashed away, slipping easily back beneath the surf, and Snips flew in after it.

Another momentary reprieve, then the otter emerged from the sea closer to where I stood, once more resuming its meal as it monitored me. When the seething crab emerged after it, I yelled, "Snips! Stop!"

The otter disappeared again, and Sergeant Snips seemed to huff as her lone eye shot between me and the ripples where the creature dove.

"Come here, Snips." She came to me, the raving bubbles tinged with confusion. "It's all right, Snips."

I bent and scratched her carapace, trying to reassure the fuming crustacean. "I don't think we could stop it if we tried, and besides, it's all right to share our land with the wildlife."

She gestured at the oyster beds, at me, and then back to where the otter had retreated, physically shaking with indignation.

"I know," I said, rubbing her top with slow strokes. "I know you want to protect our place, and it can be incredibly frustrating to be ignored, but it really is okay."

The otter emerged again, this time far away. With little regard for our existence except occasional glances, it started smacking the rock down again.

Before Snips could race off, I spoke. "Let's just leave it for now, all right? There are heaps of rocks, and plenty of oysters besides. Should we go catch some breakfast? Maybe I can get you a nice fat fish?"

She bristled but accepted my words, only flinching a little at the sound of the otter's tool descending as we walked back to the house.

"Can you carry this for me, Snips?" I asked, holding out the smaller rod and giving her a distracting task.

She nodded and took it, still clearly conflicted by having something else on the headland and actively taking from my property.

I grabbed everything else needed and began leading her up the river and further from the otter, when a voice cut through the otherwise silent air.

"Fischer! You here?"

"Hide," I said to Snips. She picked up on the urgency in my voice, dropping the rod and scuttling into the river. I saw her single peeper emerge, poking almost imperceptibly above the surface.

"Over here, Sebastian!" I yelled, walking toward the voice.

"There you are, my friend!" the lobster cultist said, stepping over the sands and giving me a broad smile.

It seemed to me the first genuine smile I'd gotten from the man, so I returned it, happy to see him in good spirits.

"Good to see ya, mate! What brings you here?"

"Coffee, of course!" he said, presenting a mug of the aromatic liquid.

CHAPTER NINETEEN

JUSTICE

"Cheers, Sebastian! You shouldn't have!"

"Nonsense!" the lobster cultist said. "I still feel terrible about the other day, and it's the least I can do."

I accepted the mug, bathing in the scent flowing from it. "I couldn't possibly say no to a free cup of coffee! Thank you, mate!"

He smiled again, wide and genuine. "You're very welcome, Fischer." He shot a look back toward Tropica. "I just wanted to drop that off—hope you have a morning as pleasant as you are."

"Thanks, mate, you too!"

Sebastian waved goodbye as he turned and made his way back toward the village. I set the mug in my bucket, keen on finding a fishing spot before indulging—my hands were full, after all.

Sebastian kept taking glances back at me, and I gave him a wave. "Nice bloody bloke, that guy . . ."

When he was gone, I returned to Snips. She'd seen the encounter from her stealthy spot in the river and came to meet me where she'd dropped the rod.

"He brought me coffee!" I said to her. "Now, let's find a nice quiet spot for some fishing . . ."

We walked until the sound of the otter's tapping was far from earshot, finding a spot on the riverbank that was deep enough to hold fish. Snips sat beside me as I cast the line of tiny jigs out. When it hit the water, I held the rod with one hand and reached to take a sip of my life-giving coffee with the other.

Snips was inspecting the bucket and mug within curiously, her body tilting back and forth as she smelled the brew.

"You wanna try some, Snips?" I picked it up, holding it down to her.

"I don't know if you'll like it, but a little caffeine couldn't hurt . . ."

She dipped a claw in, getting a single drop on her limb, then tentatively shoved it in her mouth. Her reaction was immediate and violent.

She spewed bubbles of confusion and anger, smacking the mug. It shattered in a spray of coffee and glass, leaving me with just the handle grasped firmly in my hand.

"What the hell, Snips?" I demanded, but she was already gone. She leaped into the river.

Did I piss her off . . . ? I hope she isn't going back to harass that otter . . .

She emerged again, running faster than I'd ever seen as she returned to me. She had something clamped in her claw, and as I squinted at it, a prompt populated.

Widow's Vengeance
Rare
Found in the brackish waters of the Kallis Realm, the poison of this fish is harvested for use in alchemical creations of an odious nature.

She gestured at the fish with her free claw, then at the pile of broken glass and spilled coffee. Repeating this gesture, she glared at me.

"It . . . the coffee is poison?" I asked.

She nodded her whole carapace and blew bubbles of relief as I understood her point.

"Oh, I'm sorry, Snips! I had no idea caffeine is poisonous to you! Are you okay?"

She pointed at herself, nodding, then pointed at me, gesturing repeatedly with the appendage.

"You think it's poisonous to me?"

Her whole body shot up and down, and she blew bubbles of agreement.

I let out a small laugh, shaking my head. "I'm fine, Snips. Coffee isn't poisonous to me. I really am sorry, though. You're sure you're all right? You only had a little, so I'm sure you'll be fine . . ."

She repeated the same gestures, pointing at herself, nodding, pointing to me with a claw, then gesturing between the fish and broken mug.

"I know, I know. It's poisonous for you. I'm sorry, Snips. I really didn't know . . ."

Sergeant Snips cursed her beautiful, perfect form. She couldn't form the mouth hole noises, and the master was so kind a soul as to not believe he could be a target of such nefarious plots. He was the type of man that allowed strange, furry interlopers to partake of his harvest; the type of man that would feed a crab without claws, gifting life for no discernible reason; and the type of man that was worth following. Perhaps it was for the best. She would be the one to harbor such dark knowledge and the one to deal out recompense.

Sergeant Snips will protect. I will deal with the poisoner.

After a morning of catching small fish and a subsequent breakfast by the campfire, Sergeant Snips and I spent the day together. She was shaken by the otter encounter and the belief that Sebastian was trying to harm me with coffee, an idea that still brought a smirk to my lips.

I tried to leave for the village at one point to get my complementary coffee and fantasy croissant, but she demanded I stay, pincer firmly holding on to my pants. I gave in rather quickly, content as I was to spend the day fishing and pottering around my property.

* * *

With the master soundly sleeping in his throne bed, Sergeant Snips slipped off into the night. The passing of days since she'd met the man called Fischer, the benevolent master she'd grown to adore, had brought with them understanding. She didn't know where her learning came from, seeming to come from the very universe itself. She knew of human words, of the difference between species, and of more than she could even truly comprehend.

She could have taken the time to explain to master that Sebastian, the vile poisoner, really had tried to kill him. She could have spelled the very words out into the sand, explaining that the coffee had been riddled with the poison of the fish she'd caught and showed him. This, she knew, would have been a mistake. Indeed, even the immediate reaction and accusation when she tasted the coffee had been an error.

Her master's kindness and innocence was something to be protected. It was the very thing that had spared her life and awakened her; the very thing that drew her to him, like the strange chunks of metal she found that clung to each other.

Her mind raced as she approached the village from beneath the waves, barely seeing the prey she could easily snap up in her passing. She refocused on a single thought: revenge.

She emerged from the ocean onto a stone pathway, and tasting the air, followed the scent of the man that had tried to poison her master. The trail led her to a squat house, a simple construction compared to the castle that her master occupied. She easily shoved the door open, stealing into the building in utter silence.

Her eye took in the surroundings, a floor filled with transparent cages atop wooden frames spreading out before her. She climbed one, and peering inside, saw uncountable tasty morsels within. The poisoner appeared to be farming sea snippers, their form similar to her own, but entirely lacking in beauty.

She climbed back down, returning to the hunt. The scent of the poisoner was palpable, filling the space with his hideous fragrance. It wafted from a closed door, and approaching on quiet legs, she forced her way into the room.

The target was asleep, much as her master was before she left him. He lay defenseless, his inferior shell open and inviting her claws to deliver retribution. She crested the bed he lay on, crawling along the sheets to peer at his face.

She held her claw to his neck, pulling it back, gathering force in her mighty tool of justice. Now that she was here, though, her single eyestalk looking down at the hunted man, she had a moment to think.

She'd been consumed by blood lust the entire day, her master's continued health the only thing that stayed her body from marching off and finding the poisoner immediately. Given that her claw could explode with violence at any moment, ending Sebastian's vile existence, she allowed a moment for her thoughts to expand.

The death of this man, deserved as it was, may bring down unwanted problems on her master. As with all the information the universe granted, she knew not where it came from but was certain this was the way of humans—death was not so common as in the land of water, and the occurrence of it brought investigation, heralding more retribution, misguided as it may be.

A devious plan occurred to her, and with a long glance at the doomed poisoner, her claw *begging* to snap closed, she withdrew.

She walked back out of his room, climbing the first wooden construction. She devoured each and every one of the sea snippers, going from tank to tank and scooping them up with her claws, shoving them into her devouring mouth. They had a delightful crunch. They weren't quite as good as the food her master provided, reminding her of the time before awareness. Nonetheless, her revenge was sweet, lending a complex undertone to the feast she helped herself to.

When the last tiny morsel was eaten, she walked to the wall opposite the poisoner's door and scratched a message. Her claw left behind decisive marks in the soft wood—an accusation, and a warning.

With the message soon to be delivered, and a belief that Sebastian would no longer pose a threat, Snips made to leave, but something caught her attention—she smelled another sea snipper somewhere in the building.

Walking to a crudely hidden portal in the floor, she lifted it, revealing a sea snipper of gigantic proportions. With a malicious glint in her eye, she lowered her powerful clacker—as the master so affectionately called it—and prepared to end the sea snipper's existence.

With a single command, her muscles would contract and execute one of the enemy's numbers—and yet, they didn't. She cocked her carapace in confusion. Her brain said that the sea snipper had to die; her claw didn't obey. Whether it was her master's innate kindness being infectious, her reluctant admittance of the creature's size and majesty, or some other unknown whim guiding her, every instinct told her not to kill the creature.

Another devious plan occurred to her, one that she couldn't fully articulate, even to herself.

With a nod of approval at her own deceitfulness, she slammed her claw shut, cutting through the sea snipper with ease.

Sebastian woke with a sudden gasp, perhaps having escaped a nightmare which even now evaded him. As his brain started working, the memory of yesterday's events returned and a wolfish grin spread over his face.

He had delivered justice. He'd not heard of anyone finding Fischer's lifeless body yesterday but knew it was only a matter of time before someone found the man. He'd monitored his relic the entire day, hiding in the Cult of the Leviathan's building so as to not draw suspicion to himself. That it had remained blinking the entire day was a good thing; it meant that the death was slow, a deserving fate of anyone so blatantly going against his cult's purpose.

He rose from the bed, stretched lazily, and strode over to his desk. The device lay there, and with a cruel smirk, he peered at it. The smirk died as he saw the light, still flashing red.

Wh—what? The poison was supposed to be slow . . . but this is too much. He should have passed by now. Did the alchemist sell me snake oil?

He threw his door open. "Gary! I need you to—" The words died in his throat as he caught sight of a word carved into the wall. His eyes drifted down, landing on an antenna that could only belong to a single creature. He ran and picked it up, panic seizing his heart.

"No . . ." Sebastian bolted for the trapdoor, throwing it open with reckless abandon. "No, no, no, no . . ."

He held the antenna with numb hands as he stared down at the empty tank. His life's work had been slaughtered; the fifty-year-old lobster granted to him by the capital branch upon his relocation was no more.

He felt nothing, shock robbing him of all emotions. Glancing at the tanks, he hoped, *prayed,* but no. They were all empty, each of his lovely crickets gone.

He returned his eyes to the single word scrawled in the wall, deep and exacting.

POISONER.

His stomach dropped out, and he crawled back from the message as if physically distancing himself could take back every action of the last few days.

"Woah," Gary said, pointing at the antenna. "Is that from Pistachio . . . ?"

"He-he lived through the poison—h-he killed Pistachio . . ."

"Who did?" Gary asked, leaning down to touch the words cut into the wall. "Nice handwriting, that."

Sebastian's response was filled with anger, confusion, and fear. "F-Fischer . . ."

CHAPTER TWENTY

FISH ON

I opened my eyes to the face of a rather cute crab engulfing my entire field of view. Sergeant Snips blew a single happy bubble and scuttled to the side, watching me intently with her lone eye.

"Morning, Snips." I muttered, stretching my arms to the sky and arching my back. "You seem a lot more chipper today."

She bubbled her agreement, nodding along with the sentiment.

I rubbed my eyes and yawned, enjoying the lingering calm of a good night's sleep. "What do you wanna get up to today?"

She lifted both her claws above her head, held them together there, then mimed casting out a fishing line. I couldn't help but smile at the gesture.

I threw the sheets off, slid out of bed, and gave another big stretch. "I was thinking the same thing, Snips!"

We'd spent the entire day fishing yesterday but had only gone in search of the baitfish that lived along the shoreline and riverbank.

"Shall we hunt for larger prey today?" I asked, giving Snips a sidelong glance and already knowing what her response would be. She nodded emphatically, her entire body bobbing up and down in her enthusiasm.

I barked a laugh. "But first . . ." I gave her a conspiratorial look. "Shall we check the crab pot?"

Her body rocked up and down again, this time even her claws joining in.

"Let's go!"

I had to jog to keep up with Sergeant Snips's excited pace. The predawn light was as enjoyable as ever, and a cool breeze gave me goosebumps in its passing.

We reached the shore in record time, and Snips urged me on as I pulled on the fishing line. I felt weight in the pot, and anticipation surged as the trap came into sight. I could see something in there, right in the back corner. It looked like a massive crab. It was—

It was a rock crab.

Sergeant Snips let out a hiss of incomprehensible bubbles, and the rock crab shrank into the corner. I opened the trap and let it out. My guard crab rushed over to it. She unleashed a swift barrage of her claws, giving light taps to its carapace that didn't do any damage.

The crab looked sufficiently chastised, dropping its body to the sand and blowing bubbles of embarrassment. They appeared to have a conversation, exchanging claw gestures and hiss-like sounds.

Sergeant Snips scuttled to the side, pointing at the other crab, then at a spot on the sand. The freed crab dipped its head in acquiescence, stood on the patch of sand shown, and turned its back to us, looking out at the ocean.

". . . Snips? What are you—"

In a single movement, she darted to the crab, put both her claws under its body, and flung it out to sea. The rock crab let out a notably cute *eeeeeeeee* as it sailed up and out toward the horizon, its body eventually splashing down twenty meters from the shore. She dusted her claws off, nodded, then turned back to me.

I raised an eyebrow and smirked at her. "A little discipline, huh?"

She shrugged with both claws, shaking her carapace in mock dismay.

I put another baitfish in the pot. "Would you mind placing this out into the water, Snips?"

She clacked her claws sharply, grabbed the metal frame, and dragged it out into the depths.

When she got back, I bent down, putting on my most persuasive voice.

"I know you didn't want me going into the village yesterday, but how do you feel about me grabbing a coffee and pastry before we get started on the day's fishing?"

She looked toward the village, looked back at me, appearing to consider the proposition. After a long moment, she blew happy bubbles, gesturing toward Tropica and nodding.

"All right! I'll be right back!"

She waved goodbye with a single claw.

Sebastian was a walking pillar of regret and numbness as he moved through the streets on unfeeling legs. After he found the remains of Pistachio, he had to leave the Cult of the Leviathan's Tropica headquarters.

Where do I go from here? Will he just kill more of the precious spawn if I acquire another batch of babies from the capital? Dare I request a decades-old lobster, or is that just dooming it to death by the defiler?

That thought brought on images of his giant lobster—feeding the Leviathan to be, helping it shed its outgrown carapace, giving it encouragement in the early hours of the morning when his idiotic follower was asleep, telling it of the violent conquest it would one day be the leader of.

He'd underestimated the strength of the heretical defiler that was Fischer; his growing Leviathan and his beloved crickets had paid the price.

It's all my fault. If I hadn't antagonized the man on the stairs to ascension, my children would still be alive. If only I had more knowledge, if only I'd been more patient, if only—

"Morning, Sebastian!"

Sebastian's eyes focused, and he saw the defiler approaching.

"How are ya, mate? Cheers for that coffee, by the way—it really hit the spot!" The defiler gave him a wicked smile, his entire face scrunching in delight, taunting him.

Sebastian froze, his body shutting down in the face of the man that had so easily murdered Pistachio and the crickets.

"Bad news about the mug, though . . ." Fischer grimaced, but Sebastian could still make out the smile curling the corner of his mouth, the mirth still dancing behind his eyes. "I accidentally dropped it—what does it cost to replace?"

A snarl made its way to Sebastian's face, and it continued widening. He bared his teeth at Fischer—at the audacity of the defiler who would approach so soon after such cruelty. Sebastian spun, ran, fled, needing to get as far from the murderer as possible.

It's all Fischer's *fault.* He *did this—not me. The man taunts me, rubs his treachery in, pours salt into the gaping wound in my heart.*

A resolve settled itself deep within Sebastian, and the snarl transformed into a vicious grin. He would find a way. He would be the one to avenge his precious spawn.

On Zeus's barbed lightning, on all that is holy, I swear I will take him down.

I stared in confusion after Sebastian, who was running away with a rather embarrassing gait, his tall, stick-thin frame not suited to physical endeavors.

Well, he took that way worse than I thought . . . it was just a mug . . .

I shrugged. "Weird bloke . . ."

It was still too early for most of the villagers to be out and about, with only a few of the farmers setting off for their fields. All gave me a smile, nod, or wave, and I returned each one, not letting the odd interaction with Sebastian taint my disposition.

I got my fantasy croissant from Sue first, thanking her before setting off for Lena's Café on the north side of town. No one was in line there, and the owner, presumably Lena, looked me up and down with disdain as I arrived at the counter.

"You lost, boy?"

"Uh, I don't think so, no." I gave her a smile and brushed crumbs from my shirt. "Just here to collect my coffee—I believe George organized for me to have one each day?"

She sniffed. "If you're going to be returning for the next week, I suggest wearing something more befitting the better side of Tropica." She eyed my plain clothing again. "It wouldn't do to have you scaring off customers."

My eyebrow wanted to twitch, but I carefully schooled my features. "I'll keep that in mind, Lena. Sort a coffee out for me, and I'll get out of your hair, yeah?"

She sniffed again, looking down her nose at me, but thankfully started making my coffee. I tried to watch her work, but her large body unfortunately blocked my view of the coffee machine. From what I could see, it was quite similar to the ones on Earth, but much more basic; there was a chimney attached, the water inside likely being heated by a fire somewhere within.

She spun, placing the mug down on the counter and darting her hand back as I went to grab the drink.

"Cheers, Lena. See you tomorrow!"

"There is a two iron fee if you don't return the mug."

I winced internally, getting a bit of insight into Sebastian's reaction.

Still not enough to justify that level of fury, though . . .

"No worries," I said over my shoulder, already planning what I could wear tomorrow to piss her off even more.

I'd been cognizant of the fact that getting a machine for Sue might affect the sole existing café in the village, especially with the price Sue could offer the coffee. If the rest of the north siders had the same prejudice as Lena, however, they probably wouldn't come to the south side of Tropica and mingle with who they saw as less than.

After meeting the woman, I don't particularly care if Sue takes all *of her business.*

I breathed in the rising fragrance of my mug, then took a sip of the coffee. It was delicious.

Let capitalism rise.

Sergeant Snips was awaiting me eagerly when I returned, the rising sun reflecting off her glittering carapace as she waved enthusiastically with both claws.

She'd already collected the larger bamboo rod, my bucket, and three of the baitfish from where I'd buried them in a tea towel. Her body went tense, and she cocked her head, looking between me and the fish, the question clear.

"You're allowed to eat them, Snips," I said with a laugh. "As long as we have some left to fish with, you don't need my permission."

She relaxed, almost seeming to sigh, and started snacking on one.

"You ready to go?"

She bubbled her joyous assent between bites, and I followed her down to the shore.

I found a spot on the rocks where ocean met river. Snips settled down beside me, content to watch. I placed an entire baitfish on the large hook, and breathing deep of the sea spray and wind, started whirling the end of the line round and round.

I let go, casting it out into the water. The moment between letting go of the line and when the rock hit the water was a welcome flash of silence. Only the sound of water lapping at the rocks could be heard, and we both watched the sinker and fish-laden hook arc high into the sky.

A few seconds later, they hit the water with a soft *plop,* and I held the rod out to let the line freely travel. It went taut, and I felt the thump of it hitting the sandy floor. The tide was still running out but had almost stilled, telling me the tide would soon turn.

"Dawn is a great time for fishing, as is when the tide turns," I said to Snips. "I'd wager having both at the same time gives us a splendid chance of catching something!"

She looked at the line, her eyestalk and posture broadcasting the curiosity she felt. I took a seat beside her, and we sat in companionable silence. I held my hand on the top of her carapace, finding comfort in the feel of her. I closed my eyes and bathed in the moment.

The smooth wood of the bamboo in my hand, the line taut and softly pulling when waves atop the water crossed its path; the cool, sturdy carapace of Sergeant Snips, her body seeming to radiate vigor; the sound of the churning river and ocean meeting; the calm breeze that blew fitfully, coming and going in sporadic bursts of varying intensity; and the calls of gulls and other birds singing their beautiful songs to greet the sun that shone down on me, warming my skin—all served to ground me in the moment, no thoughts strong enough to break through the all-encompassing sensations of the body.

Tug.

I removed my hand from Snips, placing it firmly around the rod to join the other.

Tug.

My eyes remained closed as I tightened my grip.

Bump . . . tug.

I heard the soft sounds of Snips standing, responding to the hits.

Tug, tug, TUG.

The fish swallowed the bait, and I roared a laugh of delight as I finally opened my eyes. The bamboo rod bent down at a ninety-degree angle, the enormous fish doing its best to swim away, thrashing its head and making the rod tip shake. Joy and excitement flooded my entire being as I shot to my feet.

"Fish on, Snips!"

CHAPTER TWENTY-ONE

EVOLUTION

Sergeant Snips scuttled in mad circles around me, an uncontrolled stream of excited bubbles following her. I held the rod firmly with both hands as the fish on the other end of the line did its best to pull it from my grip. It shook its head madly, causing the already-bending bamboo to jerk around.

I took a big step forward, leaving enough tension to keep the hook secured, but not letting the fish put too much stress on the line. The bamboo flexed and bent but stayed whole.

I walked along the rocks further to the ocean, letting the fish expend energy each time it made another blistering run. Snips followed my movements, her skittering legs and sporadically clacking claws cheering me on.

Seeing that swimming into the ocean wasn't working for it, the fish changed tack; it swam back into the river mouth, its powerful muscles keeping me on my toes every step of the way. We danced like this for what felt like an eternity, the hooked fish doing its best to escape, and me doing my best to move with it, keeping tension but not letting too much pressure hit the line.

It was a war of body and brain; the fish relying on its muscular form and sharp instincts, and me relying on my enhanced body and human ingenuity.

I breathed in the salty air, reveling in the excitement of having such a large fish hooked. As our battle waged on, the fish was losing strength, but mine was only growing—the adrenaline coursing through my veins invigorated me even more with each passing breath.

I was on the sands of the riverbank now, Snips still dancing in circles, the fish lethargic compared to how the battle began. I started moving back from the shore, one slow step at a time. The fish made another powerful run, and I took a few steps forward, letting it tire itself out. A new dance began, and for every step I let my enemy take, I took two more back, drawing it ever closer to land.

I caught my first flash of silver as the fish neared the surface five meters from shore, the rising sun reflecting off its protective scales. At this, Snips lost what composure she held, and she launched herself into the river toward it.

The joining of a sapient crab to the battle had an unmistakable effect on the fish; it took another desperate run, fleeing as best as its fatigued body could. This suited me, and I smiled to myself, knowing the war was coming to an end.

I stepped forward, letting the fish run. The attempted escape didn't last long, and as soon as it showed weakness, I took long strides back from the water.

I could see the flash of silver again as the fish swam near the surface, slow and languid as if swimming through molasses. It saw the shore and tried to make one last desperate attempt at escape. There was a flash of something beneath it, and Snips's mighty claws flicked it out of the water and onto the sand, sealing its fate.

I dashed down to it, hauling it up with one hand under the gills and one on the body. I checked its mouth, and seeing that it had no teeth, moved my right hand to hold its lower jaw, securing the victory.

I roared in delight, laughing toward the sky. "Snips! We did it!"

She nodded vigorously with her whole body, her claws moving around in chaotic happiness.

A familiar feeling nudged me, but it was blunted, much less pronounced than before.

Ah—willing the System messages to chill worked out? Take that, System, you non-functional gronk of a . . . whatever you are.

Smiling, I inspected the fish.

Mature Shore Fish

Uncommon

Found along the ocean shores of the Kallis Realm, this fish is a staple source of both food and bait.

The moment I saw it was edible, I grabbed the long nail at my side and spiked the fish, dispatching it fast and humanely.

"So this is a mature version of the baitfish we've been catching . . ." I said to Sergeant Snips. "Look how bloody big they get!"

The fish was half again as long as my forearm and hand, and Snips nodded her agreement as she eyed the giant slabs of meat.

I held it up in one hand, judging it to weigh at least three kilograms. "What do you reckon, Snips? You want to eat your share raw, or should I cook it up for us on the fire?"

In response, she tore off toward the fire pit, picking up driftwood in passing and leaving a slew of excited bubbles in her wake.

I started the fire with ease, and as the newborn flames jumped from kindling to small sticks, I turned to my guard crab.

"You okay to keep growing the fire? I need to go clean and scale this."

She nodded enthusiastically, shooing me away with both claws.

Down at the ocean shore, I took a moment to thank the fish for its meat as I removed the scales. It was a majestic creature, and its body would go on to nourish me and my beloved Snips. It was simply the way of the world that the strong fed on the weak—that was the food chain, after all, but that didn't mean I should disregard my respect entirely. I had an immense gratitude for the fish before me, both for the war it had waged and the sustenance it would provide.

Back by the fire, I rested one hand on Snips as we sat in companionable silence. The fish slowly cooked, and the smell made my mouth water.

"Where do you think our otter friend got off to, Snips? I haven't heard its telltale rock tapping since yesterday morning . . ."

Sergeant Snips went rigid beneath my hand, blowing bubbles of . . . *anger? Disapproval?* It felt like I was getting better at deciphering her communication with each passing day, but in moments of passion, her intent still sometimes escaped me.

"Now, now, Snips," I gently chided, stroking her carapace. "We have plenty of rocks, and even more oysters to share with the wildlife."

She nodded her acquiescence but still didn't completely relax.

Noted—don't bring up the otter to Sergeant Snips unless I want to ruin her mood.

I had thoroughly enjoyed seeing the furred little thing smashing open oysters in its natural habitat; I'd always loved animals, and seeing a wild otter in the flesh had been a beautiful experience. I dreamed of befriending the pawed creature, imagining all three of us sitting by the fire, one of my hands on Snips, the other stroking its no-doubt soft fur.

Maybe I can try winning it over with some fish . . .

As I relished in the rising sun, the cool breeze, and the company, I let my thoughts carry me away.

Snips clacked and drew my attention an unknowable amount of time later, and I looked between her and the fish. She blew bubbles of urgency.

"You think it's done?"

She nodded, hurrying me on with a sharp gesture.

I parted the flesh in the thickest section. It was white and flaky, perfectly cooked.

"Good eye, Snips!"

I lifted the makeshift grill from atop the flames, placing it on a wooden board to cool.

I couldn't help but smile at my impatient crab, who kept reaching for, and subsequently retreating from, the steaming meat.

When it was sufficiently cooled, I broke off a section, placing it on the plate in front of her. I grabbed my own, and with a hand almost vibrating with anticipation, I put a small amount of flesh into my mouth. It was unbelievable.

Despite the size of the fish, the flesh melted in my mouth, the flavor both subtle and notable. It had a mild fishy taste, something which I was rather fond of, that didn't linger on the tongue.

Sergeant Snips bubbled in delight, shoveling the food into her mouth as fast as she could swallow the previous bite. I picked at mine, watching my guard crab devour more and more of the fish.

The only things it's missing are salt, pepper, and a squeeze of lemon.

"Oh my god, Snips! I'm an idiot!"

She cocked her head at me, not pausing from her feast for even a second.

"I live on the beach and haven't dried out any salt! How could I have overlooked something so simple?"

She blinked her lack of comprehension at me, still shoveling food into her maw.

"Oh well . . . I'll have some salt prepared for next time. You'll love it."

She nodded, then paused.

I looked at her, unsure of what could have stopped her single-minded determination to eat all the fish in sight. "You all right, Snips? What—"

A flash of light exploded from her, and I reflexively closed my eyes against the crab-born flashbang. Something physical hit me, like air rushing from her position, but I felt it within myself, not on my skin. I opened my eyes tentatively, squinting at her. When I noticed the change, my eyes flew wide.

"What the hell, Snips? What happened?"

She sat in exactly the same position, but where she was previously only barely larger than the other rock crabs, she had just almost doubled in size.

She looked herself over with great care, her lone eye lingering on the inch-long spikes that now sprouted from each of her joints.

"Snips! You evolved!"

She clacked her delight, now-spiked claws held high above her. She bobbed up and down as she blew bubbles of contentment, but then something in her demeanor changed. She paused, as if remembering something.

Her eye slowly wandered back to the fish in front of her, and in a blur of movement, she resumed her meal with great gusto, the changes already forgotten as her improved claws threw food into her enlarged mouth.

A raucous laugh escaped my throat, and suddenly feeling competitive, I raced her. I'm not going to get outshone by my crab, evolved or not!

Gary was feeling rather morose. He'd quite enjoyed the company of Pistachio—perhaps not at the same level as Sebastian, which was bordering on some kind of perverted attachment. Even so, he had enjoyed feeding the oversized lobster, and he'd have even called the crustacean a friend.

The only friend I had in this village, he admitted to himself.

Gary had done his best to dissuade his boss from trying to poison someone, knowing that no good could come out of it, but it was what it was. Sebastian had gone through with the plan, and Pistachio had paid the price.

With a feeling the same thing was about to happen, but knowing Sebastian probably wouldn't listen, he spoke anyway. "Are you sure this is a good idea, sir?"

Sebastian looked up from the letter he was writing, staring hatred and venom at Gary. "Yes, I am sure, you half-shelled moron! By the girthy conch of Triton, how many times must I explain myself to your simple mind?"

"Well, sir, it's just that it didn't go so well last time, and I think maybe it's best to leave things alone, you know? Fischer didn't kill us or anything, and it seems a pretty reasonable retaliatory strike to—"

"You dare!" Sebastian roared. "The murder of our Leviathan, the slaying of my beloved crickets, and the intrusion by the defiler on these holy grounds—are they reasonable to you?"

"Well, I mean, you did try to poison him to death . . ."

"He is a mere human," Sebastian snarled. "The basest form of life and cultivation, and you compare his death with the defilement of our growing gods?"

Well, that went about as I expected, Gary thought.

"You're probably right, sir. Do you really think the capital branch will lend us the artifact you're going to request, though?"

"When they hear of the defiler's crimes, they will have no choice!"

As Sebastian returned to his letter, Gary shook his head. "If you say so, sir."

Barry scolded himself when his attention once more returned to the succulent morsel of crab he'd partaken in. His thoughts since that fateful moment the previous evening had been troubled, and the memory of the flavor constantly returned unbidden, as did the yearning for another taste.

He shook his head, trying and failing to focus back on the crops before him. He halfheartedly dragged his hoe through the sandy soil.

"G'day, Barry! I've been looking everywhere for you!"

Barry's head shot up, looking at the man that introduced these worries into his life.

"Oh, morning, Fischer. How are you?"

"I'm good, mate, are you all right?" Fischer raised an eyebrow at him. "You look like you've seen a ghost . . ."

"Yeah, I'm good." Barry tried to give him a genuine smile. "Didn't sleep well, that's all."

"Ah, that's no good. I was worried after you took off last night. The crab didn't make you sick, did it?"

Barry jolted and couldn't help but look around to see if anyone had heard. There was no one else in the fields, so he simply shook his head. "No, Fischer, it didn't make me sick . . ."

"That's good!" Fischer gave a broad smile and pulled a hand from behind his back, revealing a plate of something white. "Because I've brought you something to try!"

CHAPTER TWENTY-TWO

BUSINESS

"Ow! You poxed son of a whore!" Trent punched the metal leg he'd knocked his head on, then swore as he shook his hand. "You useless pieces of junk! You're lucky I don't have you melted down!"

The room of ancient artifacts he was in had become a regular haunt for Trent, and where he'd previously only used it to hide from obligations, he'd started spending more and more of his plentiful free time among the relics.

He crawled through the warren, finally finding the open pocket after only getting lost a few times—a new record. He stretched, rubbing his now-throbbing knuckles where the ancient construct had *dared* to stand in the way of his closed fist.

If Trent had even the slightest pinch of self-awareness added to the stew that was his consciousness, he would've likely recognized he'd become addicted to checking the screen on the single working artifact in the room. Being who he was, though, Trent just thought he enjoyed being there.

"Let's see what this Fischer has been up to," he said, rubbing his hands together in markedly uncognized anticipation. He slapped the screen, nodding as it came to life.

"At least one of you junkbots is subordinate enough to—*what the fuck?*" His normally dumb-looking face stared at the screen, making him appear even more vacant than usual.

He rubbed his eyes, wondering if he'd hit his head a little harder than he thought—but no, the screen remained the same. It had a single additional line of text added.

New Milestone! Sergeant Snips has reached her first stage of evolution!

". . . what in Poseidon's pickled sphincter is a Sergeant Snips?"

Barry stared down at the plate of fish, an unquenchable desire to taste it drowning out his trepidation. He tore his eyes away from it, looking up at Fischer.

"W-where did you get this?"

"Caught it just this morning, mate! It's a mature shore fish, whatever that means. I've been eating the juvenile variant for days, and I thought they were tasty!" Fischer laughed and shook his head. "This thing blows those little snacks out of the water!"

"I . . . it's okay to eat?"

"Yeah, mate, it's—" Fischer raised a finger as something occurred to him. "Actually,

I should probably mention that Sergeant Snips grew spikes after she ate some, but I'm pretty sure that's a crab thing? You have nothing to worry about . . . probably."

"Well then, I—wait, she *what?*"

"Yeah, she kind of grew spikes and doubled in size? Pretty gnarly, really—wait till you see."

Barry could smell the fragrance of the fish, close as he was. He'd always assumed it would smell disgusting if one were to cook the heretical creatures, like the smell of low tide; the chunk of white flesh on the plate smelled nothing like that. It was sweet and complex, with just a hint of sea spray. It reminded him of the crab claw he'd eaten the night before, and his mouth started watering. An insatiable need to taste it coursed through him.

"Y-you're sure it's safe to eat?"

"Yeah mate, I think the spikes were more to do with the whole 'ascended being' thing, and less to do with the fish." Fischer shrugged. "I ate almost half a fillet myself, and I feel great!"

"I-I don't know, Fischer. What if someone were to find out?"

Fischer laughed. "It's just you and me here, mate. I'm not gonna tell anyone, are you?"

Barry's mouth continued to salivate; he couldn't hold off any longer. "Maybe just a bite . . ."

Barry accepted the plate. He grabbed a corner of the meat, and a chunk fell away between his probing fingers. Before he could second-guess himself, he placed it in his mouth. The fish melted atop his tongue, the flavor delivering everything the fragrance had promised. It was much like the crab; sweet, slightly salty, and invigorating. It reminded him of the sun rising above the sea, shining its light over the land and warming his body from up high. An involuntary moan of delight escaped him.

"Good, right?" Fischer asked with a laugh.

Barry shoved another chunk into his mouth.

"Mate, if you think that's good, wait until I rustle up some salt, pepper, and citrus!"

Barry nodded, unhearing beyond the sensations he was experiencing.

"I'll leave the plate with you, mate—bring it round later, yeah?"

Barry nodded again, devouring the meal as Fischer left.

I smiled at Barry's reaction as I meandered toward Tropica. "Anyone would think the bloke never tasted fish before . . ."

I honestly wasn't sure he'd take the fish after his reaction to the crab yesterday, but the moment he'd smelled the shore fish, I knew I had him.

Winning over Barry was an important first step. I dreamed of hosting barbecues laden with freshly cooked seafood, the laughing faces of all the villagers surrounding me—well, some of the villagers. I could stand to go without the pompous north siders ruining the vibe.

Though, maybe I can rehabilitate some of them over time with the right attitude and some good food . . .

"Good morning, Fischer!" Sue called as I approached her bakery.

I returned the smile she gave me. "Morning, Sue! How's it going?"

"Good! Everyone has been abuzz over the coffee machine since learning of it—I haven't even started selling coffee yet, and business has already increased!"

"That's good to hear! Your pastries are a gift from the departed gods, so I can understand why you've been so busy!"

She gave me a sly smile. "I've already agreed to give you free pastries, Fischer. You don't need to sweet talk me any further."

I laughed. "I'm not sweet talking you, Sue—the pastries are really that good. Besides, I'm not sure Mr. Sue would approve."

Her eyes twinkled in delight. "Well, that's kind of you to say. Speaking of Mr. Sue, I'm not sure you've met Sturgill yet, have you?"

"No, I can't say I've had the pleasure! Is he around?"

"Always—hiding out back with his beloved dough, as per usual. Let me fetch him."

A moment later, a man in a black apron covered in flour was dragged from behind a dividing wall, Sue leading him with a broad smile.

"Sturgill, this is Mr. Fischer, the one I've told you so much about."

Sturgill nodded to me. "Hello, Fischer."

"Nice to meet you, mate!"

"And you." Sturgill smiled at me. "Thanks for the machine you organized—it'll do wonders for business."

"No worries, mate! I think a little coffee will pair perfectly with the delightful pastries you make!"

He nodded again, giving me another smile. "I best be getting back to the ovens—wouldn't do to have anything burning." He turned and strode back behind the dividing wall.

Sue raised an eyebrow and cocked her head at him, staring at his back as he departed.

"I'm guessing Sturgill is more the silent type?" I asked with a smile.

"That is the most amount of words I think I've ever heard him say to someone . . ." she said, still staring toward where Sturgill disappeared. "The man will not shut up when work is finished, but when there's bread or pastries to attend to, he barely utters a peep—even to me."

"Sounds like a reliable partner to have a business with! You've got enough personality to cover the both of you, and he's clearly got the wares sorted." I took a bite of the croissant. "These things are bloody delightful."

"I don't know what I'd do without him." She returned her attention to me, a smile playing on her lips. "And there you go with the sweet talking again—come back for another whenever you please, Fischer. It's the least we can do after what you've done for us."

I ate the pastry slowly as I made my way toward Lena's Café, unbuttoning my shirt as I walked. When I was one corner away, I looked at my reflection in a large window. Struck by inspiration, I reattached two of the buttons—in the wrong places, of course, making myself seem as uncouth as possible.

"Ho, Lena!" I said, swaggering up to the counter.

She turned with a slow regard, her eyes lingering on the appearance of my shirt. Her eyebrow twitched, and it took great effort not to laugh. She turned and started making my coffee, deciding not to acknowledge me.

"Are there any jewelers in Tropica, Lena?" I asked her overly large back.

"Probably not that you could afford."

"So there are jewelers, then?" I asked, voice filled with projected joy.

She sniffed. "There is a jeweler, yes, but I'm not sure they would deal with you . . ."

"Shall we make a deal?" I asked.

She turned with my coffee, placing it on the counter and staring down her nose at me. "And what would you have to offer me?"

"Well, the sooner you give me directions to the jeweler, the sooner I'll leave your counter." I beamed a smile at her, and her eye twitched again.

"One block west. Noble Star Jewelry."

"Cheers, Lena! What would I do without you?"

Before picking up the coffee, I fixed my shirt, taking the time to smooth my appearance with deliberate care.

"Bye, Lena! I'll see you tomorrow!"

With my coffee in hand, I could feel the stare she was boring into the back of my skull. With my face hidden, I let my joy show.

I tasted the drink, thoroughly enjoying the first sip. "Ah. Delightful. She may be a bit insufferable, but the lady can make a mean brew."

I probably shouldn't have been antagonizing the woman that made my coffee each morning, but honestly, I couldn't help myself.

Something about despicable behavior demands retribution, passive aggressive or not.

It probably said something about me that I felt that way, but who had time to internalize that particular lesson? There was business to conduct!

I found the jewelers easily enough; a colorfully painted sign read something illegible above a store. I was still rather illiterate to the written language of this world, but the image of a cut gem beside the words was a dead giveaway. It seemed this stretch of street was the north side version of the market, with many storefronts all smattered together.

I walked into the jewelers, finding the door unlocked despite the early hour.

"We are *closed,*" came the gruff voice of an elderly man, hunched over the counter and peering at an uncut gem through an enlarged eye glass.

"Oh, my bad, mate. The door was open. What time can I come back?"

He looked up at me, an unimpressed gaze lingering on my clothes. "That depends. What do you want?"

"Just a question answered." I rummaged in my pocket, pulling out a single pearl. "Have you ever seen one of these before?"

* * *

Julian fought down his frustration at the intruder before him.

"Just a question answered," the stranger said, rummaging in one of his filthy pockets. "Have you seen one of these before?"

Julian closed his eyes and breathed a great sigh.

Does this look like a market for trinkets? What bauble has this peasant stumbled upon, only to waste my time with—Julian's thoughts stopped dead in their tracks, and he felt his eyes go wide.

The man before him held an iridescent stone. Not just any stone, either—it was a relic of the past, one of the treasures that hadn't been found in countless years, whose numbers only diminished as pieces of jewelry were damaged or lost.

He'd seen the stones in person in the capital, only worn by those of excessive means. A single time, he'd seen a beautiful silver necklace made entirely of the precious stones, only the clasp left bare. It had been around the queen's neck, an abject demonstration of the crown's wealth.

Realizing he was staring, slack-jawed, he schooled his expression. "Ah, I cannot say I've seen such a stone before—it does seem mildly pretty, but I cannot say it would hold much worth."

"Ah, is that so?" the man asked. "Shame." He turned away. "Oh well, thanks for the info."

"W-wait!" Julian said, desperately trying to keep the man in his store. "I-I have some interest, only in a purely scientific manner, you understand? I've never seen one before and would like to examine it."

Julian shrugged, feigning nonchalance. "I must admit, my curiosity gets the better of me—I don't suppose you'd be willing to trade it for—"

"Nope!" the man said, still walking away. "Sorry mate, not interested in selling."

"One gold!" Julian yelled, desperation creeping into his voice. "I'll give you a gold coin—I'm very curious, you see—"

"I'll keep that in mind, mate." He opened the door to leave.

"*Two gold?*"

The man turned back, his expression unreadable. "Is it worth that much to you?"

"Ah—I—I'm very curious, you see . . ."

"Would you do five gold?" the man asked, face still blank.

"Y-yes! Five gold! May I see it? I—"

"Nah. Sorry, mate. Still not interested in selling it, I was just curious what it was worth to you." The man stepped outside.

"I-I'm Julian!" he yelled, doing anything to keep the stranger there. "What's your name?"

The stranger popped his head back in the door. "Nice to meet you, mate. I'm Fischer."

With that, Fischer disappeared, his head vanishing out of sight.

Julian stared at the closed door, uncomprehending.

What in Ares's calamitous spear was that?

What kind of peasant could walk away from such a vast sum of wealth? Was the man mad, or just stupid? A sudden realization struck him.

He knows what it's worth . . . ? If he knows it's worth at least twenty gold and didn't want to sell it, what purpose did he have in coming here?

The answer occurred to Julian, and it twisted his stomach with sickening ferocity.

Aphrodite's tumultuous loins! He's not really a peasant—he's a crown auditor!

The jeweler ran out the door after Fischer.

CHAPTER TWENTY-THREE

IRIDESCENT STONE

A grin made its way to my face as I left the store. Julian's reaction and increasing purchase price had been everything I needed to know.

They do *know of pearls here, and they're exceedingly expensive. He was trying to rip me off, so I'll need to find somewhere else to sell . . .*

"Fischer! Wait!" Julian yelled, throwing the door open behind me.

"I-I was only joking, you see!" He had a manic smile, his eyes wide. "Of course I know what iridescent stones are worth, as do you, right? Why don't you come back inside and we can talk properly?"

They call them iridescent stones, huh?

I looked around the empty street, the hour too early for the north siders to be out and about. "Here seems fine, mate. I can appreciate a good joke as much as the next bloke, but I didn't think you were trying to be funny . . ."

Julian wiped his brow free of accrued sweat. "A simple misunderstanding . . ." He glanced around. "I, of course, know that each stone would sell for twenty gold on their own and would be worth more if adorned in a precious metal. From your bearing, I knew you did too, and was trying to jest, you see? My wife always says I have an odd sense of humor."

I kept my expression blank as Julian rambled.

"I see—just a joke, then." I smiled at him. "No worries. If I were to come back, seeing as though you're a *legitimate* and *reputable* merchant, could I expect an honest appraisal of my wares?"

"Y-yes, sir! Of course!"

"Good to know. See ya, Julian." I turned and walked away.

"Y-yes, Fischer! Until next time!"

I pondered the interaction as I made my way back through town. Something had changed the merchant's demeanor; he seemed almost panicked when he ran out his door to meet me.

Is it that the pearl is worth much more than twenty gold, or was he worried I'd tell people about his underhanded negotiating . . . ?

I sighed, dismissing the worries.

This is exactly why I didn't want to get involved in any business dealings. I know it needs to be done, but I'd just rather be fishing.

I walked up a set of steps and knocked three times on the door.

* * *

George set his sugar-crusted pastry down, fighting the rising tide of anxiety. "Is no moment sacred to me?" he asked. "Can I not have even my second breakfast unmolested?"

"I'm sorry, dear," his wife said around a mouthful of dough and sugar. "Want me to get it?"

"No, Geraldine, it's fine."

She stood, coming to massage his shoulders with her plump hands. "I worry about your health, dear. All this stress isn't good for your digestion."

"That is the burden a lord must bear." He sighed, pushing his chair out and standing with a groan. "I'll be back in a moment."

As George walked down the stairs, the knock came again—three sharp bangs, whose strength could only belong to one man. The anxiety flooded up from where he'd suppressed it, and he stood before the door a moment, composing himself.

Wiping beads of sweat from his forehead with a handkerchief, he swung the door open and plastered a smile onto his face. "Good morning, Fischer! To what do I owe the pleasure?"

"Morning, mate! Sorry for the early visit—I had a rather pressing question for you."

"It's no problem! I am at your beck and call, good man. What was your question?"

George was rather impressed with his composure thus far and felt he was getting better at interacting with the crown agent before him.

When Fischer spoke, that composure was shattered like a lolly dropped on stone.

"What's an iridescent stone worth?" Fischer asked with complete nonchalance.

"A-an iridescent stone, you say?" George wiped the sweat pouring from his face, and he tried to keep his smile genuine. "They go for at least twenty gold on their own, but are worth more if fixed by a . . . a talented jeweler . . ."

George's voice had started to tremble, and Fischer raised an eyebrow.

"You feeling all right, mate?"

"Y-yes. Thanks, Fischer. Is that all?"

"Ah, yeah, mate. That's all I came to ask. Sure I can't help you? You look white as a ghost."

"No. Thank you." George slammed the door, his hands tingling and numb.

Triton's pointed beard—how does he know? Will this treacherous man leave no stone unturned?

George moved as fast as he could back up the stairs. When he reached the second floor, he was out of breath and light-headed. He stumbled, catching himself on the banister.

"George!" Geraldine yelled, running to his side at a respectable pace for her ample size. "What's wrong, dear?"

"The—the stones . . ." George wheezed.

"The stones? What about the stones?"

"F-Fischer knows. He knows how we . . . we've been . . . hiding the funds," he said between gasps.

"By Thalassa's lathered seahorse!" she cursed, leaving his side as she waddled toward the box of embezzled goods. "We have to destroy the evidence!"

Man, George started that interaction so well, but his social anxiety really came flying out at the end. I shook my head. *Poor bloke. I should probably stop knocking on his door—he's only getting worse.*

"Sorry, George," I said to myself. "Your anxiety served the greater good."

I breathed in deeply, relishing the fresh ocean air. I smiled as I considered how things had played out.

The pearls the crabs had gathered for me were the key to my financial freedom. If I sold even one of them, I'd have more than enough to sustain myself for the foreseeable future.

It's probably best if I only sell one anyway—I don't want to draw too much unwanted attention to myself and the crab safe haven I'm trying to establish.

I nodded to myself. *Sell a single pearl, and I'll hopefully be able to discard the business pants for a while.*

I picked up the pace as I strode to my next destination.

"Morning, Fischer!" the burly blacksmith greeted.

"G'day Fergus! How are ya, mate?"

"Always a good day at the smithy!"

Fergus put a crucible inside the forge with his oversized tongs, then set them down and walked over to me. "What can I do for you today, Fischer?"

"Mostly a question, mate—probably a dumb one."

"Nonsense!" He took his gloves off and gave me a smile. "No such thing as a dumb question, as my dad would say. What did you want to know?"

I returned the smile. "Are you capable of making or acquiring a silver chain?"

"Silver, aye?" He scratched his chin. "We can forge strips and make chains, and we've done so before, but I can't say I've ever worked with silver . . ."

"Think you're capable of it?"

"*Capable?*" He held a hand to his chest in mock affront. "Fischer! You wound me!"

"Sorry, mate," I said with a laugh. "I didn't mean it as an insult—I couldn't tell you the difference between a forge and a campfire. Forgive the ignorance."

"I jest, Fischer, I jest." Fergus crossed his sizable arms in front of his chest as he thought aloud. "I can definitely work with silver. The only reason I haven't is there's no demand for it on this side of the village. We're kept busy with the usual fare—horseshoes, cutlery, metal joinings, and nails."

"All right." I nodded, reaching a decision. "I'll need to show you something, but can you keep it between us?"

"Well, I don't keep any secrets from Duncan if it's work related, but I can assure you he's as tight-lipped as I am when it comes to requests." He leaned in, whispering. "You should *see* some of the things the north siders bring our way when they don't want their uppity smith gossiping. I won't give you names or specifics, but the things

I've had to craft, Fischer . . ." He shook his head, looking down at his hands. "Some things you can't wash off."

"I can only imagine, mate." I reached into my pocket, grabbing the pearl and holding it up to Fergus. "Do you know what this is?"

He fumbled in his pocket, withdrawing a set of spectacles. Leaning in, he cocked his head back and forth as he inspected the stone.

"It's beautiful, but what in Hades's empty glare is it? I've never seen anything of the like."

"Have you heard of iridescent stones before—"

"*IRIDESCENT STO—*" He cut himself off, glancing around and leaning further in. "Iridescent stone? That's truly an iridescent stone?" His eyes were transfixed on the pearl I held in my hand.

"You can pick it up if you like, mate."

"Y-you're sure?"

I laughed at the reverence. "Yeah, mate. Take a closer look."

His fingers pinched it with a gentleness that belied his size, and he placed it carefully in his palm, moving his head side to side as he inspected it in the light.

"It's marvelous. I never thought I'd actually see one in person, let alone be able to inspect it . . ."

"The stone is what I want the chain for."

"You're thinking of making a necklace?"

"That's the one. The jeweler Julian up north will buy it, but he said they're worth more if they're set in precious metal. I thought I could share the love a bit and spread the funds around."

"If you provide the silver, I'll happily do the work for free, Fischer. I'd love to create something with this . . ."

Fergus's head darted up, his gaze going vacant. "Take it back—one moment."

He placed the pearl in my open hand with deliberate care then ran to the back of his workshop. He came back with a box and started shuffling through it.

"I think a ring might be better suited. Here, what do you think?" Fergus held a casing in one hand, a small iron ring in the other. "While I'm confident in my ability to work with silver, a chain of the soft metal would be easily broken—a ring would be much more durable, and easier to sell."

"Mind if I look at the ring, mate?"

His hand darted forward, offering it to me.

I eyed the ring, holding it up to the light. It was smooth and absent of blemishes, its iron body basic, but still elegant. There was an empty setting in the top, with prongs outstretched—waiting for a gem or stone to be placed inside.

"You created this one?" I asked.

"Aye. The one you hold came from this mold." He indicated the casing held in one hand. "We sell them occasionally, so I always keep one spare."

I gently dropped the pearl into the casing—it fit perfectly.

"I think you're on the money there, Fergus. Tell you what—if you can create a ring exactly the same but out of silver, and you set the stone in it for me, I'll give you a gold coin."

His eyes widened, then narrowed. "You yanking my chain, Fischer?"

I couldn't help but laugh. "Nah, mate. I'm being sincere. It'll boost its value, and your skilled hands are the only set I trust to do it."

"It's still too much, Fischer. I don't want to look a gift horse in the mouth, but it is *way* too much. It's so much money that I don't want you coming back and causing an issue when you realize."

It was my turn to hold my hand to my chest in mock horror. "Fergus! My good man! Who do you take me for, a spoiled noble brat?"

He smiled at me through a wince. "It never hurts to be sure with these things, Fischer . . ."

"Okay. So, it's too much, right?"

He nodded. "Aye. Too much."

"No worries! Let's strike a deal then! I have some things I want to craft, and I'm trying to distance myself from bartering and purveying as much as humanly possible. Let's call the gold I give you a favor between friends, and the things I come and craft the same."

Fergus rubbed his hands idly in thought. "I don't think you could possibly request things to outweigh the worth of a gold coin, Fischer, but I feel the need to ask before signing up—what are you looking at making?"

I thought for a moment, sorting through my mind. "A thick metal griddle for cooking, some cogs and other bits for a fishing rod I'm creating, and some metal nails and brackets for a fence."

Fergus blinked at me. I blinked back, worried my request had overstepped his expectations.

He roared a laugh, clapping me on the shoulder. "You're a goddamn madman, Fischer—aye, I'm happy to call it an exchange between friends, but I still think I'm getting too much out of it."

I grinned at him. "Nonsense, mate. I'm getting more value from the stone because of you! Besides, friends don't count favors, and unexpected fortune should be shared."

Sergeant Snips gazed out at the squad arrayed before her. Her reliable crabs were relaying their reports of the perimeter, communicating with a series of bubbles, clacks, and gestures. A blur of brown caught her eye, and her lone stalk darted toward the interruption.

Ah—the interloper returns.

The otter swam in closer, stealing glances at their meeting as it whirled above them in the currents. Sergeant Snips fought down the rising anger. Her master had said to share their lands with the furry scoundrel, but that directive railed against her instincts.

The otter swam down closer, annoyingly intelligent eyes looking between her and the squad of crabs.

She raised both claws in warning, blowing a small stream of animosity-laden bubbles. She would tolerate the fiend's presence on the master's property, but spying on their meeting was an unacceptable intrusion.

Sensing their sergeant's animosity, the squad of crabs also raised their claws, clacking and blowing angry streams. The otter swam even closer, the warning only seeming to increase its curiosity. Its eyes lingered on the spikes now protruding from her carapace and limbs, cocking its head back and forth in thought.

Sergeant Snips clacked both of her mighty claws, sending two arcs of force out to either side of the otter. This was finally enough, and the interloper turned and swam away.

Yes. Begone, smasher of shells and stealer of meat—flee before the might of my improved form.

She lowered her claws, and with a single nod of her mighty carapace, the meeting resumed.

CHAPTER TWENTY-FOUR

PERFECT FORM

The sun warmed my skin as I walked back through the fields. Fergus was procuring the silver for the ring, my belly was still full from a feast of fish, and the future was looking bright.

What a beautiful day.

I scoured the surrounding rows of sugarcane for Barry, but he was nowhere to be seen. Instead, I found Paul, his young and enthusiastic son.

"Hello Fischer!" Paul yelled from behind me, making me jump.

"Oh, morning, mate! Is your old man around?"

"He wasn't feeling well. He went home to rest."

Damn, I hope my fish didn't make him sick . . .

"Did he, uh, look all right to you? No odd changes or anything?"

Paul cocked his head at me. "Changes? He's just a little sick, is all."

Good. No spikes, then—that would have been quite a pickle.

"Let him know I hope he feels better soon."

"I will! Here, Mr. Fischer!!" Paul held my plate out to me. "Dad said to give you back your plate and to thank you for the pastry!"

Pastry, huh?

A smile tugged at my lips. "Let your dad know he's very welcome."

"You . . ." Paul looked down, then back up at me. "You don't have any more pastries, do you?"

I laughed at the gleam in the boy's eyes. "Sorry, mate, I can't say I do. Next time, all right?"

"Right!" Paul nodded, taking the lack of baked goods in stride. "I better get back to the fields—I have a lot to do, with Dad unwell!"

"No worries. See ya, mate."

Sergeant Snips was nowhere to be seen when I got back to my shores, and I figured she was out doing crab things.

It's been a few hours, right? Surely it wouldn't hurt to check the crab pot . . .

When I pulled on the line, it felt light, and sure enough, the trap was empty, the bait inside untouched. I knew it was probably too soon to check it, but I couldn't help myself. It was just so exciting; I had constant intrusive thoughts about checking the trap.

Noted—have a little patience, Fischer, you silly goose.

I walked back to my house, sitting in the sun by the coals of my fire pit. The rays were blessedly warm, chasing away the chill from a strong breeze blowing north. The remains of the fire were still red, and I stretched my feet toward them, lavishing in the sensation on the bottom of my feet.

Probably not a good day for fishing with the wind, so what should I—"Salt!" I yelled, jumping up as I remembered my lack of seasoning. I ran to the kitchen in search of the largest pot I had.

I walked down to the ocean with what had to be a twenty-liter stockpot, waded out into the calmer waters, and filled it almost to the top. The water was freezing with the wind kicking up, but it did nothing to cool my excitement.

I got back to the fire, placed a few large logs on the still-glowing coals, and set the salt water-filled stockpot atop a rack.

I know back in the day you could just dry seawater in the sun, so heating it above a small fire couldn't hurt, right . . . ?

As for what to do with the rest of my day, I had not yet introduced myself to some of my favorite people in the village—a situation I intended to rectify while my salt water slowly reduced.

I grabbed a few berries to go, setting off with a smile.

Joel meditated, his body in a position resembling that of the perfect form. He contemplated life, the twists of fate, and the miracle that was convergent evolution. He longed for such an evolution to take him, to transcend this inferior form of flesh and its lowly, internal skeletal system. Today may not be the day, but his time *would* come.

A sense of peace and tranquility took him as he slipped deeper and deeper into his trance. A sharp knocking sounded, three loud raps shattering his focus.

Joel let out a deep sigh. *What is it now?*

His acolytes all opened their eyes, shooting similar looks of disdain toward the wooden portal, but they quickly returned to their meditations.

Swinging open the door, Joel was met by a man he recognized.

He'd seen him on the beach, watching his cult's claw ritual with great curiosity. The stranger had also interrupted the procession with raucous laughter, but that was the way of the villagers, unknowing heretics as they were.

"Can I help you?" Joel asked, raising an eyebrow.

"G'day, mate! I just wanted to come say hello!"

Joel winced at the loud tone. "If you wouldn't mind keeping it down, the faithful are currently meditating."

The man smiled in apology, dropping his voice to a more reasonable level. "Sorry, mate. I'm Fischer, and I realized I hadn't introduced myself to you guys yet—I'm a big fan of crabs myself, and I thought we'd get along like pigs in mud."

Joel looked Fischer over again with a discerning eye. He was lean and tanned, indicating he was likely a farmer.

A working man. Respectable.

"Your admiration of the crab is notable, but our beliefs stretch further beyond their perfect forms. We believe in carcinization, which is—"

"Oh, I know what carcinization is," Fischer interrupted. "The convergent evolution of different species that somehow all turn into crabs. I'm a big fan, mate—it's endlessly intriguing."

Joel had initially been annoyed at the interruption, but as Fischer spoke on, his heart swelled, his very being vibrating with the farmer's enlightenment.

He stuck his hand out. "My name is Joel. It's a pleasure to meet you, Fischer."

"The pleasure's all mine, mate." Fischer shook Joel's proffered hand, his grip firm.

And the man has a firm handshake—I may have just found our newest recruit!

"Would you care to join me for our meditation, Fischer? We are pondering the perfection of the crab's form."

Fischer peered past Joel, who had stepped aside to display the acolytes in all their glory.

"Er—it looks a little uncomfortable, mate."

Joel sighed, the comment an unfortunate reminder. "Such are the limitations of our inferior bodies—all the more reason to ponder and praise the form of the crab."

"Do I have to stay for a set time, or is it cool if I take off after a while? I have a few things I need to get to later . . ."

"Of course, of course!" Joel said, ushering him in. "We have another hour left—stay as little or long as you like."

The meditation was surprisingly relaxing, given that I was squatting down like a crab—claw hands and all.

The cultists surrounding me occasionally made little bubbling noises with their mouths, which was both hilarious and rather endearing. The first time, I thought it was an accident; when it happened a second time, I thought it was just one of the acolytes being a weirdo; when it came from a different direction the third time, I realized it was intentional and had to fight my laughter down. The sporadic mouth noises drew me from my meditation in the beginning, but as the sounds repeated, they settled into the background.

If I'm already doing a crab meditation, I may as well send it . . .

I joined in on the bubbling noises, picturing Sergeant Snips and her impressive streams as I did so.

I lost track of time as I focused on the sensations of the body. The minor aches from the odd posture faded away and melted into a single cloud of tingling and numbness. My level of zen increased, and I felt a content smile settle itself on my lips.

After an unknown amount of time, a soft *ding* sounded. I opened my eyes. Joel was standing with a tiny gong in his hands, beaming down at me.

"Thank you for joining us, Fischer. How was your first time?"

The surrounding acolytes' heads turned to me with expressions ranging from sleepy to content, two male and two female.

I stretched, leaning back to sprawl my limbs out as far as possible on the wooden floor. "That was delightful, mate. Thanks for letting me join in."

"You're welcome—come back for meditation any time you please."

I sat up, crossing my legs. "How often do you do them?"

"We do it once a week, every Fielday."

Er—Fielday? Yikes, I'd never actually thought about the days of the week here . . .

I nodded. "Right. Fielday. I'll, uh, be sure to come back soon."

Seeing no raised eyebrows or questioning looks, I confirmed Fielday was, in fact, a day of the week.

Now to work out the rest without revealing I was sent here by truck-kun . . .

Three of the acolytes packed up and left almost immediately, not lingering for longer than it took to stretch their bodies out. I remained sitting on the floor, basking in the afterglow of serenity.

"You know, Fischer . . ." Joel squatted down in front of me. "The Cult of Carcinization is always looking for more members if you're interested in expanding your piety. You already possess more knowledge than any of our previous recruits, and I'm sure Jess here wouldn't mind taking you through the scriptures."

He pointed to the single female that remained. She gazed at me with deep brown eyes, aggressively nodding.

I let out a small laugh. "I think you might find me a bit too heretical for your liking, Joel—I appreciate the offer, though."

"Heretical?" he asked, narrowing his eyes at me. "How so?"

I shrugged. "I fish."

"You . . . *fish?*"

"That's right," I said with a broad grin. "Pretty much all I do, really."

He stood and stared at me then shrugged back. "That is of no concern."

"Wait, really?" I let my confusion show. "You're not gonna call me a heretic, a fool, or something worse?"

Jess answered with her own question. "Who are we to judge you, Fischer?" She gave a kind smile. "We are all imperfect beings, after all. To err is in our nature."

Man, these crab cultists are actually pretty chill—

"Until we ascend!" Joel boomed, his eyes filled with fervor, hands clacking. "Only then, when we have achieved the perfect form, we will know the way in all things!"

Nevermind.

"Well, it's been fun, guys." I gave them a wave. "I'll see you next, uh, what day is the meditation again?"

"Fielday," Jess said, still smiling.

"Right. Fielday. See you then."

I shook my head as I headed back to my land. "I can't tell if Joel is batshit crazy, or my new best friend . . ."

The convening of the crabs had stretched on longer than the sun remained in the sky, their meeting ending just as the last bit of light fled beyond the western horizon.

Sergeant Snips dismissed her subordinates, and they all scuttled off toward their assigned positions.

After they left, she set off, heading to a cave she'd found in the deepest part of the bay. On the way there, she dispatched two small fish and carried one in each claw as she continued on her way.

When she arrived, she peered into the rocky crevice, curious to see if it was still there. A lone antenna poked out from behind a corner, moving up and down as it smelled the ocean currents. She rounded the rock, holding both fish out so their scent wafted forward.

The sea snipper emerged, larger than even Snips, lured out by the promise of a meal. The lump where its other antenna had been was completely healed, which she was glad to see.

Sergeant Snips placed both fish before it, and the sea snipper grabbed them with two humongous claws, retreating back into its hole. With a nod of respect to the unintelligent creature—a gesture it wouldn't understand, but still felt right—she began a thorough search of the bay.

It took her most of the night to ensure every nook and crevice was free of threats, and it was early in the morning when she finished. She'd been scoping out the poisoner, Sebastian, each evening since delivering her master's retribution. She clacked her claws violently—this night would be no different. Thinking of the man made bubbles of fury tumble from her mouth, and she let them flow, agreeing with the sentiment her body expressed.

In the early hours of the morning, a hooded figure draped in a king-sized black sheet crept through the streets of Tropica, large of form and short of breath. They avoided the major thoroughfares as they moved, sticking to smaller streets and alleys between buildings.

When the shadowed figure reached sections that were lit, they dashed—insofar as someone of their impressive form could dash, anyway. Silent as the night, built like a barrel, they cradled their burden with great care.

The sound of the small waves crashing against the rock wall of the shore could finally be heard, telling them they'd almost reached their destination.

A few streets and a quick dash or two later, they stepped out onto the stone walkway that separated the ocean from the houses of Tropica, only *mostly* out of breath. A strong breeze hit them immediately, almost blowing away their sheet-robe. They spun in circles, one meaty hand grabbing for the corners that threatened to blow away and leave them exposed.

"Triton's throbbing conch," they muttered, "is the world itself conspiring against me?"

They stepped up to the wall, gazing out at the ocean.

There is no other option—stashing it for later will only invite more disaster . . .

With one last look at the small chest in their hand, they closed their eyes and flung it out to sea.

A single tear ran down George's face as he watched his work of the last five years hit the water and sink into the depths.

Curse you and your devious mind, Fischer. Curse you.

A gust blew, almost taking his sheet with it.

And that damned seamstress whose clothes always shrink!

Scuttling toward Tropica, Sergeant Snips clacked a fish in passing, her arcing attack severing its head. With two halves of a fish in hand, well, in claw, she approached the village. A splash came from above, and something descended.

Danger! Attack!

CHAPTER TWENTY-FIVE

TUTOR

Sergeant Snips stretched her claws wide, gathering power in her joints. She prepared to unleash a mighty clack of the claws on whomever was foolish enough to sneak up on her.

Who dares attack the benevolent Sergeant Snips—beloved crab of Fischer?

A small object sank down toward her, and she scuttled to the side, her eye watching it with keen hesitance. It hit the bottom with a soft *thud.* Sergeant Snips waited, but nothing happened. She crawled over to it, tentatively poking it with a calcified stick of dead coral. Again, nothing. Slowly, ever so carefully, she snipped a metal padlock and lifted the lid. Her lone eye sparkled as moonlight reflected off the chest's contents.

I woke to the sight of a rather pleased crab hovering above me, tentative little bubbles of greeting coming forth.

"Morning, Snips." I stretched out, unleashing a mighty yawn. "I missed you yesterday, where'd you get off to?"

She jumped off the bed, urging me to follow her with both claws.

"Not so fast, you little scamp!" I jumped down after her, rubbing the back of her head.

"You thought you could just get away without a good scratch?"

She leaned to the side, one of her limbs kicking up and down in a rather doglike manner.

"Ohhhh, is that the spot, Snips?" I smiled mischievously, scratching the carapace harder.

Her foot tapped away on the wooden floor, a staccato rhythm to match my laughter. I released her, stretching my hands to the roof and yawning again.

"All right, what did you have to show me?"

She shook off the aftereffects of the scratch, scuttling out into the living room and leading me through the front door. I followed her, muscle memory moving my arm and grabbing my hat from a hook on the way past.

I took a moment to stare once I stepped outside. Predawn light lit the scene, small waves atop the river reflecting glimpses of the eastern sky that shone a pale pink. A claw tapped me gently, grabbing my attention. Snips gestured to keep coming, and she led me around the corner to the side patio my barbecue would one day occupy. She scuttled to a corner, gesturing at something hidden in the shadows.

"What is it, girl?" I bent down, squinting into the gloom.

It was a small chest, made of dark lacquered wood with metal casings around the corners. A padlock hung in the lock, clearly snipped by my trusty guard crab.

"You found a treasure chest . . . ?"

She nodded vigorously, gesturing with her entire body to open the lid.

I picked it up and took it out the front, wanting to see the contents in the rising sunlight. I knelt down, opening it at Sergeant Snips's eye level.

Before I could make out what it was, I saw the reflected light of the eastern sky bouncing off the contents just as it did the waves. Countless points of light hit me, and it took my sleep-addled brain a long moment to realize what I was looking at. When comprehension hit me, my eyebrows tried to leave my face.

"Snips . . . where did you get this?"

She shrugged her spiny carapace, gesturing to the sea.

I looked at her, stunned, then returned my attention to the chest. It was filled with jewelry; silver and gold rings, necklaces, and bracelets. Most of the precious-metal pieces had pearls set in them, and I struggled to grasp just how much wealth was in front of me.

I stared at it, mouth hanging open. I quickly counted the pearls; there were eleven of the orbs in total.

"Jesus, Snips . . ."

A claw tapped me again, arresting my attention. Snips peered intently at me, blowing a soft stream of questioning bubbles.

"You . . . you want to know if you did good?"

She nodded, cocking her body to the side.

"Sergeant Snips, you beautiful, majestic crab *queen*—you did *great!*" I bellowed a laugh, giving her long, stroking rubs atop her treasure-finding head. "I can't believe you brought this home! This was an insane find, Snips!"

She nodded and blew content bubbles, responding to my praise.

What in the banished gods am I going to do with all this, though . . . ?

It was entirely too much wealth, and trying to sell it would draw way more attention than I was comfortable with.

"I guess we just stash it for now . . . do you have any use for it, Snips?"

She shook her head, and I got an idea. I picked up a bracelet with a single pearl affixed, then set it atop her head.

I grinned as I eyed my handiwork. "A crown befitting a Queen, Snips!"

She bubbled her excitement, scuttling to the glass-paneled door to admire her reflection.

I knelt down behind her. The makeshift crown slid almost off as she moved, and I readjusted it to the front of her head.

"Shame it doesn't stay in place. It suits you."

She turned to me, pointing to my hat, then to her head.

"You want me to fix the crown to your head?" I rubbed my chin in thought. "I guess we could—"

She shook her entire body at my question. She took the bracelet off, handing it to me. Pointing again at the straw hat, then to her head, she repeated the gesture two more times.

"Oh!" I said with a laugh. "You want a hat?"

A stream of ascending bubbles.

"That, I can do!" I ran to the roll of string beside my drying bamboo rods. "Let me get a measurement!"

I wrapped the line around her carapace in different directions, noting the measurements. I couldn't help but brush against the hard-to-reach parts of her top carapace as I went, and she halfheartedly tried to escape my tickles by scuttling in circles.

"All right—I have a quest for today! Fetch Snips a stylish new hat!"

She raised both her claws high, a veritable torrent of happy bubbles flying from her mouth.

"But, my trusty queen crab . . ." I gave her a conspiratorial look. "Shall we check the pot first?"

She froze for a moment, then scrambled toward the shore with an astonishing pace. I ran after her, giggling at the spray of sand kicking up in the wake of her blurred legs.

"Ready, Snips?" I whispered, crouching over the line.

She nodded, her eye gleaming in anticipation.

I grabbed the line, pulling it in with constant pressure. It was heavy, and hope swelled up within me. I could see something dark in the trap and smiled as I tried to make out what it was. When I grabbed the pot and hauled it out of the water, Sergeant Snips let out a low hiss.

There were two crabs: one sand crab, and one rock crab. I reached in and grabbed the sand crab, and checking its bottom carapace, saw it was male—a big one, at that. I left the rock crab to its fate, knowing what would come next.

Sergeant Snips moved to the side with exacting movements, standing on the shore and staring out at the rising sun. The rock crab didn't need instruction. It sullenly walked over in front of Snips, turned its back to her, and awaited its discipline.

Snips held her claw to her mouth, wetting it, then held it high, checking the wind direction. She stretched both claws, limbering up. Her left claw flicked under its carapace in a blur, lifting the crab into the air. Her right claw met it midair, and with a massive overhand throw, she flung it out to sea.

EEEEEEEEEEEEEEeeeeeeeeeeeeeeeeeeeeeeeeeeeeeee—

Plop.

She shook her head at the forcibly departed crustacean.

"Same crab?" I asked, raising an eyebrow.

She nodded, then shrugged both claws, as if to say "What are you gonna do?"

"Well, at least we got some dinner!" I said, gesturing to the sand crab in one hand.

I left the crab pot on the shore as we lacked any bait to refill it, and we made our way back at a much more leisurely pace.

I filled a pot with salt water, left the crab inside the kitchen, and made my way back out to Snips. The wind had picked up again, making it, unfortunately, not a great day for fishing.

Shame—at least I have other things to take care of.

Sergeant Snips sat by the coals of the fire, staring at the pot atop them with curiosity.

"It's salt water," I said, peering inside.

The water had reduced significantly, and there was a thin layer of salty sediment on the bottom of the pot. I gave it a stir with a wooden spoon, mixing it all together.

"I'm reducing it to make salt, the flavor of the gods—" I cut myself off at a thought. "Well, MSG is the flavor of the gods, but salt is a good starting point."

She scuttled over and looked inside, blowing curious bubbles.

"Hopefully it'll reduce down completely today. Then we just need to dry it out!"

I sat down on a log, leaning back and taking in the beautiful sunrise. "I've been meaning to ask you, Snips—were the pearls you and the other crabs collected hard to find?"

She made a *so-so* gesture with a claw.

"Can you get more?" I asked.

She thought for a moment, blowing a few indiscernible bubbles. Then, with immaculate accuracy, she started drawing characters in the sand.

For a moment, I thought she was drawing me a picture, but with dawning amazement, realized she was writing—actually *writing.* I recognized some of the letters from the deed George had brought me.

I stared at the words then down at Snips. She gestured at the letters, nodding sagely.

"Uh, Snips—I . . . I can't read."

She blinked at me; I blinked back. Small hissing noises started coming from her mouth, and she shook, kneeling down and rolling in the sand.

She's laughing at me!

I roared with laughter, and her hissing noises increased. She rolled onto her back, legs kicking out as she blurted a stream of sporadic hisses and bubbles. I fell over beside her, unable to contain my mirth. We rolled in the sand, tears coming to my eyes as I lost myself to the laughter.

When my cheeks ached and I could no longer see through swimming vision, I rolled to my front, getting to my feet just as Snips did the same.

"I—I'm sorry, Snips," I said through tears and fleeting giggles, pointing down at the ruined script. "I rolled in your message—not that I could read it."

She fell backward again, her limbs quivering in delight as her hisses came bubbling back up.

"Oh, you think me being illiterate is funny?" I leaned over her, tickling under her chin with both hands.

Her kicking increased, and I moved with her as she tried to get away from my assault. Eventually, I let her go, and she got upright, settling into the sand and seeming to sigh with contentment.

After a moment of regaining her composure, she started drawing again, and this time it *was* a picture. I leaned down, seeing a rather good approximation of an oyster with a pearl inside. She wrote a word next to it.

"Oyster?" I asked.

She nodded emphatically and started drawing again. She wrote a word then gestured at everything around us with both claws.

"Area?"

She made a so-so gesture again, shaking her head.

"Everything?"

She made the same gesture, which I took to mean "not quite."

"Surroundings?"

She nodded, pointing her claw at me, then the word.

"Okay—so we've got oysters and surroundings."

She drew another word, then an "X" in the sand beside it.

"Here?"

She shook her carapace, then pointed at the word, crossed her claws in front of her, and shook her head again.

"Ohhh, no? That word means no?"

She blew victorious bubbles, nodding. She drew the word for "surroundings," then "no," and finally, "oysters."

"There are no more oysters in the surrounding area?" I asked.

She hissed with delight, her whole body going up and down.

I laughed. "I can't believe you're my language tutor, Snips—what would I do without you?"

She sidled over and rubbed against my leg affectionately. I stroked her head.

"Ah, I love you too, my literate little scamp. So you guys harvested all the oysters within a reasonable distance."

She nodded again.

"No wonder the otter has been coming to our headland, Snips—you and your crabs harvested the rest of them!"

She froze, her body going rigid as she blew tiny bubbles of comprehension.

Ah, she hadn't realized it was our fault the otter came here.

"Well, no matter." I rubbed her head again. "That just makes it easier for us to befriend it!"

She blew a single, oversized bubble of anger, and I barked a laugh.

"I know, Snips. I know."

CHAPTER TWENTY-SIX

ANIMOSITY

Ruby raised one sculpted eyebrow at me. "You're, uh, sure about these measurements, Fischer?"

I smiled back. "I am! Don't worry—it's not for me. It's for a project I'm working on."

"Some sort of pirate scarecrow?" Steven asked with a smile.

"Er—yeah, something like that. How long do you think it'll take you guys?"

Ruby tilted her head side to side. "For you, we can have it done by this evening."

"That'd be perfect!" I gave them both a genuine smile. "How much will it be?"

"Nothing," Steven said, looking down at something he was stitching. "We can make it out of scraps, and it'll give me something to do with my hands this afternoon."

"Actually . . ." I said. "I was hoping I could help you with the crafting of it."

"Oh?" Steven raised an eyebrow. "You're interested in working with leather?"

"Well, this project has sentimental value to me, and I'd feel better about not paying if I helped you out . . ."

Steven shrugged. "It's free regardless, but you're more than welcome to help me with it."

"I appreciate it, Steven, but you're gonna have to charge me at some point . . ."

"Nope!" Ruby beamed a smile, her eyes crinkling. "We're still well in your debt from the pastries. If you request something expensive, we'll gladly charge, but for now, you have an open tab."

"All right." I returned a grin with the same ferocity. "All I can do is thank you, then. I'll find a way to return the kindness."

"You know, I heard something wise the other day . . ." Steven's eyes danced above his coy smile. "Friends don't count favors."

"Morning, George!"

George went rigid in his spot in line, slowly turning to look at me.

"Oh. Hello, Fischer."

"How are ya, mate?"

"I-I'm well, Fischer—how are you?"

"I'm swell, mate! Always a good morning in your lovely village!"

The lord nodded, his face going a little tight as a silence stretched between us.

"You know, George, I've been meaning to thank you."

"Er—you have?"

"Yeah, mate. You've been nothing but helpful since I got here, even when I come bother you in your home."

"Oh." George smiled, but his eyes remained tight. "Any time, Fischer. It's no worries at all—"

"No, seriously." I shook my head with a wincing smile. "The information you've given me has really helped so far. Sincerely, thank you."

My attempt at reassurance only seemed to kick his social anxiety in more, and beads of sweat started forming on his forehead.

Thankfully, Lena saved him. "Good morning to you, George! The usual?"

"Uh—two coffees, please, but only fifteen pastries."

"Only fifteen?" A look of genuine concern crossed Lena's face. "Are you and Geraldine well?"

"Just a mild case of indigestion." George dabbed his forehead. "I'm sure it'll pass."

Good lord—I'm affecting his digestion. I really need to give the poor man some space . . .

When George collected his coffees and pastries, I simply smiled and nodded at him, not wanting to stress him out any further. He nodded back, shuffling away.

I spun back to the counter, displaying my half-tucked shirt in all its glory.

"G'day, Lena. How ya doing?"

She sniffed, refusing to speak as she looked me up and down.

My smile broadened. "Just my coffee, thanks."

Maria, Roger's much more amiable daughter, was just collecting a couple of pastries when I arrived at Sue's bakery.

"Good morning, Fischer!" Sue waved her free hand with vigor.

"G'day, Sue! Morning, Maria!"

"Oh, hi Fischer!" Maria beamed a smile at me, sweeping a loose strand of hair behind her ear. Her nose twitched, and she peered down at my coffee cup.

"What is that?"

"Coffee! This one's from Lena's—a necessary sacrifice before Sue here gets the equipment to make the best beverage in town!"

Sue rolled her eyes at my flattery, and with no words needed, walked out back to fetch me a fresh croissant.

"Does it taste good?" Maria cocked her head at the wafting scent, the strand of hair freeing itself from behind her ear once more. "It smells kind of bitter . . ."

"Not everyone likes it, to be honest. It might be an acquired taste . . ." I held the cup out. "Wanna try?"

"Oh, I couldn't . . ."

"Of course you can!" I pointed at the edge closest to me. "I've only drunk from this side—give it a taste!"

She leaned in, sniffing it again, hesitating. She placed her pastries atop the counter. Then, with delicate hands, she caressed the mug, slowly bringing it to her lips and taking a sip.

She tasted the liquid for some time, her eyebrows going up and down, and her face scrunching in adorable contemplation.

"It's . . . bitter, but not bad?"

"That's a good result for a first taste!" I accepted the cup as she held it back to me. "You'll grow to *love* it if your initial reaction isn't that it tastes like muddy water."

She let out a light laugh, covering her mouth with a hand.

"People think it tastes like mud water? I mean, it's different, but definitely not mud."

"Tell me about it." I shook my head in obvious exaggeration. "And they call *me* a heretic."

"Well, you're definitely a heretic." She gave me a kind smile, the freckles on her cheeks bunching. "But I'm still glad you came to Tropica. You've already made so much change since appearing here . . ."

"Oh, everything so far has been nothing."

Sue returned, bustling toward the counter. I accepted the croissant she held out to me, then shot Maria a wink. "I'm only just getting started."

"Fergus! How are ya, mate?"

The giant of a blacksmith held a finger up to stall me, still staring intently at his forge. He had oversized black goggles on, making him look half body builder, half mad scientist. With oversized tongs, he picked up the crucible in the forge. I recognized the small mold sitting on the cool lip of the forge, and with no small amount of excitement, realized what he was doing.

He's pouring the silver into the cast! Where did he get some so fast?

I edged toward him, not close enough to be in the way, but just enough to get a better view of the process. He swirled the crucible, withdrawing it from the heat. After a moment of looking at the molten metal within, he carefully placed it back into the heat of the forge. His attention never left his work, and I watched keenly, appreciating the years of practice and training that had created the mastery I bore witness to. The red-hot colors from the forge reflected off his goggles, and he resembled a statue as he waited, only his chest moving up and down, almost imperceptibly.

He picked up the tongs again, removed the crucible with deft hands, and swirled the contents once more—his eyes transfixed on the liquid metal the entire time. With a small nod to himself, he shuffled over to the mold, slowly pouring the silver into a minuscule opening atop it. The amount of control he had over his large body was immense; he made no wasted movements, each muscle contracting with exact precision.

The thin stream of silver slowed, eventually coming to an end. He picked the casting mold up by the attached metal vice, tapping it softly against the lip with a steady rhythm. He plunged it down into a quenching bucket. The water within bubbled and roiled, the heat rapidly dissipating from the mold and into the surrounding water. When the torrent of bubbles receded and the bucket finally stilled, Fergus reached in with a gloved hand. He cracked the vice open, let the two halves of the mold fall apart, and removed the ring.

Fergus grinned like a maniac, holding it up to me as he slid his goggles off with another hand. "It ain't pretty yet, but the forging is done!"

"How did you get the silver so swiftly?" I returned his grin, looking over the rough casting. "I thought it would take days, at least!"

Fergus winked at me. "You have to leave a man his mysteries—"

Duncan, his apprentice, snorted from the back of the smithy. "He traded a favor to the hoity-toity blacksmith on the north side of town."

Fergus leveled a glare at his subordinate. "If you weren't so big, Duncan, I'd throw you out on your ass."

Said subordinate made a dismissive noise. "Bold words coming from a man the size of a brick shithouse. A kraken couldn't throw you if it wanted to."

"How long will it take to sand and smooth it down?" I asked, interrupting before the blacksmith banter got too out of control.

Fergus returned his attention to me, then to the ring. "It'll be done in a few hours—you bring that iridescent stone around then, and we'll see about slotting it in."

"Perfect!" I grinned at how things were coming along. "I'll see ya a bit later, then—I have some other tasks to get to."

I turned to leave, then had a thought. "By the way, Fergus—is there a lumber mill in town?"

He winced. "Not anymore, lad. Not for a long time."

I nodded. "Thought so. Oh well. Guess it's on me then! Catch you guys later!"

Duncan walked up beside Fergus, watching Fischer go.

"That was just one of his odd speech mannerisms, right? You don't think he's going to actually come catch us later, do you?"

Fergus blew air out of his nose in amusement. "I hope not—I fear you wouldn't escape him, lad."

"What do you mean I wouldn't escape him?" Duncan narrowed his eyes at Fergus. "Don't you mean *we* wouldn't escape him?"

"I don't need to outrun him, lad." Fergus waggled his eyebrows. "I just need to outrun you."

"I've had a day of surprises," I said to myself, pouting, "but this might take the cake."

I peered down at the log I'd hit with my axe. I expected to split part of the felled tree—most of it, perhaps, given my increased strength. What I didn't expect was for my axe to cut it clean in half, send either side of the log flying two meters away in opposite directions, and for my fist—and the axe held within it—to create a crater as big as Sergeant Snips in the sand.

I lifted the axe from its sandy tomb with ease, moving my arm up and down in confusion. I wasn't even a little tired from the exertion. It was as if I'd just swatted at a fly, not swung down an axe with all my might.

I'll need to be careful—I could seriously hurt a villager, or worse, Sergeant Snips, with this amount of power.

I sat and thought for a second, testing if there was anything else I needed to consider or contemplate. "Nope!" I said with a laugh, getting right back to my feet. "I'm strong as hell, and that's that!" I walked over to one of the split sides, lined it up in the sand, and swung down again with a wicked grin.

I was almost finished splitting all the logs into usable palings when a hysterical crustacean came sprinting across the sand. Snips spewed incomprehensible bubbles at me, hissing as she ran to my feet. She gestured toward the headland with both claws, seething with anger.

With sneaking suspicion, I thought I knew what had got her so worked up.

"Otter?" I asked.

She nodded sharply, blew affirmative bubbles, and ran away, urging me on.

I heard a familiar tapping as we ran to the headland. The rhythmic sounds only occasionally paused when the furred friend-to-be slurped down a mollusk. We rounded the rocks, and I finally caught sight of the otter.

Damn. I don't have any fish—wait! The crab! I have a crab!

I made to run back to the house but noticed Sergeant Snips shaking with anger. I looked between her and the cause of her ire, uncomprehending.

"What's got you so worked up, Snips? I thought you were past this level of animosity."

She pointed an accusing claw at the otter, pointed her other clacky appendage at a rock on the ground, then to herself.

"It . . . threw a rock at you?"

She hissed in confirmation, her body shuddering with indignation.

"*Oh!*"

I looked at the otter, who was studiously ignoring us. I bent down, staring into Snips's eye and running a comforting hand over her carapace.

"I know it can be frustrating when others insult you, but it isn't as smart as you—our otter friend doesn't know any better."

She visibly calmed as I continued stroking her shell, and she seemed to take a deep breath, letting it out in a soft hiss. She nodded at me and blew bubbles that I took as an apology.

"It's okay, Snips." I smiled at her with genuine affection. "You don't have to be sorry for getting upset. Should we go cook our crab up? Maybe some lunch will make you feel better—we can even offer some to the otter, then it won't eat all the oysters!"

The suggestion lightened her mood further, and she nodded, blowing small bubbles of joy.

"All right. Let's go."

We walked away together, and as we were just about to leave the otter behind, I caught a brown blur of movement from the corner of my eye. I turned just in time to see the rock sailing, and with a soft *tink,* it hit Sergeant Snips in the side. She paused, slowly spinning on the spot to look at the otter. They stared at each other for a tense moment, both unmoving. With nary a warning hiss, she charged.

CHAPTER TWENTY-SEVEN

SPIKY SEA SNIPPERS

It was a beautiful day. The sun was high overhead, radiating warmth that was perfectly contrasted by a stalwart breeze blowing ever northward. Small waves crashed against the rocks of the headland, the wind causing their foamy peaks to spray and glitter in the sun. Salt was heavy in the air, its scent a constant reminder of the small joys one could find in life.

The scene was only marginally ruined by the charging, apoplectic crab. Fueled by indignation and an acutely murderous intent, Sergeant Snips shot across the rocks, a torrent of foam spewing from her mouth. The otter's sidelong glance was filled with terror as it turned to dash for the safety of open water, the sclera of its eyes starkly visible.

The creature had just learned, by hard-won experience, the age-old adage about poking the bear. In this case, the "bear" was a watermelon-sized crab, covered in inch-long spikes, possessing uncommonly agile legs and a thirst for recompense.

Sergeant Snips's claws were raised, power swelling inside her mighty joints. The otter launched itself for the water, the twin blasts from Snips's clackers striking the oyster beds from where it had just jumped. My guard crab didn't jump in after it, showing a respectable amount of restraint as she shook with fury. I walked up behind her, setting a calming hand atop her carapace.

"Nicely done, Snips."

Her lone eye turned to regard me, part of her anger melting away. She cocked her head, and I answered the unspoken question.

"I know you missed your attacks on purpose." I smiled at her. "That was good restraint, and I'm proud of you."

She dipped the front of her head down, blowing bubbles of regret for her outburst.

"It's fine—really. What do you say we go have that meal?"

She blew bubbles of assent, and we set off back for the house.

"You know, Snips . . . I think the otter was just trying to play with you."

She paused mid-bite of the sand crab leg, her eye seeming to narrow at me.

"I'm serious!" I said with a laugh. "In the very least, it wasn't trying to hurt you. It seems rather intelligent for a wild animal, and it has to know that it couldn't hurt your magnificent shell with a small stone . . ."

She preened when I complimented her shell, puffing up subconsciously. I smiled down at her, glad to see she was feeling more herself after some lunch.

I cracked the shell of a sand crab claw, and with no small amount of satisfaction, bit down on the sweet meat. Once again, the flavor of the flesh mixing with the salty water it was cooked in took my senses on a relaxing trip that was even more enjoyable with the company of the continually reliable Sergeant Snips.

It's a shame about the salt, though . . .

When I checked on the reducing seawater before cooking the crab, I found the moisture content boiled away as expected, but the sludge in the bottom was an off -brown color, telling me something had gone wrong. I suspected the water needed to be filtered somehow, or perhaps I'd made the fire too hot, burning the salt in the process.

No matter—I'll just have to try again.

The sound of Snips crunching down on her half of the crab was a comfort, and we lapsed into relative silence, both drawn in by the taste of our impromptu lunch.

A repetitive noise rang out, making both of us freeze on the spot—me with excitement, Snips with anger.

Tap. Tap. Tap.

The otter had returned.

I shot to my feet, as did Sergeant Snips. "Would you mind staying here, Snips?" I asked, voice urgent. She had already taken a step, but stopped, turning to look at me with curiosity.

"I want to try feeding it—I worry it might run away the second it sees you."

She blew a small stream of bubbles as she seemed to contemplate my request.

I bent down to her level. "Please, Snips? I know it's been messing with you, but reckon it would make a reliable ally if I can win it over with some food . . ."

She pointed at me, then herself, clacking her claws.

"I promise I'll be okay—I don't need defending from a little otter."

She considered, her clackers moving open and closed as her thoughts roiled.

With a single nod of her body, she sat back down on the sand, picking up a cooked leg and taking a crunching bite.

"Thank you, Snips!" I let my genuine excitement show. "I'll be right back!"

I picked up the remainder of my lunch and ran for the headland. Each time the tapping of the otter's rock paused, I worried it wouldn't return, the bearer having jumped into the ocean and swam away. Each time, though, the tapping resumed. I rounded the headland from the southern side, doing my best to be silent.

The otter was hitting an oyster when I caught sight of it, roughly twenty meters downwind. It saw me from the corner of its eye, and its entire body went rigid as it turned to stare at me, its white sclera clearly visible once more.

I held one hand up in a passive gesture, showing my palm. With the other, I held the crab high, letting the wind carry the smell of it toward the otter. Its head lifted, its cute little nose twitching as it breathed in the aroma of the freshly cooked sand crab.

I took a slow step forward, and it dashed farther away, stopping after three bounds and turning to watch me.

It's not going to let me approach . . .

I pointed at the crab, pointed to the otter, and with a careful underhand throw, lobbed it toward the creature. It dashed away again, wanting to be nowhere near where the crustacean landed, but turned to look at it once again.

It got on its hind legs, sniffing the air as its head moved side to side, up and down. I stepped back, body hunched and holding both palms up. It took a tentative step forward, watching me keenly for any movement. I stepped back again, hunching down even lower to make myself seem less of a threat.

It took the gamble. With a light chirp, it exploded forward, grabbed the remains of the cooked crab in its cute little chompers and dashed beneath the waves.

I stood up straight and let out a laugh. "Not bad for first contact . . ."

I let Snips know what happened when I got back to the fire. She seemed impartial, nodding sagely at my words as she snapped off the claw from her half crab. I expected her to crunch down on it, but she walked over, rubbed against my leg affectionately, and handed it to me.

"You're sure Snips? This is the best part . . ."

She nodded, blew bubbles of joy, and sat down beside me to eat her last portion.

"Thanks, Snips." I rubbed her head with long strokes. "What would I do without you?"

"How's it looking, Fergus?" I asked as I walked into the smithy.

He looked at me, slid an eyeglass from his face, and walked over with a broad smile. "You tell me, lad."

He held his hand out to me. Red light reflected from the forge, hitting the smooth angles of the ring. I accepted it, holding it up before me.

"Mate . . . it's beautiful. I can't believe you made this . . ."

Fergus snorted a laugh. "Now, lad, one could take that as an insult."

I boomed a laugh back. "No offense intended, mate—I'm stunned at your craftsmanship. Is it ready for the stone?"

He nodded. "You want to do the honors?"

I removed the pearl from my pocket, placing it between the four extended prongs of silver. It slid in perfectly, and I glanced at Fergus. He gave me another nod, gesturing to continue.

I carefully bent the prongs down, the fragile metal no match for my strengthened body. The silver hugged the pearl, and when the fourth and final sliver laid flat against the ring, a familiar tug hit me.

The System trying to spill its nonsense again? Nice try, Sys—

My eyes were drawn into the ring, and before I even knew what I was doing, I inspected it.

Iridescent Ring of Silver

Rare

A ring of precious metal, adorned by one of the most sought-after stones

found in the Kallis Realm. More than just a symbol of wealth, this ring has a multitude of purposes for those with the requisite knowledge.

What the fuck . . .

Fergus and Duncan accompanied me as I made my way back to Julian—the jeweler on the north side of town. While I wasn't sure what kind of fighting capabilities they had, it certainly couldn't hurt having the two burly blacksmiths acting as bodyguards. They were a good deterrent, if nothing else; we were going to be returning to the south side of Tropica with a sizable amount of wealth if things went as planned.

George was going through the motions, doing his best to distract himself from his troubled thoughts. He found himself stepping into Noble Star Jewelry without even realizing it.

"Good day, George," Julian said from behind the counter. "Have you come looking for more iridescent stone pieces?"

"No, my good man. Just browsing today, I'm afraid."

Julian gave him a tired smile. "You're always welcome, old friend."

George looked through the reinforced glass panels, taking in the countless silver and gold pieces of jewelry. He was just considering buying a small silver pendant for Geraldine when the door opened behind him.

"G-good day, Fischer," Julian said, his voice hesitant.

George felt pinpricks crawl up his spine, and he slowly turned. Fischer had just walked into the store, two muscular peasants walking through the door after him.

"G'day Julian, George!" Fischer gave the smile of a snake who'd cornered prey.

"G'day Julian, George!" I said, smiling my delight at them.

I focused on Julian. "I brought that ring we spoke about, mate. Is now a good time to have it appraised?"

"Yes—of course."

He knelt down behind his counter, coming back up with a silk-covered chest. He opened it up, removing something akin to a microscope.

"May I see it?"

I nodded at Fergus, who produced the ring from inside a small wooden box filled with padding.

"Would you mind putting it back in the box?" Julian asked. "Leave the stone facing up."

Fergus cocked his head but did so with gentleness belying his size.

Julian took the box and set it atop the tray beneath the eyepiece. He placed one eye to the opening, peering down as he spun the box around at different angles.

I heard the door open behind me and glanced back to see George leaving. I returned my attention to Julian.

"So . . . what do you think?"

The jeweler put a cloth glove on one hand, then picked up the ring from the box. He examined the silver sections of the ring beneath the eyeglass, too focused to answer my question.

"This is," he said, "possibly the finest ring I have ever seen. The workmanship, the symmetry, the stone itself . . . where did you get it?"

I grinned, gesturing between Fergus and myself. "We made it, mate."

". . . You really made this?"

"Aye," Fergus said, beaming with pride.

"If you were to sell this in the capital, I suspect you'd fetch at least twenty-seven gold."

I whistled. "That's a lot of dosh—how much could you pay us for it?"

"Er . . . dosh?"

"Yeah, dosh! Cash; coin; gold—same thing."

"Oh . . . right. Well, I could pay you two less gold for the trouble of transporting it. There are guard fees, you see. Not to mention the capital taxes, and that's not even considering the—"

"No need to justify it, mate," I interrupted. "That sounds like a fair price. Do you have that much gold on you?"

Julian laughed, the noise high and fleeting. "No. I hold around ten gold with my guard at a time. Any more will need to be delivered from the capital under escort."

I grinned. "How often do you get deliveries under escort?"

"They come with the merchant that visits Tropica once a month on Fielday."

I still need to work out what's going on with these weekdays . . .

I returned my attention outward, focusing on Julian. "Would you give us ten gold now, take the ring, and deliver the remaining fifteen with the merchant?"

Julian's brows furrowed momentarily, but they raised as he smiled. "Y-yes, of course!" Julian rubbed his hands together. "It's a little unorthodox, but you bear two witnesses, and I am nothing if not my reputation."

"That's fine with you boys?" I asked, turning to Fergus and Duncan.

"Aye," they both said, before squinting at each other in suspicion.

I let out a laugh. "It's a deal, mate."

I held out my hand, and after removing his cloth glove, Julian shook it.

The otter retreated further than was strictly necessary. It swam ever southward, wanting to put as much distance between itself and the sharp-clawed antagonist as possible. The scent of the stolen morsel was unbearable, and only the fear of the spiked-one following her held her powerful jaws at bay.

She had tried repeatedly to lure the crab into playing, but each time it had responded with increasing aggression—during the last of which, she had genuinely feared for her life. Spiky sea snippers were no fun, as it turned out.

She emerged onto the rocks she called home, running swiftly between a gap in the stones. She curled up in a back corner, tearing into the crab with ravenous delight.

CHAPTER TWENTY-EIGHT

LOVING INTENT

As we arrived back at the smithy, the three of us erupted. I roared with laughter, and the two blacksmiths held each other by the shoulders, yelling incomprehensibly over the top of one another.

When things finally wound down, Fergus hurried to a shelf in the corner with skipping steps. He reached to the very top, selecting a wooden box covered in a dark lacquer. He cradled it in both arms like a baby as he walked back toward us, each step exacting.

"Is . . . that what I think it is?" Duncan asked, his eyes going wide.

"Aye, Duncan. That it is."

Fergus slipped a chisel from his belt. His eyes narrowed and mouth scrunched in concentration as he cracked the dark box open. I leaned in, curious what had gotten the apprentice blacksmith so excited.

Fergus reached in and withdrew a dark bottle. It was short, reminding me almost of a maple syrup jug but with a more spherical body. Its mouth was sealed with a cork.

Fergus placed the bottle on the bench with great care as Duncan ran to fetch something else. Lacking his master's delicacy, he returned with three shot glasses and slammed them down.

Fergus reached into a drawer, removing a corkscrew. One muscular hand wrapped around the bottle while the other screwed the instrument down into the cork stopper. He pulled, the cork dislodged with a sharp *pop,* and small wisps of vapor floated from the bottle. The smith slammed his palm atop it, sealing the gas in.

I raised an eyebrow, glancing between the two excited smiths. "What is it?"

"This, my dear Fischer," Fergus said, nodding at the bottle, "is passiona wine."

"Passiona wine?" I asked. "If the husks are so expensive, that bottle has to be worth an extraordinary sum . . . right?"

"Right!" Duncan nodded. "I've been waiting *years* for this blockhead to crack it open."

"It was a gift from my grandfather," Fergus said. "He had a case of them from when he was younger—the husk never used to be so expensive, you see? It's an heirloom, and I've never had a good enough reason to crack it open . . ."

"Until today?" I asked with a smile.

"Until today," Fergus agreed.

He removed his hand from the top, swiftly half-filling each of the small glasses. He placed one hand back atop the bottle and picked up a glass with the other, holding it high. Duncan and I followed suit.

"To Fischer!" Fergus bellowed.

"To Fischer!" Duncan echoed.

"To my reliable smiths!" I cheered back.

We clinked our glasses above the bench, and I took a sip, breathing in through my nose as I did. The smell made my eyes water, but it wasn't unpleasant. The drink held a hint of ethanol, but a sweet overtone nearly drowned it out entirely. Before I tasted anything, the liquid warmed my lips and mouth. It lit me from within like a forge. The taste hit me next, and I let the rapturous expression show.

In my life on Earth, I'd tasted countless wines, spirits, and beers. I'd experienced everything from the common ales you'd find in pubs to the most expensive bottles of wine you needed to "know someone" to acquire.

The passiona wine was more akin to a spirit or fortified wine, and it was unlike anything else I had ever tasted. It was complex—sweet and tart to the perfect degree. It held the full-bodied flavor of a naturally fermented cask, and I could tell its sweetness hadn't been artificially boosted with processed sugar. Even if I hadn't been told of its origin, I would have known it was based on the fruit of the passiona plant—the taste of passiona pastries suffused the wine, the unique essence instantly recognizable.

I swallowed, and the heat spread down through my chest. I moved my tongue, circulating air around my mouth—the resulting aftertaste was even more enjoyable than the wine itself. The flavor morphed, the sweet tones flooding forward and smothering the pleasing yet notable hints of tartness.

Duncan took another sip with an exultant expression.

Fergus exhaled with a deep sigh. "I can't believe I made an entire gold piece in one job—I never thought I'd see the day."

"One gold piece?" I asked, smirking. "I was going to give you two for your contribution."

Wine sprayed from Duncan's lips like a whale breaching the surface, and he clamped a hand over his treasonous lips, keeping the liquid within.

Fergus's eyes were wide as he stared at me—he didn't even react to his apprentice misting him with a family heirloom.

"That's too much, Fischer . . ."

"Nope!" I said, taking another sip. I swished it around my mouth before I swallowed, relishing in the comfortable burn.

"You covered the silver, provided a security service, and most important of all, made the best damned ring Julian has ever seen!"

"I suspect that was more to do with your setting of the stone, Fischer . . ." Fergus said, lost in memory. "It seemed to take on a different quality when you—"

Duncan slapped him on the back of the head, not hard enough to risk knocking over any of the wine, but with enough force to halt his words. "Just thank the man, you ox-sized fool."

Fergus narrowed his eyes at his subordinate, but then sighed, turning back to me. "My loose-lipped apprentice has the right of it . . . for once. Thank you, Fischer."

"No worries, mate!" I smiled at the two men, took out the two gold coins, and handed them to Fergus. "Couldn't have done it without you."

We laughed and joked as we finished off the wine, and I noticed the two smiths slowly losing hold of their sobriety.

These two are off their bloody tits . . .

I stood, feeling my head swim a little. It somewhat steadied as I stood in place, and I exalted in the pleasant buzz.

"To Fischer!" Duncan slurred, sipping the last drops from his glass.

"Aye, to Fischer!" Fergus did the same then held the bottle out to me.

I accepted it, and giving it a light swish, felt liquid left in the bottom. "For me?" I asked.

"Aye!" Fergus roared, holding his empty glass high.

I laughed, pouring the rest of the wine into my mouth. I held it there for a long moment, the heat enveloping me. With a swallow, I sighed, my breath warming everywhere the passiona wine had touched. I looked over at the two men who were stumbling toward the back of the smithy.

"Uh, fellas . . ." I pointed to the forge. "Is it all right to leave that thing going?"

"Ah, Hestia's welcoming hearth—shutter the forge, Duncan."

The apprentice wobbled to obey, and with a single hand, slammed a metal door down. He returned to Fergus, and the two leaned against one another, muttering and laughing as they poked each other in the chest.

"Thanks again, guys!"

They didn't hear me; they swayed back and forth, joking about something. I shook my head with a bemused smile.

I tried to forget the wealth sitting in my pocket as I walked toward Ruby and Steven's tailors—*tailorors? Oh my god, not this again.* The alcohol was affecting me more than I suspected. I shook the thought away.

Seeking something to ground myself, I dipped into a gap between houses and removed a single gold coin from my pouch. I looked it over, the blue sky above reflecting off its metallic face. I furrowed my brow, cocking my head to the side.

Hang on a second . . . it couldn't be . . . could it?

With a buzz-fueled stride, I made my way toward the north side of town—a new destination in mind.

George hadn't moved from the front foyer of his spacious home. He made it back on shaky legs, and after tumbling through the portal, he had simply lain there—thinking.

Does Fischer watch me at every turn? Does he possess the devious eyes of Dolos himself?

George had moved through the streets at an ungodly hour, launching the evidence into the depths, where no one but a sea god could find it. And yet, Fischer *had* found it.

Did he follow me there? What trap does he weave, intentionally revealing his hand in this way? Are there nefarious actors watching me at every hour of the day? Oh, Fischer, bane of treats, ruiner of flavors—how you vex me.

Try as George might—applying his vastly superior, sugar-fueled intellect—he had absolutely no idea what the man's angle was.

Three loud knocks sounded above George's head.

"*Geee-OOOOOO-ooooorge!*" came the sing-song voice of Fischer on the other side of the door.

George felt the blood drain from his face, and without feeling what he was doing, got to his feet and opened the door.

"Fischer . . ."

The crown agent was just about to knock again, but when he saw George, he smiled.

"G'day, mate. I won't keep you long, I was just hoping you could clear something up for me."

The smile on Fischer's face was crooked, and George waited for the executioner's axe to drop.

"What did you want me to clear up?" he heard himself ask, his voice flat.

"Well, I just sold a ring with a pearl set in it to Julian—er, an iridescent stone, I mean. You know the man, right? You were in his store."

He knows everything . . .

George felt numb. He nodded.

"Well, Julian gave me this gold, right?" Fischer produced a coin, playing with it between his fingers. "I noticed it was different from the one I gave you. This one . . ." Fischer held the gold coin up in the light. "It has the image of a man on one side, a crown on the other."

George nodded again, his words failing him.

"The one I gave you had a face on one side and a scythe on the other." Fischer's eyes went from the coin to George, his gaze boring a hole into George's soul. "Do you still have it?"

George reached into his back pocket, producing the coin Fischer had warned him not to spend. He kept it on his person at all times, knowing the consequences to be dire if he lost it.

"Would you mind if we swapped, George?"

George knew it wasn't a question—it was an order. He held the coin out for Fischer, who replaced it with the regular coin. Fischer inspected it in the light, nodding as he placed it in a back pocket.

"Cheers, George! I have to go make a hat for a crab—see ya later!"

Fischer turned and left, and George stood in his open door, staring after the departed man. After a long while, he closed the door, his body still numb. George turned and slowly made his way up the stairs. The axe had yet to drop, but that didn't mean it wasn't coming.

Make a hat for a crab? Oh, Fischer, what game is this? What in Triton's blowing conch is that code for . . . ?

I tried to keep my wine-addled mind from the coin in my pocket as I walked toward Ruby and Steven's clothing—*shop? Yeah. Shop.* It was easier said than done.

"Steven!" I yelled, walking into the store. "Your favorite apprentice is here and ready to work!"

Steven looked up at me over his spectacles, smiling and raising an eyebrow. "My "favorite apprentice" is late. I've already got the cuts ready."

Ruby narrowed her eyes at me as I wobbled toward the front of the store.

"Fischer . . . are you drunk?"

"Uh, a little, yes, but I have a perfectly good reason."

She laughed at me, but there was no malice in it. "And what, pray tell, would that good reason be?"

I pointed out the door. "Fergus cracked a bottle of passiona wine."

"He *what?*" Ruby got to her feet, eyes pinning me down. "Is there any left?"

I shook my head. "Sorry, Ruby. They drank it all. Well, we drank it all, but I'm only a little buzzed—I reckon those two are visiting noddy land as we speak."

"Where in Hades's lightless hell did Fergus get a bottle of passiona wine?"

"You'll have to ask him in the morning! Or later tonight? I don't really know—they're both the size of a brick shithouse, so they could be sober already."

I turned back to Steven. "You don't seem too bothered by missing out."

Steven shrugged. "I'm not much of a drinker."

He set his spectacles down, picking up the strips of prepared leather. "Shall we get started?"

I grinned. "Ready when you are!"

The next half hour was a rather humbling experience. Steven was a demon with the sewing machine, which I wasn't too surprised to learn they possessed. It was foot-pedal operated, and his right leg pumped away with ease as he shifted the leather strips around. When he was almost finished, he pointed to a flap of leather, the last unsewn section of the almost complete garment.

"See this bit?"

I nodded.

"Slide this along with the needle as you go. I'll let you tuck it—just do it as I have with the other strips."

Halfway through, the needle caught, and it slipped off the leather.

"No problem," Steven said, gesturing for me to step aside.

He picked it up, and with a few swift movements, removed the incorrect stitching with a hooked needle.

"You were hitting the pedal a bit too hard."

He set it back down. "Try again. This time, use your palm to move the garment—not your fingers."

I did so, taking my time to ease it around with my palm as one leg hit the pedal with softer strikes. The strip closed up, and when my stitching started overlapping his, he put his hand on my shoulder, telling me to stop. He leaned down with a small pair of scissors, cutting the thread that connected it to the machine.

A familiar pulse rushed out.

Goddamn System, can't even let me have a wholesome moment with my new frien—

My eyes were drawn in as before, and I inspected the item without realizing I was doing so.

Leather Patch of the Fisher

Rare

A hat created for a beloved subordinate with loving intent. This hat has a multitude of attributes for those with the requisite knowledge.

What. The. Fu—

"You okay, Fischer?"

I turned to Steven, unable to school the wonder from my voice. "Yeah, mate. I'm fantastic."

He furrowed his eyebrows, a smile on his face. "Just making sure—your eyes went vacant there for a bit. I thought the wine might be getting the better of you . . ."

"I think I'm mostly sober now, but thanks for caring!"

I picked the hat up, feeling the unyielding material with both hands. "Thanks so much, mate." I stood up, stretching. "I owe you one for this."

"No, you don't." He led me out to the floor of their shop. "Friends help friends, don't we?"

I grinned at him. "That we do, mate—that we do."

As I approached my home, I pulled out the ring Fergus and I had created, inspecting it again.

Iridescent Ring of Silver

Rare

A ring of precious metal, adorned by one of the most sought-after stones found in the Kallis Realm. More than just a symbol of wealth, this ring has a multitude of purposes for those with the requisite knowledge.

I'm glad Fergus didn't realize I switched them out—that little nugget of wisdom would've been hard to explain.

I was quite proud of the sleight of hand used to keep Fergus unaware of the swap. I brought another ring with me from the stash Snips found and had placed it in Fergus's ring box before closing and passing it to the smith for transport.

My eyes wandered over the inset pearl, the afternoon sun lending itself to the stone's beauty.

I can't wait to learn about these "purposes," whatever they may be . . .

The sight of my favorite crustacean dragged me from my thoughts. Sergeant Snips was sitting by the campfire, watching the new batch of reducing seawater.

I couldn't help but break into a run. "Snips! I have a surprise for you!"

She ran to meet me, blowing bubbles of curiosity as her spiked legs devoured the distance between us. I held out my creation; her claws clacked in anticipation.

CHAPTER TWENTY-NINE

PIRATE CRAB

I adjusted the black leather strap around Sergeant Snips' carapace, her body wiggling in excitement.

"It's hard to get it in place with you moving about, Snips!"

She shifted even more to spite me, blowing bubbles of amusement.

I laughed at her antics, holding her still as best I could with one hand, the other sliding beneath her and pulling the strap through a loop. Putting both hands underneath, I pulled tight, locking it into place with the metal buckle. I took a step back, admiring the fit.

"It doesn't hurt?" I asked, looking at her now-hidden eye.

She shook her head, but both claws moved up and down in joy, making it a confusing gesture.

"Not to toot my own horn, Snips, but you look amazing."

She nodded, blowing bubbles of agreement as she felt her new leather 'hat' with one claw.

"It makes you look almost *dangerous*—you have a real air of mystique, Snips."

She squinted her lone eye, leaning into the claim and clacking her claws in an approximation of aggression.

The hat I'd made for her was a black eye patch, covering the scarred shell of her lost eye. The strips of leather acting as a strap were thick and wide, spreading out the pressure of its snug fit across her powerful carapace. I had feared it might cause her pain, but my worry was misplaced; it was *perfect*.

"It should hold up in the water, too, but don't stress—even if it wears out, I'll gladly make as many as you need."

She preened, walking beside me and rubbing herself against my leg.

I bent down to pat the top of her shell.

"I love you too, Snips—and you're very welcome."

We walked over to the fire, and I inspected the pot of saltwater atop it. I'd intentionally kept the heat of the fire as low as possible, and the liquid had reduced only minimally over the day.

"Back in a moment, Snips."

I walked inside, grabbing another large empty pot, a medium-sized pot filled with clean water, and a few tea towels. I returned to the fire, placed the tea towels atop the empty pot in layers.

"Would you mind holding these towels in place while I pour?" I asked the Sergeant.

She nodded, scuttling over to hold them down with her clawed appendages stretched wide.

I picked up the pot from the fire, the handles cool enough to grab since the fire was so low. I walked over to the pot Snips held, and with a steady pour, strained the saltwater through the tea towels. The water took time to filter through the combined mesh of layered cloth, and I waited for it to drain completely before dumping more water in.

When there was no more liquid left to strain, I inspected the top cloth in the late afternoon sun. A noticeable pile of sand sat inside it, interspersed with dark-brown flecks of other sediment.

"No wonder the last batch went bad, Snips." I pointed down at the waste.

She got up on her tippy toes, peering down at the strained materials. With a tentative claw, she grabbed a particularly large brown fleck and put it in her mouth. I furrowed my brows in abject discomfort. She tasted it for a bare moment before spewing bubbles of disgust. I laughed so hard that tears came to my eyes. I fell over, trying and failing to get comforting words out through the fleeting giggles.

"Snips—I could have told you that was a bad idea. Are you okay?"

She scuttled over to the pot of clean water, sucking some out and ejecting it onto the sand.

I held the emptied pot out to her. "Would you mind rinsing this off in the river to remove any remaining sediment? I'm gonna wash off these towels."

She nodded sharply, happy to contribute.

I took the tea towels and, placing the sediment-filled side down, washed them in the clean pot of water. Snips returned with the washed pot just as I was finishing with the cloths, and I wrung any remaining water from them.

"We'll filter it one more time then chuck it back on the fire, Snips!"

She blew bubbles of assent, setting the river-washed pot down next to the one filled with filtered seawater. I had her hold down the tea towels again and repeated the filtering process. The sediment was almost non-existent this time, telling me the seawater was mostly free of impurities.

I put the pot of salt-filled water back on the small flames of the fire.

"All right, Snips—that should do it!"

She bobbed her head, clearly as happy as I was to make some progression on the seasoning front.

"What do you say we put all this stuff away and go do a little bit of . . ."

I waggled my eyebrows, drawing out the sentence. Snips danced on the spot, knowing what was coming.

"Fishing!"

A torrent of unreadable bubbles flew from her mouth, and she sprinted as fast as all eight of her legs could carry her toward the rods. I ran behind her with the pots and tea towels in hand, giggling like a boy running after his dog.

* * *

"Looks like the wind has definitely died down—hopefully that means it's a good day for fishing tomorrow!"

Snips was so excited she let out a little squeak; my heart melted.

I had my smaller rod with metal jigs on it, and we went to our usual hole by the headland for baitfish.

"If we get plenty of bait before it goes dark, we can reset the crab pot and get right into fishing tomorrow."

She urged me with both claws, gesturing for me to get on with it.

"All right, all right," I said with a laugh. "I'm getting to it, you little scamp!"

I swung the rod overhead, the short length of line leaving the ground. With a soft flick, the rock-sinker flew out and hit the water with a *plonk.* I expected a small thump from the rock hitting the floor. Instead, the rod almost pulled from my hands.

"Woah!"

Snips hissed in excitement, her spindly legs tapping along the rocks as she ran in circles. I stepped back and lifted the rod high, the attached fish shaking its head with vicious swings. The line darted in another direction, and the bamboo pole bent over in half. I stepped in closer, not wanting to put too much pressure on the rod or line.

"Snips! Get in there! It's gonna break!"

She *flew,* her entire body launching from the spot where she stood and into the river.

I roared, half yelling, half laughing, unable to contain my joy. *This is the best!* I walked closer again as the fish on the line tried to swim away, doing my best to not let it break my equipment and get away. Suddenly, the tension eased, and I knew my trusty crab had grabbed hold of the fish. I walked backward, keeping tension on the line while still letting Snips do her thing.

Four of her legs appeared above the water, and with a heave, she threw something up onto the headland. I ran back, dragging it further onto the rocks. The fish Snips had grabbed was an eel, the same as I'd already seen.

Common Eel

Common

Found in the brackish waters of the Kallis Realm, this eel's flesh has high oil content and a strong scent, making it unpalatable food but excellent bait.

So you return, my twice-common friend.

The line tried to pull away, and I felt a moment of disorientation; the sensation didn't match the eel I saw slithering ineffectually over itself on the rocks.

Sergeant Snips hissed, pointing down into the water, and realization struck me.

There's another fish on the line!

I pulled back, slowly fighting against the strong fish.

It wasn't the eel doing most of the work—it's whatever is still in the water!

Snips cheered me on with her claws, waving them around frantically as I backed away from the edge. A flash of silver turned to orange as the fish's scales caught the light of the sunset to the east. I took one more step, pulling it halfway over the edge, and Snips finished the battle, flicking it up beside the eel. I threw the rod behind me and ran down to it. Snips held the slippery eel down, and I grabbed the other. My vision was drawn into it.

Mature Cichlid
Uncommon
Found in the fresh and brackish waters of the Kallis Realm, this fish is a staple source of both food and bait.

A mature version of the juvenile cichlids!

The fish was short and fat, just longer and wider than Snips. I grabbed it by the mouth, knowing the fish had no teeth. I reached behind me, slipping the nail from my pocket and dispatching both fish with a swift jab.

"Sergeant Snips—you beautiful pirate crab!" I looked between her and the two fish. "We got bait *and* dinner!"

She bubbled with delight.

Gary slipped inside the Cult of the Leviathan Tropica branch, casting his vision around. His boss wasn't in the main room, and he let out a sigh.

Thank Hermes's divine guidance.

Sebastian had always been a disagreeable boss, but he'd become even more verbally abusive since the murder of Pistachio and his precious crickets. There were more crickets on the way, which Gary was holding out for.

Hopefully he's a bit more agreeable once he has some little snippers to care for . . .

Gary walked through the room with padded steps, ensuring he made no noise to alert Sebastian of his presence, just in case the man was in another of the rooms. He winced as he walked past Sebastian's bedroom and glanced inside. Gary sighed again; he wasn't in there, either.

Just as he was about to leave the doorway behind, a red flash caught his attention. He dipped his head inside—the unnatural light was coming from a bag on Sebastian's desk.

Oh—just the artifact.

He was about to leave, but something drew him in. Following the pull, he stepped up to Sebastian's desk, reaching into the bag and withdrawing the flashing artifact.

"What the . . ."

The light above the approximation of a human flashed red as it always had, but something else had changed. The small bulb set below the drawing of animals also flashed at the same rhythm as the other.

He stared, uncomprehending.

. . . there's an ascending creature . . . ?

Gary reflexively went to call for Sebastian but stopped himself. He thought back on his boss's actions since discovering the flashing light. He'd ruined practically *everything* on learning of an ascendant human—what would he do upon learning there was also an ascendant creature?

Nothing good, Gary decided.

He closed the bag, taking the artifact with him as he left Sebastian's room.

"How are you feeling, dear?" Barry's wife asked from the door to their bedroom.

"Bad," he croaked from beneath the covers.

"Can I get you anything?"

"No—thank you."

She paused in the doorway, but after a few breaths, he heard her retreating footsteps.

How long can I go on like this?

After a couple days of no sleep and constant worry, Barry was no longer coping. He took a steadying breath, exhaling it slowly in an attempt to calm his fraying nerves. It worked—for a time.

He drifted off to sleep, but after what felt like a few seconds, he was violently awoken. His tormentor had returned, once more making itself known and expelling him from his only reprieve—sleep. Barry's unseeing eyes stared into space, lingering on the words before him.

Please select a name.

A line blinked after the sentence, drawing his attention with each flicker.

"Please . . ." he said, fighting off tears. "Just leave me alone . . ."

CHAPTER THIRTY

HUBRIS

I crouched, creeping across the sands as I approached my quarry. The morning was the coldest yet, an icy breeze kicking up and petering out in the predawn light, but I barely felt the chill, focused as I was on the hunt. One final step, and I was looming over my target. I reached down, a thrill running through me. With careful silence, I started tickling my guard crab.

Sergeant Snips was asleep by the fire, small flames licking up against the bottom of the pot within it. Her legs kicked out spasmodically, extending from her curled-up form as her body reacted to the soft touch of my hands. Her body went rigid, and her eyestalk sprouted upward. It turned, locking onto me. I gave her only a small reprieve before I resumed my tickling tenfold.

"Good morning, Snips!"

She hissed laughter, blowing bubbles and trying to escape my probing fingers.

I let her go, and she ran side to side on the spot, reminding me of nothing so much as a puppy woken from a dream. Kneeling down, I stroked her carapace, and she leaned into it, blowing bubbles of excitement.

"Sorry, Snips—I couldn't help myself. Did you sleep well?"

She nodded, and puffing up with pride, pointed at the flickering fire.

"I saw! Did you tend to it all night?"

She nodded again, her eye gleaming.

"Thanks, Snips. Don't know what I'd do without you." I peered into the pot, seeing the salt water at a calm boil.

"What do you reckon, Snips?" I turned to her. "Brekky first, or check the crab pot, then brekky?"

She hissed incomprehensibly, but both claws pointed to the shore.

"Aye, Snips! Lead the way, my trusty sergeant!"

Barry woke to the growing light of a predawn sky, the open window letting a breeze blow through that irritated his dry eyes. He'd had another fitful night of little sleep, and as if to punctuate this thought, his tormentor spoke.

Please select a name.

He groaned in frustration, pulling the sheets over his head.

"Dear?" his wife asked, her voice laced with worry. She pulled the covers down, staring into his eyes,

"It's not like you to let sickness keep you from the fields—what is it?"

He'd had enough; he couldn't ignore the truth any longer. "It's the System, Helen." His voice was flat, unfeeling.

"*. . . the System?*"

Barry felt her body jolt upright.

"It's come for me—it's asking me to select a name . . ."

"Oh, Barry . . ." She moved, coming to lie between the crook of his arm and chest, resting her head above his heart. "I'm so sorry."

They lay in silence, both contemplating the future.

"What are we going to do?" His voice cracked.

She sat up, determination settling on her face as she set her jaw. "Nothing. We're going to do nothing, Barry. We tell no one, and we live our life as we always have—tending the fields and our family."

Barry let out a tired noise, a mirthless chuckle. "How can you be so calm, Helen? After everything that happened with your brother—"

"Because I have to be." She put a hand on his chest, smiling down at him. "You're going to be fine, my love—*we're* going to be fine. Who knows? This could even be a good thing. Maybe you'll get some sort of farming powers!"

He laughed, this time a genuine one. It swept his worries away, if only momentarily. He raised a hand, caressing his wife's cheek. "What would I do without you guiding me, my love?"

She leaned into the touch, a smile returning her affection for him. "You'd lay in this bed until you wasted away."

She got up, throwing the covers off. "Now, let's get up and have some breakfast. I'm sure Paul would love to see your face, too."

Barry let out a long sigh, willing the exhaustion to leave him. He got to his feet, stretching his stiff body. As if to break his resolve, the tormentor returned, a blinking line demanding action.

Please select a name.

He clenched his jaw. *Barry,* he thought. *My name is Barry.*

Name "Barry" has been accepted. Welcome to the Kallis Realm.

"Are you ready, Snips?"

She nodded fervently, punctuating it with a single hiss. I nodded back with a grin and started pulling in the line. It was so heavy I thought it was lodged in the sand at first, but when the weight didn't decrease, excitement welled within me. Hand over hand, I pulled the line in toward the shore. I finally caught sight of the crab pot, a single mass of brown becoming visible beneath the ocean surface.

"No way, Snips!"

When part of the trap and the crabs within breached the surface, the line started stretching, and I had to run down and grab the handle. I pulled it onto the shore with a sliding movement, and Snips let out an excited hiss that matched my own thoughts perfectly.

The bottom of the trap was *filled* with sand crabs.

Looks like the eel was a much more effective bait than the fish . . .

The System tried to bother me, but it was only a small nudge—easily ignorable.

Not right now, System. I'm crabbing.

I counted the crabs in the pot aloud, thrilled with the haul. ". . . nine, ten, eleven!" I turned to Snips. "Eleven crabs!"

Her claw moved along with my finger as I pointed to each, and she raised her claws to the sky, clacking in victory.

I opened the trap, checking each crab's bottom carapace as I went. There were six females, and I lobbed them carefully into the waves. That left five males—a veritable feast.

"I say we put some back. What do you think, Snips?"

She looked at the five massive males in the trap, then turned to me, nodding.

"How many should we keep?"

She started drawing in the sand, cutting three lines and pointing down at the tally.

I smiled and nodded my assent. "A respectable number. Split one for breakfast and one each for lunch?"

She blew bubbles of joy, and I withdrew the two smallest crabs, setting them free.

I tied the claws of the three crabs, not wanting them to snip at each other while I took them back to the house.

"All right! Let's go get our breakfast started!"

We took the cooked crab down to the beach to watch the sunrise. The sun crested the horizon just as the crab was cool enough to eat, and we both ate in comfortable silence, me with the occasional cracking of shell, Snips with steady, soft crunching as she ate it whole.

Just as I was about to crack the body open and get to the sweet flesh inside, a familiar, adorable head breached the water in front of us. The otter stared intently at my meal, its little sniffer twitching at the aroma of the crab.

Snips got to her feet, letting out a warning hiss, but I put a calming hand on her shell.

"Do you want some?" I asked.

The otter stared between me and the food, cocking its head back and forth with a clear lack of comprehension.

I broke what was left of the crab in half with one hand, and with an underhanded throw, tossed it on the sands before me. The otter flinched back, but seeing I didn't throw anything *at* it, crept forward. One tentative step at a time, it moved like a liquid, its eyes locked on Snips. It stopped only a few more steps from the offered meal, its little eyebrows twitching as it stared at the violently capable crab.

With sudden clarity, I realized it was staring at her eye patch. It seemed intrigued, curious about the garment.

"It's called an eye patch," I said softly.

The otter took a step back, turning its attention to me.

"I made it for Sergeant Snips because she wanted a hat—I thought it was fitting of her nature, and honestly, mate, it's rather fetching."

Snips, hearing my words and understanding what the otter had been staring at, puffed herself up, blowing bubbles of pride.

"You can take the crab." I gestured at the chunk I'd thrown on the sand. "It's a freely given gift."

The otter didn't move, looking between me, the food, and my spiky guard crab, its nose twitching the entire time. Eventually, its hunger won out. It darted forward, bit down with its chompers on the morsel, and ran back to the safety of the ocean, its head turned to the side and watching us as it departed.

I smiled. *One step closer to having an otter pal . . .*

I stroked Snips's shell, once more imagining the otter on my other side, just us three versus the world.

"All right, Snips!" I got to my feet, brushing sand from my pants. "Let's get to fishin'!"

We walked the rod and associated tackle down to the beach. I cut a small section of flesh from the eel, sliding it over the sharpened hook of my larger rod with ease.

"Reckon we'll catch something good today, Snips?"

She nodded her entire body, blowing affirmative bubbles.

I grinned down at her. "One way to find out!"

I stood and looked out at the ocean. The sun was still low enough to peek beneath the brim of my hat, its soft rays covering my body in a blanket of warmth.

A perfect day for fishing . . .

I started swinging the rock, round and round until it gained enough momentum. I let go, watching the sinker, hook, and bait fly out. It hit the water with a soft *plop* twenty meters from the shore. I let it sink, and after a few seconds, I felt the tap of the rock hitting the sandy floor. I took a step back, ensuring the line went taut, and sat down on the beach next to Snips. I closed my eyes, laying back against the sloped beach and keeping one hand on the rod, one hand on Snips's reassuring carapace.

"This is the life . . ."

She hissed her agreement and settled her body farther down into the sand.

Unbidden, my mind wandered back to my time on Earth, and the air seemed to thicken around me. A life spent throwing relationships by the wayside—a life wasted on the pursuit of a goal, that when achieved, brought with it only misery.

How did I not see the emptiness of it all beforehand . . . ?

My father's words from before his passing echoed in my ears.

"This is my legacy and your birthright, son. This is what you were made for—it's your obligation, your responsibility when I'm gone."

There had been hints that it wasn't for me; my subconscious whispered to me, attempting to warn me that it wouldn't bring me joy. I had ignored them all. The weight of expectation was too much, and rather than railing against the sunk-cost fallacy, I'd leaned into it, using how many years I'd spent on training and preparing as a way to heap even more weight onto my own shoulders.

Every personal relationship was burned, cast aside for one misguided obligation or another. All the while, my father would tell me it's just "what people like us did."

No wonder my mother disappeared when I was so young . . .

At this thought, an all-encompassing resentment and anger flooded through the gates, all too happy to leap at my moment of weakness. I sat with it, and rather than process the emotions, pushed them aside.

My therapist's words rose up in response, reminding me just how futile an action that was.

"You can't push the feelings down—it's normal to have conflicting emotions when parents pass, and you'll have to work through them before you can move on and live a happy life."

I'm not ready . . .

Foolish as I knew it to be, the resentment was too much for me, and I redirected my frustrations toward the businesses I inherited—every manipulation, underhanded tactic, and unethical dealing; all of my energy, all of that *time . . .*

My father's—no, *my* corporations. I'd suspected it would be confronting, but when I took over the role of CEO, the veil had been lifted, and it was worse than I could have ever imagined. The companies squeezed every cent they could from customers and employees both. Each person's quality of life was wrung out like an old towel, sold the lie that our new product would solve all their problems—if they purchased just *one more thing.*

Safety suggestions were ignored if deemed too costly, profit set above all else—including human life and prosperity. The dispensation of poison and carnage, doled out to the masses, all with me at the head. There was a layer of separation, sure, but I knew that to be bitter consolation.

Seeing the abject evil with which they were run, I'd attempted to do it my own way. I enacted a plan, one that was far more ethical but less profitable, and was met with backlash from investors and market speculators both. The stock prices plummeted, and my name was dragged through the mud by every business publication and social media tech-bro on Earth.

The public backlash didn't affect me—my morality was a shield against such criticism. But, when the board informed me if I didn't stop they'd force me out, I took the decision into my own hands. I walked away, but not before wasting my entire life in the pursuit.

This decision didn't ease the derision—I was branded a failure, a stain on my father's legacy. I scoffed at my own hubris.

If I could take it all back—do it over again . . .

Something tapped my hand—a firm, warm touch. I opened my eyes, the world taking on a ghostly blue tinge after having them closed for so long in the sun. Snips was petting my hand as she blew comforting bubbles. I smiled down at her, her company grounding me, pulling me from within. I breathed deep, inhaling the sea spray on the air and focusing on the cool air passing my nostrils as it traveled down my throat, filling my lungs.

I'm being unfair on myself . . .

My therapist's words echoed in my head again.

"*While you're understandably upset, there's no reason to keep beating yourself up.*"

"*That feels like an empty platitude,*" I had responded. "*What was the point of isolating myself? What was the purpose of all those years wasted, dedicated to studying to be something I despised?*"

"*Perspective. Who can truly say whether something was good or bad for us? If you had railed against your father's plans, would you now be sitting before me, lamenting that you never tried?*"

She had shook her head, a kind smile on her face. "*You did what you did, and now you know what you know—living in the past and replaying long-gone decisions will only bring you misery. All that's left is to decide where you go from here, Fischer.*"

After a long pause, I'd said something that made me feel stupid at the time, but in retrospect, proved prophetic. "*You know—I've always wanted to try fishing . . .*"

My eyes cleared, and the memory faded. A smile came to my face as I realized she'd called me "Fischer" in the replayed conversion—my brain had subconsciously placed it there.

She was right—there's no point dwelling on my mistakes. Besides, it was another life on another world—none of it matters now . . .

I focused on Sergeant Snips again. She stared at me, her claw still held to my hand, concern in her eye.

"Thank you, Snips."

I felt a tear welling up, and I blinked it away, casting my eyes out to sea. I pulled her into me, and she snuggled up against my leg, deftly avoiding my soft skin with her hardened spike. I banished the unhappy thoughts, choosing to focus on gratitude instead.

I lay on my own private beach, lazing in the sun with a friend by my side—nary a care in the world.

"I'm so glad you came into my life, you beautiful pirate crab."

Snips bubbled her agreement, burying further into my side.

Something bumped the line, almost imperceptibly. My eyes shot up to the tip of the rod, where the movement was more visible.

Nibble.

Nibble.

Tug.

And then, it bit.

CHAPTER THIRTY-ONE

EXTRAORDINARY

With the midday sun beaming down, I held on for dear life. The fish on the other end of my rod swam away in a straight line, the momentum of its body gliding away above the ocean floor. Its weight felt immense.

Just how big is this thing . . . ?

The line went taut even as I stepped closer to the water, the fish coming to a slow stop as my rod held firm. At that moment, it seemed to realize something was wrong. Either the hook setting or the restriction of its movement changed the fish's behavior and the fight began.

It took off, its powerful tail pushing it through the water. Instead of swift shakes of the head, it seemed to move in broad sweeps, as if there were a person on the other end of the line, taking one long step at a time to get away.

What the hell is it . . . ?

"We got a big one, Snips!"

She cheered me on from the waterline, standing in the whitewash of small waves that crashed on the shore. Her frantic bubbling and erratic claw movements brought a smile to my face, and I let out a yell, reveling in the moment. Every time the fish tried to swim out to sea, I moved with it, letting it spend its energy. It swam to the side, trying its luck swimming toward the north instead. Again, each time it would pull on the line, I'd stepped with it, keeping the line taut but not allowing enough tension for it to snap.

I slowly took steps back from the water as we moved, allowing for enough room should it take a desperate run out to sea. This contingency proved prophetic as the fish turned and bolted, the rod sweeping side to side in response to broad shakes of its head. I stepped forward with it. Feeling the tension growing too much, I stepped faster, walking up to my knees in the waves. The water was cool on my legs, and the sensation sent a thrill up my spine, my whole body tingling with adrenaline and anticipation.

It kept going out to sea, and I moved further into the waves. I came up to my waist, holding the rod high and letting the bamboo fibers help with the stress placed on the monofilament line. Its run couldn't last forever, and I felt its body start to lag, the shakes of its head becoming sluggish and sporadic.

With great care, I walked back out of the waves, one shuffling step at a time. Tired as the fish was, it let me guide it, unable to fight off the inexorable pull toward the shore. It changed tack, swimming down to the ocean floor.

I was confused for a moment, unsure what it was doing—but then I felt it stick in place. It had pressed its body into the sand, and when I pulled the line, it moved only millimeters at best.

Is it some sort of stingray? That could explain the weird movements . . .

Unperturbed, I resumed the battle. It hadn't gone completely limp; its body felt rigid, as if it had used muscles to suck itself down against the sands. That meant one rather important thing: the fish would continue to tire, whereas I had what felt like an endless fountain of energy.

Millimeters and centimeters at a time, I pulled it toward the shore, ever onward. Snips tapped my leg, and blowing questioning bubbles, offered to go in and help.

I shook my head, smiling down at her. "Not yet, Snips. We want to make the fight as fair as possible."

She nodded, accepting the words without issue, and resumed her cheerleading from the whitewash.

From waist to knee, from knee to ankle, I withdrew from the waves, bringing my quarry with me ever closer to the shore. A dorsal fin poked above the water ten meters from the shore, light brown and gigantic.

"Holy shit, Snips! You see that?"

She hissed her agreement, jumping up and down on the spot.

Is it a shark?

Whatever the thing was, it was tired. There was barely any fight left in it, and with each passing swing of its great tail, it grew more and more lethargic. It was only a few meters from the beach now, its dorsal fin raised high, a long tail moving ineffectually to escape the shore.

"All right, Snips, go—"

I didn't have time to finish my sentence.

Sergeant Snips flew from where she stood, taking off like a rocket. She landed on the other side of the catch, disappearing beneath the swell. I knew Snips was underneath it when the fish turned, was lifted above the waterline, and emerged from the ocean with eight crab legs visible underneath it.

Snips's mighty carapace was hidden by the fish's body, leaving the creature looking like some sort of eldritch horror—the hiss Snips was emitting from beneath it didn't help the situation. Before I could laugh at the sight, my eyes were drawn in to inspect the catch.

Mature Shovelnose Ray

Rare

Found in the coastal waters of the Kallis Realm, the flesh of this ray is prized for its unique and desirable flavor. Sought by anglers everywhere for its powerful body and difficulty of catching.

The shovelnose ray was over a meter long, a third of its body made up of a shovel-shaped head, the rest composed of a powerful, shark-like tail. It was, quite literally, half ray, half shark.

I felt the System nudge me, but by now the sensation barely lingered in my mind. Snips hissed her victory as she crawled out from beneath the shovelnose ray. I stepped toward it, dispatching the creature with my trusty nail.

"No wonder it was so hard to catch, Snips! Look at this bloody thing!"

She danced on the sands, responding with her body.

"Can you inspect the fish we catch?" I asked, raising a brow.

She cocked her carapace and blew bubbles of intrigue before shaking her head.

"Well, I can—and guess what it said about the shovelnose ray?"

Picking up on my conspiratorial tone, she leaned in, her curiosity palpable.

"It said it was prized for its . . ." I trailed off, grinning and building suspense.

She leaned in closer, her lone eye sparkling.

". . . *unique* and *desirable* flavor."

Snips clacked her claws to the sky, hopping from side to side in excitement.

I smiled at her. "I thought we'd have crab for lunch, but what do you say we cook this up instead?"

She braced herself as a slew of affirmative bubbles came flying from her mouth with such velocity that her carapace shot backward.

"If you collect some wood and get the fire going, I'll prepare the ray—deal?"

She didn't bother responding, simply tearing off across the sands toward the house, a dust cloud of sand kicking up in her wake.

This thing is gonna be way *too big for cooking whole—filleting it is.*

Before beginning, I laid my hand on the top of its head, thanking the magnificent creature for the nutrition it would provide us. I didn't take joy in ending its life, and even though I was a willing participant in the food chain, I still thought it an important step to show my gratitude.

I took my time processing the shovelnose ray, taking care to get every bit of flesh possible from its frame. I was surprised to find a cartilaginous skeleton rather than a bony one, but that meant there weren't any pesky pin bones running down the length of its body. When I'd finished, I walked toward the fire my ever-reliable Snips was no doubt building, fillets on a board in one hand, the head and frame of the ray in the other.

On the way back, I separated the head and the rest of the frame, throwing the cartilage in the river out front of the house, and taking the head back with the fillets. I had a devious plan, and I grinned at the potential of it coming to fruition.

The otter was searching for clams off the shore from its den. The meal she'd managed to steal from the angry snipper and its two-legged pet had been a welcome treat, but she found that it only filled her body with the energy and desire to find more food.

She dug up a clam, and swimming to the top of the water, cracked it open with her favorite rock. She ate the flesh within. It was tasty, sure, but it just didn't hit the same spot as the stolen crab had. Since when had clams, her favorite food after oysters, become undesirable?

She was just contemplating this anomaly when an aromatic scent hit her nostrils. It held the promise of a tasty meal, with an added flavor to it that was unrecognizable. With a start, she realized the unknown smell was akin to the scents that sometimes wafted from the two-legged animals' village.

With the hunt for clams forgotten, the otter swam in search of the source, her curiosity and hunger too piqued to ignore.

Sergeant Snips and I lounged in the midday sun, the scent from the cooking fillets making my hunger grow by the second. I hadn't managed to lure my target in yet, so I'd taken a bit of flesh from the ray's cooking head and thrown it into the river beside the frame.

Hopefully that's enough to bring in my adorable quarry . . .

I cast the worry aside. If the otter came, neat. If it didn't, I'd get to have a delicious lunch with my favorite crustacean.

I renewed my petting of Sergeant Snips's shell, and she bubbled contentedly.

As the meat grilled atop the flames, the smell grew more and more irresistible. The rising steam and smoke danced languidly in the midday sun, only somewhat distracting me from the coming meal.

Movement down at the water caught my attention, and I squinted against the light, trying to make out what it was. A small brown head poked up above the water, staring intently at Snips and me. Butterflies churned within my stomach, and I held my mouth closed as a wide grin spread across my face.

It worked!

Sergeant Snips had noticed the otter too, and she'd stiffened before forcing herself to relax again.

"It's okay, Snips," I whispered, stroking her carapace reassuringly.

The otter emerged from the water, its nose sniffing the air as it skulked up the bank toward the grilling food. I slowly stood, not wanting to spook it. The creature paused, frozen on the spot. I picked up the head of the ray with a pair of tongs. It had already cooked through, flat as it was, and I walked with small steps down toward the otter. It backed off, retreating into the water.

I continued moving forward, and the otter swam out into the river, its head held above the surface—watching me and the food intently. I knelt down on the shoreline, and with glacial movement, placed the piping-hot head into the water.

It'd be no good to burn the poor thing with food fresh off the fire—the water should cool the fish down enough, hopefully.

I walked backward up the bank, watching the fish's head moving in the small waves hitting the sand. The otter crept ever forward in my retreat, and just as I'd gotten halfway back to the fire, it burst forward, grabbed the head, and swam away just as quick—well, it tried to, but the ray's head was both an awkward shape and as long as the otter was, making it a rather awkward and endearing withdrawal.

"Cute little bugger . . ." I said aloud, watching it disappear from sight.

* * *

It took the otter much longer on the return trip than the way there, overburdened as she was. The entire time, she could feel her mouth salivating, the taste of the stolen food driving a desire to stop and eat it on the spot. Despite her need, she knew it to be unsafe; the aroma of the fish would doubtless bring in scavengers, and it would be much safer to consume within her den.

She pushed the head up onto the rocks before her home, shuffling up beside it to drag the meal back and into the safety of her cavern. Her claws skittered across the rocks, but driven by the taste she'd already experienced, her small muscles convulsed, all working together to achieve her goal. With a final heave, the head made it up and over the rocky shore, and she scrambled backward with the momentum, dragging the stolen meal all the way back into the den.

As soon as she reached the back wall, the feast began and she lost herself to the experience.

Each subsequent mouthful was better than all those before it, and the indescribable and incomparable flavors seemed to build upon themselves. The meal filled her with energy, renewing the effort spent in getting the fish home.

Just as she ate the last bite, with her stomach filled almost to bursting, something extraordinary occurred.

CHAPTER THIRTY-TWO

FISCHER'S COOKING

Trent, the first in line to the throne of Gormona, wiped his sweaty palms on his velvet pants. It didn't help. He sat in a waiting room, his slow brain churning at an entirely unusual speed. There weren't many things in this world that could unsettle his rock-like intellect, but ever since discovering the powered-on artifact in his favored room of hiding, it had been steadily becoming a common occurrence.

Poseidon's oiled back hair, how long is he going to make me wait?

Trent had mostly kept his calm at all the messages flowing from the relic hidden in his warren of constructs, but upon checking it the previous day, there had been two more additions that shattered his composure.

At first, he'd tried to pass off the messages as those of the ancients, the screen somehow relaying advances that occurred some time in the distant past. With each new advancement and with the sporadic times between them, however, another possibility had become unignorable. This "Fischer" had somehow taken steps on the path of the ancients and was steadily gaining more and more powers.

Trent thought back to the printed lines, his reluctant brain once more rolling into thought.

New milestone! Fischer has learned jewel crafting!
New milestone! Fischer has learned tailoring!

With those new additions, Trent had left his room of hiding, uncaring if the dreaded decorum tutors found him. It was time for Trent to take action.

The only question is: What can I get out of it?

A man opened the door and walked into the waiting room, clearing his throat. "The king will see you now, prince."

Trent stood and nodded at the dignitary, wiping his hands once more. It still didn't help.

Augustus Reginald Gormona, the reigning king of Gormona and lord of these lands, let out a sigh. Light shone in through the stained-glass windows high above, painting the white walls and pillars of his domain in a sea of colored fragmentation.

He slouched on his throne, easing the tension from his lower back while there was no one present. "Just what does this idiot son of mine want?" he asked himself aloud, genuinely worried about the no-doubt moronic request his progeny had.

The outer door of the antechamber groaned in protest at being opened, and Augustus sat up straight, projecting regal majesty across the still-empty throne room. The inner door opened, and in stepped a dignitary, followed closely by his biggest source of disappointment.

"What can I do for you, son?"

Trent stepped up, glancing back at the dignitary and waiting for him to leave the room. Augustus noticed his son wiping his hands on his overly flagrant pants, and he raised an eyebrow.

What has him so nervous? I swear, if he asks for more serving girls . . .

With the dignitary closing the door behind him, leaving only the two royals in the room, Trent turned and cleared his throat. "Father. I have a request for you."

"Yes, Trent—I gathered that when you asked to meet with me." The king rolled his eyes and made a hand gesture for him to get on with it. "Speak your mind."

Trent took a deep breath, letting it out as he forced his eyes up to meet his father's.

"I wish—er—request that I be allowed to leave the capital, Dad . . . uh, *sire.*"

Augustus sighed. *Eros's quivering sack—It's definitely about more serving girls, isn't it? The boy has an insatiable taste for those lowborn peasants.*

"And why do you wish to leave the capital, Trent? I thought we already spoke about the girls—"

"N-not the girls, Dad—sire!" Beads of sweat visibly sprouted from Trent's forehead, but the lackadaisical youth, balling his fists at his side, continued. "I want to go on a cultivator hunting trip."

Augustus Reginald Gormona, the king and father of the boy before him, physically recoiled at the statement. "You . . . want to go out on official business? On your own merit?"

Trent nodded, his eyes firm. "Yes, sire."

Augustus stared at Trent for a long moment. Then, something unexpected occurred. He gave his son a wide smile as a tear came to his eye.

Maybe this wayward son of mine has finally discovered his direction as a man . . .

The otter paused mid-chew, an odd tingling suffusing her entire body. She panicked. Was the fish poisoned? It hadn't smelled so, but could it have been noxious, nonetheless? The tingling in her limbs seemed to crawl inward, radiating toward the center of her body. Time seemed to freeze as she imagined it reaching her organs, getting to the vital parts of her body, shutting them down, seizing—

The tingling flooded back out, transforming into a pleasant sensation as it flew from her body. The world brightened, and she had to squeeze her eyes shut. A loud *pop* rang out, seeming to come from her. She felt her body *change.* It seemed to expand out, ballooning in size, her senses being overwhelmed by the experience. Her claws grew long, and she could *feel* how sharp they became, like the edge of the sheerest rock. Just as fast as it had come, however, it was gone, and her body shrank down to its usual size. She looked at her front paws, inquisitive eyes lingering on the tips of her claws.

They did become sharper . . . they still are . . .

Her head reeled back with the realization that she had done something entirely new, and that somehow, she knew what it was.

I am having . . . thoughts?

A trickle of understanding continued to flow through her, the sensation both unsettling and filled with awe. She cocked her head at the interactions she'd had with the two-legged creature as they played through her mind unbidden.

No, not a two-legged creature—a human. I wasn't stealing the food . . . he was giving it to me of his own free wi—

She snapped her eyes to movement in the opening of her den, and her hair stood on end. Two scaled heads were in the entrance, a pair of forked tongues tasting the air of her cavern. She froze, willing them to find nothing and leave, but the smell of the cooked fish still lingered in the air and they slithered further inside.

She caught sight of their bodies, the red, white, and black stripes causing base instincts to well up from within; the venom would prove fatal if their fangs found purchase. Hissing and growling, she buffed her body up, trying to scare them off.

The sea snakes were unaffected by her warning, their heads moving closer and closer toward her and the back of the den. Their tongues continued darting out, tasting the air and searching for the source of the delicious smell.

The otter pressed herself against the back wall, still trying to appear as large as possible. She hissed louder, the noise echoing off the stone walls of her safe place—her home. The thought of these intruders invading her dwelling filled her with an emotion she wasn't sure she'd ever felt. Rage.

She darted forward, lashing out with a paw as her fury demanded. The movement was instant, and as her sharpened claws collided with the head of the first snake, they extended, and power exploded from within her.

Five lines of silver light arced out from her, fading from existence as fast as they had come. The snake she'd hit flew backward violently, seeming to unravel as it did so. The second snake stopped moving, and after staying upright for a mere moment, it fell into pieces.

The otter looked down at her claws with great curiosity. They were still extended, poking out over half the length of each digit. She flexed her pads, and they retracted, going back to their regular size.

I am . . . strong.

She started eating the venom-free chunks of snake absentmindedly, her focus still on the never-ending stream of information pouring in. The snakes didn't taste anywhere near as good as the cooked fish.

"Are you ready, Snips?"

She nodded her agreement, blowing impatient bubbles.

I picked up a section of the cooked ray, laying it on the sand in front of her. The first bite was a slow thing—a testing of the waters. She chewed it, tasting the unique flavors. Then, with two-clawed enthusiasm, she started shoveling the food in.

I smiled down at her. *Guess it passes the Snips test, then . . .*

With the tongs, I grabbed the same amount of ray for myself, and settled down next to Snips on the sand. Before I could even taste it, my mouth was watering. The aroma seemed to surround me, filling my body with vigor before even sampling it. The flesh itself had a unique texture. It was neither as firm as crab, nor as delicate as fish; it settled somewhere in between.

As I lifted a chunk to my mouth and placed it inside, I lost focus on the world surrounding me. The flavor drew me in, caressing my taste buds with its warmth and distinctive taste. Much like the texture, the flavor also seemed to be an amalgamation of crustacean and fish, its sweet and savory combination a one-two punch that made me think of the colorful sunsets so prevalent in my new world.

It'll be even better with a little more salt—I can't wait *until that seawater is done reducing . . . hopefully it doesn't burn this time after all the filtering.*

I sighed contentedly. "Snips . . . I think this is my favorite meal yet."

She didn't stop eating as she nodded her agreement, the lone eye above her carapace squinting in bliss.

I finished my portion of ray without even realizing it, the meal warming me from within just as the midday sun warmed my legs and arms. I lazed back on the sand, content to relax before helping myself to even more.

"Hello, Fischer," came an unexpected but welcome voice.

I turned my head toward the voice, smiling at the new arrival.

"Barry! How are ya, mate? Glad to see you up and about. I was worried that fish made you ill—it didn't, did it?"

Barry winced. "No, Fischer. It didn't make me ill, I was just feeling a little under the weather . . ."

Barry trailed off as his eyes locked on the cooked ray, and I could see his eyes widen a little as the scent of it hit him.

"In that case . . ." I grinned at him. "Care to try some shovelnose ray? Sergeant Snips and I reckon it's the best catch we've had yet."

Snips bubbled her agreement from where she lay half-buried in the sand, delighting in the meal.

Barry swallowed and nodded almost imperceptibly. "Aye, Fischer, that'd be nice."

I smiled at him. "Let me serve you some, then!"

As I passed the plate to Barry, I was expecting the same hesitation as the previous times I'd given him food. Instead, he accepted it with a radiant smile and intent eyes. Without pause, he started eating it, and didn't stop until all of it was gone.

"That was delicious, Fischer. Thank you."

"No worries, mate! Can I do anything for you, by the way?"

Barry cocked his head.

"Do anything . . . ?"

"Yeah! Not that I mind you coming round here, but I thought you might need something—you're usually working your fields this time of day."

"Oh, no, nothing like that, Fischer." He stood and brushed off his pants. "I just wanted to thank you for the fish you gave me the other day, but now it seems I have to thank you twice . . ."

"No worries, mate," I said with a laugh. "Come around whenever you want—Sergeant Snips and I are always happy to see your face."

Snips bubbled her agreement, nodding from her hole in the sand.

"Well, thank you regardless. The meal was delicious, but I'd better get back to the fields—plenty of work to catch up on after my time in bed."

"No worries, mate! Catch you later?"

I waved goodbye as Barry left, then turned back to Snips.

"So . . . you ready for more ray?"

She jumped from her place of relaxation in excitement, a stream of bubbles flowing.

Barry walked away from the fire, his thoughts a cloud of implications and possibilities.

There's no doubt in my mind—it's Fischer's cooking that facilitated my awakening.

His acceptance of that fact came easily, like the last stone of a wall settling into place. Fischer was some sort of nexus for advancement, and his arrival on their shores meant both change and a great potential of harm would be coming the way of Tropica Village.

What can I do to make sure we keep the harm at bay?

CHAPTER THIRTY-THREE

COLLAR

"What in Apollo's delicate lute are you planning behind that toe-like face, Trent?"

Trent, first in line to the throne, and only marginally resembling a toe by his reckoning, closed his slackened jaw. He turned away from the parapet he leaned over, facing the speaker.

His sister Tryphena stood behind him, blocking his way down from atop the wall. Her usually schooled and beautiful features were scrunched in an ugly scowl, her derision clear.

"Nothing, sister," Trent replied. "I've simply decided it's time to step up as a man and the future king."

She snorted, a noise their decorum tutors would no doubt disapprove of.

"We both know that's not true, so why don't you cut the malarkey, Trent?"

"Maller key?"

Trent felt his jaw drop open again as he tried to parse the unknown words.

"What's that, and why would I cut it?"

Tryphena laughed, loud and condescending. "You're a moron. I don't know what you're planning, but I suppose it doesn't matter—you're more likely to get yourself killed by the cultivators you're taking with you than to succeed."

Trent's eyes narrowed in anger. "They won't be able to hurt me with the collars on. You know that."

"You'll still find a way to mess it up." Tryphena turned, walking down the stone steps and out of sight. "I have complete faith in your lack of ability."

Trent's eyebrow twitched as he realized she'd gotten the last word—again.

Mock me all you want, overconfident sister of mine.

He reached a hand into his pocket, removing the artifact his father had given him for the search. It was a simple thing compared to the room of relics he usually hid in, able to fit in a single hand. There were two sides to the handheld artifact, one depicting a human, the other a group of animals. Each side had a small bulb that would light up when within range of an uncollared cultivator.

With this, I will find and bring in whoever this "Fischer" is.

A rather disgusting smile crossed Trent's face, one that was usually reserved for the girls he paid to come to his chamber.

I'll collar Fischer, and I'll torture his secrets out of him.

* * *

I sneezed, covering my mouth with an arm so as to not hit the ray I was storing for later. I felt Snips tap my calf, and I smiled down at her.

"Thanks, Snips. Someone must be talking about me—only good things, I hope."

She nodded sagely, unable or unwilling to entertain any other possibility.

I stretched. "I think I'll head into town, Snips—I have something planned that should take our fishing adventures to the next level."

She froze, and after only a moment of thought, started ushering me out the door.

"All right, all right," I said with a laugh. "I'll get going, then. Meet me back by the fire at sunset for a ray and crab feast?"

She blew happy bubbles, and I beamed a smile at my enthusiastic guard crab.

"Hey, mate. Are you Bradley?" The man carving the back of a wooden chair looked up at me, his eyebrows subtly raising.

"I'm Greg—Brad is my brother, but if you're looking for a woodworker, I can help you just as well as he can. We run this place together."

I smiled. "Well, pleasure to meet you then, Greg!" I held out a hand. "Name's Fischer, and I am indeed looking for your woodworking expertise."

He shook my extended arm with a heavily calloused hand. "Ah, Fischer. I was wondering when I'd meet you—I've heard your name thrown about the past week like sugarcane during the harvest."

I laughed. "Only good things, I hope."

Greg let out a light chuckle. "Aye, mostly good things. You're some sort of benevolent ascendent if the praises can be believed, but with an odd penchant for heretical activity."

He stretched, arching and rubbing his lower back as he stood straight. "What can I do for you then, Fischer?"

I grinned at his "heretical activity" comment.

Not entirely wrong, but I'm glad he's still happy to work with me . . .

"I'm looking for something a little unconventional."

I passed the schematic I'd carved into a wooden plank to him, local measurements helpfully provided by a certain literate crustacean.

Greg looked it over, his brow furrowing in consternation. "Is it some sort of wheel? It shouldn't be a problem . . ."

"Not a wheel—it's a reel to help me with that heretical activity you spoke of."

His eyebrow raised for a moment but quickly dipped back down. "What do you want it made of?"

"Strong wood, and I'd like it oiled or waxed with something that helps keep water out."

"Something that keeps water out, eh?" Greg rubbed his chin. "Ironbark wood treated with linseed oil is probably your best option for keeping water out."

Huh. They have linseed here. Neat.

"Ironbark and linseed oil sounds good to me, mate. Do you mind if I help with the reel, or at least watch you create it?"

"Called a reel, is it . . . ?"

Greg trailed off as he eyed me up and down, his gaze lingering on my arms. "I suppose it wouldn't hurt to try your hand at woodworking—you look like you have the strength for it. So long as you agree to step back if I think it's not working, I'm happy for you to help."

I nodded. "Works for me, mate—if I'm ruining the reel, tell me, and I'll move aside."

"Deal."

"What will it cost me?"

"Hmmm. With these materials and dimensions . . . let me just check if we have any ironbark offcuts."

He strode over to a back shelf laden with different planks and slabs of wood, rummaging through the pile.

"Ah, you're in luck, Fischer!"

He picked up a gray-tinted chunk of wood, hauling it back to the bench with little effort.

"This is just big enough, and should bring the base cost down—does two iron coins sound fair to you?"

My eyebrows raised a little at the cost. "Is the wood rare? That seems quite expensive for a bit of wood compared to most things I've come across in the village."

He gave me a wincing smile. "It is, aye—the trees don't grow in these parts, and it's hard to work with, hence the name. We can use another material if that's too much for you . . ."

I shook my head and smiled at him. "Nah, mate, I want the best material I can get—I'm building this reel to last."

I felt a moment of desire to bargain Greg down, but quickly quashed it.

Fergus said he was trustworthy when I asked for a local woodworker, so I'll believe him. Besides, I have plenty of coin and it doesn't feel right leaning on villagers that are already doing it tough.

"Well, my mates at the smithy recommended you, so I'll take your word for it, Greg. If you say two iron coins are fair, I'll pay it." I held my hand out, and Greg shook it.

"Are you free now, Fischer? I'm ahead of schedule with our work orders, and we can probably finish your job today if we start now."

I rubbed my hands together as a grin spread across my face. "I certainly am, mate. Let's get into it!"

"You're, uh, sure you haven't done this before, Fischer?"

The man looked up at Greg, cocking his head in confusion before smiling. "Nah, mate—never worked with wood before. How am I doing?"

Greg looked at the astonishing amount of wood Fischer had already managed to shave off the hardwood section.

I was just going to let him have a go . . . but this . . .

Fischer was shaving it down faster than even Greg could, slowly taking the corners off and rounding the square slab.

"Uh, Greg . . . you right, mate?"

Greg jolted, realizing he'd been staring in silence. "Oh, s-sorry, Fischer. Yeah, you're doing well—keep going."

Fischer grinned and laughed. "That I can do!"

He bent down over the vice again, shaving down the ironbark once more.

Unbelievable . . . just how strong is he? He's carving through that slab like it's made of pine . . .

Just as impressive was the precision. He didn't stick to a single section for too long; he shaved an area down, then opened the vice, spun the wood, closed the vice, and resumed shaving away.

There's no way he hasn't done at least a little woodworking, is there?

There's something so satisfying about doing physical work with your hands.

I let my thoughts get drowned out by the steady movement of my arms, the rhythmic planing of the wood a meditative process. Slivers of wood shaved off with each push and they flew from the plane in my hands, hitting my forearms before falling to the floor. I lost myself, removing thin ribbons with sweeping movements before spinning the ironbark wood in the vice and attacking the next area.

Before I knew it, I'd reached the mark on the wood, and with a final arc of force, the initial shape was done. I turned to Greg, who was watching intently, eyes focused on the finished wood.

"All right—what's next?"

His eyes seemed to clear, and a discerning gaze settled on me. "Next, we chisel out the concave section you wanted—do you want to give it a go?"

"Mate, if you think I won't ruin it, I'm happy to have a crack."

Greg nodded. "All right, you can start, and I'll step in when you get to the intricate sections."

Greg handed me a pointed chisel with a ninety-degree angle between two cutting edges, followed by a wooden mallet.

"Start in the middle. That way, if you take too much off, we can smooth it out."

"No worries, mate. I'll give it a shot—just pull me up if necessary."

I set the chisel to the middle of the reel and raised the mallet high.

Brad, Greg's brother and business partner, walked into his workshop to a flurry of banging and wooden chips. There was a man he'd never seen before chiseling away at a slab of wood, presumably pine with how fast he was working. He stepped up beside his brother, who was watching intently.

"Who's this then, Greg?"

Greg jumped, then turned to his brother. "This is Fischer—the one we've been hearing so much about."

Brad nodded. "Well, that explains why I've never seen him, but why is he hammering that wheel of pine like it ran away with his sister?"

Greg raised an eyebrow. "Pine? Look again, brother."

Brad did, not sure what he was looking for.

What other wood could someone be chipping through so easily?

The mallet swung down again and the expelled sliver of wood bounced along the floor, landing at Brad's feet. He bent down to pick it up, and as he brought it up to the light, his eyes went wide.

"Hephaestus's rock-hard anvil," Brad whispered, "is that ironbark wood?"

Greg nodded vehemently.

"Right? He's shaving it down like it's made of butter and hasn't slowed in the slightest."

"Gods above—his muscles must be screaming in protest . . ."

A small smile made its way to my face as I chiseled away patiently at the wood. It didn't seem as hard as Greg made out, but it was certainly stronger than the logs I'd split for my fence.

I guess that could be my improved body coming in clutch again, though . . .

I'd gouged out most of the section that would house the fishing line, so I started chiseling smaller sections, shifting from shaping to smoothing. After ten minutes, I pulled back, inspecting my handwork.

There's no more I can do with the chisel—I'd guess it's time for sandpaper, or whatever equivalent they use in this world.

I turned back to Greg but saw another man beside him. "G'day, mate—I presume you're Brad."

"Y-yes. You're Fischer, right?"

We shook hands, and I turned to Greg, who was looking a little unwell.

"How'd I do, mate—er, are you all right?"

Greg gave me a smile that was incongruous with his pallid features. "I'm fine, Fischer, just a little shocked. You did marvelously. Here." He held out a curved file.

I accepted it. "You don't have sandpaper?"

Both men gave me a funny look.

"Sand . . . paper?" Brad asked, voicing the question for both of them.

Add that to the list of creations I can bring to this world.

I made a dismissive gesture with my hand. "Forget about it—the file is all I'll need." I returned my attention to the almost finished reel and started filing.

With a furrowed brow, Greg watched Fischer use the file on his reel. Each stroke was that of an expert, and with each movement his confusion only increased.

Brad nudged him in the side, leaning in to whisper. "I never expected another woodworker to come to the village, let alone someone so experienced . . ."

Greg leaned over, whispering back, "He claims he's a novice . . ."

Brad snorted softly. "That's not possible, right? Do you think he's—"

Brad cut himself off, and Greg's eyes went wide as the reel shrunk and morphed before them.

CHAPTER THIRTY-FOUR

FUN

As I took one last sweeping stroke with the file, the reel seemed to transform. It shrunk and smoothed out infinitesimally, the change so minute that I hoped the brothers wouldn't notice. Along with the transformation, the System tried to send me another message that was, thankfully, suppressed. What wasn't suppressed was my eyes being drawn into the reel, as with my previous creations.

Ironbark Reel of the Fisher
Rare
Crafted of ironbark, this reel has a multitude of attributes for those with the requisite knowledge.

Again with the vagueness, System, you belligerent calculator?

"Hephaestus's chisel!" Brad yelled. "What was that?"

I schooled my face before turning to Greg and Brad, taking in their shocked expressions.

"What was what?" I asked, feigning ignorance.

"That damned thing just smoothed and shrank!" Brad answered, his eyes wide, still yelling.

"Did it?" I cocked my head as I turned back to the reel. "It looks the same to me . . ."

I ran my hand over it, feeling how smooth and hard it had become. There was no doubt about it; the reel *had* transformed.

"Well," I said, opening the vice and picking up my creation, "I need to go about sorting out a bearing for this thing—you said two irons, right?"

"Yes, but that was for me to do the work . . ." Greg said with a vacant expression. "You did most everything . . ."

"No worries. Chuck in some linseed oil for me to take and we'll call it square. Deal?"

"Y-yeah, that sounds fair . . ."

I withdrew the coins from my pouch, placing them in Greg's hand. Brad walked to a bench, bent down, and picked up a small tin of what I assumed was linseed oil. He placed it before me with a thoughtful expression, staring off into space.

"Well, thanks for the help, guys! It was a pleasure meeting you both!"

I turned and strode from the shop, heading for my next destination before they could ask any more questions.

"All right, what was that?" Brad asked, turning to his brother. "Are you pranking me? Is he some secret master from the capital?"

"No . . ." Greg said, still staring at the door Fischer had departed through. "I have no idea what that was . . ."

"Well, he's either a master at woodworking, or he's a cultivator from one of the stories—who else could have so much aptitude with a profession they've never done before? We might have to tell someone . . ."

They looked at each other, and after a moment's pause, burst into laughter.

"Yeah, a cultivator of old," Greg said through his mirth. "Next thing we know, he'll be shooting lightning from his crotch and beams of water from his fingers."

"Still," he continued, "I believed him when he said he'd never worked with wood before. Did we imagine the reel changing?"

"Who knows?" Brad shot Greg a wink. "All I know is, we just sold a chunk of ironbark wood and a tin of linseed oil for a great price."

Greg scowled at his brother. "Don't say it like that—it makes it sound like I overcharged him."

Brad rolled his eyes. "You know what I mean. It would have taken either of us the rest of the day to do what he just did in less than an hour. Besides, he was the one to offer the same price despite him doing all the work."

Greg leaned against a bench and looked back toward the door. "I don't know what to make of him . . ."

Brad walked over and sat on the bench. "No use overthinking it. Whatever he is, he's bloody good with wood, despite not even realizing what he did."

What the fuck was all that? I'd made a wooden version of something famous back home—an Alvey Reel. Though, I'm pretty sure Alvey is just the brand—what the hell kind of reel would you even call this thing?

It looked like a hand reel, but with the addition of a metal bracket, I should be able to attach it to one of my bamboo rods. I rolled it over in my hands, admiring the smooth surface. It was like polished stone, the finish entirely too fine for the toothy file I'd been using. Even the sections I didn't file down had flattened, their edges and faces becoming uniform. I'd noticed something similar with the other things I'd created that the System assigned names to. Even Fergus took note that something with the ring changed when I put the pearl in the setting, but it had been a much more subtle affair. The transformation of the reel was, frankly speaking, astounding.

Even with my improved body, I could tell the wood was incredibly tough. Compared to the common trees I'd been felling near my property, the gray-tinted wood was something else entirely. The hardwood was, all at once, compacted and compressed. It ended up looking like it was made on an assembly line from Earth before being sanded by the finest grit sandpaper possible.

I felt the smile coming to my face, and it spread so wide my cheeks started to ache.

Who cares about the details? I have a reel!

"You certainly look happy, Fischer," a welcome voice called from behind.

I turned, beaming a smile back at Maria. "I am! I just created this nifty new reel for fishing."

I held it out, letting her inspect the creation.

"Wow. It's so smooth . . ."

Her eyes sparkled as she inspected it. Her head cocked, freeing a loose strand of hair from behind her ear.

"Can . . . can I touch it?"

"Of course! Wanna hold it?"

I held it out, and she picked it up, her core bracing as she hefted its weight.

"Wow, it's heavier than I thought it would be!" She moved it around in her hands, feeling the sides and concave indent with deft fingers.

"Ironbark, right? How on Kallis did you get it so smooth? I've never seen ironbark with such a fine finish—it must have taken days."

"Something like that," I said with a smile. "I have Brad and Greg to thank for the workmanship. Those two seriously know what they're doing when it comes to wood."

"I figured those two would have been behind it, but it's still impressive." She raised her eyes to meet mine, her gaze filled with curiosity. "So what does it do? How is this going to help your fishing?"

"See the concave bit?" I pointed at the outer ring. "That's for winding line around. I'm going to attach it to a fishing rod, and with a handle and bearing in the middle that Fergus is gonna help me with, I'll be able to reel in fish when they get hooked."

She looked back down at the reel. "It's so beautiful, it almost seems to be a waste to use it on heretical activities." The gleam in her eye and the playful smile let me know she was teasing.

"Oh, absolutely!" I grinned. "Alas, what else is a heretic like myself supposed to do with it?" I winked at her. "I'm nothing, if not consistent."

She laughed, genuine joy spilling out. "Well, I'm glad your activities are going well, if nothing else."

"What about you and Roger? How goes the farming?"

She grimaced. "Honestly . . . not great."

"Oh? Sorry to hear. Anything I can do to help?"

"Not unless you can fix soil," she said with a sigh. "We're struggling with crop rotation. We simply don't have enough land to plant the crops we need to fix the levels in the soil while still farming enough wheat and sugarcane to make a living."

I winced. "That's a pickle. How much land do you have to farm on, if you don't mind me asking?"

"We only have four standard fields. Dad thought we'd be able to afford much more when first coming here, but we could only buy three at the time. With the cost of living and operating, we've only been able to expand to a fourth field in recent years."

"Damn, margins are that tight?"

She nodded, giving me a rueful smile. "They really are. But listen to me, harping on and ruining your good mood." She handed the reel back to me. "I'd better get back out to Dad, he's churning soil out there by himself."

"You didn't ruin my mood, Maria—always happy to be a sounding board."

She grinned, hiding her troubled feelings.

"Well, I'll see you later, Fischer."

"See you next time!" I said as she turned and left.

As I strode off toward the smithy, possible solutions started churning through my mind.

Maria glanced back at Fischer as she left, seeing the man already off and moving with purpose-filled strides.

"Maybe we need to take up some heretical activity of our own . . ."

She laughed at herself with a shake of the head, causing her hair to tickle the sides of her face. "It might actually be worth it with how carefree Fischer always seems . . ."

Her troubled thoughts returned as she made her way back to the fields.

How are we going to get out of this mess?

She had underplayed the situation they found themselves in to Fischer; the levels in the soil were getting so bad that if they didn't find a way to improve the crops soon, they'd be in serious financial trouble.

She caught sight of her father attacking the soil as she stepped past a neighbor's flourishing field of cane. He was taking his frustrations out on the barren field, using overhand strikes to plow the earth.

"Dad, you're going to hurt yourself if you keep up at that pace," she gently chided.

Her dad glanced at her, then stood back, leaning on the haft of his hoe. "It'll hurt me more if we can't get these damned fields sorted. We just can't keep up with the cost of operating and the price of the medicine your mother needs." Her dad's eye twitched as he reminded himself of the medicine, and in a single movement, he stepped back, grabbed the plow, and threw the head high.

With a grunt, he slammed it down into the ground.

"Damn this bloody village!" He slammed it down again. "Damn the bloody lord!"

Using his whole body, he rammed it home in the soil a final time before letting go of the haft.

"And damn Demeter's fickle bloody heart! God of farming, my ass!"

Maria rushed to him, knowing he would only spiral if she couldn't drag him out of it. She wrapped her arms around him, ignoring the sweat and grime on his work-slickened body.

"It's okay, Dad. We'll work it out. We always do."

Her father relaxed in her arms, if only a little, and he wrapped an arm around her. Despite her words, Maria's heart sank.

What are we going to do . . . ?

* * *

The otter swam through the waves of the ocean in search of her target. She knew the general area the crab resided in but couldn't find her anywhere. Struck by inspiration, she approached the rocky headland, and after selecting a choice rock, started banging.

She brought the rock down on the oysters, delighting in the speed and strength the changes to her body granted her. She was able to work through them with a previously unseen speed, and she slurped the delicious treats down. After a few, she stopped, tasting the oyster on her tongue.

Taste . . . not good.

The texture and flavor were still there, but after experiencing the food the human had provided, her body seemed to crave more. She struggled to come to terms with a dissonance coloring her mind; the trickle of information received was not yet enough for full comprehension.

Movement caught her eye, dispelling the half-formed thoughts. She spun to look at the side of the rock, half a crab and a lone eye visibly poking around the side of the headland. The otter, not knowing what she was doing or why, waved. Blinking and scuttling to the side, the crab revealed more of her body. The otter waved again and took a few steps forward. With one raised pincer, the crab slowly waved back. The otter took more steps, closing the distance and tilting her head back and forth as she took in the crab.

She'd not before realized just how different the crab was, but since whatever happened in her den, she could now see just how distinct its form was. It wore a black piece of . . . *cloth* on its eye, something only humans usually did. The crab was also larger than normal and covered in vicious-looking spikes.

The otter walked forward more, and trying to display her own intelligence, nodded at the crab. The crab, its entire body now visible, nodded back, and with a final wave of a dangerous-looking claw, turned to leave.

Seeing an opportunity, the otter snuck closer on silent legs. She picked up a spherical rock and slowly raised her arm. With a swing of her empowered forepaw, she launched the stone at the crab's back. It sailed through the air, and excitement swelled within the otter as it approached the mark.

Tink.

The otter chirped in delight as she turned and dashed for the safety of the water. The crab hissed in fury behind her, and eight hardened legs struck the rocks as it tried to catch her. It was too late; the otter dove and slipped beneath the small waves on the shore, gliding away.

Fun.

Crab is fun.

CHAPTER THIRTY-FIVE

INSUFFICIENT POWER

Sergeant Snips, best friend and protector of Fischer, huffed on the shore as she glared at where the otter had disappeared, daring it to show its face once more. The otter seemed different, and Snips suspected the creature had experienced some sort of awakening, just as she had. It was, as some might find surprising, not at all incongruous to Sergeant Snips's expectations.

She has eaten of my master's food—it was a matter of time.

What she hadn't expected, however, was for the otter to still demonstrate such juvenile behavior after gaining the information awakening brought along with it.

Maybe the otter isn't as intelligent as I . . .

This thought brought with it a sense of calm, her superiority washing away the anger.

That is also to be expected—a mere otter could never be as intelligent as I, chosen of Fischer.

She walked back toward the campfire, intent on resuming her watch; the seawater would be boiled and reduced to perfection.

I will do as my master has requested—I'll endeavor to forgive the otter its shortcomings, various as they may be.

"G'day, Duncan!" I called as I strode into the smithy. "Is Fergus about?"

"Back here, Fischer!" the head smith called, walking from behind the forge. "How did it go with Brad and Greg?"

"It went better than expected, mate! Check it out!" I held up the reel, and Fergus came over, accepting it from my extended hands.

"Damn, how did you get it so fast?"

"Little bit of hard work on Brad, Greg, and my part, mate!"

Fergus raised an eyebrow at me as he handed the reel to Duncan. "Something tells me that's an understatement . . . but I'll take your word for it."

"Hephaestus's girthy legs, I've never seen ironbark refined so smoothly . . ." Duncan said, his eyes squinting as he rotated the reel.

"So, what do you two reckon—could you help me out with the metal parts I requested?"

Fergus crossed his muscular arms. "I have some good news and bad news on that front, Fischer. We could make the bearing you asked for, but I think for your purposes, we might be better off waiting for the merchant, Marcus, to come. I recommended you make the internal hole that size for a reason, and it'll likely last longer if you have a pre-prepared bearing set in it."

My hopes dropped momentarily, but I cast the disappointment aside. "Damn. I was stoked to fish with it today or tomorrow, but it's all good. When is Marcus set to come to Tropica?"

"He'll be here on Sunday."

One of my eyebrows shot up. *They have Sunday? I really need to work out these weekdays . . .*

"Right. Sunday. What day is it tomorrow, again? I've been so busy lately I've lost track."

"It's Winday tomorrow, so you'll only have to wait three days—Marcus should have that coffee machine with him then, too."

Winday? So I have Winday, Sunday, and Fielday so far. God, I hope there are seven days—that'll make things so much easier.

I smiled as Duncan passed the reel back to me. "Well, thanks anyway! I couldn't have made the reel in the first place without your recommendation. Waiting a few days won't kill me."

"You're welcome, Fischer . . . seeing as you're here, though, I don't suppose you feel like working the bellows for an hour?"

Fergus gave me a sheepish smile. "I wouldn't usually ask, but we're running a little behind after we changed the plans on your—"

"Mate! Say no more! I could use the exercise!" I strode past the counter and toward the forge. "Let's get this training montage started!"

"This, er, what?"

I laughed, unable to keep it in. *Why is it so fun saying things the locals don't understand?*

"Forget it. Let's begin."

Fergus wiped the sweat from his forehead as he watched Fischer leave after only a half hour working the bellows.

"Is he getting even stronger?" Duncan asked from beside him, also watching the friendly yet strange man depart.

Fergus grunted in agreement. "I almost ran out of energy trying to keep up with him. If he went any faster, the damned forge itself might melt."

Duncan scoffed. "The bellows would break before then, but I take your point—he'd be terrifying if he wasn't so . . ." he trailed off, gesturing for a word that wouldn't come.

"Goofy?" Fergus asked with a smile.

Duncan laughed. "Yeah, goofy."

Joel, the leader of the prestigious Cult of Carcinization, sat in the meditative pose of his desired form. A heavy knocking came at the door, and frustration blossomed, shattering his calm.

I was just getting lost in the trance . . .

He stood, his elbows and knees complaining at the return to his inferior, two-legged posture.

Walking awkwardly over to the door, his eyebrow twitched as the knocking came again.

Hold your damn crabs—I'm coming.

Joel opened the door, a considerable amount of effort going toward keeping his features calm. The man standing on the other side of the door washed away his annoyance.

"G'day, Joel! How are ya, mate?"

"Oh—Fischer! I'm well, I'm well! Come on in!" He stepped aside, ushering the potential recruit inside the cult headquarters.

Fischer stepped inside, looking around the mostly empty room.

"You here alone today, Joel?"

"I am. Unfortunately, our cult doesn't have the funding of some other organizations—we have to work our fields to sustain ourselves."

"Your fields? You all share a farm?"

Joel nodded. "That's right. We pooled our resources to buy the headquarters and requisite farmland before relocating here."

"I'd assumed you were all funded by, I don't know, followers or something?"

Fischer trailed off, rubbing his chin in thought before continuing.

"So, are you guys the only branch of the Cult of Carcinization, then?"

"Not at all!" Joel puffed his chest out in pride. "There are four branches, five if you include the main temple we originated from on the outskirts of the capital. Each branch starts there, then when the members gather enough funds, they relocate to a coastal town—where better to await carcinization, after all?"

"Huh. Neat. So there are three other headquarters on different coasts? Are they close?"

"There's one a few days south, but the other two are on the west coast. We communicate via merchants and travelers, but so far, none have made any breakthroughs."

"Well, I find it admirable you all work and make your own way while still following your beliefs. At least you get to escape the farming. That's something."

Joel laughed. "No, it's not like that. It's my turn for meditation, but I'll be heading out soon to take over Jess in the fields."

Fischer raised both eyebrows. "Even more admirable—I respect that, Joel."

Joel felt his pride swell even more but tried not to let it show.

"We do our best to not be like some of the other cults. There are a lot—and I mean *a lot*—of really shady practices with some of them."

Joel smiled, letting some of the pride show. "Our followers are real believers, and I'm truly proud of each of them and their commitment."

Fischer didn't respond, simply looking around the room as he seemed to consider.

"Well," Joel said, "listen to me prattling on. What can I do for you, Fischer? I don't suppose you came to inquire about joining? We're always looking for more members . . ."

Fischer gave a kind smile. "I think I'm still a little busy at the moment to give your cult the devotion needed, but I'll keep it in mind, mate. I did come to ask about your meditation, though! You said it was Fielday, right? I've lost track of time—what day is it again?"

Joel tried not to project his disappointment at the refusal. *At least he wasn't directly opposed to it—maybe we can win him over with time.*

"That's right, we do it every Fielday. It's Crafday today, so it'll be another five days until the next group meditation."

Fischer smiled at the mention of the next meditation, causing Joel's stomach to flutter with excitement.

He's that excited for the next meditation . . . ? Oh, I'll recruit you yet, Fischer . . .

I let out a small chuckle after departing the headquarters of the Cult of Carcinization.

Thank God there are seven days of the week here, too. That makes things simpler.

I let out a sigh before smiling at the afternoon sun.

So we've got Crafday, then Winday, an unknown day, Sunday, another unknown day, Fielday, and finally, another unknown day.

I cocked my head.

Weird damn names, though . . . other than Sunday, of course!

I walked back toward my property, delighting in the smell of salt on the air and the warmth of the sun on my exposed skin.

Barry swung his hoe down with reckless abandon, a wild smile plastered across his visage. The energy of Fischer's food still coursed through his veins, fueling his single-handed assault on the field.

"Go Dad!" his son Paul yelled from the side.

Barry grinned in delight at his son's excitement, glancing to see how far the young lad had gotten in the neighboring field. He was only a quarter of the way through a single lane, a respectable distance for his son, given how much time he'd been working it. Compared to Barry and his awakened body, however, it was night and day; Barry's own field was almost complete, most of the soil already tilled and aerated.

Out of habit, he went to wipe sweat from his brow, but there was none. The day was hot, the weather not yet turned from the reliable heat of summer, and yet, he'd not perspired a single drop.

He shook his head, laughing at himself.

I can get used to this . . .

A sensation came forth unbidden, drawing him in.

[Error: Insufficient power. Superfluous systems offline.]

The message filled him with excitement, and the ever-present grin he'd had since eating what Fischer called a "shovelnose ray" spread even further across his face. It was the third message he'd received, all of them stating the exact same thing.

I wonder what the System is trying to communicate . . . ?

He began hoeing again. The familiar movement—now boosted by a previously unknown strength—filled his mind and body with ease.

Something related to farming? I know there were farming cultivators in the distant past . . . will it help my crops—

A sharp crack rang out, and he paused, staring down at the wooden shaft in his hand. He'd broken his trusty tool; the handle snapped off a handspan from the metal head.

"Woah, Dad!" Paul yelled. "You went so fast you broke it!"

Barry looked between the two pieces of his favored tool, and a laugh rushed forth. "Your old man is getting strong, lad!" Barry called across the fields. "You'll have to put in the work if you want to catch up to me!"

Paul nodded, a serious demeanor wiping away his excitement, and he resumed tilling the sandy soil.

Barry threw the handle aside, bent down to pick up the head of the hoe, and continued his work, one hand swinging down again and again, easily parting and shifting the earth beneath him.

The improvements to his body were still fresh enough to be alien, so he couldn't help but marvel at the way he could simply force the iron head of his broken tool all the way into the ground with a single hand.

My entire life, I've needed to use my whole body in an overhand swing . . .

Hunched over, he worked his way down the last of the field, the sandy soil tilled and ready for planting in his wake. Thoughts of his future plans came through as he lost himself in the labor, and he milled over the decisions he'd settled on. Excited as he may be, Barry knew the importance of proper consideration and planning; he would sit with his thoughts for a few days, letting them grow and mature like sugarcane beneath the summer sun.

One thing is certain—I'll need to rely on her, *no matter what path I take . . .*

CHAPTER THIRTY-SIX

SOLUTION

As was becoming a welcome part of my morning routine, I woke up to a crab looming over me.

Sergeant Snips tapped my nose delicately with her claw, blowing bubbles that were instantly recognizable as a mix of excitement and pride. Her soft touch tickled, and I wiggled my nose.

"Morning, Snips." I said around a yawn.

I rubbed the top of her carapace, causing her to sway with delight.

"What has you so excited this early?"

She made the gesture of shaking salt, a move I'd shown her to help our communication.

"The salt water is finished reducing?"

She nodded intently before jumping down from the bed.

I threw the sheets back and stood, enjoying the sensation of stretching the sleep from my body. "All right, Snips! Lead the way!"

I followed her out of the house, pausing a moment to take in the beautiful scenery as we exited the door into the predawn light.

Sergeant Snips, knowing my mind and habits, paused before I did, taking in the river mouth before us with her lone eye.

There was a soft wind blowing, cooling my skin and causing small waves to kick up along the surface of the water. Gulls and pelicans flew above, coasting on the winds up high, letting their extended wings catch the updrafts and take them where they needed to go.

I breathed deep of the ocean spray in the air, sighing as I let it out with a growing smile. "What a beautiful morning, Snips."

She bubbled in agreement, the rising sunlight causing her carapace to reflect a calming shade of pink.

"All right, let's see this salt!"

She led me down to the fire, her steps slow and calm after our moment of mindfulness.

The flames were small, licking up from smoldering coals Snips had helpfully added.

I peered down in the pot. There was a white slurry in the bottom, and I stirred it with the spoon left by the fire; it was thick, most of the water having evaporated.

"This looks perfect, Snips!"

She bubbled happily as I praised her, petting the top of her head.

"All we need now is some trays for it to dry in . . ."

We went to the kitchen, collected four large baking trays, and returned to the campfire.

I picked up the pot of salt slurry and poured a quarter of the mixture into each tray. I dispersed it on the trays with the spoon, ensuring each layer of salt was uniform in its thickness.

"In a few days, we should have salt to add to our meals, Snips!"

She stared down at the trays with curiosity, her eye blinking as she contemplated my words.

"Should we go check the trap and see if we have some breakfast?"

She nodded vigorously, taking one last look at the trays of salt before we took off for the headland.

George, the lord of Tropica Village and all its surrounding lands, let out a weary breath as he finished swallowing his seventh pastry of the morning. His wife, Geraldine, rubbed his back with one hand, attempting to ease his troubled mind. George looked at her, and she sucked the sugar from the voluptuous fingers of her other hand before speaking.

"It's going to be fine, George. We'll make it work, as we always do."

"I know, my love, it's just . . . the future seems bleak, each option as unpalatable as the last."

"We just take it one day at a time."

She stood and walked behind him, rubbing his shoulders. "If we break the problem down into manageable bites, anything is possible. What's troubling you now?"

George laughed hoarsely, the outburst sounding harsh to even his ears.

"Everything. Fischer is an existential threat and his plans seem as intricate as the finest of glazing."

"Nonsense," Geraldine said, her voice kind and soothing. "If he wanted to oust us, he would have done so already."

"I know you keep saying that, but I'm just not so sure . . ."

She leaned down, resting her head atop his.

"Are you calling me a liar, George?"

"Never that, my love, it's just . . . I don't understand why he wouldn't take our power."

"Who knows? Whatever his plans are, they don't involve removing us. We just need to focus on the things we can control."

George sighed, leaning back into his wife.

"What can we even do?"

"Well, the first thing that comes to mind is the tithe. Fielday is our next collection, right? We need to adjust the tithe."

"What if that's playing right into Fischer's plans? What if that was the goal of letting us know? How can we—"

Geraldine cut him off by leaning around and raising an eyebrow. "Maybe that is what he wanted, dear husband, but it won't hurt us. The choice is between continuing to over-collect, or adjusting the tithe to the correct amount, as laid out by the crown."

She caressed his cheek with a hand, her eyes turning fierce.

"We just have to play by the rules . . . for now, at least. That is what we can do."

He nodded, but his stomach still twisted and churned, stirred by uncontrolled thoughts of Fischer and his machinations.

With a belly full of crab and the sun rising about the eastern horizon, I walked between rows of sugarcane. I held my hand out as I passed, letting the long leaves flow over and around my hand. It was grounding, and I focused entirely on the sensation as I looked for my neighbor. I had no path in particular; I knew I'd find him eventually, and I was happy to wander through the fields of sugarcane.

An odd sound broke through my trance as I traveled, and I paused, cocking my head. Following the sound, I walked between rows, eventually stepping out into an open field. Barry was hunched over, shuffling backward as he slammed a single hand down into the soil repeatedly. As I got closer, I realized he had some sort of one-handed hoe, and he was shifting the soil at an impressive speed.

"Damn, Barry! You got some moves!"

He jumped, spinning his head to stare at me. "Oh, Fischer! You startled me!" he said with a laugh.

I smiled back. "Sorry, mate. Didn't mean to spook you."

"It's okay." Barry straightened up, stretching his back. "To what do I owe the pleasure of a morning visit from our heretical fisherman?"

I laughed at the title and walked closer to join him.

"I actually wanted to ask you a favor."

"Oh? What's that?"

"Well, I spoke to Maria yesterday—she said they were struggling to make ends meet with their limited fields."

Barry nodded, a morose smile coming to his face. "Aye, crop rotation issues? I was worried when I saw them planting wheat and cane again . . ."

"Yeah, mate—that's what she said."

Barry wiped his brow despite not seeming to have a single drop of sweat on him.

"What do you want my help with? I'm happy to assist where I can, but we don't really have enough fields to spare with how many mouths we have to feed . . ."

"Oh, no, not that!" I held my hands up in a halting gesture. "I don't want you to sacrifice, but I had another idea that might work."

Barry cocked his head, his brows furrowing.

"What is it?"

"Well, you said you could help me grow crops on my sandy soil, right? Now, I'm still as heretical as ever, and have absolutely zero interest in doing so, but I thought if I offered for them to use my land . . ."

"Oh!" Barry's eyebrows shot up in comprehension. "You want me to help them with setting up the fields? I—"

"I know," I said, cutting him off before he could voice his inevitable concerns. "It's a lot to sign you up for, but I'd be happy to help you with—"

"Fischer." Barry cut me off right back, shaking his head with a laugh. "I'd be more than happy to help them do that. I think it's a brilliant idea."

Gratitude flooded me, and I let my genuine feelings take over my face.

"Thank you, Barry. You're a good bloke."

He raised an eyebrow. "A good bloke . . . I'm going to assume that's a good thing?"

A laugh burst from my throat. "Yeah, it's a good thing."

He grinned back at me. "That's good—I was worried I'd have to chase you off my land."

I shook my head, smiling back. "There is one issue with my plan, though . . ."

"Yeah? What's that?"

"Roger."

Barry nodded and winced, clearly understanding. "Best to go through Maria, then—explain yourself to her and let her worry about Roger."

"Good idea, mate. I'll go grab a coffee and pastry now and see if I can't find her."

"A good plan. I'll be in this field or the one behind me if you need any help."

"Cheers, Barry—I'll come back later and let you know how it went."

"G'day, Sue!"

The woman at the bakery spun, giving me a beatific smile. "Fischer! What will you have this morning?"

I held up the mug of coffee I'd already retrieved. "I reckon my usual pastry would pair perfectly with this!"

She nodded along with a conspiratorial smile. "I think you may be right . . ."

She bent down, grabbing a croissant and putting it in a paper bag.

"You know, Fischer, I won't be offended if you still drink the coffee from the north side when the machine gets delivered. I understand my coffee might not be as good as theirs . . ."

"Sue!" I held a hand to my chest in mock affront. "I'm appalled! I'll be having your coffee exclusively, thank you very much!"

She smiled, but her brows remained tight. "I'm just saying, I don't want you to feel you have to, even if it's not as good . . ."

"Listen, Sue, if your coffee has even a tenth as much love put into it as your baked goods do, it will be the best coffee this world has ever seen."

Her knitted brow relaxed. "You flatter me, Fischer."

"It's not flattery if it's true, Sue. I think your coffee is gonna be a massive hit."

She passed me the pastry, and I took a bite. It was still warm, and the buttery layers melted in my mouth, causing me to let out a groan of pleasure.

"Good lord, Sue—your husband is a wizard with his hands."

She grinned lasciviously. "You have *no* idea . . ."

I coughed, choking on the pastry. I had to wash it down with coffee as Sue's cackle rolled out over the street.

"Sue! How indecent!"

"Ah, thank you, Fischer. I needed that laugh."

I shook my head, taking another sip of coffee to soothe my throat.

"Have you seen Maria this morning, by the way?"

Sue quirked an eyebrow and looked behind me. I spun to see Maria, her own eyebrow raised high, her lip curling into a smile.

"What's a girl to think when she's being asked about after the conversation you just had?"

I sighed dramatically. "You're both as bad as each other!"

They both burst into laughter, Maria's giggle light and lilting compared to Sue's boisterous roar.

"I wanted to talk to you about something," I said, "but it can wait until after you get your breakfast."

Maria stepped up to the counter, her eyes sparkling with mirth as she shot me a sidelong glance. "Just the usual please, Sue."

Sue collected two pastries from beneath the counter and handed them to Maria.

"Are you okay to be left alone with this scoundrel, Maria?"

Maria gave me an assessing look. "I think he can be trusted . . ."

I rolled my eyes, smiling at the theatrics.

"Well," Maria said, "thanks for the pastries. I'll see you tomorrow, Sue."

"See you then!"

I gave Sue a nod as Maria and I left, and she shot me a wink.

"So?" Maria asked as we walked west toward her crops. "What did you want to ask me?"

I took a sip of coffee, delighting in the flavor and warmth.

"I've been thinking about what you said yesterday, and I think I may have a solution of sorts."

She glanced at me, a slight bit of suspicion crossing her features. "What did you have in mind?"

"Well, I have a lot of unused land, right? It's sandy and not ideal, but Barry offered to help me try farming it if I wanted to. I only care about fishing, so I don't, but if you want to . . ."

She stopped walking, blinking rapidly.

"Are . . . are you suggesting what I think you are?"

"Well, that depends—if you think I'm saying you can farm the land for free, then yes. If you're thinking I'm offering for you to join me in maligning yourself to the absent gods and fishing, then also yes, but I get if that's not your—"

Maria slammed into me, hugging me tight and stopping my river of words in their tracks.

CHAPTER THIRTY-SEVEN

NEIGHBORS

Maria's body struck mine, whisking my thoughts away. I hadn't realized how much I'd been missing physical touch, and my heart seemed to jump at the impromptu embrace. Her toned form latched onto me like a lost sailor clinging to a life raft, and she buried her face in my chest. I hugged Maria back, matching her fierce grip and resting my chin atop her head.

"Can I take that as a yes, or . . . ?"

I lost track of time as we held onto each other. Eventually, she pulled away, taking a step back.

A single tear dripped down each cheek, and her lower lip shook.

"Maria—are . . . are you okay?"

She nodded wordlessly, averting her eyes as she wiped them. "I'm—I'm sorry. It's been really hard . . ."

I felt the need to rush to her, to wrap her in another hug and make it all better. Instead, I tried to convey my comfort with a smile.

"You don't need to apologize, Maria. It's human to have powerful emotions, especially when your family and livelihood are at stake. Besides—I'm a hugger. I'd gladly hug anyone, even that grouch of a dad you have to deal with."

She laughed, the sound a breath of fresh air. "Wow, you really must be a hugger."

I nodded sagely, trying to uplift the mood. "Right? Speaking of, he's probably going to fight the offer of farming my land tooth and nail, won't he? Do you think you can convince him?"

She nodded, freeing the strand of hair that always slipped so easily from behind her ear. "He'll come around—we have my mother to care for, and she may be the one thing that makes him cast his pride aside."

"Your mother? Is she okay?"

Maria grimaced, shaking her head. "She's really sick. Her pricey medicine is the main reason we've been struggling."

"Maria . . . I have money. How much is it?"

She shook her head again.

"You've done enough already, Fischer. It wouldn't be right to rely on you for that."

I shook my head. "If someone's health isn't good enough to spend it on, what is? Think of it as self-serving—I won't sleep well knowing someone is sick when I could make a difference."

She gave me a tight smile. "Thank you, but we can cope for now. If it truly gets dire enough that we can't afford it, even my dad wouldn't be too proud to accept your generosity."

"If you're sure . . ."

"I am. Do you think farming the sandy soil will work, though?" she asked, not-so-subtly changing the subject.

"I do, or at least Barry reckons we can." I shrugged. "They've made their crops work, and my land is only a little worse than theirs. I'll be happy to help out, too—I have no interest in farming for myself, but if it can help you guys . . ."

She took a deep, steadying breath, looking toward the light of the western sky as she breathed it out. "My pride wants to say no, but at this stage, I'd accept any help if it gets us more fields to work . . ."

"Done," I said. "Do you want me to come and let Roger know with you, or do you think it's better if you go?"

She let out a soft laugh, shaking her head. "It'll be much smoother if I go alone, I think."

I nodded, and seeing she was still struggling to compose herself, laid a hand on her shoulder.

"I really am sorry, Maria. I can't imagine the pressure you've been under. It's all going to be fine, though. I promise."

She nodded and turned back to me.

"Thank you, Fischer. I can't express how much I appreciate it."

I barely heard the words. Her eyes were puffy, but that didn't detract from her beauty. The sun rising behind me highlighted her freckles and reflected in the tears still threatening to fall. She smiled and tilted her head, and I felt the need to rush to her once more, to hold her until everything was all right. Again, I smiled instead.

"Don't mention it. That's what neighbors are for, right?"

She nodded, wiping a tear that formed as she blinked.

"I'll go talk to Dad. Should I come find you after, or . . . ?"

"I'll be waiting with Barry in his fields. Take your time, okay? I'm sure we can find stuff to have a yarn about until you can convince your old man."

Her smile spread wider as she nodded again. "Okay. I'll go find him."

She turned and strode away, and I watched for a moment before spinning to head back to Barry.

Damn, I have a serious savior complex going on. I need to rein that in before I go embarrassing myself.

"Fischer!"

I turned back, peering down the street toward Maria.

"Thank you!" she called, bouncing on her heels as she beamed a toothy smile at me.

She turned and jogged away, her hair bouncing with her hastened steps.

That's not helping the complex, Maria . . .

* * *

Barry and I raced down his last field to be tilled. His technique was honestly impeccable—much better than my own; the speed at which he moved was *wild,* considering I had an enhanced body, and he was only a little slower than I was. I emulated his movements, taking care not to exert too much pressure and snap the full-length tool that Paul had given me.

I reached the end of the last lane and waited for Barry to finish his. When he got there, he stood and stretched his back, his hunched-over method with the broken hoe evidently not an ideal posture to till with.

"You sure you've never done this before, Fischer?" he asked, giving me a grin.

"Never, but I can't say I don't see part of the appeal—there's just something about physical work that clears the mind, ya know?"

"Does that mean you'll set your heretical fishing ways aside for some farming?" Barry wiggled his eyebrows and gave me a smile, already knowing my answer.

I laughed. "Nope—unless it's to help out others, of course!"

Barry shot a glance behind me, and I turned to see two people approaching. The first was a vision of glee, her steps bouncy and short. The other looked like he was chewing nails, a scowl firmly settled on his face. They both stopped before us.

"Fischer. Barry," Roger said, giving us a small nod.

"Hey, guys!" Maria said, her excitement palpable.

"Perfect timing!" I smiled at both of them. "Barry and I just finished up here. Should we go scope out the fields?"

"I don't know what scope out means," Barry said, "but if you mean you want to go have a look at the fields, I've already picked the perfect spot to start."

"Yeah!" I smiled. "That!"

Barry laughed. "Follow me."

We walked between the fields of cane as Barry laid out what his steps were for preparing sandy soil.

"The issue with sand all comes back to a single aspect: moisture. Water drains through sand too quickly, not letting the roots absorb enough before it disappears."

"Is the key watering more often, then?" Maria asked.

"Yes and no." Barry made a so-so gesture with his hand. "More water is important, but if you simply water the sand without changing the composition of the land, the water will drain away any nutrients you've added. So, you can't simply water it more and hope for the best."

"How do we change the composition, then?" Roger asked, speaking up for the first time since their arrival.

I glanced to the side, seeing the same get-off-my-lawn style grimace plastered across his face, but his eyes held curiosity and intrigue.

We'll win you over yet, Roger.

"It's actually simple, if a little physically intensive," Barry answered. "You need to add nutrient-dense soil to the sand."

"Wait, just adding soil?" Maria cocked her head to the side in confusion then swept the always-escaping strand of hair back behind her ear.

"If it was that simple, we'd see more people farming the sandy flats," Barry said with a grimace. "It's taken *years* for our fields to reach the point where we can farm them without constantly having to add soil from the forest. You'll find it much more difficult than simply adding nutrient-rich soil a single time, and the first few harvests will probably be stunted, yielding little."

Roger nodded, the ever-present grimace disappearing as he rubbed his chin in thought.

"That makes sense. If the water washes the nutrients away, each time we water the fields, the soil will be forced further down into the ground, and will start to build up beneath the taproots, correct?"

"Right," Barry confirmed. "The washed-away sediment will settle underground, and eventually, will build up and enrich the land."

I'd reached the same conclusion, but I let the farmers talk it out.

Anything to distract Roger from dwelling on the fact he had to accept help from others.

There was little in my past life more powerful than the stubbornness of an older man, and this world seemed exactly the same in that regard.

"Well," Maria said, "Even if the yield is small, anything is better than nothing. Thanks for your help, Barry. And you, Fischer."

She turned to give me a small smile. "I know I've already thanked you—probably too much—but really, thank you."

"Don't mention it," I said.

Barry nodded. "As Fischer keeps reminding me, that's what neighbors are for, right? You don't owe me a debt, and I'm happy to assist."

From the corner of my eye, I saw Maria elbow her dad in the ribs, none too gently. He glared at her, but under her continued stare, Roger cleared his throat.

"Thank you, Fischer. Thank you, Barry."

"You're welcome!" Barry and I shot back, then turned and grinned at each other.

We stepped from between two fields, finally arriving on the sandy stretch that marked the beginning of my land. There were seven wooden pegs stuck in the ground by Paul, who was waving enthusiastically from the far side as he wiggled an eighth peg into the sand. He'd marked out two fields, with a meter of space in between each other and Barry's existing crops.

"I was thinking right here," Barry said. "It's far enough from the coast to not be too salty, but the added salt content of the ground should aid sugarcane in growing. It's also close to the forest, and therefore, the soil we need."

"Sounds good to me, mate. Shall we get started?"

As I dug another spade worth of soil from the earth, I smiled at the hole I was forming. Barry, Maria, and Roger were all taking wheelbarrows filled to the brim back to the fields, Paul having returned home to assist his mother. I'd nominated myself for the shoveling, knowing my body could easily carve through the soil. I felt bad about making them travel further than was strictly necessary, but after explaining my reasoning for digging where I was, they were happy to oblige.

We were on my land, closer to the river than the north end of my property line.

I could have just dug another hole in my free time, but it seems destructive to create two holes when I can only disturb the forest with a single one . . .

With each shovel of dirt, and with each soil-laden wheelbarrow carted away, my bonus project came closer to completion.

It was a staggering amount of earth we were moving, but even when Maria and Roger poured with sweat, and their breaths came heavy, nary a complaint was whispered; we were all focused on the task at hand, and the sooner we completed the fields, the sooner the farming of them could begin.

"Two more trips each should do it, Fischer!" Barry said, his brow only a little sweaty.

Damn, my man has some serious cardio skills going on . . .

"No worries! My hole is almost the perfect size!"

After I loaded all of their carts for a final time, we took a moment to sit and rest in the shade next to my creation.

"Your heresy . . . really knows no bounds . . . Fischer," Maria panted out, drinking from a gourd of water she'd slung over a shoulder.

"It really doesn't, does it?" I answered, beaming a smile.

Roger's scowl was well and truly back as he stared down into the roughly three meter by three meter hole. "And what do you call this monument of stupidity, heretic?"

The words only made my happiness swell. "This, my good man, is called a pond."

CHAPTER THIRTY-EIGHT

SOFT FUR

"A *pond?*" Roger spat the word, turning it into a curse.

"That's right—a pond."

Maria peered down at the hole, curiosity etched on her features.

"What does it have to do with fishing?"

"Well, while you *can* fish in a pond, I don't intend to use this one for fishing—I want to use it for bait."

". . . Bait?" Maria asked. "You use bait for catching fish?"

They really have no knowledge about fishing, do they . . . ?

I smiled, happy to answer any questions she had.

"That's right! To catch the larger fish I target, you have to put bait on a hook. I want to fill this pond with some freshwater fish, let them grow and live in here peacefully, and in exchange, I'll use some as bait."

"You put them on the hook when they're still alive?" Maria asked, scrunching her nose. "I know they're from the domain of the traitorous gods, but still, that seems a little . . . cruel."

"While that's a valid method some use where I come from, I also think it's cruel—I dispatch the fish humanely before using them."

I shrugged. "I know even that might seem a little rough, but at the end of the day, it's part of the food chain. It's no different from a human eating meat, or a larger fish eating them in the wild."

Maria still stared down at the beginnings of my pond, and she nodded slowly to herself. "You do everything you can to reduce their suffering . . ."

She turned to me, giving me a brilliant smile. "That's admirable, Fischer—even if you're a heretic."

Roger scoffed. "Still a heretical fool at the end of the day."

Maria slapped him on the back of his head. "A heretical fool that is selflessly letting us use his land to expand our farming."

Roger scowled at her. "A fool, nonetheless."

"I'm not offended by being called names," I said to them with a smile. "It's all a matter of perspective, and while it may seem odd to you all, I'm really enjoying my *heretical* life in this beautiful world."

"I have to admit, Fischer," Barry said, "I was worried for you only a week ago, but now, I wonder if the prejudice we have against living from the water is misplaced."

Roger snorted. “See, Maria? *This* is why heresy is dangerous—it can be contagious.”

“Dad, you keep calling Fischer a fool, but *you're* the one insulting the two people actually helping us right now.”

Barry laughed, the sound filled with genuine joy. “I'm not insulted, Maria.” He turned to Roger. “Keep speaking your mind, Roger. My assistance doesn't rely on you praising me.”

Roger glared between Barry and me, daring either of us to spout more “heretical” nonsense.

I'm glad my initial assessment of Barry was correct; he's a good man, and I'm lucky to have him as my next-door neighbor.

“Couldn't have said it better myself, Barry,” I said, smiling at him.

I stood from the side of my pond, stretching out my back, which was a little tight after so much digging, improved body or not.

“Well, I feel refreshed—should we start mixing the fields together?”

I did my best to not burst out laughing at the expression on Roger's face as he glared at us. Maria and her father sat in the shade, needing a moment to recover as Barry and I continued to mix the forest soil into the sandy fields. Roger's look was somewhere between astonishment and frustration, but definitely leaned toward the latter.

It can't be a fun experience to be outperformed in farming by a “heretical fool,” can it?

“You don't need . . . to keep . . . going, guys,” Maria said between pants.

“If I stop, Barry will catch up to me!”

Barry laughed from beside me. “If you keep talking, I'll catch you, you heretical bastard!”

I roared a laugh and sped up, mixing the soil at a blistering speed to keep ahead of Barry.

All four of us were working the last bit of the first field when Paul came running out from between the rows of sugarcane to the north.

“Mom and I brought food!” he yelled.

A woman stepped out from behind Paul, a tray of sandwiches in her hands as she smiled down at her exuberant son.

“Afternoon, Helen,” Roger said, wiping sweat from his brow.

“You haven't met my wife yet, have you, Fischer?” Barry asked.

“I can't say I have.” I smiled at Helen. “It's a pleasure.”

She returned a radiant smile, the corners of her eyes crinkling. “The pleasure is mine, Fischer. Paul told me what you were all up to, so we brought some afternoon tea.”

“They're salad and ham!” Paul yelled. “I made some of them all on my own!”

Helen nodded, grinning down at her son.

“He did, and I daresay, they're even better than mine.”

Paul beamed, revealing a gap-toothed smile.

“Did you lose a tooth, Paul?” I asked, walking over to the shade.

“He did,” Helen confirmed. “His last baby—”

“My last baby tooth!” Paul bellowed, cutting his mother off.

"Wow, your last one? Now that's impressive!"

"Yeah! That means I'm not a kid anymore!"

I raised an eyebrow and shot a look at Barry, then Helen; the former shrugged and smiled, the latter shook her head and rolled her eyes good naturedly.

I picked up a sandwich and took a bite after everyone else had grabbed a triangle. There was a thick slice of ham accompanied by lettuce, tomato, and cucumber, some sort of tangy sauce binding the flavors together and making them sing. As refreshing as the ham and salad sandwich was, it didn't compare to the feasts of fish, as basic as they were.

Fish and salad sandwiches, though . . . maybe I need to recruit Barry for some ingredients in exchange for a sanga . . .

"These are delicious, Helen!" Maria said before taking another bite.

She let out an *mmph* of delight, her eyes closed as she savored the taste.

If she thinks that's good, wait until I convince her to try some seafood . . .

It was a beautiful afternoon for my dreams to come true. The sun was setting as Sergeant Snips and I sat by the fire, sitting in comfortable silence while our dinner of sand crab boiled atop the campfire. A warm wind blew from the north, tousling my hair and causing a small smile to spread across my face. My body was tired after a day spent shoveling and mixing soil in the sandy fields. Barry and I had done most of the work on the second field, just as the first.

The look of mixed astonishment and frustration that had been etched on Roger's face was still firmly held in mind, a continued source of entertainment for me to reflect on.

As we sat and waited for our dinner to finish cooking, a small form slunk from the river, drawing both of our attention. The otter walked toward us with clear trepidation, taking slow, easy steps as it approached.

Snips blew small bubbles of anger and hissed under her breath, and I rested a hand atop her hard carapace, doing my best to radiate calm reassurance toward her.

The otter came to the fire, its head swaying back and forth as it glanced between Snips and me.

I nodded to it. "Hello. Have you come to have some dinner with us . . . ?"

It cocked its head, chirping softly. It crawled further, and with its eyes firmly fixed on the violently capable guard crab next to me, put one paw into a pouch at its side. With a slow movement, it removed a shellfish, placing it on the sand and sliding it toward me.

I raised an eyebrow, and looking down at the offering, my gaze was drawn into it.

Ridged Clam

Uncommon

Found along the ocean shores of the Kallis Realm, this mollusk is prized for its subtle flavor.

"For us?" I asked, looking back at the otter.

It nodded, and with another dip into its pouch, placed another Ridged Clam on the sand, sliding it toward Snips. It repeated the move, removing one more and placing it before itself.

It chirped, cocking its head and looking between us, the clams, and the pot.

"Ohhhhh, you want us to cook it?"

It dipped its head again, sliding the two offered clams further toward Sergeant Snips and me.

"I'll let the crab finish cooking, then I'll cook them in the pot, all right?"

It cocked its head and chirped, appearing to think for a moment before sitting down in the sand.

The second the otter sat down, my right hand started twitching. It was within petting range, and I kept shooting it glances, each time fighting the urge to reach over and scratch its cute little ears. I held my hand atop Snips's carapace, taking comfort in her armored body.

Patience, Fischer . . . patience . . .

After what felt like an hour, but was probably five minutes, I stood to check the crab.

When I took the lid off the pot, steam billowed out. The otter ran back a few meters, arching its back up like a startled cat.

"It's—"

A noise cut me off, and I looked down at Snips. She rolled in the sand, her legs kicking out spasmodically as hissed laughs poured out of her. I shook my head at her but couldn't help but share in some of the joy.

"It's just steam—it happens when you boil water," I explained to the otter, who was glaring at Sergeant Snips. It pinned its ears back, squinting at Snips in accusation. The human-like reaction was confirmation of something I'd been suspecting since it offered clams.

The otter has evolved—just like Snips.

The realization gave me a rush of euphoria, and my mind once more pictured myself sitting by the fire, Snips on one side, the otter on the other.

"You understand me, don't you?" I asked, voice soft.

It returned its attention to me, and with a small chirp, nodded once.

"Since you ate the shovelnose ray I gave you?"

Again, a single nod.

I sat down, back to the still-open pot, staring off into the distance of the western horizon.

That settles it—my food can, most likely, awaken animals. What are the conditions? It has to be my seafood, right? What about targets? What animals will it work on?

Sergeant Snips tapped my leg with a clawed carapace, drawing me from my thoughts.

She blew questioning bubbles, checking to see if I was okay.

"I'm all right—thank you, Snips."

I rubbed her head. "What would I do without you?"

She sidled up against my leg, glaring at the otter with her eye, which I couldn't help but smile at.

Jealous, Snips?

I returned my attention to the boiling pot behind me, and with my large tongs, removed the crabs from the water. I'd added some of the still-drying salt to the pot, increasing the sodium content of the cooking water. I was conservative with the amount but wasn't sure if I added too much.

"Sorry if it's a little too salty—it's a work in progress."

Snips blew bubbles of disbelief and made a gesture with her claws that told me she couldn't even entertain the idea of a mistake on my part.

I laughed. "I'm not infallible, Snips, but I appreciate the trust."

I set half a crab down on a plate for me, put a half in front of Snips, and went to place another beside me toward the otter, but paused.

"Do you want a plate?"

It made a soft noise, seeming to consider, then shook its head, pointing at the portion in the sand before Snips. I nodded, setting the crab down on the ground before it.

I grabbed the three clams and went to place them in the boiling pot, but again paused.

Carefully placing them on the coals instead, I turned to the otter, who was already cocking her head in question.

"It just occurred to me that if I boil them, the flavor might get completely washed away by the salty water. I've seen clams cooked in a fire—well, I've seen a video of them cooked on a fire, but I think this will make them taste better."

The otter chirped, the intent of the noise indiscernible to me. It crept forward, staring at the sand crab I placed on the sand, its nose twitching adorably as it sniffed the air.

I sat down between Snips's and the otter's portions with my plate in hand. Snips started crunching happily, and the otter walked up beside me, tentatively touching the hot crab with a paw.

"It might be too hot for you yet. It'll cool in a moment."

It looked at me, cocked its head, and sat down, smelling the crab intently.

Personally, I couldn't focus on the food; my mind was filled with a compulsion to pet the otter. I reached out absentmindedly, my eyes locked on the soft fur of the creature beside me.

CHAPTER THIRTY-NINE

APPROVAL

I stopped my hand before it got too close to the otter as I realized what I was doing. Noticing my outreached hand from the corner of its eye, the otter turned from the crab, giving me a questioning chirp.

"Is . . . is it okay if I pet you?"

It made no move, staring between me and my extended hand. It gave a small, almost imperceptible nod.

Slowly, keeping my hand as steady as possible, I placed my fingers on the fur of its upper back. I scratched the otter, my fingers easily parting the soft fur. It was wet still from its passage through the waters of the river, and some sort of slippery film coating its fur.

The film didn't bother me. Its body was warm, radiating enough heat to ward off the chill I'd expected to find. It leaned into my touch, arching its back so my fingers were more firmly pressing into its body. I continued scratching, moving my hand up toward the rear of its neck.

Snips hissed, grabbing my attention, and I paused my petting, glancing at her. She wiggled her back, pointing to the top of her carapace with her free claw.

I smiled. "Of course—sorry, Snips."

I started petting her with my left hand; my right resumed scratching the otter. Snips bubbled happily, and the otter bent down so my fingers dug into the back of its head. It let out a happy chirp, and I started rubbing the area around its ears. Its head lifted, again making my fingers dig in harder. I closed my eyes, bathing in the sounds of happy chirps and joyous hisses.

I wish this moment could never end . . .

Both of my animal pals looked at me when I reluctantly withdrew my hands.

I pointed down at the crab in front of the otter. "It won't be as tasty if it gets cold. By the way, sorry if this is rude to ask, but are you male or female?"

Sergeant Snips let out a sharp hiss I took as a snort of amusement, and I turned to her.

"Don't be rude, Snips—I had to ask you the same thing."

She froze, peering at me and dipping her body in apology.

I shook my head with a smile as I returned my attention to the otter. It pointed to Snips, then to itself—*no, herself.*

"You're female."

She nodded in a matter-of-fact way, not taking offense at my question.

"All right, thank you."

Her eyes locked back on to the waiting meal. Extending both forepaws, she tested the heat by tapping the crab rather adorably with rapid-fire touches. Finding the temperature acceptable, she removed a rock from one of her pouches, and with a swift *crack,* smashed the joint of the claw and body. She took the claw in both hands, tasting the sweet, exposed flesh with tentative licks.

The events of the next second were a blur; she held the claw in one hand, smacked her rock up and down its length, and lapped up any juices that threatened to drip into the sand. With dexterous purpose, she discarded smashed sections of shell, biting and sucking the meat revealed within. She was a storm of movement, and I couldn't help but stare in amazement. Snips was watching too; she took it as a challenge.

Crunching came from my left, surrounding me with a symphony of noise. I smiled and cracked the claw in my hands.

I love my life.

Trent, first in line to the throne of Gormona, and, by his estimate, quite a ladies' man, stared down the two cultivators accompanying him. He focused on the first cultivator, a man with short-brown hair.

"Come on! It's not *that* far out of the way to stay in a tavern."

The cultivator shook his head. "No. It's too far."

"You'd rather spend the night in a forest? There are *ladies* in a tavern. You're a man, aren't you? I could just order you to do so, cultivator. Then you'd have to."

"Why? So you can be shot down again? You didn't have your fill of rejection in the last village we passed?"

Seeing red, Trent slapped him, causing his head to jerk to the side. He expected a reaction; anger, sadness, anything. The cultivator merely straightened out, his cheek already reddening as he stared back at Trent.

"I was told by my handler that our mission was to locate cultivators, not harass every serving girl we come across."

Trent's face heated, and he tried to make the cultivator submit with a rather potent glare—the cultivator looked back with practiced calm, not responding in the least to Trent's implied threat. The other cultivator, a man with long blonde hair, stared into space, not even registering the conversation.

Eyebrow twitching, Trent tried to take a steadying breath, but gave up halfway through, releasing his lungs with a frustrated groan.

"I'm the leader of the expedition, so you need to listen to my orders. I'm a *prince!*"

Trent pointed at the collar around the impudent man's neck. "That alone should remind you of your position, *cultivator.*" His gaze was, again, unmoving.

"You are the leader, yes, but that doesn't mean you get to change our orders. We are to follow and assist you in finding cultivators, so that's what we'll do. Spending the afternoon and night in an unrelated town goes against the parameters of our existing orders."

"If you don't listen, cultivator, that collar will detonate. Is that what you want? You want to—"

"It won't detonate because I'm following my orders. If I were to attack you, to place you in danger, then yes, my life would be forfeited. Seeing as though I'm not doing that by insisting we stick to the mission, I suggest we leave this town behind and continue our search." The infuriating man's countenance didn't change, even in mentioning the possibility of his own death.

Trent snarled and turned, not wanting the cultivator to see how affected he was. Not that Trent realized *why* he turned away, of course—he was as ignorant as he was repugnant.

"Fine. I've decided the girls of this town are beneath my attention, anyway. Let's go."

Trent climbed back on his horse and spurred it on, not even hearing the sound of the cultivators' footsteps falling in beside him; he took it as a given that they would follow.

This mission will be even more boring than I thought if I can't even look at the local girls as we go . . .

Sebastian, leader of Tropica's Cult of the Leviathan branch, grinned. Gary, his trusty apprentice, watched the smile grow, cringing at the malice it held. A runner had come with an urgent missive, the communication deemed important enough to not wait for the merchant's monthly visit.

"Good news, boss?" Gary asked, already dreading the answer.

"Great news, Gary—no, *perfect* news. The main branch agrees with my assessment and will be sending an artifact I can use to deal with Fischer—once and for all."

"I know artifacts exist, but is there really one strong enough to deal with someone immune to even the deadliest of poisons? Are . . . are you sure it's a good idea, boss?"

Sebastian's grin turned to disgust as he peered at Gary, somehow looking down at the taller man, even from his seated position. "Yes, I'm sure it's a good idea. What makes you say otherwise?"

"Well . . . it's just that we don't even have the new baby lobsters yet—"

"They're called crickets, Gary! Crickets!" Sebastian yelled, a vein bulging in his neck.

"Er, right, crickets." Gary forced himself to meet Sebastian's furious eyes. "We haven't even gotten them yet, and maybe further antagonizing Fischer is a bad idea . . ."

Sebastian's stare flattened, his expression becoming one of indifference. "Are you a coward, Gary?"

"N-no, sir."

"Have you so easily forgotten Pistachio, Gary?"

Gary clenched his jaw. "No, sir."

"Then cease your incessant chattering. The crimes against our cult and Pistachio demand retribution. The next time you voice such concerns, leave, and don't bother coming back."

"Yes, sir."

Gary left the home that served as their headquarters, stepping out through the back door into the waning light of the setting sun. He knew better than to continue a conversation with Sebastian after his mood had shifted. His thoughts swam as he walked along the cobbled stones connecting to the breakwall. Stopping absentmindedly, he stared out at the eastern skyline, the beautiful colors bringing a touch of peace. Still, his mind whirred.

How do I steer Sebastian off this path of vengeance . . . ?

"This is what I made today!" I said, gesturing at the pond. Snips blew curious bubbles, and the otter chirped in consideration. "It's called a pond, and fish can live in it."

Snips crawled down into the hole, making the sign for salt as she cocked her carapace questioningly.

"No, I was thinking fresh water—if salt water leaks out from here, it could ruin the soil, potentially even killing the surrounding grass and trees."

Snips pointed down, then mimed eating, small questioning bubbles coming forth.

"Not for eating, no—well, that's not what I planned, at least. If we stock the smaller fish in here, it will be an easy source of fresh bait for us to use. This is just a test pond to see if it works. If it does, we could even create a brackish one for stocking the common eels that are such good bait."

Sergeant Snips's carapace swayed back and forth in thought as she considered my words. She started drawing in the soil. The word for water, then the word for leaving, both of which she had taught me since discovering she was literate.

"Will the water drain out through the ground?"

Snips nodded.

"Well, maybe. If we get it lower than the water table, which I'm guessing is about the level of the river with how close we are to it, then the water will remain. Otherwise, we'll have to line the ground with something to stop it draining."

I shrugged. "That's all assuming the water drains at all—it's not sandy this far back, but I've never made a pond before. We'll have to work it out together."

The otter joined Snips in the hole, walking around and testing the soil with her claws. As I watched them inspect the earth, I smiled at the curiosity they both held.

They're more alike than Snips would care to admit—man, I hope they grow to become good friends.

My eyes went distant, and I started considering the most important task I had at the moment.

The otter needs a name . . .

When Fischer retired for the evening—after making the otter and her swear they wouldn't attack each other when left alone—Sergeant Snips, chosen of Fischer and defender of his land, turned to the new recruit. They stared at each other, Snips with a tinge of frustration coloring her expression, the otter with an infuriating calm. Snips took the first step toward peace. She gestured for the otter to follow, and not caring to see if she did or not, set off.

It's to be expected that my master would accrue more followers. He's too kind to request work, so it's my responsibility to ensure any recruits contribute to his land.

The otter's paws padded through the sand behind her.

Good. I shouldn't have to force obedience.

Snips eyed the landscape as they moved north. She already had an idea for the ideal spot but kept an open mind as they traveled toward it.

Not seeing any better positions, she stopped on the sand fifty meters northwest from the headland. It was in a small dip of the sandy mounds, protected from the strong southerly winds by the headland, but not so close that they would hit rock.

Snips pointed at the sand and dug her claw through it, then pointed toward the forest, where Fischer had shown them his pond. The otter cocked its head and chirped, clearly not understanding.

Great—it's a moron.

Snips scuttled out from the center and began dragging her claw through the sand as she drew a large shape. She walked all the way around the hole she envisioned, its size and scope much grander than that of the small pond Fischer had dug.

The otter let out a sharp chirp, walked into the middle of the soon-to-be pit, and nodded. She started digging, and Snips nodded her approval.

CHAPTER FORTY

CLAWS

Barry sat straight-backed, his legs crossed before him as the sun started to peek over the eastern horizon.

"This was such a good idea, Barry," Maria said.

Roger harrumphed from the other side of his daughter. "It's lovely, but we have fields to work."

"Dad, you are such a grump—we have all day to work, and Barry even offered to help us. The least we can do is take a few minutes to enjoy the sunrise with him."

Barry smiled at the two, then closed his eyes, focusing on the cool wind blowing fitfully from the south.

"You aren't obligated to join me; I'll help you two with your field, regardless. I invited you to join me because this is the best way to start the day."

"Well," Maria said, "I, for one, am glad you suggested it. We've been so busy lately. I can't tell you the last time we took a moment to appreciate the beautiful village we live in."

Roger grunted, somewhere between agreement and annoyance at what he perceived to be a waste of time.

Should I ask them now? Barry thought.

He took a deep breath, exhaling it slowly.

No time like the present, I suppose . . .

"I'm sorry if this is overstepping, but is it all right if I ask you about your mother, Maria? It's Sharon, right?"

"What does my wife have to do with this, Barry?"

Roger's tone was hard as a rock, and Barry opened his eyes to peer at the farmer. Roger glared back, his eyes flinty, his expression flat.

"Fischer told me she's been having some health issues. I just wanted to know what her ailment was, because I might be able to help her."

Maria covered her father's face with a hand, pushing him back lightly.

"Geez, Dad—can you drop the hackles for one second? You keep assuming the worst of people."

Roger turned his gaze on his daughter. "Maybe you're just too trusting, Maria—you take after your mother."

Maria nodded. "That's a good thing, you stone-headed oaf. What on Kallis could Barry do with the knowledge that Mom is sick?"

"What could he do to help with that information? Last I checked, you're a farmer too, Barry—what can you do that we can't?"

Barry held his hands up, trying to diffuse Roger's anger. "Please, indulge me. We've dealt with a lot of odd ailments in our family, all of which we cured with natural remedies," he lied.

Roger's scowl deepened, and Maria sighed.

"Forgive Dad. He's overprotective."

"There's nothing to forgive. Would you share with me, though?"

Roger stood. "I'm going back to the fields. Say what you will, Maria."

He turned and strode away, swiftly retreating from the shore.

Maria rolled her eyes after he'd left. "I swear, that man . . ."

"It's not a bad thing to be overprotective," Barry said. "I can empathize with where he's coming from."

They lapsed into silence, both returning their attention to the rising sun.

Eventually, Maria started talking. "Mom's sickness is something you can't see. It began with bouts of dizziness and weakness. Over time, it got worse, and for the last year or so, she's been bedridden."

"I'm sorry. That must be hard . . ."

Maria nodded as she continued staring out to sea. "It is. After some searching, we found an alchemist operating out of the village, and we've been buying elixirs from him. She doesn't seem to be getting worse, but she's also not getting better."

Barry couldn't stop both his eyebrows from shooting up.

"The Cult of the Alchemist is in Tropica?"

Maria nodded again, wiping a tear from her eye.

"They are—one of their members is, anyway. It's extremely expensive, and even with the best elixirs he can craft, she's not improving."

"I'm truly sorry, Maria. I'll ask my wife and see if any remedies we've used in the past may be of use," he lied again. "Her father was a member of the Cult of Growth, and he passed down knowledge of herbs and plants that might be able to help."

"Thank you, Barry. I'm not sure it'll help where the alchemists can't, but honestly, we're willing to give anything a go."

Barry smiled at her as he stood. "Don't mention it. Should we get back to the fields? We don't want to keep that rock-headed old man of yours waiting."

Maria laughed, wiping another stray tear from her cheek. "Yeah, we'd better. I'll never hear the end of it if we linger any longer."

They walked back toward Fischer's fields in silence. Maria may have taken Barry's lack of talking for awkwardness, or perhaps kindness, following her difficult recounting. Neither were true. Barry was planning.

I woke to the light of dawn peeking through my open bedroom door. There was a chill in the air, and I pulled my covers up, relishing the warmth they provided.

"Good morning, Snips," I yawned.

I extended one arm from the comfort of my nest, feeling for my trusty guard crab. Feeling nothing, I lifted my head, peering out at the room. Sergeant Snips was nowhere to be seen.

Huh.

I'd become accustomed to being awoken by a crab blowing happy bubbles, and I felt a moment of loneliness from her lack of presence.

Maybe she's out tending the campfire . . .

In a single movement, I threw the bedding aside and stood, stretching my body. I felt much better after a night's sleep, the minor aches and sore muscles of the previous day already a distant memory.

As I stepped out my front door, I gazed east. The sun was already above the horizon, the purple and pink light of the predawn already long banished by the orange hue of the day to come. I breathed in deep through my nose, the cool, salty air both calming me and banishing the sluggishness of waking.

"Where has that crab of mine gotten off to . . . ?"

A thought startled me, and my eyes went wide.

Not just my crab—my otter, too!

I grinned as excitement and joy coursed through me.

An otter I have to name!

First, I checked the campfire; the coals had died overnight, untended as they were. Next, I made my way around the headland. I walked from the south, finding neither carapace nor hair of my animal companions as I followed the coast. I walked for the crab pot, intending to check it, but a flicker of movement caught my eye. To the northwest, a pile of sand climbed high above the flat landscape. I felt my eyebrows furrow as my partially sleep-addled mind tried to make sense of what I saw. At least a shovel worth of sand shot up over the side of the mound, adding itself to the hill.

"What the . . ." I walked toward the anomaly, unsure of what I was going to find.

As I got closer, I noted the sand cresting the mound was wet. I walked up the side and found myself speechless. It wasn't a hill—it was a hole. A *massive* hole, and my two friends were within.

The otter was beneath the water that filled the hole, swimming in circles and dredging up impressive amounts of sand. Snips was on the inside wall, taking the dredged-up sand and flicking it up and out of the excavation site.

"Woah . . ." I said aloud, my speechlessness overcome by shock.

Snips and the otter both paused, as if caught in a nefarious act. They peered at me with inscrutable looks, then as one, rushed me. Snips blew a trail of happy bubbles, gesturing at the surrounding creation with chaotic movements of her claws. She tried to encompass everything at once with her erratic pointing. The otter made a half-chittering, half-squealing noise, her body gliding through the water to reach the side closest to me.

They both reached me at the same time, a hard carapace and a furred body running around my legs and rubbing up against me.

I giggled in delight. "Good morning, ladies!"

They both pulled back, stared at me in a moment of silence, then blurted out indiscernible hisses, bubbles, and chittering chaos. They glared at each other, the silence returning with their accusatory stares.

"I'm happy to see you guys, too!" I said with a laugh. "What have you two made? A saltwater pond?"

They nodded vigorously, Snips with her entire body, the otter with rapid-fire head movements.

"It's *huge!*" I raised my eyes to take in their creation now that the mystery of its existence was solved.

It was at least ten meters across from east to west, and twenty meters from north to south. The walls were three to four meters tall, and the bottom of the pond was already filled to the halfway point with salty water seeping in through the sand.

"Did . . . did you two work all night?"

Again, they nodded, now with more calm.

"I . . . can't believe it . . ."

I bent down, patting them both to let my elation out. "You two are amazing! I don't think I could have done this myself in a single night!"

Snips bubbled happily and closed her eye as I scratched her.

The otter extended her head into my rubs, staring at me with big golden-retriever energy.

"Are you done, or do you plan to make it bigger?"

Snips and the otter reacted as one again, stretching both their forelimbs out wide.

I couldn't help but laugh. "What do you two say to some breakfast, first? You don't have to finish it all right now, and I'm sure you both need some rest after a full night of digging."

They both nodded, their eyes gleaming.

If I was being honest, I was still a little unsure of the name I'd offer my otter pal when I woke up. I hoped it would come to me as I lay in bed, but I'd fallen asleep the moment my head hit the pillow. I knew, however, that it would come to me.

My food sat untouched as I watched Snips and the otter devour theirs. If the average villager were to walk by and catch sight of the decimation before me, they'd probably be horrified. Me? I was ecstatic they were enjoying themselves and my cooking.

As usual, Snips ate the crab whole, carapace and all. The otter had started by using her trusty rock, but after a pause, did something astounding. She held a paw out, and with a small flex, extended five ridiculously sharp claws. She swiped down, obliterating the cooked crab in front of her. Her head cocked back, seemingly startling herself with her own strength and efficacy. The astonishment only lasted a brief second, and she quickly started collecting chunks of crab meat with her agile paws, shoveling them into her mouth.

At that moment, I was struck with inspiration, and her name came to me.

. . . it can wait until after breakfast.

I started eating too, and the wonderful flavor swept me away. Adding salt to the water was a game changer. The increased salinity clung to the shell and seemed to spread throughout, adding a rich depth to the sweet meat within. When I sucked the cracked limbs, salty juices joined the flesh and a groan of contentment escaped me.

"Oh, man, this is unreal," I said around a mouthful.

They both nodded, Snips crunching away, the otter chewing adorably.

Before I knew it, I was finished, and I let out a sigh after eating the last bite. "How was it, ladies?"

Snips bubbled happily from the sand. The otter let out a soft chirp, lounging on my other side, and I turned to her.

"I wanted to ask—do you have a name?"

She glanced up at me lazily, shaking her head.

"Do . . . do you want one?"

She sat up, her eyes considering me with a spark of intelligence.

She gave a single nod.

"How do you feel about the name Corporal Claws?"

Blinking, she shot toward me. She leaned her upper body against my leg, nodding and chirping incessantly.

I smiled and let out a small laugh. "I'm glad you like it!"

I stroked Corporal Claws's head, causing her to close her eyes and lean into me.

I felt Snips press up against my other side, and before she could complain, I started petting her, too.

My little family has grown . . .

CHAPTER FORTY-ONE

ANOTHER TASK

With Sergeant Snips and Corporal Claws napping peacefully in the sun, I made my way toward the fields.

Those two really did a number on themselves by working all night.

As soon as the food had settled, they both started falling asleep, and I stroked them until they passed out.

The passage toward the fields was pleasant; the sun warmed my skin, perfectly contrasted by a cool breeze blowing from the east. When I arrived, the work was well and truly underway. Maria and Roger were working on the field closest to the ocean, once more mixing the soil and sand, as per Barry's instruction. Barry, the madman that he was, occupied the other field, doing the same amount of work as the other two.

"Morning, guys!"

"Morning!" Maria and Barry both called, while Roger simply nodded at me.

I walked toward Barry. "What's the plan for today, chief? Want me to jump in and mix up some dirt with you guys?"

"Sounds good to me, Fischer! Unless you have plans, of course . . ."

"Nonsense, mate. I'm happy to help. I did want to run an idea past you though . . ."

"Oh? What's that?"

"Well, that totally depends on what you can tell me about the fertilizer you use."

Barry shot a look at the other two, and seeing they weren't listening, leaned in and spoke softly. "Are you suggesting what I think you are?"

I grinned. "If you're thinking I want to catch a fish for food and use the inedible parts of its body for fertilizer, you're bang on the money, my friend."

Barry glanced toward the others again before returning his focus to me. "I'm all for it, but I don't think Roger would take too kindly to the idea."

"Yeah, I figured." I shot him a wink. "That's why I'm asking you, not him. What do you guys usually use for fertilizer?"

"Most farmers in Tropica use cow manure from the pastures to the north, but I think blood-bone fertilizer is more suitable as a jumpstart for these fields—I have plenty of it to spare, as we often replenish the soil every few harvests."

Not sure what I was expecting, but that seems pretty similar to Earth.

I let out a soft chuckle at myself.

What did I expect, magic fantasy dust?

Barry raised an eyebrow at my mirth, but I shook my head.

"Don't worry, mate—just had a giggle-worthy thought."

I peered at the fields, taking in their size. "I can't say I'd be able to get anywhere near enough for the entirety of one field, let alone two. What do you reckon about me catching something, and we test it on a small patch?"

"That sounds prudent—if you catch it today, we can fertilize the field with it tonight when they leave."

"Sounds like a plan, Barry! I'll get to it!"

I walked over to Roger and Maria on the way back to my shores.

"How are you guys going? Looks like you're killing it."

They both gave me odd looks.

". . . killing it?" Maria asked.

"Er—sorry, I mean that you guys are doing a good job."

Roger snorted, muttering something under his breath. Maria shot him a chastising look, then turned back to me.

"We're doing good. Thanks again for letting us use your land. How are you doing, Fischer?"

I beamed with genuine excitement. "I'm doing great! I have something to take care of today, so I won't be able to help in the fields—it looks like you have things covered, though!"

Roger snorted again and shook his head, causing Maria to let out an exaggerated sigh.

"Don't mind him—what he means to say is thanks for letting us use your land, and for all your help so far. Right, *Dad?*"

Roger grumbled something inaudible as he continued tossing soil.

"You're welcome!" I said, making him scowl further. It only increased my enjoyment of the interaction.

I let out a content sigh as I breathed out a lungful of salty air. "What a beautiful day."

Birds were circling high above me, their calls barely audible over the wind and the soft crashing of waves against the shore. I held my trusty fishing pole in hand, and I watched the tip intently, waiting for a fish to take the bait.

If I can catch one more, I'll get even more fertilizer.

I'd already caught a mature cichlid; it was wrapped in a wet towel beside me.

I can have one fish for me and my animal pals and can gift the other to Barry as thanks for all the—

My thoughts cut off as something bit the line, and the bamboo pole almost jerked out of my hands.

"Woah! Fish on!"

I walked forward, moving with the pull of what had to be a massive fish. The rod trembled violently as it shook its head, doing everything it could to get away. I walked all the way down to the shore, but with nowhere left to go, held firm. I leaned back away from the water, not intent on taking an impromptu dip in the river mouth. The fish pulled; I leaned back with all I had. All at once, the line went slack, and I fell back onto the rocks with an involuntary *oof.*

"Heavens, what was *that?*"

I wound the line in, hand over hand.

Did it snap the line . . . ?

I caught sight of the sinker and hook, and with one last tug, I lifted them up.

Woah . . .

The hook, even as large and thick as it was, had bent. Whatever had taken the bait was so large that it completely bent the hanger, letting it slide out of the fish's mouth.

I guess that's what I get for using a wall hanger for a hook . . .

It was greedy of me to try for a second fish, and I paid the price.

Just like Icarus, I flew too close to the sun. More like Fisharus . . .

A sharp laugh burst from my mouth, half at myself, half because of the joy and purpose having another task brought me.

Guess I'll have to go see Fergus . . .

Processing the fish I'd caught was a slow endeavor; I took the time to remove every bit of edible flesh possible, showing respect for the life taken as best I could.

"Thank you," I whispered aloud as I scaled its entire body, collecting all the scales in a pot.

The obvious cuts to remove were the fillets on either side of the fish, and I did so with small, exacting slices.

Following the example of a cliff-fishing Aussie I'd watched in my previous life, I removed other bits of flesh. First were the cheeks, two small muscles on either side of the head that the fish used to open and close its mouth. Next, I removed what said fisherman had called "wings." It was a long strip of flesh that ran beneath the fish, including both its pectoral fins. Even having watched a video on doing it, the process was a little confusing. Still, I was glad I made the attempt; I did a respectable job, by my estimate, and I couldn't wait to try them.

Because I took so long to process the fish, a crowd of onlookers gathered. The seagulls must have spotted the fish from above, and four of them stood on the nearby rocks of the headland, watching me with hungry eyes.

"Sorry, fellas—I don't have any scraps for you today. My friends need the leftover frame."

They didn't respond, of course, other than to continue staring between me and the morsels just out of their reach.

I placed the wings in a smaller pot with the cheeks and fillets and started breaking down the leftover skeleton. My sharp, System-produced knife and my improved body made short work of it.

I turned to the birds, giving them a sheepish glance. "Sorry, guys—next time, okay?"

I made my way back toward the house. My heart melted as I passed Snips and Claws, both of whom were releasing soft snoring sounds, and I petted them gently before taking the pots inside.

* * *

"G'day, Fergus!"

The large smith turned from his hammering, giving me a broad grin. "Hey, Fischer! With you in a moment!"

I walked over to the anvil, not invading his personal space as I watched him work. With each swing of the hammer, the bar he was shaping got closer and closer to its intended form. He started hammering harder, and the muscles of his arms bulged with the effort.

Who needs to hit the gym when you're hitting metal all day? My man is jacked!

The hammer fell one last time, and Fergus took a deep breath as he inspected the bar. His eyes ran up and down the length as he checked for any defects or mistakes. Nodding to himself, he dropped it in a quenching pit filled with oil.

"To your liking, mate?"

He grinned at me. "Aye, not that digging bars need a perfect finishing touch—still, it never hurts to pour care into something you make."

I smiled. "Couldn't agree more, Fergus. What day is it, by the way? I've lost track."

"Resday."

So Crafday, Winday, then Resday today, and Sunday tomorr—

"So, what brings you here?" Fergus asked, interrupting my thoughts. "Other than my beautiful face, of course." He wiggled his eyebrows at me, causing a laugh to escape my throat.

"Purely selfish reasons for my visit, I'm afraid—I wanted to see that beautiful mug of yours. Oh, and craft some things."

He roared a laugh as he took off his gloves. "You're only human, after all! What did you want to make?"

I pulled out my bent hook, holding it toward him. "I've been sharpening wall hangers to use for my heretical activities, but as you can see, they stand no chance against my foes."

Fergus raised both eyebrows after accepting the bent hook, and his eyes narrowed as he tried and failed to bend it with his hands.

"What in Hephaestus's hammer bent this . . . ?"

"Big bloody fish, mate."

His eyes met mine. "Do I need to be worried? Can you even handle something strong enough to bend this?"

I gave him my best reassuring smile. "A fish is still a fish—they're as good at fighting on land as you'd be fighting underwater."

"Just a normal-looking fish? How does it bend metal?"

"You'd be surprised how much force they can exert underwater; their bodies are built for swimming. It felt like the biggest thing I'd hooked so far, but don't worry—I'll keep my heresy to my little patch of sand."

"Still . . ." His eyes roamed back over the bend in the hook. "I'm a little awed by the strength . . ."

"I am too. That's why I wanted to try my hand at crafting my own hooks!"

Fergus rubbed his chin in thought and turned to peer at a shelf in the back of the smithy.

"One moment."

He returned with a box filled with casings similar to the one we'd used to create the silver ring. "You can start with these molds; it'll save you some time."

"They're the ones you use to create the wall hangers?"

"Aye. You can reshape them as you need after you take them from the mold . . ."

Fergus looked back at the shelf then gave me a wide smile. He walked over to it, grabbed a smaller box, and brought it over to me.

"If you use these hooks I've already made, you can heat and shape them, then use the reshaped hooks to create your own casings."

"Mate. You're too good to me."

He shook his head. "You've helped me plenty—it's the least I could do."

"Well, thank you. I appreciate all the help. Any advice on the best way to go about it?"

"I can do better than that, *mate!* I'll help!"

I grinned at his use of "mate"; he gave me a coy smile back.

"I can't turn down that offer, my man! Are you free now?"

"For you, Fischer?" He set his gloves down. "Always."

CHAPTER FORTY-TWO

PULSE

I removed the hanger from the forge when it glowed red, just as Fergus had suggested. He passed his pliers, and I started shaping it. I started with a smaller hanger, not wanting to waste any of the smith's metal if it went poorly. The metal bent easily, and I turned the round curve into a shape approximating an Aberdeen hook. I made the bend slightly squared, then straightened the shank out and used the needle-nose pliers to create the small eye I'd attach my line to. Finally, I turned my attention to the tip of the hook. I raised it right before my eyes, carefully pinching and molding the tip into as sharp a point as possible.

"Quench?" I asked.

"Aye, when you're happy with the shape."

I inspected the tip one more time then checked the eye. I bent the metal as close to the other end of the hook, intent on leaving no space between where the end of the eye met the shank. Happy with the shape, I plunged it into the oil.

"That'll do," Fergus said. "It's thin; it'll be cool already."

I removed it, testing the heat with my finger; he was correct. "Should we make a casing with this one, or make the rest of the hooks . . . ?"

Fergus nodded at the forge. "Do the rest of the hooks, I think. We can make all the molds later."

I set the hook down on the anvil and grabbed the next hanger.

Fergus watched Fischer intently, professional curiosity overcoming his aversion to anything heretical. He'd watched Fischer create four types of hooks already; the first one with a long shaft, and three rounded hooks of varying sizes that Fischer had called "circle hooks," only one of which had an eye at the end.

The one Fischer was now placing in the forge was the weirdest yet. The fisherman had created three of the medium-sized circle hooks and tied them together with thin wire at the blunt ends. The tips splayed out in even intervals, the three needle-like points facing outward.

Fergus's intrigue grew as he watched the thin wire melt, fusing the three hooks together. When the amalgamation was glowing red, Fischer removed it, immediately getting to work with the pliers. He pinched the shafts together, fusing the metal into a single form.

While Fergus rarely worked with such small objects in the forge directly—usually only doing so to create casings—he couldn't help but feel a kinship with Fischer's attentiveness and care in creating the hook, heretical as it may be.

Fischer pinched the joining bits of metal meticulously, taking particular care around the eye to remove any imperfections or sharp edges. When he was content with the shape, he drove it down into the quenching pit, swirling it around. He withdrew the hook, inspected it with a discerning gaze, and nodded. Then, something unexpected occurred.

A small pulse hit Fergus, resonating between his stomach and lungs. He reeled, taking a few steps back in confusion.

"W-what was that?" Fischer's eyes went wide, but quickly returned to normal.

Did I imagine that . . . ?

"You right, Fergus?"

"Yeah . . . I just . . . I thought I felt something."

"Is my smithing that impressive?"

Fischer smiled and waggled his eyebrows.

"Blown away by my skill and expertise in heretical matters?"

"That must be it . . . what do you call that hook?" Fergus asked, trying to change the subject.

"It's called a treble hook, mate. I don't think I'll use it anytime soon, because they're usually attached to lures, but thought I'd try making one and see if it was possible."

". . . lures?"

Fischer laughed, his face broadcasting delight. "It's something made to look like a fish out of wood, plastic, or metal—basically, you pull it through the water to imitate a baitfish swimming, and when a bigger fish tries to eat it, the treble snags them no matter what direction they come from."

"Metal? Do you want to try creating one?"

"I'll gladly come back to do so another day, but after making the casings, I wanna get back and help Barry and the gang on the fields we're making on my land."

Fergus nodded, leaning into the conversation to distance himself from thoughts of the pulse.

"I heard about your fields—good business, that."

Fischer shrugged. "Just the right thing to do, mate. I'm not charging them or anything, and I'm not using the land, so I'm happy for them to have a crack at farming it."

"Aye, but you don't need to help them."

"You're right; I don't. Again, though, it seems like the right thing to do."

Fergus smiled, his thoughts momentarily swept away by feelings of gratitude for Fischer's arrival.

"Well, if you want to get back to the fields and help them, let's get started on the molds."

An almost predatory grin spread across Fischer's face, and he nodded.

"Let's."

* * *

The early afternoon sun and an accompanying breeze felt cool on my skin as I walked back toward the fields.

Man, what a productive day!

I'd managed to create hooks and moldings, catch dinner, and even prepare fertilizer for mine and Barry's nighttime activity.

I laughed at myself.

Might want to rethink the phrasing on that one . . .

Fergus had given me a leather wallet for the hooks, and I removed it from a back pocket, peering inside at my new creations. I only had the ones I'd made for the moldings, as I wanted to get back and help before the day was through.

"With any luck, I'll only need one of each for a while."

The memory of the pulse that had radiated through me returned, the sensation so strong I could still feel the echoes of it.

Fergus nailed it on the head—what was *that?*

It had felt like the pulls from the System I'd previously felt but was accompanied by a physical sensation in my core. The power seemed to rush from within, blooming, then disappearing as fast as it came.

Is that this world's version of a breakthrough . . . ? Like the ones in the stories I read on Earth?

Following an impulse, I willed my notifications back on and was met with an absolute barrage of regret.

[Error: Insufficient power. Superfluous systems offline.]
[Error: Insufficient power. Superfluous systems offline.]
[Error: Insufficient power. Superfluous systems offline.]

It stretched on, madly scrolling down.

Welp. Nevermind.

I willed the notifications back off. Just as I did so, I walked out from between the last of Barry's fields to find my neighbors taking a break in the shade. They sat around a tray of sandwiches, Maria and Roger looking absolutely wrecked, Barry looking like he was just sitting down to make them feel better.

"I leave you guys alone for *one* minute, and you all start slacking off?"

Maria and Barry smiled, and Roger scowled.

"Mind if I join you?" I asked, pointing at the sandwiches.

"I don't know . . ." Barry tried to hide a smile, but failed. "The wife might get upset if we share the food she made for hard workers with a freeloader . . ."

I nodded seriously, not bothering to hide the grin forming.

"That's a good point! I'd feel just *terrible* if I had to share the fish I caught today with one of my friendly neighbors."

Barry's eyes sparkled, and he slid the tray forward.

"Let me get this straight," Roger said. "You had *business* to attend to today, and you couldn't help in the fields, because you were . . . *fishing?*"

"Oh, not just fishing, Roger!" I sat down, picking up a sandwich. "I also saw Fergus and crafted some new hooks—to improve my fishing, you understand?"

Maria nodded along with a smile, ignoring her father's unimpressed expression.

"A truly productive day, then! May your heretical activities be ever fruitful!"

I raised my sandwich in a toast. "And may your fields be ever bountiful!"

I took a bite of the sandwich, enjoying the taste but again wishing it had a little seafood added. I chewed it slowly, as I swallowed turned to Barry.

"This is delicious, mate—make sure you thank Helen for me . . . especially for showing hospitality to a freeloader such as myself."

Barry's eyes still sparkled after my mention of fish, and he smiled.

"I will. I'm always complimenting her food, but I'm sure she'll be delighted to hear it from you."

"So," I said, "where are you guys up to with the fields? If there's more churning and mixing to be done, I'm ready to roll."

"We're all done with the mixing," Maria said.

She leaned back on her hands, letting out a weary yet content sigh. "We're up to the planting."

"Why don't you guys take the rest of the day off and let Barry and I handle it?"

"We're not children, Fischer—we don't need coddling," Roger growled.

I help my hands up placatingly. "I only suggested it because Barry and I have some other stuff to do." I turned to the man in question. "You're still up for helping construct my fence, right?"

Quick-witted as ever, Barry nodded. "Aye, Fischer—I never forget a promise."

"So?" Roger demanded. "You think we're incapable of planting stalks?"

"No, but you *can* do stuff in your fields, right? You're really trying to tell me you have nothing to work on? Last I heard, you had a field with improper levels that desperately wants a stabilizing crop planted in it . . ."

Roger's lips moved as his pride warred with his financial pressures.

"Dad." Maria shook her head lightly, a stray strand of hair falling from behind her ear.

"There's no shame in accepting kindness—you'd do the same if they needed it, wouldn't you?"

" . . . *I would,*" he reluctantly admitted.

"So let them help. Now that we have other fields to plant crops in, we can fix the nitrogen in our own. The sooner we plant them, the sooner we can resume growing sugarcane or wheat."

Roger averted his eyes and nodded a single time.

"And what do we say when people help us, Dad?"

He glared at her. Standing, he muttered as he turned to walk away.

"I didn't hear you, Dad!" she yelled after him.

"I said thank you, dammit!" he called over his shoulder, still marching.

Maria let out a deep sigh as she turned back toward Barry and me. "I swear, that man . . ."

I shook my head with a small laugh. "Old codgers are the same everywhere. If you ever met my dad, you'd think Roger a saint."

She raised an eyebrow. ". . . *codgers?*"

"Yeah, you know—codgers, fellas, old blokes. Same thing."

She gave me a bemused smile.

"You have the oddest way of speaking, Fischer."

I beamed a grin. "Thank you!"

She playfully rolled her eyes at me. "Still, I find it hard to believe that your father could be worse than mine . . ."

"You'll have to take my word for it. He's passed now, but he was an abrasive bloke at the best of times."

"Oh, I'm sorry . . ."

"It's all good. He did everything he wanted in life, and his only regret was probably yours truly."

Barry and Maria both blinked at me, concern flooding their expressions.

"Err . . . that came out worse than I meant it to. I'm okay—really."

Maria gave a kind smile as she stood, brushing her overalls off. "Well, sorry to leave it on a sad note, but I'd better get back to Dad before he takes his anger out on our sacks of seed."

I stood too. "Not at all—sorry if I brought the mood down."

She smiled again, and clearly unsure of what to say, waved and set off.

"Damn," I said to Barry. "Think I might have killed the vibe there."

Barry grimaced. "It may have reminded her of her mother's, well, mortality."

I facepalmed, groaning at my stupidity. "I'm an *idiot.* I didn't even think about that . . ."

"It's fine. I have a feeling that Sharon will get better soon."

"I didn't even know her name was Sharon. I'm a terrible neighbor . . ."

"If you were a terrible neighbor, Fischer, you wouldn't be helping them create a farm on your property for free."

Barry stood, collecting the almost empty tray of sandwiches. "Let's focus on what we can do. You caught a fish?"

Barry was right, of course.

There's no use in dwelling—I can make a difference in their situation, so that's what I'll do.

I grinned. "You ask *me,* the heretical Fischer, if I caught a *fish?*" I shook my head in mock dismay. "My good man, who do you take me for?"

CHAPTER FORTY-THREE

LEMONS

In a long-abandoned room, high in the capital city of Gormona's castle, a construct sat among a sea of similarly forgotten relics. Despite there being no one present, not a single pair of eyes there to witness its efforts, it sprang to life. Text typed itself out on the screen, a single line intended to inform the long-departed rulers of this land about a cultivator's advancement.

New milestone! Fischer has advanced to fishing 25!

"About this deep, you reckon?" I asked.

Barry nodded. "Aye, Fischer—that should be the perfect depth for the sugarcane's roots."

I threw a chunk of fish into the hole.

"You want to put a bit of dirt on top," Barry said. "Like so."

He threw a handful of soil atop the fertilizer, and I nodded.

"And we just plant the stalk of sugarcane right above it?"

Barry removed one from the satchel over his shoulder, holding the stalk out to me.

I accepted it. "I still can't believe you propagate sugarcane like this . . ."

Barry raised an eyebrow, smiling at me. "Did you think it grew from seed?"

"Well . . . yeah. It really just regrows itself if you don't pull the stalks out?"

"It does, yes, but as Maria and Roger have shown, if you leave the field for too long without planting something else, the soil quality will worsen. You have to occasionally rip the entire stalk out and start the cycle over."

I held up the palm-length section of cane. "Yeah, but we can just chuck this thing in the ground and it'll grow? That's wild, Barry."

He laughed, loud and full of joy. "There are plenty of plants like that, Fischer—they're called perennial, meaning they grow for a long time with the right conditions, if not indefinitely."

I shook my head, still amazed. "Man, you almost make farming sound interesting."

He laughed again, even more jubilant than before. "It's never too late to abandon your heretical ways for a life of farming, you know."

"Oh? And where would you get your seafood fix if I wasn't living the life of a heretic?"

Barry's eyes sparkled as I brought up the food.

"You, uh, have any of that fish you can spare for your favorite neighbor . . . ?"

"But of course! How else could I repay the kindness of Helen's sangas?"

". . . sangas? That's what you call sandwiches where you're from . . . ?"

"Struth, mate."

"All right, you lost me again."

We grinned at each other, and I placed the sugarcane stalk inside the hole.

"Do I cover it with loose soil, or do I pack it down?"

"Pack it down a little. You don't want any air pockets, but you also don't want the soil too constricting."

I pressed down after filling in the hole, taking care not to use too much strength because of my improved body.

"Good?" I asked.

"Perfect—let's move on to the next one."

We repeated the process with small chunks of fish fertilizer in the northwest corner of the western field—the closest to Barry's home.

"Shall we do the rest of the fields without fertilizer, or do you have somewhere to be, Fischer?"

I grinned. "Wanna race?"

Barry stared at me, and in a single movement, dumped half the satchel of stalks on the ground and sprinted for the eastern field.

I roared a laugh. "You're on, Barry!"

Unlike our previous races, Barry was annihilating me. It wasn't a test of strength or endurance; the planting required care and precision. If anything, my empowered body slowed me down, and I took much longer than Barry each time I pressed down the soil atop the stalks.

"What's the matter, Fischer?" Barry called, taunting me. "Can't handle a little farming?"

"Hey!" I yelled back, laughing. "I'm doing my best!"

In less than an hour, Barry was finished and he came over to join me.

"Oi! I don't need help from a goody-two-shoes farmer like you!" I joked.

"Two shoes?" Barry raised an eyebrow. "How many shoes do you usually wear?"

I chortled, the question catching me off guard.

"Never mind. I can't lie; I'd appreciate your help with my share of the field."

I passed him half the remaining stalks, and we finished the field together, Barry still excelling well past what I could accomplish.

"Whenever you're finished, *mate,*" Barry taunted.

"Whatever, *nerd.*"

"Do I want to know what that means?"

"It means you're smart."

Barry cocked his head. "And that's an insult where you come from . . . ? That sounds more like a compliment to me."

I snorted. "That's exactly what a nerd would say."

I glanced over with a cheeky grin; Barry just shook his head with a confused smile.

* * *

When I'd planted the last stalk, I stood and stretched my back. "Ah, man, that was harder than I expected!"

"But how do you feel now that you're finished?"

I rubbed my chin in thought. "I feel good. My body is a little sore, but I helped my friends, and that gives me the warm fuzzies."

Barry sighed. "Warm fuzzies?"

"Yeah! The warm, fuzzy feeling of helping someone out, or seeing a cute animal and petting their hard shell."

"I'm not sure if that's wholesome or horrifying . . ."

"Was the hard shell imagery too much?"

"A little . . ."

"C'mon!" I gave him an incredulous look. "You're really telling me Sergeant Snips isn't a beacon of cuteness?"

"Cute isn't the word I'd use, but I can see where you're coming from . . ."

"Speaking of, there's someone I need to introduce you to . . ."

With the afternoon sun setting to our right, Barry and I made our way toward where I'd last seen Snips and Claws. When I caught sight of the campfire, my trusty guard crab stood tending it, placing small logs into the flames. Sergeant Snips heard us approaching, and she spun. She scuttled at us with incredible speed, her spindly legs making short work of the distance. A stream of joyous bubbles greeted us, and I bent down, petting her head.

"Good afternoon, Snips—or should I say good morning? Did you sleep well?"

She nodded, leaning into my touch.

"Hello, Sergeant Snips," Barry said, bending down to be closer to eye level.

She tilted her head in thought and wrote in the sand.

Barry's eyes went wide.

"You . . . *you can write?*"

She nodded, dragging her claw through the sand to underline whatever she'd written.

"Snips? You mean I can call you Snips?"

She nodded once, happy her decree was understood.

Barry smiled. "Of course. Whatever makes you happy."

She bubbled her approval and started walking back to the campfire. I noticed she'd retrieved the pot with fish in it from the kitchen; it sat on the sand by the fire.

"Oh! Did you want to try cooking, Snips?"

Her head jolted back, she shook it emphatically, then pointed at me with her claw. I couldn't help but laugh at her insistence.

Guess she really likes my cooking, huh?

"Of course, Snips! I'm always happy to cook."

"So," Barry said, "who was it you wanted me to meet?"

As if called from the depths, a four-legged creature sprinted from the river. She ran straight for us, her mouth open and tongue lolling as she approached. Her eyes caught sight of Barry, and her body went rigid. She skidded to a stop, leaning back and staring at Barry with clear trepidation.

"He's a friend!" I called, urging her on with one hand. "I brought him here to meet you!"

With narrowed eyes, she resumed her approach, now walking rather than sprinting.

"This," I said to Barry, "is Corporal Claws."

His shocked expression was a joy to behold.

"She's . . . like Snips?"

"Sure is, mate."

"Two creatures on the path to ascension . . ." Barry shook his head. "Unbelievable . . ."

"What can I say?" I shot him a wink. "I have a way with the ladies."

"Please don't ever say that again when talking about animals—awakened or not."

"Get your mind out of the gutter, Barry. You're worse than webnovel commenters demanding that stories devolve into harems—joking or not."

He gave me his most confused look yet, and I chortled for the second time that day.

Corporal Claws reached us, and I bent down to pat her, delighting in the cute little chirps she gave.

"This is Barry, Claws—he's a neighbor and a good mate of mine."

She gave him a nod, and Barry, still looking rather out of his element, nodded back.

"Is it all right if Barry pets you?" I asked Claws.

She instantly nodded, not needing a second to consider it. Barry stared down at her as she stood on her hind legs, offering her head up for a good scritching. Barry looked at me, looked back down at Corporal Claws, and made no move. Claws mimed scratching behind her head, giving an insistent chirp. Obeying the order, he bent, scratching the spot behind her ear that Claws had indicated. He started softly, but as she leaned further into the scratches, he once more obeyed, fingers pressing firmly into her coat. Corporal Claws chittered and cooed, broadcasting her enjoyment to the world.

"Your fur is so soft . . ."

Claws nodded slowly, making Barry's fingers scratch different parts of her head. She pulled away, shaking her entire body, which caused her legs to spread wide so she didn't fall over. She looked like nothing so much as a dog shaking water off, and I couldn't help but smile at the joy flourishing within me.

Barry had an awestruck expression, and I spoke to bring him back to the present.

"I assume you don't mind if Claws joins us for dinner?"

His head turned slowly, as if moving through honey.

"N-no, of course not . . ."

"Didn't think so, but thought I'd make sure—I'll start cooking!"

Claws chirped to grab my attention, and she began fervently rummaging around in both pockets.

Her paws withdrew, holding two rock-like objects in each.

". . . oysters?" I asked.

They were large—bigger than the ones I'd seen on the shore, anyway. Claws nodded, and she walked forward on her hind legs, holding the four oysters out to me.

"Where did you find them . . . ?"

With her forelimbs now free, she chirped and started drawing in the sand. She drew a checkered pattern, an open hatch, and a bunch of oysters within.

". . . the cages off the shore?"

She nodded, chirping in the affirmative.

The oyster cages had oysters in them already? Of that size . . . ?

"Were there more in there than those?"

She pointed at the oysters in my hand then made a minimizing gesture with both paws.

"Smaller ones . . . ?"

Affirmative chirp.

"Huh . . . that's surprising."

"Uh, I don't mean to butt in," Barry said, "but you can understand what she's saying?"

"Yeah, mate—you can't?"

He shook his head. "No, Fischer, certainly not."

"Same as Snips then, huh?" I petted the crab in question, making happy bubbles come forth.

"Do you have lemons, Barry?"

"Er—lemons . . . ?"

"Yeah, you know—citrus fruit, yellow and kind of egg shaped, tastes sour?"

"I know what lemons are, but no, I don't have any lemons on me . . ."

I barely heard the end of his response.

They have lemons here!

"Are there any in Tropica?" I demanded, not caring to hide the desperation in my voice.

"Tropica? I doubt it, unless one of the north siders has some stashed away—they're exceedingly expensive, just as with passiona."

My excitement died; my stomach dropped. "Let me guess—the seeds are engineered to not reproduce?"

"Just so," he said.

This fantasy-land Monsanto is really killing my vibe. I need *lemons.*

I let out a great sigh. "Ah well, I supposed that'd make things too easy on us, huh, Snips?"

Sergeant Snips nodded, definitely not understanding the nuance of my frustration, but still supporting me unconditionally.

I petted her again, taking solace in her company.

"Well, no matter—they'd have gone really well with the oysters."

Barry furrowed his forehead so much that his eyebrows almost touched.

"You're planning on eating those . . . rocks . . . ?"

I blinked; Snips blinked; Claws's head spun and glared at him.

Snips was the first to break. A low noise came from her, transforming into a churning hiss of bubbles and laughter. She fell on her back, kicking her legs up in the air. I joined in. I didn't know when I hit the ground, but I found myself sitting, one hand bracing against the sand, the other wiping tears from my eyes.

Corporal Claws didn't find it as entertaining as Snips and I did, but she still let her amusement out in little chitters as she glanced between all of us rapidly.

"They're—they're not rocks, Barry. They're a type of shellfish."

Barry shook his head, laughing at himself. "So you *do* plan on eating them?"

"I reckon you should try one too, mate—they're best served fresh."

Without further ado, I held them back out to Claws. "Would you open these for us?"

She nodded as she ran toward me, collecting the oysters and setting them down on a log used for sitting. Claws flexed her paw, and five of her namesakes sprung out, sending Barry's eyebrows flying up.

"You're gonna get wrinkles if you spend too much time around us," I said, giggling.

With a series of adept movements, Claws unhinged each oyster and discarded the lids.

She passed one to me and Snips first, then gave one to Barry, and finally, picked up her own and slurped it down with glee.

"After you, mate," I said to Barry.

He stared down at the mollusk, and after gathering his courage, poured it into his mouth, copying Claws's action.

His face immediately transformed.

CHAPTER FORTY-FOUR

THE PLAN

Barry's face scrunched in obvious disgust as the oyster's flavor and texture hit him. He bit down a single time, and his disappointment only deepened. He swallowed it whole, his whole body trembling.

"Yeahhhhhh," I said, "they can be a bit much for the uninitiated."

"W-water," he begged.

I pointed toward the house. "Inside."

He nodded and all but ran away, likely not wanting to offend me by sprinting.

Snips and Claws both stared after him in confusion.

"Raw and unseasoned oysters don't taste great to everyone—it can be a bit of an acquired taste."

Sergeant Snips shrugged, accepting my words, but Corporal Claws looked like Barry had just slapped each and every one of her ancestors.

"Forgive him," I said. "He didn't mean to offend you—in fact, I think he schooled his reaction pretty well."

I raised my oyster to my lips, enjoying the salty taste that washed through my mouth.

When Barry returned, I was just placing the fish on my makeshift grill.

"You right, mate?"

He nodded, grimacing. "Sorry—I don't think oysters are for me . . ."

"They rarely are the first time you try them. I'll cook them up in something tasty for you next time."

He nodded, the lingering grimace telling me he didn't believe I could turn them into something palatable.

Just you wait, Barry—I dare you to knock back my Oysters Kilpatrick once I get the spices and seasonings of this world worked out.

"This fish didn't actually have wings . . . right?" Barry asked, staring down at the bit of fish I removed from the grill.

"Nah, mate—just a term for this cut of meat."

I removed the cheeks too, placing them beside the wings on the wooden board. I walked over to a tray of salt, and finding it mostly dry, I grinned.

One more day of sun, and it'll be finished and ready for jarring.

I pinched some from the surface, sprinkling the coarse rocks of salt over the wings and cheeks.

"This will be a taste of what's to come," I said, placing the board on the floor and cutting the bits of meat into sections.

"Try the cheeks first," I said to everyone, pointing at the small bits of flesh I'd cut in half.

Snips and Claws grabbed them without delay, happily digging into the bite-sized morsels. I held the board out to Barry, and he eyed them with trepidation.

"I promise it'll taste better than the oyster. In fact, it might taste even better after eating something you deemed gross."

"Gross might be a strong way of putting it . . ."

"You don't have to lie, Barry," I said, smiling. "I remember my first oyster as a young man, and I can't say I composed myself as well as you did."

He winced, reaching out for the fish cheek. I watched as he placed it in his mouth. The moment he did, his hesitancy evaporated.

"Mmmm," he groaned, closing his eyes in delight.

I ate mine too, and I had to agree with his assessment. The salt had been what was missing; the umami boost was sublime in combination with the fish's flavor.

"Next, the wings."

Everyone grabbed a chunk as one, Snips and Claws just as excited as before, and Barry having all his trepidation swept away by the cheek's taste.

"Careful of the bones," I said. "Eat around them."

I held a pectoral fin and bit into the meat, carefully testing for bones as I bit down. The flavor hit me like a truck—and believe me, I'd know what that felt like. The flesh was darker than the cheeks and held more of a fishy taste than the lighter meat. I didn't shy away from the stronger flavor, and if anything, the contrast between the two only improved the experience. I felt it regenerating my spirit; it invigorated me.

Barry let out an *mmph* as he ate, and I smiled, happy he was enjoying himself. Sergeant Snips finished first—unsurprising, given her lack of aversion to bones. Corporal Claws, Barry, and I all finished around the same time after working around the cooked bones.

Barry let out a content sigh. "That was *delicious,* Fischer."

I smirked at him. "Glad I could redeem myself after the oyster."

"Well and truly," he said, taking a deep, relaxing breath.

"If you liked that, wait until we have the main course."

"Goodnight, Fischer," Barry said.

"Night, mate!"

Fischer made his way to the house, accompanied by Corporal Claws. Barry sat by the fire, and he reflected on the meal just gone. It was hard for him to sit still; his body radiated energy, seeming to demand he use it. Sergeant Snips sat in the sand beside him, but where Barry felt like he had to run, she dozed, her body pressed to the ground.

Barry had intended to sit on his plans for at least a week, but after spending even more time around Fischer, he'd reached his decision.

Still, I hope this isn't a mistake . . .

He swallowed, his throat all of a sudden dry and tight.

"Snips . . . I wanted to talk to you about something."

She opened her eye, looking at him lazily. She blew a small amount of bubbles and tilted her body in what Barry took for a question.

His heart pounded in his chest, and the words wanted to stay within, to not be spoken. Barry clenched his jaw, and unsure where to begin, just started speaking.

"You know that Fischer is . . . *special,* right?"

She perked up, nodding.

"What you might not know is just *how* special he is. Are you aware that he caused your awakening?"

She nodded, the gesture as much a dismissal as an answer.

"You . . . aren't bothered by that?"

She shook her head. *No.*

"And you also know he probably caused Corporal Claws to awaken, too . . . ?"

She nodded again, her lone eye locked on Barry.

"I have to confess something that you might find a little shocking—I know I still can't believe it, anyway."

She blew bubbles, but Barry couldn't understand them, so he continued.

"He caused me to take steps on the path of ascension, too . . ."

Snips jolted upright, standing on her spiked legs as she looked at him and blew more indiscernible bubbles.

"I know . . ." Barry said with a wince. "I wasn't really happy to learn about it, given how this world treats cultivators, but I've come to accept it over the past few days."

She made no move, simply listening and watching.

"The reason I'm telling you this is because it places you and Fischer in danger—"

Barry's eyes went wide, and he stopped speaking. Snips's claw was held around his throat, its cold and firm touch sealing his words. She'd moved so fast he hadn't seen it; she may as well have teleported, given Barry's inability to respond or even notice. She stared at him with her inhuman eye. She tightened her claw, sending a chill down Barry's spine.

Trent, the first in line to the throne of Gormona and possibly the most repulsive man Leroy had ever met, scowled down at him.

"What gives you the courage to display such petulance, *cultivator?*"

Leroy sighed, accepting that he had to repeat himself. "We have orders from our handler in the capital, and you soliciting "fun" from serving girls hurts our goals. Besides, given your looks, it'll probably cost more coins than you have."

Trent's face scrunched in fury, and he slapped Leroy. Leroy let the blow land, rolling his eyes before turning his head back toward the garbage human before him.

"You can strike me as much as you want, Trent—"

He slapped him in the same place. "It's "prince" to you, *cultivator!*"

Leroy sighed as he straightened out again. "Very well, prince."

Leroy's lack of outrage seemed to stoke Trent's own even more, and the sorry excuse for a leader snarled.

"How will having consensual fun with a local girl hurt our quest? Any girl would be lucky to experience a man such as myself!"

"Despite how dubious consent may be with the power imbalance between you and a villager, even if we assume that it's completely consensual, word will spread of your actions, and the cultivator we're looking for could flee."

"How?" Trent demanded. "How can you know that word will spread and that it will hurt our goals?"

"Let's say you're right, and that they're lucky to be with such a man as yourself—they'll brag, or her coworkers will spread nasty rumors out of *sheer jealousy* at not being chosen by such a *strong, manly,* no-doubt *flawless* lover—"

Trent slapped him again, and as Leroy turned back to look at him, he smiled at the prince.

"Let's say you're wrong, though—that the girl finds your touch repulsive, but feels threatened by the presence of two cultivators. What happens when her father or lover learns that you defiled her with your *disgusting* body—"

Trent screeched as he slapped him, and Leroy simply straightened and smiled again.

"Does that make you feel better?"

Trent lashed out again, harder than ever, but this time Leroy held his head firm. Trent's eyes went wide as he struck what must have felt like a stone wall, and he took a step back, his jaw quivering.

"Y-you can't attack me—your collar will detonate!"

"Do I look like I'm attacking you, *prince?*" Leroy spat the last word, but the look of fear remained on Trent's face; not a bit of anger showed.

Trent turned to the blond-haired cultivator, who was staring off into space, as ever. "What about you? You'll let this man threaten me—your prince? You should punish him for his insolence!"

Surprisingly, the other man actually turned, appearing to have heard Trent's words. "If I were to hurt this man, I'd be placing the mission in jeopardy and my collar could detonate."

Trent shook, his anger finally winning over his fear, and he spun.

"Fine! We keep moving, then! See how you traitorous fools feel after a night of running without sleep!"

Trent jumped atop his horse as awkwardly as ever, and after an embarrassing amount of time getting situated atop the saddle, he spurred it on. Leroy followed, finally letting his frustration show now that Trent had turned his back.

The collar around his neck was a constant reminder of his servitude, and for a moment, he let his hatred toward his captors roil within him. His blood boiled, and he felt the need to lash out, to wipe Trent from the face of Kallis.

"You know," the other cultivator said, "you could kill him in a single blow—you should."

Leroy glanced at the man, still shocked to find him speaking. The look in the blond-haired man's eyes drove a spike of cold understanding through Leroy's awareness. He'd seen that expression before, especially among cultivators that had been slaves for too long. Something had broken within the man; he thirsted for blood and would take any excuse to witness violence.

Leroy looked forward, ignoring him. Instead, he tamped the swelling fury down, focusing on his guiding star, his lodestone that was the only thing that kept him going.

Getting myself killed is a betrayal of those I love.

Leroy had people to return to.

I have to find a way back to my family. No matter how long it takes, or how many injustices I have to live through.

Barry raised both hands slowly, trying not to let them shake.

"I'm on your side, Snips—you're not under threat from me, and killing me will only hurt your safety."

Sergeant Snips weakened her grip, and after staring into Barry's soul for a long moment, she pulled away and started drawing letters in the sand.

"Explain."

Barry nodded, rubbing his neck where Snips had held him.

"The danger comes from Fischer's ability to create more ascendant beings. If the wrong person or creature were to awaken, their actions could bring down the weight of the crown upon us."

Snips started writing again.

"*Then you are a threat.*"

He shook his head again, not insulted by the claim. "I'm not—I want to help Fischer ascend."

Snips sat unmoving, watching Barry with her inhuman eye. After a tense minute, she scuttled to the side and pointed at the first word she'd written.

"Explain."

Barry nodded. "I need your help to do it, which is why I came to you."

Barry took a deep breath, letting it out slowly as he tried to calm his nerves. "This is the plan . . ."

CHAPTER FORTY-FIVE

TAPROOT

Sergeant Snips scuttled beneath the waves surrounding Tropica, searching. The moon high above shone its light down atop her, brightening the sea floor. Despite the myriad benefits of her new body, it also had its detriments. She no longer looked like a simple crab, and the moment any fish caught sight of her steady movement through the water, they fled. A new tactic was necessary.

She traveled to a large boulder she knew was just east of her position. The moment the fish using it as cover saw her, they fled. Her legs worked their way down into the loose sand, digging until her large and rather impressive carapace was resting atop the ocean floor. She sat and waited, unmoving. Her thoughts returned to the conversation with Barry, and a few bubbles escaped her mouth as she considered.

It is well I didn't have to kill him—that would have caused master grief.

Snips was also fond of Barry, but should he turn out to be a threat, she would harbor no regrets at having to take his life—other than the negative emotions her master would feel as a result, of course.

Sergeant Snips had been shocked at the revelation that Barry had also taken steps on the path of ascension. If she had known that to be a possibility, she would have insisted he didn't eat.

And, if he did, I would have ended him before he awakened; such is the threat he possesses.

Luckily for Barry, he was a more-than-reasonable human, and not only were his plans largely good, but also beneficial. Snips couldn't enact them without him, and so, he had proven himself. Most surprising of all was that a simple farmer had reached so many correct conclusions and devised sound plans with them. *Well,* sound after Snips's corrections, but that superiority was to be expected of Fischer's first chosen.

Movement caught her eye, and a large fish lazily swam toward the rock. Snips remained still, allowing it the illusion of safety. Even with no threat visible, it approached warily, its eyes and body darting around and scanning each section of sand it crossed. She kept her eyestalk still, not needing to move it around to track the fish. It swam behind her, and she lost sight of it—still, she didn't move. Her anticipation rose; even with her awakening, base animalistic instincts remained.

The fish rounded the boulder in front of her, and it looked down at her, its eyes darting around rapidly as it took in what must have looked like a rather odd rock. It swam closer; its curiosity sealed its fate. Her claw moved faster than an unascended creature could register, clacking sharply and shooting an arc of water outward.

It severed the fish's head; her aim was true, ending its life in an instant—as was Fischer's teaching. She collected both pieces of fish and set off for the cave. When she arrived, she found an antenna poking out of the entrance.

The previous times she'd visited, the sea snipper lay further back in the cave, hiding in a hole that barely fit its size.

Good, she thought, nodding to herself. *It gains confidence.*

She approached, holding the bits of fish before her so the scent wafted on the ocean current. The sea snipper, catching the scent of slain fish in the water, crawled toward her, its remaining antenna moving up and down. Two smaller antennae below the larger one moved around rapidly, enticed by the meal.

Sergeant Snips dropped the fish on the sand, intent on making the sea snipper come further from its cave to collect the gift. As it stepped out, she caught sight of the nub where its other antenna had been. The appendage appeared to be regrowing, but the base was still notably scarred. She rubbed her eyepatch, touching the spot where she'd lost an eye.

The fight that caused her to lose it was lost to time, her memories from the before fleeting and unreliable.

Will my eye one day regrow, too?

She shrugged to herself, and the sea snipper darted back a meter, spooked by her gesture.

No matter, she thought, stepping back from the cave a few steps to encourage the sea snipper forward.

If it regrows, I will still wear my master's gifted garment.

The creature walked forward once more as she retreated, tentatively picking up the large section of fish with one gigantic claw. It made to take it back to its cave, but realizing that a section of head remained, it scooped that up too in its other forelimb. With both bits of fish secured, it withdrew, already holding the head to its mouth and crunching on it.

Barry walked beneath the full moon, its light showing him the way home. Despite the late hour, he didn't feel tired. The cool night air was invigorating. He and Sergeant Snips had talked for hours, and after explaining himself and what he had planned, she'd been more than willing to work together.

While he knew creatures on the path to ascension were said to be smart, he wasn't prepared for just how intelligent she was. Being literate and able to communicate with written language was one thing; her insight and input were another thing entirely.

Busy as his mind was, the trip back home took no time at all. He stepped inside; the air was warm and the smell of his wife's curry still lingered.

As he approached their bedroom, a sense of dread welled up when he saw candlelight peeking beneath the door.

Why am I more scared of my wife than an ascendant crab . . . ?

He reached out and grabbed the door handle, pausing as indecision washed over him.

Is this really the right move . . . ?

Barry shook his head.

Snips and I already set things in motion—if I can't trust Helen, who can *I trust?*

The door creaked, cutting through the night's silence.

"Barry!" Helen said, sitting up. "I almost came to find you; I was worried sick!"

He sat down on the bed beside her, wrapping his arms around her and squeezing tight. She went rigid, surprised by his embrace, but melted into the hug immediately after, fiercely embracing him back.

They held each other there, both taking solace in their touch. The only noises Barry could hear were the wind blowing cane leaves around outside and his own pulse beating in his ears.

"Are you well, husband?" Helen asked, still holding him to her.

"I am—I'm just thankful to have you here."

She pulled him closer, squeezing him with all her strength, then let go, leaning back to look into his eyes.

"Are you sure you're okay?"

He nodded. "I am, but I have something to tell you."

She smiled at him, and Barry's heart somehow felt even more love for her. He took a deep breath, letting it out slowly before beginning his tale.

"It's about Fischer . . ."

Sergeant Snips, having ensured the sea snipper's continued survival, set off toward Tropica.

She had been keeping her eye on the poisoner and his follower at least once each day, and this day was no different.

As she was almost at the rocky wall that marked the village, a mumbled conversation could be heard. Snips cocked her head, filled with intrigue at who could be outside and talking at such a late hour. She carefully walked up the rocky wall. Her head poked above the waterline beneath a wooden dock, and she listened.

"What did I say last time, Gary?" the poisoner demanded.

It took all of Sergeant Snips's will to not blow a slew of furious bubbles. She felt the desire to ascend the wall, to end the coward's life once and for all, but she quashed it.

Patience, Snips . . .

The poisoner's follower, Gary, let out a sigh. "You said the next time I question you, I should leave and never come back, boss."

"And yet, you question me?" Sebastian demanded in a hiss.

"No, boss. I don't question you—I merely asked if dwelling on the past was stopping you from sleeping."

Footsteps sounded atop the wall at a clipped pace.

"That is questioning me, Gary!" Sebastian grunted in annoyance. "How can you *not* lose sleep after Fischer murdered Pistachio?"

"Please let go of my cloak, boss. I miss Pistachio just as much as you, but for me to be an effective member of the cult, I know how important sleep is . . ."

The poisoner grunted again, and Snips heard receding footsteps, followed by the creak and slam of a door. She peeked out past one of the pier's wooden poles.

The one called Gary leaned against the low wall surrounding the village, his shoulders hunched and head hanging low. He reached one hand into a pocket, hefted his arm back, then threw something out over the water.

"You brought this on yourself, Sebastian," he whispered to himself, then turned and left the wall.

Snips bridled with curiosity, and she immediately dipped below the ocean's surface, heading for the discarded item. When she got to it, her confusion only increased. It was small and rectangular, but the shape wasn't what made it so intriguing. On one side there was a drawing of a human, a drawing of myriad animals, and two red bulbs, constantly blinking. With the object clutched in one claw, she scuttled under the softly crashing waves.

Despite talking into the early hours of the morning, Barry woke early. He kissed his wife Helen on the forehead before stealing out into the predawn dark. The full moon was over the northern sky, its reflected shine lighting the way. Even with not much sleep, he felt refreshed.

Helen is right—I never should have kept it all from her for so long . . .

A smile came to him, and he let gratitude for her wisdom and strength flow through him.

Where would I be without that woman?

Barry resumed walking, holding his hands out to touch sugarcane leaves in his passing. His mind was dragged away, mulling over plans, possibilities, and outcomes. He barely registered stepping out between his crops, and his eyes cleared as something unexpected appeared. Barry cast about, checking to see he was where he thought.

Fischer's sands stretched out before him, the two new fields making two brown rectangles on the yellow and white landscape. In the corner of one of the fields, the one to his right that Fischer had fertilized, sat a section of fully grown sugarcane.

"What in Demeter's harvest . . ."

His legs walked toward the anomaly unbidden, his mind unbelieving despite the proof being directly before his eyes. He reached out, grasping one of the stalks.

It wasn't just fully grown—it was the largest stalk of cane Barry had ever seen.

"*Huh . . .*"

A small laugh bubbled from his throat, and he shook his head with a smile.

"And he doesn't even like farming . . ."

With this discovery, the plans in Barry's mind shifted. He walked toward the closest sugarcane stalk and pulled it from the ground—well, he tried to. The cane held firm, so he redoubled his efforts. A grunt escaped him, and he felt the roots beginning to give. Finally, with a last tug, the stalk came free.

He stumbled backward as the last root snapped, then took a few steps back as he regained his balance. He lifted the sugarcane, inspecting the roots; they were the thickest he'd ever seen, looking more like the roots of a sapling than those of Tropica's staple crop.

A taproot sat in the middle of the tangle of nutrient-gathering tendrils, wider than one of Barry's stout fingers.

He grabbed it in his hand, assessing its sturdiness. "No wonder it was so hard to pull out. . ."

It was firm, once more reminding Barry of a tree rather than a crop. Barry smiled to himself.

With this, the first stage of our plans should be easy as sowing seeds.

Barry placed the sugarcane on the ground, walked over to the next stalk, and braced his legs.

He started tugging.

Helen cracked an eye as she heard the front door close. Getting up with a grace belying her age, she scurried to the window. She peeked her head around the corner, watching her husband disappear between two rows of sugarcane. With a smile, she wished him all the luck in the world.

Helen knew that if Barry had known she was awake, he'd likely have stayed and spent time with her. As much as she liked that idea, she also knew he'd work through his complicated emotions quicker if he got outside among his treasured fields.

You're a simple man, Barry—and I love you for it.

Helen also couldn't sleep, excited as she was. Her whole body seemed to hum with the information it now held, the energy making rest and relaxation an impossibility.

She made her way to their back door and collected a bucket before heading to the well. She'd known Barry was hiding something but waited for him to tell her when he felt comfortable doing so. The awakening wasn't enough to have unsettled him, after all.

Barry was a pragmatic man, and they'd already discussed what they'd do should one of them happen to awaken—nothing, of course. They'd tell no one and change nothing. It had been a hard lesson to learn, having lost her brother to the capital. The thought immediately brought her down, so she redirected her thoughts.

With these plans . . . if things go well, maybe we can one day rescue him.

She tied a rope around the bucket's handle and lowered it down into the well. Perhaps because she was still waking up, or maybe due to the scope of their plans, negative thoughts blossomed.

What if he's already dead? What if he was too pigheaded to be a slave, and they got rid of him . . . ?

The moment she recognized she was catastrophizing, she cut the thought off at the root.

No. He would never give up. Wait for us, brother. We'll come for you.

CHAPTER FORTY-SIX

FLOOD

I woke from a wonderful dream, one in which I was surrounded by a veritable sanctuary of animals. My legs were inexplicably warm, and I opened sleepy eyes, glancing down toward them.

Corporal Claws slept atop my bed, letting out soft snores each time she inhaled. I stretched my arms, doing my best to not move and wake the peaceful otter. This proved a pointless gesture.

At seeing my raised arms, a crab leaped from out of sight, landing on my legs between the otter and me. Snips stared at me, her body shaking with excitement at seeing me awake. We made eye contact, and she rushed me. She hissed as a stream of bubbles flew from her mouth, and I petted her sturdy carapace with both hands.

"Good morning, Sni—"

A furred head darted beneath Snips's carapace, chittering and rubbing up against my chin and face.

"G-good morning, Claws!" I said, laughing as the two fought to get closer to me.

They reached an unspoken agreement after a little jostling, Claws nuzzling one side of my face, Snips sidling up to the other, blowing joyous bubbles.

"You too, Snips! Did you guys sleep well?"

They both nodded, a storm of hisses and chirps ringing out.

"Happy Sunday, ladies!" I said, sitting up and arching my back. "Not that I know what Sunday entails . . ."

I stood, stretching my hands toward the roof and delighting in the feeling of sleep falling away.

"What do you say we go rustle up some brekkie?"

With one hand on a crab, the other on an otter, I sat and watched the sunrise to the east. There was a red haze on the horizon, and as the sun crested higher, it painted the world an otherworldly color. A deep red turned to a light pink as the sun went higher and higher, slowly banishing the haze beneath its warming light.

"This might be the most beautiful morning yet . . ."

A soft chirp and hiss answered.

"I'm going to help out Barry again in his field today. What do you ladies have planned?"

Snips and the otter looked at each other, the former blowing questioning bubbles, the latter making a chirp of assent.

I cocked my head, but before I could ask, Snips pointed toward the saltwater pond.

"Ah. More excavation?"

They both nodded, and I smiled.

It's nice having friends so willing to help you create stuff . . .

"All right," I said, slowly standing. "Shall we go cook up these crabs? We'll all need energy for today's work!"

As I approached the fields after collecting a coffee and pastry, Barry, Maria, and Roger were already working. I glanced toward where we'd fertilized the crops and didn't notice any difference; the sugarcane stalks were still mostly hidden by the surrounding soil.

Duh. It's not like they'd grow overnight, Fischer, you goose.

Each had a hoe or shovel and were digging furrows between the rows of sugarcane.

"Is this for that watering method you mentioned, Barry?" I asked.

He gave me a broad smile. "Mornin', Fischer! It certainly is!"

"Where are my manners?" I said. "Good morning, everyone!"

"Good morning, Fischer!" Maria beamed.

Roger nodded in greeting and returned to his hoeing.

"So, what can I do to help?" I asked.

Barry pointed to the side. "There's an extra shovel over there if you want to help dig!"

"More than happy to, mate!"

Following my neighbors' example, I dug lines through the soil between the rows. We made short work of our field, and when the last furrow was finished, Barry called me over.

"Do you want to help and see how it works, Fischer, or do you have somewhere to be?"

"Mate, I'm fueled by coffee and a fantasy croissant right now—you point me at a job, and I'll smash it out."

Barry laughed. "I think I got about half of that, but I'll show you what to do."

Before following Barry, I turned to see Maria and Roger's progress.

Maria smiled and waved, so I waved back, while Roger studiously ignored me.

"So," Barry said, "we've dug the furrows between the rows, but now we need to dig a ditch connecting these fields and the well."

"Oh, *that's* what you meant by doing the watering with a well."

He raised an eyebrow. "What did you think I meant?"

"I, uh, kind of thought you'd dig up a well next to the field . . . ?"

Barry stopped walking and turned to me. He made a confused expression before bursting into laughter.

"Hey! I'm a fisher, not a farmer, remember—don't be surprised when I get things wrong."

"I-I'm sorry," he said between giggles. "It was just . . . unexpected, is all. Why did you think we were digging the furrows?"

"I don't know, man—that we'd dig that well, then collect water from it and pour it in the furrows somehow?"

I tapped his forehead lightly. "You're the thinky one; I'm the doing one."

He smiled and rubbed where I'd touched him. "All right, that's fair—at least when it comes to farming, anyway."

He led me on a path through the fields, and after not much walking, we arrived at a well behind Barry's house. It was the first time I'd seen their house, and I found myself entranced by its quaintness.

It was constructed of the same stone and mortar as in town, but unlike most houses, it had wooden detailing, lending it a much cozier feel.

"Love the house, mate."

Barry turned to me, radiating contentment.

"Thank you. Helen and I put a lot of work into it; it's our pride and joy. Well, Paul is our pride and joy, of course, but our home is a close second."

"Speaking of Paul, where's that little scamp been?"

"He's been helping his mom and tending to our fields while we work on yours. Speaking of, we should get to it—Roger and Maria won't take too much longer."

Barry led me over to a stone well, and I peered down. It was deep, only a glint of light reflecting off the water's surface around fifteen meters below.

"Barry . . ."

"Yes, Fischer?"

"That's pretty far down . . ."

"Yeah, the water table is low here—it's a real pain to pull so much water up with a bucket, but that's the method."

"That bucket . . . ?" I pointed at the bucket sitting atop the well's wall—it looked like it could hold five liters.

Barry nodded. I raised an eyebrow at him, looked at the bucket again, then back at Barry.

"Look—I know you're the farmer here and I'm in over my head, but something tells me pulling five liters out at a time isn't gonna . . ."

I trailed off as I noticed Barry's lip twitching. "You're fuckin' with me, aren't ya?"

He burst into laughter, holding the well for support. "Y-yes, Fischer," he said, still laughing. "I'm fracking with you, whatever that means."

I snorted at the butchered swearing.

Probably best to not correct him on that one . . .

"Man, you're getting better at that, Barry; I almost didn't see your lip twitching."

"My lip twitched?" He grinned. "Thanks for the tip—I'll work on it."

I shook my head, smiling and rolling my eyes. "Where do you keep the pump, Barry?"

He narrowed his eyes. "How did you know it was a pump?"

"Unless you guys have some sort of water-magic shenanigans going on, a pump is the only thing I know of that would get enough liquid up from this well to water fields. Need me to help you grab it?"

"I got it," he said. "Back in a moment."

Barry returned with a cart on wheels, the pump atop it looking surprisingly sophisticated for the semi-medieval tech of this world. The body of the pump was well crafted.

I eyed the long section of pipe attached; it seemed to be made of a brown, flexible plastic.

"What's that made of, mate?"

"You've never seen plastic?" he asked, genuine confusion crossing his face.

I considered how to answer. "I have," I said after a moment. "The line I use is made of plastic, after all—I just haven't seen it that color before. What's it derived from?"

"Your plastic line would be made of the same material, as far as I know. They crush linseed and refine the oil into this somehow."

"Huh. Neat . . ."

He shot me a look, but then shook his head, dispelling his thoughts.

"Would you be happy working the pump?" he asked, pointing at the wooden lever atop the main body. "I'll dig a trench and connect the fields."

I nodded. "Of course, mate—if you think you can dig faster than I can pump, that is . . ."

His eyes sparkled at the challenge, and without hesitation, he grabbed his hoe and started digging.

I walked over to the pump and turned the cart, facing the spout toward where Barry had begun his trench. I untied the pipe, and unrolling it as I lifted, dropped it over the side of the well. It fell, unrolling as it went and dropping into the water below with a soft splash. With a tentative pull, the lever of the pump came up; it was well oiled and made no noise or scrape.

I glanced to the side, saw Barry's trench almost rounding the crops closest to his house, and with a competitive grin, started pumping.

Good luck outpacing the torrent coming your way, mate . . .

"Frack me!" Barry said to himself, trying to incorporate Fischer's curse word. He picked up the pace as he saw the flood approaching, spilling over the sides of his trench he'd assumed to be deep enough. He had assumed wrong.

One step back at a time, he drove his hoe down into the ground and dragged it toward him, causing the earth to spill to either side. If the water were to reach him before he connected the trenches, it could flood his other fields, potentially killing off swathes of established plants by over watering.

Demeter's sharpened sickle—challenging Fischer was a mistake.

Barry had thought it was a safe bet; the water would soak the surrounding earth of the trench as it went, and only when the ground was sodden would it continue traveling further toward the fields. He didn't account for just how much water a single pump could displace when someone with Fischer's strength attacked it.

The water was gaining on him; Barry increased his pace again, working his entire body to dig as fast as he could. He checked over his shoulder; he was almost at the new crops, but the water was almost on him.

"Just . . . a little . . . more!"

He yelled the last word, slamming the hoe into the ground and dragging it back as hard as he could. His back foot fell in the lanes already dug into the crop and relief suffused him.

The relief was short lived, quickly replaced by discomfort. Just as he connected the trenches, the torrent of water hit him, spilling over his legs and throwing dirt and sand into his boots. He stepped aside and watched the water hit the rows dug between the sugarcane stalks; it spread out evenly, the flood dissipating between the multiple lanes. The sight of the water bringing life to the field washed away his annoyance, and he relished the calm it brought him. This calm, just as his earlier relief, was short lived.

Maria and Roger hadn't yet finished their field, and if the water in the first field had nowhere to go, Fischer's flood would wash the stalks—and all their hard work—away.

Barry sprinted, his shoes making squelching noises as he ran to finish the rows and connect the two fields.

"What is that fool doing?" Roger demanded, sweat pouring from his brow.

"He challenged me to a race!" Barry answered, digging a deep trench between the two fields.

"I think he's winning!" Maria said.

"Nope!" Despite the worry of all their work being swept away, Barry couldn't help but grin. "I won!"

"If these stalks get washed away," Roger said, "we all lose!"

"Best dig and stop talking then, Dad!"

Roger grunted, listening to the advice, but clearly not happy about it.

Barry connected the two fields and began digging another trench between the sugarcane stalks. A full third of the rows weren't yet dug, and unless they could get them done before the water spread this way, the earth would need to be reshaped, the stalks replanted.

We might actually need to get more soil and start over if it gets too out of control . . .

Despite their best efforts, the torrent of water was overwhelming. It flooded the first field in less than a minute and began flowing down the trench Barry had dug. They all continued digging as fast as they could; if they couldn't curb the flooding entirely, at least they could minimize the damage.

The water reached Barry, once more flooding over his boots and filling them with sediment. His fears had come to pass; the water started flowing up and over the sugarcane, carrying much-needed soil away with it.

Barry tried to focus on digging the trench, on minimizing the damage as much as possible, but as he saw the first stalk floating past on top of the water, his skin prickled with anxiety.

How many days will this set us back? Roger and Maria have no coin, and they need *these crops to sustain themselves . . .*

Barry's eyebrows furrowed, and he paused in confusion as the water seemed to dissipate, soaking into the surrounding soil.

Had Roger and Maria managed to lead the water off somewhere? He glanced at them, seeing them absolutely exhausted, but similarly confused.

A voice called out, and Barry breathed a sigh of relief.

"Did I win, Barry?"

CHAPTER FORTY-SEVEN

CONFRONTATION

"No, Fischer—you lost!" Barry called back, exulting in the relief of knowing the fields wouldn't wash away. He bent down, picked up the single stalk of sugarcane that had been lifted from the soil, and pressed it firmly back down.

"You fool!" Roger spat, stomping toward Fischer with sodden steps. "Do you know what you almost did? Do you know you almost ruined everything? Bloody heretical bloody idio—"

"Dad! You—" Maria began but was similarly cut off.

"Roger!" Barry boomed, the strength of his voice making Roger pause mid-step.

He walked toward Roger slowly, adopting a softer tone.

"Come with me for a moment."

"You know what he almost just did! Are you really going to—"

"*Roger,*" Barry said, something in his tone bringing Roger up short. "Walk with me."

Barry turned and strode away, and with only a little grumbling under his breath, Roger followed.

As Barry passed Maria, she raised both eyebrows at him, clearly impressed by his wrangling. She spun away, pretending to not notice her father walking after him as she studiously inspected the head of her shovel.

"Damn—Barry can be pretty intense, huh?" I asked.

"I've never seen him like that—neither has Dad, I'm guessing. That's probably why he listened to him . . ."

I shrugged.

"Guess he finally cracked it over your dad's attitude."

Maria winced, shooting me a furtive glance. "I really am sorry for that, you know—I try my best, but he never listens to me."

I waved her apology away. "It's all good. You have nothing to say sorry for. I've dealt with worse, and I know it's all probably stemming from the stress over your situation."

"Oh, no—he's always been a giant prick."

I snorted a laugh at the unexpected confession.

"Though," she said with a smile, "I have to admit he's been way worse since Mom got sick."

I nodded, figuring that to be the case.

Humans are volatile at the best of times, let alone when their loved ones—and very pride—are on the line.

"I'll win him over eventually—until then, he can call me whatever he wants. Sticks and stones."

She cocked her head. "Sticks and stones . . . ?"

"Yeah. You've never heard that? Sticks and stones may break my bones, but words will never hurt me."

"Wow—is that a common saying where you're from? It's quite profound . . ."

It was an effort not to laugh at the profundity of a children's rhyme. I hid my mirth by nodding sagely with pressed-together lips.

Roger glared his anger at the back of Barry's head. The leader stopped on the spot between rows of sugarcane, turning a calm gaze on Roger. Roger's face contorted at being ordered to do anything, and he fought down a snarl.

"Why are we letting this fool get in the way? He—"

"Roger," Barry said, cutting him off with a flat look. "I haven't known you for my entire life, but I think I've taken your measure pretty well over the years you've been here. The way you're acting now, lashing out at a man that's done nothing but help you, is entirely unlike you."

Roger felt a moment of guilt, but it quickly drowned beneath the weight of unbridled fury.

"He flies in the face of the gods themselves, Barry," he spat, leaning into whatever he could to justify his petulance.

"That's not what you're upset at, Roger. You know it, and I know it—I suspect Fischer knows it too, which is why he's giving you so much leeway with your constant insults."

"Then what am I upset at, Barry?"

"We both know what's got you so out of sorts, Roger. You're under an immense amount of—"

"*Say it!*" he yelled, cutting him off. "If you're going to challenge me, be man enough to speak it!"

Barry's mask of calm remained, and he slowly nodded.

"All right. You're lashing out because Sharon is sick, and you're financially—"

"Dying," he corrected, his face trembling. "My wife is dying, Barry. I expect you'd be angry too if Helen wasn't long for this world."

"I would," Barry said, "which is why we're having this conversation, and why Fischer hasn't told you to leave, and still helps you—even through your outbursts."

The reminder of his actions, alongside voicing his wife's true condition, made guilt, hatred, and self-pity join the raging flames of fury within him. He growled deep in his throat, picked up his hoe, and swung it with all his might. The tool traveled through Barry's almost mature sugarcane, snapping stalks and sending leaves flying. He swung again and again, each strike wiping out swathes of the crop. Finally, he swung it down into the ground, planting the hoe deep within the soil.

"So what do I do, Barry?" His voice was soft, his emotions deadened. "What would you do if it were your wife?"

"I don't know, Roger, but I think you need to work that out. I don't want you to come back until you've worked through your—"

"You'd cut me off? What will we do without the fields? We—"

"No," Barry answered, holding up a hand to forestall him. "Maria and I, and sometimes Fischer, will continue farming the land. I don't want you to come back until you've worked through your emotions—until you can genuinely thank Fischer and be around him without lashing out, I don't want to see you working his land."

"What gives you the right? Was this his idea? Is he not man enough to talk to me directly?"

"Again, no. Fischer is too kind, and would just let you continue insulting him endlessly. This is coming from me. Go spend time with your wife, Roger. Get your mind right. Then, and only then, should you come back."

Roger glared, wishing more than anything that Barry would swing at him. He craved violence, any outlet for the fire within. Barry's face remained calm, and, if anything, held compassion. Roger spat on the ground and strode toward Tropica.

Barry returned alone. I raised an eyebrow.

"No Roger?"

"No Roger," he confirmed. "I asked him not to come back until he sorts his feelings out. I've had enough of him lashing out at you."

"Oh—er—you didn't have to do that, mate. It's really all right—"

"No." Barry shook his head, his lips forming a line. "It's not all right, and I think he knows that too."

Maria sighed. "Maybe that's what he needs. Sorry you had to deal with it, Barry. It shouldn't be your problem."

He smiled at her. "It's fine. I'd expect him to do the same if I were acting out of character as much as he's been. We're neighbors, after all—right, Fischer?"

I grinned, my eyes crinkling. "That we are, mate."

"Well," Maria said, picking up her shovel, "should we get back to finishing these trenches? Maybe I'll go pump the water, though . . ."

She squinted at me; I grinned back. "Yeahhh. Maybe I should stick to digging . . ."

"I'll go work the pump," Barry said. "Are you two okay to finish the rows?"

I smiled at Maria. "You reckon you and I can handle a little labor?"

She nodded, then swept the loose strand of hair back behind her ear as she looked at Barry.

"I'm sure we can manage. Don't worry—I won't let Fischer ruin anything else in your absence."

"Like that, is it?" I leaned back in mock affront. "Looks like the bad attitude might be a family trait . . ."

"Oh, too far!" She slapped my arm playfully. "Don't compare me to that old grouch."

"I'll leave you to it," Barry said over his shoulder. "Though don't spend too long being handsy with each other—the water will start coming as soon as I get there."

Maria blushed an adorable shade of pink, the blood visibly rising beneath her tanned skin.

"You know, you're pretty cute when you blush."

"Don't tease me!" She slapped my arm again, harder this time, but still playfully. "Is harassing innocent young ladies part of your heretical doctrine? Not sure I'd have farmed your land if I knew you were not only a heretic, but a deviant, too."

She did pretty well at hiding her smile, but an echo of it teased the corner of her lips, and I beamed a genuine one back at her. "That's precisely the point! Hide your true nature until it's too late."

She let out an exaggerated sigh. "Well, it *is* too late to turn back now, I suppose. You win this round . . . *deviant.*"

She winked at me before picking up her shovel.

"I think that should be more than enough for the first watering," Barry said as he inspected the soil.

"Looks good to me, too," Maria said. "The stream you sent down was much more manageable than Fischer's river."

"Oh, c'mon! It can't have been that bad."

Barry took off his shoe and shook it; handfuls of sand and soil fell out, splattering wetly to the ground. Maria did the same, and I frowned at them.

"Well, you're not supposed to walk in it. That's user error."

"We didn't!" Maria pointed at me. "A certain *someone* sent so much water our way that it flowed over the trenches and into our shoes!"

"That just tells me you were digging too slow and weren't fast enough to get out of the way."

She blinked at me. "Barry."

"Yes, Maria?"

"I think I'm beginning to agree with my dad."

He nodded. "I'm certainly starting to see Roger's point of view."

Roger held his wife's hand as he thought of the distant past, of times when she was healthy, their family whole. The sickness was a slow thing, yet in hindsight, had come on so quickly. It seemed like one day she was fine, the next, she was bedridden.

She slept most days away after ingesting the alchemist's elixirs; today was no different. She was so thin now, and as Roger held her hand in his, his heart broke anew. The very world was wrong without her presence, and he longed for nothing more than her laugh to once more echo off the walls of their home. The hand not holding hers balled into a fist, and he clenched his jaw.

It wasn't fair. None of this was as it should be.

Barry's conversation flitted through his mind, causing his thoughts to wander toward Fischer, and his lip to twinge involuntarily. He had been taking out his emotions on Fischer—that, at least, he could admit—but wasn't it deserved? Weren't the other villagers the ones in the wrong for readily accepting a heretic?

He looked down at his wife, took in her gaunt face and pitted eyes. The flame within Roger roared back to life.

The moon was mostly full, but a thick carpet of clouds blocked out its white light. With the sun long ago set, and as darkness spread over the land, Barry began his work. Before he could process his harvest, he had to oil and repair the machine. It had sat unused for the last few years after one of its internal shafts snapped, and something had always stopped Barry from repairing it—until now.

He opened up the side, replaced the metal shaft with the one he'd bought from Fergus, and began oiling. He was careful with his application, removing each component and lubricating only where strictly necessary. When he was finished, he closed the side panel again.

He picked up a stalk of sugarcane, wound the crank on the machine's side, and fed the stalk into it. The sound of fibers snapping and metal cogs turning rang out through the night. A soft trickle joined the symphony of sounds as the first drops of sugarcane juice fell from the juicer, collecting in an empty pitcher.

In the capital city of Gormona, in a seldom used room, a screen blinked to life. Once more, there was no one present to turn it on, nor anyone there to witness the anomaly. Still, it printed information out, screaming the words into the void.

New milestone! Barry has learned leadership!

CHAPTER FORTY-EIGHT

DECORATION

Sergeant Snips, first chosen of master Fischer, sentinel of these lands, and de facto leader of the local rock crab population, collected some rather lovely looking rocks. She'd picked them for their pretty color, and as she inspected the opalescent stones already piled up, she nodded.

Master will like them.

She and her squad of crabs hadn't collected many. Well, she supposed that was relative, but for her project, she needed much more than the meager collection piled before her.

Another of her crabby subordinates walked from the crevice and dropped two more of the rocks onto the pile, nodded to Snips, and walked back toward the cave.

They were located on Fischer's land, in a little-explored area of the southern coast. One of the rock crabs had flagged it for Snips herself to check in on, and her initial annoyance was quickly replaced by wonder, perhaps even a little gratitude. Not that she would tell the masochistic crab that—it was the same one that kept getting itself stuck in the crab pot, and she'd started to suspect it was doing so on purpose.

With a bubbled sigh, she set off into the crevice to look for more of the rocks—the sooner they collected enough, the sooner she could return and get started on the construction.

Making her way down into the hole, she pushed past three other crabs making their way up with stones, each of them cowering before her magnificently spiked body.

She followed the curve down to the left, opposite the tunnel to the right she'd taken earlier; the rock crabs were going that way, and she didn't want to squeeze past them.

As she followed the crevice, she found more of the opalescent rocks, each of which she picked up. Her mind wandered elsewhere as she moved.

She was thinking of how much she loved the master, and of ways to get Corporal Claws back for the stones she constantly threw, when she found it.

As Snips rounded a bend, she arrived in a large room. There was some sort of lump in the back of the space, and as she peered at it, light exploded, blinding her in the dark depths of the crevice. She fell back and peeked at it through the gap of her claw, squinting to block out as much light as possible.

An opalescent rock stood in the middle of a cavernous room, glowing with a spectrum of different colored lights and bathing each wall in its splendor.

Unbidden, her legs scuttled forward, drawing her in toward the stunning sight.

Different aspects of light reflected from the rock, moving through churning water and causing the colors to dance.

Her eye adjusted to the shift in brightness, and with a start, she realized the light wasn't coming from the rock; the sun was high above, its light beaming down through a crack above and bouncing off the opalescent boulder. The realization struck her with a sense of awe, and as it did so, the light faded, returning the world to darkness.

This stone, this source of such beauty, had sat here for untold years, undisturbed and unmolested. She had come along at the perfect moment, the single glimpse of time each day that the sun would hit the stone and reveal the hidden magnificence of this place. She couldn't wait to steal it.

Master will love it.

Corporal Claws was lazing in the sun, dreaming of the perfect rock. Her mind's eye imagined a quintessential stone, almost perfectly spherical, but with a small dip in one side that made it fit the paw *just right.* If anyone had been watching her sleeping form, they would have seen her whiskers quiver in unbelieving delight. As it so happened, someone was.

Sergeant Snips upended the pot of seawater, pouring a steady stream of the cold liquid over the corporal's illustrious face.

"*Glbgglgblblgglb,*" Corporal Claws said, the stream of water flooding her mouth when she tried to screech in outrage. She opened her eyes, and through the stream of water assaulting her, saw a crab blowing rather self-indulgent bubbles.

Diving to the side, spluttering and reaching into her pocket, she withdrew a rock. Before she even hit the ground, her forepaw slung out, the stone flying and colliding with Snips's forehead.

Tink.

Snips rubbed her carapace, and Claws prepared for the crab's retaliatory charge, but it never came. Instead, Sergeant Snips gestured her over with a claw as she walked toward the ocean. Corporal Claws, expecting a trap or some such underhanded tactic, followed at a safe distance, bristling at the rude awakening.

Snips lead her to the south. They passed the river mouth and continued further on. They had almost reached the mountains to the south, but before they could, the treacherous crab turned toward the rocky shore.

Corporal Claws chirped to herself in confusion when she caught sight of the other crabs. They were outside a great crack in the underwater cliff of the shore, surrounding and protecting a gigantic pile of pretty rocks.

At the sight of the treasures, she swam past Snips, intent on inspecting the treasures. They were reminiscent of the stones held within oysters but were larger and of poorer quality. Still, in other ways, they were *better* than the tiny oyster stones. For one, they were large, about the size of the rocks she favored; she knew she could use one to crack open shells, bonk predators, or even as a projectile against her shelled nemesis, Snips.

One crab scuttled forward, clacking its snippers at her.

She cocked her head.

Crab wants to fight?

Before Corporal Claws could act, Sergeant Snips approached the crab, chastising it with a tap on the head. The assaulted crab scuttled back, dipping its head in apology. The otter nodded, accepting the show of deference. In her magnanimity, she only pocketed two of the stones out of respect for the crab's showing of respect.

Sergeant Snips led her into the crevice, and they followed a winding path deep into the cliff face. The ambient lighting got dimmer as they went, the only source of said light coming from thin cracks in the crevice above.

Snips rounded a bend, and stopping in place, gestured for Claws to move past. For a moment, Corporal Claws thought she had made a mistake, and that she'd walked right into the crab's trap. That brief bout of paranoia disappeared when she saw the rock in the middle of the room.

A crack in the crevice above had been recently widened; debris of the slate stone was piled to one side of the space. The light of the day above highlighted the boulder, and her eyes went wide.

Before she knew it, she was at the opalescent stone, and she ran her paws over it. It was . . . beautiful.

Each day since she'd awoken, Corporal Claws had understood more of the world she occupied. It was an entirely alien experience, yet completely welcome. She felt more whole, like each bit of information brought her a bit closer to completion. Alongside her growing awareness, she understood more of Sergeant Snips's bubbles and gestures each day.

So when Sergeant Snips joined her by the glittering stone and blew a stream of bubbles, accompanied by a slew of gestures, Corporal Claws understood her.

She wants my help to lift the rock out . . .

Claws nodded, chirped, swam to the surface to get a lungful of air, then darted back down through the column of water.

With both powerful pincers, Snips hefted the stone out of the sand and walked toward the wall. A full half of its size had been obscured beneath the ocean floor, and Claws swam under it, helping her hard-shelled rival get to the sheer rock.

When they got to the wall, Snips started climbing it, her spindly legs digging deep into its surface and easily taking hold. Corporal Claws helped hold it steady, her powerful body pushing it further toward the surface. The boulder stood no chance against their combined efforts, and they easily pushed it up and over the side of the crevice above.

They both crawled up beside it, and Corporal Claws couldn't take her eyes off their resplendent haul. The sun shone through the rock, sending rainbows of light out to color the surrounding slate. She held a paw to it, taking comfort in its sturdy touch. She pulled a rock from her pocket, one of the ones she'd requisitioned from the pile below. Holding it up, the light did the same thing to the stone, just on a much smaller scale. Snips blew reprimanding bubbles, and Claws just chirped, shrugging.

What was she supposed to do—just leave the rocks? That went against everything she knew.

To change the subject, Claws gave a questioning chirp.

Snips nodded, and together, they moved the rock back toward the ocean.

From atop her glittery throne, Corporal Claws reassessed her opinion on the brown-looking crabs that served under Sergeant Snips. Despite their relative inadequacy, they had their uses—such as carrying the opalescent boulder currently serving as her chair.

Snips walked alongside the other crabs, her lone eye diligently roaming the seascape for any threats. As they traveled, Snips explained her plan, and Claws couldn't help but admit it was a good one.

Her moment of leisure ended when they returned to Fischer's shore; both Claws and Snips headed for the saltwater pond.

As per Snips's plan, they resumed their excavation, making the hole deeper and altering its shape. As they worked, the crab squad collected the rest of the iridescent rocks, making a pile of them on the sand.

With a clack and a bubble, Snips told Claws to stop, and they both climbed the wall, peering down at what they'd made so far. The pond was significantly deeper, the sand having been scooped up and out by their combined efforts. Before, the sand had filled in over time, and the hole had, hour by hour, gotten shallower. So began the next step of Snips's plan.

Using previously collected rocks—those of the normal, bland variety—they laid a bed of stones along the bottom and side of the pond. At first, the placement had been haphazard, but as the normal rocks diminished, each stone was placed with deliberate care.

Next, Snips gestured at a collection of larger rocks, all plain, but much bigger than the others. Claws's head tilted all the way to the side as she considered the stones.

She let Snips place most of them, unsure of what she intended to create, but jumped to help in lifting the largest few—they were bigger than the massive opalescent boulder, and even with Snips's impressive strength, their size made them unwieldy.

Finally, it was finished, and they appreciated their accomplishment together. The entire pond was lined, a mesh of dark stones holding back the sand. In the center, Snips had created a cave, the stones placed ingeniously to make a tunnel that was deep and winding yet structurally stable.

Claws wondered about its purpose, but she didn't have long to consider; it was time for Corporal Claws's favorite part of the plan, after all: *decoration.*

They collected the opalescent stones, and with careful deliberation, spread them intermittently over the carpet of rocks. They glittered in the afternoon sun, casting colorful reflections. The darker stones drank in the light, but that didn't diminish the scene's beauty.

Snips tapped Claws on the shoulder, and when she turned to look at the crab, Snips pointed toward the ocean, where the boulder awaited them. Together, and with help from the squad of crabs—who were largely ineffective but tried their darnedest—they walked the opalescent boulder to the center of the pond.

Snips had left a dip in the top of the constructed cave; the boulder easily settled into it, a final testament to Snips's planning prowess.

The sun, high above, came out from behind a wispy cloud, transforming the world. Its rays beamed down, hitting the boulder and painting the landscape. The colors were contained within the walls of the pond, the shifting spectrum of light a stark contrast to the sandy vista beyond.

Snips took a moment to appreciate what they'd built. She hoped her master would love it, and that its other, more important purpose would be achieved.

At that thought, she felt a pulse from the pond's center, right where the giant stone sat. She peered at it, trying to make out what it was.

Then, her concentration was shattered by a voice behind her.

"W-what?"

Claws and Snips both turned, eyes widening.

CHAPTER FORTY-NINE

MEDICINE

W-what?" I asked, rather dumbly, by my estimation. Corporal Claws and Sergeant Snips both turned to me, their eyes going wide. They had excavated the pond further. It was twice as deep as the last time I'd seen it and was lined with dark rocks. Semi-opaque, opalescent stones broke up the tedium of plain rocks, the sun's rays hitting them and casting rainbow colors. In the middle of the pond sat a boulder; the prismatic reflections coming from it were overwhelmingly pleasant.

Claws dashed for me, running the length of the wall to reach me. She rubbed up against my leg, chirping happily. Snips also approached, but with a hesitant gait. She looked almost bashful, her eye averting and flicking back to me as she moved.

"You two did all this?"

Claws nodded vigorously; Snips nodded shyly.

"It's . . ."

Snips looked up at me, blowing bubbles of hesitation.

"It's *beautiful!*"

Her bubbles paused, and her body froze. She blew a tentative bubble of questioning, asking if I meant it.

"Snips . . . how could you think I'd dislike this? This is *amazing!*"

She slowly nodded to herself, and as the realization sunk in that I wasn't upset, she rushed to me, all her trepidation replaced by a stream of happy bubbles and hisses. I petted her carapace as she rubbed a spike-free section of it against my leg.

Corporal Claws chirped, demanding the same attention. With a laugh, I obeyed, delighting in their affection. I cast my eyes back up to the pond, the sea of light on the black and gray floor filling me with awe.

"How did just the two of you do this so quickly . . . I was only gone for half a day . . ."

Snips gestured at part of the pond and made a so-so gesture. I looked closer; five rock crabs sat at the bottom, apparently resting. I hadn't noticed them before under the barrage of visual stimuli.

"They helped?"

Snips shrugged, repeating the same 'kind of' movement with her one claw.

I walked down into the water. It was cool, and without a second thought, I stripped off my outer clothes and sat down. The water came up above my shoulders, and I let out a sigh. My companions joined me, both fighting for space in my lap.

I let out a contented noise. "This is just what I needed after a morning of labor."

From my position, I noticed the cave for the first time. The pearl-like boulder was nestled atop large black rocks, and on this side of the pile, the entrance was visible.

"Is . . . is that a cave, Snips?"

She nodded, blowing proud bubbles.

"What's it for?"

She considered for a moment, but instead of telling me, blew an anticipatory steam.

"I have to wait and see?" I asked with a grin.

She nodded.

"All right—keep your secrets."

A soft breeze blew, its temperature perfectly matching the moon's light shining down from above. Sergeant Snips, chosen of master Fischer, entered the house. She approached the master's room, finding her target within. She poked it. Claws let out a sleepy chirp as she raised her head, half-lidded eyes opening to peer at Snips. She gestured for Claws to follow, holding one pincer to her mouth, telling the otter to be quiet. Corporal Claws glanced at Fischer, and seeing him still asleep, took Snips's meaning.

Corporal Claws couldn't contain her curiosity, but each time she chirped in question, Snips simply gestured for her to keep following. Her sleepiness had long since dissipated, and the further they got out into the bay, the less she could contain her growing anticipation.

Snips remained silent until they arrived at a cavern deep below the water of the bay. With a small stream of bubbles, she told Claws to wait. The crab produced a small fish, scuttled toward the entrance to the cave, and threw it just outside. Then she settled down beside it, holding completely still. Corporal Claws sat, watching with swelling curiosity.

Is Snips . . . hunting?

Something poked out of the cavern, and Claws's eyes focused on it sharply. An orange stick poked out, moving up and down in the water. It extended further out, slowly, inquisitively, and a realization struck Claws. It was a sea snipper—a *giant* sea snipper.

The thing continued walking out, lured from its home by the fish Snips had placed. One of the sticks on its head had been cut off recently; a nub remained of the severed appendage, which had only grown back slightly.

Snips is going to kill it?

The sea snipper's body was entirely out of the cave now, the moonlight from above showing all of its form. It was twice as long as her own length, its body thrice larger.

Claws imagined the taste of the giant creature, and just how much flesh must be held within its mighty shell. Her mouth salivated.

The sea snipper drew closer to the fish, and its doom. The remaining stick atop its head—and two smaller ones below it—moved chaotically in every direction, tasting the water and watching for predators. Snips bided her time; she moved not a muscle, intent on waiting for the sea snipper to get even closer.

It reached the fish, lazily picking it up with a massive claw and drawing it to its mouth. The giant crustacean took a single step back toward the cave, and Snips attacked.

Faster than Claws could even register, Snips's pincer shot out, clamping and releasing a shockwave that could be felt from her position ten meters away. Sand flew from Snips's position, a small cloud billowing from the detonation site.

Claws's eyes went wide as a newfound respect for Snips's power took root deep in her psyche. She'd assumed previously that even if Snips were to attack her, to catch her despite their speed differences, that they'd be on equal footing if it came to a fight. She had assumed wrong.

The sand began to settle, revealing Snips under the giant sea snipper. The creature was unharmed—unconscious, but whole. Claws cocked her head in confusion, and Snips gestured for her to help. Following the instruction, Claws approached, also getting under the limp body. Snips pointed, and with blooming understanding, Claws knew where they were going.

The lobster's awareness—as limited as it may be—returned in the blink of a compound eye. It scanned its new surroundings. It was within a cave, and following base instincts refined over millions of years, withdrew further into it.

The water here was acceptable, and there was a delicious smell present. Its antennae moved without thought, locating the source of the food—it was in its claw. Content, it brought the claw to its mouth, happily chewing on the fish it found there.

Barry took a deep breath, willing the cool morning air to wash away his remaining sleeplessness.

It worked partially, but his nerves were still frayed. The first sign of light had just begun to poke over the eastern sky, the rays heralding the sunrise to come. He'd hoped that first light would increase his wakefulness; it only made his eyelids heavier.

After his work last night, he'd found himself unable to sleep, his mind trapped in a storm of thoughts. He breathed the breath out, knocking on the door before him as he did so. Before he finished exhaling, the door was thrown open, and a pair of similarly sleepless eyes narrowed.

"What do *you* want?" Roger demanded. "If you've come to demand an apology, you can shove it right up your—"

"I'm here for Sharon, Roger," Barry said, cutting the diatribe off at the root.

He held up his satchel. "Helen and I prepared a concoction of herbs and roots. This has nothing to do with yesterday."

Roger's nostrils flared, his mouth tightening, but then he stepped aside.

"Maria!"

His daughter poked her head around a corner. "Yes, Dad? Oh, Barry! Good morning!"

"Good morning, Maria," Barry said, stepping inside. "I've brought some medicine for Sharon."

"Oh! Come with me!"

At least one of us is chipper this morning, as Fischer would say, Barry thought.

Maria led him to a bedroom door across from a basic kitchen, opening it gently and entering.

Barry followed, his heart breaking as he saw Sharon. He'd never known the woman personally but had seen her around the village when the family had first arrived in Tropica.

The person he saw laying in the bed was a shadow of the memory he had in his mind. She was stick thin, her body that of a woman decades older than her actual age. The ever-present smile he had pictured in his mind was gone, her visage sunken and gaunt.

"Mom, I've brought Barry to see you."

Sharon opened her eyes, peering up to look at him. Her gaze seemed to shift right through him, her eyes unable to focus.

"Barry . . ." she said, a mere repeating of the word, rather than a name that held recognition.

"He's brought medicine for you, Mom."

Sharon blinked, unresponsive, and Maria's lip quivered. As soon as the despair appeared, the daughter swept it away.

"I'll help you sit up. Here."

Maria bent, easily lifting Sharon upright with one arm as she placed pillows behind her back with the other.

"It's good to see you, Sharon." Barry opened his satchel, removing the container that held the juiced sugarcane. "My wife helped me prepare some medicine to help you heal."

He popped the lid, kneeling down to be at her height. "You don't have to drink it all, but anything you can get down will be of great help."

He held the open container to her mouth, and whether by cognizant effort or instinctual reaction, Sharon pursed her lips and brought them to the opening. With great care, Barry poured a little of the juice into her mouth.

Sharon swallowed the first trickle, the muscles of her throat and chest clearly visible beneath her paper-thin form as they worked to ingest the liquid. Trickle by trickle, swallow by swallow, Sharon drank the juice.

It was a long process, but all involved were patient, and Barry didn't want to rush her, lest she cough up a single drop.

When most of the liquid was gone, only a quarter of the juice remaining, Sharon shook her head and closed her eyes.

"Tired . . ." she whispered, leaning away and back into the pillows.

Swift as a flood, Maria removed the pillows and eased her mother down onto the bed. Sharon stirred, opened her mouth to say something, but her eyes glazed over, then closed. Maria pulled the blanket up, tucking her mother in. She kissed her on the forehead and smoothed her hair back.

Barry stepped from the room, waiting for Maria to join him. When she exited, her face was pointed down, and she breathed out a sigh. Barry went to put his hand on her shoulder and console her, but then she turned. Her eyes welled above a happy smile, and as she looked up at him, a tear fell down her freckled cheek.

"She hasn't drunk that much of anything in weeks, let alone medicine. What was in that, Barry?"

"It's of Helen's making, but you don't need to worry about what's in it—as long as Sharon drinks it, we'll make more and bring it over."

She nodded, a strand of hair falling from behind her ear that she immediately swept back.

"Thank you, Barry."

"No problem at all."

He glanced toward the door. "Well, I'd better get back to the fields. I'll see you out there?"

She nodded again. "See you out there."

As Barry was leaving, a hoarse voice called his name. He turned back to see Roger, who was looking out a rear window, his back turned.

"Thank you."

Barry smiled at the man's back. "You're welcome, Roger. I'll be back with more tomorrow."

He left with hope in his heart.

Please work . . .

He shook his head.

No. It will *work.*

CHAPTER FIFTY

LOBSTER

I'd seen Snips excited before, especially when waking me up, but the fervor with which she woke me this morning was at a previously unseen level. She and Claws both led me toward the saltwater pond, running ahead of me on the sand and urging me on with varied noises, gestures, and bubbles. The sun had not yet risen above the eastern horizon.

The landscape slowly lightened, the growing brightness a promise of the day to come. A cool breeze tickled my body as I jogged to catch my two over-enthusiastic friends. As they both once more turned and sprinted, flicking up sand in their wake, a smile came to my face and gratitude swelled up, suffusing my entire being.

We arrived at the pond, and I looked down in confusion. It appeared the same as the previous day, if a little dimmer because of the lack of sunlight hitting the opalescent stones. I wondered about our purpose here.

Do they want to watch the first rays of daylight hit the stones together when the sun rises?

"What has you two so excited?" I asked.

Corporal Claws ran in circles, only pausing intermittently to stare at me in anticipation. Sergeant Snips's entire body shook, her excitement unable to be held within. She scuttled to the far wall, the one closest to the ocean, and picked something up. She held it high above as she ran back to me, and I looked down at it, my brow furrowing. It was a dead fish with a vicious line in its head that told me Snips had ended its life in an instant.

"Er—is that breakfast? You want to cook and have brekkie here?"

She shook her whole body in the negative, a slew of bubbles streaming. With her eye locked on me, she threw her claw up, launching the dead fish high into the air. It arced backward, plummeted toward the pond, and hit the water with a large splash.

I blinked.

What . . .

Corporal Claws sprinted to the side of the pond, her head darting between me and where the fish had landed. Sergeant Snips hissed bubbles of joy and scuttled beside her, urging me on with one clacker.

"Uhh, you guys know that fish is dead . . . right?"

They stared at me in confusion, so I continued.

"That fish can't live in there—it's already dead . . ."

Claws chirped, Snips hissed, and each of them pointed at the water where the fish had landed.

Curious, I stepped up, squinting to make out the fish. It had sunk to the bottom of the pond—it sat there before the cave entrance, unmoving and most definitely dead.

What do they expect me to—

Movement from the cave's mouth cut off my thoughts, and what looked like a stick poked out. It waved up and down in the water, searching for something.

Is that . . .

The creature emerged further from the cave, and my suspicions were confirmed.

It was a lobster—a *giant* lobster. The thing's body was enormous, as round and long as a large dog. It had pincers like Jaws of Life; the claws had grown humongous in what had to have been a long life.

The lobster slowly left its den, making its way toward the dead fish. One of its pincers reached out, grabbed it in its vice-like grip, and ponderously made its way back to the cave.

Just as the lobster disappeared from sight, the sun rose high enough to crest the walls of the pond. A trickle of refracted light spread from the opalescent boulder, but the sun continued climbing, and in a matter of seconds the entire pond was bathed in a colorful, swirling rainbow.

I sat down atop the wall, my feet dangling down toward the water.

"W-where the hell did you find it . . . ?"

Corporal Claws pointed out at the bay, and Sergeant Snips nodded.

The first thing I thought of was Sebastian and the Cult of the Leviathan.

They would lose their minds over such an old lobster, and it isn't like the lobster has ascended or evolved or whatever . . .

I shook my head.

No. Sebastian is too unstable, and I can't trust him to not harm such a magnificent creature.

I nodded to myself, and a broad grin spread across my face as I imagined the giant lobster joining us by the fire.

It will stay here with me—with us.

I bent down to pet both Claws and Snips.

"You two are amazing, you know that? Is this why you built the cave in the first place, Snips?"

She nodded, happily bubbling as she leaned into my touch. Turning, she stared up at me, blowing questioning bubbles and tilting her carapace to the side.

"Yes, Snips, I was pleasantly surprised—thank you."

She shimmied as I scratched her head again, my joy resonating with hers.

I turned to look back at the pond and its radiant color.

"Man, I could just look at this all day."

Both animals nodded beneath my touch, agreeing with the statement.

I let out a content sigh as I stood. "All right. I have some more farming to do today unfortunately, so I'll have to get a move on. Should we have some brekkie first, though?"

Snips hissed her assent; Claws chirped hers.

I ruffled my shirt, and struck by inspiration, made my straw hat sit askew atop my head.

Nodding to myself, I crossed my arms and joined the line. It moved quickly, small as the line was, and I met the owner's glare with a proud smile.

"What it do, Lena? How's ya week been?"

Her glare deepened into a scowl at my gibberish, and she pointed at the counter.

I placed the mug there, my grin not disappearing for even a moment.

"This is the last one," she said, turning her back to me.

"Oh, I'm well aware! I'm going to miss your bubbly personality, but it'll be nice having coffee even closer to home."

Her body went rigid, and she looked at me over her shoulder.

"Coffee closer to home . . . ?"

"Oh, George didn't tell you? I organized a coffee machine for Sue, so this is the last one I'll be buying from you—your business is well established, after all, and I'd feel morally better about supporting a smaller business."

I had all of Lena's attention now, and her nostrils flared as she stared down at me. "There's another café opening in Tropica?"

"Kind of?" I shrugged. "It's a bakery, but they'll be adding coffee to the menu with the machine's delivery tomorrow."

Lena snorted, then unleashed an ugly laugh.

"A *bakery?* Good luck making a profit with coffee on the peasant side of town."

She shook her head and turned back to her machine.

My grin broadened. "Oh, I'm sure it'll be easy for Sue to make a profit—she received the machine for free."

I'm not sure a bolt of lightning could have had more of an effect on Lena than my words did.

She visibly jolted, her body shooting upright. Her arm shot forward, and the milk intended for my coffee spilled all over the machine. Her body spun at a speed I didn't know she possessed, her eyes going wide as she looked at me.

"What do you mean, 'she received the machine for free'?"

"Yeah, I thought the productivity of the workers would go through the roof if they had caffeine, so I organized it for her. She should be able to offer it at prices even the 'peasants' can afford. Exciting, right?"

"C-caffeine?" she asked, her face going white.

"Yeah, you don't know what caffeine is? Not gonna lie, Lena, that's a little embarrassing."

I raised an eyebrow, unable to stop myself from taking the little dig at her. "It's the molecule in coffee that gives it the stimulating effect."

"R-right . . ."

"Yeah, anyway, I really have to get back and help some of those peasant farmers out today—would you mind getting my coffee ready . . . ? The day is wasting, and all that."

She nodded, her eyes far off as she turned and started mechanically making my beverage.

Did I go too far . . . ?

I shook my head, taking a sip of my coffee and delighting in the energy even its flavor seemed to grant me.

Nah. That felt like just the right amount of sass.

I took a bite of the croissant I'd collected from Sue; it was buttery and flaky, cooked to perfection. I demolished the croissant, and just after taking my last sip of coffee, walked from between two of Barry's fields.

"Good morning, guys!" I called to Barry and Maria, who were both unloading a cart.

"Morning, Fischer!" they both replied, smiling at me.

"So, this is the mulch we're using?"

"Aye." Barry pulled a bale down from the cart. "Sugarcane mulch. It's good for most soils, but especially handy for the sandy soil in these crops."

I nodded. "What day is it today, by the way?"

"Trueday," Maria said, beaming. "Only one more sleep until Fielday."

I added the information to my mental calendar.

"I am *so* excited about Fielday tomorrow. I won't need to head to the north side of Tropica or deal with that toad Lena anymore."

Maria raised both eyebrows at me, and I cocked my head in question.

"You know, Fischer," Maria said, "I think that's the first negative thing I've heard you say about anything or anyone since arriving here."

I grimaced. "Yeah, that was decidedly unwholesome—my bad. I've been responding to her personality with unerring positivity, but I think it took its toll on me over time . . ."

"Well, one thing is for sure," Barry said. "If Fischer says she's a toad, I believe him."

Maria snorted a laugh; the harsh sound coming from her small frame brought me immeasurable joy.

"What about you guys?" I asked. "Aren't you excited about having coffee?"

Maria's jubilation turned somber in an instant, and Barry glanced at her, his mood similarly shifting. I looked back and forth between them.

"Er—what am I missing here?"

Barry gave me a half-hearted smile.

"The day when the merchant comes is the day we sell our goods."

"So . . . you get money? I'm not seeing the issue, mate."

"It's also the day we have to pay our taxes to the village—they've been increasing every other month, and an increase tomorrow could be disastrous for some."

The medicine . . . I realized. *Roger and Maria are still struggling, and if their income is brought any lower . . .*

"Well, you never know, guys." I tried to give a reassuring smile. "Maybe the taxes will go down—regardless, I've already offered to help with the medicine should you be unable to afford it, Maria."

"It's not that," she said. "It's just that market day is a painful reminder of the rising cost of living and doing business."

She shook her head, forcing a grin onto her face as her hair slipped from behind an ear. "I'm hopeful that Barry's medicine will have more of an effect than the expensive elixirs, anyway."

"Wait, Barry's medicine?" I asked, raising a brow. "You made medicine?"

He shrugged. "Helen's father was a member of the Cult of Growth, and he passed down a great amount of knowledge of herbs, roots, and their natural uses."

"The Cult of Growth . . . ? They're not trying to raise a sentient tree, are they?"

Barry shook his head with a smile.

"No, Fischer—though I think they'd be beyond pleased if a tree somehow ascended. They believe that with the cultivation and study of plants, they can use that information to create medicine to help humans ascend."

"Huh," I said. "That might be the most sane sounding cult yet."

"They mostly focus on using their knowledge for good—they provide remedies to common ailments at a fraction of the cost that the Cult of the Alchemist does."

I turned to Maria.

"Do you think the medicine helped at all?"

"I think so! She managed to drink most of it. Oh! I forgot to tell you, Barry—Mom did something amazing after you left."

"She did?" Barry asked, his eyes gaining an intense gleam. "What happened? Tell me everything."

CHAPTER FIFTY-ONE

WILLPOWER

The air thickened around me. The chill morning breeze stilled, and the warmth from the sun seemed to vanish as if a cloud obscured it. I glanced up, seeing not a single cloud in the sky, then looked back at Barry. His eyes were fixated on Maria, and she stood like a mouse beneath a predator's gaze.

"B-Barry?" she asked, the word soft.

As soon as the air had shifted, it changed back, and Barry shook his head.

"Sorry. I'm just really interested in the medicine's effect. We might be able to adjust the recipe if something happened when Sharon drank it."

Maria swallowed, giving him a half-hearted smile.

"I-It's fine, Barry. After you left, she sat up and asked for food. She'd fallen asleep by the time Dad brought her food, but still, that she requested it is a great sign—she hasn't done so in months."

Barry rubbed his chin in thought, and he stared into space, clearly thinking of adjustments he could make to the medicine. With the quiet, I let my brain process what had just happened.

What in the anime protagonist, Xianxia master's aura was that? Did I imagine it, or did Barry's stare actually make the air change?

I blew air from my nose, smirking at the idea.

Who cares? As long as no evil sect or big bad enemy guy shows up, it won't change my way of life.

"What do you think, Barry?" Maria asked. "Is it as good a sign as it seems?"

"It is," he said, still rubbing his chin and staring into the distance.

"Do . . . do you think you need to change the recipe at all?"

He looked at her, seeming to come back to himself.

"Oh, uh, yeah, I think it'll need to be adjusted. I'll talk to Helen about it tonight, and we'll bring some of the new recipe around tomorrow morning."

Maria smiled and nodded, the effect of Barry's aura-adjacent shenanigans long forgotten.

"Well, if you can deal with all that later, should we spread the mulch?"

Barry sighed, looking at the sky and smiling as he did so. "Yeah, that's a great idea." He turned to me.

"You know, we probably don't need you here anymore, Fischer. We can handle this menial work if you have something else to take care of . . ."

"Nonsense!" I walked toward the cart. "I'm here now, so I'll gladly help out!"

* * *

We spread the final bale together, each taking some to shake loose and layer around the stalks of sugarcane.

"You know, Barry," I said, "it's a real shame not everyone is as fast as you and I. I'm happy to help, but when someone else in the field isn't carrying their weight, it's just a little disappointing having to—"

A wad of mulch hit me, exploding against the back of my head and sending yellow plant material and dust particles everywhere. Surprised as I was, I breathed in through my nose, and immediately regretted my doing so. I ran from the cloud, coughing and spluttering. I squinted through narrowed eyes, not wanting to get any dust in them. Barry was trying to hide a smile, and Maria had her hand held to her mouth, trying and failing to keep the laughter from bubbling up.

"I . . . I . . ." I sneezed. "I have—" I sneezed again.

"Ahhh!" I yelled, rubbing my face all over and blowing out through my nose. I stepped back, trying to get as far as possible from any more particles, and caught my heel on the last half bale. I fell over, and when I opened my eyes, all I saw was the blue sky above. Maria's giggles grew, and Barry was making a whining noise as he tried to hold his in.

"Oh, that's funny, is it?"

I got to my feet with vengeance in my heart. I picked up two handfuls of mulch from the bale and turned my squint on Maria.

"How fast can you run?"

She fled, her laughs rolling out over the fields as I chased her down.

"You're sure I can borrow it, Barry? You don't need it today?"

"I'm sure, Fischer. Just bring it back by nightfall—I'll need to water the fields with it tomorrow morning."

I bent down, picking up the handle of the cart Barry's pump sat atop with one hand, lifting the wheelbarrow and shovel onto my shoulder with the other.

"Thanks, mate. I appreciate it."

I set off toward the forest with a growing smile.

Do those two think they're the only ones that can prepare a surprise?

When I loaded the last barrow-full of dirt, the sun was high overhead, its rays peeking through the forest canopy as wind blew the leaves and branches. I pushed the wheelbarrow back toward Barry's, my mind swimming with how I'd landscape my creation.

Should I only partially decorate it in case the water drains?

I picked up a handful of soil from the wheelbarrow and squeezed it, condensing the mass into a small ball. It was cool and moist, reflective of the forest's environment. I smiled to myself.

No, if I want to surprise Sergeant Snips and Corporal Claws, I'm gonna have to go all out.

I continued walking, a myriad of possible materials and layouts running through my cerebrum.

I placed the last rock down and stepped out of the pond. My head tilted back and forth as I walked around the hole, assessing my landscaping from every direction.

Inspired by Snips and her saltwater pond, I'd increased the size of the hole I'd previously dug. It was almost double its original size, only just a little smaller than the one my animal pals had made.

With how much dirt I excavated, roots had become visible. They were thick and sturdy, and I took care digging around them so they weren't damaged. They looked like natural logs extending from the walls of the pond and down into the floor, and I knew the fish I moved into here would appreciate the cover they provided.

I just have to remember where they are, so I don't get snagged . . .

Similar to Snips's and Claws's pond, I'd lined the floor and walls with stone. Unlike theirs, I didn't use slate rock from the coast, or the opalescent stones they'd discovered; I used river rocks, wanting the environment to be as natural as possible for the fish.

In the middle of the pond, I'd placed a gigantic log. It was propped atop a large river rock on one end, its natural curvature sending that side of the log poking up above where the water level would be.

The pond looked good, but it was missing . . . something—other than water and fish, of course. I knelt down and leaned my head against one hand.

"What am I miss—*oh!*"

I shot to my feet.

"It's missing plants!"

My eyes lit up as I caught sight of a small plant growing in the shallows. I rolled my pants up and walked down the riverbank. The water was cool against my legs; it was a welcome sensation after a morning spent moving soil, stones, and a particularly large log.

I stepped on the uneven river rocks with care, slowly approaching the plant's green underwater mass. It was thirty centimeters tall and wide, its leaves spreading out and moving languidly in the softly running water of the shallows.

I slowly reached both hands in, and gripping it firmly at the base, pulled with soft, testing tugs. The plant came free easily, and I lifted my prize from the water. It was much less impressive when removed from its wet habitat, but I knew it would appear beautiful again when I filled my pond with water.

I grinned. *Let's see what else I can find . . .*

My clothes were drenched and my arms were full as I made my way back to the pond, a veritable forest of underwater plants held to my chest. I was fueled by both excitement and anticipation as I traveled, and I reached my ongoing creation in a matter of minutes.

I set my load of plants down and began separating them into the different species. Along with the original type of plant I'd found—the one with long, billowing leaves—I found three other types.

The first grew in single strands, with small leaves fanning out from its stem. Each plant looked like a fox's tail when underwater, but looked like a rather sad asparagus when removed. I'd collected literally hundreds of the plant and couldn't wait to decorate with them.

The second was a plant that grew chaotically; its stems branched off in every direction, each individual section sprouting multiple others. The leaves of the plant looked like small blades of grass, and I suspected it would provide safety and cover for smaller fish and invertebrates.

The third, which may have been my favorite of the four collected, was what looked like a small moss. They grew in tiny patches—about ten centimeters in diameter. Despite their small size, they were beautiful, and when submerged, reminded me of the centuries-old moss you could find in damp rainforests.

I picked up the first species of plant, and with contentment radiating through me, made my way down into the pond.

"Well—that looks terrible." I looked down at the arrangement I'd settled on.

Without water, the plants I'd placed looked like someone had boiled spinach and thrown it around haphazardly; it was a rather sad sight.

I rubbed my hands together and glanced at the pump.

"Guess it's time to add the water and hope for the best."

I put one end of the flexible pipe at the bottom of the pond where there was no dirt visible, weighed it down with a rock, and made my way toward the river. I pulled the pump off the cart when I arrived, walked it down to the water, and placed it on a rock. Making sure the intake was far beneath the surface and free of obstruction, I began pumping.

On my third trip to check the water level of the pond, I was finally happy; it was almost completely full, only a small section of river stones poking up above the surface. The water was a little murky, and while I'd been hoping it poured clear, I knew that was an impossibility. Still, it wasn't anywhere as dirty as my worst fears, so I counted it as a win.

I appreciated the view for a moment longer, happy with the placement of the plants now that they were once more submerged. The green—even seen through slightly murky water—provided a welcome relief from the dark tones of the rocks, roots, and log.

"All right!" I said to myself, standing up and stretching. "There's only one more ingredient . . ."

I skulked through the sand, my heart beating and eyes roaming. If I were to be seen—to be found out at this pivotal part of the plan—my efforts would all be for naught. I slipped into a shadow, walking along wooden boards with silent steps.

A sound broke the silence, and I stopped, my whole body freezing. The sound came again, and I peeked around the corner, my eyes gazing out toward the sunbathed landscape.

Snips and Claws were sleeping by the campfire, the latter wrapped around the former's carapace. They were both snoring softly, one sounding like a dog, the other like a monster from the depths—I still found Snips's noises adorable, though. A smile came to my face unbidden, and I had no choice but to allow a moment of appreciation for just how damn cute they were.

"Not now, Fischer," I chided under my breath, "you've got fishies to catch!"

I resumed sneaking toward the rods.

I rushed toward the pond with my bucket of fish, knowing full well that they'd easily survive the trip, but finding myself unable to slow down. It was all too exciting.

I reached the pond and immediately bent down, carefully pouring the fish in. They disappeared instantaneously, darting off in every direction to parts of the pond where I couldn't see them. I dropped to my knees, held my hands up in prayer, and closed my eyes.

"Please don't die. I'd feel terrible if your lives were wasted."

I wished nothing but health and vitality for the pond and its occupants, and I took a deep breath, willing it to be so. I opened my eyes slowly, just in time to see the world shift.

CHAPTER FIFTY-TWO

TRANSFORMATION

In a room long since abandoned by the god that created it, something miraculous occurred.

A construct whirred to life. For centuries, this creation had lain dormant, lacking both the energy and parameters to perform its tasks. Well, except for a single instance in the recent past, but that was, most certainly, an anomaly.

Another construct—a harvester—had facilitated that single occurrence, and its profound ambition had destroyed it, making that task its last.

This time, the construct that even now whirred into life was operating on its own merit. Someone had met a set of intricate parameters on the world below, and so, it tried to complete the task set by its creator, harnessing what little energy remained.

The world the construct occupied had long been absent of the energy needed for it to operate, but when it reached out for energy, for the lifeforce needed to complete its task, it found wisps of power. If a machine could feel surprise, it would have.

The strands of energy were but a faint echo of what the world once held, yet the construct latched onto them, breathing in each bit of power it could tame. The lifeforce gathered in its crystal core, condensing then pulsing as the energy tried to escape its confines. The construct held true to its nature, continuing on with inhuman tenacity.

When the energy was condensed enough, and with a single effort of will, it funneled the growing power into a different segment of its machinery. The lifeforce shifted when it arrived there, turning into something physical.

The construct gathered one last wisp of power, harnessing and using it to send the physical manifestation spiraling down to the world below. With its task complete, the machine powered down. It lay dormant, waiting, and silence once more returned to the room.

The entire world pulsed a single time, as did my body. If I hadn't already been on my knees, I would have fallen down; I braced my hands against the ground, holding myself steady.

"Wh . . . what was that?"

I glanced up at the pond. The pulse had seemed to originate from it, as if it radiated from the log in the middle. What I saw was even more shocking than the pulse. The pond had transformed.

It was even larger than before, now taking up more area. It occupied the space where trees had stood, and somehow, the trees had been shifted to the side, roots and all. The previously muddy water was now crystal clear, allowing me a full view of the underwater landscape. The roots had grown in size, the rocks had changed to be uniform in shape, and the plants . . . *the plants!*

Each of them had grown an unbelievable amount, at least tripling in size. The foxtail plants drew my attention, their long stalks swaying hypnotically in the current.

Wait . . . the current?

Not just the foxtail—all the plants were moving, shifting in a current that didn't exist.

I felt the spot above my stomach where the pulse had hit me—the exact position where the same sensation had struck me at Fergus's forge.

"What the frack was all that?" I asked, stealing Barry's lingo.

I smiled to myself, letting out a quick breath.

"This world is too much . . ."

I leaned forward, looking for any fish.

I hope they didn't die from the pulse—I'm hundreds of times larger than them, and it rocked me.

There was a fish hiding near the log, its dark body standing out against the pale wood; it looked the same, and I breathed a sigh of relief.

The fish are safe. Good.

As I stood and got to my feet, I felt an unexpected weight on my belt. Kneading my pouch with one hand, I found something heavy. I squeezed it, and my eyes went wide.

"No way . . ."

I slipped it off, opened it up, and stared inside. Twenty-five gold coins stared back at me. They appeared exactly the same as the ones I'd received upon arrival in the Kallis Realm. One face showed a crown, the other a scythe. I bit one; it was gold.

I sat back down, hitting the ground with a thud. My eyes darted back and forth between the gold coin in my hand and the pond.

"What the frack . . ."

Corporal Claws was running through the sand, chasing a giant oyster. The mollusk was terribly fast, and each time she almost reached it, it would dash away, somehow escaping her grasping paws.

Something hard hit her in the head, and she opened her eyes, a sense of disorientation overwhelming her. She was face-to-face with a rather angry crab that was omitting soft *tap tap tap* noises.

With a glance down, Corporal Claws saw her back legs still trying to run after the mollusk, making the soft tapping noises where her pads hit the crab's carapace. Sergeant Snips bonked her on the head with a pincer again, and Claws darted away, putting distance between herself and the cantankerous crustacean.

She reached a paw into her pocket, withdrew a stone, lifted it high overhead, and . . .

A distant yell caught her attention.

"Snips! Claws!"

Her head spun toward the sound, cocking to the side in confusion. Fischer was sprinting toward them, both arms waving high to get their attention.

"Snips! Claws! You've gotta see this!"

Their impending brawl forgotten, they glanced at each other, back toward Fischer, then raced off through the sand toward him.

Corporal Claws had experienced a moment of anxiety at Fischer's arrival, but upon realizing how excited he was, her worry morphed into anticipation. Snips blew bubbles of curiosity as they ran through the forest, and Claws chirped her agreement.

Fischer had a wide smile plastered on his face.

"You'll have to wait and see!"

They passed countless trees as they ran over the grass, the fading sunlight above taking the day's warmth with it. Claws noticed a clearing ahead, and her eyes locked on it. They emerged from the trees, and Claws's eyes were drawn down from the gap in the canopy above toward something entirely unexpected.

There was a body of water in the clearing, the type that Fischer called a "pond." She walked toward it, bending down to peer within. The water was crystal clear; she could see everything beneath the water's surface. It called to her, demanded her presence. Without a second thought, she slipped beneath the surface.

She swam between plants, delighting in the way small fish darted from her. She chased one, not intending to catch it, but exulting in the emulated hunt. The fish swam under the log in the center, and she let it go, turning her attention to the plants instead.

A patch of one that looked like a series of animal tails swayed hypnotically, and her body stilled as she took it in. There was something small moving on the leaves, and she moved forward slowly, filled with curiosity at what the tiny thing was.

A crustacean was nestled between the leaves. It had a long body like a sea snipper but lacked the giant pincers. Small appendages worked feverishly to remove specs of algae that it then shoved in its mouth. It was entrancing, and she watched the creature work for a long moment.

Something to the right called to her, as before when she was outside the pond, but even more insistently. She swam toward it, touching both front paws to the log. It offered something to her, something unexplainable and alien, yet it seemed . . . benevolent.

She climbed atop it, walking its length toward the water's surface. Emerging from the pond, she walked to the top of the log and nestled between forking branches. It was as if it was made for her; it caressed her form, taking all the weight of her body.

Both energy and a deep lethargy hit her, the conflicting sensations not at all unwelcome, as one might expect. She looked at Fischer and chirped a single time, letting her eyes close.

I'll rest for a moment, then I'll go have dinner with master . . . and the . . . crab . . .

* * *

I watched Corporal Claws gliding beneath the surface of the pond. I could tell she was enjoying herself; she moved languidly, played with a fish, and inspected the plants with great curiosity.

She swam toward the log, climbed it, and sank into the nest of branches at the top. Her body almost took on the properties of a liquid as she melted into the branches, like a cat finding the perfect sleeping spot.

Her eyes became lidded, and she let out a single chirp. She closed her eyes, and her head dipped down. Within seconds, she was snoring, the soft sounds slow and measured.

I looked down at Snips, whose eye hadn't stopped roaming since our arrival. I sat down beside her, resting a hand atop her head.

"What do you think, Snips?"

She turned to me, blowing bubbles of awe.

I smiled at her. "Glad I could surprise you back. Something crazy happened when I finished building it . . ."

She cocked her carapace in an unspoken question, and I told her what had happened. She looked thoughtful, her mouth moving slowly, as if tasting my story.

When I'd finished, she carefully stepped into my lap, lowering herself down to sit. I rested my hands atop her head, taking comfort in her affection.

"Do you think I need to worry?"

She shook her head minimally, blowing small, sincere bubbles. I hadn't even realized my body was holding tension, but my shoulders relaxed at Snips's reassurance, and I breathed out a sigh.

"With this, we have access to easy bait, and I have a feeling the fish are going to be thrilled living here."

She nodded, somehow nestling even closer to my legs.

We sat in silence, both embracing the calm that the pond granted. It wasn't just the view; the body of water seemed to radiate a soothing aura.

The forest grew cooler as the sun started setting over the eastern mountains. The gap in the trees above let us see the sky, and it slowly transformed from light blue to shades of orange and pink.

"Should we go get dinner, Snips?"

She stood, placidly lifting herself from my lap. With a scuttle toward the pond, she gestured at Corporal Claws, clacked one pincer, and blew questioning bubbles.

I smiled. "Nah, let's let her rest—she looks way too comfy to bother right now."

Snips appeared a little disappointed that she couldn't wake the otter, but accepted my words, and we both set off for our campfire with a leisurely gait.

Corporal Claws, for the second time that day, was having a rather odd dream. Unlike her chase of the oyster earlier, however, she knew she was dreaming. She walked through a place of blackness, ever drawn on toward some unknown source of power that called her. Her passage seemed never ending, yet it wasn't a frustrating endeavor.

The pulsing energy drew her on, ever promising a satisfying conclusion; this journey couldn't be rushed, and was not only beneficial, but absolutely necessary.

An unknowable amount of time later, she caught her first glimpse of it. On the far horizon, a brilliant source of light became visible. Spurred on by how close she was, she picked up the pace, trotting toward her destination. As she drew even closer, she realized she hadn't truly seen the source that called to her earlier—she merely saw the light it emitted. The nearer she got, the larger it grew.

By the time she reached it, the radiant orb was towering above her. A great sphere, bigger than anything she'd ever seen, engulfed her view. The surrounding area was white, the darkness long since banished. The orb pulsed incessantly, its power immutable, irresistible.

Corporal Claws paused, but only for a moment; she stepped into the orb's perimeter, allowing it to pull her in. Lifeforce flooded into her, and her eyes went wide as she was banished from the dream, returned to her throne above the pond. The power flooding her concentrated, and the transformation began.

CHAPTER FIFTY-THREE

FIELDAY

Corporal Claws felt, more than saw, the changes to her body. Her entire being expanded, shifting her perspective as it did so. Her claws grew, teeth sharpened, and muscles bulged, filling her with new strength. With a soft *pop*, her body condensed again, and her vision cleared.

She took in the surrounding scene. She was back on her perch atop the pond, the branches caressing her body. Moonlight shone down from above, bathing the scene in its blue-white light.

Corporal Claws wiggled her body, leaning back into her throne. While the log's peak was still comfortable, she didn't fit it as she did before. She held a paw up before her face and, with a mild flex, extended her claws. They were thicker, sharper, longer, and her instincts told her they were stronger, too. With a testing movement, she scraped her tongue along her teeth. They, too, were enhanced in the same way.

She chirped, and it sounded deeper, richer; the noise vibrated her chest and cut through the silence of the night. She wanted to go to her master to show off her new form. Almost as urgent was the need to show that dastardly crab that she, too, had an improved body. More pressing than both these needs, though, was a weariness that seemed to suffuse her.

Her body felt heavy, her eyes hard to keep open, her breathing slow. Before she knew it, sleep took her, and soft snores rang out through the evening.

I woke with an explosive burst of excitement. I threw the covers aside and jumped out of bed, stretching as an afterthought.

Fielday! It's Fielday!

The merchant was arriving today, and with him came things I'd been counting down the days toward.

"Coffee machine!" I yelled as I stretched.

A yawn escaped me, and I let it out in all its glory.

"And a bearing for my rod . . ."

Neither of my animal pals were in the room, so I made my way outside to look for them; I didn't have to go far.

Sergeant Snips was tending the campfire, adding wood and stoking coals. The predawn light of the sun bathed her in its reflected light, giving her spiked body a pink hue.

"Snips!"

She jumped and spun on the spot, facing me as she landed. Feet scuttled and sand flew as she ran to meet me.

"Morning, Snips!"

I bent to rub her carapace, and she blew content bubbles at my touch.

"Did you sleep well?"

She nodded, hissing her affirmation.

We were staring down at each other, both enjoying the comfort of the other's touch, when we were interrupted. A far-off sound echoed off the sandy flats, smothering the ever-present noise of waves crashing and birds calling. I spun toward it, and as I squinted into the distance, a grin spread across my face. Corporal Claws was inbound, a cloud of sand in her wake as she tore through the distance between us.

"Snips . . . ?"

She hissed in question.

"Does Claws look . . . bigger to you?"

I glanced down at my stalwart crab, and she cast a suspicious gaze toward the approaching otter. I returned my attention to Corporal Claws.

She was almost at us, her entire body somehow wiggling in delight as she ran, aggressively chirping.

"Yeah, she's definitely bigger."

When she was within rock-throwing distance, she launched.

"Claws—"

She collided with my chest, and I flinched back but easily caught her in my arms. I laughed as she writhed, rubbing her body against me and speaking in chaotic chirps I didn't understand.

"Claws! What happened?"

She was almost twice as big as the last time I saw her. She put both forepaws on my chest, leaned back, and peered down at me with obvious pride. I caught sight of her teeth; they were longer, sharper, vicious looking.

"Your chompers, Claws! They're bigger!"

She jumped down, puffing out her chest as she peered at Snips. Sergeant Snips scuttled up to her, cocking her carapace as she inspected Claws's improved body. Snips nodded a single time, giving her approval.

"Claws—did you evolve? How?"

She puffed her chest out even more, lavishing in the attention, then nodded a single time, gesturing back to the forest with one paw.

"The pond?"

Again, she nodded.

I bent down, unleashing a laugh as I picked her up. "You're amazing, Claws!"

She rolled onto her back in my arms, letting me scratch her belly. Her back paw shot out, kicking the air, doglike.

"Oh, is that the spot?"

I scratched harder, and her leg kicked harder. As it did, the claws extended from her rear paw, and my eyes went wide.

"Woah. . ."

Just as with her teeth, they had transformed, and I ceased my scratching, feeling the needle-like extensions.

"These are ridiculously sharp . . ."

With a flex, they withdrew, and she chirped in the affirmative before shooting a glance at Snips. Snips glared back, radiating indifference.

"Now, now, ladies."

I set Claws down, petting both her and Snips's heads.

"Don't be like that. I love you both, and you're both the guardians on this patch of land."

I looked at Snips. "You should be happy that our friend evolved and got stronger."

Snips dipped her carapace, blowing apologetic bubbles.

I looked at Claws, who had once more puffed her chest out.

"And you, ya little scamp—it's good to be proud of your accomplishment, but don't let your head get too big. Snips is your friend, and you don't need to show off."

Claws, too, dipped her head, letting out a sad chirp.

"It's fine—you don't need to apologize. I just want you two to remember that we're on the same team, that's all."

They looked at each other and both made begrudging noises of agreement.

"Good girls."

I rubbed both their heads, smiling down at them. "Now, before I head off to Tropica to see what this Fielday has in store, should we see what those new daggers of yours can do, Claws?"

Her eyes got a dangerous gleam, and she bared her teeth in the approximation of a smile.

Marcus, bringer of goods, taker of coin, and merchant extraordinaire, looked into the far distance with an expression that projected both wisdom and opulence. He had company this fine morning, and joined by such a grand associate, felt the need to inflate his own self-worth.

Marcus wasn't conscious of said inflation, of course; he merely felt bad when around the crown auditor. Artificially boosting his worth—even if in his own head—dulled the inferiority complex buried deep within; gifted as he may be as a merchant, his ability to read others didn't, unfortunately, extend to his own psyche.

He squinted a little, wondering if it lent his visage an extra air of mystery and contemplation. Unbidden, his thoughts drifted to something productive: there was a man awaiting two deliveries in Tropica Village. Marcus had never heard of him, yet this mysterious man, this "Fischer," was the receiver of both a coffee machine and no small amount of gold from the jeweler's guild. If the stranger was a noble, receiving fifteen gold wouldn't be too notable. But Marcus had done his research; there was no "Fischer" among any of the noble families. Whoever he was, he was either a noble with a false name or an upstart commoner who was business savvy enough to carve himself out a decent position.

Marcus grinned. Either way, it could present an opportunity for him to make gold. He would have to find a way to get on the man's good side.

As the sun peeked over a mountain, its warm glow drew him from his thoughts. From the corner of his eye, he saw the crown auditor watching him, so Marcus looked into the far distance once more, squinting and pouting to project his wisdom.

Theo looked at the overlarge merchant sitting beside him, trying not to laugh at the haughty expression he was putting on.

I wonder if he's aware he looks like he needs to go to the bathroom . . . ?

With a smile, he turned away from Marcus, focusing on the rising sun instead. It crested the mountains to the east, directly above the well-worn road their carriage traveled. With the sun came a welcome warmth, and he couldn't wait for the dew of early morning travel to evaporate under its glare.

Theo glanced to the side, seeing if Marcus still wore the same expression—he did.

"How long until we reach the next village, Marcus?"

The merchant didn't respond, still projecting his stupid face into the far distance.

". . . Marcus?"

"Ah, sorry, Theo." Marcus breathed out an exaggerated sigh. "The scenery of these distant areas can be breathtaking. What did you say?"

"I asked when we'd reach the next village."

"Ah, yes. Tropica. We'll arrive within the hour. Once we climb the forthcoming hills, we will see it."

"An hour, huh?"

Theo hadn't seen the ocean in years, and the thought of glimpsing its hypnotic movement brought up a surge of joy.

I'll have to soak in its beauty while I have the chance.

In afterthought, he remembered his responsibility to the crown, and he let out a small sigh.

After auditing the village, of course.

I stared wide-eyed at what remained of the log I'd buried in the sand for Corporal Claws to test her new body on. It hadn't merely been cut by the improved claws—it had been obliterated. Splinters of wood flew everywhere from the attack, and they now littered the ground all around us. She stared down at her paws, her eyes sparkling.

"Good lord, Claws . . ."

Snips let out a hiss of appreciation, nodding her approval at the powerful strike. She gestured with one claw at another log, tilting her head at me in question.

"You want to try, too?"

She blew bubbles of confirmation.

I grabbed another log and twisted it down into the ground, the sandy soil no match for my strength. Stepping back, I nodded for Snips to go for it.

Without hesitation, her right claw extended. A sharp crack split the air, and a white arc of energy shot from her. The aura attack traveled so fast I could barely see it, and when it hit the log, the world transformed into a shower of wood and splinters. Just as with the first log, this one wasn't cut; it was all but disintegrated.

"Unbelievable . . ."

Corporal Claws looked on with an assessing gaze, and after only a moment's pause, also nodded her head in acknowledgment.

I smiled at them, glad they could find some mutual respect.

"All right, girls—as much as I'd love to spend the rest of the day hanging out, I really have to get going."

My smile widened as they both waved goodbye, each as adorable as the other.

"I'll be back later, okay? I don't think it should be too eventful."

George, the lord of Tropica, took a deep breath, doing his best to calm frayed nerves. It was going to be an eventful morning.

"It'll be fine, George," his wife, Geraldine, said.

He wiped his hands on a cloth, unsure if they were sticky from sugar, sweat, or both. Probably both. She pressed her face against his back and wrapped her meaty arms around his impressive girth. He leaned into the touch.

"What would I do without you?"

"You'll never know, husband—I'm not going anywhere."

George took another deep breath—as deep as he could breathe, anyway—and let it out slowly.

"All right. Let us go address the peasants."

She patted him on the back. "There's my husband."

I joined the milling crowd gathering in the middle of Tropica. I couldn't help but raise my eyebrows at just how many were present. It was nearing hundreds of people, most of whom I didn't recognize—I wasn't even aware there were so many farmers living in Tropica.

I guess there are plenty of people that just keep to themselves . . .

"Fischer!"

I turned to see Maria striding toward me through the crowd, and I beamed at her.

"Morning, Maria!"

I glanced behind her, seeing a grumpy-as-ever Roger in her wake. "G'day, Roger. How are ya, mate?"

He nodded and grumbled something indiscernible, but I didn't let it kill my mood.

"I've been wanting to ask you something, Roger."

He narrowed his eyes at me.

"Yeah? What's that?"

"What day is it tomorrow?"

He squinted even more, which was genuinely impressive. I wasn't aware such a feat was even possible without closing them entirely.

"It's Fielday today . . ."

I nodded.

"Very true, but what day is it *tomorrow?*"

"Were you dropped on your head as a kid?"

"Dad!"

"What?" he demanded, turning to Maria incredulously. "That's the dumbest question I've ever heard, and he has asked some incredibly inane things."

She swatted him on the shoulder, and I laughed.

"Just humor me, Rodge—can I call you Rodge?"

"No."

"To humoring me, or to calling you Rodge?"

"Both."

Maria sighed.

"It's Moisday tomorrow, Fischer."

"Thank you. That's the last one I—wait, what? Moisday? I don't like that at all . . ."

So, I thought. *The days of the week are Sunday, Trueday, Fielday, Moisday, Crafday, Winday, and Resday . . .*

"See?" Roger said, gesturing at me with both hands as I rubbed my chin in thought. "Dropped on his head—there's no doubt about it."

I beamed a smile at him and Maria rubbed her temples, shaking her head.

"Have you heard the news, Fischer?" she asked, not-so-subtly changing the subject.

"What news?"

"George has a special announcement. We—"

"Thank you for coming, everyone!"

I turned to see George, standing on a box overlooking the crowd.

"I bring tidings that I believe you'll all find most welcome . . ."

Barry held the cup to Sharon's lips as she slowly drank the sugarcane juice. He'd insisted that Roger and Maria go on ahead to the village meeting, and after convincing them his hand was necessary to administer the medicine, even Roger eventually capitulated.

"Your husband is a stubborn man, Sharon."

Her eyes were still staring into space, but she continued drinking, downing the juice sip by sip.

"Your condition has him acting even more stubborn than usual, but I suppose any man would act the same. I'm not sure what I would do if Helen were sick."

She pulled back from the cup, having had her fill. Following Maria's instruction, he put the cup down and tried to ease her back onto the bed.

As he lowered her to the pillows, her body went rigid. Her hands scrabbled, finding purchase on his arms. She blinked, her mouth moving inaudibly as she gripped him. Her head turned, and she looked up at him. As he stared down into her eyes, they held recognition.

". . . Barry?"

CHAPTER FIFTY-FOUR

ECCENTRIC

The sun was midway through the morning sky, its warm touch and a cool breeze highlighted by the silence that spread over the crowd. George cleared his throat once more, closing his eyes to collect himself.

Poor bloke, I thought. *For someone with debilitating social anxiety, addressing all these people must be a nightmare . . .*

He started speaking, his voice shaky and hesitant. "As you all know, taxes have been progressively increasing in the past months . . ."

A soft murmur came from the crowd, a large collection of the present farmers both agreeing and lamenting the fact.

"I assure you, this was as the crown willed, and I understand your pain. No one has felt the pinch of decreased funds as much as I. You . . ." He spread his arms wide, encompassing the crowd. "The farmers of Tropica—you are the people that keep the village afloat through your hard work. The knowledge that you have been doing it tough has filled my heart with despair, and my every waking moment has been tormented by your plight."

As he spoke, George seemed to gain more confidence. His voice grew deeper and clearer, his body language more robust. Another murmur came from the crowd, this time with a notable tinge of hostility.

"But!" George yelled over the crowd's growing displeasure. "Today, we have news of tax relief!"

The murmuring shifted as people turned to their neighbors, whispering excitedly.

"Yes! It's True!"

George waited, letting the conversation swell and die down.

Man, he's actually pretty good at public speaking when he gets over his nerves. You go, George!

When the crowd returned to silence, he continued.

"It is with great pleasure that I tell you, the workers—nay, the very backbone of Tropica—that the taxes will be returned to the level of three years prior. You will now—"

The gathered farmers erupted. People yelled, whooped, hugged, and turned to each other, unbelieving. I glanced at Maria; she embraced her father. Roger held his daughter as she bounced on her toes, unable to contain her joy.

His lip curled in a smile, and I joined him, happy to see anything break through his exterior shell. His eyes locked onto mine, and seeing my mirth, his scowl returned, so

I laughed and looked away, not wanting to ruin their moment. Similar scenes played out throughout the square, and I bathed in everyone's excitement.

George waited patiently atop his makeshift podium, a benevolent smile fixed on his face. There was still an underlying hint of his anxiety, but it was mostly buried.

It looks like he genuinely enjoys delivering the good news. It's heartwarming to know the village's lord actually cares about the farmers' well-being.

When the noise died down again, he continued.

"That's right—your taxes will be one-third of where they'd climbed to. My contacts in the capital have also assured me that, going forward, the taxes will remain stable at that reduced rate for the foreseeable future."

Again, the crowd erupted.

". . . Barry?"

Barry's heart tried to jump from his chest, and his eyes went wide as he stared down at Sharon.

"Sharon . . . you . . . recognize me?"

A smile teased the corner of her lips, only slightly diminished by her gaunt frame. "Of course I recognize you, Barry. What an odd dream, though."

"Sharon . . . you're not dreaming."

She shook her head lightly, finding the idea humorous. "The System asking me to pick a name says otherwise. Usually I dream of Roger and Maria, but your face isn't unwelcome."

While the speed of her recovery was astonishing, the news of her awakening didn't shock Barry; that had been his plan, after all.

"Sharon . . . you're not dreaming. This is all real."

He leaned down, picking up a pastry Roger had left, and the rest of the sugarcane juice.

"Try to eat and drink as much of this as possible. You've been unwell for a long time, but I suspect you'll recover quickly."

She smiled and nodded, picked the pastry up with one hand, and bit into it.

As the sensations hit her tongue, her eyebrows furrowed. Her eyes looked at the pastry, around the room, then back up at Barry. She blinked rapidly, clearly processing the fact that this may not, in fact, be a dream.

He nodded. "It's real." Barry gestured around the room. "*This* is real."

He pointed back down at the croissant and cup of sugarcane juice.

"While you eat and drink, let me tell you the story of how this all came to be . . ."

Theo, the crown auditor, walked ahead of where the merchant caravan was setting up. He could hear voices in the near distance, both yelling and cheering. Intent on finding the source of such joy, he strode through the winding streets of Tropica, following the sounds of jubilation.

The houses and storefronts he passed were quaint, made of basic materials. Despite their rudimentary construction, he knew this to be the standard way of things outside of the capital, and just because they weren't as opulent as some of the mansions in Gormona, the families that lived within still experienced all the happiness, tragedy, and everything in between that came from existence.

If the inhabitants are always as happy as they sound now, Tropica might be my favorite village on this trip . . .

The sounds grew louder and louder, and he finally rounded a corner to find the crowd. People were still cheering and yelling, and they hugged each other, showing their love through embrace.

A person stood above the crowd, smiling down at the people. Theo took him in and noted the hint of fear hiding behind a mask of magnanimity.

His training as an auditor was extensive, as was the standard that said profession was required to uphold. He could read people better than most, and this person towering above the others—the village's lord, if his attire could be believed—was a curiosity.

I'll have to interview him and get to the bottom of it . . .

The village lord cleared his throat, commanding everyone's attention.

"That is all I had to say, and I thank you for your attention and continued hard work. I trust that the reduced taxes will benefit you all, and I am truly blessed to be able to deliver such good news."

Theo's eyebrow rose and he squinted at the lord.

Reduced taxes . . . ? What's going on here?

As if in afterthought, the lord raised a hand like he just recalled something; Theo saw through the act.

"Oh! I just remembered! As you all know, the merchant caravan will be arriving today, and with it comes a boon for the peasant—er—farmers and common folk of Tropica."

The gathered crowd grew quiet again, and the lord let the silence spread.

"I, George, have bought and paid for a coffee machine for your very own Sue to have—free of cost! Some of you may not even know what coffee is, but I hope that its affordable pricing, as well as its stimulating effect, will increase productivity and make even more money for your farms and families."

The crowd started murmuring, but only a few of them were making noises and gestures akin to surprise.

"I believe the merchant should be setting up west of the village even now, so I will leave you to your business." George gave a flourishing bow. "Thank you for coming."

The lord stepped down from his raised position and disappeared behind a building.

Theo watched the crowd as they once more turned to each other, almost as one. They discussed, speculated, and celebrated. One man in particular caught Theo's attention.

Among the crowd, there was a single person that stood out like a weed among the roses. He wore the basic clothes of a farmer, yet where others excitedly spoke of the event just passed, the anomaly simply stood and smiled at those around him.

He's happy for those around him, but not for himself?

Theo cocked his head, trying to work out why he stood out so much.

It's his garb, he decided. *He doesn't look like a crafter or merchant—he looks like a farmer. If a noble, merchant, or crafter were to experience compassion for others, that I'd understand—but another farmer?*

Too curious to leave it alone, Theo strode toward him.

I was so happy that my heart might explode. I smiled at everyone surrounding me, especially Maria and her father. Roger had repositioned himself to not face me, but I could still see the smile spreading across the side of his face while he hugged his daughter tight.

Not wanting to stare, I cast my eyes around, looking at the rest of the people. I found Helen and Paul off to the side, but there was no Barry in sight.

Huh. Maybe he's with Sharon, giving her some of that medi—

My thoughts stopped in their tracks as I felt a pair of eyes locking me down. I glanced to the side and found a man approaching, his gaze pinned on me. He wore clothes that presented a humble front, but they were anything but. Though constructed of basic materials, the cut and hem were immaculate, and no doubt prohibitively expensive.

My eyebrows furrowed. *What kind of person would buy such expensive clothes, then make them appear cheap? I have to—*

"Something confusing you, friend?" the man asked, giving me a genuine smile.

"Yeah—your clothes! They're made to look cheaper than they are, right? I don't get why?"

The man smiled and nodded. "You have a good eye. Are you perhaps a merchant? Is that why my attire offends you?"

My eyebrows shot up. "*Offends?*"

I laughed. "Mate, I want a full wardrobe for myself!" I tugged at my linen clothing. "These can be scratchy, but I don't want to buy the good stuff and stand out from my neighbors, ya know?"

The stranger paused, cocked his head, and just when the silence was getting unforgettable, he chuckled.

"I approached because you confounded me and I wanted to understand why, but all you've done is give me more questions."

I grinned. "Yeah, sorry about that, mate. I seem to have that effect on people. What did ya wanna ask? I'd be happy to help if I know the answer."

His face tilted in confusion at my vernacular, but that was intentional—I just couldn't help myself.

He pointed down at my shirt.

"Well, I wanted to know about your clothes, actually. You dress like a farmer, but you're not one, are you?"

"Nope!" I extended a hand. "I'm Fischer, by the way."

He took my hand and shook it. "Theo. It's a pleasure to make your acquaintance, Fischer."

"Pleasure's all mine, mate. But yeah, I'm not a farmer."

"What do you do, then?"

My curiosity for Theo grew as our conversation stretched on. He was trying to present this as a conversation, but it was anything but—it was an interrogation. I considered my response and decided lying would be a bad idea.

Theo seems exceptionally smart.

"I do heaps! Recently I've helped in the tailors, the smithy, made some jewelry, and now that I think of it, I *did* do some farming. The fields are on my land, but they're not actually mine—I'm letting a neighbor use them to supplement their income."

As Theo's eyes weighed me, they gave nothing of his intent or thoughts away. Finally, after what felt like too long a moment, he smiled and clapped me on the shoulder.

"It's truly a pleasure to meet you, Fischer—you seem like a good person."

Relief flooded me as I passed whatever test that was, but I paid it little mind.

"Likewise, Theo—what about you? What do you do? I also find myself a little confused by your getup."

"Oh, I can't tell you yet. I hope I'll see you later, though."

"Ahhh, you too . . . *mate* . . . ?"

Theo was already gone, having pushed through the crowd toward the north side of Tropica.

I crossed my arms, watching where he'd gone.

"Weird bloke . . ."

Theo let the positive emotions from his interaction with Fischer linger, genuinely enjoying having met a kind soul.

He's clearly some sort of eccentric noble or heir to a house.

He smiled at Fischer's odd speech and eclectic range of activities.

Whatever else he is, he's kind. That's all that needs to be said.

Theo pulled out his map, and after scanning the streets scrawled on the parchment, pinpointed his location.

Straight, then left, then right after two streets . . .

As he strode away, he banished the echoes of his interaction with the friendly eccentric.

It's time to ask the lord about these "reduced taxes" . . .

CHAPTER FIFTY-FIVE

CREMA

George closed his door behind him, letting out a sigh of relief. Geraldine rushed him from behind, wrapping her meaty arms around him.

"That was wonderful, George—absolutely perfect!"

He kissed her on the forehead, delighting in the way her plump skin pressed back against his lips.

"Thank Poseidon's girthy shaft that it's over—we can get back on track with managing the village."

She nodded and pulled back, looking up into his eyes. "Was Fischer there?"

The mention of his name made George's stomach twist, but he pushed the rising anxiety down.

"He was."

"Did he react at all to the news?"

"No—well, he did, but he only seemed to project joy at those surrounding him."

Geraldine glanced to the side, considering, and George knew what she was about to say before she even voiced it.

"So, have you put much thought into my theory?" she asked.

"Of course, my love. I'd dismiss nothing you said without giving it proper consideration."

"And?" she asked, cutting right through his platitudes. "Are you still convinced that Fischer is an agent of the crown?"

"I'm . . ." George paused for a moment to plan his words carefully before continuing. "I'm still unsure. What you say has some merit, of course, and it could all be a string of coincidences . . . but my gut still tells me there's more to it."

George caught her annoyance; her lip twinged minutely, but she swiftly schooled her expression.

"All I ask is that you give it more thought, husband. I still think his actions make little sense for a crown agent. If he were to truly be one, I don't think we—"

"You don't think we'd still be in power," George finished, smiling kindly so his words delivered no sting. "I know. His actions make no sense if he's a crown agent, but the things he seems to know, and the way he's conducted himself . . ."

George sighed, running his overly large fingers through thinning hair. "I just don't know what to think of it all."

She rested a hand on his arm. "Do you think you're scared of the possibility, because then we'd have discarded wealth for nothing?"

George's mind railed at the thought, but he'd be lying if he said that wasn't the case.

"That may be part of it, but it's mostly the feeling I get when interacting with him—it's like looking down a speeding cart. Not to mention his *wealth.* Where could anyone but an agent of the crown acquire the materials for his house, let alone the gold coin he presented me?"

Geraldine leaned into him, and he took solace in her touch.

"I know. He's shrouded by murky water, and none of it makes sense, but it's a vast world we live in, George. The gods may have abandoned Kallis long ago, but there are still plenty of mysteries to be unraveled."

A knock came at the door, causing both of them to jump. The three knocks were loud and firm, spaced out at even intervals. Geraldine shot George a look, then she moved to the side, hiding from sight.

Speaking of Fischer . . .

George took a steadying breath, and after letting it out slowly, opened the door.

Theo knocked three times. There was a long pause of silence before the door swung open and the well-endowed lord appeared in the doorway.

"Hello, Fisch—*oh.*"

George blinked.

"Sorry, I was expecting someone else. Can I help you, my good . . . uh, my good . . . ?"

The lord of the village's eyes grew wide, and his words failed him as he caught sight of Theo's outfit.

As expected of nobility—he knows the garb of an auditor. They gossip and rumor among themselves like old crones on Fielday.

"Hello, George. My name's Theo."

Theo held his hand out, and the lord took it without looking, his eyes still locked onto Theo's outfit.

"I caught the end of your announcement to the villagers. It was a rather enlightening speech."

Small beads of sweat sprouted from George's forehead like morning dew.

"It . . . it was?"

"Yes, very much so!"

Theo gave him a grin, and George withered beneath it.

"As you've no doubt guessed, I'm a crown auditor, and I've been sent here by the king to, well . . ." Theo flourished his hand, gesturing at the opulent house and the lord before him. "Audit."

"Y-yes," was all George could say.

"Do you mind if I come in?"

"N-no, please . . ."

George opened the door, and Theo stepped inside. He caught movement to the side, and he spun, finding the lady of the village. She was dusting a set of lavish curtains with her . . . *hand?*

She turned to him. "O-oh! We have a guest! Let me just . . . get some tea!"

Abandoning the curtains, she rushed toward and up the stairs as fast as her large frame could travel.

So you were listening in, huh? Good. That will make my job easier.

"Please, allow me to escort you to the lounge," George said.

Theo turned to look at him, noting his pallid complexion and the sweat now dripping down his brow.

He smiled at the lord. "Lead on."

I couldn't contain my excitement as we walked between fields of sugarcane and came upon the merchant caravan. I don't know what I'd expected, but it wasn't the scene that met us.

There were six wagons in total, each with their sides folded down and their wares displayed in organized rows. Villagers were already there, bartering and trading with the men working each shopfront.

As we got closer, the air smelled of horses, and I caught sight of a veritable herd of them tied up behind the merchant's setup. Five of the wagons were around the size of a medium-sized camper van from Earth, and the last one, likely the one belonging to the merchant, Marcus, was the size of a bus.

I eyed the wooden vehicle, marveling at its size. An open side provided a massive area to display goods, and a large man testing the weight of a crate caught my attention.

"G'day, Fergus!"

"Morning, Fischer!" the smith called back.

He walked toward us, turning his attention to Maria and Roger. "The tax cuts—I heard! Congratulations!"

He shook both their hands, and even Roger granted him a smile.

"Thank you," Maria said, beaming. "I can't express how welcome the news is."

"I can imagine." Fergus gave them a kind smile. "I know how bad things were getting, and I'm hoping this news will let the entire village breathe a breath of fresh air. Well, listen to me harping on—I'm sure you guys have some business to take care of."

He turned to me. "I'm in need of those arms of yours—I might need your help carrying Sue's new machine to the bakery."

My eyes lit up.

"Is that what's in the crate?"

He nodded, and I rubbed my hands together. "Let's go!"

Sue followed along behind us, a crate of wooden cups gripped in her hands.

"Are you sure you're good to carry those, Sue?" I asked.

"You're worse than my husband, Fischer. Just because I'm of the fairer sex doesn't mean I can't carry a few wooden cups."

She tucked in her chin, putting on a fair approximation of her husband, Sturgill. "*I'll go get the crate. You couldn't* possibly *lift such* heavy *wooden cups.*"

"I don't sound like that." Sturgill said, hefting his crate of coffee beans and sounding eerily similar to Sue's mocking tone. I snorted at the good-natured bickering.

"Did you only purchase one crate of coffee, Sturgill?"

"That's right—just the one."

"Did they have more?"

Fergus snorted. "I saw at least ten crates of the stuff in the back of one wagon."

"Can you afford more?" I asked Sue and Sturgill over my shoulder.

"We can," Sue answered. "You think we need more?"

"Oh, yeah. The merchant doesn't come back for another month, right? I'd buy *at least* two more crates."

"You really think we'll sell that much?"

"Think? I *know* you'll sell that much!"

After unpacking the coffee machine, I looked down at the parchment that held what were most probably the instructions. Despite Sergeant Snips's ongoing lessons, I still had no bloody idea what a single word said.

"Hey, uh, Sue?"

"Yes, Fischer?"

"Would you mind reading the instructions to me? I'm feeling a little dumb today—my eyes don't want to work."

She raised an eyebrow and smirked at me, but happily took the parchment.

"I suppose we can't all be blessed with the gift of perfect intellect."

She winked at me, and I laughed.

"I know, I know, I used all my genetic luck on my ridiculous good looks and unflappable attitude."

"And your humbleness," Fergus said as he fitted a pipe.

"That too!"

I rubbed my chin with great exaggeration, humming in thought. "Not to mention my flawless personality and chiseled abs."

A metal clang sounded as Fergus fumbled the pipe he was fitting, and he looked up at me incredulously.

"Please tell me you haven't been chiseling yourself."

I bounced on my toes as Sue turned a knob for the first time. Pressurized steam came out of the wand, and my excitement swelled.

"This is the one for frothing the milk, right, Fischer?"

"Yeah! It looks like that part works, now we just need to test the *really* important ones."

She held up the portafilter that would hold the grounds. "Fill this up, right?"

I nodded, gesturing at the coffee grinder.

The grinder was attached to the coffee machine, and she put the portafilter where the diagram had shown. She turned the crank, and the sound of coffee being ground was music to my ears.

She pointed at the group head—where the hot water would come from the machine and filter through the grounds—and cocked her head at me.

"I just attach the portafilter here, and turn this knob?"

"Yep! If we've done everything right, it should work."

She twisted the portafilter into place, and with one last look at me, turned toward the machine. One hand reached up, turning the knob so the water could rush forth.

The machine groaned as pressure was released and transferred; Sue's eyes turned to me, panicked, but I smiled and nodded at the machine. She turned back to it, and a moment later, the first drips of espresso fell into the cup below. The flow increased, and the crema-laden liquid dripped out, its golden hue making my heart sing.

"About now, Sue."

She turned the water off, removed the now-spent grounds, and held the cup to her nose, smelling it.

"Give it a taste," I said, hoping to see the look of glee on her face.

She held the cup out to me instead. "I think you should try the first cup, Fischer."

"Me? It's your coffee machine!"

"We wouldn't have the machine without you," Sturgill said, poking his head from the back of the bakery.

"Besides," Sue added. "I'm not sure anyone else would even know what coffee is supposed to taste like."

Even I had to admit that was a point—still, testing the fruits of her labor before she could felt . . . wrong.

"But it's the first one!"

"Exactly." Sue held it up before my nose. "No one else is more entitled to the first cup than you are. Please, Fischer. Let us show our gratitude."

I narrowed my eyes at her, smiling to offset the harsh expression.

"Using guilt now, are we?"

"Whatever gets the job done."

I laughed, accepting the cup as I shook my head.

I looked around at the arrayed faces—Sue, Fergus, and Sturgill, still poking his head from around the back, giving me a thumbs up and a smile. Maria had arrived not long ago, joining us after selling their goods. I wasn't surprised Roger was absent—he'd likely go home to check on Sharon. Despite that, and his grumpy demeanor, I still wished he were here.

"To all of you." I held the cup up in a toast. "My friends."

I received smiles in return, and I brought the cup to my lips.

The espresso, along with the rich crema, covered my taste buds. The coffee was still hot, its heat enhancing the flavors. It was nutty and flowery, with a hint of vanilla and chocolate. It was mildly acidic, with an even more subtle hint of bitterness.

It was neither the smoothest coffee I'd ever had, nor did it bear the most complex flavor profile. Despite these shortcomings, it was the best espresso I'd ever experienced. It tasted of friendship, opportunity, and new beginnings, and I drank the rest in a single mouthful, breathing out through my nose and aerating the flavors with my tongue.

I let out a long sigh. "Sue, that was the best coffee I've ever had."

* * *

Theo sat down at the table, scrutinizing a pastry George had set before him. It was covered in sugar and looked like just the type of thing the nobility back in Gormona would enjoy.

He brushed some of the sugar crystals aside and took a bite. The pastry beneath was buttery and flaky, and his eyebrows rose.

Not bad . . .

George pulled out the chair opposite Theo, fumbling it against the floor with his nervousness.

Theo stared at him, letting the silence stretch as he set the pastry down. The lord opposite him dabbed his brow, trying ineffectually to remove the perspiration.

"So, George, I take it by your reaction that you know why I'm here?"

George slowly nodded.

"I'm a crown auditor—you knew that by my outfit, correct?"

George nodded again, looking like a condemned man before the executioner.

"So, as I said when I arrived, I caught the tail end of your meeting with the villagers of Tropica."

Theo crossed his arms, pursing his lips as if considering how to put his next words. He looked around the room, letting George's anxiety morph into panic.

"Let's talk about the taxes, and how you've managed to lower them."

CHAPTER FIFTY-SIX

INTERROGATION

Theo stared the man down, waiting for a response. George cleared his throat.

"Well, you see, the thing is . . ."

George gesticulated, searching for the correct word or phrase; Theo was happy to let him squirm.

While Theo rarely liked the reputation his profession held—that of inscrutable and ruthless investigators—he didn't mind leaning into the stereotype when it got him what he wanted. And right now, what he wanted was to learn what was going on with Tropica's taxes. He kept George pinned down with his glare, and he steepled his fingers, leaning his elbows on the table.

His wife walked into the room carrying a tray laden with a porcelain tea set. She bustled over to the end of the table and set the tray down between the two men.

"Excuse my rudeness," Theo said. "I'm not sure I caught your name."

"I-I'm Geraldine."

"A pleasure. I'm Theo."

Her hands shook as she reached for the porcelain. "Would you like a cup of tea?"

"Please."

He looked between Geraldine and George, watching for any hidden communication. They studiously ignored each other, Geraldine pouring two cups of tea, and George accepting his with a small nod to the table. She crossed her hands behind her back, trying to hide their trembling from Theo.

"Can I get you anything else?"

"No, Geraldine. Thank you for the tea."

Theo picked up his cup and sipped it. It was black tea, mixed with passiona husk and something that tasted of vanilla. He breathed out a content sigh, happy to indulge in a more expensive blend of tea after traveling through small villages for over a week.

Geraldine left the room, once more leaving George alone with him.

"So, where were we?"

Theo tapped the table. "That's right! You were going to tell me how you managed to lower taxes. How did you manage that, George?"

George set his jaw and began talking.

"Well, the thing is . . ."

Seeing that George had collected his wits, Theo sought to scatter them again.

"Oh! I forgot a formality. You are aware of what a crown auditor is, right, George?"

"Yes . . ."

"And you're aware of the extensive training we're required to undergo, yes?"

George gulped. "Y-yes . . ."

"That's good. It means I'll have to explain a lot less to you. The formality that I'm required to tell you is this: I will know if you lie to me. If you conceal facts, twist words, or otherwise attempt to mislead me, things will only get worse for you."

The latter sentence, that of knowing about attempted misdirection, was a lie—it was entirely possible for people to slip information past an auditor if they were clever enough, but George didn't need to know that.

Theo leaned back, shaking his head and smiling to himself. "It's only an issue if you have something to hide, of course, which I'm sure you don't."

George nodded and smiled, but it held no real mirth.

"So," Theo said. "Feel free to explain the taxes. Sorry for interrupting you." He shrugged. "You know how the crown can get with the formalities."

George took another sip of tea, his hand shaking as he put the cup back on the saucer.

"Yes, well, the thing is, we raised the taxes temporarily."

Theo nodded, keeping his face unreadable.

"I figured that to be the case. Are they now lowered to the base amount?"

"Y-yes!"

Theo pulled a notepad and pencil from his pocket, scribbling down notes.

"Good . . . that's good."

He looked back up at George. "How high did they get?"

"Triple . . ."

Theo scribbled more notes, keeping his face still. "Triple. Got it."

He set the pencil down, crossing his fingers on the desk in front of him.

"Did you know that I was coming to Tropica? Is that why you lowered the taxes today?"

"N-No! I swear on my life!"

Theo watched him closely, analyzing his words.

He's telling the truth . . . fascinating.

"How long have the taxes been raised?"

"Th-three to four years . . ."

Theo drew on his pad, set the pencil down again, and stared into George's eyes.

"Was it triple the rate of tax for all those years?"

"N-no! It was only the last two months that it was so high."

"The skimmed taxes—what did you do with them?"

George reached for his handkerchief, wiping the bullets of sweat from his face.

Theo could tell he was stalling—thinking of how to word it while still telling the truth. He let him.

"Well," George said, then took a drink of tea to ease his dry-sounding throat. "It went toward many things. Most recently, I bought a coffee machine for the village to use. I organized for the owner of a bakery to sell the coffee at a rate affordable for all the peasants."

"That's good," Theo said, drawing again. "Using extra taxes to benefit the common folk isn't unheard of . . ."

George jumped at the lifeline.

"Right! We took extra money, but we've been putting it all back toward the village."

Theo raised an eyebrow. *That was a lie, but that's hardly surprising . . .*

He said nothing, knowing silence to be the most effective tool in an interrogator's arsenal.

George, no doubt realizing he'd been caught in a lie, rushed to continue.

"W-well, not all the funds have been given back toward the village. Much was invested in commodities that we speculated would go up in price . . ."

Theo waited to see if George would continue; he didn't.

"Are you still in possession of these investments?"

George's eyebrow twitched, and a muscle in his neck tensed for a fraction of a second, a hint of genuine anger breaking through his anxiety.

"No. They were lost to the sea."

Theo's brain went into overdrive following the lord's words. They were true.

They invested in something they speculated would go up in price, and they lost them at sea?

"What were these . . . commodities?"

George drank from his cup, stalling. "Pearls," he eventually said, anger creeping into his voice. "As they're a non-renewable precious stone, we believed they would only go up in price."

"I see."

Theo drew on his notepad some more, making precise and measured strokes with his pencil.

He set the writing utensil aside and looked back up at George.

"Have you spent any of the taxes on personal expenses?"

The village lord set his jaw and cast his gaze down.

"Yes."

"What did you spend them on?"

"Upgrades to our home, and pastries."

"It's not his fault!" Geraldine called, bursting into the room and rushing to George. Theo watched her calmly as she gripped her husband's shoulders with shaking hands.

"Explain."

"I—I wanted more! It was my fault! If you have to drag anyone back to the capital, take me!"

"Geraldine!" George pushed his chair back and stood, his eyes going wide.

"I'm the lord of Tropica, so if anyone has to take the fall for my mistakes—"

Theo cleared his throat, slicing through their objections.

"Why don't you both take a seat?"

George sat back down immediately, and Geraldine pulled out the chair beside him. They held hands, and with his wife beside him, Theo could see George's anxiety recede, if only a little.

He looked between them, keeping his gaze neutral. "From what I've heard, there's no reason for anyone to be punished at this stage."

George opened his mouth to speak, but nothing came out, and his brows knitted together in confusion.

"There isn't?" Geraldine asked, her eyes wide as saucers.

"Not at this stage, no."

He opened his notepad again, looking over what he'd jotted down.

"You'd hardly be the first lord of a small village to misappropriate funds . . . but let me be clear."

Theo put just the right amount of judgment into his voice. "Your actions have gone against your oath to the crown, and should you be caught doing so again, the full weight of His Majesty's justice will be brought down upon you. In fact, had you not put so much of the taxes back into a service for the village, both of you would be coming with me back to the capital. In chains."

Geraldine's jaw trembled, and she gripped her husband's hand harder.

"A s-service?" George stammered.

"Yes. A service."

Theo glanced down at his notepad.

"The coffee machine. I believe it will both benefit the villagers, and potentially increase the future tax yield for the crown. It was a savvy move, one that demonstrates your care for your charges, and your commitment to His Majesty."

"O-of course!" George all but yelled. "Even before you arrived, we recognized that our past actions were wrong, which is why, with the delivery of the coffee machine, we lowered the taxes to the amount set by the crown."

Theo nodded at the statement, hearing the truth it held. "Good to hear."

He stood, collected his things, and gave them both a small bow. "That should be all for today. I'll be staying in the village until the caravan leaves, so I may come see you again tomorrow morning."

Geraldine stood in a hurry. "Y-You're staying? Do you need somewhere to sleep? We have plenty of spare rooms, and you're more than welcome to spend the night with us. It might not be up to the capital's standards, but you'll find it more accommodating than staying with the mercha—"

"That would be lovely," Theo interrupted, walking out of the room. "Thank you."

"We'll prepare a room!" George said, also rushing to stand.

Theo hurried down the stairs and stepped from the home into the morning air. He stood on the step, inhaling the fresh, salty air.

Thank Themis's scales that's over. I'm glad I didn't have to arrest anyone today.

A smile came to his face as he started walking, going to see something he'd been waiting to see the entire time spent with the caravan.

I'm finally *going to see the ocean.*

As Roger opened his door, he was filled with a field's worth of mixed emotions. The taxes had come down, which was more than welcome.

We won't have any issue paying for Sharon's medicine.

With that thought, though, came the knowledge that she was still sick. He quietly closed the door behind him, not wanting to disturb her rest. With soft footsteps, he made his way toward their bedroom. And he heard talking.

Roger froze, confused. Then, realizing that Barry had brought someone else into his home without permission, he marched for the open bedroom door, his conflicted emotions all channeling toward his misplaced fury. He rounded the corner.

"Barry, you—"

The words froze at what he saw, and he barely recognized Barry standing in the room.

His eyes were fixated on a single thing—the rock that held their family together, the source of both his life's joy and his recent misery. Sharon. She was awake.

He didn't feel himself move, but he was at the bed in the blink of an eye, taking his wife's offered hands.

"Sharon . . ."

Tears fell, and he made no effort to hide them.

Barry stepped from the room, giving the couple the space they deserved. Before he could make it from the home, he heard soft cries that were definitely not Sharon's, and he felt a spark of guilt for having heard such a raw moment.

As he closed the front door behind him, the emotions of it all hit. Without Fischer's arrival, and without Barry's intervention, Sharon would have continued wasting away, afflicted by an illness that would have proved fatal. Because of his actions, she was free of the illness and would make a full recovery. He laughed, the sound turning harsh and choking as tears started to fall.

"This is amazing, Fischer," Maria said, taking another sip of coffee.

I nodded, taking a drink of my own. "Wait until the caffeine kicks in—that's when it gets *really* good."

She put the cup to her lips again, letting out a content sigh as the flavors assaulted her.

"You're sure you want to help us carry our crops to the merchant, though? It'll take us a few trips without you, but you've already done so much."

I shook my head.

"I'm happy to help. Besides, I'm already coming to your home—there's no way I'd miss the look on Barry and your dad's face when they have their first coffee."

We each held an extra cup of the golden liquid, and I couldn't wait to see the farmers' reactions.

Maria smiled. "I know I've thanked you already, probably too much, but again, thank you. I'm so glad you chose our little village to settle in."

I returned the smile. "There's nowhere I'd rather be. I'm surrounded by water to fish in and the best people I've ever met."

She swept hair behind her ear as best she could with a cup of coffee already occupying her hand, and I marveled at her beauty. Realizing I was staring, I cleared my throat and looked away.

We stepped from between two fields of cane, and as we caught sight of Maria's home, we both came up short. Barry stood at the front door, tears streaming down his face.

Maria dropped both her cups, one empty, the other full.

"No . . ."

CHAPTER FIFTY-SEVEN

SHE'S AWAKE

"No . . ."

Unbidden, my hand shot out, discarding my almost empty cup and catching the full cup of coffee with a single lightning-fast movement.

"No . . ." Maria said again, her voice tinged with grief.

Barry looked up at her second utterance, his eyes red with tears. His face transformed. A smile of the purest joy swept away any hint of sorrow, and he beamed at Maria.

"Your mother," he said, his voice hoarse.

He pointed to the door. "She's awake . . ."

Maria ran, and I hurried behind her. She flung the door wide and made to follow, but Barry reached for my arm. His grip had no chance of halting my enhanced body, but I stopped.

"Give them a moment," he said, wiping tears from his face.

I stared through the open portal, my mouth moving inaudibly.

"She's . . . Sharon's really awake? Is she okay?"

Barry nodded, clearing his throat. "She's going to make a full recovery."

I set the cups of coffee down, sprang back up, and wrapped Barry in a hug. "Mate—you're amazing."

He clung to me, laughing as his body shook with small sobs. I held him as he let his emotions out, happy that I could be there for him.

I heard small but fast footsteps approaching. As I looked up, Maria collided with us, wrapping her arms around both of us. She buried her face into Barry's shoulder, and the convulsions of her tiny body made me want to fix every problem she'd ever face. As she let go, she turned her face up to Barry, tears flowing freely, her lip trembling.

"Thank you . . ."

She hurried back inside to her family, and Barry sobbed as he watched her go.

I squeezed him tighter. "You did good."

He nodded, unable to get any words out. He took a few deep breaths and exhaled them slowly before easing his grip around me.

"Sorry, Fischer. This is embarrassing."

I let go of him, leaving one hand on his shoulder as our embrace ended.

"You have nothing to be ashamed of, mate. It's a lot."

He looked up at my own tear-streaked face and smiled.

"Wow, I didn't know you were the emotional type. Maybe go see Sergeant Snips next time you need a good cry—I can't always be here to support you."

We both laughed at the light-hearted jibe, Barry with a hearty chuckle, me with my head thrown up toward the sky.

"Yeah, sorry about that. Here, I bought you something in apology for my outburst."

I bent and picked up one of the coffee cups, holding it out to him. Both his eyebrows shot up.

"From Sue?"

"Yeah—we brought one for you and Roger."

Barry accepted the proffered drink, holding the cup in both hands.

"You just . . . drink it?"

"Yeah, mate," I said with a laugh. "As if it were a cup of delicious, motivation-inducing water."

He took a tentative sip then scrunched his face. "It's sort of bitter."

"Yeah, if it doesn't taste good your first time, don't worry—it'll grow on you."

He took another sip, swishing it around his mouth. "It's not bad, just not what I expected."

"Wait until the motivation I mentioned hits you—that's where it really shines. I have a feeling today is going to be wildly productive for the village."

"You weren't lying about the coffee, Fischer—I feel like I could do everything right now!"

"Right? Feel free to get going if you wanna put that energy to good use—I'm waiting here to help Maria and Roger take their sugarcane and wheat to the merchant, but if you wanna get going . . ."

He shook his head. "No, I'll wait to make sure everything is fine with Sharon."

Barry and I sat on the small porch, looking out over the fields.

"I still can't believe your medicine was so effective . . . that was only the second dose, right?"

"It was, though I don't deserve any thanks—it was because of someone else's efforts, I just delivered it."

"Nonsense, mate. I know it was Helen's recipe, but you brought the medicine yourself, and I bet you'd have kept doing so for as long as it took, right?"

He gave me a wry smile. "I would have. I knew it would help, so I'd have kept bringing it as long as it took for her to recover."

Someone knocked on the door frame behind us, and I turned to see Maria looking at us.

"I'm not interrupting, am I?"

"Not at all." I held up Roger's coffee. "You should get this to him before it gets cold."

"Oh! The coffee!" She took it in both hands and rushed it inside to her father, returning a moment later.

She sat down beside Barry, looking out at the blue sky. "I don't have the words for how thankful I am, Barry . . ."

"You don't need to thank me. That's what neighbors are for—right, Fischer?"

I grinned. "Right. I'd have done the same if I had any medicinal knowledge."

She shook her head, the movement freeing a strand of hair that was immediately swept back behind an ear.

"We are forever in your debt."

Barry made to say something, no doubt a refusal of any debt owed, but a set of heavy footsteps cut him off. Roger emerged, his eyes red, the usually omnipresent scowl nowhere to be seen.

"Barry. Thank you."

He strode to Barry and held out his hand. Barry stood, shaking it with a smile. Roger shook Barry's hand, using both of his with a vigor that would be comical if not for the situation.

"A million times, thank you. I'll never be able to repay you for returning Sharon to us."

"There's no need for thanks—"

"There is," Roger insisted. "Anything you ever need is yours—if you want our fields, they're yours. If you want our land, it's yours. By Asclepius's serpentine staff, I'll be your slave if that's what you wish."

Barry laughed as Roger let go of his hand, shaking his head.

"No—I don't need anything. If I think of something, I'll let you know, but the medicine was freely given."

Roger nodded, turning as another tear fell. With his back to us, he wiped his face and cleared his throat.

"Sharon asked to speak to you alone for a moment—I believe she wants to express her thanks."

"All right. I'll go see her."

As he moved inside, I turned to Maria, not wanting to make Roger feel embarrassed for showing emotion.

I know how those old codgers can get about showing what they perceive as weakness . . .

"Do you want me to take your stuff to the merchant? That way, you two can stay with Sharon."

"No!" She held up both hands in protest. "I'll come with you—I don't want you doing our work."

"It's really no problem," I tried, but Roger turned to me.

"I'll go with you. It wouldn't do to have you go by yourself, and I don't want to leave Sharon alone. You can stay with her, Maria."

She looked between us, and with a small smile, nodded.

"Okay. I'll leave it to you two."

Barry barked a laugh from inside, and I couldn't help but smile. She's already feeling well enough to joke.

* * *

Barry stepped into the room to find Sharon waiting for him.

"How are you feeling?" he asked.

"Much better, thanks to you."

He smiled down at her. He wasn't sure if it was because of speaking with Roger and Maria, but she already looked healthier than the last time he'd seen her.

"I'm glad I could help."

He sat down on the end of the bed. "So . . . I know your mind was probably occupied, but have you put any thought into what I said?"

She gave a single nod. "That's what I wanted to speak about. It didn't require much thinking, and I've decided."

"Oh. Okay. What did you decide?"

"Your plan is audacious, cunning, and more than a little foolhardy."

She gave him a mischievous smile. "I'm in."

He grinned back at her. "I knew you'd agree, but it's still good to hear."

"I wouldn't miss it. If nothing else, it'll be quite a show to see unfold—win or lose."

Barry barked a laugh. "You're not wrong, but I don't plan on losing."

Roger raised an eyebrow at me as I hefted three bunches of sugarcane over my shoulder. I could have carried more, but I figured carrying any extra toward the merchant's caravan would have drawn too much attention. He picked up two, putting one on each shoulder before setting off.

I walked behind him through the fields, the passageways too thin for us to walk side by side. The midmorning sun was high in the sky, and I basked in its warmth, shifting the bails to my other shoulder to better expose my body to its heat.

"Fischer . . . I believe I owe you an apology."

I raised an eyebrow that Roger couldn't see as he marched ever onward. "You do?"

Silence stretched between us as the ground passed underneath, and I gave him as much time as he needed.

"I've had some harsh words for you, and while I still think you're a heretic, I went too far. I'm sorry."

I smiled at his back, knowing that couldn't have been easy for him to voice.

"Thank you for the apology, mate. It's accepted, and all is forgiven. I know you were under an unimaginable amount of stress while Sharon was unwell, and I'm beyond glad that she's making a recovery."

He dipped his head in acknowledgment, our footfalls the only sound against the dirt path.

"I owe you an apology too, Roger."

He halted mid-step, but then kept on walking, so I continued.

"You weren't in the wrong for having a go at me when I pumped too much water out into the fields. I didn't stop to consider the consequences of my actions, and I was treating my foray into farming as a fun activity."

I shook my head at myself.

"I acted as if it were a game, but to all of you, farming is anything but. It's your way of life, and at the time, the income from those fields was needed for Sharon's medicine. You have my permission to chew me out if I do something so dickheaded in the future."

Roger stopped, spinning to look at me.

"Dickheaded?"

"My bad. It means stupid and irritating, like a bloke that cuts in line or does something similarly annoying, whether by malice or incompetence."

He tilted his head, tasting the word. ". . . it was pretty dickheaded of you."

I snorted a laugh. "It was, mate. I'll do my best to rein it in, but yeah, call me out if I lapse back into dickheadedness."

He nodded and spun back, continuing toward the caravans. We lapsed back into silence, the previous tension having melted away.

After the third trip to the merchant with their goods, I said farewell to Roger—I had some things to buy.

I approached the largest of the wagons and looked through the wares as the merchant spoke to a farmer I didn't recognize. All manner of objects were arrayed, but I had eyes for only one thing. Lemons.

There was a small basket of the fruit on a back shelf, too far for anyone to grab. I waited patiently, and when the farmer was done, the merchant came over to me.

"Hello, friend! I have not seen your face before—are you a new farmer?"

He held his hand out, and I shook it.

"G'day, mate! Not a farmer, but I am new around these parts. Name's Fischer."

As soon as he heard my name, his eyes lit up, but he quickly schooled his features.

"Ah, Fischer! I have heard of you. I am Marcus—the humble owner of this caravan. That coffee machine was for you, correct?"

"It was for the whole village, but yeah, I'm proud to say I organized it for them!"

"Someone of your means is most welcome to my humble array of wares." He gave me a coy smile. "I actually have something for you."

He passed me a small leather pouch, and as soon as I held it I knew what it was: the rest of the gold from selling the pearl ring to Julian.

With how eventful life had been, I'd totally forgotten. I slipped the pouch into a pocket, not wanting to display the wealth.

"You don't wish to check the amount?" Marcus asked.

"Did you take any?"

"Of course not, my friend! My good name is all I have!"

"No worries, then. I trust you, mate."

His eyes sparkled again, but I didn't have the faintest clue why.

Marcus gestured at the surrounding goods. "What did you want to buy, then? I have all manner of wares."

"A couple things—I heard you sold bearings?"

"Bearings—of course! One moment."

He whistled, and a man at the caravan to his left looked up.

"Bearings, Jager!"

The man in question ran a tray over and handed it to Marcus before returning to his customer.

Marcus sorted through the tray, plucking things from it and placing them in his palm.

"We have bearings of four different sizes—which would best suit your needs?"

I looked them over. The smallest was the size of a pea, the largest about the size of a gold coin.

"How much are they, mate?"

"Five, seven, nine, and twelve coppers, respectively."

"Can I buy three of each?"

"But of course, my friend!"

He laid them out on the lowest shelf and set the tray of bearings aside. "What else would you like?"

I tried not to let my need show, lest the savvy merchant overcharge.

"You know, I haven't had lemons since coming to these shores . . . I see you have some."

"I never leave the capital without a selection of them!" He rubbed his hands together. "How many would you like?"

"How much are they?"

"Five silver coins each."

My eyebrows shot up.

Damn, they are expensive. . .

Marcus gave me a wincing smile. "Yes, my friend, they are more dear than in the capital, but it costs to transport and keep them fresh, you understand?"

"Hmmm. I was hoping to buy three of them, but a gold and a half? That seems excessive."

He leaned in, a conspiratorial look on his face. "I'll tell you what, my friend. If you keep it between us, you can have them for four silvers each, and I'll throw in the bearings for free. This price is only for you, as you are such an esteemed member of this village."

I looked through the other things he had on offer as I thought, and my eyes froze as I found a hidden treasure.

"Tell you what, mate. That sounds like a deal—if you're willing to chuck in some of those spices."

Marcus glanced at the rack I'd pointed to, and when he turned back to me, smiled.

"Nothing would make me happier, friend."

I couldn't believe my luck as I made my way home. I had a tray laden with bearings, lemons, and an assortment of each spice the merchant had in stock. Some of the spices I'd recognized—powdered garlic, onion, paprika, and sage, to name a few. There were a number that I'd never heard of, and upon smelling them, they weren't recognizable.

I'll have to experiment with their flavor profiles when I get the chance . . .

A grin spread across my face.

But first, I have a fishing reel to construct.

I turned the screw one last time and looked down at my handiwork. I'd attached the metal bracket to the rod, and as soon as I set the bearing in the reel, I could fix it in place. Along with the metal bracket, I'd pushed a number of wall hangers into the bamboo to act as eyelets for the line to run through. They were crude looking, but I hoped they'd stay in place and function correctly.

"Almost done . . ."

I took the reel, and picking out the second-largest bearing, I put it inside the central hole. Well, I tried to—it was too tight, but only just.

This is probably the right bearing—I might need to widen the hole a little, though . . .

I tried pushing the bearing in, and it slid in a fraction, then wouldn't go further.

"Maybe with a little lubrication . . ."

I retrieved the linseed oil I'd gotten from Fergus, carefully dripping some into the hole. The wood absorbed most of it immediately, the dark fibers going an even richer shade of brown. Anticipation welled up, and thoughts of fishing with my new reel flooded my mind. With a smile, I picked up the bearing and set it against the opening once more. With care not to force it and break the bearing, I pressed down with my thumb and it slid even further in.

My stomach filled with butterflies as I realized this was going to work. I set the reel against the ground, and with both hands, pushed down against the bearing with all of my weight. It slipped into place, and a *thunk* rang out as it hit the back side of the housing.

"Yes!" I yelled, picking up the reel.

I put it on the bracket and spun it; the bearing performed its job perfectly. As the reel turned, a familiar feeling rushed up from within me, and the rod transformed before my eyes.

CHAPTER FIFTY-EIGHT

DIVINE INTERVENTION

My eyes went wide as the reel and rod transformed. A rushing of power came from my core, along with an almost unnoticeable nudge from the System, no doubt trying to spew incoherent nonsense at me. The rod seemed to blur, then sharpen. The bracket, which wasn't yet properly attached to the reel, secured itself. The metal warped and grew, sprouting a section on the side closest to me that flattened out, holding the reel firmly in place. The wall hangers I'd pushed into the rod to act as eyelets also changed, becoming whole and fixed into the bamboo fibers.

Finally, and most notable, part of the reel bulged out, quickly morphing into a handle to turn.

A split second after the transformation was complete, my eyes were drawn into it.

Bamboo Rod of the Fisher

Rare

A bamboo rod paired with an ironbark reel. This fishing rod provides boosts to both fishing and luck.

+10 fishing

+2 luck

I blinked.

"Holy frack . . . stats?"

My joy couldn't be contained as I sprinted along the sands, my rod and everything I needed to fish in hand. A wide smile stretched across my face, and I breathed deep of the afternoon air.

The first thing I'd done upon seeing an actually useful item description was to turn my notifications back on, but once again, I was greeted with a wall of 'insufficient power' nonsense.

I had no idea *why* the System decided to be useful all of a sudden, so I paid it no mind—instead, I focused on my destination. I was headed somewhere I'd eventually intended to fish but hadn't yet had the guts to try—the break wall along the shores of Tropica.

I'd been too worried about setting off the villagers with my heretical activities, but riding the high of my new rod, along with knowing I'd earned a certain amount of goodwill with the coffee machine's delivery, I was willing to push it.

The jetty extending from the village had long since caught my eye, and I knew the structure it provided could grant a hunting ground for species of fish I'd not yet encountered.

I looked around as I neared the rock wall; there was no one in sight, so I started setting up my rod. I'd already transferred a length of line to the reel, and I strung it through the transformed eyelets running the length of my bamboo pole.

Cutting a small length of the plastic string, I tied a rock to act as a drop sinker running off the main line. To the end of the line, I tied a medium-sized hook and placed a small slice of eel on it.

I lifted the rod, hefting its weight. As I drew the rod back over my shoulder, I took a moment to soak in the surrounding landscape and my flourishing emotions.

The bay was calm, and the soon to be setting sun bathed the sky in a palette of pastel colors.

I took a deep breath, and with a radiant sense of joy, cast out the line.

The rod flexed as I flung the tip toward the jetty, and my hook and sinker flew, arcing high over the softly lapping waves. The moment seemed to stretch on forever, and I watched its trajectory as it crested over the shore. With a splashing of water and a soft *plop,* it hit the water right by the jetty and sank toward the bottom.

Theo walked along the shore to the north of the village, and he basked in the beauty of the late afternoon. He had always been a fan of the sun rising and setting, but it'd been a long time since he'd been able to see it happen over the ocean.

He paused and looked out at the protected bay, transfixed by the water's movement as it languidly shifted with almost imperceptible grace. With a sense of immense calm, he took a deep breath, the salt in the air flooding his lungs. Theo breathed out, the air hissing past his pursed lips.

I bet the sunset will look glorious from Tropica's break wall . . .

An unexpected urgency filled his steps as he headed back south.

George wandered the north side of Tropica, his mind a wash of contradictory thoughts. Following the meeting with the auditor, Theo, he'd felt a need to move—it always helped him process, loathe as he was to exercise like a common peasant.

Despite the auditor's reassurance, he still felt like the axeman's blade was hanging over his neck, just waiting for the right moment to cut down. The most annoying aspect of his thoughts was that Theo wasn't even the main focus as he assumed they should be—Fischer was.

Since the man's arrival in Tropica, things had flipped end over end, more often than not landing facedown, like a glazed donut's sugar-crusted top hitting the dirt.

Did I really invent all his machinations and trickery? Were they a figment of my imagination, as Geraldine suggests?

Admitting that was true may free his mind of the metaphorical axe hanging over his head but could replace it with something just as psychologically damaging—the knowledge that he had been wrong and had invented the entire situation.

Most people would be glad to admit they were wrong in order to free their consciousness of impending doom, but George—and more importantly, his ego—were not most people.

He let out a deep sigh, his legs subconsciously wandering along the paved road.

Theo climbed a set of stairs and stepped onto the stone walkway atop the break wall. Its firm surface was welcome after walking so long on the sand, and he approached the low wall, leaning on it as he looked out to sea. The air turned cold, and he glanced back, seeing the sun was blocked by the tall walls of the north side homes.

"Well, that won't do."

He moved south, intending to find a patch where the sun peeked over the smaller buildings on the southern side of Tropica.

I caressed my finger against the line, waiting for the telltale bump of something nibbling my bait. Even if I didn't catch something, I didn't care—just this feeling, this meditative state of waiting for a bite, was just what my soul needed after such an eventful day. I lost myself to the hunt; the sounds of waves lapping the shore, and birds calling from above, pulled me into a state of zen.

Theo saw the perfect spot from which to watch the sunset. The most southern point of the wall would let him see the sun setting over the western mountains, and he strode toward it, excitement bubbling up from within.

As he reached the corner, he intended to look toward the mountains, to see the sun's descent in all its glory, but something else caught his eye. A person was down on the shore, looking out to sea with something long held before him. He squinted, curiosity getting the better of him. It only took him half a second to realize what the man—Fischer, who he'd met earlier—was doing.

"There's no way . . ."

The more George wandered through the village and sorted through his churning thoughts, the more Geraldine's theory seemed to make sense. With the arrival of a confirmed agent of the crown, Fischer also being one made less and less sense.

Sending two of them to a minor village in the far reaches of the kingdom for something as minor as misappropriated taxes seemed unlikely. Even having one of them visit Tropica would be an anomaly, which was why George assumed the crown would never discover his tax theft in the first place. If Fischer was just a regular citizen, though, George's assumptions and actions were an embarrassing mistake.

He let out a snort of derision.

Did I create the entire narrative in my head? What kind of madman would do such a thing?

He replayed every interaction they'd had, sifting through the memories for a glimpse of understanding. The ancient coin, the house appearing from nowhere, the conversations and comments that presented as threats—each could be individually seen as innocuous, but together, they painted the portrait of a devious man hellbent on George's downfall. Fischer's arrival had brought confusion, turmoil, and worry into George's life.

But, if not for Fischer, I'd never have bought the coffee machine. The real *crown auditor would have found increased taxes, a box filled with embezzled pearls, and no benefit added to the villagers . . .*

Perhaps he could reframe the webs that seemed to bind him, to choose gratitude for the actions he'd assumed to be a curse, but in the end, were a blessing in disguise.

Is this what they call divine intervention? Wisdom from the heavens?

George's subconscious latched onto the possibility; better to be subjected to the whims of divine beings than the abject chaos of existence. If Fischer were merely a vessel for the actions of divinity, it would also explain the mystery surrounding him. He could have easily come upon an ancient coin and the materials for his grand home if it were a lingering god pulling strings behind the scenes. It also explained his odd mannerisms, statements, and general lack of decorum. If a god was directing Fischer, it all made so much sense.

But what god could be doing it? Which one makes the most sense for—

George's eyes went wide, and his thoughts stopped in their tracks.

"No . . ." he heard himself utter aloud.

Fischer was a *heretic!* If any god were directing him, acting as the puppet master behind the strings, it would be a god of the sea.

". . . he's a fisherman . . ."

George's mouth went dry, his tongue leaden.

"N-not Glaukos. Please . . . not that . . ."

George squinted as he stepped out from between buildings; the light of the setting sun lit the scene before him. He'd arrived at the break wall without realizing it, and he stumbled forward, grabbing the stone wall with both hands as he rested his weight upon it.

The attention of such an entity was a worse fate than anything the crown could do to him. As he stared out to sea, attempting to make sense of his doom, a figure caught his attention. He hadn't noticed before, self-absorbed as he was, but there was another person atop the stone walkway. Theo stood at the southern corner, his body erect at attention as he stared at something out of sight. The crown auditor sprinted down the stairs and disappeared from sight.

What could have Theo so transfixed?

With curiosity overcoming his existential dread, George dashed toward Theo's previous post, intent on having a peek.

Sergeant Snips, having heard of Corporal Claws's ascension atop the freshwater pond, scuttled toward the saltwater construction with great anticipation. Through chirps and chitters, the otter had communicated the way the pond beckoned to her, and the awakening she'd experienced after heeding the call.

Sergeant Snips recalled the pulse she'd thought a figment of her imagination upon the pond's completion. She'd believed the warmth radiating from the opalescent stone atop the sea snipper's cave was also in her head—a sense of accomplishment that came from having built something useful to her master. After hearing Corporal Claws's retelling, she hoped both signs meant something more exciting. She intended to find out.

When she got to the pond, Snips took a moment to appreciate its beauty. The light of the setting sun lit the large stone seemingly from within, and it reflected the usual rainbow colors, but overshadowed by a soft purple hue.

The same feeling of warmth radiated from the boulder, calling to her. It didn't seem as strong as the otter made the call of the freshwater pond sound, but there was *something* there, and she listened to it.

Her body slipped beneath the cool water. She scuttled across the pond floor, and climbing the sea snipper's cave, found an underwater nook that was perfect for her body. She nestled into it, the back of her carapace resting up against the shiny boulder. Sergeant Snips closed her lone eye, focusing on the stone's resonance.

The top half of George's head poked up above the wall. He caught sight of Theo immediately, running across the sand toward another figure. Fischer stood at the water's edge, soft waves washing over his feet. He had a fishing rod in his hand, and George felt a myriad of emotions as he realized what the heretic was doing.

He's fishing, and a crown agent has spotted him . . .

An ugly smile crossed George's face as schadenfreude flooded him.

Play with my fate, Glaukos? See what becomes of your vessel.

A deep calm flooded through me as I focused on the sensations of my body. The water lapping at my legs, my steady breaths, the calls of birds from above, and my finger held to the line, waiting for a fish to bite—all grounded me to the present moment.

The sound of footfalls on the soft sand jarred me from my meditation, and I glanced aside. The man I'd met earlier, Theo, was running toward me, his eyes wide and brows furrowed.

Oh—that's not great . . .

He reached me, his eyes darting between me and the rod in my hands.

"Fischer—you're . . . *fishing?*"

I tried to give him a disarming smile.

"Er . . . yeah. I know it's a bit odd, but I—"

He cut me off, the words coming from his mouth shocking me to my core.

CHAPTER FIFTY-NINE

BEST FRIEND

Theo's entire face lit up. "I *love* fishing!"

"I—wait, you what?"

"I love fishing!" he repeated, half yell, half whisper. "I've never come across another angler—you're doing it so openly!"

I blinked rapidly, a smile spreading across my face. "Theo, mate—you've just been upgraded from acquaintance to friend."

He let out a laugh and clapped me on the shoulder. "You too, Fischer—it was Fischer, right?" His lip curled up into a smirk. "An apt name . . ."

"Not wrong, mate."

He cast a furtive glance at our surroundings. "Aren't you worried someone will see?"

"Not really. The villagers were super hesitant about what they call my 'heretical activities,' but they've gotten past it . . . mostly."

I shrugged. "What about you? Where do you go fishing?"

"When I get the chance, I go up into the mountains and fish creeks and ponds. I'm part of a fishing club—we get together and exchange tips and locations."

"There's a fishing club?"

"There is," he said with a smile. "We only have five members, but we meet as often as possible when we're back in Gormona."

"You're all from the capital? I'd never expect such heresy from citizens so close to the king." I waggled my eyebrows, and he laughed again.

"Yeah, we keep it pretty quiet for obvious reasons. I think most of the water aversion is overblown, though. The gods are gone, right? What's the harm in a little fishing and relaxation?"

I gripped his shoulder, beyond happy to find a kindred spirit. "Theo, my man, you just earned best-friend status."

George watched over the rock wall as Theo sprinted through the sand. He reached Fischer, halting on the spot. George's grin turned savage as the confrontation began.

Fischer's eyes were wide, and he uttered something with a numb face, a spike of panic no doubt driving into his body.

Will he take him back to the capital for punishment? Will Theo remove this heretical thorn from my side?

George watched on with glee.

Clap the god's pawn in chains, take him from these lands, subject him to the king's—

Fischer's shock turned into . . . *joy?*

He said something, and Theo let out a loud laugh, clapping him on the shoulder. George's mind tried to make sense of the scene unfolding before him.

"What in Triton's girthy conch is going on?"

The two men by the shore started talking again, hands moving chaotically as they laughed and joked.

"Th—they know each other?"

Theo glanced around, and George threw himself to the floor, knocking the air from his lungs.

Did they see me?

He felt the need to run, to get as far from this place as possible, but he had to know—he had to glean as much information as possible. He poked his head back up slowly and saw them once more conversing, focused on each other. George continued scouting, looking for insight.

Theo gave me a broad smile. "Best friends it is!"

He peered past me, his gaze locked on my rod. "Wow. What is *that?*"

"Er—a fishing rod?"

"I know what a fishing rod is, but this . . ."

His hand reached for the reel, a single finger extended, then his head snapped back toward me. "May I?"

"Of course!"

I held the rod out; he took it with care. He held the rod's handle in one hand and ran the other along the reel and bracket.

"Is this ironbark wood?"

"Yeah! The local woodworkers helped me craft it."

"It's beautiful . . ."

His hand ran up the reel and along the bracket. He lifted it before his face, eyebrows knitting as he tried to comprehend the metal arm's purpose.

"I've seen nothing quite like this reel. How does it work?"

"It's called an Alvey reel. You can twist it like so when casting." I spun the reel ninety degrees. "That way, the line spools out freely."

Theo's eyes went wide as saucers, and his head rapidly moved to me, to the reel, and back again.

"Fischer . . . this design is genius! I have to write this down!" He pulled a notepad from his pocket. He flicked past the first page and went to start writing, but I put a hand on the notepad, stopping him.

"Theo! You drew that?"

"I did. I just had a rather straightforward meeting with the village's lord, so I did some doodling to pass the time."

He flipped back to the first page and spun it toward me. A vivid landscape was sketched onto the page, depicting a man holding a fishing rod and standing before a calm river. The strokes were rapid but exacting, and the artist's skill was easy to see, despite how fast the lines had been drawn in.

"Mate, you really made this? It's beautiful."

His eyes lit up. "You think so? It's a part-time hobby, and before I found fishing, was my favored source of relaxation. Do you want it?"

"I'd love it! I have some friends who I reckon would enjoy it as much as I do."

With a careful tear, he removed the page from the notepad and held it out to me. I accepted and slid the sketch into my back pocket, making sure to not bend or crease it. When I looked back up at Theo, his attention was back on the rod.

"We use reels too, but you can't cast very far—does letting the line 'spool out,' as you said, let it go further?"

"Yeah, mate—it lets you cast *really* far." I pointed out at the jetty. "I didn't use all my strength, and easily sent my bait and sinker out to the end of that dock."

". . . you're joking, right?"

I grinned. "Wanna see?"

George watched the men, his stomach sinking, his thoughts roiling. Fischer passed Theo the rod, and the crown auditor's eyes poured over it as he touched different parts of it with his hands.

Is . . . is Theo simply a heretic also interested in fishing? Did I jump to conclusions in assuming he was in cahoots with Fischer about our interrogation?

These thoughts planted a seed in George's mind.

Is fishing somehow linked to the power the crown and its agents hold? Why else would a crown representative—not just *a crown representative, but a crown auditor—be interested in something forbidden by the crown?*

Theo's next action swept George's assumptions and introspection aside. He reached into his back pocket, withdrew the notepad he'd been writing in during the interrogation, and held it out before Fischer.

George may have reasoned, whether through careful deliberation or mindless self-preservation, that Theo was simply showing Fischer something else in the notepad—if not for Fischer's actions. He reached out, placing a hand on the notepad and bringing Theo up short. The heretic, the man that was the source of all his life's discomforts, presumed to touch a crown auditor.

Rather than striking the man down, or clapping him in chains, Theo flicked back a page and held it up before the heretic. Fischer peered at it intently, scouring over the notes Theo had jotted down. They spoke as Fischer continued looking over the information. Then, with practiced movement, Theo tore the page out and handed it to Fischer.

George fell back, rolling awkwardly as his rotund and powerful frame hit the stone walkway.

He crawled away from the wall with numb limbs, his brain too overwhelmed to register his body's sensations.

When he reached the far corner of a building, he leaned against it, using it to get to his feet.

I was correct . . .

This knowledge didn't bring George satisfaction; it set a convulsing pool of uncertainty and existential dread into motion.

Fischer isn't just a crown agent—he's the direct superior of a crown auditor.

George stumbled between rows of buildings, eyes unseeing as the light of the day bled from the sky.

This is worse than I could have possibly imagined.

He lurched, almost falling over as the weight of his discovery settled on his shoulders.

Okeanus's tempestuous waters—what storm do I find myself adrift in?

"What on Kallis is *that?*" Theo pointed at the rock and sinker, his face scrunched.

"A sinker, mate—a bit of weight helps cast the line out and keep it still on the ocean floor."

He gave me an askew glance. "Doesn't it scare away the fish? It's pretty . . . *noticeable.*"

"Not at all, my man! I love fish as much as you or any of your fishing club members, but even you have to admit, they're pretty dumb. I call this one a 'drop rig'—you can even add more lines coming off the main one. More hooks, more bait, all represented at different levels in the water—that only increases your chances of catching a fish, right?"

"That . . . doesn't scare the fish away either?"

I shook my head. "The opposite, mate. I've only used drop rigs with multiple hooks on smaller baitfish, but it's not uncommon to catch multiple fish in one cast. When a fish gets hooked, its movement catches other fish's attention, and they go for the other hooks."

Theo almost threw the rod at me in his haste; I took it with a smile as he rushed to jot down a sketch in his notepad. When he finished, I held the rod back out to him. "Have a go at casting it."

Theo flipped the reel to its casting position, and I grabbed the line with one finger, holding it to the rod so it didn't unspool.

"Hold the line against the rod like this before you're casting—let go just as you cast it out, and the line will flow freely."

He nodded and did so with an intense look of concentration. "How, uh, how hard can I throw it?"

"As hard as you want, mate. Maybe start with a small throw to get a feel for it."

I stepped back to give him space, and with an overhead flick, he sent the bait out over the ocean.

It traveled about half the length of the jetty, hitting the water with a soft *plop.* Theo's smile was a beautiful thing to see, and he let out a soft chuckle.

"Amazing! It feels so solid—this rod is something else, Fischer!"

He flicked the reel back into its natural position. It made a soft *click* as it did so. He started reeling, and pure joy swept over his face.

"And the reel feels so smooth! Fischer—I can't believe you made this!"

My heart sang with the purity of the moment, and I bathed in Theo's childlike wonder.

"That cast was perfect. This time, send it as far as you can."

"You're sure?" he asked, not looking away from the rod as he wound the line in.

"I'm sure, mate—I doubt you can mess it up. Just let go of the line as you did before when you cast it."

With Theo's exuberant winding, the sinker and hook came from the water in no time at all.

He flicked the reel back into the casting position and flung the rod back over his shoulder.

"Wait!" I said.

He paused, giving me a questioning look. I flicked the reel back into the standard position and eased the rod down from above his shoulder.

"You have a bit too much line free. Wind it a couple times so the hook and sinker are closer to the tip of the rod—you'll cast it much further."

He did so, giving the reel a few turns.

"Is this better?"

"Perfect, mate."

Theo nodded, mostly to himself, and tried the cast again. With the reel in the casting position, the rod over his shoulder, and a finger held to the line, he flung as hard as he could.

As the hook and sinker arced high over the waters of the bay, a faint nudge came from the System, the subtle blip telling me it was no doubt sending through another error message.

I quirked an eyebrow.

For showing someone how to fish? Odd . . .

In a room high atop the castle of Gormona, a relic blinked to life—an exceedingly rare occurrence that was becoming more and more commonplace. There was no person there to witness the anomaly, yet the artifact still completed its task, printing words out onto its screen.

New Milestone! Fischer has become a fishing trainer!

CHAPTER SIXTY

SOMETHING COLOSSAL

With the sun setting at our backs, Theo and I watched the hook and sinker as they flew over the languidly shifting ocean. It flew further than the jetty, hitting the ocean half again the dock's length from the shore. A great splash sprang from the sinker and the line meeting the ocean's surface, so far away that we couldn't hear the sound it made.

"Wow!" Theo yelled, his voice tinged with awe. "It went so far!"

"Mate, that's further than even I've sent it—you've got a serious throw on you!"

It wasn't a lie—I hadn't tried casting my new rod as far as I could—but I didn't want to tell Theo that and ruin his moment.

"Reel it in if you want to have another try."

He gave me a grimace. "Are you sure? I feel bad for interrupting your fishing time. I don't want to be an annoyance . . ."

"Not at all!" I clapped a hand on his shoulder. "I'm beyond content letting someone who shares my passion try out my equipment. Have as many casts as you want."

He gave me a kind smile, his eyes crinkling.

"You're a good man, Fischer. I'll have one more try, then I'll let you get back to—*woah!*"

The rod bent almost in half as something colossal struck the bait and took off. Theo held the rod, his eyes going wide.

"H-here!" He tried to hand me the rod, but I pushed it back into his hands.

The reel was spinning freely, the giant thing on the other end of the line forging a path from the shore.

I pointed down at his hands. "Reel! You've got a big one!"

"But it's your—" he tried.

"Nonsense! You cast it, you catch it!"

I watched acceptance roll over him, and a grin came to his face as he braced himself and set his hand on the reel's handle.

"Don't hold the reel firm—wind backward so the fish can take some ground. This thing is massive, and you'll want to tire it out."

He nodded, doing as I said. Theo leaned his entire body back as the weight of the fish tugged on the line. His hand rotated backward quickly, having to let out long lengths of the line so it didn't snap.

"Do—do I just keep letting it take line? Won't it get away?"

"You're doing perfect, mate. Fighting big fish like this is a dance. Let it take line now, but keep the line taut if it changes direction—"

As if listening to our conversation, the fish arced to the left, then dashed back toward the shore.

With the lack of force pulling on Theo, his body was off balance, and he crashed to the sand, one of his hands falling from the reel to brace his fall.

"Wind it in!" I urged. "You need to keep tension!"

He sprang to his feet and gripped the reel again, winding as fast as he could. As he kept reeling the line in, I held out hope the fish was still hooked, but soon realized it was too late—it had gotten away, unhooking itself while the line was slack.

Theo grimaced. "It's gone, isn't it?"

"Yeah, I think so, mate—that was a good fight, though!"

He let out a sigh as the hook and sinker came up onto the shore.

"I'm sorry, Fischer. I should have given it to you."

I put a reassuring hand on his shoulder and shook my head. "Not at all—that was a great learning experience. You'll dance better next time."

He shot me a questioning look. "You're really not annoyed? That was a *colossal* fish . . ."

I laughed. "Not at all. It's more about the experience than the result, right? Otherwise it'd be called catching, not fishing."

"You've got a point there," he admitted, looking sheepish. "Still, I can't help but feel it was my fault."

"Hold the rod still a second—I'll show you something."

I pinched the top of the free line in one hand and carefully grabbed the hook with the other.

"Flick the reel into the casting position."

Theo did so, despite his obvious confusion at my request.

"It's partially my fault." I pulled the hook toward him, the line unreeling itself. "See this hook? Do you and the other fishermen in Gormona use barbed hooks?"

He nodded, his eyebrows knitted together.

"I use barbless hooks," I continued. "If you let even a bit of slack into the line, it's easy for the fish to unhook itself and get away."

"Why do you do it, then?"

"I think it makes for a fairer fight, and more importantly, it causes less harm to the fish. The barbs can tear and hurt the fish when you remove them."

"I see . . ." He gestured at the hook. "Do you mind if I have a look?"

"Have at it!"

I held it out to him, and he took it carefully with two fingers. Theo blinked as he held it up in the fading light, inspecting it.

"Did . . . did you make this, too?"

"Yeah, mate! With help from the local blacksmith, of course."

"Wow . . . the quality is unbelievable. One of our members makes all of our hooks, but he's no smith."

He winced. "The barbs on our hooks are vicious-looking things—I feel bad for the fish now. You must think us barbaric."

I held both hands up. "Oh, I'm not judging you at all for your methods. I do what I do based on my own morality, and what you choose to use is your prerogative."

He felt the tip of the hook, pricking a layer of skin on his thumb.

"It's so sharp . . ."

He peered at me, his eyes hopeful.

"Do you have any you could sell to us?"

"I'm afraid I don't—I only have one of each size so far."

A look of disappointment crossed his face. "Oh. I understand. Maybe I can organize for the merchant to purchase some from you next time he comes to the village?"

I gave him a conspiratorial grin. "When are you leaving?"

"Tomorrow morning with the merchant . . . why?"

"At daybreak?"

He shook his head. "No. Marcus usually stays for a few hours following sunrise to sell more wares. What are you planning?"

"Well, if you have some spare time in the morning, Fergus at the smithy might let me make you some more."

His eyes lit up. "You'd do that? I'd be happy to pay whatever price you request!"

"Mate, I'd be more than happy to do it—free of charge, of course! I already have moldings made, so it shouldn't be too hard."

"Free?" Theo held his hands up this time, showing his discomfort with the idea. "I couldn't possibly . . ."

"Hey now, I thought you agreed we were friends!"

I clapped him on the shoulder.

"What are friends for, if not for sharing the love of fishing? You can think of it as me pushing my morality onto you if it makes it any easier—think of the poor fish and what your barbaric hooks are doing to them."

I waggled my eyebrows at Theo, showing I was only joking, and he smirked back.

"And here I was thinking you were just a nice person—I knew there had to be an ulterior motive for your selflessness."

He shook his head with a soft laugh. "I suppose I can agree to your help—for the fish, I mean! It has nothing to do with me wanting your quality hooks for my friends and I."

Theo let go of the hook and passed me the rod, then extended his hand.

"I'd better get going, but it was a pleasure meeting you, Fischer. I'm glad we crossed paths."

I clasped his proffered hand. "Likewise, Theo. I'll see you tomorrow morning at first light, yeah? Do you know where the smithy is?"

"I'm staying in the village lord's house tonight—I'll ask him or his wife for directions."

I raised an eyebrow. "I knew you were well-off by the cut of your clothes, but I had no idea you walked in such prestigious circles!" I shot him a wink and gave a bow. "Thank you for blessing me with your presence, my lord."

He rolled his eyes at my feigned deference. "I'm only here on business." He adopted a posh intonation, his words clipped and grandiose. "I am but a pawn in the crown's game, a mere vessel for His Majesty's greatness."

I laughed at his approximation of nobility. "Well, I'll see you bright and early tomorrow—if Your Excellency can find it in his heart to indulge this lowly one, of course."

He rolled his eyes again and turned away.

"See you then!" he called over his shoulder, giving me a wave.

"You're sure, George?" Geraldine asked. "He passed him the notes from our meeting?"

"I'm sure." George leaned back in his plush couch, wishing he could sink into it and disappear. "We are undone . . ."

She laid a hand on his. "We aren't undone, my love. If anything, this is fantastic news."

He raised his head, looking at her through half-lidded eyes. "How is this anything other than a disaster?"

"Because they can't be here for us! Don't you see? Theo said it himself: it's not uncommon for lords and ladies to steal—uh, *misappropriate* funds. If Fischer is a crown auditor's handler, he must have another goal in mind."

"Who else could it be?"

She squeezed his hand. "I have no clue, but it can't be us—think about it. If the goal were to remove us from power, to drag us back to the capital and make us pay for our actions, he could have just done so. You said Fischer was in Julian's jewelry shop, right? Maybe it's something to do with the jeweler association, or the Cult of the Cut Gem."

George just shook his head. "I don't know, my love. I cannot think at this moment. My thoughts are addled, my normally unflappable pragmatism shattered into a thousand pieces."

Geraldine picked up his hand, squeezing it between both of hers. "Why don't you go get some rest, dear? It can't have been easy discovering what you did."

She kissed his hand and held it to her cheek. "My brave, courageous husband—you did so well scouting out the two vile crown agents. I'm so proud of you."

George was about to agree with her suggestion of rest when three loud knocks came from the front door.

Geraldine stood. "I'll get it."

"No."

George peeled his immense girth from the couch and began straightening his clothes. "I can handle one more confrontation for the day. There is nothing either of them could say to shake me further."

She rested her head on his chest, blinking up at him seductively. "My big, strong husband."

It stirred nothing within George, numb as he was.

"I shall return."

* * *

When George answered the door, Theo raised an eyebrow.

"Are you well, George?"

"Y-yes."

Lie.

Theo cocked his head, looking at the village lord and his pallid complexion. "Are you sure?"

George's eyes went wide as he no doubt remembered Theo's ability to detect lies. He nodded, averting his eyes.

"I'll show you to your room."

When George walked up the stairs to the second floor, he leaned heavily on the railing, further stoking Theo's curiosity. Whether it was in his nature, or a result of his years of training, Theo found the unresolved mystery unbearable.

He opened his mouth to start a line of questioning that would eventually sniff out the root of the cause, but after letting it hang open for a moment, closed it again.

I have something more important to do . . .

They traveled in silence, both men's thoughts elsewhere.

"This is your room," George uttered, opening a door. "The bathroom is two doors down."

"Thank you, George."

Theo stepped into the room and withdrew his notepad. George started to speak, but a choked noise came out, so he cleared his throat.

"I-if you need anything, just call for Geraldine or I."

Theo gave him a broad grin. "Thanks, George—I will. I think I'll turn in for the night, though—I have to meet Fischer bright and early at the smithy."

Theo closed the door and got out his pencil, intent on formulating his plans, then paused as part of his training sprung up from within.

He threw open the door, and was about to call for George, but the lord was still standing there, staring into space.

George blinked as his eyes refocused. "Y-yes, Theo?"

"I just remembered something—you've met Fischer, correct?"

George's neck twitched.

"Yes . . ."

"What is your opinion of the man? Is he what you'd call a good person?"

George's face was a mix of emotions, and small muscles beneath the surface moved continuously.

". . . George?"

"Forgive me—I've had a rather stressful day."

Theo gave him a disarming smile, nodding at the words. "I apologize, George. We auditors can have that effect on people." He put a hand on the lord's shoulder, intending to comfort, but George flinched.

"Could you answer my question, though? Would you call Fischer a good person?"

George paused while formulating his answer, and eventually, he spoke in a flat tone.

"Fischer has had a resoundingly positive effect on the villagers and seems to bring joy and prosperity to those he calls his friends."

Complete truth, but he skirted around his own opinion . . .

"And what of you, George? What do you think of Fischer?"

He took another moment to formulate an answer.

"He is endlessly intriguing and shrouded in mystery."

The truth, but likely only a half truth . . .

If it were any other time, Theo would have dug into the misleading answer, but with more important things to consider, the lord's answers would suffice.

"Thank you, George. That's all I wanted to know. Goodnight."

Theo closed the door and moved to the bed as he started jotting down thoughts. He sat down, letting out a content sigh.

Despite his feelings of friendship and gratitude for Fischer, his training had kicked in, demanding he check the opinions of those around him. As vague as George's personal opinion had been, knowing his effect on the villagers—and, more importantly, those he called his friends—was more than enough to set his mind at ease.

His hand was a blur as he started planning.

CHAPTER SIXTY-ONE

IMBALANCE

Sergeant Snips woke beneath the water. She stretched out her limbs, shuddering as each muscle loosened. Blinking her lone eye, she peered at her surroundings with blurred vision. Predawn light filtered down from above, bathing the pool in orange and pink light.

Her missing eye, which was still a minor annoyance at times, itched beneath her prized eye patch. She scratched the top of the patch absentmindedly while her thoughts slowly churned into motion.

I slept for the entire day and night?

No awakening had come from her slumber, but she felt renewed, her body filled with vigor. Scuttling out of the pool, she headed for the scheduled meeting.

"G'day, Theo!"

"Fischer!" He strode toward me, and we clasped hands. "Did you sleep well?"

"I always sleep well here, mate. Tropica is a little slice of paradise."

He looked up at the sky and its blend of colors, letting out a content sigh. "I can see that. Being so close to the ocean is a blessing—I'm beyond jealous."

"Hey, you could always move here. Bring your fishing club down and set up a little clubhouse."

"If only—I have commitments in the capital, unfortunately."

"Well, there's always a spare bed available in my house if you come visit. You're welcome anytime."

He shook his head with a laugh. "You're too good to me, Fischer." He quirked an eyebrow. "You're sure there's no ulterior motives?"

I held up my hands. "You got me, mate—I'm trying to lure you into a life of fishing and heresy."

"Jokes on you—I'm already well past that line." He yawned. "Before we get started on this selfless hook-crafting lesson . . . are you a coffee drinker? I want to try out that new coffee machine."

I grinned. "I was gonna ask you the same thing."

"Good morning, Fischer!" Sue yelled, a bead of sweat on her brow as she rushed to keep up with the coffee orders.

"Mornin,' Sue!" I called from the back of the line.

Some people in line turned, giving me smiles, which I happily returned.

"Is it always this busy?" Theo asked.

"Not usually, but I think it's only gonna get busier when people get a taste for the liquid of the gods."

"Understandable. I still can't believe George organized affordable coffee for the masses—in retrospect, it's a genius idea, but I've never seen it implemented in any of the other towns or villages I've visited."

I grinned at Theo's assumption but was happy to give George the credit—he'd been having a tough crack of it lately.

"Do you travel much?" I asked. "You never did tell me what you did for work."

"I travel around a lot. It comes with the territory, unfortunately. Not every place I visit is as idyllic as Tropica."

He pursed his lips. "I suppose I can tell you what I do for work, but can you promise to keep it to yourself?"

"You're not some crime lord's muscle, are you?" I asked with a laugh. "You seem a little too wholesome to be a hired thug."

He gave me an askew glance, smirking at my words. "I'm sorry to get serious for a second, but I need your word that you'll keep it to yourself. If you share what I do, there may be . . . consequences."

"Wait, you aren't really a crime lord's enforcer, are you?" I kept the smile on my face, showing him I was still joking. "Mate, I wouldn't tell anyone even if there weren't consequences—that's not what friends do."

Theo nodded at my words, accepting them as the truth. "All right." He leaned in, speaking softly. "I'm a crown auditor. Do you know what that means?"

"I don't," I whispered back, "but I can sort of guess just by the job title. You check up on villages and businesses to make sure they're playing by the rules, yeah?"

He nodded. "That's right."

"Well, that certainly explains the clothes—why the mystery, though? Is it that important to protect your identity?"

"It is. If people knew who we were, every time we were spotted on the road, someone could run ahead and warn other villages of our impending arrival. We tend to operate by going on long excursions, hitting every stop on the way."

"Ah, got ya. That makes sense."

I snapped my fingers. "That's why you came with the merchant! You can just slip into the caravan, becoming just one more of the workers, right?"

He grinned. "Exactly right. I have one more thing to mention, though."

"Yeah? What's that?"

"I tell you this in the spirit of friendship, so there isn't an imbalance—well, as little an imbalance as possible. I need your word you won't speak of it."

"Of course, mate. I'd never share anyone's secret they wanted to keep, let alone a friend." I leaned in closer, filling my whispered words with exaggeration. "*Or even worse, a dreaded crown auditor! I've heard those blokes can be ruthless!*"

He gave me a flat stare but couldn't keep his face straight for long. "All right, what I wanted to tell you is this: we have the ability to detect lies when people speak to us."

Both my eyebrows shot up. "Wait, for real? How?"

"Years of training. Some nobles speculate that we're hidden cultivators, harnessing the power of the long-dormant System, but it's something much more simple. We can read body language and hear the truth of words after years of painstaking study."

"Er—is it okay to tell me all of this?"

"It is—you promised me you wouldn't speak of it, right?"

"Oh my god, you read me when I promised that?"

He grimaced. "I did. I see you as a friend, Fischer, which is why I told you this. I understand if you don't want to associate with me anymore, but I'll need your word again that you won't tell a soul."

"Mate, that sounds *exhausting* for you. Knowing the truth all the time can't be easy, right?"

He gave me a sad smile. "It has its drawbacks . . ."

"Well, it doesn't bother me, my man!" I put an arm around his shoulder. "And, to set your mind at ease, after learning about your psychic-power shenanigans, I still won't ever tell a soul. Your secrets are just that—yours."

"Sorry about the wait!" Sue called.

We'd reached the front of the line without even realizing.

"Two coffees?" she asked.

"And two of your finest croissants, please!" I said.

"Coming right up!"

"Damn. This is good," Theo said, appraising the coffee's crema with a practiced eye.

"Mate, I'm offended! Did you think we would make a bad coffee?"

"We?" he asked, smiling sidelong and raising an eyebrow.

"Yeah! Sue and I are best friends! You insult her coffee, I might just come out swinging!"

I mimed a few punches toward him with my freehand, and he snorted.

"I thought you and I were best friends?" He pulled a hand back to his chest, the very picture of indignation. "Fischer—have you been seeing other friends?"

"Frack me, you're so controlling. I can't do this anymore, Theo." I took a breath, exhaling it with a dramatic sigh as I put my head in my hands. "It might be time we see other people."

Theo made a choking noise, so I looked up, my eyebrows furrowed in confusion. "Mate?"

He was choking back a laugh, and as the confusion on my face grew, he pointed over my shoulder. Maria stood behind me, her eyes wide and jaw slightly open, darting looks between us.

Heat rose to my face, and I could tell a furious blush was overcoming me.

"Er—it's not what it sounds like . . ."

Theo couldn't contain it any longer. The laugh burst from him, loud and full of elation. He buckled, leaning on his knee with one hand, the other pointed at me.

"Y-your face!"

"This is why it'll never work between us, Theo! You never take me seriously!"

He crumpled onto the ground as his laughter grew, the coffee placed on the street so it wouldn't spill.

My composure dissolved, and I soon joined him on the cobbled street. Wiping tears from my eyes, I glanced at Maria. She still looked flummoxed, but the corner of her mouth was curled up in a smile.

"Ah, I needed that," I said, standing. "This is my friend, Theo. Theo, this is Maria."

"A—a pleasure," Theo said, his voice high and strained as he fought off his mirth.

He approached and extended a hand, which Maria shook in a firm grip.

"You two had me worried there for a second." Realizing what she'd said, she raised both hands. "N-not that there's anything wrong if you guys were . . . you know . . ."

Theo wiped his eyes. "While I admit Fischer is quite a catch, he's just not my type, sadly."

"Playing hard to get, huh?" I asked.

". . . is it working?"

"Sorry, mate—I think we should just be friends."

"Ahhh," Theo lamented as he stood. "Unrequited love."

"Uh . . ." Maria said. "Are you sure you guys aren't . . . ? It's fine if you are."

"No," I blurted, realizing we'd taken it too far.

"W-we're only joking," Theo said at the same time, coming to a similar conclusion.

Maria was trying to hide a smile but failed spectacularly.

Theo shook his head. "Young lady! *I have never!*"

"Sorry," she said, her laugh finally escaping. "I couldn't help myself."

I took a deep breath, exulting as I stretched and let it out. When I finished, I turned to Maria.

"How's Sharon doing?"

She beamed. "Mom is doing really well, Fischer. I came to get a coffee for Dad and me. He stayed up all night, refusing to leave her unwatched for a moment—despite her protests."

"Well, we'll leave you to it, then. We wouldn't want to keep your poor Dad waiting."

She nodded, her hair flowing with the movement. "I might see you later, then. I'm sure Mom would love to meet you at some point."

She turned to Theo. "It was nice meeting you."

"Likewise, young lady. It was a pleasure."

After Maria was long gone, Theo raised an eyebrow at me.

"Her mother was unwell?"

"Yeah, mate. Really sick. Even elixirs from the Cult of the Alchemist weren't working, but another villager performed a miracle with some herbal concoction."

"Really? Alchemist elixirs didn't work, but an herbal remedy did?"

"Yeah. I have no doubt she'd still be unwell if it weren't for Barry's intervention."

"Fascinating . . ."

* * *

"Have at it, Fischer!" Fergus called from the back of the smithy. "You need a hand? I'll be busy back here a while, but if you're not ready to do it yourself . . ."

"Nah! I've got it!"

Fergus flicked his goggles back on and returned his attention to the molten slag before him.

"Give me a yell if you get stuck!"

Theo gave me an odd look. "You do it yourself? I thought you said the smith helped you make them?"

"Well, yeah! He helped me make the castings and showed me how to do, well . . . everything. It's super simple though, so I can fly solo now. Here, I'll show you."

Theo watched with growing amazement at Fischer's aptitude.

I know he said the smith showed him how, but his hand is so steady, his movements so exact. I'd think he'd been a blacksmith for years if he didn't tell me otherwise.

Theo shook his head, returning his attention to Fischer and the metal he was currently melting in the forge. Thick muscles bulged from Fischer's forearms as he gripped the tongs.

Even his body looks like he's been a blacksmith for years . . .

Fischer withdrew the crucible, and in a single flowing movement, swept it to the molding and began to pour. A thin line of molten metal poured directly into the hole, and at what looked like the perfect moment, he moved the crucible to the next casing, not losing a single drop of metal to the table.

When the last casing was poured, he set the tongs and crucible down, scooped up all the molds, and carried them toward the bucket of . . . *oil?* Theo's knowledge of smithing was rudimentary at best, but he was *pretty* sure they used oil in the forging process.

"Are you all right if I step outside for a moment, Fischer? I just need to go speak to Marcus about the departing time."

"No worries, mate," Fischer replied, still focusing on the casings.

No worries? Theo thought. *He has such an odd way of speaking sometimes . . .*

"I'll be back in a moment, then."

I barely heard Theo's words, completely focused as I was. A state of flow had overtaken me, my work all consuming. I dropped the molds into the oil, then reached in and flicked the latches open. The oil getting on my skin didn't bother me in the least, and as the metal swiftly cooled, I reached into the bottom and plucked up the hooks. I pulled them up just in time for all four hooks to transform as one.

CHAPTER SIXTY-TWO

LUCK

The forge radiated a calming heat, making me feel at ease. My eyes widened as the change started.

As the hooks transformed, a familiar feeling welled up from my core. The hooks expanded, then contracted, and they drew my vision in.

Small Barbless Circle Hook of the Fisher

Uncommon

A small hook used for catching fish. The design causes fish to hook themselves when attempting to escape. This hook provides boosts to both fishing and luck.

+2 fishing

+1 luck

The description and stats were the same for all three circle hook variants, the only change being the size listed: small, medium, and large. Then, it gave a description for the last hook.

Small Barbless Shank Hook of the Fisher

Uncommon

A small hook used for catching fish. The design of this hook makes it easy for smaller fish to eat the hook, and the long shaft protects the line from being severed by sharp teeth. This hook provides boosts to both fishing and luck.

+2 fishing

+1 luck

"Fischer..."

I looked up, worried I'd see Theo watching me. Instead, Fergus had a flat stare leveled at me.

"That was you again, wasn't it?"

"I, uh, have no idea what you're talking about?" My voice trailed off at the end of my sentence, leaving the last word hanging.

He smiled and shook his head before returning to his work at the back of the smithy.

Real smooth, Fischer. Real smooth.

I returned my attention to the hooks, and more notably, their stats. Just as with my new rod, I could actually read the stats listed. My previous creations—Sergeant Snips's eyepatch and the pearl ring—had simply said something about needing "requisite knowledge" to see the benefits they gave.

Is that because I've leveled a fishing skill enough to have the requisite knowledge?

It lent further credence to a suspicion I'd long since held but had no way to prove: the System messages were trying to tell me about advancements, but lacked the power to do so.

"There's enough power to continue advancing me, but not enough to tell me about it? Who coded this damn thing?"

"Who whated what thing?" Theo asked from behind me.

I jumped and almost sent the hooks flying. "Frack me, mate—you scared the piss out of me."

Theo raised an eyebrow, glancing down at my pants. "You . . . wet yourself?"

"What? No." I waved the question away. "It's a figure of speech, my man. I'm saying you scared me enough to wet myself."

"That's . . . an odd thing to say."

I sighed, waving my hand again. "Forget it. It's normal where I come from."

I considered if I should show the hooks to Theo. I trusted him, but he worked for the crown. Would it make him realize I was ascending, then lead to me being taken?

There's no Xianxia Liam Neeson to come save me if I'm kidnapped.

Smiling at the inner monologue, I shook my head.

He already held my rod and that didn't cause any issues . . .

"Fischer? Are you all right?"

I looked up at Theo, smiling. "Yeah, mate. I finished the first batch of hooks."

I held my hand out, and he opened his palm. When the hooks landed, he held his hand up before his face, inspecting them with an unwavering gaze.

"They're so smooth."

"Just like me with the ladies." I waggled my eyebrows, drawing a laugh from Theo.

"You mean like before with Maria, when your face went pink as a watermelon?"

"There's watermelon?" I yelled.

"What? Here? No." He leveled a finger at me. "Stop changing the subject—I saw the way you two looked at each other. Is she your lady friend?" He wiggled his eyebrows back at me, but excited as I was, I barely noticed.

They have gods damned watermelons! *I* need *some! It'd be hard to grow in sandy soil, but with enough watering—*

"Fischer . . ."

"Huh?"

He shook his head at me. "I mention Maria once, and you get dragged off into your head. You like her that much, do you?"

Heat rose to my face. "Maria and I are just neighbors—er—*friends?*"

"You're blushing!"

"Leave me alone, Theo! The forge is hot!"

* * *

After another hour, and a few threats to cease production if Theo didn't stop bringing up Maria, I finished the twentieth set of hooks. All were the same, and thankfully, none brought on another pulse of advancement that may have been hard to explain.

"I insist," I said.

"And I refuse," Theo answered.

"I can make more!"

"Twenty sets and a leather pouch are too many for me to take without payment."

"You already paid me!"

"How?" he demanded.

I gave him my best jazz hands, singing my response. "*Friendship!*"

". . . I'm not sure I want to be friends with you anymore."

"It's too late—you're stuck with me. Take the hooks before I start singing again."

He scrunched up his face but held out a hand, and I happily placed the small leather pouch into his hand. He peered inside, and despite his hesitancy to accept, a wide smile spread over his face.

"Thank you, Fischer."

I beamed. "You're most welcome, my man. I'll walk you out."

I turned my head back to the workshop, yelling. "Thanks, Fergus!"

"You're done?" he called back.

"Yeah, mate! All done!"

The burly man walked around from the back of the workshop, removing goggles and gloves as he went.

"Sorry for my rudeness—I've got an urgent order to replace an axle bearing for Marcus."

Theo snorted. "He told me he would happily wait as long as I wanted—now I know why."

Fergus gave a rueful grin. "He's tricky, that one."

He glanced at me. "Who's your friend, Fischer?"

"Oh! Sorry! Fergus, this is Theo. Theo, Fergus."

Fergus held out a meaty hand, and Theo clasped it.

"Thank you for letting us use your forge, Fergus. It's a pleasure making your acquaintance."

"*Acquaintance?*"

Fergus's hand pumped up and down. "Any friend of Fischer is a friend of mine!"

As we wandered toward the merchant caravans, a comfortable silence stretched between us. My eyes were drawn to the western mountains, the blue skies above them heralding the beautiful day to come.

Theo let out a content noise. "I'm loath to leave this place, Fischer. The scenery and the people are as lovely as each other."

"You know, I offered for you to stay . . ."

He shook his head.

"I still have my commitments—I did have a proposition for you, though."

"Oh? What's that, mate?"

Theo chewed the inside of his lip as he considered how to word his offer.

"Why don't you come back to the capital with me?"

I raised an eyebrow. "What do you want with me in the capital?"

"I know you have a good setup here, but I thought you might want to be closer to people with an appreciation for your . . . activities. I'm sure the rest of the fishing club would love to meet you."

"Sorry, Theo—I have commitments here as well."

"If it's work, I can get you a job in the capital. Whatever it is you do here to get by, I could find you a better-paying job. Something with low hours so you can spend as much time fishing as possible."

I smiled at him. "Thanks for the offer, mate, but it's not a financial obligation. I have friends here, and as nice as it'd be to meet some fellow heretics, this is the place for me. Right back at you, too—if you ever change your mind and want to move out here, or even come for a holiday, come ask for me. I live on the southern shores, and most people can point you my way."

Theo nodded then produced his notepad. "I figured you'd say that. Here."

He tore out a page and held it out to me. Neatly written words covered both sides—none of which I could read.

"The first is my address if you ever change your mind. The second is the fishing club president—Josh's—address. Last is the address of the tailor where you can get clothing like mine prepared. Her name is Sammie, and if you mention my name, she'll be happy for your business."

I neatly folded the page and put it in my back pocket.

"Thanks, Theo. You're a good bloke."

His eyebrows knitted together. "You have such an odd vernacular, Fischer. May I assume 'bloke' is a good thing?"

"It is," I said with a laugh. "Just another word for a man."

"Cheers . . . bloke," he replied, testing the words. "Did that sound right?"

"Nailed it."

We walked between the last two fields of cane before the merchant caravans, and we both came to a stop.

"Well," he said, "I guess this is goodbye for now."

He held out a hand, and I looked down at it. "You a hugger, Theo?"

He smiled, so I grabbed his hand and pulled him into one.

"Until next time, mate. We're bros now, so don't be a stranger."

"Er—*bros?*"

I let out a loud laugh as our embrace ended.

"Short for brothers."

"Same to you . . . *bro.* Come see me in Gormona any time."

"I might take you up on a visit soon—I have some things I think I can only get in the capital."

He flicked the sleeve of my shirt, a wry smile on his face. "Like a decent set of clothing?"

"Hey! There's nothing wrong with my clothes . . . but I might visit Sammie the tailor while I'm there, just to peruse her wares, of course—I worry they might be a bit too lavish for a mere peasant."

Theo winced. "I was only joking."

"I know. Just yanking your chain."

He let out a prolonged sigh at the unfamiliar idiom. "Do I even want to know?"

I held out my hand. "See you soon, Theo."

He clasped it. "See you soon . . . *mate.*"

After providing Sharon with another dose of the sugarcane juice, Barry rushed through the forest on the west side of Fischer's property. His steps were clipped, late as he was. He caught sight of the blue-tinted tree, and as he got closer, saw his accomplice was already there—he jogged toward her.

"Sorry I'm late, Snips—I had to dispense more medicine for Sharon."

Sergeant Snips stood on eight spindly legs, shrugging as she stretched her claws out.

Barry began making his report.

"The first test was a complete success—the sugarcane juice required little processing. As we hoped, but didn't dare expect, the produce grown from Fischer's power was enough to awaken Sharon, and she's making a full recovery from her sickness."

Snips nodded as she drew words in the dirt.

"Not needing to use master's cooking is good—it makes our goals much easier to accomplish. What did you mean by little processing*?"*

Barry nodded vigorously, unable to contain his excitement. "I thought we might need to refine the juice into sugar, then have her eat the granulated essence, either straight or baked into food by someone with the baking skill. Having the juice work directly saved days—if not weeks—of testing."

Snips blew what Barry thought was a happy stream of bubbles.

"Did she agree to the plan?"

"She did! Just as we expected. She took it even better than I'd imagined, and she offered to join us before I could ask."

Snips nodded again, claw once more drawing.

"Good."

She paused, rocking her carapace back and forth in thought before her writing resumed.

"Should we go over the plan again? We may improve it."

"I thought the same thing! That we don't need to process the sugarcane opens up a world of possibilities. How do you feel about making rum?"

Snips cocked her carapace, clearly not understanding the word.

Barry's eyes gleamed. "I'll bet Fischer will love it."

Sergeant Snips, having heard all she needed to be convinced, nodded her agreement.

CHAPTER SIXTY-THREE

PROPOSITION

On my way through the village, I picked up another croissant. I was feeling rather peckish after a morning of smithing, minor as the work may have been. Naturally, I grabbed a second coffee, too.

"Thank you, Sue!"

"Thank *you,* Fischer!" she called, once more a blur behind the coffee machine.

I bit into the flaky pastry as I walked, the buttery flavor washing over me and pairing perfectly with the coffee.

That Fielday was even more productive than I'd hoped.

I stopped in place so abruptly, my coffee almost spilled. I cocked my head, my face scrunching.

Why does it feel like I'm forgetting something, though . . . ? I'm pretty sure I did—

"Shit!"

I ran through the streets of Tropica.

As I knocked on the door, I plastered an apologetic smile on my face. There wasn't a sound from the other side, and just as I started thinking no one was home, the door creaked open.

A single eye peered out at me.

"Fischer."

"G'day, Joel. You, uh, you all right, mate?"

His single visible eye didn't move, and he let out a sharp sniff.

"I'm fine."

Seeing he was most certainly not fine, I rushed to speak.

"I wanted to come and apologize for missing your group meditation yesterday. I know I promised I'd come, but some wild things happened, and I just didn't have the time." In truth, I'd forgotten, but he didn't need to know that.

The door slowly swung all the way open, and Joel stood before me, putting on a smile. "Would you like to come in?"

Joel forced a smile onto his face as he opened the door. "Would you like to come in?"

"I'd love to, mate," Fischer said, easily striding inside.

"So, *wild things* kept you away yesterday? What kind of *wild things?*"

"I mean, there was the merchant, the coffee, a new friendship, and all tax-break shenanigans—but all that was nothing before Sharon's recovery."

Joel's heart fluttered, and all his feelings of rejection melted away like all life before the inevitability of carcinization.

"*Sharon has recovered?*"

"Er—yeah." Fischer raised an eyebrow, but it was quickly swept away by a full-faced smile. "I wasn't aware you knew her."

"I do—we do, I should say. The Cult of Carcinization meditates on the health of sick community members, channeling our will toward their ascension." Joel sniffed again. "You'd know that if you showed up for the group meditation yesterday."

Fischer furrowed his brow. "Just to clarify, mate—you meditate with the express goal of turning sick people into crabs?"

Joel nodded seriously, content that Fischer was so quick to comprehend. "Precisely. If carcinization were to claim them, they would leave behind the weak flesh of the body, and with it, all illness and ailment." Joel snapped his attention to Fischer. "She didn't show any signs, did she?"

"Er—signs?"

"Of carcinization."

Fischer pressed his lips together, and Joel's hopes soared.

Is it possible?

I pressed my lips together; it took every ounce of my will to not laugh in Joel's face.

"Nah, mate," I forced out, keeping my expression schooled. "Sorry to be the bearer of bad news, but she didn't show any signs of evolving into a crab."

Joel sighed, long and exhaustive. "As expected. I know it likely won't happen in our lifetime. Even so, I hold out hope that carcinization will occur in our sleepy little village."

"Hope is a powerful thing, Joel! You never know what will happen."

I turned and strode toward the door.

"Well, I've got a bunch of stuff to get done—thanks for the hospitality!"

"Y-you're sure you have to go? We could do a meditation together if you please."

"Sorry. So much to do, so little time. I'll see you next Fielday for the meditation, though, yeah?"

"Of course. I'll see you then, Fischer."

As I walked outside, I finally let my smile out. A meditation actually sounded quite nice, but if I spent one more second in the Carcinization headquarters, I couldn't have stopped myself laughing at Joel and his hope that Sharon sprouted claws.

Man, he would absolutely lose his shit if I introduced him to Snips—I wonder if he can be trusted.

I'd have to consider it more; I still didn't know him well enough to make that call yet.

With my sincere apology delivered, I made my way toward Maria's.

* * *

"I've brought someone to meet you, Mom."

Maria led me into the room, and Sharon peered at me with a focused gaze.

"G'day, Sharon—I'm Fischer."

Roger cleared his throat. "That's his way of saying hello."

"Barry told me of his colorful words, husband." Sharon smiled up at me. "It's a pleasure to meet you finally—I heard you've been helping out my family, and I find myself in your debt."

I held up both hands. "I was just helping out where I could. You owe me nothing."

Sharon nodded, accepting my words. "Would you mind giving us a moment of privacy, Roger?"

He shot a look at her, then at me, his eyes narrowing.

"My goodness, Dad." Maria walked over and grabbed his arm. "Show Fischer a bit of trust, would you?"

"No funny business," he said in passing.

Roger's warning was entirely undermined by him being dragged from the room by his daughter, and Maria rolled her eyes as she removed him.

The door clicked closed behind them, so I returned my attention to Sharon.

"What did you wanna speak about?"

"I wanted to know more about you." She sat up straighter, resting her hands on her lap. "You showed up on our shores only weeks ago, and from what I've heard, you've had an overwhelmingly good impact on everyone in Tropica—my family included."

I sat down on the end of her bed. "Hearing that makes me happier than you know, Sharon. I came to Tropica for two reasons: fishing and making friends. Knowing I've had a positive impact on those around me is all I could ask for."

She nodded, a kind smile spreading across her face. "Where did you come from?"

"Really, *really* far away. It may as well be another world with how different it is."

She nodded again, and her eyes held an intelligent gleam as she stared into mine. "Are you from this world, Fischer?"

"Uh . . . *yes . . . ?*" I responded, the words unconvincing, even to myself.

I let out a soft chuckle, trying to hide my shock at the abrupt question. "What makes you ask something so wild?"

Sharon shrugged. "I'm only joking. I remember stories my parents used to tell me as a young girl—tales of fancy where people would appear from another world and flip the Kallis Realm on its head with their very existence."

My skin prickled, and her look seemed to pin my feet to the floor.

She let out a quiet laugh. "They're just stories, of course. Since the gods fled and the System stopped working properly, such things are impossible, wouldn't you agree?"

I leaped at the extended olive branch, nodding along. "I couldn't agree more. Those stories do sound rather romantic, though—someone just appearing from another world and helping people out." I shrugged. "I'm from Kallis, too, unfortunately."

"*Helping?*" She shook her head with a smile. "We must have heard different stories as children. More often than not, in the ones my mother used to repeat, new arrivals swiftly gathered power and started taking over vast swaths of land before a hero finally stopped them."

"O-oh . . . right . . ."

"That only further cements you as a fellow native of Kallis—all you've done is help others, after all."

"I gotta say, I never heard those stories as a kid. Were there any tales of people who arrived and didn't want to conquer?"

Sharon tilted her head back and forth. "There were a few, but they always ended up becoming tyrants in the end. Power corrupts, as they say."

I grimaced. "It does seem to have that effect . . ."

"Well, if one shows up, maybe you can be the hero that saves the world." She gave me a wink. "Thank you for indulging my questions, Fischer. I just wanted to get a better idea of the man that was my family's lifeline while I was unwell."

I tried to give her a confident smile, but it felt shaky. "You're welcome, Sharon. It was a pleasure to meet you finally."

"The pleasure was all mine."

She stretched, letting out a yawn. "Would you mind sending that overprotective husband of mine back in? I have some tasks to take his mind off me."

"Has he always been so . . . intense?"

Her eyes sparkled. "Always. It's what I love the most about him, but it can get stifling at times."

"All right. I'll send him your way." I shot her an exaggerated wink. "Good luck."

Sharon laughed, the sound light and fleeting, reminding me of her daughter.

"I'll certainly need it . . ."

Roger made a sound that, by some stretch of the imagination, could be equated with a noise of gratitude. He turned and strode into the house.

Maria sat on the porch, lazily dragging a stick through the dirt below. She looked up at me.

"So? What did Mom want to speak to you about?"

"She just wanted to thank me in private for letting you guys farm my land while she was sick."

Maria smiled halfheartedly, then returned to drawing in the dirt. I sat down beside her.

"How are you feeling?"

She pressed down on the stick; it snapped in half. "I don't know how I feel." She picked up both halves, probing the broken ends. "I'm beyond happy that Mom has recovered, but I feel . . . useless?"

"What makes you say that?"

Maria sighed. "I feel like I should do something, but she's already back to her sharp self. Dad is by her side every minute for the small things, like bringing food and water, but I can tell she's feeling smothered by even that."

I glanced at Maria; she stared at the ground, lost in the thoughts of uselessness. I knew the sentiment well, and I wished at that moment I knew the right words to say; the magical combination of sounds that would set her heart free.

Instead, I said something cliché. "Isn't just being there enough?"

She shrugged with one shoulder. "I feel like I'm intruding when I'm with her and Dad. They have so much history, and it feels like I'm interrupting their conversation."

She snapped one of the sticks, discarding the shorter end in the dirt. "I don't know. I feel like I just need to do something to distract myself, but there isn't really much to do with the fields right now."

The seed of an idea planted itself in my mind, and after a moment of trying to suppress it, the seed sprouted. "You know . . . you could always try fishing . . ."

Her gaze shot up to me, and I smiled at her. She scoffed, so I raised my eyebrows, my smile growing. Upon realizing I was serious, her mouth dropped open and her eyes widened.

"You're serious? You'd show me how to fish?"

"Yeah! Why not? You're looking for something to keep you busy, right? A new hobby sounds like just the thing."

I tried to keep the desperation from my voice.

Keep it cool, Fischer. Don't scare her off!

"Is . . . that something you'd be interested in?"

"If you'd asked me a couple weeks ago, I'd have rejected it offhand, but after getting to know you . . ." She shrugged. "The idea doesn't seem so bad."

While I was thinking of what to say next, she continued.

"I don't think I could, though—can you imagine how Dad would react? The silent treatment wouldn't be worth it."

My mind raced for a way around the roadblock that was Roger.

"What if we went on a trip?"

"A trip?" she asked. "What do you mean?"

"Have you ever been camping?"

"Fischer . . ." She laughed, the sound free and jubilant. "I have no idea what a trip or camping is."

"Oh, right. Sorry. A trip is like a holiday and camping is staying outdoors. There's this place I saw on the way here that I've been meaning to go back to. It's a couple of days away, but we could camp overnight in the forest."

"Hmmm," was all she said, then she stared off into space.

Damn, did I come in too hot? I really just want someone to fish with after meeting Theo, and it feels like just the thing to keep her distrac—

"Let's do it, Fischer."

CHAPTER SIXTY-FOUR

INTENTIONS

I blinked at Roger, and he scowled back at me.

"What are your intentions with my daughter?"

"*Dad!*" Maria yelled, running out of the house after him. "You are *so* embarrassing! Fischer invited me to go camping because I've been feeling down!"

Heat rose to my face; I felt poleaxed by the accusation in Roger's voice.

"Uh, yeah, that. Maria said she needed something to keep her busy, and I thought going on a trip would be a welcome distraction . . ."

"Uh-huh. Just you and my daughter, right? Alone? In the forest?"

"*Dad!*"

"Roger!" came another voice.

Where Maria's complaints had no effect on him, Sharon calling his name made Roger go bolt upright. She leaned against the doorframe, glaring out at him.

"Dear," she said, her voice sickly sweet. "Could you come speak with me for a moment?"

Roger audibly swallowed and started walking into the house.

"You shouldn't be out of bed . . ."

"I wouldn't need to be out of bed if a certain someone wasn't . . ." Sharon's voice trailed off as they retreated farther into their home.

Maria covered her face with a hand. "I am *so* sorry."

Glad to be rid of the belligerent father, I breathed a sigh of relief.

"It's fine. You're his only daughter, so I understand him being overprotective."

"Leto's modest veil—he's *so* embarrassing."

"You know, I think it's kind of sweet."

She shot me an incredulous look. "I've heard my dad called a lot of things when he wasn't around, but sweet was never one of them."

"Just to be clear, I'm talking about his actions, not the man himself. It shows he cares about you. Better to be overprotective than not care at all, right?"

She shook her head, pouting. "If he could keep his caring to himself instead of embarrassing me, that'd be great."

I grinned at her petulant expression; it was inexplicably adorable.

"So, when do you want to leave?"

She turned to me, her petulance forgotten.

"As soon as possible."

"Like . . . today?"

She nodded. "As soon as we're packed."

We were discussing what we needed to bring with us when Roger reappeared. He cleared his throat, leveling a moderately cowed glare at me.

"No fishing."

"*Dad!*"

"That's enough, Maria. I can accept that you're old enough to choose your own company, but the idea of you eating food that goes against the gods is where I draw my line in the sand."

I gave Roger a disarming smile. "You know I can't promise that, mate."

Roger's eyebrow twitched, and he opened his mouth to call me something choice—likely some creative mix of heretical and foolish—but I cut him off.

"I understand you're just trying to protect your daughter, so why don't we meet in the middle—any fish I catch will be returned to the water. I won't force Maria to partake in any heretical food."

Roger's glare deepened, and he made to speak, but was once more cut off. Sharon poked her head out the doorway behind him.

"That sounds like a lovely compromise, Fischer."

Roger started and spun. "Sharon—you agreed to go back to bed!"

She smiled sweetly at him, but her eyes held a gleam of danger. "And we agreed that you'd let our daughter make her own decisions, sweet husband, yet here we are."

Roger took a deep breath, letting it out in a rush as he turned back toward me. "You swear to not let her eat any fish?"

He extended a hand, and I winced. "I can't shake your hand on that, Roger."

His blank stare transformed into a mask of indignation. "And why is that?" he asked, his words clipped and halting.

"Because it'd be treating Maria as property to be bargained upon. I give you my word that I won't force her to do, well, anything. I won't force her to *not* do anything either, though. She's her own person, and she has complete autonomy over her choices—even if her choice is to catch and eat fish."

Roger's eye twitched, but before he could blurt anything out, Sharon spoke.

"Well said, Fischer." She gave me a beatific smile. "The only thing we ask is that you keep her safe. Isn't that right, Roger?"

A vein in Roger's forehead pulsed with such intensity, I worried it might explode. He nodded his acquiescence to Sharon's words.

"That, I can promise." I extended a hand. "I'll protect Maria with everything I have."

Roger grasped my open hand, and judging by the way his wiry muscles knotted, he was squeezing rather aggressively; I couldn't really tell, given my improved body.

"Well, I have some things to organize before we set off—you still want to leave today, Maria?"

I turned to her as I voiced my question, and her expression brought me up short.

Maria stared down at the ground, her face hidden. The skin I could see—that of her cheek and neck—were a bright pink, even through her sun-kissed tan. She nodded, making a small noise of assent.

Ah, damn. I embarrassed her . . .

I grimaced at my stupidity. "I'll see you soon."

"Sergeant Sniiiips!" I called, having looked almost everywhere for my favorite crustacean.

"Where has that little scamp gotten off to?"

Corporal Claws chirped her own confusion from atop my shoulder.

"Have you seen her at all today?"

Claws shook her head from side to side, letting out a soft coo.

I rubbed my chin in thought. "If I were an adorably cute, yet violently capable crab, where would I be?"

Sergeant Snips sat beneath the pool in a state of complete calm. She was neither awake nor asleep, existing in a state of limbo that she found entirely enjoyable. She'd thought she may have been imagining it previously, but now, she was sure: there *was* a power coming from the opalescent stone.

Faint wisps of its magic poured into her even now. She knew not where they went, yet it felt right; the slow accumulation made her more whole.

Something tugged at her awareness, so she slowly opened her lone eye. Light flooded in, and she held a claw up as a shield. Her missing eye itched under its patch, and a spike of annoyance ran through her at the interruption. But then, the real source of her alertness made itself known.

A muffled voice called from above.

"Hey! I can see you down there, Snips, you scoundrel! Stop ignoring me!"

Her entire body tensed.

Master is here!

She caught sight of him on the side of the pond, peering down at her. She bent her legs, and in a single, full-bodied effort, launched.

With my hands on my hips in mock affront, I stared down at the inattentive crab.

"You might need to go in after her, Claws. I think she's asleep . . . wait, what is she—"

Snips flew from the pond, her orange carapace aimed directly at my chest, a stream of water and ecstatic bubbles trailing in her wake. My improved body easily caught her, and I spun around, letting the movement absorb her momentum. Corporal Claws jumped from my shoulder, puffing up like an indignant cat as she hit the sand. Snips simply ignored the otter, rubbing her hard shell against my chest as a stream of joyous bubbles continued flowing.

"Where have you been, Snips? I've been looking everywhere for you!"

She gestured at the pond, then out to sea, then back at the pond again.

"All over the place, huh? Well, I'm glad I found you before I left."

Both Snips's and Claws's heads darted back, their eyes going wide, so I held my hands up placatingly.

"I'm only going on a trip, girls. Don't stress. I'll be back in a few days."

Snips blew bubbles of firm curiosity, demanding where I was going.

"I'm going on a little fishing and camping trip with Maria. She needs some time away, so I'm gonna go with her."

Snips narrowed her lone eye, pointed at herself, Corporal Claws, then me.

I shook my head. "Sorry, girls. I don't know how she'd react to learning of you. You're so strong and graceful, after all—she needs a break from life, and I'm not sure learning of sapient mini-gods would help."

They both stared hard at me, but after a moment, nodded their acquiescence.

"By the way, Snips—who's your friend?"

She cocked her head in confusion, so I pointed down into the saltwater pond.

"That's one of your rock crabs, right?"

She scuttled over, peering down into the water. Just below where she'd been sitting, a hint of brown could be seen. The crab was doing its best to hide from sight, huddled into a crevice as it was, yet it was still quite visible.

Snips took a few steps down to the water and slapped her deadly snipper on the surface. The crab didn't respond, so she cocked her claw back, ready to shoot an aura attack down at it—the crab responded immediately. It sprinted from the pond, prostrating itself on the sand before Sergeant Snips. She glared down at it, imperious. With one claw, she spun it around. Letting out a hesitant squeak, it lifted its body from the sand.

Poor thing has accepted its fate, I thought.

Snips released a hiss and a gout of angry bubbles as her right clacker shot under the body of the crab, and with a swift uppercut, launched it out to sea.

EEEEEEEEEEEEEEEEEEEEEEEEEEEEeeeeeeeeeeeeeeeeeeeeeeeeeeeeeeeeeee
eeeeeeeeeeeeeeeeeeeeeeeeeeeeeeeeeeeeee—

Plop.

"Damn." I raised an eyebrow. "Nice arm, Snips."

She shook her head and shrugged, blowing bubbles of reluctant acceptance.

"It's hard being a leader, huh?"

She nodded.

I bent down and stroked the top of her head. "You're doing good, Snips. I'm proud of you."

She preened—an impressive feat for a crab—and sidled up to me. Corporal Claws joined on my other side, rubbing her body up against my leg. I sunk my fingers into her fur, a deep well of contentedness enveloping me as I pet them both.

"I know it'll only be a few days at most, but I'm gonna miss you two."

A hiss and a chirp answered me as they returned their feelings.

"Oh—I just remembered!" I reached into my back pocket and withdrew the drawing Theo did. "Check this out."

I placed it on the sand between them, and they both leaned in, curiosity overcoming them.

"I got it from a man I met yesterday. His name was Theo, and he found me fishing on the shore near Tropica."

Snips's eye darted up at me; it held a dangerous gleam—I'd explained how frowned upon fishing was, and she knew the risk it presented.

"Don't worry, Snips. He was also a fisherman and was beyond pleased to find a kindred spirit—as was I! He even gave me this little drawing so I could show you guys."

Her worry assuaged, Sergeant Snips's attention returned to the sketch.

"Impressive, right? Theo said he drew it while in a short meeting. It would take me an entire day to make something so detailed, and it would look *way* less impressive."

They both nodded, transfixed by the piece of paper.

"Maybe I'll store it in the house so it doesn't get ruined, but feel free to have a look whenever you like! Our home is sorely missing some decorations, and I'd love to collect some art to spice up the place."

I stood and stretched. "Have you fed the lobster today, Snips?"

She shook her carapace, still looking down at Theo's drawing.

"Are you okay to keep feeding it while I go on my trip?"

She nodded, and spurred by my request, scuttled toward the ocean, a stream of confident bubbles flowing in her wake.

Snips returned not even a minute later, a large fish held in one pincer. We walked over to the side of the pond, and with an underhand toss—er, under*claw* toss—she lobbed the fish out over the water. It hit the surface with a belly flop that made a loud *slap.* The sound was enough to spur the enormous lobster within, as its single long antenna soon exited the cave.

As it came further from its den, I raised an eyebrow.

"Is it just me, or is the severed antenna healing?"

Where before there was only a small nub, a ten-centimeter length of the appendage had grown back.

Snips leaned in, getting a closer look. One claw rubbed her eye patch absentmindedly, and with a tentative tug of the other claw, she slipped the leather strap off. I stared down at the revealed section where her other eye had been. My mouth dropped open.

"No way . . ."

CHAPTER SIXTY-FIVE

DEPARTURE

The morning gave way to day as the sun rose ever higher in the sky. A soft breeze blew, the perfect counterpart for the day's heat. I felt neither the kiss of the sun's rays, nor the pleasant gouts of wind coming and going, though—all my attention was on the ascendant crab before me.

I blinked as I took in Snips's healing eye. She shielded it from the sun with one claw, and I bent down, getting a closer look. It was small, like a limb denied blood flow, but I knew that to be anything but the case—the eyestalk wasn't shrinking; it was *growing*.

"Snips! Your eye!"

She blew entirely incomprehensible bubbles, her other eye turning to the side to look at the recovering appendage.

"Can . . . can you see out of it?"

Her good eye blinked, and she made a 'so-so' gesture with her claw.

"You can see a little?"

She nodded, and small, awe-filled bubbles came from her mouth.

Corporal Claws chirped in excitement, darting around Snips's body to get a look from every angle.

"That's amazing, Snips! I didn't know you could regrow an eye!"

Even with how animated Corporal Claws and I were, Sergeant Snips remained calm, thoughtful. Looking at me with her good eye, she pointed to her healing one with a claw, then pointed down at the pool.

The pieces clicked into place in an instant: Snips's eye, the lobster's antenna, and the common denominator—the saltwater pool.

". . . really, Snips?" I cast furtive glances between her and the body of water. "The pool healed you?"

She made the same "maybe" gesture but nodded.

"You're almost positive?"

Nod.

"Huh . . ." I stared out at the opalescent crystals scattered around the pool, my eyes lingering on the boulder in the middle. "Is it something to do with the stones?"

Again, she nodded and made the same gesture.

"I wonder if it only works on sea creatures, or if it will work on other animals—even humans?"

It was a startling discovery, but a welcome one. Combined with Barry and Helen's knowledge of herbs, the pool Snips and Claws had made may just be something the villagers could benefit from.

Realizing both my hands were each still on one of my animal pals, I rubbed one and scritched the other.

"You two are amazing—you know that? You girls made something that can *heal!*"

They both leaned into my touch.

"I know I'm repeating myself, but I'm gonna miss you two."

They chirped and hissed their agreement as I continued petting them.

I bent down and opened a kitchen cupboard, rummaging for my treasure hidden within.

"I know you'd do it anyway," I said to Claws, "but I need to ask. Please watch the house, and in particular, keep this chest safe."

Looking down at the sturdy box, Corporal Claws nodded, her eyes steel as they returned to meet my gaze. I reached out and rubbed her head.

"Good girl."

I opened the chest one final time before my departure, peering inside. All the jewelry was held within, along with all the gold coins I'd collected so far. Following a whim, I inspected the pearl ring I'd made with Fergus's help.

Iridescent Ring of Silver
Rare
A ring of precious metal, adorned by one of the most sought-after stones found in the Kallis Realm. More than just a symbol of wealth, this ring has a multitude of purposes for those with the requisite knowledge.

Still just "requisite knowledge," huh?

I shook my head and placed the ring back in the chest before closing the lid. I'd hoped for a more forthcoming description following the stats listed by my new fishing rod, but I guess that was too much to ask.

I slid the chest into the back of the cupboard, once more hiding it behind my copious amounts of pots and pans.

With more than a little excitement, I strode back to the table and checked the contents of my bag one last time.

I'm glad I bought a bag from Ruby and Steven, but I wish I had the foresight to buy some sort of canvas for a tent.

I cocked my head in thought.

It's not too late—should I go look around Tropica for something . . . ? Nah. Building makeshift camps will be something for us to do, which is exactly what Maria needs right now—busy work.

With a prolonged scritch of Corporal Claws's cute little head, I slung the bag over my shoulder and headed outside.

* * *

Sharon peeked into Maria's room, overwhelmed with pride. While Maria was a grown woman, she had spent so much of her life tending to their farming and helping around the house. Sharon was happy for her daughter to take a short trip away, and with Fischer, of all people.

Maria had out every piece of clothing she owned, all arrayed over the bed. In the short time Sharon was watching, she'd seen her put every item of clothing in her bag, then take it out again.

"Have you got everything you need?"

Maria jumped, her head spinning toward the door.

"Mom—you scared me!"

"Sorry, dear." Sharon stepped into the room. "Do you need help deciding?"

"Yes." Maria sat down on the bed and sighed. "Why is it so hard to pick what I need?"

"Because you're going away, so you'll want to take everything, but you can't possibly fit it all in such a small bag."

Maria looked over the sea of clothing atop her blanket, frowning at it.

"Fischer says we're only going for a few days, so I need little, but what if I get too far away to turn back and realize I forgot something important?"

"I'll help, dear." Sharon picked up her daughter's folded underclothes. "You'll need these no matter what, so we'll put them in first."

"Right. Thank you."

Sharon neatly placed them in the corner of the bag as she considered how to approach the conversation. Deciding it was best to just get it out, she spoke.

"Is it hard to decide because you want to impress Fischer?"

Maria froze, and her eyes looked everywhere but at her mother.

She nodded once, sharply.

"Well, that's nothing to stress about, dear. You're a beautiful young woman, and I'm sure Fischer would be enthralled, no matter what you wore."

Maria covered her reddening face with both hands. "Mom, can you be a little more subtle?"

Laughter bubbled from Sharon's throat, and she lay a hand on her daughter's shoulder.

"You know I'm a blunt person, Maria. Wanting to impress a man is nothing to be embarrassed about."

"You're not helping, Mom," Maria said, her hands still covering her face.

Sharon selected clothes one by one, slowly packing the bag. "I'm not trying to embarrass you, dear, but I have to ask an uncomfortable question."

Maria's hands fell away, revealing a look of sheer incredulity.

"You have a question that's even *more* uncomfortable?"

Sharon laughed again, and Maria joined her, her nervousness falling away.

"Come here, Maria." Sharon wrapped her in a hug, and she returned it, squeezing her mother gently.

"All right," Maria said. "Ask your question before I get unnerved and run away."

Sharon took a breath, relishing the fact that she could once more embrace her daughter.

"Are you romantically interested in him?"

Maria's body shook as she chuckled softly.

"By the gods, that *was* an uncomfortable question."

She pulled away from the hug, averting her eyes.

"I don't know, Mom. He makes me feel . . . safe."

"And he's attractive."

Maria shot a glare at Sharon's bouncing eyebrows before looking away again.

"He's attractive, yes, but I don't know how I feel about him."

Sharon smoothed her daughter's hair, sweeping a loose strand behind one ear.

"That's fine, dear. You don't have to know one way or the other. Call it a mother's intuition, but I take him to be a good man."

Maria sighed. "Is this the conversation where you tell me it's time I find a man and start a family?"

Sharon winced. She *did* want Maria to pursue such things, especially after learning of Fischer's . . . nature, but she would never force her only daughter into something she didn't want with her whole heart.

"Not at all." She lifted Maria's chin with one hand, and her daughter reluctantly met her eyes. "He's a good man, but that doesn't mean you need to settle down with him. I love you more than words could ever say, Maria, and above all else, I want you to be happy. If happiness for you is living with your father and I for the rest of your life, you'll always be welcome."

Maria gave one of the smiles that always made Sharon's heart melt, then wrapped her in a fierce hug.

"I love you too, Mom. Thank you."

Sharon returned the hug, rubbing a soothing hand on Maria's back. "For packing your bag, or for being the best mother in the world?"

Maria shook with laughter. "Both."

As I strode up to the door, hesitance hampered my steps.

Why am I so nervous?

I shook my upper body, trying to physically dispel the unease. Taking a deep breath, I let it out slowly and knocked on the door. The moment my knuckles hit, the entry flung open.

I'd been excited to see Maria's beautiful face, which made the appearance of Roger's best scowl yet rather jarring.

"Fischer."

"Uh—oh. G'day, Roger. Is, uh, Maria ready?"

"Maria!" he yelled, not breaking eye contact with me.

"Coming!" she called from within, and a moment later, she appeared.

As she came into view, I fought to stop my eyebrows from raising. Usually, she wore basic clothing akin to my own; simple linen, perfect for working the fields. Today, she wore a dress. It was short, with neatly hemmed edges that wouldn't get in the way. She wore pants underneath that came to just above her knee, made of a thick, durable material. It wasn't intended as an outfit of pure beauty; it was also utilitarian, perfect for traveling, but that didn't subtract from her charm.

"Wow . . ." I heard myself say, and I quickly clamped my mouth together as a flush crept over my face.

Roger's nostrils flared, and his scowl deepened even further, but Sharon clearing her throat kept his lips firmly pressed together. Maria gave me a shy smile as she swept her hair behind an ear, and she rushed past her father.

"Are you all ready to go?" she asked, shifting her bag from one shoulder to the other.

"Ready when you are!"

"Make good choices," Roger said, his eyes glancing between Maria and the rod I held in one hand.

Maria sighed. "Yes, Dad."

Sharon stepped up beside her husband, resting one arm on Roger's lower back. "Keep our daughter safe, Fischer."

I nodded. "I will."

"We'll be back in a few days, right?" Maria asked.

"We will—a few days at the latest." I turned to her parents. "I promise I'll bring Maria back in one piece."

Roger grunted, and Sharon gave me a pure smile. "We're counting on it."

She ushered Roger back inside with practiced grace and started closing the door. "Have fun, you two."

The front door closed with a soft *click,* and I turned to Maria.

"Anything else you need to pick up from Tropica before we go?"

"No, I'm all ready!"

"All right." I gave her a broad grin. "Let the holiday begin."

Sergeant Snips, maiden of the pond and protector of master's land, opened her uncovered eye as something disturbed her slumber. She glared around, searching for her rock crab subordinate, who had no doubt returned to the pond to meditate.

Maybe I should let him stay, she thought.

Whether it was the calm the pond lent her, or her begrudging appreciation of the masochistic crab's companionship, she knew not.

Snips glanced around the pond, unsure what she'd do when she found the uninvited guest. To her surprise, though, he wasn't there. She scratched at her eyepatch absentmindedly, questing further for whatever had woken her.

She peered into the cave's entrance, pitying any crab fool enough to get close to the sea snipper's oversized claws. Not expecting to find anything, her claws twitched as she caught sight of what her master called a "lobster."

Its body was flickering, increasing then shrinking in size repeatedly. She tried to focus on it, but something about the sea snipper's shifting form made it hard to look at. A source of light fluctuated from somewhere within its giant body, and in an instant, the light exploded out, turning the world white.

CHAPTER SIXTY-SIX

HOLIDAY

With a loud *pop,* the lobster's vision was engulfed by white. He opened and closed his trusty pincers as a sense of unbridled confusion grew. Taking in the surrounding landscape, he slowly shifted to glance all around him as color returned to the world.

Walls of rock were on either side, and a single opening lay ahead that let in light. He recognized the cave—his home—from memories that felt distant, yet from only a moment ago. A slow trickle of information chipped away at his confusion yet brought with it more questions than he could fathom.

His vision cleared further, and from the entrance to his domain, he saw an enemy. He scuttled back reflexively, wanting to get further into the safety his cave provided, but as the lines of the creature before him snapped into focus, a spark of recognition took hold.

I know . . . crab?

Memories flashed through his mind; the crab checking on him, repeatedly bringing him food, and, most pleasing of all, bringing him to this wonderful, safe place he called home.

With claws extended, the lobster inched his way toward the light, eyes locked on the creature beyond.

Maria and I followed the setting sun; its passage toward the western mountains heralded our journey. A cold wind blew at our backs, a tailwind that made it seem like the world itself urged us on.

"So, have you traveled in this direction much before?" I asked.

She shook her head, eyes trailing the retreating sun. "Not really, no. There was the time we traveled to Tropica for the first time, of course, but other than that, I've never really left."

While I knew life as a farmer in my new world was a different experience to living on Earth, something about that statement really nailed home how distant I was from my previous existence.

Life here is a constant battle to survive for the common folk. There might not be bandits, roaming wolves, or goblin attacks as I worried about upon my arrival here, but that doesn't mean life isn't filled with challenges.

Growing enough food to survive and keeping her family healthy without the aid of modern medicine, was challenging enough that, by her account, she'd never—in her entire life—had a holiday. It was a sad realization.

"Well," I said, "hopefully that makes this trip all the more enjoyable."

She grunted, shifting her bag from one shoulder to another.

"Do you want me to carry that?" I asked.

"Oh, no. I'm fine—I may have overpacked a little, though . . ."

"Are you sure? You can hold the rod, and having a bag on each shoulder will even me out."

She shifted her weight again, the physical load warring with her desire to not be a burden.

"Please," I urged. "It'll make both our loads easier."

She frowned, her lips pressed together.

I pressed the advantage. "Besides, I'm an absolute klutz, and I'm likely to break my favorite rod by getting it caught on something. You're much more coordinated, so it'll be safer in your hands."

She turned and squinted, but a barely concealed smile threatened to take over. "Fine, we can swap." She grinned at me, raising an eyebrow. "But only because I won't be able to fish if you break the rod."

I laughed and held the rod out to her; she offered her bag in exchange.

"Thank you, Fischer. You're sweet."

I bowed at the waist. "Anything for my lady. I'd not be able to face your lord father if any damage came to your person."

"Hestia's maternal urges—don't even joke about that. I wouldn't want my *lord father* to remove that handsome head of yours."

I straightened up, the weight of both bags nothing before my improved body.

"I have a handsome head?" I glanced at her, delighting in the blush I saw peeking through her tanned and freckled skin.

"There!" I said, pointing at my discovery. "I knew it was around here somewhere."

"Wow," Maria said, "you weren't wrong—it held up pretty well . . ."

I walked up to my shelter, the last one I'd built before heading into Tropica for the first time.

It's probably big enough for both of us to sleep under, but a little more room would be best.

"All right, let's begin."

Maria cocked her head. "Begin what?"

I smirked. "The renovations, of course!"

"Are these leaves okay?" Maria asked.

"They're perfect—thank you!"

I grabbed the palm-like fronds and put them next to the pile of leaves I'd removed from the frame. "Let's split these fronds in half, like so."

I pinched the thick end of one, and with a smooth movement, split it in two. I then wedged a fingernail under one side, and gripping the long fibers, pulled a strip off to use as string. With a smile, I held the rope of fibers up to Maria.

"I brought string to tie the frame together, but if you're ever lacking the correct materials, you can make string out of plants you find in the forest—like these."

She raised an eyebrow at me. "Where did you learn to do that?"

"Trial and error," I lied, unsure how to explain the concept of tutorial videos.

I held up an unsplit frond. "You try—it's not as hard as you might think."

As she tried splitting a palm lead, I picked up the sticks I'd gathered. They were longer than the ones I'd used previously—a necessity for the increased floor space this new shelter would have. Planting two of the sticks firmly in the ground, I held the tips together, overlapping each other by a few centimeters. I waited patiently as she split the frond, then removed a length of fibers as I'd shown her.

"Like this?" she asked.

"Exactly like that. Bring it over here and try tying the frame with it—loop it around where the sticks connect."

She did so, deft fingers easily looping the handmade string back and forth over the sticks.

"Keep going?" she asked.

"Yep, until you've used almost all of it."

She stopped when a small length of the line remained, and I grabbed her hand, guiding the end of the fibers under the last loop she'd made.

"Pull it tight," I said.

She nodded, holding the knot steady with one hand as she pulled the end, cinching it into place.

I shook the frame lightly; it held firm. Raising an eyebrow, I grinned.

"You're sure you haven't done this before?"

She shrugged. "I have an excellent teacher—besides, I've always been good with my hands."

"Maria! Phrasing!"

She cocked her head in confusion, but upon realizing what she'd said, her cheeks went beet red. I laughed uproariously, ducking the thrown stick.

I woke in the middle of the night to an unexpected nudge in the side. With bleary eyes, I blinked, taking in my surroundings. The dying embers of our campfire gave the inside of the tent an orange glow, and it took me a long moment to remember where I was. An icy breeze blew into the shelter, even more frigid than usual after the sun's departure.

The nudge hit my side again, and I cast about, searching for Maria. I expected to find her awake, warning me of some danger, and a spike of panic began welling up. My thoughts vanished as the nudge came one more time, and I looked down.

Maria was asleep, curled in on herself and shivering slightly under the chilly breeze. She stirred, still not awake, her body subconsciously searching for heat. I lifted the end of my blanket and tucked it over her, giving her another layer of warmth. As the blanket hit, she rolled over, her back coming up against my side. I froze, my body reacting to her touch.

Her head tilted back, coming to rest on my shoulder, and I put my head back on my pillow, breathing shallow breaths so as not to wake her. She shuffled back again, her body craving the heat mine was exuding.

After a few breaths that felt like a lifetime, I tilted my chin toward her, softly resting it atop the back of her head. My heart raced as the floral scent of her hair consumed my world. I wouldn't get much rest that night—or so I thought; before I knew it, I'd drifted back to sleep, thoughts of her running rampant through my mind.

When I opened my eyes, the rising sun peeked over the trees, bathing my surroundings in its welcome light. I stretched my arms up, unleashing a yawn.

"Did you sleep well, *princess?*" Maria asked, voice laden with mirth.

I lifted my head, glaring out at her. "*Princess?*"

"You certainly sleep like one—well, except for the snoring."

"Snoring?"

I sat bolt upright. "*I snore?*"

She cackled, leaning back from where she stoked the fire. "No—well, kind of. You make soft noises, but I wouldn't exactly call it snoring." She shook her head with an exaggerated shrug. "Your reaction to learning you snore doesn't help the princess attitude, though . . ."

I stepped from the tent, squinting against the sun's light as I stretched as high as I could.

"Can you give me five minutes to wake up before you start teasing me? I don't even know where I am right now."

She pouted. "Absolutely not! Your wits are too sharp when you're awake, so an early morning ambush is just good warfare."

"*Good warfare?* What have I gotten myself into?"

She giggled, the sound lilting and soft. "Being the daughter of a career soldier turned grumpy farmer has its benefits."

I walked over to my pack and collected my bundle of treasure.

"What's that," she asked?

I smiled. "Brekkie."

She gave me a flat stare."Can I assume that means breakfast?"

I sat down beside her, untying the cloth bundle. "You can."

I spread the cloth wide, revealing a pile of golden croissants, and a bottle of brown liquid.

Maria made a surprised noise. "Is that what I think it is?"

I nodded, giving her a knowing smile. "What's a good brekkie without some of Tropica's finest coffee?"

I bit into a warmed bun, my eyes going wide. "Wow—it's sweet."

The soft bun, combined with a pleasant amount of sugar, reminded me of the sweet buns I'd tried in Japan a lifetime ago.

Maria quirked an eyebrow at me. "You know we're sugarcane farmers, right? What did you expect?"

"Touché . . ." I said around a mouthful of the pillowy dough. "Don't tell Sue, but your buns might be even better than hers."

Maria smirked at me. "Who needs to watch their phrasing now?"

I opened my mouth to say something, but my brain betrayed me, and I closed it again, lost for what to say.

Maria laughed at me, shaking her head. "Wow, you really are defenseless first thing in the morning—I'll have to keep that in mind. I can't take the credit for the pastries—Mom made them."

"Well, pass her my compliment," I said, forging past her comment, and my lack thereof. "These things are delicious."

We had a croissant and bun each, and I took a bite of my croissant, relishing in the contrast its flaky and buttery texture gave. Seeing the enjoyment on my face, Maria followed suit, and she let out an appreciative *mmm* as she chewed.

Wisps of steam started rising from the saucepan atop the fire, so I reached over, stirring it with the wooden spoon. I kept it moving, wanting to keep the liquid inside from burning. I didn't know if it could burn, to be honest, but I didn't intend to find out.

When the steam was billowing up from the surface in a steady stream, I removed it from the fire. I carefully poured it into our cups, then passed one to Maria.

"Coffee's ready."

"Thank you," she said, putting her plate down and accepting it with both hands.

"Careful—it'll be scorching."

She held the cup to her nose, breathing deep of the rising vapor. "It smells strong . . ."

I took a whiff of my own cup. "Yeah, it will taste a lot stronger without any milk. I had Sharon water it down—this is what you'd call a long black where I come from."

"You never did tell me where you're from, Fischer. You have the funniest names for things."

I took a sip of my coffee, savoring its bold flavor. My go-to drink was a flat white, but there were periods in my previous life where long blacks were the drink of choice. I breathed out a content sigh, the heat of the coffee making me blow a cloud of vapor.

Maria followed suit, and her face scrunched as she tasted it. She swallowed and took a quick bite of her croissant.

"That's not as nice as the coffee with milk . . ."

I smiled at her. "Yeah, black coffee is more of an acquired taste. Still, better than no coffee at all, in my opinion."

She took another small sip, once more chasing it with a bit of pastry. She chewed it slowly before swallowing. "They're quite nice together . . ."

I nodded. "Some people like dunking their croissants in coffee."

She raised an eyebrow, looking between her food and drink. She dunked a corner of the exposed croissant and bit into it; her face immediately transformed into disgust. She chewed and swallowed as fast as she could.

"Yeah, that's not for me."

I fought down a smirk. "It's usually done with milky coffee, to be honest."

She picked up a stick and threw it at me. "You could have told me that *before* I tried that horrid combination!"

Her outrage removed the stopper on my mirth, and I let out a loud laugh. "Sorry—it wasn't intentional."

She shook her head, hair swaying around her face. "So, you avoided the question of where you're from pretty smoothly, but I'm still curious. I think you might owe me the information after that *cruel* and *intentional* prank . . ."

She wiggled her eyebrows, but I knew her words held a hint of truth; she wanted to know.

How much can I tell her without putting either of us at risk?

"What do you know about places other than the kingdom you live in?"

"Not too much, to be honest. I know there's another kingdom called Theogonia that Dad fought against when he was still in the army. Other than that, I know other places exist, but they're far, *far* away."

I nodded, slowly coming to a decision.

"I come from a place called Earth."

CHAPTER SIXTY-SEVEN

VESSEL

Earth?" Maria asked. "I've never heard of it."

"Yeah . . . it's a long, *long* way away, on an entirely different continent."

It wasn't a lie, but I still felt bad misleading her.

It's safer for both of us if I keep the full truth to myself for now . . .

"Another continent?" Her eyebrows shot up then furrowed in thought. "Like another kingdom?"

"Kind of like that, yeah."

"How did you get here?"

"It's a long story."

A silence stretched between us before she spoke again.

"I knew you were from far away, but I still thought it'd be within the kingdom of Gormona."

"Yeah, that's my fault—I've been intentionally vague." I gave a rueful smile. "People already have enough reason to avoid me with my fishing ways—no need to add fuel to the fire."

"That makes sense . . ."

She took a bite of her bun, washing it down with a mouthful of coffee.

"So fishing isn't considered heretical there, right?"

"Yeah, it's totally acceptable there."

She chewed her lip, clearly lost in thought. "Sorry if this is a dumb question, but if you can fish there, and fishing is all you do . . . why did you come here?"

I couldn't help but laugh.

It wasn't exactly a choice to come here, but it was a good question from her perspective.

"I wasn't always into fishing—that's actually quite new. I came here to start over. My old life became . . . well, unrewarding. I realized I'd wasted it, and I wanted to get as far away from my mistakes as possible."

She gave me a look filled with compassion. "Wasn't it hard leaving your friends and family behind?"

The question, and the memories it brought up, were as a physical blow. My family, or lack thereof, was something I hadn't spent time ruminating on since I'd arrived in Tropica, and the thought's resurgence made a wave of sorrow wash over me. It must have shown on my face because Maria quickly spoke, holding up both hands.

"Sorry, Fischer. You don't have to tell me . . ."

"You have nothing to apologize for." I forced a grin across my face, but it felt empty. "It's a bit of a rough subject for me."

"Well, forget it then. Another time, if you feel like getting it off your chest." She stood, smirking at me as she brushed her hands free of crumbs. "Should we pack up and get going? I'm excited to have a fish at some point today."

I nodded, a genuine smile coming over me.

"Let's."

"This is it," I said, pointing down at the creek that had originally led me to Tropica.

"Wow!" Maria leaned closer, squinting. "You caught fish in such shallow water? I can't see any . . ."

"Well, not here exactly, but in the same creek, yeah."

Having caught movement in the shallows, I pointed.

"Can you see those guppies?"

"Uhhhh—what are guppies, and where are they? I can't see a thing."

I smiled. "Let's sneak closer—keep your body low or they might swim away."

I led her forward, slowly stepping down the raised bank. She knelt down beside me, and I leaned in, whispering as I pointed.

"Just there—beside that large rock."

Ten or so of the tiny fish were milling around by the bank, flinching and darting away from shadows. A sharp intake of breath told me that Maria had spotted them.

"They're . . . *they're so cute!*"

I glanced at her, marveling at the wonder her eyes held; they sparkled with the morning's sun.

"Are they babies?" she asked, leaning in closer and causing her hair to fall from behind an ear.

"They might be the baby versions of what we'll be fishing for, or they might just be a tiny species of fish. We could try to see, but it might hurt them."

She nodded seriously. "Best to leave them be, then. It'll have to remain a mystery."

"Should we move further upstream?" I asked. "The sooner we find a deeper body of water, the sooner we can start fishing."

"After you, my heretical teacher."

I blew air from my nose, smirking at her as I turned to walk back up the bank. From behind me, I heard the scrape of rocks, and Maria made a startled noise. Without thinking, I whirled, my hand darting out to grab hers. She stabilized immediately, and a look of sheer panic disappeared from her face with a sigh.

"Thank you, Fischer."

I barely heard the words, transfixed as I was on her touch. Despite the callouses from work, the skin covering her small hands was smooth, soft. The sensations drew my mind back to the previous night, and I pictured her small frame pressed up against mine. The warmth and comfort she brought—

"Um . . . *Fischer?*"

My eyes went wide as I returned to the present. Maria's head was cocked to the side. She looked down at our hands, then back up at me.

"Everything okay?"

"*Er* . . ." was all I could say as heat rose to my cheeks. I pulled her up the bank, letting go of her hand.

"Yeah, sorry, I was just thinking of . . . er, fishing stuff."

She raised a slender eyebrow. ". . . fishing?"

"Yeah. Fishing."

A corner of her mouth curled up. "Holding my hand makes you think of fishing?"

"Yep! You and fishing are my two favorite things about my new life here, after all."

She giggled, covering her mouth with one hand. "*Smoooooth.*"

"If you think that was smooth, wait until you touch a fish, my inexperienced student."

She snorted. "Lead the way, then, oh wise trainer."

Gary, the single follower of the Cult of the Leviathan's Tropica branch, peeked out of his room to see what his master was doing. Sebastian had risen early and was tending to the new batch of baby lobsters that the merchant from the capital city had delivered.

Er, I mean crickets, he thought, trying to lodge the name for them firmly in mind, lest he incur Sebastian's wrath. Gary took a deep breath, gathering his wits, and then stepped from his room.

"Good morning, master. How are the crickets faring?"

"They're not well, Gary," he responded, not taking his eyes from his babies. "The merchant treated them poorly, no doubt. Not to worry, though, my precious little crickets—I'll nurse you back to full health in no time, won't I?"

Sebastian leaned down to one of the tanks, all but pressing his face against the glass.

"Yes I will, my beautiful, innocent newborns," he said in a tone like you'd use on actual children.

Sebastian's obsession with the tiny creatures would cause most people distress, especially considering they were from the sea, but to Gary, it was a relieving sight.

Hopefully he'll forget his foolish pursuit of vengeance against Fischer now that he has something to tend to . . .

"Did the merchant deliver the artifact you requested, master?"

It was a testing question, one to see if Sebastian was ready to move past his foolhardy intentions. Sebastian failed the test spectacularly.

"Oh, I didn't show you?" His face twisted into a vicious snarl. "Look upon the vessel of our retribution, Gary."

Sebastian reached into his robe, removing a dark cube etched with red symbols and held it out. "I had to pull a lot of strings to get this here, but now that we have it, his demise is all but assured."

Gary was glad Sebastian hadn't removed his eyes from the baby lobsters—*er, crickets*—because otherwise, he would have seen the sweeping disappointment on Gary's face.

"How does it work, master?"

"We must meditate on it, Gary. The fools at the capital tried to tell me it wouldn't work—it hasn't since the times of old, after all—but given my, no, *our* devotion, I know it will work. It *must*."

Gary breathed a sigh of relief.

I wish he'd abandon his thirst for vengeance entirely, but if he's going to spend time on this broken relic, that's less time he can spend trying to poison Fischer again.

"Now," Sebastian said, peeling his eyes from the baby lobsters to look at Gary. "Let's begin the gathering of power. Who knows how long it will take to collect enough to take down Fischer."

Gary nodded, keeping his face neutral despite the sinking feeling in his stomach. "Yes, master."

The sun must have been extra hot today, because as I stepped out of the shaded forest and crossed the road, I sneezed.

"Bless you," Maria said.

I rubbed my nose. "Thanks!"

A sense of excitement grew as we crossed the road and made our way farther through the forest. I knew the perfect spot was just ahead, and as we rounded a bend in the creek only minutes later, we came across it.

"Oh, wow," Maria said. "It's beautiful . . ."

A small lake stretched out before us, fed by a meter-high waterfall. The sound of splashing water was calming, and I breathed deep, the moist air of the forest cooling my nose.

I turned to Maria.

"Are you ready?"

She bounced on her heels, unable to contain her anticipation. "I am *so* ready!"

I set down our bags, rifling through mine. I removed my little tackle box, opened it, and removed a knife.

"Should I be worried?" Maria joked, eyeing the clade.

"It's for the line—I need to replace the tackle," I answered, shaking my head at her. "See this hook and sinker?"

"I do . . . what's wrong with them?"

"They're way, *way* too big. I was using these to fish in the ocean with a mate of mine. For a calm little pond, a smaller hook and sinker will be much better."

Maria scrunched her nose.

"Fischer—you were fishing with someone else?"

She held a hand to her chest, leaning back. "*How could you?*"

I laughed at her fake affront. "Yeah, I was fishing with Theo, the bloke you met with me in the village."

She rubbed her chin in exaggerated thought. "I *knew* he was a rival . . ."

I raised an eyebrow. "A rival, huh? You trying to keep me all to yourself?"

"Of course—how else would I learn to fish?"

I grinned, then cut the line, putting the hook and sinker back in the tackle box and collecting a smaller set.

I really need to make actual sinkers when I get back to Tropica . . . the rocks work, but metal sinkers would be so much better.

With slow movements, I showed Maria how to tie a drop rig.

"Do you want to try tying the hook?"

Her eyebrows furrowed. "What knot do you use?"

"It's called an improved clinch knot." I handed her the hook. "Hold that still—I'll show you."

She pinched the hook between her thumb and forefinger, and I slid the line through the hook's eye, twisted it around itself eight times, fed the line back through the original loop, then back through itself, completing the knot. I bent down and wet the line with my mouth.

"Uh, Fischer, why are you kissing it?"

"If you wet the line . . ." I held her hand steady on the hook, pinched the line's tag with the same hand, then pulled it tight. "The knot will get tighter because of the reduced friction."

As I pulled, the knot slid into place, and Maria's eyes went wide. "Oh. Wow."

"Do you wanna try?" I asked. "I can cut it off if you want to have a crack."

She shook her head. "No—I don't want to waste the line—I'll try next time, okay?"

"No worries."

I rummaged in the bag again, removing a small package. "You might want to lean back from this one. The eel we're using for bait can be a bit, uhhh, *aromatic.* I'll put it on the hook for you."

I cut a slice of the flesh off, setting it aside as I wrapped the eel back up. Despite my words, Maria reached for the eel and picked it up, gingerly sliding it on the hook. I raised an eyebrow, and she smiled back at me.

"I'm a farmer, Fischer—not a noble lady. I don't mind getting my hands a little dirty."

She wiggled the eel into place, then looked up at me.

"Do I want the pointy bit of the hook poking out, or in the meat?"

I grimaced at her. "That's a bit of a debate between different anglers, but personally, I don't think it matters too much. Do whatever feels best."

She cocked her head, her lips pouted in thought, then moved the bait so a tiny bit of the hook's tip poked out.

"There. That feels right."

"Well done—it's ready to go."

She looked down, rubbing her fingers together and frowning at how slimy the eel left them.

She lifted her hand toward her nose.

"It can't really smell that bad, right? It's only—*EUUUUGHHHHH!*"

She threw her head back and her hand forward at the same time, trying to put as much distance between the two as possible. "That *stinks!*"

I collapsed immediately, bracing myself on the forest floor as my body shook with choking laughter as Maria ran down to the water's edge to wash her hand.

"Like this?" Maria asked, holding the rod before her with one finger on the line.

"Just like that. Twist the reel left, then cast."

She rotated the reel, held out the rod, and with a look of sheer concentration, flicked the line and sinker out into the pond. It made a small splash as it hit the water, and I reached over, pushing the reel back into position with a soft *click.*

"Reel it in so the line is tight."

She slowly did so, and something tugged on the line.

I squinted. *Was that a fish, or a snag?*

Maria had stopped reeling, and the line bumped again. It was definitely a fish.

"Wait for it . . ." I said.

Her head darted to me, then back at the water, her entire body tense.

Tug.

Tug. Tug.

Nothing happened, and I worried the bait might have been stolen. Then, the rod bent down as the fish took the bait, hook and all.

CHAPTER SIXTY-EIGHT

THUNK

The fishing line darted to the side, cutting through the water toward the small waterfall. Maria held the rod firm, watching its tip bounce and move with the fish's attempted escape.

"What do I do?" Her entire body was tense, her shoulders hunched, and knees slightly bent.

I smiled and set a hand on her shoulder. "First, take a deep breath. Relax."

She rolled her shoulders and inhaled shakily, her body loosening.

I pointed at the reel.

"Good. Now reel the fish in, just as I showed you. Keep the line tight, but don't reel too fast. You might hurt it."

She released the breath and stood upright, her body much more relaxed. Putting one hand on the reel, she wound in the line with controlled movements, her eyes fixed on the fish's path under the water. As the line between us and the fish reduced, we started catching flashes of silver where the sky reflected from its scales.

Maria's face was caught somewhere between sheer joy and nervousness, and I couldn't help but feel a shadow of the same emotions—such was the excitement of fishing.

The fish darted toward the shore—a last desperate attempt to escape its fate—but Maria was prepared. She deftly wound in the line, keeping it taut so the fish couldn't spit out the hook.

"W-What do I do now?" she asked.

Before she could finish the question, I was moving down to the water's edge. I grabbed the line in one hand and pulled the fish up and onto the bank. I grabbed it by its toothless mouth and lifted it. It was just longer than my hand and had a soft brown tinge to its scales, reminiscent of the environment it lived in. I held it up for her to see, a broad grin spreading across my face as my eyes were drawn into the unfamiliar fish.

Juvenile Jungle Perch
Uncommon
Known for its delicate flesh and subtle taste, this is prized among the freshwater fish of the Kallis Realm.

A high-pitched squeal greeted me as my vision cleared, and Maria was hopping foot to foot while staring down at the fish.

"I caught a fish! I actually caught a fish! That. Was. So. *Exciting!*" Her eyes sparkled. "Can we do it again?"

I laughed uproariously, beyond happy with her reaction. "We have to decide what to do with it first. We didn't actually discuss if you wanted to eat any fish on this trip."

She looked at the fish then up at me.

"What do you think we should do?"

I rubbed my chin in thought. "This fish is a juvenile, so I think we should let it go and try to catch its big brother."

She nodded vigorously. "Yeah, let's do that!"

I smiled and shook my head at her energy. "Do you want to let it go?"

"That depends. Does it stink like the eel?"

I laughed again. "No, it doesn't. It'll be a bit slimy, though . . ."

She stepped forward.

"How do I hold it?"

I had one thumb held in its mouth, and one supporting the weight of its body.

"I'll hold up the fish, and when I let go of its lip, you grab it. Some fish have teeth, but for the ones that don't, the safest way for both you and the fish is to hold it by the mouth with one hand while supporting its weight with the other."

She nodded seriously, coming closer.

"Ready?" I asked.

"Yep!"

I tightened my grip around its body and removed my hand from the mouth. Maria quickly grabbed it with deft fingers.

"Now," I said, "support its weight from underneath. Each of its fins has sharp spines on the end, but as long as you control the head, you shouldn't get pricked."

I removed my hand, leaving her to hold the fish all by herself. She bounced up and down on her heels, then side to side on each foot, letting out another high-pitched sound.

"I have a fish!"

I grinned. "And you caught it all by yourself!"

"Demeter's nourishing food—*this is so exciting!* It's. So. *Cute!* Is it okay out of the water? Can it breathe out here? How do I put it back?"

Pure happiness spread across my face at her rapid-fire questions.

"It can't breathe air, so we should put it back as soon as possible. Lower it gently into the water, and it'll swim away."

"Right! Sorry fishy!"

She moved to the pond in a blur, bent, and put the fish underwater in the shallows. As soon as it was submerged, its body flicked side to side. Maria made a startled noise and let it go, her backside falling onto the rocky shore. The fish disappeared into the depths of the pond in less than a breath, vanishing from sight.

She twisted her body and looked up at me. "Can we do it again? Like right now?"

I smiled. "We absolutely can."

At the friendly crab's request, Pistachio walked up the side of the pond he called home. Despite the growing catalog of knowledge somehow steaming into his consciousness, his base instincts wanted to crawl back into his cave and hide. He tamped the inclination down; it didn't serve him at the moment.

He peered at his claws as the day's sun shone off them, marveling at their size. He had flashes of memories from the time before awareness, and while some were confusing and somewhat sorrowful, he was certain of a few things.

One thing he knew, and was positive about, was that he had grown. The cave he called home was now a much more snug fit, his enlarged form no longer easily slipping between its walls. Rather than make him feel confined, the cozy cave made him feel safe, secure.

Another thing he knew was his name—Pistachio. He recalled the name from sorrowful memories, so he pushed them away, not ready to confront them yet.

The crab hissed his name, interrupting his rumination, and he looked up at her, ready to listen.

Sergeant Snips watched the attentive sea snipper, and with a single claw, stroked the top of his head, just as her master was wont to do. She remembered how dissociating an experience it was to awaken, and how welcome her master's attention had been when trapped in such a turbulent time. With Fischer on a trip, it fell to Snips to support the sea snipper, and she was more than happy to do so.

Corporal Claws, who had until now been watching with curious eyes, dashed over and tapped rhythmically on the lobster's head, assisting in the only way she knew how.

The lobster looked up at them, unaffected, not reacting in the way she or Corporal Claws had when receiving the master's blessed scritches. Snips and Claws persisted anyway, resolved to be the emotional support animals that this newly awakened soul no doubt needed.

Come, she hissed.

The lobster's antennae moved up and down, clearly not understanding her words. She scuttled along, instead gesturing with one claw for the lobster to follow.

Pistachio knew not what the crab was trying to say, but when she moved away and made a gesture, he understood. He followed her, enjoying the ease with which his legs carried his impressive size.

The otter, who had been tapping his head with rapid yet soft touches, jumped astride his carapace. He swiveled his eyes, peering to ensure the creature was not intending to attack. She spun in circles before lying down and rolling onto her back, rubbing herself against his mighty shell.

Reassured, he returned his attention to the crab, who glared at the otter with what he thought was . . . *annoyance?* Seeing that he had resumed his march, the crab also continued, leading him further away from the ocean.

They crossed a large stretch of sand, and Pistachio took in the unfamiliar sights. From what he remembered of his time before awareness, he had never walked atop land. His instincts told him it was not a safe place to be, but he fought down the urge to return to his favored cave, reminding himself that he no longer had to listen to such impulses.

They approached a sea of trees, and the crab led him over the sand and beneath their cover.

The calls and chirps of unknown creatures could be heard all around, their songs shrill yet welcome.

He spotted one of the creatures opening a beak and calling out as it hopped from perch to perch, hiding then reappearing from behind patches of green.

It is called a bird . . .

And the green things trees are covered in . . .

He cocked his head.

. . . leaves?

Yes. That was the word.

The trees' leaves moved in a soft . . . *breeze,* their limbs and attached greenery shifting pleasantly, more chaotic than the movement of ocean-borne plants.

With each word he correctly identified, he felt a sense of . . . *accomplishment.*

That word also brought on a pleasing sensation, and his mouth, unbidden, made a sound of delight.

The crab looked back at him, nodded her agreement, then blew a small series of bubbles.

Pistachio understood their meaning—the crab was also experiencing joy.

They moved ever onward between the trees until they had traveled far from the ocean. The smell of salt had dissipated significantly, making way for the alien scents of wood, earth, and terrestrial vegetation.

The crab stopped when they reached a group of thick trunks. She looked at Pistachio with intent, pointed to her claw, then at the tree. Her claw cocked open, and she placed it up against one of the trees. Faster than he could register, the claw clamped shut, and the loudest sound Pistachio had ever heard rang out through the forest, like two colossal stones colliding together.

He flinched back and closed his eyes, unprepared as he was for the attack.

A great crashing sound followed, and he hunkered down, protecting the vital point of his body. The otter atop him once more tapped her paws on his head, and he finally understood what her purpose was—she was trying to reassure him.

He slowly opened his eyes to steal a glance, but the sight before him made them fly open.

The tree lay on the ground, felled. A sizable chunk from the base had been obliterated; splinters strewn across the ground were the only thing that remained. Beyond the tree's base, a curved slice had been cut into the soil, as long as Pistachio's body, and hewn deeper than an attack from such a small creature had any right being.

She is . . . strong.

The crab scuttled closer, once more rubbing his head as she had before.

She also wants to reassure me . . . ?

She stepped back, and with a slow gesture, pointed to his claw, then at another tree. He cocked his gigantic head, causing the otter to stop tapping and hold on, lest she fall off. With one impressive claw, he pointed to his other, then at the tree. The crab nodded a single time, stepping aside.

He ambled toward the trunk, holding one claw out. His claw slowly opened, and as it reached its apex, the hinge made a *click,* locking into place. He wanted to release it, slam it closed just as the crab had, but something felt . . . *wrong.*

Absentmindedly, he held his other claw forward too, opening it until another soft *click* was heard. He held his open claws to the tree, and with a single command, his body released both.

Corporal Claws resumed her comforting taps on the lobster's head, showing her love and affection for the gigantic thing. Unlike her general desire to mess with Sergeant Snips, she felt a need to protect the magnificent creature. He was a babe in this world, and although he was many times larger than her, she felt a maternal urge to keep him safe, to show him everything was going to be okay.

She paused her rhythmic tapping as his opening claw made a *click,* but then resumed again as he slowly opened the other. With her improved body, she would be safe from any attack coming from the lobster. From her position on his back, she could also protect him from the falling tree should he cut through it.

I doubt it can sever the tree upon awakening, but better to be safe than sorry.

She squinted at his claws, intent on seeing just how much damage they could do to the wood.

A sort of power built in the claws, and she leaned in closer, drawn in by the odd gathering. As she made to step closer, the claws slammed down with a deep *thunk.*

The next thing Corporal Claws felt was open air as she was launched from her perch atop the lobster, expelled by the force of the attack.

Oh . . . was all she had time to think.

She struck something hard, and all thought disappeared.

CHAPTER SIXTY-NINE

NICE

Sergeant Snips uncurled her body, her ears ringing from the sea snipper's blast. She had felt the power welling and, unlike the overly curious Corporal Claws, had known an explosion would follow. As Snips's lone eye cleared, she gaped at the carnage.

The lobster had both claws held before him, an intense gleam in his eyes as he surveyed the vessels of destruction. Where the tree had previously been, only a hole and debris remained.

Unlike her attack—which was precise, directed—the lobster's attack was all-encompassing, the force exploding out. It had been slightly directed, as he still stood atop solid ground, but everything beyond was . . . gone.

The hole left by the blast was twice as long as the lobster and almost as wide. All that remained of the tree was a collection of branches strewn through the hole. A tree beyond had also been destroyed, only its top half remaining on the forest floor.

Snips scuttled over to the lobster, who still looked at his claws, an obvious look of confusion set on his features. Claws peeled herself from the base of a tree, shaking her head with a small chirp, then also moving to the sea snipper's side.

With one claw, Snips rubbed his head.

He's strong—immensely strong.

She blew bubbles of approval.

Master will be pleased.

"Nice!" I yelled.

"I did it!" Maria called back, lifting her prize. She held another of the juvenile jungle perch, which she had caught and removed from the pond all by herself.

I smiled, delighting in her enjoyment. "You're a natural!"

She giggled as she bent down, releasing it back into the water.

"Bye, fishy! Thank you!"

It darted beneath the surface, swiftly melding back into the camouflage of the pond.

"This pond might be a bit small to hold any larger fish," I said. "Should we travel deeper?"

"There are bigger ponds?" she asked, her eyes going wide.

I nodded. "At least one I've seen other than the big one we're heading to—we might not reach it today, but if we leave now, we'll get there the following day."

She picked up the hook, put it through an eye on the rod as I'd shown her, and wound the reel, pulling the line tight and keeping it in place.

"What are we waiting for, then? We've got bigger fish to catch!"

"Are you sure you don't want to sit?" I asked, biting a croissant as we moved.

"The sooner we get where we're going," Maria responded, "the sooner we can catch more fish, right?"

I smiled at her keenness. "You've really caught the fishing bug, haven't you?"

She paused, looking over her body. "Please tell me I don't have a bug on me."

I laughed. "Don't tell me you're afraid of bugs—I thought you were a tough farmer."

She leveled a flat glare at me, making me laugh harder.

"Sorry, it's just a turn of phrase. Saying you've caught the fishing bug means you've got the urge to do it more."

She resumed walking, her eyes narrowed at me playfully.

"I wouldn't say I'm afraid; I'd say I have a healthy aversion to things with entirely too many limbs."

I wonder if she'll fear Sergeant Snips, then?

I smiled to myself.

Nah. Snips is entirely too cute and lovable to be afraid of.

"Can I tell you something, Fischer?"

Maria's question drew me from my meditative state, and I glanced up lazily. We sat at the side of the creek, resting our legs after coming across another of my abandoned shelters.

"Of course. You can tell me anything."

She kicked her legs, making the shallow water of the creek swirl around them.

"Promise not to laugh?"

With an exaggerated *hmmm,* I rested my chin on a closed fist.

"I can't promise I won't laugh, but I swear to you if I do, there's no ill intent behind it."

She dipped her hand in the creek and flicked droplets of water at me.

"Not good enough. I need your word."

I held my hands up. "All right, all right—I promise."

Her gaze went wide as she stared down at the moving water, so I looked away, not wanting to pressure her.

She took a deep breath, sighed, then the words flew free. "I don't really like farming."

I raised an eyebrow. "You don't?"

"No." She shook her head, making her hair bounce softly against the sides of her face.

I gave her time to continue, but she didn't.

"What makes you say that? You always seem so lost in the process when I've seen you working the fields."

"Don't get me wrong—I don't hate it . . ."

She kicked her legs again, the water languidly moving around her feet.

"Working outside isn't bad; I get a sense of accomplishment when a field is tilled or planted. It's just . . . overall, you know? I like the idea of growing our own food, of living off the land, so to speak, but being out here, exploring . . ."

She leaned back, looking up at the sky.

"I probably sound silly—forget it."

"No, Maria, you don't."

She cocked her head at me, brows slightly furrowed, and I continued.

"I'm following you so far. What is it that bothers you?"

She lay back on the rocks of the shore, her hands behind her head.

"I feel, I don't know . . . pushed into it? Like it's what my family does, so that means that's what I have to do. It's all I've really known."

I lay beside her, looking up at a cloud slowly shifting across the sky through a gap in the trees.

"I get it. Believe me. I spent years doing what my family wanted me to do, knowing deep down it wasn't what I wanted, but telling myself it would make me happy."

A silence stretched between us, both lost in our own thoughts.

After a dozen breaths or so, I turned my head toward her.

"If money wasn't an issue, and you could follow your passion, what would you do?"

She shook her head, eyes closed as she let out a self-deprecating laugh.

"I have absolutely no idea. It feels silly complaining about my work when I don't even know what I'd rather be doing."

"Not silly at all—that's normal."

"If you say so . . ."

I sat up. "I mean it, Maria. You're what . . . twenty?"

She opened her eyes, narrowed them at me, and smiled.

"Are you trying to flatter me, Fischer?"

I held up both hands. "I would never attempt such base flattery on you, *my lady.*" I grinned. "I really have no idea, and you could easily pass for twenty."

She rolled her eyes playfully.

"I'm twenty-seven."

I nodded, more to myself.

"You know, I heard something once that really stuck with me: some of the most interesting people you'll ever meet didn't know what they were doing with their life until they were well into their thirties or forties. It's normal to feel lost, and you shouldn't bash yourself for not knowing what your passion is in your twenties."

"You're just saying that to make me feel better."

"Nope. I mean it."

She raised an eyebrow at me. "Well, what did these 'interesting people' do, then?"

I shrugged. "Everyone is different, but I'd bet they all had one thing in common: they took many steps down the wrong path."

I shook my head.

"The 'wrong path' isn't correct, because those missteps are exactly what led them to what they truly wanted to do. You just need to have a little faith in yourself. If you keep an open mind and try different things, I promise you'll find your passion. The universe always provides."

She sat up, peering over at me. "You always say the sweetest things, but I'm still not convinced."

"I'll help, then. What if we try brainstorming?"

". . . *brainstorming?*"

I laughed at her obvious incredulity at the unknown phrase. "Yeah—brainstorming. It means just throwing out ideas and seeing if anything sticks. It's particularly helpful doing it with someone else."

She glanced at me, still unconvinced, but after a long moment, nodded.

"All right. How do we start?"

"Which of these sounds the most enjoyable to you: running a business, making art, or working with animals?"

She perked up. "Animals? What do you mean by working with animals?"

I raised an eyebrow, hearing the interest in her voice. "There are plenty of things you can do with animals. What about raising them?"

"I had thought of breeding cattle before like some farmers in Tropica do . . ." She winced. "I hate the idea of growing animals just for them to be eaten, though."

"Good—that's perfect. So you like animals, but you don't want to farm them for food. What about farming them for other reasons, then? Chickens for laying eggs; animals for companionship, like dogs or cats; or animals for use, like oxen or horses to pull carts—er, you have all those animals here, right?"

She looked thoughtful at my words until my last question, which made her smirk.

"Yes, Fischer—we have all those animals." She squinted at me. "Just how far away is the Earth kingdom?"

I scratched the back of my head, grimacing. "I was just making sure—I hadn't seen some of them yet since coming here. Do any of those ideas sound tempting to you, though?"

She lifted a hand to her head, playing with a loose strand of hair as she thought.

"As much as I'd love to work with those animals—if I could ever afford any, that is—I'm not sure breeding them is the right move for me. We had a puppy once when I was younger. It was really expensive, and Dad bought it on our way to Tropica. He wanted to have something to alert us of anyone approaching in the night."

Maria gave me a sad smile. "She ate something she shouldn't have while we were traveling with a caravan. She got sick and passed away, and that was the last pet we ever owned. I know I was young, but having something so small and innocent die in my arms . . . I'm not sure I could handle that part of breeding. It's an inevitability, after all—not every animal is going to be healthy and make it past adolescence."

"I'm sorry . . ."

She took a deep breath, sighing it out. "It's okay. It was a long time ago, but the memory of it still stings."

I snapped my fingers as a thought came to me.

"Do you have vets here?"

"Like . . . veterans?"

"Nah, not veterans," I said with a laugh. "Veterinarians. Animal doctors."

"*Veterinarian* . . ." She spoke the word slowly, tasting it. "Yeah, I'm just gonna keep calling them animal doctors. We do have them, but they're too expensive for a small village like Tropica. Most farmers just have to do it themselves."

"That's even better—you'd have no competition! You would have to deal with some animals . . . *passing,* but at the same time, you'd be the one responsible for saving heaps more." I shrugged. "Something to consider, anyway."

She twirled her finger, the strand of hair twisting around and around as she stared at the pond in thought. "I will . . ."

"Well, while you're doing that, I'm gonna fix up this disaster of a shelter I left behind."

She stood and stretched. "I'll get a fire started for dinner, then."

Leroy gazed at the mountains stretching toward the horizon before him, wondering if they could be the same landmarks that could be seen from his family's home.

They do look similar . . .

Trent, first in line to the throne of Gormona, snapped his fingers indignantly.

"Faster, cultivator. It's in the brown bag. Make haste."

Glancing at the long-haired cultivator, and seeing he was staring off into space as usual, Leroy sighed. The collar around his neck was an unignorable weight as he stepped forward to unclasp the prince's bag.

"Not that brown one!" Trent screeched in his annoying voice. "The other brown one!"

Leroy felt his eyebrow twitch as he moved to the other satchel, and with deliberately slow movement—and a secret hope that the tyrant atop the horse would have an apoplectic fit and fall to his death—he flicked open the clasp.

"Hurry up!"

A soft whistling sound was the only warning that the prince had struck out. The end of his whip cracked down, striking his hand. At his flinch, Trent giggled.

"That's what you get!" The prince snapped his fingers again. "Now pass me the package wrapped in cloth, plebeian."

Clenching his jaw, he removed it and offered it up. Trent snatched it.

"That's what you get for being such a spoil sport the entire way here." He adopted a mocking tone. *No, Trent, we can't go find some ladies. No, Trent, I'd rather sleep in a forest with leeches and bugs.* I swear, you cultivators are—"

Leroy was preparing a retort about the prince's unsightly face, or perhaps that one serving girl that had laughed in his face when Trent asked for a kiss, but when the prince's words cut off mid-sentence, Leroy glanced up.

Trent's eyes were wide; he stared down at the artifact in his hands. A wicked smile spread across the prince's countenance, making his already ugly face all the more detestable.

"We've found him . . ."

CHAPTER SEVENTY

TEMPEST

The world was cold and gray when I woke the following morning. Maria had once again rolled into me while we slept, and despite the blankets separating us, her slender form radiated a welcome warmth.

I yawned as I took a moment to reflect on my gratitude for her companionship. Then, with no small amount of reluctance, I carefully extracted myself from the tangle of blankets, intent on waking her with breakfast and the blessed taste of coffee.

Just as I snuck from the shelter, a powerful gust slammed into me, sending the surrounding trees' leaves into a frenzy. I glanced up as my eyes cleared, seeing a sea of gray beyond the frenetically shifting canopy above.

"Of all the times for a rainy day . . ."

I stretched, unleashing a mighty yawn."Oh well, at least it won't be hot, I guess."

A soft yawn from behind me ended in a cute sigh, and I turned, seeing Maria glancing from the tent.

"Sorry," I said. "Did I wake you?"

She smiled at me with sleepy eyes then glared at the surrounding trees.

"Not unless you control the wind. I was having such a pleasant dream, too."

"Oh? What about?"

"I can't tell you that—it might not come true."

I raised an eyebrow but lacking the requisite caffeine to fuel early morning banter, I just smiled at her.

"I'll get the fire going—you can stay comfy in the blankets if you like."

Seeing the offer as a challenge, she threw the blankets aside and emerged from the tent.

"Many hands make light work."

She cut off as another breeze kicked up, immediately sending her body into a full shiver.

I smirked at her. "Maybe those 'many hands' should wear a blanket while collecting wood?"

She glared at me, but the curl of her lips betrayed her intent. She bent and snatched a blanket, then, cocking her head, bent and grabbed another.

She held it out to me, and I raised an eyebrow.

"I'm not sure I need it."

"Nonsense," she said, waving it in my face. "If my servant catches a cold, how will he be able to serve me? I demand that you stay warm."

A laugh shot from my throat at the look on her face; it was full of petulance, the perfect approximation of entitlement.

I grabbed the offered blanket. “You know, your acting is a little *too* good . . .”

“That’s the secret, Fischer.” She gave me a haughty expression, but the corner of her lip tugged up, threatening to shatter the facade. “It’s not acting.”

She whirled, hiding her face and striding into the forest. “Follow me, manservant! Your liege demands kindling!”

The steam wafting from the pot hit my face as I poured our coffee. Its heat joined the warmth radiating from the campfire, and I closed my eyes as I poured the last drop into Maria’s cup, bathing in the moment.

She cleared her throat. “Faster, servant. This lady requires her morning coffee.”

“Of course, my liege.”

I held the cup out, bowing as low as I could without spilling the drink. She accepted it with both hands, her lilting laugh joining the passing currents of air.

“Thank you, Fischer.”

I beamed. “You’re most welcome, my lady!”

She took a sip of the coffee, letting out a satisfied sigh. I held my cup to my lips and drank. The hot liquid warmed my mouth, and as I swallowed, I felt its passage down my throat, a welcome heat traveling to my core.

After a bite of a croissant, I smiled at the world. “I could eat this every morning without getting sick of it.”

“I couldn’t agree more,” Maria responded, a similarly content smile on her face.

I took in our surroundings, seeing the clouds above getting darker, not lighter. “Are you sure you don’t want to turn back?”

She shook her head. “I’m not scared of a little rain.”

“Of all the times for the weather to turn bad . . . I haven’t seen a drop of rain since coming to Tropica, and the moment we go camping, the universe threatens us with a storm.”

“Don’t worry—I’ll protect you from the rains if a storm rolls in.” She winked at me. “I take good care of my servants, after all.”

I barked a laugh. “What would I do without you?”

With the threat of rain ever-present, we traveled at a swift clip beneath the forest’s canopy. We came upon a camp just after midday, and as Maria caught sight of it, she stopped on the spot, turning to raise an eyebrow at me.

“This is one of yours?”

“Uh, yeah . . . *why?*”

“You weren’t always great at making them, were you?”

I snorted, looking at the haphazard shelter. One side was lopsided, having collapsed since I used it.

“Hey, this was only the second shelter I tried to make, all right? Besides, I bet it was only knocked down by the wind.”

I recalled making it; it wasn't the wind that caused it to fall—I just hadn't built it well.

"If you say so . . ." she said, smirking at me.

"My construction skill aside—"

"Or lack thereof," she cut in.

I narrowed my eyes at her.

"*Or lack thereof*—do you want to camp here, or should we try to get to the big lake today?"

Her eyes lit up. "The big one? Where you saw the massive fish that snapped your line?"

"That's the one."

She gave me a broad grin. "Let's keep going."

A bolt of thunder split the sky above us, flooding the world in white. Through the blinding light, I caught sight of Maria slipping forward, her body pitched to the side. My hands shot out, one looping around her waist, the other gripping her wrist so she wouldn't get hurt. I lifted her with ease, setting her back on solid ground.

Her eyes were wide, and I watched as her tanned complexion was almost immediately washed out by a deep red blush.

"Er—sorry. I didn't mean . . ."

"No—I'm sorry. I tripped over my own feet." She set a hand on my shoulder, her face hidden and eyes averted. "Thank you, Fischer."

Her slight touch, innocuous as it was, made my heart leap from my chest. I stood there for entirely too long, my brain failing me as it reached for what to say. Her head was still dipped down, and I thought she might have leaned a little closer.

Was it my imagination?

My hand moved by itself, reaching to pet the top of her head—half out of a want to reassure her, half out of a desire to be closer.

A drop of water flew down, smacking into my hand and shattering my trance. I looked up at the sky just as more droplets started falling. They came slowly at first, but in the space of seconds, more and more flew down, crashing against my face and arms. I took my extended hand and ran it over her head, smoothing her hair down.

"Let's go—we'll get soaked if we don't get to the next shelter."

She nodded stiffly, still looking down.

What in Hades's gloomy abode was that? Maria thought, chastising herself.

Fischer's arm wrapping around her waist had caused her senses to leave, and playing it over in her mind again, heat rose to her face. She knew he was strong, but he'd caught her so easily. Not only that—despite his strength, he'd used such care when catching her. His arms felt strong enough to snap her wrist with a simple squeeze, but they'd delicately held her in place before leveraging her back to her feet.

Why did I reach out and touch his shoulder? What are you doing, Maria?

Her hand had moved out unbidden; averting her face was the only action she felt in control of. If his grip around her waist and wrist had sent her thoughts into disarray, his soothing hand moving over her hair had made her thoughts a veritable tempest. If Fischer hadn't suggested they keep moving, she may have stood there indefinitely, just waiting and hoping for another touch.

The sprinkle of droplets had turned into a deluge as they traveled, and the surrounding trees now roared as wind and rain assaulted them. Her entire body was soaked, but she barely registered the sensation.

Another crack of thunder exploded above, and her foot caught on something. She stumbled, but before she even had the chance to trip, something caught her arm, holding her upright. She glanced over, seeing Fischer holding her upper arm and giving her a beaming smile.

"You good?" he yelled over the rain.

Maria nodded.

He nodded back. "Let's go!"

They took off again, both lost in introspection.

She must be freezing, I thought, glancing at Maria through the torrential downpour. She looked shocked after I caught her the second time, her body stiff.

"We're almost there!" I called over the storm, trying to reassure her.

She nodded at me with a smile; it looked forced. I returned my eyes to the surrounding forest and the creek we followed. It all looked the same.

I hope we reach the pond and shelter soon . . . I'd feel terrible if she got sick on what's supposed to be a relaxing trip . . .

By the time we reached our destination, the pelting rain and winds had receded into a calm sprinkle. I guessed that Maria was feeling better, because as the storm diminished and we could hear each other speak again, we intermittently talked and joked about small things.

"Are you okay?" I asked, turning from my still-standing shelter to look at Maria.

She smiled at me. "Other than being drenched?" She wrung the bottom of her top for emphasis. "I'm good otherwise."

"You're not too cold?"

"No. I wouldn't complain if we got a fire going, though."

"I'm glad I decided to pack some kindling and sticks in my bag. I hope they stayed dry."

I took the packs off and walked over to the shelter, opening up mine as I handed Maria's to her.

Please don't be soaked . . .

To my joy and surprise, only the outer blankets were a little wet—everything else within managed to stay dry.

Maria let out a long-suffering sigh and started emptying her bag. Her pack was completely soaked through. Blankets, clothes, food—*everything* was wet.

As if to rub it in, the rain had stopped falling, and the clouds above seemed a little lighter. Maria's body shivered, the cold overcoming her now that we'd stopped running. I dipped my hand into my pack, removing a shirt, pants, and a towel.

"Here," I said, holding it out to her.

She took them, then cast around, looking for somewhere to change. I wiggled the shelter's sticks from their holes in the earth and tipped it up on one side, making a screen.

"Get changed out of those wet clothes and I'll start a fire. We can dry all your wet stuff afterward."

She smiled up at me, an unreadable mix of emotions crossing her face.

"Thank you, Fischer."

"No worries!"

I winked. "What are servants for?"

Leroy felt numb as they walked through the tempest—it had nothing to do with the temperature. As the rains grew even steadier, they crested the top of a hill; they were greeted by a stunning vista.

A bay stretched out between two headlands, one of which had a river on the other side connecting with the ocean. A village sat right at the center of the cove, a sprawling mess of houses, buildings, and crops that stretched out into the surrounding lands.

A gust picked up, hitting the crown prince's parasol. It turned it inside out, and as he wrestled to get it back under control, the rain splattered into him, making dark spots appear on his royal clothing.

"By Poseidon's soaked beard—one of you help me!"

The long-haired cultivator let out a snort of amusement, one of the rare sounds he'd made since they started traveling. Leroy looked at him, noting the look of joy at their handler's discomfort. Unlike his long-haired acquaintance, he was unable to feel any mirth. All he felt was a murky mix of hope and dread.

With each stretch of road they crossed, and each step further east, his suspicions at their destination grew. Now, both his fear and hope were confirmed.

He'd arrived back in Tropica, his home, and the rogue cultivator that the artifact sensed was one of the villagers—perhaps even a member of his family.

He clenched his jaw, not hearing the expletives pouring from Trent's mouth.

What twisted working of fate is this?

CHAPTER SEVENTY-ONE

LIGHTNING

How do I look?" Maria asked.

I had my back to where she'd been changing, so I half turned, keeping my hands held out before the small fire. When I caught sight of her, I stood, forgetting the campfire entirely.

My clothes were oversized on her; the pants were rolled up just above her ankle, the shirt hanging down well past her waist. Where it may have looked ridiculous on another, it was entrancing on her, and I couldn't peel my eyes away.

Her half-wet hair was tied back, revealing her freckled nose and the pleasing lines of her face. With my prolonged attention, she blushed, and realizing I'd been quiet for too long, I said the first thing that came to mind.

"B-beautiful."

She covered her face, letting out a nervous laugh. "Don't tease me, Fischer—I know I look ridiculous."

"I mean it. Maybe you should have them." I pointed at the clothes. "They look better on you than me."

She laughed again, walking over and taking a spot by the fire.

I held out a blanket. "Here."

"Thank you," she said, wrapping it around herself.

"I'm gonna get dressed into something dry, too."

I narrowed my eyes at her, smiling. "No peeking."

She rolled her eyes and let out an exaggerated sigh. "Lucky for you, I'm too cold to leave this fire."

"Be right back, then."

With a dry set of clothes on, I returned to the campfire, drying my hair with a towel. Maria sat staring into the embers, her hands extended toward the growing flame.

"I'm gonna get some sticks to make a drying rack."

"I'll help."

She stood, but before she took more than one step, a full-body shiver took her.

I shook my head. "You stay warm. If I take you back to Tropica with hypothermia, Roger's gonna have a fit."

"I'm fine," she said, then shook all over.

I laughed. "Please. Let me do it."

She raised an eyebrow. "You're really not cold?"

"Nope—not at all. You sit and get comfy, and I'll sort out the clothes, all right?"

"Hmmm. I guess that is what servants are for . . ."

I grinned. "Exactly!"

I walked through the surrounding forest, picking out sticks long enough to construct a rack. When I had an armful, I returned to the fire. I'd found some dry wood, too—a thick log that had been protected from the rain by the trunk of a fallen tree. I held the log at an angle, stomping down to crack it into smaller bits. When I looked up at Maria, her face was full of incredulity.

"What?" I asked, picking up one of the longer sticks.

"What are your legs made of?"

I pushed the stick into the ground and picked up another.

"Er—same as you . . . I think."

"If I just did what you did to that log, I'd be more likely to break my foot than the wood."

"What can I say?" I wiggled my eyebrows at her as I pushed the second stick into the soft earth. "Fish are full of nutrients that make you grow big and strong."

She raised an eyebrow at me. "If you say so . . ."

"I do."

I finished hanging up the last bit of clothing, all of it easily fitting on my makeshift rack.

"Have you tried the berries that grow around water, Maria? The ones all around this pond?"

She looked up at the patch growing on the far bank. "They only grow by water, so Dad always said eating them would be . . ."

"Heretical? Going against the gods?" I finished.

She nodded, rolling her eyes. "Exactly."

"Well, they grow in the ground, so I don't feel bad introducing you to them. More importantly, they're delicious and full of sugar, which you no doubt need right now."

She cocked her head to one side. "Why would I need sugar?"

"Because you're shaking so hard you might start an earthquake. We'll need to replenish that energy you're losing."

I bent and grabbed a pot from beside the campfire. "Back in a jiffy."

I picked my way around the pond, stripping berries by the handful. Intending to only get enough for a snack, I ended up filling the pot entirely.

I brought it back to Maria, and as I got closer, I saw her shaking had gotten worse. Her teeth chattered, and she looked a little white.

"Are you okay?"

She nodded, but even that action made her shake more. I set the pot down in front of her then grabbed another blanket. I sat on the log beside her and draped the blanket over us both. She went to pull her blanket closer around herself, and her hand brushed up against mine. It was ice cold.

"You're—"

"You're so warm!" she interrupted.

I was getting worried, so I grabbed the corner of her blanket and opened up her cocoon, throwing the blanket over both our shoulders so my body could warm hers. As she felt the heat radiating from me, she sidled closer. Her small body shivered; my heart thundered in response. Her hand brushed up against my arm, and she withdrew it immediately, as if burned by my touch.

"Sorry," she said. "I didn't mean to—"

I grabbed her hand, holding it between both of mine.

"Oh . . ." She put her other hand atop mine. "You're like a furnace."

". . . Are you calling me hot?"

She laughed hard, her body shaking with shivers that made the laugh halting. She accidentally snorted, then held one hand up to her mouth, her eyes going wide.

"Why am I so embarrassing?"

"I think you mean endearing," I said, grabbing her hand and pulling it back beneath the blanket.

With one of her hands held in each of mine, we sat and stared at the fire, a comfortable silence stretching as her shivering slowly receded.

Barry ran across the sand flats of Fischer's domain, only stopping once he reached the covered awning of his home. He removed his hat, shaking it free of the water atop it.

"Usually I like the rain, but this downpour is a bit much."

Snips shrugged, standing in the rain with her eye half closed, clearly enjoying the drops hitting her carapace. Beside her, similarly enjoying herself, was Corporal Claws. Unlike Snips, however, her eyes were filled with anticipation.

"Is it all right if I grab a towel from inside?" Barry asked.

Snips nodded her acquiescence, gesturing for the door.

Barry walked inside, and after only a little searching, returned to the creatures outside, drying his hair.

"All right . . . where should we start, Snips?"

The crab shrugged, blowing indifferent bubbles. As they left her mouth, they were hit and popped by the sheets of rain. She scowled at the sky, stepped under the roof, then blew bubbles of annoyance, followed immediately by the indifferent variety. Barry laughed, and Snips cocked her carapace, clearly questioning him.

"I always find it funny how, well, *human* you are. We're told stories of ascending creatures as kids, and none of them involve annoyance when rain pops their bubbles."

Snips shrugged again, as if to say, "*So?*"

Claws dashed under the roof and let out an indignant chirp.

Corporal Claws, first of her name and cutest of Fischer's disciples, grew tired of the meandering conversation. She dashed out of the rain, making her frustration known with a sharp chirp and accusatory glare.

She'd been waiting a long time for the revelation of Barry and Snips's plans. Every time she asked what they were doing, Snips would reiterate two things: not yet, and don't tell Fischer—both of which were as anger inducing as the other. What reason could they have for keeping master in the dark, and why couldn't she know?

With Fischer gone on a trip with the speckle-faced human, Snips had told her they would let her in on the secret—*finally.* That was *two days ago!* Claws was a patient and magnificent otter, but there was only so much waiting she could handle. She chirped again, frowning at Barry and Snips in turn.

"You're right. Sorry," Barry said. "You've been most patient, Claws, and we've decided it's time we brought you in on the plan—well, plans. There's a lot to go over."

She nodded, chirping her agreement with just how patient she had been.

Much more patient than Snips would have been in the same situation.

"All right . . . where to begin?" Barry tapped his chin in thought. "Perhaps we should start with why we're keeping this all a secret from Fischer . . ."

The rain battered his face as Leroy ran, but he neither shielded his eyes nor closed them for a moment. They traveled down the main road toward Tropica, and with each step, his confusing emotions churned and billowed.

Trent was giggling to himself, muttering something about women and going home with a cultivator, but Leroy barely heard it, consumed as his thoughts were. He had dared to hope he'd one day return to his family, to shed his chains and come back a free man.

To come back like this, though . . .

The village grew closer with each step they took.

"Stop!" Trent yelled, pulling up short.

He glanced down at the artifact in his hand, spinning around on the spot. When he was facing to the southeast, he looked up, a vicious snarl on his face.

"This way."

Trent, crown prince and leader of the expedition, glared at the two cultivators.

"Well? Lead the way, morons! I'm not cutting through this field!"

The long-haired cultivator shrugged and stepped into the field of cane, knocking aside swaths of the crop with haphazard swings of his arms. The other cultivator stared into space, looking at the village with an unreadable expression.

"Go!" Trent screeched, stepping toward the man. He looked at Trent, blinked rapidly, then walked behind the longer-haired man after a long moment.

I swear, Trent thought, *these idiots would be lost without me. Look at how they take turns staring into space—each cultivator is as mad as the other.*

As he followed them through the demolished crop, Trent reached into his bag and removed one of the spare collars.

His grin returned as he looked down at the relic. It was blinking rapidly, showing that the cultivator in question was in the direction they traveled. Soon, he'd return to the capital with this 'Fischer' in chains, added to the ranks of cultivator slaves. The kingdom would grow stronger, and his father, the king, would reward him for his efforts. He would have riches, accolades, and all the serving girls he wanted.

With one more swing of the cultivator's arm, the way forward was clear; no more crops remained to hamper their way. A house stood before them, directly where the artifact was pointing. Trent stepped past the cultivators, striding toward the home.

"Follow me."

"No . . ." came a soft voice from behind.

Trent whirled, glaring hate at the short-haired cultivator.

"No? You dare say no to me even now? This isn't about going to stay in a tavern—this is our mission!"

Trent slapped him. The cultivator's face didn't move, the strike shaking nary a drop from his head, still as it was.

"Useless!" Trent snarled, turning back toward the house.

As he approached the front door, he looked down at the artifact, then stopped; the blinking light had slowed. He turned to the right, then to the left; the blinking increased. Confused, he looked up in the direction he was facing, seeing sandy flats before him. The artifact wasn't pointing at the house—it was pointing past it.

"Fischer isn't in there!" he yelled over the rain. "With me, gentlemen—er—cultivator scum, I mean!"

He marched off toward the sand, and a sharp tone cut through the storm like a knife. Knowing what the sound meant, Trent dove forward. He crashed into the sand, scrambling to all fours. He glanced up, his eyes going wide, expecting the cultivators to descend upon him. But that wasn't the case.

Instead of attacking, the short-haired cultivator had stepped toward the home, his arm outstretched. The light on his collar was glowing red, threatening to detonate if he continued going against orders. The long-haired one looked between them with a grin of the purest joy.

Trent had assumed one or both of the cultivators had attacked him from behind, and he'd meant to get as far from the subsequent death-inducing explosion as possible.

He got to his feet, channeling every ounce of indignation—*his clothes were covered in sand and dirt!*

"One more step toward that home and you'll die, you idiot! Your collar is beeping!"

The cultivator ignored him, staring at the closed door. Before he could say something, the door flew open, and a woman stepped outside.

"Leroy?" She fell to her knees. "It's really you?"

"Helen . . ." the short-haired cultivator replied, his whimper barely heard over the storm.

After an impressively short amount of time—by his estimation—Trent finally understood. The short-haired cultivator and this woman knew each other.

A flash of lightning lit the sky above the mountains, highlighting the stricken lines of the woman's face. Trent grinned, baring his teeth at the short-haired cultivator the woman had called Leroy.

"Punch her in the face."

That seemed to snap Leroy back to reality, and he turned toward Trent.

" . . . What?"

Trent grinned. "Remember all the insults on our way here, cultivator? All the times you refused to escort me to a tavern? All the nights spent in leech-infested forests? I order you to punch that lady you know. In the face."

"That . . . would be going against our handler's orders. It could hurt the mission."

An idea occurred to Trent, and he grinned even wider. He threw one of the collars to the long-haired cultivator.

"Put that on the woman. She can come with us back to the capital. I bet our lover boy Leroy here would just *love* that."

The cultivator gave a cruel smile and exploded into action, moving as a blur for the woman, one arm extended with the collar spread wide. Trent watched the collar closing, his own smile growing wide.

CHAPTER SEVENTY-TWO

THUNDER

Leroy flew into action, catching the other cultivator's arms as the collar was closing around Helen's neck. The two sides of the collar were only centimeters from sealing Helen's fate, and Leroy flexed his arms, pulling it open and away from her.

"Run!" he yelled, his voice sounding hysterical to his own ears. "Once the collar is on, you can never remove it!"

Helen was frozen, tears in her eyes as her gaze lingered on him.

"Leroy . . ."

The collar around his neck vibrated, once more making the harsh sound that warned of an impending explosion.

"What the hell are you doing!" Trent demanded. "That was your last warning! It won't beep next time—it'll detonate! You want to die so badly?"

Leroy leaned in closer to the other man, setting his collar against his.

"Rescind the order, Trent! If it goes off now, we'll both die, and you'll have lost two cultivators rather than gaining a third!"

"Y-you dare order me?"

Leroy glanced at Trent, forcing a smile. "You dare return to the capital having lost two cultivators?"

Trent's face twisted. "Fine! I rescind the order! Follow me—now!"

Leroy let go of the other man's arm, watching him closely.

The long-haired cultivator shook his head. "Shame. That would have been fun."

As he turned back to look at his sister, Leroy's eyes were hot. Tears ran down his face, mixing with the rain.

"I love you, Helen. Please don't follow me."

Her lip quivered, and she nodded a single time, her own tears falling.

Maria popped a berry into her mouth and slowly chewed. A pleased noise escaped her.

"Thank you, Fischer."

I squeezed her hand. "For what?"

"Everything." She leaned against me with her back, turning her body away. "For the berries, for bringing me out here, for keeping me warm, and for being so kind."

"It's easy to be kind, especially to people deserving of it."

"If only the world were so . . ."

She put her head back against mine, and I leaned into it. Her hair was soft and smelled of flowers; the scent was bewitching.

"You know . . ." I said. "If you're warm enough, we can try for another fish before it gets too late."

She bolted upright, spinning to face me. "*You mean it?*"

I couldn't help but smile at the intense gleam in her eyes.

"Yeah—I mean it. We should probably remake the shelter first, but that shouldn't take too long."

"Let's do it!"

She shot to her feet, blankets discarded as a burst of energy hit.

"Would you mind looking for sticks?" I asked. "I have something I want to try."

"Yeah!"

She all but sprinted into the forest, and I watched her go, the smile never leaving my face.

I collected some of the short sticks I'd gathered earlier and connected the ends together in a tepee shape, then tied them together with string. It was just tall and wide enough for my purpose, so I placed it over the fire. With another length of string, I tied one end to the pot's handle and the other to my makeshift frame's peak.

The flames licked up, now and then touching the bottom of the pot, so I shortened the line, raising it higher above the flames. I added a dash of water to the berries, then stepped back, nodding to myself.

Maria tore from the forest, her face almost manic, a handful of long branches under one arm.

"I got the sticks, Fischer! They should be long enough! Let me know if they're not, but I think they're fine! I'm ready when you—*woah!* What's that?"

I laughed at her excess energy. "Those sticks look perfect." I gestured at the fire. "I made a rack to try cooking the berries down into jam."

"Oh, jam! That's a great idea—they're super sweet!"

"Yeah, I thought it would pair well with our breakfast pastries." I waggled my eyebrows at her. "Or even a fish—if you manage to catch one."

She bounced on her heels. "Let's make the shelter! Fast! So we can go fishing!"

I smiled. "Nothing would make me happier."

With our combined efforts, the shelter came together in no time at all. I leaned down, looking at the small gaps between the leaves.

"I'm gonna weave in an extra layer of the palm fronds in case the rain comes back. I'll just go collect some."

It took me less than a minute to find the palm-like trees again, and after stripping a handful of their greenery, I returned to the pond. What I found there brought another smile to my face.

Maria held the rod under one arm, had cut a small strip of the eel, and was putting it on the hook. She had a large leaf in her hands acting as a glove, and her head was extended as far from the bait as possible, avoiding the stench.

Happy to let her work it out, I wove the leaves in between the others of our shelter with deft hands. Just as I was finishing up, Maria let out a little squeal. I glanced over, and she was bouncing from foot to foot, the rod held in her hands.

"Cast it out," I said.

She stopped, staring at me.

"You're sure?"

"You remember how, right?"

She held the line under one finger, flicked the reel forward, then raised a questioning eyebrow at me.

I nodded. "Go for it—I'll be there in a sec."

I was weaving the last leaves in and tying them down when Maria's voice arrested my attention.

"F-Fischer!" she whisper yelled.

My eyes shot up, just in time to see the tip of the rod dip down as a fish nibbled the line. The shelter forgotten, I dashed to her, eyes pinned on the tip of the rod. It bit again, a small, testing nibble. Maria tensed and squeaked a quiet, high-pitched sound.

"Not yet," I said. "Wait for the big bite and then strike."

She nodded, her eyes watching the water under the fading light of the day.

Tug. Tug.

She tensed again, so I laid a hand on hers.

"Wait for it . . ."

She nodded again, her body trembling with anticipation.

Tug.

Tug. Tug.

The rod bent almost in half as the fish took the bait.

"Now!"

She reefed up the rod, attempting to set the hook.

Corporal Claws could never have envisioned a situation where leaving her master in the dark was justified. Yet, with her growing understanding of Barry and Sergeant Snips's plan, one such situation was made known. Not only was it vital that Fischer did not know yet—nothing would protect her master so much as enacting the plan.

"So," Barry said. "I have to ask—do you agree?"

Barry's question drew Claws from her rumination, and she looked up at him, her eyes clearing. She nodded.

Master must be protected.

Snips nodded from beside her and blew bubbles of approval, clearly already knowing what her answer would be.

Barry smiled down at her. "Good. Now, let's go into the fine details, and what I'd like you to do for now."

Leroy felt hollowed out as he strode through the storm. The wind had no chance of knocking his cultivator body over, yet he felt fragile before each localized squall, like they blew right through him. He fell to his knees, staring down at the sand beneath him.

"Get up!" Trent screeched, but Leroy barely registered it. In his mind's eye, all he saw were the faces of his family.

"Drag him with you! Don't let his collar detonate!"

Leroy heard a grunt and was then hauled to his feet. He felt his feet move, and he stumbled across the sandy flats with the help of the long-haired cultivator.

Trent spat, glaring his annoyance at the two cultivators. Seeing the sand on the cultivator's clothes, Trent looked down at his own pants.

One of his favorite purple outfits, of which he only had ten sets of, was ruined. Sand, water, and muck had infiltrated the fibers, and no amount of cleaning would repair the lavish garment.

A growl rose from deep within him. All he wanted was to catch another cultivator for his father, earn some goodwill, and perhaps have fun with some busty serving wenches on the way. Was that too much to ask?

He returned his attention to the artifact in his hands. He spun on the spot, and when he pointed it toward a dark mass in the distance obscured by the surrounding storm, the light blinked faster yet. A smirk came to his face, and he strode toward the shape.

There was still time to salvage the trip. He would catch this "Fischer" and take him back to the capital. With the money his father would give him, he'd be able to buy even *more* outfits.

"With me, fools."

"All right," Barry said, "that's about all that I think you can do right now, Claws. Do you have any tho—uh . . . Snips?"

She had spun on the spot in an instant, staring at the rock of the headland.

"What's wrong?"

Corporal Claws, who at first peered at Snips with similar confusion, suddenly looked as if struck by a bolt of lightning, and her head darted to stare at the same spot as Snips. A shiver ran down Barry's spine, and he looked at the rock, uncomprehending.

Both creatures took defensive stances in the sand, Snips hunkering down and Claws arching up like a startled cat.

Barry returned his attention to where they gazed, willing his focus to join theirs. Unexpectedly, he felt . . . *something.* A power, or a source of power, was approaching from beyond the rock. He squinted, his brow furrowing as he delved deeper into the sensation.

It wasn't a singular source of power; a trickle of resonance came from two points, both right beside each other, but definitely individual points.

"Hide," Barry said.

Snips shot him a look, and he nodded.

"They're cultivators, and neither of them is Fischer—hide and wait to see what happens."

* * *

Trent heard a laugh come from behind him, and he whirled, glaring daggers at the long-haired cultivator.

"What?"

The man gave a wolf's grin. "There are two of them."

Trent, his eyes going wide, stared at what he could now see was a large formation of rock.

"Two of them?"

The cultivator nodded, his eyes going vicious. "There are two cultivators behind that rock—close."

Trent returned a grin of his own. He fumbled in the bag, and with his mouth growing wider, removed a second collar. He salivated at the thought of bringing *two* cultivators back to the capital. His father would be most pleased and would reward him accordingly.

"Walk close to me, and no matter what, don't kill them—they are to be captured."

In the decade that Robert had been chained, he'd found ways to enact his violence without going directly against orders. He flicked his long hair, sending the wet strands away from his face.

After all, he thought, *if I'm a little too slow to act, and my handler gets attacked, it's only natural that I'd save him by killing the attacker.*

As they stepped closer to the rock outcropping, his anticipation grew. He could feel the two cultivators; both of their bodies resonated with his. Only others on the path to ascension could cause such a sensation.

As they stepped around the last rock, he barely felt the weight of the cultivator he held—if you could call the coward that. What good was a cultivator with attachments, after all?

I'll have to find a way to kill that sister of his before we leave . . .

His mouth watered at the prospect.

As Trent stepped around the rocky headland, he caught sight of a man. The person, dressed in farmer's garb, stood with arms behind his back, a calm expression on his face.

"So," Trent screeched. "We finally meet, Fischer."

The man raised an eyebrow. "You come looking for Fischer, then? I'm sorry to say, but he's not here."

"Hiding him won't work, you idiot! I can detect both of you!"

Trent looked down at the artifact, and moving it side to side, saw that the light blinked faster when pointing at the house's front door.

"He's inside, isn't he?" Trent glanced up at the man, seeing his eyes wide, his jaw slackened.

Happy to see his words had the intended effect, he continued. "If you come easily, I won't do Fischer any harm. If you don't, though . . ."

Trent trailed off when he realized the man wasn't gaping at him; he looked behind and to his right.

". . . Leroy?"

Trent looked back just in time for the short-haired cultivator's wits to return. His eyes cleared, and he looked up at the farmer.

"Barry?" His face twisted, contorting with grief. "No . . ."

The long-haired cultivator let go of the man and stepped forward, closing and opening his hands.

"It's not him."

Trent spun. "What do you mean, it's not him?"

The long-haired cultivator stared at the farmer, his brow furrowing, then eyes going wide.

"Wait . . . he *is* a cultivator, but he's . . . weak."

Trent only felt a moment of confusion before elation overrode the emotion. *Three cultivators!* He'd return with *three* cultivators!

He threw one collar toward the farmer; it skidded to a stop at his feet.

"Put that on, then go get the others from inside. If you do, I'll make this pleasant. Make this hard for me, though . . ." Trent gave a mischievous grin. "Well, then you'll see just how brutal I can be."

"They're not inside," the long-haired man said from behind him.

"What do you mean, they're not inside?" Trent stared down at the artifact, seeing it was still blinking incessantly when facing the door. "Where are they, then?"

The man, his gaze unwavering, pointed down at a spot in the sand with one hand, and an upended pot near the front door with the other. As if on command, a fountain of sand exploded skyward, and the metal pot was shredded to pieces. Trent fell back, stumbling over his feet. The revealed cultivators didn't attack, though, so he squinted at the shrinking cloud of sand.

On the sand between them and the farmer stood an otter and a crab. The otter was large, with extended claws and fangs. The crab was covered in spikes and wearing . . . *is that an eyepatch?*

Trent's amazement was washed away by dawning horror. He looked down at the artifact. The light below the drawing of a human was blinking, and the light below the series of animals was blank.

Creatures . . . ascendant creatures that have grown powerful enough to no longer be recognized as animals . . .

Like cupcake frosting beneath the midday sun, his hopes of returning to the capital with three cultivators melted away. Such beings couldn't be controlled.

"K-kill them!" he screeched, crawling back from the abominations.

At his decree, the world exploded into violence.

CHAPTER SEVENTY-THREE

THE STORM

Robert dashed toward the crab, his fists prickling with sparks of deadly energy. He drew deeper from his core, knowing he wouldn't need so much power to kill lowly creatures, but wanting to see the carnage he could weave. He'd never killed an ascendant creature before, and he couldn't wait to see how it felt, to feel this crab's carapace crack and shatter between his fingers.

He swung his arm up and around, moving faster than the creature could register. With a single kick off the sand, he changed his trajectory, delighting in his body's superior speed. He leaned his torso over the crab's back, then, with wide eyes and a vicious grin, he let the punch fly.

His fist slammed into the ground. A gout of sand shot in every direction, creating an obfuscating cloud of grit and particles. As he felt the sensations of his fist striking the earth, and the stark lack of anything crunching underneath, he experienced a wave of disappointment. He'd used too much power, and the crab had disintegrated beneath his falling fist.

Oh well, he thought. *At least it might have made a cool splatter on the sand.*

He blinked as the sand cleared, and when his vision returned, his eyebrows furrowed. The sand he'd struck was just that—*sand.* There was no coloring to mark the crab's annihilation, neither flecks of carapace, nor limbs flung askew.

Where did it go . . . ?

Something hard tapped him on the shoulder, so he turned, and his entire field of view was swallowed by a terrifying sight—the crab's mouth blowing a steady stream of bubbles, its face more smug than a crustacean had any right being.

It was at that moment, on his knees in the sand, face to face with an ascended creature, that he felt fear for the first time in over a decade. Faster than his eyes could see, the crab thrust him in the air with the slap of a claw, knocking the air from his lungs.

As soon as the cultivator dashed, attempting to "surprise" Sergeant Snips, Corporal Claws paused, watching with curiosity. The cultivator's closed fists intrigued her; they seemed to radiate the energy of the heavens above, emitting small crackles of lightning. The energy resonated with her—*called* to her.

With a small chirp, she shrugged. She could revisit that later. The cultivator would reach Snips soon, and there were things to be done. She spared another fraction of a second to assess the cultivator's speed.

Pathetic, she decided.

She zoomed behind the other two men, appearing in the blink of one of their eyes. The one that Barry knew stood unmoving, his body trembling. The other, the one in a purple outfit—that would *probably* need to be eliminated—stared at the charging man. She watched them, seeing if either made a move.

The long-haired cultivator reached Snips's position, striking down with a pitifully sluggish strike. Claws watched him get flung high in the air, and a smile spread across her furred face. He looked like a bird, flapping his arms around in an attempt to fly—to no avail, of course.

The uncollared man turned to the other, snarling.

"W-what are you doing? Do you want your collar to explode? Attack, moron!"

The collared man, the one Barry had called Leroy, didn't respond, simply looking between Barry and the airborne fool. The collar beeped, and a spark of power began swelling within it.

Stumbling back, the purple-fabric-wearing man's eyes went wide. The look on his face, the comment on the collar exploding, and the swelling of power told Claws everything she needed to know.

The world slowed to a crawl as she bent her legs, gathering strength. From all around, she drew in force, the essence of the very storm heeding her call. A prickling sensation climbed her legs, but it wasn't unpleasant. Like scratching an itch, each pinprick was more satisfying than the last. Her muscles bulged, and her lips spread into a grin, revealing her sharp teeth. With one last contraction of her legs, she hunched and grasped for more power. Then, all at once, she released it.

Barry had worried about how the confrontation would play out, but after Snips so easily flung the overconfident man like a pebble, his worries were assuaged. Until, that is, the noble spoke.

"W-what are you doing? Do you want your collar to explode? Attack, moron!"

His heart sank, and he stared at Leroy, horror dawning. Leroy locked eyes with Barry, and even through the falling rain, Barry saw his brother-in-law's tears fall. Then, the collar detonated, shooting a bolt of lightning that tore through Leroy.

With his cultivator eyes, he saw it happen in slow motion. Saw the lightning seem to start from the sand and tear right toward Leroy's neck, connecting his body with the ground below.

Before he could register the grief that should follow such a sight, he realized something was . . . wrong. He squinted his eyes, only able to follow the movement because of his awakening.

The strike didn't condemn Leroy; it removed the collar from his neck, throwing it to the side.

As the collar flew to the side, moving faster than a mortal could see, it detonated in truth. A small explosion that sounded like another blast of thunder was unleashed, just far enough from Leroy to do any damage.

Then, the bolt of lightning released a chittering, high-pitched cooing as it flew past Barry, smiling madly at him and maintaining strong eye contact in her passing. Corporal Claws, having harnessed the power of lightning, continued on, shooting toward Sergeant Snips.

As Robert shot high into the air, unable to breathe and not comprehending what was happening, he reached the apex of his impromptu flight. With his descent back to solid ground, he matched the speed of the falling rain, and even in his state of confusion, the sight of suspended raindrops drew him in with its oddity.

An explosion rang out, signifying that the cowardly cultivator's shackles had detonated. If Robert had been in his normal state of mind, he would have celebrated this occurrence—reveled in the deserving death of a man brought down by familial attachments. As it was, though, he felt no such joy; all he knew was terror.

He looked back down at the ground rushing up to meet him, absorbing the scene in slow motion. The crab waited, one claw pulled back, its lone eye fixed on him. In its gaze, he saw death.

Corporal Claws felt *alive.* She'd reached for the storm, and the storm answered, caressing and guiding her passage. On a bolt of lightning—no, *as* a bolt of lightning—she shot for Sergeant Snips. She didn't necessarily *need* to make a stop by the powerful crab, but having harnessed a power that Snips hadn't, she felt it only prudent to show off a little.

As she flew directly for Snips, she chirped, drawing the Sergeant's attention. In a fraction of a mortal's heartbeat, Snips's eye shot toward her, went wide, then narrowed in suspicion. Claws chirped a laugh; she could see Snips's annoyance etched on her carapaced face. It made Claws's laugh increase, pouring out with her sheer joy at the situation. Snips reluctantly held out a claw, understanding Corporal Claws's intent.

The corporal hit the claw, gathering power before kicking off with lightning-enhanced legs. Snips hefted up simultaneously, sending her skyward at the speed of sound. She bared her teeth in a smile as she shot at the airborne cultivator.

Robert watched as a bolt of lightning struck the crab, and he felt a moment of hope.

Did that coward not explode? Has he somehow harnessed the power of lightning better than I? Will—huh?

The bolt of lightning sat for a moment, collecting on the crab's extended claw, then shot up to him. It flew past him, making an odd chirping sound as it went. He spun, subconsciously wanting to see where it went. As he faced the sky, he came face to face with the storm.

An otter's head, surrounded by lightning, its face split in a vicious grin, stared down at him.

It spun in a figure eight, gaining speed and making the same chittering sound. The noise increased as it gained speed, and all Robert could do was watch.

It flew wide, spun up and away from him, then, faster than he could register, slammed down into his chest. The power of the lightning the creature held allowed only a single thought before it reached his brain and blackness took him.

So much . . . power . . .

Snips glared up at Claws, disapproving of the way she played with their quarry.

Though, she supposed, *I could have ended him immediately instead of throwing him up into the sky . . .*

She shrugged.

Oh well. What's done is done.

The cultivator's body flew down at incredible speed, and she held her claw back, waiting for the perfect moment. As it arrived, she swung out, using all the force she could muster. Her claw struck the man with a hideous *crack,* his improved physique the only reason his body wasn't torn apart.

Water turned to mist from the impact, and his limp form flew out to sea. Despite the modicum of strength held in his body, the man was no more; his soul had departed his body before it struck the open water of the ocean.

The rock crab sat beneath the waves. He was supposed to be keeping an eye out for any intrusions yet was constantly being distracted by what his spiky-shelled leader was doing. From what he could tell, complex thoughts were a recent occurrence for him. Rather than be worried or disoriented by them, however, he marveled at their novelty, finding it wonderful that he could think about the other crab when she was not present.

Something hit the water above, crashing down at terrifying speed. The crab held up his clackers, prepared to fight off whatever interloper dared invade his designated patch of sand.

The thing slowly sank to the ocean floor, giving off a smell like the cooked food his spiky-shelled benefactor occasionally brought tastes of.

The thing hit the ocean floor, and seeing that it was very much not moving, the crab scuttled over.

Food.

He nodded to himself, copying the gesture from his beloved leader.

Good.

Trent, first in line to the throne of Gormona, and bane of serving girls everywhere, fell to his knees in the sand. The body of the long-haired cultivator had been beaten and thrown around like one of his sister's dolls. Worse, the creatures had ascended beyond any reasonable level. One of them had even harnessed the power of lightning—its strength beyond anything he'd ever seen.

He'd witnessed the power of many a cultivator, ordered to show off their powers at dinner parties to impress one noble family or another. Trent remembered them fondly. Gouts of flame shooting from fists, sparks of lightning enhancing body parts, blades of water shooting from palms, even one cultivator that could grow trees and plants. All of those abilities were small things, though. Impressive to the average person, and indeed, a terrifying prospect to even him, a crown prince.

Compared to the power of that otter, though . . .

He shuddered, remembering the way it had wrapped itself—*become* the lightning.

To think there were ascendant creatures, let alone ones this advanced . . .

Forget the kingdom—the *world* was lost if they weren't brought to heel. There were only a few people Trent knew of that could hope to contend with that power, but unleashing them was a death sentence in itself.

What am I going to do?

A soft *click* came in answer, and a weight settled around Trent's neck. His hands scrambled, finding the object he'd known he would find, yet still hoped he wouldn't.

A collar.

Someone stepped in front of him, and he looked up, glaring daggers.

"Cultivator scum. You think you can enslave *me—a crown prince?* You think you'll get away—"

The man in the farmer's garb slapped him, almost haphazardly, but the strike was enough to make Trent's head spin and ears ring. He fell to the sand, and as he tried to get to his feet, the farmer grabbed his chin, forcing his head up so their eyes met.

"It's a pleasure to meet you, *prince.*" He spat the last word with venom. "My name is Barry, but you can call me *master.*"

CHAPTER SEVENTY-FOUR

REUNION

D-did it work?" Maria asked, her voice shrill. The tip of the rod bent down, moving with the fish's head shakes.

"It did!" I answered, watching the water, my gaze unwavering.

The fish on the line gave a valiant fight, but it didn't stand a chance against Maria's farm-hardened physique and my new rod.

Within a few breaths, silver flashed at the water's edge, and Maria bent to pick up the fish.

Maybe I should have brought a smaller rod for this freshwater fishing trip.

As I saw the catch, my suspicions were confirmed. It was the same juvenile jungle perch as we'd caught so far.

"Is this as big as they get?" Maria asked, looking down at the fish with furrowed eyebrows.

I smiled at her. "Nah, they definitely get bigger."

She bent back down, lowering the fish under the water.

"Good, because I really want to try fish, but I don't want to eat one of these little babies."

The fish kicked off, leaving ripples in its wake as it disappeared into the depths.

"Still," she said, "even catching these little ones is so much fun!"

I smiled. "I couldn't agree more. Wanna try for a bigger one right now?"

She nodded, beaming.

Barry led Barbara along the earthen track between two fields of sugarcane.

"What is this about, Barry? You're worrying me . . ."

"It's something good—" He shook his head. "No, something wondrous. You'll just have to trust me."

"Well, tell me where you're taking me, at least."

"We're going to my house."

Barbara gasped. "Is Helen pregnant? Am I going to have a new niece or nephew?"

Barry couldn't help but laugh.

"No, it's not that, but it is something just as miraculous."

"Something as wondrous as making life from nothing?" The skepticism was obvious in her voice. "If you say so . . ."

They stepped from between the last two fields of sugarcane, catching sight of his house.

He turned to smile at her. "You'll see soon enough."

Her eyes narrowed in return. "Your level of excitement is making me even more concerned . . ."

Barry laughed. "Go inside, Barbara. There's someone waiting to see you."

With one more glare, she stomped off, and Barry followed. She threw open the door as if it were her own home, her hands quickly going to her hips as she cast her eyes around.

Soft voices from inside halted as Barbara made herself known.

"All right, what's the big deal, Helen? What am I—"

She froze, and Barry slowed his approach. She stood for a good five seconds, a statue in the doorway. Then, a whimper escaped her throat, and she stumbled inside and out of sight.

Barry made it to the doorway just as Helen appeared, ushering their son Paul before her.

They walked outside, and Barry softly closed the door behind them. The last thing he heard was Barbara's sobs and Leroy's reassuring voice, but he tuned them out, not wanting to intrude on the reunion.

Helen had tears in her eyes, and Barry felt his own well up. He wiped them away and scooped Paul up in his arms.

"Why don't we go for a stroll down to the ocean? The rain has finally stopped."

"Dad . . ." Paul said. "Why is everyone sad about Uncle Leroy coming home?"

"We're not sad, my little love," Helen said, hugging them both. "We're overjoyed."

I watched Maria cast out the line, marveling at her form—er, the form with which she cast the rod, I mean. The bait flew over the water, splashing down on the other side of the pond. With no prompting, she reeled in the line a little, pulling it further toward us and into a deeper section of the pond. She turned to raise an eyebrow at me, and I nodded in response.

"Perfect."

She held her finger to the line, waiting for a bite. Her chest expanded as she took a deep breath, then contracted as she closed her eyes and exhaled.

A soft breeze kicked up, blowing the cool, humid air against my skin. I closed my eyes too, breathing deep of the frigid environment. The air entering my nostrils held the smell of earth and trees, and though it was in stark contrast to the scents of my shoreline, it was entirely welcome.

It brought with it a sense of calm and tranquility, and as I slowly breathed in and out, a smile spread across my face.

This is pure bliss . . .

"Oh!"

At Maria's exclamation, I opened my eyes. She watched the tip of the rod, and I raised my eyes but didn't see anything.

Did a fish steal the bait or somethi—

A fish struck, and Maria's body tensed, holding on to the rod. Its bamboo shaft was bent almost in half, and she held the reel firm, leaning back to keep her balance.

I stepped up beside her. "Let some of the line go."

She spared me a glance. "Y-you're sure?"

"Positive. Just give it a little room to run but keep the line taut—it'll tire itself."

She nodded and wound her hand backward, letting some of the line out. The fish happily took it, swimming to the far end of the pond before darting back toward us.

"Reel!" I yelled, but it wasn't necessary. Maria had seen the fish's change of direction, and had quickly wound the line in, keeping it tight.

"On it!" she replied, not taking her eyes off the water for a moment.

Unlike the previous battles, the hooked fish provided a suitable challenge for Maria. There were no snags to bust itself off with, but it used every trick it had to get away, constantly darting and shifting directions with its body. Maria rose to the challenge, responding with swift precision each time it tried to escape. Eventually, the fish tired, and we caught our first glimpse of silver from beneath the surface. One thing was for sure: this fish was *not* a juvenile.

"Woah!" Maria yelled, her voice jubilant. "*It's huge!*"

"You're almost there!"

It dashed away again, but it was clearly exhausted, the run tiny in comparison to its previous efforts. Maria quickly recovered the line, and with a few more winds of the reel, the fish was at the side of the pond.

"Yes!" She roared a laugh as she bent and picked it up, holding the fish with both hands. "I did it!"

As always, my eyes were immediately drawn into the fish.

Mature Jungle Perch

Uncommon

Known for its delicate flesh and subtle taste, this is prized among the freshwater fish of the Kallis Realm.

"It . . . it's the same kind of fish, right?" Maria asked.

"It is! An adult version!"

I looked down at the fish again, assessing its size. It was just bigger than my extended hand.

I guess the fish doesn't get much bigger than this . . .

Maria let out a high-pitched noise and danced from foot to foot.

"How do we cook it?"

I laughed at her exuberance.

"I'll dispatch it first—do you want to see how?"

She nodded, holding out the fish. I went down to the bank, and with a single thrust of my spike, it was done.

"That was fast . . ." Maria said. "Is that the spot for every fish?"

"Yeah, the same general area behind and above the eye. It's the most humane way to do it."

She bent down beside me, peering at the lifeless fish.

"Thanks for your sacrifice, fishy."

I smiled at her, happy she had the same instincts as I did.

"Me, too, fishy. Thank you for the sustenance."

I walked back to the fire and put the fish in a pot.

"Before we gut and cook that fish, do you wanna try to catch another?"

She cocked her head. "Do you think we'll need another?"

"Hmmm, they're pretty small, so if you want a good meal, I think another couldn't hurt."

Her smile grew.

"Let's do it!"

"Are you sure you're okay with keeping him here, Leroy?" Barry asked, peering at his brother-in-law. "I don't want his presence to interrupt your reunion."

Leroy smiled at him, genuine joy on his face.

"There's nothing that could ruin our coming back together, Barry." He sighed, his smile growing. "I still can't believe everything that's happened."

Barry rubbed the back of his head. "I can't either, to be honest. We still have a lot to tell you, but if you like, we can take care of that later."

Barbara put her arm around Leroy's waist. "Now is fine, Barry. I can't speak for you . . ." She leaned up and kissed Leroy on the cheek. "But I'd rather have it all out in the open."

Leroy nodded, peering down at his wife before returning his gaze to Barry.

"Aye. Couldn't have said it better myself."

Barry looked between them, his eyes crinkling and heart singing. There was a moment there—when seeing Leroy on his knees in the sand, his eyes unseeing—when Barry had worried about the man's mental state. That worry had evaporated the moment he'd collared the slaver prince. With the removal of Leroy's shackles, and the sudden realization that he was free, his eyes had cleared—mostly, anyway.

He could tell there was still lingering pain there—some remnant of the ordeals he must have experienced.

I hope he can heal up, given time . . .

"All right," Barry said. "I'll explain everything. Then I'll give you some alone time. Well . . ." He nudged the unconscious prince with his heel. "As much alone time as you can have with this monster hanging around."

"It's no worry," Barbara said, a dangerous gleam in her eye. "I've heard all about what he's done, so if he gets lippy, I'll sort him out."

Barry nodded. "Good. I'll get right into it, then. This story all starts with the arrival of Fischer . . ."

* * *

"Are you sure, Barry?" Helen asked.

He looked down at his wife, nodding. He'd passed by their shed on the way home from Leroy and Barbara's, collecting a cup of a certain liquid.

"I'm sure. It's too risky to not give it to you, especially after yesterday . . ."

He cut himself off, clenching his jaw as rage threatened to overcome him. He'd heard all about the prince's actions, including his order to collar Helen. Barry's face twisted, unable to contain the emotion.

"If he wasn't of use to us . . ." The sentence was ground out between clenched teeth, and he took a deep breath, willing himself to calm.

Helen wrapped herself around his waist, and though it didn't entirely clear the storm, some clouds dissipated with her embrace.

"It's okay, my love. I'm safe." She pulled back, looking up into his eyes. "If you think it's the best course, I'll trust you."

As their eyes met, Barry thanked the gods for the umpteenth time that they'd seen fit to send this woman his way.

He held out the cup of sugarcane juice, and she accepted it. She took a tentative sip after lifting it to her mouth.

"Oh." She giggled. "It's *delicious!*"

She downed the rest of the cup.

As Maria cast the line out again, I fetched the fish-laden pot.

"I'll show you how to process the body—er, it can be a bit much, actually. Do you *want* to see?"

She nodded seriously. "I do. I won't turn my back to the reality of it."

I smiled up at her.

Why is everything she says so . . . perfect?

"Is there something on my face?" she asked, smirking.

"Oh, uh . . . sorry. I was lost in thought."

I walked down to the shore and took the fish from the pot.

"All the bits we discard are beneath the skin here." I pointed at the belly, running my finger along where I would cut. "When a fish is big enough, it makes sense to remove the fillets from the frame. For a fish this size, though, I'd say we should just cook it whole after scaling and gutting."

She nodded, eyes watching the fish intently as her hands gripped the rod.

I quickly cut and processed the fish, throwing the inedible parts out into the shallows for the pond's denizens to feast on.

"The scales are easy to remove if you rub from tail to head with something blunt."

I ran the back of my knife against the fish, sending translucent scales flying. Maria's brows were furrowed, focused as she was on the lesson.

Given I was looking at her, I saw the exact moment the fishing rod was almost pulled from her firm grip by a *massive* strike.

"W-Woah!"

CHAPTER SEVENTY-FIVE

LADY OF THE LAKE

"It's huge!" Maria yelled, her eyes wide as saucers.

I jumped to my feet and lobbed the half-scaled fish into the pot. "It is! You've got this."

The rod was bent in half, constantly lurching further down as the fish's tail swept back and forth through the water. A smile slowly grew across my face as I recognized the movement.

This is the same species—if not the exact same fish—that busted off the rod I made when arriving on Kallis.

Maria let some line out, doing her best to not let the behemoth of a fish snap the line.

"I-I think you should take it!"

"It's okay," I said. "You've got thi—"

"No," she interrupted. "I *want* you to take it! Here!" She thrust the rod into my hands, and I had no option but to catch it.

"Why?" I asked, reeling the line in to take up slack.

"I've already caught plenty." She grinned at me. "It's your turn for some fun."

I grinned back at her before returning my attention to the water and the battle taking place beneath it.

The fish took another run, dashing from my left to my right. With each massive kick of its tail, the rod dipped down; each pull sent adrenaline shooting through me. My heart raced, my breathing was fast, and despite the cold, my body felt like it was burning.

"I love this!" I laughed uproariously, unable to contain what I was feeling. "Fishing is the best!"

Maria giggled at me, but I kept my eyes forward, focused on the fight. It swam toward me, seeming to come almost to the bank, but with the fading day's light, I saw no flashes of silver, despite how close it came. The line went rigid, and I tugged, but nothing happened. I had a moment of doubt, thinking the fish had managed to get snagged somehow—then, it took off.

With massive, sweeping kicks of its body, it swam at top speed toward the far bank. It caught me off guard, and I couldn't wind the line out fast enough, so I stepped toward the water's edge, reducing the strain on the line with my movement.

It repeated this action a few more times, seeming to rest on the floor of the pond before tearing off in another direction. I got better at judging the movements, and each time I was a little less caught off guard.

The fish's odd behavior reminded me of the shovelnose ray I'd caught from the beach. The ray had sucked itself to the ocean floor, making it impossible to budge, just as the hooked fish seemed to be doing now.

It began to tire, and bit by bit, I reeled it closer to the shore. The fish was so large that I had to pull the rod up slowly, then reel swiftly to take up the line as I dipped the rod back down, similar to videos I'd seen of deep-sea fishing. I continued this method, pulling the fish to me one reel at a time.

The line entered the water right before me, and I leaned closer, trying to catch a glimpse. I saw a swirl, and I squinted, leaning further in. All I saw was a *monstrous* tail resembling that of an eel.

"What is *that?*" Maria yelled.

The fish must have heard Maria, because it took off again. The water roiled in its wake, displaced by its massive body. I slowly turned to look at her, my eyes wide and mouth open.

She had the same expression, and we blinked rapidly at each other.

"I have no idea . . ." I said, returning my attention to the water.

I pumped the rod again, reeling as I dipped the tip back toward the water. This continued for a few more minutes, the fish taking another run each time it got to the shore. Finally, it was too exhausted to swim away.

I passed Maria the rod. "Keep the line tight until I get it out of the water!"

I strode into the shallows, put a leg on either side of the monster, then dipped my arms under its body. I lifted, pulling it to my chest and holding it tight. If it weren't for my enhanced body, I'd have had no chance of lifting the creature without slipping a disc.

Maria flicked the reel open, and the line went slack.

"What in Poseidon's salted sack is *that?*"

"His *what?*" I asked, laughing.

"That . . ." She pointed at the fish in my arms. "What on Kallis is that thing!"

I looked down at the fish as I strode from the water, seeing a mouth that, if I were to try, could fit my entire head within. It had fleshy whiskers growing from around its lips, each as long as the mouth was wide. My eyes were drawn into it the next moment.

Ancient Freshwater Catfish

Rare

For those that know how to prepare the flesh of the freshwater catfish, it is prized as the best-eating of all freshwater fish. The females of this species grow to monstrous sizes and can single-handedly provide the spawn to sustain entire ecosystems.

The fish squirmed, its muscular body doing the best it could to get away. It was so long that even with its head at my chest, the base of its tail slapped my ankles. I'd already seen everything I had to.

I walked back to the water, quickly putting it back beneath the surface. I moved it back and forth, forcing water—and therefore, oxygen—through its gills.

"You don't mind if I release it, do you?" I asked Maria, not looking up.

"Of course not. What makes you want to release it, though?"

"This thing is . . . old. It's a breeder, which means taking its life would lead to the loss of countless fish."

"How do you know it's a female?"

"Er—from its size."

It wasn't a lie—I knew it was a female from its size, but only because of the System's description.

Maria walked down to the water, running her hand along its back as I continued moving oxygen through its gills.

"Wow. *Wow!* It's so big and slippery!"

"She's a beaut, isn't she? I wonder how old she is?"

Maria touched the fish's head, withdrawing her hand as it kicked.

"How many years have you been living here, lady of the lake?"

She turned to me, her head cocked. "What does moving it like that in the water do?"

"Big fish can get exhausted when you catch them. After the fight this old gal gave us, I was worried that she'd suffocate if I just let her go. Moving her like this forces water through her gills, which lets her breathe."

Maria put her hand against the catfish's head again, rubbing it slowly.

"When will you know she's ready to go?"

I smiled up at her. "When she swims away."

As if in response to my words, the catfish kicked its tail, ponderously gliding away from the shore. I watched it disappear back into the depths of the pond with an immeasurably deep sense of gratitude.

"Thanks, lady of the lake," I said, copying the title Maria gave.

"Thank you!" Maria called, her hands cupped to her mouth.

I'm so glad I didn't catch her when I first arrived in this world, I thought. *Given my lack of food, I would've eaten her, robbing this land of a majestic creature.*

"Wow," Maria said, sitting down. "I don't even know what to say. That was . . ."

"Unbelievable."

She nodded. "Yeah . . . that . . ."

I walked over to the pot, removed the half-scaled fish, and resumed my cleaning.

"I didn't know fish got that big," Maria said.

"I've caught a similar-sized fish from the beach before, but that was a first for such a small lake."

"What?"

I glanced back at Maria, whose eyebrows were raised almost off her face.

"What do you mean, '*what*'?"

"You've caught something that big from the beach? The beach where you live?"

"Uh, yeah. Why?"

Her eyes got a dangerous gleam, and they bore down on me. "Tell me."

"About the fish, or how I caught it?"

"Everything. Tell me *everything.*"

Trent, the crown prince of Gormona, awoke from a terrible dream. He'd been running for his life, trying to escape a monster. Each time, he'd almost escape, but just at the last minute, when he was thrashing free of the shackles confining him, more would wrap around him, cinching tight.

As he stirred further into the waking world, he yawned and tried to roll over. His sheets were too tight, and he scrunched his eyes closed, grunting as he put his entire weight into it.

Damned servants, putting too many sheets on—

The lavish coverings dug into his skin with his effort, and he opened his eyes in terror.

"Ah, you're finally awake," a voice said.

"Who . . . who's there?"

Trent squinted in the dim light, comprehension still evading him. A man stepped closer, stepping into the light of a candle. Recognition hit, and with it came Trent's memories. The blood drained from his face as a spike of terror shot through his core. Leroy knelt down in front of him, his jaw set in a firm line.

"It's time we had a little conversation, Trent."

"Is it hot enough?" Maria asked.

I smiled at her. "I'll show you how to test it!"

Maria had brought some beef tallow with her, so I'd put a decent amount into the pan currently heating over the campfire. Well, I'd instructed Maria to do it, anyway.

As misguided as I thought Roger's requests were, I wouldn't go back on my word. I would not be cooking any fish on this brief camping trip, and though adding fat to a pan might not technically count, I wasn't going to push it.

"You can check the temperature of the fat by putting some breadcrumbs in."

Maria took a pinch of the leftover crumbs, dropping them into the tallow. It hissed and bubbled immediately, and I nodded at her.

"It's ready. You can chuck the fish in."

Maria picked up the crumbed fish carefully, not wanting to disturb the layer of pan-dried and crumbled bun that covered it.

"Watch your fingers," I said, urgency in my voice. "Don't drop the fish in—lower it down while holding the tail."

She did so with deft fingers, dropping the tail at the last possible second.

I raised an eyebrow at her. "You're sure you haven't shallow fried a fish before? You've kind of already mastered it."

She rolled her eyes at me, a smirk on her lips. "Don't patronize me, Fischer."

"Woah," I said, holding up both hands. "I was being serious!"

She pouted, squinting at me as if to decipher my intent.

"As I said before, I've never heard of shallow frying." She pointed at the pan. "I still contend that this is *entirely* too much fat to cook in."

"Yeah, it's a bit excessive, but beef tallow is good fat, and wait until you taste the fried fish—you won't regret it."

"I'll have to take your word for it."

"You won't need to when it's finished. Flip it over when the crumbs are golden and crispy."

I leaned over, looking down into the pot of berry jam I'd removed from the fire. I'd not long removed it, and steam rose from the surface. I dipped my pinky in and tasted it. My face scrunched involuntarily as its flavor assaulted me.

"Did you bring any sugar?"

Maria leveled a flat glare at me.

"I don't care what you say—I'm *not* adding sugar to the fish, and neither are you."

"Not for the fish," I said, laughing. "For the jam."

"Are you sure you need it? The berries were already super sweet . . ."

"Just a pinch or two. Some were unripe, and it's a tad bitter. I'll set some aside to try with the fish, but for the jam we use on our pastries tomorrow morning, I reckon a little sugar will go a long way."

With another glare, presumably warning me not to add sugar to the fish, she walked to the shelter and removed a small pouch before returning and holding it out.

"Thank you." I said, accepting it.

Peering inside the pouch, I saw a handful of granular sugar inside.

I grabbed a cup and poured some of the jam, setting it aside to try with the fish. I carefully added some of the sugar to the remaining mixture and began stirring.

"Is this crispy enough?" Maria asked, grabbing my attention.

I stood and leaned over the pan as she lifted the fish. The underside was golden brown, and the fish's flesh had a slight curve.

"Looks perfect to me. Flip it over."

The tallow hissed and bubbled when the uncooked side hit it, and the scent of the fish rose from the pan.

"Mmm," Maria said. "That smells amazing."

"If you think it smells good, wait until you taste it."

I stirred the jam absentmindedly as the fish finished cooking, unable to focus on anything else. Maria watched it intently; I found her focus entrancing. She had eyes for nothing else, occasionally sweeping a loose strand of hair behind her ear.

She cocked her head to the side to see under the fish as she lifted it, and like clockwork, the hair fell back down, only to be swept back behind her ear.

Sensing my gaze, her eyes darted to me. "What?"

"Er—nothing. I have to get some condiments for the fish. One second."

I strode to the tent, my face going hot. I rummaged around in my bag, found the last ingredients, then returned to the fire.

"I think it's ready," Maria said. "What do you think?"

She lifted the fish, and the bottom was the same golden brown, cooked to perfection.

"Looks like it to me! Put it on the board and we'll check the thickest part."

She removed it from the tallow and placed it down. "What are we checking for, exactly?"

I used a knife and fork to split the fillet in the center; the flesh was flaky and white.

"See how the flesh has turned white? Fish can make you really sick if it's not cooked properly."

Maria nodded. "Same with all meat. The texture is like nothing I've ever seen before, though . . ."

"Yep—fish's flesh is unique, both in texture and flavor."

I poured some salt from my pouch onto the board, then put the other ingredient down beside it, causing Maria to hiss a sharp intake of breath.

"Is . . . is that what I think it is?"

I smiled over at her. "It is. Nothing goes better with fish than lemon."

"But . . . are you sure you want to use it? Isn't it really expensive?"

"Price is relative, and some things are worth more than coins."

To cut off any more debate, I grasped a knife and sliced two wedges from the citrus. I took a large pinch of salt, sprinkled it over the fish, then squeezed one of the lemon slices over it.

"After you." I pointed at the fork in front of Maria. "It'll be hot."

As she pressed the metal prongs into the crumbed fish, it made a sharp *crack* before sliding into the soft flesh below. She lifted the portion, blew on it a few times, then popped it into her mouth. She bit down, and her eyes went wide.

CHAPTER SEVENTY-SIX

THERAPEUTIC

Gary, the lone disciple of the Cult of the Leviathan's Tropica branch, looked out over the ocean. The storm had passed, and he stood atop the breakwall, staring out at the roiling ocean. The sea was chaotic following the tempest, and white waves continually rolled in, crashing against the wall beneath him.

He had long found solace in the sea and its chaotic movement, and the view from behind the cult's headquarters made the spot he occupied on the wall his favored perch.

"Gary!" came a muffled yell from the building behind him.

With his momentary peace shattered, he let out a long-suffering sigh.

"Back to work, I suppose . . ."

He turned and strode toward the door and reached out, grasping the handle. Pausing, he took a deep breath, releasing it slowly as he swung open the door.

"Gary! Where—oh! There you are! Good!"

"Yes, Sebastian?"

Sebastian turned from staring at his beloved baby lobsters and raised an eyebrow. "What did you call me?"

"Sorry, master. What is it?"

Sebastian nodded. "Better. The time has come for Fischer's demise. His downfall is nigh."

Gary tried not to let his disappointment show. "Yes, master. What would you like me to do?"

"Come with me to the roof. I'll show you."

He followed Sebastian up the stairs, a cold wind blowing into the building as his master threw open the door to the roof. As he stepped outside, Gary's eyebrows furrowed.

A mess of rocks had been scattered around the roof, and as he looked closer, they appeared to be arranged in some sort of pattern.

"Over here," Sebastian said, walking to the center.

Gary followed, eyeing the swirling patterns as he carefully stepped over them—he knew there would be hell to pay if he disturbed the arrangement.

Sebastian stopped, pointing at one of two circles amid the haphazard creation.

"Sit here, disciple."

Gary nodded, sitting cross-legged.

Sebastian sat in the other circle then removed something from his robe. It was the artifact he'd been sent from the capital, the same one that everyone was convinced wouldn't work—including Gary.

As before, it stood inert, looking more like a lump of rock covered in scratched runes than an ancient relic of the distant past.

At least it won't lead to any harm . . . Gary thought. *Tremendous waste of time, though.*

"Now, repeat after me, Gary. In Hades's name, I call to thee . . ."

"Before we start, master—how long will this take?"

Sebastian scowled, the lines of his face turning sharp.

"As long as I damn well say, Gary! Repeat the words!"

He sighed, no longer caring to hide his discontent.

"In Hades's name, I call to thee . . ."

Maria put the fish into her mouth and bit down. The moment the flavor hit her tongue, saliva flooded her mouth. Her eyes went wide as she slowly chewed the morsel. The flesh seemed to melt, disintegrating all by itself. A section of fried crumbs crackled between her teeth, and she couldn't help but release a soft noise of delight.

She closed her eyes as her mouth watered, the fish's taste overwhelming all other senses.

Something crunched between two molars, and by the flavor that covered her tongue afterward, she guessed it had to be a lump of salt. The salt melded with the rest of the tastes assaulting her, somehow taking the fish to another level. Covering it all was an almost sour taste. It cut through the fat she'd fried the fish in, making the entire mouthful of food seem . . . lighter.

She pictured herself lifted above the treetops, soaring through the cool night air, warmed from within by the unbelievable flavors suffusing her awareness.

Fischer spoke, returning her to the ground. "I take it that means you like it?"

She swallowed, her mouth salivating for more the moment it was empty. "Fischer . . . is this a dream?"

He laughed, the sound filled with delight. "While fish is pretty dreamy, I don't think you're dreaming right now, no."

"That sour flavor . . . is that the lemon?"

"It is." He smiled at her. "What did you think?"

"You were right—some things are better than coins."

He laughed again, louder this time. With a deft stab, he grabbed a section of fish and brought it to his mouth. He closed his eyes and leaned back, a soft *mmph* escaping as he chewed.

"Oh my god, Maria. This is the best food I think I've ever eaten."

Normally, she'd have rolled her eyes and called him a flatterer. This time, however, she agreed. This was the best food she had ever eaten. She took another forkful, placing the delicate fish in her mouth. Another soft noise left her throat, louder this time, not caring how it made her look. The salt, and what she now knew was lemon, melded with the fish, playing a concordant melody across her taste buds.

"Oh!" Fischer said. "I almost forgot!"

He grabbed a cup and shook it, causing a dollop of the dark-purple jam to drop onto the board.

"It should be cool enough judging by the consistency—try dipping some fish into it."

They did so, both placing the jam-dipped flesh into their mouths simultaneously. The berries hit her tongue first; the strong and somewhat bitter taste was jarring. Then, the rest of the flavors joined the fray.

"Mmmm," they both said, lost for words before the war of sensations.

The berries added a complex flavor that intertwined with the others, creating a unique blend.

Calling it "better" than the fish without it wouldn't be correct; it was a different version, one that had a more pleasant, relaxed feeling to it. She swallowed, letting out a contented sigh.

As the food hit her stomach, she felt a burst of energy. It was in complete contrast with the refreshing undertones of the jam, and she cocked her head to the side, her brow knitted. The power surged from her core, crawling down each limb.

"Woah . . ."

"Good, right?" Fischer asked, his eyes still closed. As fast as the energy hit, it dissipated, melding inward. She shook her head, her hair bouncing against her face.

"That was something else . . ."

"Try it again without the jam," Fischer suggested, and she did, once more losing herself to the savory blend. Fischer did so too, a pleased smile spreading over his features.

"I don't know which one is better."

Maria nodded. "I feel the same. Neither is better, but they're both so . . . different."

"They really are, aren't they?"

Fischer took one last bit of flesh from the fish, then flipped it over, exposing the other, untouched side.

With the fish eaten, they sat by the fire, and a warm feeling radiated from Maria's core, easily keeping the night's chill at bay.

"That was unbelievable, Fischer."

He glanced at her from the fire, where he was toasting a croissant.

"I can't tell you how happy it makes me that you enjoyed it. You're a natural at fish—both catching them *and* cooking them."

She leaned forward, resting her head on her hands. "I was just following your instructions."

"Even so. Some people just got it, ya know? You're one of those people."

She rolled her eyes at him, and he laughed.

"Yeah, yeah, I know—you think I'm flattering you." He stood, removing the croissant from the flames. "I mean it, though. Do you cook much at home?"

Maria nodded. "I do, especially while Mom was unwell. She's always been best in the kitchen, but I'd say I'm a close second."

Fischer bent down and cut the croissant in half, spread some of the sweetened jam over each portion, then held one out to her. "Here. Let me know if it needs more or less sugar next time."

Maria sniffed it; the scents of buttery pastry mixed with the tart jam was irresistible, so she took a bite. The flavors mixed as she chewed, and when she swallowed, the same feeling of energy resonated within, then spread through her body.

"Do you feel that?"

"Feel what?" Fischer asked around a mouthful.

"That . . . *energy.* Each time I eat some of the jam, it's like I've had a mini coffee."

His eyebrows creased as she slowly chewed and swallowed. "I mean, it's delicious, but I wouldn't say I've had a mini coffee . . ."

He shrugged. "It's only natural for your body to feel enlightened after eating some of my world-class jam." He winked. "I'm not surprised in the least."

She laughed, covering her mouth. "At least it's not only me you're flattering."

"I'm nothing if not consistent. And humble."

She snorted. "Oh, yeah. I've never met someone more humble."

He beamed a smile at her, and it made her heart sing. They ate the rest of their dessert in silence, enjoying the warmth and crackling sounds coming from the campfire.

"There's just something about camping and watching a fire." Fischer said.

She felt herself nodding. "It's my first time camping, but I couldn't agree more. I almost don't want to go back to town . . ."

"Yeah, I've heard many people have a comedown when returning home from a trip."

"You've heard?" Maria cocked her head. "You don't get that?"

He gave her a sheepish smile. "I've never actually been camping before."

"Oh . . . I'd assumed you had."

"Yeah, I mean I've heard a lot about it, but I didn't really have the time in my previous life."

He picked up a small twig, touching its rough surface absentmindedly. Maria leaned back and looked at the trees above. Their swaying leaves were dimly lit by the fire below, lending them an orange tinge.

Whether it was the energy from the jam, or the serene surroundings, she didn't know, but the courage to ask about his previous life came to her.

"Would you tell me more about your life before coming to Tropica, Fischer?"

A quiet moment stretched, interrupted only by the sound of a twig snapping. Maria darted her eyes toward him; he stared down at the two halves of the twig, his eyes distant.

"Sorry," she said in a rush. "You don't have to . . ."

I stared down at nothing, lost in memory. My hands moved over the stick as a barrage of thoughts sped through my mind, consuming my attention. Maria said something, and I shook my head, dispelling my introspection.

As much as I thought I'd improved my ability to not get drawn in by memories that made negative emotions flourish, it was so easy to fall into old habits. I'd have to keep working on it.

I looked up at Maria. "Sorry, I didn't catch that."

Her lips made a line and she gave me a wincing smile.

"I said I'm sorry, and that you don't have to tell me—if it's too painful, I mean . . ."

My therapist's words bubbled up to greet me.

"*I want you to try and open up to someone this week, Fischer. Talking to me is good, but the ability to be vulnerable around those you care about is an important skill to develop.*"

Before I had the chance to do so, to even find someone I felt comfortable opening up to, truck-kun had sent me on a cosmic adventure, and I'd kept my cards close to my chest since arriving in this new, strange world.

"I shouldn't have brought it up, Fischer. Sorry."

I looked up at Maria, forcing a smile to my face.

"No. It's okay. Maybe talking about it would be therapeutic for me."

She didn't respond, giving me time to formulate my thoughts.

Where do I even begin?

I took a deep breath as my hands, seemingly of their own accord, snapped a twig in half.

At the beginning, I suppose.

I opened my mouth, and the words came trickling out.

CHAPTER SEVENTY-SEVEN

FURY

The rock crab, having had his fill of the feast, scuttled along the ocean floor, his movement lethargic. Once he'd started eating, he hadn't been able to stop. There was something about the flesh that, with each bite, only increased his hunger, and that was the meat's *least* remarkable aspect. He'd somehow consumed all of it in a single sitting, despite the body being many times bigger than his own.

Even now, retreating to his favorite hiding spot for a good rest, he didn't feel full. He *did* feel bloated, but it wasn't with food. Each bite had brought with it a trickle of power that seemed to swirl through his body, circulating around each limb before eventually reaching his core. Then, it would get sucked into . . . *something.* That *something* was what felt distended—pushed to its very limits.

He'd been vaguely aware of the void within his body over the last few days but had never physically felt it as he did now. When sitting beneath the cool waters of the pond the sea snipper occupied, and trying to avoid the attention of his spiked leader, he'd experienced glimpses of the same sensation—a drop of essence, swimming through his body before settling deep within.

If not for the time spent in the pond, and his burgeoning awareness, he wondered if he'd have been able to consume all of what he just had.

With a shrug—a gesture he'd copied from his beloved leader—he continued his trek toward the crack in the earth. Why or how were irrelevant; the only things of consequence were that he *had* eaten the food, and what he would do with this overflowing power.

Before he realized it, he'd arrived at the crevice, and a warm stream of water flowed out toward him. It was a stark contrast to the cool water of the bay; the heat called to him, and he slipped inside.

His body held low, he crawled deep into the crack. He followed the winding path, passing many of the holes and corners he'd previously used to rest while letting streams of hot water pass by his trusty carapace.

The heat beckoned him more than it ever had before, and he listened, following his instincts to crawl deeper and deeper. With each stretch of winding tunnel he traversed, the water grew hotter, the strength of the torrent increased. Though his passage slowed, it never stopped, and he crawled ever down. He was lost in a trance, his eyes unseeing, when a change in the surroundings arrested his attention.

An orange glow came from up ahead, immersing the tunnel in a soft light.

Gripped by curiosity, he took over the subconscious movement of his legs and scuttled forward, each step filled with intention. He rounded the corner, and he froze on the spot.

A large cavern greeted him, filled with torrents of bubbles that swept up and into holes in the ceiling. His tunnel had come out halfway up the cavern's wall, so he was spared any of the air.

On the floor of the space, a carpet of black, orange, and red roiled. Sheets of black rock rose and fell back down, exposing the red and orange liquid beneath.

No, not liquid . . . rock.

He knew not how, but he could tell—it was super-heated rock. When the colored sections touched the water, they cooled, forming black sheets that hardened, then fell back and were consumed by the molten rock below.

He spared the scene another glance, then he sat, wiggling his body to find a hold amid the black silt on the tunnel's floor. He closed his eyes, bathing in the warmth. Within seconds, his awareness faded.

The moonlight filtering down from above was a calming presence. A cool breeze suffused the entire area, and I focused on it as I cleared my throat.

"The situation that predicates everything else is—*was*—my father."

Maria didn't respond for a long moment.

"He's passed?"

I nodded softly. "He has. A blood illness."

"I'm sorry, Fischer."

I smiled at her, but it felt hollow.

"Thank you. Our relationship was complicated, which only makes my feelings toward him more confusing."

She chewed her lip, thinking before responding. "Why does he predicate everything?"

"My father was a . . . singularly minded individual. His businesses—and his empire—were more important than everything else. Family included."

"Your mother?"

"Left when I was still a baby—never knew her." I gave a half smile. "Pushed away by my father, no doubt."

"Fischer . . . I'm so sorry."

I'd been holding the tears at arm's length, hidden behind a thin veil of bravado. With Maria's words, a crack formed in the dam's wall.

I looked up at the moon as a single drop rolled down my cheek.

"Oh, Fischer . . ."

Faster than I knew she could move, she was beside me, a hand resting on my back. My lip quivered, and I took a deep breath, forcing it out through pursed lips.

"Sorry." I let out a short laugh, shaking my head. "This is embarrassing."

She rubbed my back, her hand moving in a steady circle. "There's nothing to be ashamed of. Your response is completely warranted."

"Still." I sniffed, wiping my eye. "I bring you out here for some time away, then I throw a pity party . . ."

She moved her hand side to side between my shoulder blades, the warmth and touch a welcome comfort.

"I asked about it, and you never have to be sorry for being genuine with me. I'd rather comfort someone than deal with a false mask of indifference."

I nodded, still looking up to avert my eyes, and she pulled me into a side hug.

"I'm here if you want to talk about it more, or we can drop it for tonight. Totally up to you."

I took another deep breath, my roiling emotions calming somewhat as I exhaled it slowly. Seeing as though I'd already come this far, I continued.

"My entire life, my father molded me to take over his empire when he passed. It was . . . vast. His companies and holdings made him the richest man on the continent by far."

Not a lie, I thought. *If a bit of an under exaggeration . . .*

Maria said nothing. She'd removed herself from the hug and resumed rubbing my back. She waited for me to go on when ready.

I snapped another twig in half.

"Whether or not it was his version of showing love, it doesn't make it any easier. I wanted for nothing, except attention." I laughed at myself. "I probably sound like a spoiled brat—"

"Not at all," she said, immediately cutting me off. "I'd rather live the life I have with parents that loved me rather than a life of riches without—"

Her hand went stiff on my back.

"S-sorry. I didn't mean that your parents didn't love you. I—"

I smiled at her. "It's okay. I know what you meant."

She let out an awkward laugh. "I'm not doing a great job of comforting you. Sorry."

We lapsed into silence again as I stared into the campfire, taking solace in its dancing flames.

"If your dad was busy running the companies, who raised you?"

"A never-ending roster of staff, nannies, and tutors. They never stayed long—my father saw to it that I didn't grow too comfortable."

"That's horrible . . ."

"Yeah, it wasn't great. I held a lot of anger and resentment for my father as a result. I didn't even realize how messed up it was until I was much older. It was all I knew. From a young age, I was taught all I needed to know to be an effective leader. I didn't even go to a regular school with other children. I just had tutors come to me, molding me into the perfect corporate machine."

"So, what happened when your father passed and you took over?"

I shook my head.

"I proved how much of a waste of time it all was. For all of Dad's record profits, the companies were, in my mind, horrible for both employees and staff. Everything was run to extract as much from everyone involved as possible, while funneling all the profits to the top. Honestly, it was the epitome of capitalism, and as far as 'business' is concerned, all of my father's endeavors were immensely successful."

Maria said nothing, simply rubbing my back as she had before.

I sighed and continued. "When I took over, I sought to make some changes. They weren't even that substantial, just minor adjustments to improve the lives of employees and customers. I axed some subscription services that should have been included and weren't even that profit—"

Realizing Maria likely had no idea what a subscription model was, I cut myself off, shaking my head.

"It doesn't matter. The parent company still would have been the most profitable on that continent with the changes, but even that small reduction was too much for the stakeholders, so I was given the choice to leave or be fired."

"From your company?"

"Honestly, it should have been a blessing. Leading a company would never have made me happy. I stuck with it because I'd sunk so much time into it, and despite my anger and resentment toward my father, I still wanted his approval. Even after his passing."

The memory of our final conversation played in my mind, as it had so many times before.

"Does Mom know you're dying, Dad? Do you really not have any way to contact her?"

He scoffed. *"She was weak. I have no desire to speak to—"*

He cut off, a wet cough racking his body. When it subsided, he continued.

"I never regretted your mother leaving, Fischer. I did what I had to do, and she did what she had to do. Not everyone can handle a man's greatness."

He shook his head.

"This is all we are good for, son. Don't be sad that you can't accomplish anything else—there is nothing greater. You're my son, after all—this is what you were born to do."

From his prone position, lying in the best private hospital bed money could buy, he still managed to seem like he looked down on me.

"I've left you orders in your new office. Not that you need them, but it never hurts to over-prepare—you know that."

His powerful presence was gone, replaced by a skeletal frame. Despite his "perfect" diet, extensive exercise regime, and all the money he'd thrown at stem cell research and experimental procedures, the end of his life was mere hours away.

The white walls of his suite felt suffocating in their brilliance, the antithesis of the man before me.

"Why do you have that look in your eye, boy? It's unbecoming of a wolf."

I set my jaw, tried to firm my emotions, but it only made him more scornful. He shook his head, a look of disappointment etched on his features. Then, he'd said the last four words he would ever speak to me.

Those words made my soul burn with fury then, just as they did now, and I blinked as I returned to the present. I looked over at Maria.

"Do you know what the last thing he ever said to me was?"

My lip twitched, and I clenched and unclenched my jaw before speaking them.

"'Just don't disappoint me.' Not 'I love you.' Not 'I'm proud of you.' Not 'Be happy.' 'Just don't disappoint me.' And despite all that, even after he was gone, I just wanted to make him proud."

With the stopper removed on my anger and self-loathing, they poured out, flooding my body.

I clenched my jaw, and unbidden, my lip curled into a half snarl.

Maria's hand still rubbed my back, but all the comfort it lent was gone.

I got to my feet.

"Fischer?"

I barely heard Maria; my legs moved, the growing outrage within demanding an outlet.

"It's okay, Fischer . . ."

I shook my head, lost in remembrance.

This is all we are good for, son.

I strode around the campfire, eyes unseeing, my body growing hot.

I don't regret your mother leaving. I did what I had to do, and she did what she had to do. Not everyone can handle a man's greatness.

My face convulsed, and a great well of darkness opened up in my core.

Why do you have that look in your eye, boy?

All the thoughts, all my emotions, every ounce of indignation swirled and built, climbing atop each other.

Just don't disappoint me.

I couldn't breathe. The condensing pit of darkness was cloying, choking.

Just don't disappoint me . . .

"Fischer . . . you're scaring me . . ."

Just don't disappoint me!

Stumbling forward, I wrapped my arms around my core, fingers digging into my sides. My entire body tensed, trembled. All at once, I unraveled, and I sprang to my feet as the void within threatened to overflow. A scream tore from my throat, the raw bellow of a beast. All the pain, the anger, the loathing; everything exploded from the pit within, flying through my body, up my arm, and then out as I uppercut the air. A glistening line of thread extended from my hand, piercing through a trunk, branches, and leaves before going straight up into the sky. Then, the thread expanded; if not for my improved body, I wouldn't have seen it. The thin line, in the blink of an eye, became wide as a car, perfectly cylindrical in its destruction. It resonated a blinding light, white as the walls of my father's hospital suite.

Fwoom!

The forest tree the blast had hit was completely gone, providing a spherical window to the night sky. I blinked, not believing my eyes.

Nothing remained of the trees, branches, and leaves affected; anything touched by the light had been removed from existence—nary a splinter remained.

I bent and touched the trunk before me, only half a meter remaining where once had been a proud tree. The branches—those that had been outside of the blast—fell to the forest floor around me.

A scrape sounded behind me, followed by a muffled thump. I whirled, seeing Maria on the ground, having tripped in her attempt to back away. Her eyes were wide, her face white, and she crawled back a step, getting further away from me.

CHAPTER SEVENTY-EIGHT

SPECIAL

Maria moved her arm backward, getting further from me; a fist gripped my heart and squeezed.

My father's words sprouted in my mind, tormenting me.

This is all we are good for, son.

Releasing the blast, whatever it was, had hollowed me out, emptied every ounce of anger and frustration. Into the yawning void, despair rushed.

"I'm sorry," I uttered, a hoarse whisper. I fell to my knees, my head down, unable to meet that horror-filled gaze. My core felt scoured raw, and I wrapped my arms around my stomach.

"Please . . . don't leave. I get you might not want to see me again, but I promised I'd get you home safe. It might be dangerous if you run in the dark—"

Maria's tiny frame crashed into me, her arms encircling me. At first, I felt nothing.

"It's okay, Fischer," she whispered. She held one hand against the back of my head, petting my hair.

Still, I felt nothing.

She squeezed me, and despite my enhanced body, her grip was firm, unrelenting. A spark of emotion stirred, like metal hitting flint.

"You're okay, Fischer," she said, rubbing my head.

The spark took hold, and an ember flared.

"Dad was right—maybe I'm worthless."

I breathed in shakily, my lip trembling, and all at once, the cinder bloomed into a bonfire.

Grief gripped me, and my body heaved with sobs. I lacked the strength to hold the tears at bay, so they flowed forth, finding the cracks in the dam's wall and winding through them, blowing the hole wide open.

"You're not worthless," Maria whispered. "Only a fool would think so."

My hands fell from around my waist, and Maria seized the opening, wrapping her arms around my abdomen and pulling herself into my chest.

I encircled her small body with my arms and clung for dear life, like a shipwrecked sailor clinging to flotsam. We didn't speak for what could have been minutes or hours.

Beside the pond, beneath the stars peeking through the destroyed canopy, we simply existed, holding each other close enough to become one.

My heaving breaths slowed with time, both the tears and Maria blunting the edge of the knife twisting within. I breathed deep, held it, then exhaled all at once, a calm blanketing me.

Maria, sensing my despair had shifted, hugged me tighter, then rubbed my back with both hands. She said nothing—neither did I, feeling the vague numbness that follows tears. It was a welcome sensation following my breakdown, like a weighted blanket on the soul.

Maria pulled back, looking up at me. I turned my head down, conscious of my red, raw eyes, but she caught my chin in one hand. She hadn't the strength to stop me if I tried, but I let her guide my face. I squeezed my eyes shut, then, tentatively, opened them, seeing the world through blurred vision.

Maria stared up at me, her own eyes red and watering. She blinked, and a tear rolled down each cheek, reflecting the campfire's light. She slammed into my chest again, squeezing like a vice. I held her back, and as she did for me, rubbed her back, attempting to give comfort.

"I'm—"

My voice was like two stones grinding together, so I cleared my throat.

"I'm sorry, Maria."

She shook her head. "You have nothing to be sorry for. Stop apologizing."

I nodded, not trusting my voice.

She removed her arms from around me and shifted to the side, her hands around her knees as she leaned up against me. I rested my head on hers, easily encompassing her tiny form with my body.

"So . . ." she said. "You're a cultivator, huh?"

I blew air from my nose.

"Yeah . . . I guess I am."

"How come you're so terrible at cultivating crops, then?"

I paused, my addled mind not hearing the joke at first. Then, I barked a laugh. It dragged on, transforming into a choking wheeze as I let go of Maria, leaning back to brace myself. Her musical laugh joined in, and it, too, escalated, a couple of snorts showing up for the performance.

She wiped her eyes, tried to start talking, but another giggle took her. With one hand on her stomach and the other wiping away tears, she let out a content sigh.

"I needed that."

I smiled at her, my vision clouded by tears of laughter.

"So did I."

"How long have you been . . . you know . . ."

"A cultivator?"

She winced at the word, but nodded, looking up at me.

"Yeah."

"It happened after I met you."

"Does anyone know?"

"Only Barry—maybe his wife, Helen. I don't imagine they keep any secrets."

Maria's eyebrows shot up. "Barry knows? I guess it makes sense he'd keep your secret after what happened to Leroy."

"Leroy? Is that his brother-in-law? The one that got whisked off to the capital?"

She gave me a sad smile. "Yeah—that's the one. I can't believe you've been dealing with that the entire time you've been here."

"Well, 'dealing with it' is a generous description. I've mostly been putting my head in the sand and pretending it doesn't exist."

"Still, even ignoring it, it must have been a weight."

She shook her head, letting out a light laugh. "You came here for a relaxing life, and you almost immediately unlocked the System. This world is too cruel."

"Oh, it's not cruel at all. I wouldn't trade anything to have not become a cultivator, or whatever I am now."

"Really . . . ?" She pulled to the side, giving me an unbelieving glance. "Why not?"

"I wouldn't have made the friends I have."

"Um . . ." She raised an eyebrow, smirking at me. "I'm pretty sure the villagers would have liked you, regardless."

"Oh, I don't mean the villagers. I'm talking about my sentient animal companions. Or are they awakened beasts? Creatures on the path to ascension? I can't recall—Barry has called them a few different things, but basically, I have animal pals."

She rolled her eyes at me, shook her head with a smile, but it slowly came to a stop.

"Please tell me you're joking."

"Okay. I'm joking."

She closed her eyes, took a deep breath, and sighed. "What on Kallis have I gotten myself into?"

"Yeah . . . being into fishing is only the tip of the iceberg with me, I'm afraid."

Maria snorted and put her head in her hands, shaking it. "My dad thinks you're a heretic for *fishing*. If he knew you're harboring ascendant creatures . . ."

I watched her closely, not missing the lack of tension in her body.

"You're taking this remarkably well."

"Yeah . . . I should probably be freaking out."

She shrugged. "Maybe it's being around you, but I don't feel threatened. If you say they're 'friends,' or whatever, then they're probably good people—*er, animals* . . . right?"

I smiled at her. "They're the best."

"What are they? What kind of animals, I mean?"

"A crab and an otter."

"A crab?" She blinked rapidly, then dipped her head, resting it on her open palms. "The Cult of Carcinization members are going to *lose. Their. Minds.*"

"Yeah, her name is Sergeant Snips."

She leveled a flat stare at me. "Who left you in charge of choosing names?"

"What makes you say it was me?"

She raised an eyebrow. "Who else would call an ascendant creature Sergeant Snips?"

"Yeah . . . fair call. I totally named her."

"What's the otter's name?"

I beamed a smile at her. "Corporal Claws."

She rubbed her temple with one hand. "I'm becoming less and less sure that I trust your judgment about them."

"Wait until you meet them—you'll understand. They totally fit the names."

"I can . . . meet them?"

"I mean, yeah, if you want to. Do you?"

She tossed her head side to side, weighing her thoughts. "Yeah. I think I do."

"I'm sure they'll love you—they're both super cuddly."

"Okay, now I can tell you're messing with me."

I held up both hands. "No—I'm serious. They're both really affectionate."

She blinked at me, and seeing I was sincere, sighed her acceptance.

"The otter I can understand, but the crab?"

"Well, you have to avoid her spikes, but she's very careful with them."

Maria leaned back on her hands, staring up at the night sky through the hole in the canopy.

"I'm not totally sure this isn't a fever dream of some kind. Were those berries hallucinogenic, and I'm currently passed out by the fire?"

I spun, joining my gaze with hers to stare up at the stars. "It's real, I'm afraid. I just kamehameha'd an innocent tree."

"You what?"

"Nevermind. Something from where I'm from."

I glanced at her. "I'm surprised you didn't keep backing off and run away after that, by the way. I think most people would assume me a monster and retreat."

She shook her head. "I wasn't backing away from you, Fischer. *Despite* what you did to that innocent tree, it wasn't you I was scared of, but the . . . what did you call it? Karma-farmer-hah?"

I barked a laugh, and she shrugged. "The blast, I mean. My body reacted to the blast—that's all."

I tilted my head, smiling at her before returning my attention to the stars above, glimpsed through the hole I'd created.

"You're a special person, you know that?"

She scoffed. "Says the man that turned trees into toothpicks with a single punch, and has not one, but *two* ascendant beasts as friends."

"Woah, you guys have toothpicks here? Tight."

I glanced at her, delighting in her scowl.

"You're so weird sometimes."

Her pronouncement held no malice, so I smiled. "So are you."

She nodded. "Thank you."

We both looked up at the stars above, the foreign celestial bodies both intriguing and soothing. We'd so easily slipped back into our playful dynamic, but my outburst still hung heavy on my mind.

Maybe it's time I confront some of the things I've been avoiding . . .

* * *

The crab was dreaming, and somehow, he knew it. He could see his body from above, as if a third-person spectator of his own form. His carapace was translucent, allowing glimpses of channels winding below. A red light shone from within them, pulsing from an orb of unbelievable brilliance located deep within his cephalothorax.

Wait . . . my what?

He shook his spectral head.

Nevermind.

His burgeoning awareness was growing at an alarming rate, yet it didn't hold a candle to the changes he knew were happening within.

The red channels were as the molten rock on the cavern's floor, and like the sheets of black rock that crumbled and were consumed, the winding veins did the same thing within him. Parts of his body—his very being—were burned away, devoured and replaced by more of the glowing channels.

Unlike what one would expect, the process didn't bring pain, but a sense of elation; each section scoured away made him feel more whole, closer to his true nature.

With growing anticipation, he saw the channels expand, climbing down into the ends of each limb. The passages going to each claw were thicker and much more numerous, and he watched intently, absorbed in the hypnotic expansion. The core within pulsed all the while, each thump radiating from it, reaching out and along the glowing-red veins.

As the process wound on, his carapace started to shine with the same hue. The channels carved deeper, and with each wave of energy, his body grew more and more brilliant.

Despite being outside of it, he could feel his body's senses, and he delighted in the warmth that increased with each passing moment. The power held within his core seemed to be running out with each flash, and suddenly, the process shifted. The pulse no longer originated from the core, instead radiating from the channels themselves, sending essence pouring back toward the orb. The pleasant sensations disappeared; all that remained was pain.

He tried to scream, but his ghostly form had no mouth, no method with which to broadcast his terror. The light coming from his carapace altered, turned from something light to something dark. He could no longer see the channels beneath as his entire form glowed molten red. Just as the rock below, sections of his body grew black, bulged, and cracked.

He panicked, tried to run, to flee, but he wasn't in control. Excruciating pain washed over him, and just as a white light started to glow from the gaps in his armor, his consciousness faded before the onslaught. The blackness took him.

CHAPTER SEVENTY-NINE

SMOOTH

The crab stretched as he woke from a delightful dream. A pleasant, continuous torrent of warm water washed over him, holding his body down against the floor. Memory of his dream was already fading, and only hints of its feel remained.

He moved his joints, each creaking a little after his slumber. With eyes still closed, he stood, stretched—and collided with the roof. He blinked his confusion, and the scene below brought a moment of vertigo. A roiling sheet of red and black was beneath him, folding into and swallowing sections of itself with unerring sluggishness.

The vertigo was cleared away as his memories returned. The veins of molten red, the orb of power hidden within, and above all else, the searing pain. He peered down at his claws, opening and closing them, the sight giving him a bout of dissociation—they weren't his claws.

No . . . he thought. *They are mine, just . . . different. Bigger.*

Continuing to clack them softly, his awareness melded with his new form. He marveled at the strength they held, and, extending one out above the pit of lava below, he slammed one closed. An explosion of noise shot out, followed by a destructive force. Quick as it arrived, it dissipated, washed away by rising water columns from below.

He nodded to himself.

I can't wait to show my leader . . .

He turned and started his passage back to the surface.

"Fischer."

My sleep-addled mind barely registered the word, and I pulled the blanket up, delighting in its warmth.

"Wake up, sleepyhead," a sing-song voice called, warring with my body's attempt to fall back asleep. A soft weight rested on my chest, and I opened my eyes, blinking through blurry vision at the beautiful sight.

Maria knelt between me and the daylight streaming into the shelter, her head cocked to the side as she smiled at me, her hair falling around her face. One hand was resting on my chest, and she patted me softly. I covered my mouth and yawned, stretching my other arm above my head.

"Good morning. What time is it?"

"It's midmorning," she said kindly. "I made you breakfast, but you can go back to sleep if you need more rest."

I shook my head, pausing to yawn again. "I'll get up. I've already slept too long."

She nodded and left the shelter, and after one more yawn, I threw the blankets aside and stepped out into the daylight.

The sun shone down from above, warming my skin pleasantly. I stretched my arms up, breathing in as I bathed in the sensations. The air was still cool as it passed my nostrils, the canopy above still holding a portion of the night's chill.

A welcome scent drew my attention, and I smiled.

"Mmm. Coffee," I said.

Maria giggled. "I said I made you breakfast, didn't I? What's a brekkie without coffee?"

I smiled at her use of *brekkie*; despite my overall joy with this new world, it gave me an unexpected bout of comfort whenever someone used Aussie slang.

"Too fracking right," I said, walking toward the campfire.

A plate and cup awaited me, so I sat down behind it.

"Thank you, Maria."

She beamed from her spot beside me.

"You're welcome. I figured you needed the rest after last night, so I let you sleep in."

"About last night—"

"It's fine," she said, cutting me off.

I gave her an awkward smile. "I won't blame you if you want to run away now that you've slept on, well, everything you learned."

She shook her head. "Nope. I'm good. I'm not sure why, but you being a hidden cultivator kind of makes sense."

I looked up from spreading jam over my croissant, raising an eyebrow at her.

"It does?"

"Yep." She took a sip of her coffee. "The amount of things you've accomplished since coming to Tropica is kind of staggering, and I already felt there was *something* about you, even before learning the extent of it."

I took a bite of my croissant, unsure of what to say. She took a bite of a bun, making a pleased sound as the jam hit her taste buds, then washed it down with another sip of coffee.

"How are you after last night?"

I swallowed my food and took a sip, appreciating the bitter contrast to the sweet jam as I considered how I felt.

"Honestly . . . I'm confused. I've never lost control like that, let alone used any sort of cultivator power before—other than my improved strength, I mean."

She smirked at me. "You don't usually go around shooting beams of light through trees?"

"No." I shook my head with a smile. "I can't say I do. It's kind of worrying, though. That could have seriously hurt someone if they were in the path, and I wasn't exactly . . . myself at the time."

"I seriously doubt you would have unleashed that toward someone by accident, but I take your meaning. It took out a tree—a person wouldn't have stood a chance."

I nodded, chewing my cheek. "I think I've been in denial about a lot of things, and touching on my past opened the floodgates."

I sighed. "I do feel much lighter, though. I needed to get that conversation out—perhaps the beam of light, too."

She giggled. "Yeah, it can't have been comfortable holding a pillar of pure light in like that. Sounds bad for your health."

I gave a half smile. "Anyway, thank you for listening last night and being so attentive. I appreciate it."

"It was my pleasure. I owed you for bringing me on this trip."

She took another sip of coffee. "Next time you unleash an unsolicited blast at the heavens, though, you'll owe me one."

"Deal."

I held out my hand, and after looking at it for a second, she shook it, both of us smiling.

"By the way," I said. "What would you like to do? Stay here longer or head back to the village today? It's your trip, so it's your call."

"We should probably head back. I wouldn't want my dad to track us down and challenge you to a duel for my honor—now that I know you could slap him into oblivion, I mean."

I winced, but she laughed and touched my shoulder. "I'm only joking, Fischer. I'm not worried you're going to hurt him. If anything, I'm reassured, because even if he decides to attack you with a farming tool, you'll be fine . . . probably. He does have one hell of a swing."

"I'll endeavor not to piss him off enough to start swinging at me, then. I hope I didn't actually bring your honor into question by bringing you out here."

She snorted. "As much as we joke about me being a noble lady and you being my loyal servant, I'm no such thing. Dad may be overprotective, but they know I can take care of myself, and they trust you."

She moved her head from side to side, weighing her words. "Well, Mom trusts you, and Dad knows better than to call her judgment into question."

"A wise man," I said, laughing.

She grinned. "Only sometimes. So, should we pack up and leave after brekkie? I haven't even mentioned the main reason I want to get back to the village."

"Oh? What's that?"

"I love animals, Fischer. You told me last night that you have some rather cute and friendly animals in your possession."

Her eyes narrowed playfully, all but shining with her intensity.

"I intend to give them *all* the pats."

Sergeant Snips, first chosen of Fischer and protector of his lands, led a procession across the sandy flats. They headed south, toward the distant mountains and far from the citizens of Tropica.

If someone were to spot the motley crew, they'd no doubt run and alert the first person they saw—if they could run fast enough to escape, that is.

The sea snipper walked beside her as the annoying otter darted around them, occasionally wreathing her limbs in sparks and shooting off at outrageous speeds. Despite her frustration with the overly enthusiastic creature, she couldn't help but appreciate the power she'd somehow harnessed.

Anything that benefits our master is a welcome addition, she thought, attempting to remain objective and, therefore, not annoyed at the toothy ball of fur showing off.

Snips felt the now-familiar power surging again, and knowing what was about to happen, let out a bubbled sigh. The next moment, Corporal Claws shot in front of them, a chirp of pure joy heralding her passage. Snips shook her carapace, failing to keep all the frustration at bay.

Unlike Snips, the lobster tracked Claws's body with keen curiosity. He appeared to hold no annoyance, only a sense of wonder—perhaps awe—for the otter's new ability.

They passed over the rocky shore where they'd found the opalescent stones, and Corporal Claws dashed into the hole, disappearing beneath the water.

Snips urged the sea snipper on, and they continued—she knew the troublesome creature would catch up. Sure enough, she reappeared not long after, flying past them with a surge of electricity, an opalescent stone held in each forepaw, and a toothy grin plastered on her face.

With a disapproving shake of her body, Snips picked up the pace toward the distant mountains.

They reached the forest at a mountain's base before the sun had reached its peak in the sky. She gave them directions, and they set off to explore.

As Snips scouted the area, her thoughts drifted to the male crab that kept sneaking into the saltwater pool. When she'd woken that morning, she had searched for him, suspecting to find him tucked away somewhere beneath the waters. He hadn't been there, and she'd found herself almost . . . disappointed.

Realizing she needed to focus on the task at hand, she banished any thoughts of the vexing crustacean and resumed her scouting.

When they reconvened a half hour later, Snips, Claws, and the lobster nodded to each other; the area was clear.

Snips pointed at herself, then the otter. The lobster scuttled back, making space. Corporal Claws knew the ability to harness lightning would bother Snips, which was the exact reason her furred rival had been taunting so flagrantly.

Despite the annoyance, the development was welcome, and Snips had learned a rather important detail as a result: battle and struggle aided growth.

Snips blew questioning bubbles, and Claws nodded, sparks crackling around her legs. The air stilled, growing thick with tension.

As one, they attacked.

As Maria and I disassembled the camp, I found myself surprisingly excited. Packing up after a trip was said to be a morose endeavor; a prelude to the return to reality. I felt no such thing. I couldn't wait to get back home and see my animal pals.

"Ready to go?" Maria asked, nudging me from my thoughts.

She stood in her washed and dried clothes, the same set she'd worn when we left Tropica, and I got lost in the view of her, marveling at her allure.

She tossed her head to the side, sweeping hair back behind an ear. "What is it?"

"Nothing," I said. "Just appreciating how beautiful it is here."

She snorted. "Smooth."

I laughed. "I have my moments. Let's go."

The next two days were an enjoyable trek. We took our time, taking in the scenery as we joked and talked. We fished, we laughed, and we ate, our conversation never straying back toward my outburst.

At the end of the second day, the sun was just setting as we neared where I knew the road would be.

"As excited as I am to get home," Maria said, "I feel like I could just do this forever."

I smiled at her. "I know what you mean. It's—"

A twig snapped somewhere to our left, and I stopped on the spot. Maria looked at me, then toward the bush I was staring at.

"What—"

I held up a hand, cutting her off. "I heard something."

I walked between her and the bush as the creature disturbed leaves on the forest floor, the sound clear as day to my enhanced hearing. With careful, quiet steps, I crept forward. I reached the bush and, sweeping branches aside, peeked between the leaves.

When I caught sight of it, I froze.

Is that—

"What is it?" Maria whispered, leaning over my shoulder.

When she saw it, she took a sharp intake of breath.

"Oh, no."

CHAPTER EIGHTY

REMORSE

Sitting on the forest floor, doing its best to hide beneath the leaf litter, was a tiny, cinnamon-colored bunny. One of its rear legs was held out to the side, and when it tried to nuzzle beneath the leaves, that leg didn't move. As it noticed Maria and me looming above, it froze.

"Is . . . is it okay?" Maria asked.

"I think its leg is hurt."

"What can we do?"

I turned to her. "You said there weren't any vets in Tropica, right?"

"No . . . none."

I unslung our bags and, bending down, rummaged through mine. I pulled a blanket out, the softest one I owned that I'd removed from my bed, and folded it. With deliberate slowness, I lowered it down over the bunny.

Pressing the blanket up against the bunny's sides, and taking care not to hurt its injured leg, I scooped it up. I held the blanket-wrapped bunny out for Maria to hold, and she gripped it tenderly, pulling it and holding it to her chest. She moved the blankets aside so the bunny's head was poking out. The moment she did, it buried its head back out of sight, hiding from us.

"Oh, you poor darling," Maria said.

"I might have something to help it at home."

She covered it in the blanket once more, looking heartbroken. "Should we travel through the night to get it there? I don't want it to suffer."

I shook my head. "We might trip and fall, hurting it more. I think we should camp for the night, then get it back to Tropica in the morning."

"Okay. You think it will survive the night?"

"Other than the leg, it looked healthy. If it had an open wound, I'd say we should risk it and run through the night, but as it is . . ."

She nodded. "Okay. Let's get to the camp as fast as possible."

The crab's eyes twitched as he came to another constricting section of tunnel. The last two days—despite having just attained a new body, and more intellect than he'd previously fathomed—had been infuriating beyond belief.

What good is a new body, he thought, *if it's too big to get back to my spiky mistress?*

He'd chipped away at the first few roadblocks slowly, eventually carving his way through.

At the fourth or fifth one—he couldn't remember, given how many he'd passed—he was fed up, and had unleashed a mighty clack at the walls.

The subsequent explosion of power had been a mistake. The cave-in had robbed half a day of his time, and ever since, he'd been carefully excavating each narrow section of the tunnel.

Blowing bubbles of resignation, he began cutting into the newest hurdle in his way.

The last two days, Sergeant Snips reflected, had been infuriating beyond belief. This thought was punctuated by a strike to the head. All eight of her legs crumpled beneath the blow, and the bottom of her carapace hit the sand. She got back to her feet as she blew bubbles of annoyance, shaking sand from her undercarriage.

In response, her rival unleashed a chittering laugh. No matter what she or the lobster did, neither could match the speed of Corporal Claws's lightning power, and the otter was all too pleased with herself. Said otter puffed her chest out, preening with the victory.

Where the goading would cause some to quit, to desire a reprieve from the torment, all it did to Snips was make her more resolved. She glanced at the sea snipper, but he was still exhausted from previous bouts; his overlarge form—and his status as a newly awakened—left him unable to keep up with the constant training.

So be it, Snips thought. *I'll keep going until I can shut her up.*

She readied herself, and with her eye locked on the abrasive otter, she charged.

I gathered sticks and kindling for the fire as Maria sat with the bunny, cradling the bundle like it was a newborn. All I could hope was that I could heal it when we got home; any alternative wasn't worth lingering on.

I had to go far to find sticks, as we'd collected all those nearby on our last visit. In my travels, I picked some berries from a nearby bush, holding them in one hand as I returned to the camp.

When I got back, Maria was hunched over and whispering to the bundle in her arms, and I couldn't help but smile.

"I got some berries—I thought we could try feeding them to the bunny."

Maria raised an eyebrow. "Do bunnies eat berries? I thought they ate grass."

"I'm pretty sure everything likes berries. They're full of sugar, so they're super nutrient dense."

In truth, I'd seen videos of bunnies munching down berries with fervor back when I was on Earth, but that was too difficult a concept to explain.

Maria unwrapped the blanket, exposing its head once more. Before it could bury itself back within the folds, I held out a single berry in front of its head.

At first, it didn't move, but then its cute little nose started twitching. It leaned in closer, and after a few more rapid-fire sniffs, bit into the berry. A soft, high-pitched noise came from Maria's throat, and I couldn't help but agree—the damn thing was adorable.

As it chewed, purple juice spread around its mouth, making an absolute mess of its cinnamon-colored fur. Being such a small creature, it was a slow process, but Maria and I watched with rapt attention, unable to take our eyes off it.

After the last bite, it sniffed the stem held in my fingers, its pink nose blowing wisps of air on my fingertips. It raised its head, its nostrils twitching nonstop.

"I think it's looking for more," Maria said, and I nodded.

I held out another berry, and the moment it was within its field of view, the bunny's head snapped to it. I moved the berry down, and it stretched its neck out, snatching a mouthful.

"It's getting more comfortable," I said.

Maria grinned like a child seeing her first puppy.

"Gods above, can we keep it?"

"I mean . . . maybe?"

She shook her head, still smiling. "I'm just dreaming aloud. It's a wild animal, so it wouldn't be right to have it as a pet."

She lowered her head, her hair draping down. "It's just so damn cute—I want to squeeze it and never let go."

The bunny looked up at her, sensing her looming presence. It didn't look away, staring up at Maria as it chewed with an open mouth.

"What do you think, little one?" she asked.

It lifted its head, seeming to hear her words.

"Do you want to stay with us . . . ?"

The bunny leaned closer, then took a bite of Maria's dangling hair. A small length, two centimeters long and wide as a bunny's mouth, was cut from her hair in the blink of an eye.

"Oh . . ." she said as the bunny put its head back down, chewing the stolen mouthful.

We burst into laughter. Maria shook with mirth, trying to hold it in to not spook the bunny, and I did the same, not wanting to roar with laughter and scare it. Trying to keep it in only increased the hilarity, and before I knew it, my eyes were swimming with tears. My legs gave in, and I fell to the ground on all fours, convulsing with soft laughter. Maria braced herself with one hand, having to keep upright with the bunny in her lap.

"I thought it was looking at my face," Maria squeaked out through fits of laughter.

I tried to respond, but my words failed me, and I fell to the floor, rolling onto my back.

"I think it wants more berry, Fischer," Maria said, her voice shaky.

I rolled to my front and braced myself, holding an arm out for the bunny to have some more.

"You sure it doesn't want another taste of your hair?"

Maria snorted, and the bunny happily bit into the proffered fruit, completely unaffected by our laughter.

"Oh my god," I said. "I needed that laugh. I think it's safe to say the bunny isn't too sick—it has a healthy appetite."

"Yeah, no kidding."

* * *

A wave of elation washed over the crab. It had taken hours, but it finally cleared another section of blocked tunnel. It blew happy bubbles and strode on, content to finally have a stretch of path to traverse with its sturdy, reliable legs.

The crab rounded a corner, and it froze. Right in front of it, not even one crab-length away, the tunnel constricted again, becoming entirely unpassable. The crab's eye twitched and, with a slew of dejected bubbles, its body dropped to the tunnel floor.

It sat there for a few breaths and gathered its wits, letting the frustration build. The spiky mistress, with her eyepatch and impressive carapace, drifted into his thoughts.

He got to his feet, shaking his body as if to dispel any annoyance.

I must continue. The sooner I leave, the sooner my leader can see my improved form.

He flexed both clackers as his resolve firmed, and with a steady scrape of his mighty claw, he began clearing the tunnel.

Sergeant Snips dug deep for the energy to continue. Even her nemesis, the flagrant and braggadocious Corporal Claws, was growing tired, her taunting chirps having silenced an hour ago.

Snips got to her feet as she rallied her strength, and she blew small, meaningless bubbles. The otter, heaving air and shoulders slumped, locked eyes with her. They both nodded, and the battle began anew.

Claws lead with her lightning ability, but the sparks were diminished, as was her speed. They met in the middle of the sand, and a loud clap rang out through the forest as claws met, one covered in shell, the others extended from a furred paw.

Both flew back, then darted forward with explosive movement, meeting once more with another exchange. This time, a blur of strikes shot between them, but all were blocked.

When an opening presented itself, Snips jumped back, eyeing the otter. Her exhaustion was immutable, and she thought she may come out with a single victory if she could bait the otter into expending too much of her similarly dwindling reserves.

With each of Claws's ability-powered attacks, Snips had grown more accustomed to the patterns. She would feint an attack from the front, and when Snips attempted to block it, she darted above or around, attacking from behind before Snips could react.

If I can trick her into doing that again, now that her attacks are slower . . .

Snips's pride needed—no, *demanded*—at least one win. She felt the lightning gathering before it started to wreathe Claws's legs.

The blue-white lines sparked into existence, and with the amount of energy expended, Snips knew her trap had worked. Corporal Claws shot over the sand, eating the distance with a manic grin on her face.

Just as the otter was about to pivot and strike from behind, Snips twisted, opening her claw as she spun. She felt the explosion of Claws's redirected energy; the bait had worked perfectly.

She clamped where Claws would appear, right where her neck would be. Snips wouldn't injure her, of course, but a firm grip of the throat would secure a victory. As her claw clacked together in empty air, Snips registered her folly.

Corporal Claws hadn't appeared behind her. Snips spun, but it was already too late. Claws was arcing down from the front, having spun in a loop at blistering speed. Snips didn't have enough time to turn, let alone block the attack. Rather than instill a sense of defeat, it bolstered her fury.

This pup dares outclass me?

She reached deep, grasping for more power, and the ever-flowing current of time seemed to still. A hint of something immense bloomed, but like vapor on the wind, she couldn't grip it. The vast power was out of reach; too abstract for her to comprehend. Despair and anger washed over her, and defeat approached with unerring finality.

No, she thought.

The single syllable held more weight than any word had a right to, and its echoes reverberated throughout her. She channeled all the frustration, all the fury, into her claw, and with the potent appendage, she grasped for the power again.

It was like water, moving around and avoiding her grip. It pulled her in, and she plunged down into a never-ending abyss. As the power hit her carapace, she realized the truth. It wasn't like water—it *was* water. She was within a bottomless sea, plummeting toward a floor she'd never find.

With that enlightenment, the water poured into her, suffusing her entire being. Thick torrents of it penetrated deep, pouring into a place within. An orb of vitality stretched, threatening to burst, yet didn't.

There was no pain, only acceptance and an understanding deep as the immense well of power. She opened her eye, returning to the present.

Water flowed from her body, creating billowing pockets of light-blue energy all over. They collected along the lengths of each claw, and she flared the one to her left, using the momentum to spin her toward the still-charging otter.

The toothy grin across Corporal Claws's face melted when she spotted the change, but she was traveling too fast to stop. Snips's right claw snapped out, faster than Corporal Claws's lightning-powered body could react to.

As her claw shot forward, power gathered on the hinge. It swelled from that place within, traveling through her and coalescing at a single point. She pulled back, sending some of the power back within; she didn't want to kill the otter.

Her claw clacked closed, and an arc of razor-sharp water shot out, angled for Claws's body.

It reached her at an unbelievable speed, and when it hit, Snips's eye went wide. It was too much; she hadn't held back enough. The power sliced through a blocking claw, severed the otter's matted fur, and bit deep into the flesh below.

An explosion rang out as it connected, and Snips was sent flying back, filled with remorse and grief.

CHAPTER EIGHTY-ONE

INTRODUCTION

Pistachio, even exhausted as he was, had felt the welling power within Sergeant Snips and knew it was too much. If it were to hit Corporal Claws, she'd be hurt, if not killed.

The moment the water started pouring from Snips, he extended a single claw and unleashed a blast at the two creatures. All he could do was hope it was fast enough.

Snips moved as a blur, barely visible to Pistachio's eyes even with his enhanced body. The shotgun of force shot from his pincer, blasting into both of them.

As it engulfed them, an arc of blue light shot through it, warping and twisting, dissipating as it went. His blast knocked both of them to either side, and they flew free of a giant cloud of sand that flew up.

Claws rolled to the sand, coming to her feet. Her eyes were wide, and she stood on her hind legs, inspecting her stomach.

As Pistachio approached, he saw a small cut there. A trickle of blood came from the wound, pooling on her fur.

Sergeant Snips, having landed in the opposite direction, tore across the sand with a stream of bubbles flying from her mouth. Pistachio wasn't yet fluent in their meaning, but he caught hints of sorrow, apology, and regret.

She reached Corporal Claws, hissing emphatically as she inspected the wound. The otter still appeared shocked, her eyes wide and staring into the distance now that she knew she hadn't been seriously injured.

Pistachio reached them, leaning in to inspect them; neither had been injured by his blast—only misplaced. He let out a hissing sigh as his anxiety receded.

Snips grabbed Claws by the shoulders, slowly shaking her until her eyes cleared. She looked down at Snips, and as her shell-shocked expression disappeared, a toothy grin spread across her face. She put her paws atop Snips's clackers and unleashed a verbal torrent of excited hisses and chirps. Snips blinked at the barrage, then joined in on the conversation, hissing and bubbling too fast for Pistachio to comprehend.

While he didn't really get it, he understood the general sentiment; they were both ecstatic at Sergeant Snips's new ability.

The mighty crab stepped back, and in an instant, blue liquid sprouted from her limbs, forming into billowing clouds of water that shifted languidly of their own accord. Each spike on her powerful body was tinged blue, covered in a thin layer of power. She pivoted, extending a claw out into open space.

* * *

The feeling of sorrow and regret instantly evaporated as Snips extended her claw and gathered power. She drew from deep within, and the source of the strange power answered, sending a twisting torrent of energy spiraling out through channels within. They coalesced at the hinge of her claw, but unlike the previous attack, she didn't push any power back within, calling forth all that she had. She began to lose control of the flow, so before it could go awry, she slammed her claw closed.

A blue arc of energy—half again larger than the previous one—tore over the sands. It made a distorting sound as it went, like it sliced the air itself in its passing. Sand swirled behind it, and it continued on, slamming into a raised section of earth toward the mountain.

Snips glanced at the others; Claws blinked, her toothy jaw unhinged; Pistachio blew bubbles of awe, staring at her with wide eyes. As one, they sped for the collision sight, intent on seeing the damage.

When they reached it, Snips pulled up short, confused. Claws ran forward, putting her head only centimeters from the mound as she wiggled around, seeking the entry point. Snips could have sworn it had hit right there but saw no hint of damage.

Claws chirped, gesturing down at the mound. Snips leaned in closer, and as she squinted, she saw it. It was only visible because of severed blades of grass. A line was cut across the entire section of earth, thin as a razor.

Claws hissed in appreciation, and Snips blew bubbles of shock. A giant claw extended from behind, tapping each of them on the head. They spun, and the lobster rubbed both of their heads, a gesture of approval.

Claws smiled between the other two, and Snips hissed her appreciation. They may have been entirely different species, and even rivals sometimes, but they shared one unifying goal. The protection of these lands—of Fischer's lands—was the most important thing.

Any of them increasing in strength was a source of celebration, and Snips felt a fluttering deep within her carapace as she realized the other two were proud of her.

She blew questioning bubbles, and they both nodded, so they began the trek back toward master's home—*their* home. Snips hoped he would return soon. Her eye gleamed in the fading light of day. She had a lot to show him, after all.

I woke the following morning to a soft muttering within the shelter.

"Did you sleep well, little bun-bun?"

I smiled and peeked out through a squinted eye. Maria crouched in the corner by where we'd stashed the bunny. She peered into the nest we made, peeling back layers of blanket to reveal a cinnamon-colored head.

"You are just. So. Cute!" she whispered, thinking I was still asleep.

"Thank you," I said, causing Maria to jump and make a startled sound, which made the bunny go alert, raising its ears.

She glared at me. "You scared our child!"

I laughed, pushing back the blankets as I stretched.

"I think it might have been you jumping that scared her, not me."

"Her? How do you know it's a her?"

I cocked my head.

"Uh—I don't know, actually. She is a her, though."

"If you say so . . ." Maria said, her brow furrowed. "I always wanted a daughter."

"Are you, uh, still planning to return her to the wild?"

She sighed. "She's a free spirit, so yes, but that doesn't mean I can't love her while she's healing."

"Speaking of—how about I get some brekkie sorted so we can head off?"

"Yeah! I'll, uh, hug the bunny. It's important we keep her . . . comfortable, you know?"

"Thank you for your hard work," I said, laughing.

As we crested the final hill, a beautiful sight met us. The sun was low in the morning sky, and it reflected off the bay surrounding Tropica. Birds wheeled high in the sky above the village, circling on unseen currents as sunrays warmed everything they kissed. A soft breeze blew from the east, hitting our faces with its cool touch.

Maria's eyes were closed, and she gave a small smile as the wind swept her hair back from her face. She hugged her bundle a little tighter, taking comfort in our rescue's presence. Joy swelled in my heart, and I watched her for a long moment, basking in the scene.

"Let's go," I said.

Maria turned toward me and nodded, her smile turning beatific.

Sergeant Snips, first student of Fischer, and maiden of the salty pond, luxuriated beneath the water's surface. She'd woken early that day, going to meet her squad of crabs at the designated spot. The one crab wasn't there, and with the thought of his continued absence once more permeating her consciousness, she felt a moment of concern.

As soon as it came, she swept it away; he was a foolish and insubordinate creature, but he was reliable. He would live.

He's probably off getting some shiny bauble to bribe his way into my beloved pool, she thought, shaking her head. *It had better be extra shiny to make up for his disappearance.*

She returned her focus to the pond, bathing in the resonance coming from the surrounding opalescent stones. It made her eye itch, and she was absentmindedly rubbing her patch when something joyous entered her sphere of awareness. She leaped from the pond, flying clear over the wall as she launched herself at it.

"That's the pool," I said, gesturing at Snips and Claws's construction.

"If we're lucky, we might find Sergeant Snips within—"

The water *exploded,* spraying upward as something large—and rather spiky—flew from beyond the pond's raised wall. Snips, in all her glory, and expelling a torrent of ecstatic bubbles, landed on the sand before us.

With my enhanced body, I'd seen her expression change midway through her leap—she'd seen Maria, but it was too late for her to cancel her jump once she was already airborne.

She blinked at us, then with slow, testing steps, started backing up, returning toward the pond.

"Snips!" I said, dashing forward and scooping her up. "It's okay—I told Maria."

I hugged her tight. "I *missed* you!"

She looked at me, then at Maria, then back at me. A jubilant hiss escaped her as she gripped my arms and chest with her legs, pulling herself into me.

I roared a laugh, hugging her tight. "I'm happy to see you, too, Snips."

"H-hello, Snips," Maria said, her eyes wide.

Snips waved a single claw, blowing bubbles of greeting at her.

"She says hello back," I said. "Do you want to pet her?"

Maria swallowed, blinked, then nodded. She walked over and, clutching her bundle of blankets to her chest with one arm, extended a hand, gently petting Snips's head. Snips extended her carapace toward the touch, making Maria rub harder.

"She loves scritches," I said.

Maria's face was smothered by awe, and her lips curled up into a smile. "Unbelievable . . ."

"I told you she's friendly. Wait until you meet the other—"

Snips froze, bubbles ceasing as she looked back at the pond. She extricated herself from my grip and jumped to the sand, then gestured for us to follow as she scuttled toward the pool.

"Er . . . Snips?" I asked.

She just gestured us on, more urgently this time. Maria and I exchanged a look, and I shrugged.

"She has something to show us."

We both approached the pond, and Maria let out a gasp. "Hestia's growing bust—it's beautiful."

The morning sun was hitting the opalescent boulder in the center, shining a full spectrum of rainbow light in different directions. It bounced off the smaller stones, making the colors refract and build off each other.

"I know, right? This was Snips and Claws's creation. They—wait . . ."

Something came from the cave, its giant form even larger than the last time I'd seen it.

The lobster, now somehow even bigger—I don't know how it even fit within the cave, to be honest—strode toward us.

I looked down at Snips.

"Did he . . . ?"

She nodded and blew small anticipatory bubbles.

"No way."

Maria spotted the shape approaching and took an involuntary step back.

"It's okay," I said, putting a reassuring hand on her shoulder. "It looks like I've gained another friend."

The lobster emerged from the pond—well, its head did, anyway. It glanced up at us, intelligent eyes bouncing from Snips, to Maria, then to me. Its eyes unwavering, it nodded to me, and I nodded back.

"Nice to meet you, mate."

It—no, *he* blew bubbles of agreement. I wasn't sure how I knew his gender, but I did—the lobster was *definitely* a he.

I bent and scratched his head. He didn't respond as Snips and Claws would, simply looking back up at me as I gave him my best scritch.

"Not a fan of pats, hey? No dramas, my man. We—"

I cut off as I felt power welling up from behind and to my left. I whirled, stepped in front of Maria, held out my hand to protect her, and paused.

What the . . . ? Is that . . . ?

Corporal Claws exploded from her spot on the sands. Lightning—gods damned *lightning*—wreathed her body, and she slammed into my chest. I caught her, bracing for an electrical strike that never came. Claws was a storm of hisses and wiggles, twirling over and over in my arms as she kept glancing up at me.

"W-what?" I said, dumbly.

The lightning still wreathed Claws, but it didn't zap me; it tickled, like a vague sense of pins and needles everywhere it lashed out to touch me.

"You . . . you control *lightning?*"

She let the power go, returning to her normal form as she shrugged and puffed out her chest. She chirped, as if to say, *yeah . . . so?*

I laughed and hugged her tight. She leaned up, pressing her head firmly into my chin as she slid it back and forth hard enough to injure anyone without an improved body. I turned to Maria, showing off my friendly neighborhood otter.

"Maria, this is Corporal Claws. Corporal Claws, this is Maria."

Her eyes were wide, her mouth slightly open as she stared at Claws, no doubt impressed by the lightning—damn, I really could not get over the gods damned *lightning.*

"Do you want to hold her?" I asked.

"Is . . . that okay?"

"Be gentle, okay?" I said to Claws, using a stern voice. "Maria doesn't have an enhanced body."

Claws chirped her agreement and saluted, then jumped to the ground.

I grabbed the bundle from Maria's arms, and before she could bend to pick up Claws, the otter leaped. Maria caught her, making a surprised noise.

Claws sat on her crossed arms, put a paw on each of Maria's shoulders, and chirped her greeting.

"H-hello, Claws."

Claws rolled onto her back, exposing her belly.

Maria giggled, her face awestruck. "You're so cute . . ."

Claws nodded, agreeing wholeheartedly.

A presence caught my attention, and given my creatures—including the newly awakened lobster—were all present, a spear of fret wedged itself deep within me. Everyone but Maria felt it too, and we shot out our heads toward the ocean as another ascendant being approached.

CHAPTER EIGHTY-TWO

GANG

The crab wasn't even relieved when he finally crawled free from the hole; he radiated fury. A hole—a damn *hole* had kept him prisoner, delaying his magnificent reunion with the spiky mistress.

Finally free of the constricting tunnel, he sped toward where he suspected he'd find her, intent on venting his indignation. He arrived at the shore within a matter of minutes, the distance not standing a chance against his improved body, even exhausted as he was. He tore up the sands, hissing and gesturing emphatically with both claws. Across the pond, standing in a group, was his beloved mistress.

Good, he thought. *More beings to listen to my unfortunate tale.*

He increased his speed, sprinting toward them.

I watched the crab tear toward us, a moving tornado of hisses, gestures, and indignant bubbles. As soon as I saw him, I recognized him; it was the crab with a penchant for being flung into the ocean.

He reached us but had eyes only for Snips, ignoring the rest of us entirely. As his impressively vitriolic diatribe dragged on, I raised an eyebrow. All I got was hints of the tale, but it sounded full of struggle.

The relief Snips felt at seeing the missing crab return was dissipating at an impressive speed.

He was rattling off a self-absorbed story of his awakening and subsequent imprisonment beneath the ocean floor.

The story had some interesting points she'd like to delve into later, but the melodramatic embellishments of the tale were leaving a bad taste in her multi-segmented mouth. Worse, this was the first time he'd met their master as an awakened being, and he'd ignored their benefactor entirely.

She let out a sharp hiss, cutting the crab off. With one claw, she pointed at the crab, then to Fischer, gesturing at him repeatedly as she hissed a warning, giving the crab a chance to atone for his mistake. The crab looked at their master and shrugged, then resumed his story where he'd left off. Sergeant Snips, first chosen of master Fischer, and leader of the rock crabs, saw red.

Following Snips' chastisement, the crab glanced up at me, shrugged, then continued hissing.

I smirked.

Cheeky little bugger . . .

Snips, taking much more umbrage with his dismissal of me than I did, trembled. Water seemed to pour from her body, churning out and undulating in a non-existent wind. She shot toward him with one claw pulled back, and as she reached him, it scooped under his carapace.

The blue liquid . . . *er, was it energy?* Whatever—the blue stuff flared from the joint of her claw, propelling it with unbelievable speed as she swung it up. The rock crab never stood a chance, and his body flew out to sea as if shot from a trebuchet.

"Eeeeee—" was all he had the chance to say before he left hearing range, spinning chaotically as he soared toward the horizon.

Snips, releasing whatever power she'd used, returned to her normal, crabby self. She rubbed her claws together and shook her carapace, the very picture of disapproval.

"Uh . . ." Maria said. "Is that crab going to be okay?"

Snips shrugged, and I nodded.

"He'll be fine—he's awakened now, after all. Forget that, though! You unlocked a new power, Snips?"

She nodded, lifting her body from the sand in obvious pride. The blue ability flooded from her again, and she extended a claw. Power swelled from deep within her, collected in the claw, then shot out with a sharp *clack.*

An arc—the same color as the ability wreathing her body—sliced out. Sand flew up behind it, dragged in the impressive attack's wake as it flew out to sea. It kept going, only dissipating when it was far, *far* away.

I dashed and scooped her up, laughing as I spun.

"Hot damn, Snips! You're amazing! How did—" I shook my head. "Never mind. We can handle that later. Everyone—this is Maria."

With their attention turning to her, her face flushed and she hugged the bundle in her arms tighter.

"H-hi, everyone."

"You've already met Corporal Claws and the ever-reliable Sergeant Snips I told you about. This . . ." I gestured at the lobster, mouth moving but no sound coming out. "Er—he doesn't actually have a name yet."

The lobster blew bubbles of . . . *reproach?* They were different to Sergeant Snips's, but definitely had a negative flavor to them.

Seeing my confusion, he pointed at himself and nodded.

"Uhhh . . . you mean you *do* have a name?"

The lobster nodded again. He ambled forward, his massive body climbing over the pond's wall. With one giant claw extended, he drew something into the sand. I looked down at it, my brow furrowing.

"Pistachio?" Maria asked.

The lobster nodded.

"Er . . ." I said. "Your name is Pistachio?"

It nodded again, blowing bubbles that brooked no nonsense.

"Okay, then . . . odd name for a lobster, but I can dig it."

I snapped my fingers. "Private Pistachio! What do you think, buddy? Can you get behind the rank of 'private,' or would you rather just 'Pistachio'?"

The lobster—Pistachio—didn't move for a long moment. His mouth slowly undulated, chewing the words. Then he stepped forward with finality, drawing another word in the sand.

I raised an eyebrow and glanced at Maria, whispering.

"Just checking—he wrote 'private' in the sand just now in front of 'Pistachio,' right?"

She nodded. "Yeah, he—wait, you can't read?"

"No, but that's not important right now. Focus, Maria."

I smiled at her, and she squinted back at me, her lips pursed in confusion. I stepped toward the creatures arrayed before us.

"We have a new friend, and that's all that matters!"

I held a fist out toward Private Pistachio, seeing as though he wasn't a big fan of scritches.

He stared at it, lacking even a modicum of comprehension. I mimed fist bumping it with my other hand. Blowing bubbles of sheer bewilderment, Pistachio reached a meaty claw out and bumped it against my fist.

"Welcome to the gang, Pistachio. It's a pleasure to meet you, mate."

He nodded back at me, blowing bubbles of agreement.

"It's nice to meet you, Pistachio," Maria said.

He bobbed his head.

Then, unsurprisingly, Corporal Claws lost her composure. She let out an indignant chirp, crossing her arms across her chest.

"Claws, you goose," I said, shaking my head. "I already introduced you. Don't get all pissy."

Corporal Claws, looking like nothing so much as a petulant child, raised her chin and looked away.

"You're gonna have to pet her," I said to Maria.

"I . . . will?"

"Yes, I'm afraid. Better to indulge her than deal with the silent treatment."

Claws still looked away, but I caught the smile curling the corner of her lips.

I held out my arms, and Maria passed me the bunny-laden blanket. She stepped toward Claws, bent, and pet her across the head. Claws made an effort to appear indifferent—it lasted all of two seconds before she was leaning into it, unleashing a sing-song series of chirps.

"Well," I said, clapping my hands together. "Now that introductions are taken care of, we have something important to tend to."

Maria snapped upright, and Claws almost fell over with how hard she'd been leaning into the pets.

"Oh. Sorry, Claws." She bent and patted her head in an attempt to dispel the otter's glare. "We have an injured friend."

At the last statement, Claws's scowl disappeared, and she cocked her head, looking between the both of us.

I nodded, unwrapping the bundle in my arms. I squatted down, and all three of them approached—even the stoic Pistachio. They peered down, and the cinnamon bunny lifted its nose, sniffing the air. Then, she glanced at Pistachio, who was leaning in rather close, and swiftly buried her head back into the blankets.

"It has an injured back leg," I said, covering her head back up. "I thought the pool might be able to help it."

"Uhhhh," Maria said. "The pool?"

I gestured at the saltwater pool with my head.

"Yep. It has some sort of healing power, far as I can tell?"

She blinked at me. "You're serious?"

"Maria. In the last five minutes, you've seen an otter riding lightning, a crab using water ninjutsu like some kind of anime protagonist, a lobster that can write his own name, and a sentient rock crab get turned into a frisbee and launched out over the horizon, which, I might add, he's going to survive."

She raised an eyebrow, then she nodded.

"All right, yeah, that's true. I don't know who Anna-Mae is, but you've got a good point."

I barked a laugh. "Don't you worry about Anna-Mae. We won't be seeing her on this world—er—continent. We won't see her on this continent."

Forging past the verbal whoopsie, I strode for the pond and carefully stepped down the wall.

Maria followed, walking right behind me.

I unwrapped the blankets, exposed the bunny's hurt back leg, then carefully drizzled water from the pond over it. The entire limb was soaked after only a few palmfuls, and I sat back, wrapping the blankets back over its body.

Maria sat down beside me, peering at the bundle. "Do you really think that will help?"

"Snips," I called over my shoulder. "How's your eye doing?"

She scuttled down between us as she removed the eyepatch, and her healing eyestalk poked up.

As I stared into it, I realized *healing* wasn't the correct word—it was *healed.*

"Snips! Can you see out of it?"

She nodded, her body poised, proud.

"Why do you still wear the patch, then?"

She pointed at me, the eyepatch, then blew bubbles of adoration.

"Aww, Snips. I love you too, but wouldn't it help you see better if you removed it?"

She shrugged.

"Well, whatever you want to do, I support you."

Maria arrested our attention by clearing her throat.

"I . . . don't get it."

"Oh. Right . . . sorry. When I came across Snips, she was just a regular ol' rock crab. She was covered in scars and half-healed wounds, one of which was a missing eye." I pointed at the healthy-looking appendage now standing firm.

"Stepping on the stairs to ascension, or whatever it is that Barry usually says, didn't heal her eye—sitting in this pond did."

Maria sighed, then chuckled as she shook her head. "This is all too much for me to take in, but if it can heal our little bunny friend, I'm willing to try anything."

"There's something else we can try," I said, "but I'd rather not talk about it unless we have to use it."

Maria raised an eyebrow but didn't press the issue.

"Well, hopefully this works, and we won't need your secret method."

I smiled. "I don't see why it wouldn't, to be honest. It—"

The bunny kicked from within the blanket, and I raised an eyebrow.

"Did you see that?" I asked Maria.

"No . . . ?"

I peeled open the back of the blankets, revealing the bunny's rear legs. The right one was planted firmly on the blanket resting against my leg. The left leg—that which was injured—still sat at an odd angle, but as we watched, it twitched, kicking out spasmodically.

My animal pals, having realized something exciting was occurring, had all crawled into the water. They peered up at us and the bunny with curiosity clear in their eyes. Maria and I both looked at each other; her eyes went wide, and I smiled.

"Movement has to be a good thing . . . right? It didn't move at all before."

Maria nodded fervently.

"Pour more water on!"

I beamed at her. "Exactly what I was thinking."

I cupped my hand in the pond's warm water, then dripped it over the leg, taking care not to get the blanket wet.

When the leg was once more soaked, I wrapped it back up, holding it tight.

"Will you try something with me?" I asked.

Maria's head tilted to the side, causing her hair to hang down.

"What is it?"

"So, I'm pretty sure this world—and the System—functions, in large part, on will."

"How do you know that?"

I shrugged. "Just something I've picked up."

"You want to use our will to help the bunny?"

I nodded. "I could be wrong, but it couldn't hurt to try, right?"

"Okay . . . how do we do it?"

"Well, it's worked previously by closing my eyes and meditating on stuff. Come closer and put your hands atop the blanket."

She shuffled over, her small hands resting on the bundle. I put my hands over hers and closed my eyes.

"Focus on sending waves of healing down into the bunny. Imagine it becoming healthy and whole."

I cracked an eye open, locking eyes with Snips, Claws, and Pistachio. "Would you guys help, too?"

They all agreed with various bubbles, hisses, and chirps, then joined us, leaning over us to put claws and paws atop the blanket.

"Okay. Let's do it."

I closed my eyes, willing the bunny's body to repair. I pictured green light radiating from my hands and those of my friends. In my mind's eye, the beams pulsed into the bunny below, permeating and taking hold deep within.

"Good job, everyone," I whispered. "Keep it—"

Something surged from my core, zooming up my chest, down my arms, and through my hands in an instant. The System tugged at me, sending me a notification. It had done so multiple times during our trip away, but they'd been growing muted, ignorable—this pulse was anything but. I shuddered and opened my eyes.

"What . . ." Maria's hands tensed under mine, and she pulled them to her chest as if burned. "What was that?"

I pulled my hands back, and Claws, Snips, and Pistachio followed suit, eyes locked on the blanket. I started to peel back a corner, hesitated, then unfolded it. When I caught sight of the bunny, my jaw dropped open.

CHAPTER EIGHTY-THREE

HUMBLE

The moment I opened the blanket, the change was visible. Its leg was bent to the side still, but as I freed it from the surrounding blankets, she stretched the limb back, testing it. The bunny put weight on it, pushing down against my thigh, and after a moment of hesitation, launched herself from the blanket with a powerful leap.

"No you don't!" I said, snatching her from the air.

I put her back into the blanket and bundled her up.

"What are you . . . ?" Maria asked, her voice full of awe and confusion.

I sprang to my feet. "We've gotta get her to the forest!"

I took off, running just slow enough for Maria to match my pace. Snips and Claws dashed off ahead, a trail of sand in their wake, and Pistachio plodded along behind us, happy to follow.

We reached the trees and continued on, going right to the edge of my property. I turned to Maria, whose skin was flushed and forehead pricked with sweat after what had to be a sprint to her.

"Do you want to let her go?"

"You don't want to?"

I held the bundle out. "I insist. You should be the one to free her."

She accepted the package, hugging it tight and whispering into it. "Goodbye, little bunny. Live a happy and long life."

She knelt and unwrapped the top layer, exposing the bunny to the cool forest air. She raised her head, ears twitching as she looked around. Then, she leaped from her arms, landing softly on the loamy earth.

She paused there a moment, but upon seeing there was no danger—other than the two humans that had kidnapped it, and three ridiculously large, rather violent-looking creatures by our side—the bunny dashed off into the forest, her cute little feet a blur of movement as she disappeared around a trunk and out of sight.

"Bye, Cinnamon!" Maria called after her.

"Cinnamon?" I asked, raising an eyebrow.

She nodded. "Yep—Cinnamon. That's her name."

"A fitting name." I cupped my hands to my mouth. "Bye, Cinnamon! Make good choices!"

Maria elbowed me in the side, recognizing her father's words from when we left for our trip.

"Not funny."

"Hey—it's solid advice. I want her to make good choices."

Maria scowled, but the hint of a smile was on her lips.

"You're a big meany, Fischer."

I grinned at her. "Only to those I like."

Barry carried his prized possession from town, his stride firm and core muscles engaged.

"Are you sure you're okay with that, Barry?" Fergus asked behind him.

"Yeah, I'm sure, mate. It's pretty fracking heavy, though."

"All right . . ."

Barry glanced back to see Fergus and Duncan exchange a look with each other. He returned his attention to the earthen ground, smiling to himself.

Let them think what they want, he thought. *It's more likely to help my mission than hinder it.*

He led them ever on, through the cane fields and further from the village's buildings with each step.

When they arrived at his house, he walked around the back, heading for the shed. They followed silently, focused on the contraptions they bore. Barry reached his shed and bent at the knees, setting the metal pot down on the sandy soil.

"Just here will do, guys. Thanks for bringing it over."

"No problem, Barry," Fergus said, eyeing him with a discerning gaze. "Happy to be of service."

"So, uh, Barry . . ." Duncan said, running his hands together and looking away. "When you finish making a batch, do you think we can have—"

Clap.

"Ow . . ."

Fergus raised his hand, threatening to slap his apprentice on the back of the head again.

"We were paid for the work, Duncan. No asking for extras."

Duncan rubbed the back of his head—overacting, by Barry's estimate; the slap hadn't been hard.

"That's abuse, you know," the apprentice said. "I could have you taken to the capital and whipped like the show pony you are."

"Ohhh!" Fergus said, laughing. "Feeling mouthy today, are ya, lad?"

Duncan grinned. "I learn from the best."

"Yeah? Well, you can learn to clean out the forge when we get back—it hasn't had a good scraping in a while."

"No doubt. You do a half-assed job every time, unlike—*kidding! I'm kidding!*"

Duncan held his hands up, warding off Fergus's raised hand.

Fergus grinned at Barry. "Sorry about the lad. He gets his manners from me, unfortunately."

"It's no problem." Barry turned to Duncan. "I'd be happy to give you some when it's finished. It's the least I can do after all this work."

"See?" Duncan said. "It doesn't hurt to ask!"

"Doesn't make it right, lad," Fergus responded, scowling, then turned to Barry. "We'll be off, then. Forges to clean, apprentices to abuse—I mean discipline. You understand."

Duncan grinned widely at his master, then at Barry.

"Bye, Barry! Can't wait to try some of your—"

Slap.

He rubbed the back of his head, the smile never disappearing.

Barry chuckled at the two. "Until next time. Thanks again."

The smiths turned and left, and Barry spun to focus on his new toy.

"Now . . . let's get started, shall we?"

The first thing he moved inside was the pot—a large, bulbous contraption made of pure metal. He placed it in the back corner of his shed, atop the brick stove he'd built. The stove was just far enough from the wooden walls that any radiating heat wouldn't threaten to catch the entire shed afire.

The pot alone must have been almost a hundred kilograms, and he knew that, if not for his awakening, he wouldn't have been able to lift such a preposterously heavy object, which was likely the reason Fergus and Duncan had been exchanging looks on their way to his shed.

Thankful for his empowered form, he lifted the pot still neck, the object the burly Fergus had been carting. It was a metal chimney that would allow the vapor rising from the pot to travel up and away from the fermented mash. It slid into place with ease—Fergus's work was exactingly precise—and Barry pushed it down, cementing the seal.

Next came the swan neck, which he attached to the still. It was a long chimney for vapor that ran perpendicular to the ground. As with the previous seal, it slid into place, the measurements flawless.

Last came the jacket and the worm condenser that wound within it. The jacket was a metal box to hold water, and the worm condenser looked like a hollow spring.

He gazed over his construction, admiring the work. When the fermented mash was put inside the pot, and the brick stove below was lit, vapor would travel through the still, eventually coming out as pure rum.

He looked to the side, seeing the barrels of mash he'd prepared earlier. They'd been sitting for long enough and should be ready.

"Only one way to find out, I suppose," he said aloud.

He bent and picked one up, intent on finding out.

Maria stepped up to her porch, the midday sun lending an orange tint to the world. A light breeze blew from behind her, wicking away any hint of sweat before it had a chance to form.

"Well," Fischer said from behind her, "it looks like I got you home safe—just as promised."

She turned, smiling at him from atop the porch. They were at the same level, and as their eyes met, her heartbeat quickened.

"Thank you, Fischer. I can't tell you how much I needed that little holiday."

He gave her a wincing smile. "I'm glad you still feel that way. I thought after finding out . . . well, everything, you'd be more stressed than when we left."

Maria shook her head softly.

"Not at all. I feel . . . I don't know. Excited? Thank you for telling me and trusting me with everything."

Fischer laughed. "I didn't really leave you much of a choice."

"No, you did." She stepped closer. "You had to explain your blasting of a tree or two—that little show was hard to ignore—but you didn't have to tell me about Snips, Claws, and Pistachio. You didn't have to tell me about the pond, and you certainly didn't have to show me the bunny's healing. Still, you did all those things, and I appreciate your trust."

As Maria spoke, Fischer slowly nodded along.

"Yeah, you know what? You're right. I'm kind of a good dude, huh?"

"And humble."

He nodded, a glint in his eye. "And humble—that's my most prevalent virtue."

As my mouth ran its course, as it so often did, most of my attention was fixated on Maria. Her blonde hair, moving silently in the breeze. Her blue eyes, like the sunlit ocean on a clear day. The freckles—chaotic, yet perfectly placed, as if the magnum opus of a career artist.

A silence stretched, and my heart quickened, thumping in my chest. Her lip twitched, almost imperceptibly, and she leaned closer. It was a minute shift, yet it made my heart hammer even more.

She darted a look at my lips and then back up at my eyes. I took a half-step forward, drawn into her. She slipped toward me, paused, then leaned in.

Maria couldn't hear. She couldn't think. Her breathing felt too fast, and her heart pounded in her ears as she stared at the strange, enthralling man across from her. He'd revealed so much, things that should have made her want to run and hide, and yet, she didn't; she wanted to be by him—she wanted to help him.

He took a step forward, and she shuffled closer, her legs only half obeying the command. She leaned in, eyes locked on his lips. Fischer froze, his eyes darting to the side as his head jarred backward.

Someone cleared their throat behind her, the sound gruff and loud.

"*Ahem,*" Roger said, getting both of our attention. It was almost a yell, and the admonition was clear. My stomach convulsed, the butterflies turning into a volatile storm.

"Dad!" Maria whirled, letting out an awkward laugh. "I'm, erm . . . *back?*"

He nodded, his eyes locking me down. "I'm glad. Come inside and I'll help you unpack."

"There's no rush," Sharon said, poking her head out the open door. "Right, dear?"

Roger didn't take his eyes off me, and I stared back dumbly, like a fox caught in a chicken coop.

"Right," he agreed, his jaw clenching. "We'll be . . . inside."

Sharon ushered him back in and closed the door, leaving us alone on the porch. She appeared in the front window, looked between Maria and me, winked, and drew the curtains closed.

Maria shook her head, letting out a soft sigh. "Sorry."

"It's fine," I said, my heartbeat pounding for an entirely different reason than earlier.

Before I could move, she wrapped her slender arms around my neck and pulled me into a hug. My hands moved around her waist, and I pulled her tight against me.

Despite how small and frail she felt, and how powerful the cultivation shenanigans had made me in this world, our bodies fit together—two puzzle pieces made for one another. My chest hammered, and I could feel her soft heartbeat racing as we held each other there, frozen in time.

"Thank you again, Fischer."

I squeezed lightly, pulling her even closer.

"Thank you for coming. I had such a nice time."

She pulled away, so I let go. With her hands on my neck, her arm extended, she leaned in and planted a kiss on my cheek, the touch soft as a feather. Even with my enhanced cognition, I couldn't have dodged if I tried; my body was suspended, overwhelmed by her.

She danced backward, putting her hands behind her back.

"I'll see you soon?"

I nodded, blinking. "Yeah—see you soon."

She smiled, her eyes crinkling as she took one last look at me before turning for the door.

"I don't like it, Sharon!" Roger hissed, keeping his voice low.

His wife let out a small sigh, nodding. "I know you don't like it, my love, but that doesn't mean it's right for us to interfere."

He felt his mouth form a line and eyebrows scrunch together as he thought of what to say, but Sharon spoke first.

"Do you not remember how we met, Roger? I seem to recall a strapping young man sneaking me from my window of an evening . . ."

"This . . . this is different, Sharon. She's—"

"She's our only daughter. I'm well aware, my love, but that's all the more reason to let her make her own choices."

Sharon smiled at him, and her face held such adoration for Roger that his complaints died in his throat.

"She's not an object for us to defend," Sharon continued. "We made her, yes, but that doesn't mean we own her. We're not some noble family that treats their daughters as bargaining chips for power—is that what you'd rather be?"

At the rebuke, Roger's pained expression melted away, and he shook his head.

"You know I detest them more than anything else. It's just . . . she's our only daughter, Sharon."

She put a hand on his chest and stepped in, leaning her head against his sturdy frame.

"I know, my love. You just want what's best for her, but she still has to make her own choices. She isn't livestock for us to herd."

Roger sighed, deep and long. "You're right, but I still don't like it."

Sharon laughed, her small body shaking with mirth as he wrapped his arms around her.

"You don't have to like it." She pulled back, patting his chest. "You just have to grin and bear it."

The door made a soft click and opened, letting in the midday light. Maria stepped through, beaming brighter than the sun outside.

Sharon turned to Roger. "Would you mind going and getting some supplies from town, husband?"

Roger gave her a deadpan look but nodded.

"Been meaning to go for a walk, anyway."

He stomped to their room, presumably to get his things.

Sharon ushered her daughter over; Maria all but ran. She grabbed Maria's hand and dragged her to her room, closing the door behind them.

Now that they were alone, Maria's smile widened, and Sharon's did the same. She leaned toward her daughter, whispering as she bounced on her heels.

"Tell me *everything.*"

CHAPTER EIGHTY-FOUR

RECONNAISSANCE

My hand went to my cheek absentmindedly as Maria closed the door behind her. The touch of her lips lingered, and I replayed it over in my mind. I shook my head, dispelling the rumination—not because I wasn't enjoying it, just didn't want someone to come outside and see me standing there like a weirdo.

"Maybe it's time for Operation Sweet Tooth . . ." I mused aloud as I wandered back toward my home.

An arc of blue energy shot from Sergeant Snips and sliced through the log with ease, hit the sand beneath it, and made a ground-shaking *thump*.

The wood split in two, and as I collected the two halves, I leaned down, squinting between both. They were cut as if by a sawmill; the line was straight and free of imperfection.

Sergeant Snips had cocked her head at my request—and the code name—yet happily joined my undertaking.

I smiled over at her. "You're unbelievable, Snips—you've got some serious cutting power."

She puffed up and nodded as she hissed her agreement.

"All right, could you do the same, but right here, this time?"

I marked the spot I wanted with my fingernail, then set the wood down and stepped back.

Snips cocked her claw back as her ability engulfed her.

Then the claw slammed shut, and power shot forth.

I stroked the rather content crab in my arms as I strode for the forest. When we stepped beneath the forest canopy, the temperature almost immediately dropped ten degrees as the midday sun's baking heat made way for the forest's cool air. I breathed deep, enjoying the moisture-laden oxygen that chilled my nose.

"There's just something about the forests here, Snips."

She shrugged.

"I guess you're more inclined to the ocean, aren't you?"

She nodded, leaning her head into my hand. Realizing I'd stopped scratching her, I laughed and resumed.

We arrived within minutes, and as I gazed at the tree, I smiled.

Insects flew in and out of a hollow, the bees looking healthy and active.

"This is why I want to build something, Snips."

She cocked her head, blowing questioning bubbles. She leaped from my arms and scuttled toward the tree, her head moving back and forth adorably.

"Remember when I told you about these guys? That feels so long ago, but it's been what . . . weeks?"

She turned and hissed at me in agreement before returning her attention to the bees coming and going.

"So, bees make honey, but I'd have to destroy this hive to harvest it, which I don't want to do. I might just make some hives, leave them next to this one, and hope for the best. That way, the bees might expand, or another queen might make the new hive her . . . home?"

I shook my head. "I have no damn clue how bees work, and I'd be more likely to kill them off by accident than to move them successfully. I just wanted to see if they were still here before I wasted wood, and more importantly, time."

I looked at the tree again, enjoying the chaos of so many bees darting about.

"All right. They're here. Let's see how we go with the build."

She nodded, blowing happy bubbles as we pottered back toward the beach.

"If I were a bee," I said, "I'd not only avoid moving into this thing—I would also move my existing hive as far from it as possible."

Snips, my ever-supportive friend, made a so-so gesture with one claw as she looked over the abomination.

"I guess not measuring wasn't my brightest idea."

In my head, having slightly different lengths for each plank would lend the otherwise-square hive a rustic look. In reality, it made it, well . . . not a square. The oblong shape sat there on the sand, taunting me. I grabbed one corner and pulled it apart, the nails standing no chance against my enhanced strength.

"Let's try this again."

After a few cuts from Snips, I started over. I nailed sixteen different planks into a rough square. It was rickety and would twist under the slightest amount of pressure.

I sighed. "I mean, it will probably work."

Snips nodded, having entirely too much trust in my woodworking ability.

"If I'm going to do it, I may as well do it right. Let's cut some more planks, then I'll take a little trip into Tropica."

Snips bubbled along happily, always pleased to help out.

"G'day, Brad. How are ya, mate?"

Brad, one of the woodworking brothers, looked up from his workbench, startled from his focus.

"Oh . . . hello, Fischer." He looked at my armful of wooden planks, raising an eyebrow. "What can I do for you?"

"I was hoping I could make use of your tools for a bit. I'm happy to pay."

He set his chisel down and smiled at me. "As long as you don't break anything, you're more than welcome to use the space."

I smiled at him—the people in this village were just too damn wholesome.

"Thanks, mate. In exchange, just let me know if you need any help down the line. That's what mates are for, yeah?"

"Sounds good to me, Fischer."

He pointed at the other end of his long desk.

"Take up a spot wherever you want."

I took up position behind one of the four vices atop the workspace, on the far end from Brad—I didn't want to impose.

After collecting a chisel, handsaw, ruler, and a pencil, I started measuring.

Brad continually glanced up from the slab of wood he was planing, checking up on Fischer's progress. He'd figured it was a basic box given the materials he'd brought, but when Fischer started marking down measurements on the ends, his curiosity grew.

Given Brad's experience with woodworking, it didn't take him long to understand Fischer's intent—he was making dovetail joints. Brad said nothing, only keeping a tentative eye on the project from afar.

Fischer checked all the measurements repeatedly, double-checking his work, and Brad nodded to himself.

Measure twice, cut once—clever.

As with the reel he'd crafted in their workshop, Fischer's speed was infuriating, and Brad once more found himself wondering if he was some hidden woodworking master.

He shook his head, smirking at himself.

What in Hephaestus's rock-hard chisel would a woodworking master need to hide from?

Fischer finished chiseling the joints of one plank, nodded to himself, then put it against the ends of another, checking to see if the measurements needed adjusting. He smiled to himself, then picked up the saw.

"Wait!" Brad yelled when he saw where Fischer placed it.

I jumped, Brad's unexpected yell surprising me, and my head shot toward him.

He strode toward me, smiling. "Sorry, Fischer—I didn't mean to startle you."

He pointed down at the saw in my hand. "You were about to make a mistake."

I blinked. "Really?"

I glanced at the wood, the saw, and cocked my head, uncomprehending.

"Don't think I was, mate."

He grinned as he reached me, then nudged the saw's blade to the other side of my mark.

My eyebrows furrowed as I tried to work out what he was doing, then it hit me, and I laughed.

"Well, that's embarrassing."

I'd put the saw on the wrong side of the line and would have wasted a plank of wood with my mistake—not the end of the world, but I would have had to go home and fetch a replacement if not for the timely intervention.

"Nothing to be ashamed of," Brad said. "I'd be lying if I said I never made simple mistakes like that, even ten years into owning my own workshop."

He gave me a kind smile and patted me on the shoulder.

"If anything, you should be proud—those joints look perfect so far."

"Minus the one I almost just ruined."

"Aye," Brad responded, laughing. "Except for that one."

"Well, feel free to jump scare me if you notice any other mistakes. Thanks, mate."

Brad walked back toward the slab of wood he was carving away at, grinning at me over his shoulder.

"That I will."

With all the pieces carved—and with no mistakes, thanks to Brad—I started assembling the beehive. It was a simple thing, with only two boxes—one for the bees to make honey in, and one for the queen's . . . hangout area?

What was the non-harvestable area called again? The part where the queen lives?

I smirked to myself.

I'm just gonna call it the "queen bed." New world; new rules. That's assuming I have to collect another hive of bees. Anyway—with any luck, the existing hive will use both boxes.

I constructed the queen bed first, all the pieces easily slotting together with a bit of elbow grease. I recalled it was normal to place a screen between the queen's area and the rest of the hive, but I didn't want to spend time weaving wire, and figured a little wooden paneling would do the trick.

Next, the honey collecting . . . area?

I'm just gonna call it the busy-bee box, I decided, the goofy name bringing me entirely too much joy.

I started putting together the aptly named box, and the wedged joints slid together after a little fist-hammering.

With both of the boxes complete, I started putting together the frames where bees would build honeycomb. I'd cut a single dovetail joint into the ends, and they slid in with ease. There were fourteen frames in total; seven for each box.

I'd brought my own nails, and now that all the wooden pieces were put together, I picked up the hammer and got to work. With two hits to each nail, the boxes and frames were complete. I looked down at my handiwork as gratitude and accomplishment spread a smile across my face.

I slotted the frames into the boxes, and they held firm against the bracing I'd hammered to the boxes' inner walls.

Lifting the top box, I set it on the bottom one, and made to pick them both up and head out.

Instead, I froze as the System nudged me, and the beehive transformed. Time halted as each wall of the boxes went fuzzy, expanded—doubling in size—then shrunk back in and solidified once more.

It didn't lower all the way down, and as the boxes' lines sharpened, I realized something startling. It had created another box from thin air; there were now three.

Handles had appeared on the boxes, and I felt the need to open them up, to see if the internal frames and overall structure had also altered, but then I remembered I wasn't alone.

My eyes darted to Brad. His back was toward me, his body hunched and muscles bulging as he planed the slab of wood atop his bench. I scooped my beehive up and all but ran from the building.

"Cheers, Brad! Catch ya later, mate!" I called over one shoulder, concealing the boxes in front of my chest.

"See ya, Fischer!" Brad yelled back, his breath heavy from exertion.

As the sun set over the eastern mountains, Brad and his brother Greg made their way through the streets of Tropica.

"You're absolutely sure, Brad?"

He nodded, not turning to look at his brother.

"Aye, Greg. I'm certain."

No response came, and they strode in silence, headed for their friends' home. Their steps were hurried, and they reached it in no time. Brad knocked on the door in their usual pattern.

Tap. Tap, tap, tap. Tap.

They could hear something heavy set down inside, and a moment later, the door swung open.

Steven, one of the tailors, and one of their closest friends, beamed a smile at them.

"Hey there, guys. Come on in, it's good to see . . ."

He trailed off as he looked between them. "What's wrong? Has something happened?"

Brad nodded. "Can we talk inside?"

"Of course . . ."

Steven swung the door wider, inviting them in. As Brad stepped inside, the warmth of a stove burning replaced the cool air of fading sunlight, but rather than being a comfort, it felt oppressive to his sweat-pricked skin.

"Oh, hello boys," Ruby said from where she stirred a pot.

When she saw the look on their faces, her demeanor immediately changed.

"Is everything okay?"

The door closed behind them, and Brad took a deep breath, letting it out slowly before launching into his tale.

"Fischer came by the workshop today . . ."

"You're sure you don't mind?" Barry asked Corporal Claws.

She chirped in response, delighted with the task, and Barry nodded his thanks.

"You're most suited for reconnaissance, so I'm glad you agree."

Sergeant Snips bubbled her agreement, and the otter puffed up in pride. She *was* the best for such things, given her speed, lithe form, and vastly superior intellect.

Without further ado, she chirped a goodbye and ran across the sands, her paw-pads falling soft and silent across the landscape.

Corporal Claws grinned to herself as she reached Tropica; she was the night. With the fading daylight, she climbed a building, excited to start her watch. Following the cultivator incident, and how unprepared they had been for it, they'd realized their, uh . . . *folly? Mistakery? Indis . . . cretion?*

Claws shook her head. Words and definitions were for the less-smart of their number, and it didn't befit the most intelligent of them all—the fast, speedy, clever, and *agile* Corporal Claws—to worry about such things.

She dashed across the rooftops, pausing in the shadow of a chimney as she scouted her domain. Most of the citizens of Tropica had already returned to their homes and started cooking; scents and flavors drifted through the air, none of which held a candle to her master's food.

Given the lack of people traversing the streets, it was notable when two forms, both large men, made haste between the buildings, heading somewhere to the east. Corporal Claws, master of the rooftops and traverser of tiles, leaped to another building, trailing them.

When they reached a house and knocked on the door, the two men were ushered inside, so Claws clambered down the wall, wedging herself between a pipe and the stones that made up the home. She closed her eyes, focusing all attention on her enhanced hearing.

CHAPTER EIGHTY-FIVE

FISTICUFFS

Corporal Claws pressed her ear to the stone, feeling and hearing the vibrations from within the home.

"Fischer came by the workshop today," came the voice of a man, "and it happened again."

There was a long pause as no one spoke, and Claws pressed her ear against the cold stone.

"You're sure, Brad?" a female voice asked.

"Yeah—I'm positive," Brad responded.

Another male voice spoke up.

"Did you see it too, Greg?"

"No, Steven," a deep voice, clearly belonging to this "Greg" said. "I was out getting materials."

So, the men are Greg, Brad, and Steven, Claws thought.

She grinned to herself—she was *so* good at this. *What had Barry called it? Recompense? Rent-on-a-scent?*

She shook her head.

Whatever—I'm really good at this sneaky-sneaky stuff.

The conversation resumed, snatching Claws from her self-satisfaction.

"What was it this time?" the female asked.

"I have no clue—just a couple boxes with hollow frames inside. I was trying to look busy, not alert him I was watching."

Another silence stretched. Then, the voice of Steven broke it.

"So, what are we going to do about Fischer?"

Claws's self-centered pleasure was shattered like a clam beneath an opalescent rock, and her lips spread to reveal razor sharp canines. It took all of her significant willpower to not explode through the wall.

The female sighed. "I don't know. I hate knowing that he might be a cultivator. Fischer is such a nice person, and has been nothing but a boon for everyone since coming here . . ."

"On the other hand," Steven said, "he might bring the crown down on us."

"Or worse," Brad added, "he's working for the crown. I don't know how powerful or well connected a cultivator would need to be in order to have his shackles removed, but whatever the answer, it's bad news."

"Well, whatever we do," the female said, "I don't want to put Fischer in danger, but I also don't want anyone else being put in danger."

Grunts and murmurs of agreement came from the others, and Claws's lips fell back into place, once more hiding her vicious teeth from the world. She continued listening.

I stretched my legs and rolled over, curling myself beneath the luscious blanket. For a moment, I'd expected to wake beneath a shelter, Maria beside me—but the illusion was shattered as I felt just how comfy I was. As nice as it was waking up beside her while we were camping, I had to admit I'd missed sleeping in my bed.

I threw the covers back, stretching my arms high as I unleashed a mighty yawn. A smile came to me at a realization—I could once more indulge in Sue's coffee. I made my bed in a hurry, then rushed out the door.

I basked in the daylight creeping between buildings as I strode through Tropica, my steps fueled by the thought of my first love—blessed, ever-dependable caffeine.

I'd thought it my imagination when out camping, or perhaps a side effect of sleeping beneath the trees, but the night appeared to be getting cooler, and a chilly breeze blew between the buildings, waging a battle on my skin against the sun's warming rays.

I rounded a bend, and my heart climbed in my chest as I caught sight of the bakery. Sue was behind the coffee machine, working herself into a tizzy.

With how late I'd slept, there was a sizable line, and I raised an eyebrow. My surprise held not even a hint of annoyance at having to wait; I was happy that more villagers had caught onto the blessing of coffee.

"I hope Sue is making a killing," I said with a smile and joined the line.

As I waited for my turn, my thoughts went toward the beehive I'd made yesterday—I still couldn't believe it had changed so drastically.

When I'd opened the boxes up, they had transformed even more than the outsides. The frames had been made without any wax or plastic sheeting to show the bees where to build honeycomb, but sheets had materialized from nowhere, filling in the spaces between each frame. Not only that, but the extra box had been an exact clone of the others, filled with seven frames, all of which had the same sheets affixed.

I'd taken it to the bees in the tree hollow immediately, placing it on the flat ground right next to their home. I felt a desire to go check it, but worried I might scare the bees away from using it.

Better that I just leave it alone for a while, I thought.

Anticipation welled up inside me; I hoped the bees would find it suitable and expand their nest.

A gruff voice spoke from behind me, pulling me from my thoughts.

"Fischer."

I spun, and when I saw who it was, beamed.

"G'day, Roger. How are ya, mate?"

"I'm well."

He paused a moment, then continued awkwardly. "How are you, Fischer?"

"I'm great, thanks! Camping was really fun, but there's nothing quite like Sue's coffee."

I couldn't read his intention as he clenched his jaw, but then he spoke.

"I was hoping to talk to you about some things."

A spike of anxiety rose at the request, and I gave him my most disarming smile.

"Of course. We can speak now, if you like . . ."

He shook his head. "No, I'd prefer some privacy, and the ladies back home are waiting for their breakfast. Can I come see you later?"

"Er—yeah, that shouldn't be a problem. I'll be building some stuff on my property, and I imagine it will take me most of the day, so come by whenever."

"Morning, Fischer!" Sue called, and I turned to her.

"G'day, Sue!"

She planted her hands on her hips, narrowing her eyes with a smile.

"And where have you been, young man? Not getting your coffee fix elsewhere, I hope!"

I laughed.

"I told you I was going away for a couple days! That's why I wanted all that coffee!"

She sniffed, playing up her annoyance as she moved to the coffee machine and started preparing a cup.

"That was more than a couple days, Fischer. You had me worried my coffee wasn't to your liking anymore."

"Your coffee," I said, bowing grandly, "is the best in Tropica—nay, the best I've had in this world. I beg your forgiveness, request that you make this humble customer your finest of brews, and pass him one of your most delicate pastries, my lady."

She smirked. "How could I turn down such a request? I suppose I can forgive you just this once . . ."

I finished the last bite of croissant as I got back home, and cast about, looking for my animal pals.

I didn't have to look far. Snips, Pistachio, and Claws were all sitting by the fire. Unexpectedly, they had a guest—the rock crab that Snips had launched out to sea yesterday.

They all greeted me in their usual ways; Snips and Claws rushed me, Pistachio raised a claw, and the rock crab blinked at me, as indifferent as he was yesterday. I caught Claws as she leaped at me, and Snips followed suit, latching onto my arm with her legs.

"Good morning, ladies! Did you sleep well?"

They hissed and bubbled, rubbing their heads against me. Snips glanced back at the rock crab, and upon seeing his complete lack of a greeting, hissed an order. I thought the order was for the crab; I was wrong.

Claws dipped a hand into her pocket and removed a pretty stone. With a blur of speed and a spark of lightning running up her arm, the stone flew like a rocket.

Tink!

It slammed into the crab, and he let out a startled noise as he flew backward, landing on the top of his carapace.

Snips and Claws cackled with laughing hisses, and I joined in as the crab's legs sought purchase, finding only air.

"Does he have a name, Snips?"

She shook her head as she jumped to the ground, blowing bubbles in the negative. She scuttled to him and flipped him upright with one claw. The rock crab glared at Claws as she retrieved her prized pocket-rock, and Snips bonked him on the noggin. Sufficiently chastised, the crab settled into the sand, looking everywhere but at us.

"I've thought of a name," I said, and everyone's eyes—including the insubordinate crab—turned toward me.

"Your name is Rocky, my friend, because you just keep on getting up."

Snips blew questioning bubbles, and I shook my head in response.

"It seems like he is here to support you, not me, so I don't think he needs a title like sergeant, corporal, or private."

I smiled down at the rock crab, enjoying the way his eyes sparkled at being given a name.

"You don't have to serve or support me, Rocky. Every creature here does so of their own accord, and if your only purpose is to serve Snips, you're more than welcome to chill with the gang."

He nodded at my words, and then gazed at the fire and the pot of crabs boiling atop it.

"Thanks for making brekkie, by the way. You guys are the best."

I strode toward the fire. "I'll need you all to hide out somewhere today. Roger is coming by at some point, and I don't think he's ready to meet a gang of sentient creatures."

They all agreed with myriad nods, hisses, and bubbles.

I peered down at the boiling water; the sand crabs' shells within were red and pink, ready to eat.

"All right. Let me serve up breakfast and add some seasoning before you all take off for the day."

The flavor of crab, lemon, salt, and assorted spices lingered on my taste buds as I waved goodbye and left to collect the materials I'd need for the day.

Snips had prepared all the lumber when I left for the woodworking shop yesterday, and I felt another wave of gratitude for my violently capable crab.

Guard crab, snuggle buddy, friend, and now lumber mill, I thought, shaking my head with a smile. *What doesn't she do?*

I grabbed all the poles first. They were saplings cut in half lengthwise and would serve as the foundation for my construction.

I marked a spot in the sand, lifted a pole high, then slammed it into the ground. After a few twists, the pole was firmly in the ground, and I leaned against it, pulling and pushing to assess its stability; it held firm. I measured the length between poles with one of the wooden slats, then slammed another pole into the ground and started twisting it down.

I nailed the first paling between the two poles, and seeing it stayed strong, did the same with the rest of the wood.

As I finished nailing the last paling to the panel, I saw someone approaching from the corner of my eye. Roger marched across the sand, making a beeline for me; he arrived in no time at all.

"G'day, Roger. How did the ladies like their brekkie?"

He nodded his greeting.

"They enjoyed it. I must admit that coffee is a bit of a winner in our household."

"Glad to hear it! I feel exactly the same . . ." I trailed off, not really knowing what else to say.

"So, what did you want to talk about, Roger?"

He clenched and unclenched his jaw, looking at my in-progress fence. Then his eyes darted up, and his gaze focused.

"Thank you for taking Maria, and for keeping her safe. She had a good time, and I'm told you were respectful."

A weight lifted from my shoulder as he spoke, and I let out a breath. I'd been worried he was gonna challenge me to fisticuffs, and I hadn't been looking forward to the prospect of holding down an old soldier until he stopped trying to swing at me.

"And, you were right," he continued. "Maria is her own person, and she can make her own choices. I hope you don't look down on me for being protective of her. She's my only daughter, and I love her more than life itself."

I smiled at his admittance of affection; I suspected it was the sappiest thing I'd ever hear from the rugged farmer.

"You're welcome, Roger. I know we've had our differences, but I hope you know by now that I'm a trustworthy bloke. I'd never do anything to hurt her."

As I spoke, his eyes returned to the fence, and with every word, his face grew more annoyed.

"Er . . . something wrong, mate?"

"Is that supposed to be a fence, Fischer?"

I looked at it, furrowed my brow, then blinked at him. "I mean, it is a fence . . . but yeah, why?"

"It looks like shit."

CHAPTER EIGHTY-SIX

SMITTEN

"It looked like shit," Roger said, his annoyance morphing into disapproval.

I roared with laughter at the conversation's shift in tone.

"I thought it looked pretty good," I said, wiping a tear from my eye.

He shook his head. "You've done it all wrong—attaching the palings directly to a pole makes it less sturdy, and given time, the nail will warp out of the pole you've driven them through."

"Er, thank you . . . I think? What should I do to make it better?"

He cocked his head and nodded as he reached a decision.

"I'll go get my tools. I think you'll need more help than a bit of instruction."

Without another word, he turned on his heel and marched off. I blinked at his back as he strode over the sandy flats.

"My man doesn't pull any punches, does he?" I whispered to myself.

I looked back at the fence.

"It's not *that* bad . . . is it?"

When I spotted Roger returning, I couldn't help but grin; he'd brought helpers. Barry and Maria walked behind him, the former easily keeping pace, the latter having to take hurried steps with her much shorter legs.

I'd brought over the rest of the materials for the fence, and I organized them into piles as my soon-to-be-helpers got closer. Maria reached me first.

As she approached, I worried about how to act in front of Roger, but she settled that internal debate for me. She wrapped her arms around my neck and pulled me into a hug, getting to her tiptoes. I wrapped my arms around her waist, matching the strength with which she gripped me.

Her tiny body fit mine, and as she pulled closer, I could feel her heart fluttering—mine hammered in response.

"Morning, Fischer," Barry said, raising an eyebrow and smiling at me.

"I missed you," Maria whispered, squeezing my arm as she withdrew.

The comment brought me up short, and I let go of her, blinking at nothing before returning my attention to Barry.

"Uh, g'day mate."

His eyebrow raised higher, and he shook his head with a smile.

"How was the trip?"

"It was *great!*" Maria answered for me. "We went fishing, ate a bunch of tasty food, and even rescued a little bunny. It was an eventful few days."

As Maria mentioned food, I could have sworn Barry's eyes sparkled.

"Jealous that someone else had some fish, mate?" I asked. "I'd be happy to have you around for some more later, if you like."

"I'd be a fool to turn that down, Fischer." Barry turned to Maria, a glint still in his eye. "So, what did you think of his cooking?"

"Oh, I did the cooking, but the fish was *so* tasty!" Her eyes darted to her father. "Oh, uh, sorry, Dad."

Roger set his tool bag down and shook his head. "I don't wanna know anything about your heretical activities. I'm here to fix this abomination of a fence."

I held up both hands. "Abomination seems a little harsh . . ."

Roger ignored me, picked up a hammer, and strode for my glorious, definitely-not-abominable fence. He put the claw behind a paling and shoved the handle, removing the nails in a single movement.

"You're missing the supporting structure."

He moved on to the next one, removing the paling with a similar push—flexing his dad strength on us mere mortals.

"Running one of these palings from side to side will make the entire fence stand against a storm. This thing . . ." he said, kicking the bottom of my fence, "wouldn't stand up against time, let alone an ocean front."

I glanced at Barry, who nodded his agreement. Maria shrugged at me, as clueless as I was in the mystical art of wooden dividers.

"C'mon, Fischer," Barry said. "I'll show you how to do it. Maria can learn from Roger."

I smiled at her as I followed Barry, and she grinned back, giving me a quick wave.

By the time the sun had crested the horizon, half of the fence was erected.

"All right, you guys may have had a point about my previous work," I admitted.

Roger gave me an unreadable look.

"Does that mean you're willing to admit your fence looked like sh—"

Maria slapped his arm. "Play nice."

He turned his unimpressed face toward his daughter, and I laughed.

"I'll freely admit the fence wasn't the best, but hey, it wasn't the worst for a bloke that's never built one before."

We stood in the shade of a tree by the edge of my forest, having a quick break. Roger and Maria had worked up a sweat in the day's heat, but Barry and I, having been on the receiving end of some otherworldly System shenanigans, were unaffected.

"There you are," a feminine voice called.

I turned to see Sharon and Helen walking along the tree line with trays in hand. Paul walked behind them, all his attention focused on the pitcher and cups in his hands.

From the corner of my eye, I watched Roger; the way his face transformed at seeing his wife was magical. I hadn't seen a smile from him all morning, yet at a single glance of his beloved wife, hard lines melted and corners of his mouth relaxed, curling up.

"Finally, some good company," he said. "Maria and I have been boxed in by buffoons all day."

I raised an eyebrow. "Roger! Was that a joke? If you're not careful, people might assume you're having a good time."

The lines on his face firmed again, and Sharon burst into laughter.

"Don't dish it out if you can't handle it, husband. Come now, I've brought some lunch. You boys can return to your barbed words after you've had a bite to eat."

The ladies reached us, setting down their food vessels, and Helen helped Paul lower his burden to the ground.

"Wow!" Paul exclaimed, his attention finally free to observe the fence. "It's so long! Is it gonna go all the way to the tree line?"

"Why don't you go have a closer look, Paul?" Helen suggested. "Let these hard workers have some rest."

Not needing any more prompting, Paul sprinted across the sand, holding his straw hat firmly to his head with one hand.

One of the trays was layered in sandwiches, the other in cut fruit, and I grabbed a slice of salad sandwich as I accepted a cup of juice from Sharon.

"What's this?" I asked, peering at the light-yellow liquid.

"Cane juice," Helen replied. "We've rediscovered it lately after Barry brushed off the old juicer."

I took a sip, and the cool, sweet liquid was a remedy I didn't know I needed.

"Wow. That hits the spot."

Helen tilted her head to the side, but before she could ask what that meant, I answered.

"That means it tastes delicious. Thank you."

She smiled. "You're most welcome."

Despite not being exhausted, the food, drink, and company were a welcome break, and with the sun descending from high in the sky, we resumed our work on the fence. Maria and Roger worked toward the coast, while Barry and I made our way along the tree line, heading for the river shore.

Despite our enhanced bodies, the father-daughter duo was keeping pace, only slightly helped by Barry and I constantly messing with each other. It was during one such instance, my arm held back, about to throw a nail I was aiming to land in Barry's shoe, when Roger cleared his throat.

I turned, my arm still held high.

"Oh. Hey guys."

Roger glared, and Maria smiled at us, shaking her head.

Still looking at them, I threw the nail, and a moment later, Barry let out a groan.

"That is so annoying, Fischer!"

His arms held a paling flush against the wooden bracing as he lifted one leg high, shaking it to free the nail.

Maria and I laughed at the sight, but Roger cut in.

"We're finished with our section. Maria and I will make the gates while you two waste time."

"You don't have to make the gate," I said. "I'm more than happy to do that later if you have places to be . . ."

"Nonsense. If I don't make it, you'll just stuff it up, then I'll have to come fix it later."

As much as Roger hid his helpfulness behind a thin veneer of aggression, I smiled at him.

"Thanks, mate. I appreciate it."

As Roger turned and marched away, he grumbled something under his breath that I wasn't supposed to hear.

I waved goodbye to Maria, who flashed me a brilliant smile, then I turned to Barry. His lips were held firmly together, his face going red, and as the pair rounded the corner of the fence, we both burst into muffled laughter.

"Wow," Barry said, keeping his voice low, "I've never heard something so vulgar from him."

"Yeah, I didn't think he had it in him."

Barry gave me a smirk. "I wonder if it has anything to do with your trip away."

"Good chance."

"So," Barry said, turning back to the fence and pointedly looking away from me. "You and Maria, huh?"

At his words, my face grew hot, and butterflies took wing in my stomach.

"I'm not one to kiss and tell, mate."

"Ooooooh, you kissed? That's sweet."

"What? No. I mean, she kissed me. Wait, no, don't give me that look, Barry, you degenerate. She kissed me on the cheek."

He burst into laughter. "You must really like her—I've never seen you so flustered."

I sighed, accepting my fate as a red-faced, stammering fool.

"Yeah, I think I do."

Barry held up another paling and hammered a nail in.

"Well, I'm glad. You're both wonderful people."

We left it at that, putting all our focus on completing the fence, only committing a paltry amount of tomfoolery on one another in the following hours.

I held up the gate as Roger hammered in the nails with swift strikes. The sun was low in the sky, casting a long shadow on the fence's other side. With one last swing, the final nail took hold, and Roger stood back, admiring his handiwork. I did the same, and even I had to admit the gate was pretty damn good.

I couldn't have done better . . .

Well, I probably could have, but only because of System-related upgrades, but it wouldn't do to have such a visible landmark turn into ironbark wood.

Imagine if it upgraded into stone—that wouldn't be a fun one to explain.

With the gate's addition, the fencing was complete, and I grinned at it. The wood ran from shore to riverbank, not encompassing my entire property, but a sizable chunk of it surrounding my home. There were two gates leading out, one facing Tropica and one on the other length, leading into the forest.

I turned to my helpers, giving them a broad smile.

"Thank you so much, everyone. I couldn't have done it without you.

"You're welcome," Maria said.

"Happy to help," Barry added.

Roger just grunted, which I took to be Roger-speak for, *I'm happy to help you any time, my stalwart, handsome, and humble neighbor.*

"To show my appreciation, what do you all say we have a little feast tomorrow night? I'd be happy to do it today, but we probably don't have enough time."

Maria and Barry's eyes lit up, and a scowl sprouted on Roger's face.

"I won't be partaking in any heretical food, Fischer."

I held up my hands. "Who said anything about heretical food? I can make plenty of things that don't involve fish, if that's not to your liking."

"We can all bring something," Maria said, bouncing from foot to foot. "Mom and I can make your favorite stew, Dad!"

Roger glanced askew, his face going shrewd.

"With lamb?"

She nodded. "Of course! We even bought some of those spices you like from the caravan."

His face calmed. "I suppose that would be nice . . ."

"I can bring rum!" Barry said.

We all turned to him.

"You have rum?" I asked. "Where did you get rum?"

He beamed. "I made it from sugarcane juice. I've been experimenting with it over the last week, and the boys at the forge helped me make a still."

"Hot damn, Barry! I'm not much of a drinker, but who can turn down a glass or two at a celebration?"

Barry nodded his agreement.

"All right then—it's settled. You guys sort out the food, and I'll handle the drink. I suspect Helen will want to make a dish, too."

I grinned. "It's a date."

Roger's scowl returned, and he glared at me.

"It is *not* a date."

"It's a figure of speech, Dad," Maria said, rolling her eyes as she grabbed him by the arm. "Come on, let's get back to Mom. She'll need a hand with dinner."

"Er . . . Sebastian?"

Sebastian, the leader of the Cult of the Leviathan's Tropica branch, cleared his throat.

"Uh, master, I mean," Gary corrected.

"Yes, disciple?"

"It looks like Fischer has put up a fence."

Sebastian stomped to the edge of the roof, narrowing his eyes at the distant structure. He started laughing. It was soft, fleeting, but it grew as it continued, transforming into an unhinged cackle.

Gary openly winced at his boss's villainous activity.

"Does that mean we should stop trying to summon a—"

"Dare not finish that sentence, Gary!" Sebastian spat, his laughter cutting off in an instant.

"We know not who could be listening to such words."

Gary nodded. "Yes, boss."

"Besides, do you really think mere wood can keep our plans at bay? A single sheet of thin tree, versus a creature of sheer and utter darkness?"

"I thought you didn't want us to say such words."

Sebastian blinked at him then snarled.

"Sit in the circle, Gary! It's time to meditate."

Gary sighed. "Yes, boss."

As the sun set in the sky, the creature emerged from her burrow. She was still growing into her body, and her instincts knew it was safer to eat when the brightness of the day had disappeared.

Her head poked from the hole, and she froze, watching her surroundings for a long moment.

Seeing no movement, she emerged, bounding twice before freezing again.

This process repeated, and by the time she felt sure of her safety, the sun had left the sky. She was chewing on a blade of grass in the shadow of night when an alluring scent crossed her path.

She stopped, her senses overwhelmed by the smell. She raised her nose up, and it twitched fast as she breathed more of it in.

With how thick it was, she could almost see the trails of scent that called to her. With bounding leaps, and making sure to watch her surroundings, she heeded the call.

Between trunks, over grass and fallen logs, and beneath bushes, she traveled onward. The smell grew stronger, and as she caught sight of the source, her mouth salivated.

A field of green stalks grew from the ground, the soil below them brown and free of grass. It was surrounded by trees, hidden deep in the forest.

She glanced around, and after seeing no movement, she could control herself no more; she dashed for the stalks, running between them and toward the field's center.

As she was deep in the patch, she bit into a stalk without hesitation. It was sweet, similar to the dark berries that grow on bushes in the forest. Losing herself to the flavor, Cinnamon took another bite, absolutely smitten with her grand discovery.

CHAPTER EIGHTY-SEVEN

EXPLANATION

Into the early hours of the morning, Cinnamon ate. The tall plants were a fresh experience to her, and with each bite, sweet liquid flooded her mouth. The fibers of the plant were stringy, wooden. Somehow, she knew they held no sustenance, so she spat the fibers out after drinking all the delicious juice within.

No matter how much she consumed, her body craved more, and within the safety of the crop's center, she was happy to oblige.

If she were an awakened creature, she would have recognized how odd the experience was—she never grew full, never became satisfied. Alas, she was not, so she chewed along, ingesting entire stalks, bite by tiny bite.

The first light of the day to come swelled in the sky above her; Cinnamon knew she should return to her den. Leaving now, though, felt . . . wrong. Something was building. The urge to stay warred with her animal instincts, so she drank faster, rushing to consume as much as possible before the daylight grew.

Pink and purple started leaching into the sky, and Cinnamon took one last bite. She took a single hop away, still delighting in the juice flooding her mouth when light exploded out of her, making a soft *pop*.

Cinnamon froze. As the light dissipated, strands of knowledge trickled in. She'd not lived a long life, but it had been filled with terror, pain, and the unknown. These emotions flooded her, and she dropped to the ground, trying to sink into the earth.

Then, flashes of something else joined the fray, adding color to the sheer-black memories. Two creatures, tall and terrifying, wrapping her in a blanket. She'd thought them attackers at the time—predators waiting for the perfect time to strike and end her.

With her burgeoning awareness, she knew better. They had swathed her, protected her, fed her, then . . .

My leg, she thought.

Cinnamon extended the healed appendage, feeling neither pain nor hindrance in the joint.

They . . . fixed me.

They'd repaired her broken leg. Then, instead of killing and eating her, they had let her go.

Her head darted up, her ears twitched—she could feel him. The tallest one, the male . . . *human.* He was close, and his presence drew her on. She bound off toward him, following her senses.

The sky was painted in purple and pink hues as I stepped outside, and I took a deep breath of the cool morning air, a smile coming to my face. There were small waves cresting the river mouth, and their movement drew my attention. Each moment was as a new picture; the ocean would never again be in that exact shape, the water creating a brand new configuration with every passing millisecond.

The thought hit me as profound, and it gave me a new appreciation for the vista. Then, something physical hit me.

Corporal Claws squealed as she slammed into my side. She scrambled up my body, hugging herself against my chest, so I made a cradle with my arms, which she happily fell into. We grinned at each other.

"Morning, Claws. Did you sleep well?"

She chittered her joy at seeing me, and I rubbed her cute little head.

"I missed you too!"

I returned my attention to the predawn landscape, and she joined her gaze to mine, body going soft as she leaned into my arm and watched the shifting waters.

"Are you up to anything today?"

No, she chirped.

As one, we both paused, our eyebrows narrowing. Synchronized, we turned our heads to the side. A creature approached, her form radiating the softest trickle of power I'd ever felt.

No way . . .

I recognized her immediately—it was Cinnamon. The bunny hopped along the sand at a leisurely pace, ears held high and eyes locked on me. I blinked dumbly as she approached.

Claws was similarly lost for words, nary a chirp or hiss escaping her mouth as Cinnamon reached us.

"Er . . . Cinnamon? Is that you?"

The bunny raised her head toward me and nodded a single time, her gaze filled with intelligence. There was no doubt in my mind—she had awakened.

And I'm pretty sure I know how . . .

Pushing aside my annoyance, I bent down and pet her head. Her fur was like velvet, and she leaned to the side as I scratched behind an ear.

"It's nice to meet you properly, Cinnamon. My name is Fischer, and this is Corporal Claws."

Claws jumped from my arms, timidly approached, and reached out her front paws, giving Cinnamon testing pats on the body. The otter's paws tapped away, as if feeling a hot surface. When Cinnamon didn't protest, Claws let out a curious chirp and stroked one forelimb across the length of Cinnamon's back.

Claws's eyes went wide, sparkling with the sensation, and she started cooing as she ran both paws through the bunny's fluffy fur.

"Be gentle," I said, laughing. "She's tiny."

Unlike the other awakened creatures, Cinnamon hadn't appeared to grow in stature, and was still only the size of my hand.

"Would you come with me, Cinnamon? I need to go speak with someone, and I think you might need to be there."

She looked at me curiously, perhaps not understanding what I said. I held out my palm, and she hopped atop it. Her body was so warm for such a small creature, and I held her close to my chest.

"Would you go get Snips and Pistachio, Claws?" I asked.

Claws gave me a curious look but nodded.

"Thank you. I'll meet you back here, okay?"

She nodded again and dashed off toward the saltwater pond.

Sergeant Snips was having a wonderful dream. Fischer had prepared a feast, and her entire squad of rock crabs was invited. She knew not what was cooking, but it smelled delicious, and she salivated at the scents in the air.

Fischer walked toward them with his trusty pot and set it down between the crabs. He removed the lid, and the meal's flavor flooded out, engulfing them all. It was some sort of soup, filled with chunks of fish, clam, crab, and other unknown morsels.

Her master poured some into a bowl and set it down before her. Vapors rose from the pot, permeating her senses, and she leaned in, grabbed a portion of fish with one claw, raised it to her mouth, and—something tapped her head.

She shook her carapace, ignoring the interruption. She had to taste this meal. She needed to . . .

The tapping increased, and a loud chirp cut through her consciousness.

Sergeant Snips opened her eye, and as the blurred world came into focus, she glared her annoyance at Corporal Claws. The otter was playing her head like a drum, tapping incessantly with her infuriatingly furred paws. Snips knocked her hand away with one claw, bubbling with frustration.

I was so close to tasting it . . .

Claws let out another chirp, sharp and insistent. She gestured toward the pond's wall and darted off toward Pistachio's lair.

Snips let out a bubbled sigh as she walked from the water and into the predawn light. Rocky followed her, having also been woken by the boisterous otter.

A cool wind struck Snips as they waited for Claws and Pistachio. They both emerged a moment later, Claws swiftly, and Pistachio with lumbering steps.

The otter immediately launched into a panicked stream of hisses and chirps, and worry blossomed within Snips. She bubbled a question, and Claws nodded—she was sure.

Pistachio, ever silent, simply watched and listened, taking in the conversation.

Snips let out a sigh, and she pointed at Rocky.

Stay here, she hissed.

They turned to leave, and at hearing Rocky's legs hitting the sand, she whirled on him.

Go back, she bubbled, pointing at the pond.

Rocky stared at her, unmoving.

No, he hissed.

Her worry morphed into anger at the insubordinate idiot, and power flooded from her. She launched at him, water billowing from her body as her ability-powered claw shot forward.

Checkmate, mistress, Rocky thought as he soared over the ocean. It was an unlosable position—either he could join the meeting, or he got sent flying; both were acceptable.

As he arced high over the ocean—elevated above the ground as he was—he caught sight of the rising sun. Rocky blew a stream of joyous bubbles, the small orbs shining in the light of day.

He took in the scenes below and above, his vision flashing between both as, following the spiky mistress's toss, he spun chaotically. The ocean was calm and flat and the sky above was a stunning pink; both were beautiful. If not for his improved body, he'd not have been able to appreciate the sight. Gratitude flooded him.

The sea rushed up to meet him as he descended, and he extended his limbs, anticipating the slap to come.

This is the life . . . he thought.

With Cinnamon wrapped in a shirt, I walked across the sandy flat toward Tropica. I wasn't looking forward to the conversation but knew it to be necessary.

I held my hand atop Cinnamon's shirt-covered body, taking solace in the warmth she exuded.

The sun was just cresting the horizon behind me when I knocked on the door. I heard shuffling from inside, and after a moment, Helen peered out at me.

"Oh, Fischer," she said. "Good morning. What can I do for you?"

"Morning, Helen. Is Barry in?"

"Um, yes, he's just waking Paul up. Is everything all right? You don't seem yourself . . ."

I hadn't realized I was frowning, so I smoothed my features.

"Yeah, sorry, everything's fine. I just need to steal Barry for a bit. Could you ask him to meet me back at my place?"

"Sure, I can do that."

"Thanks, Helen. I'll see you later."

I turned and left, headed for the next home.

I knocked on the door, my anxiety spiking. The portal flew open, and Roger's scowling face greeted me. I forced a smile onto my face.

"G'day, mate. You all right?"

"I knew it would be you. I'm fine. Maria is still asleep."

"I'm actually here to see Sharon."

His eyes widened then narrowed again.

"Fischer?" Sharon called from inside. She joined Roger at the door, giving me a smile.

"Good morning. What did you need me for?"

"I need to steal you for a moment." I turned to Roger. "We won't be long—we just need to have a little chat with Barry back at my place."

At Barry's name, Sharon's lips formed a line for a bare second, then went back into a smile—it was tense, and didn't entirely reach her eyes.

She petted Roger on the shoulder. "I won't be long, dear."

Roger clenched his jaw but said nothing, staring his suspicion at me as Sharon stepped past him and outside.

Barry stepped through the gate and found Snips, Claws, and Pistachio waiting.

"Is this about what I think it is?"

Snips nodded but made a *maybe* gesture with one claw.

Barry sighed, casting his gaze toward the rising sun.

"Well, there's nothing we can do about it now. I guess we just have to wait and see. Did you learn anything else last night, Claws?"

The otter shook her head, letting out a negative chirp.

Unlike the night gone, Claws now held no excitement when he brought up her scouting; worry knitted her features.

He knelt down, waving for the ascendant creatures to get closer. "Let's get our story straight."

"So, what's this about, Fischer?" Sharon asked from beside me as we walked past fields of cane.

"Just something I need to clear up—I'll wait until we're all present."

We walked in silence the rest of the way, and as we stepped through my fence's gate, Sharon inhaled a sharp intake of breath.

Snips, Claws, Pistachio, and Barry all stood there. Barry was kneeling, talking to the others softly, but he stood as he noticed us.

"Good morning, Fischer."

"Morning, mate."

Barry gave me a smile, but it seemed strained.

"What did you want to see us about?"

Without preamble, I unwrapped the shirt in my arms and held out the adorable Cinnamon.

Seeing them all, she cocked her head, her long ears flopping to one side.

"Care to explain this, Barry?"

CHAPTER EIGHTY-EIGHT

CONFESSION

Care to explain this, Barry?"

Everyone assembled gazed at Cinnamon, their eyes going wide.

"I'm guessing Maria told you about Cinnamon, Sharon?"

She swallowed and gave a small nod.

"I hadn't noticed her before, but looking at her now . . . is she . . . ?"

"Yes. Cinnamon here has awakened."

Barry cleared his throat. "That's . . . odd."

"Is it, mate?" I gave him a flat look.

"Do you have any idea how a wild rabbit, living in the forest behind my property, could have taken steps on the path of ascension, or whatever it is you usually say?"

Barry opened his mouth, but said nothing, so I sighed.

"Fine. I'll begin, then. I know much more than I've been letting on. I've been here for what . . . a few weeks? In that short time, I've become surrounded by awakened animal pals, have a body that can shoot gods damned laser beams, and when I build or craft things, they turn into magical items with stats and numbers like I'm some sort of progression fantasy protagonist."

I took a quick breath, then dove right back in.

"I know you're a cultivator, Barry."

Barry's face remained calm.

"How long have you known?"

"I'd already suspected it was the fish I caught making creatures awaken, but then I made the whoopsie of feeding some to you. When you got 'sick' after eating fish I made, and then suddenly had the stamina of an ox, I had my suspicions. When you got a little stronger, I could feel it when I was around you, and I knew."

"I'm sorry I kept it from you."

"It's fine—that's not the issue here." I stared into his eyes. "I know about your secret field of sugarcane, Barry. That's what Cinnamon here got into—she's covered in it. I'm guessing the juice from that same sugarcane is what healed you, Sharon?"

"How did you know?" she asked, her voice barely above a whisper.

"I can smell a half-eaten croissant from a hundred meters away, and just like with Barry, I can feel that you're a cultivator. When Barry brought you a cup of what should be bitter or root-smelling medicine, it was pretty odd that it smelled sweet and refreshing. It could have been just a coincidence, but when I smelled the sugarcane juice Helen brought us yesterday, I knew it was the same." I shook my head. "The most obvious part, though, was you immediately healing from what I'm pretty sure was some kind of Xianxia-land cancer."

"W . . . what?"

"Forget it. I meant that your sickness was something you shouldn't have bounced back from in a day or two by drinking root and herb juice."

Barry cleared his throat again.

"I . . . I can explain . . ."

I held up a hand. "I haven't brought you here to grill you, mate."

I chewed my lip, thinking of where to begin. Eventually, I let it all spill out.

"I'm telling you all this because something happened. When Maria and I were away, I had an . . . episode of sorts. I lost my composure when recounting my past, and I accidentally *annihilated* a tree with a pillar of light. I think my denial of everything around me contributed to the outburst, and I realized it was time I confronted what I've been pretending didn't exist—for the safety of those around me, if nothing else. If that blast had hit anyone, it would have killed them. So, here I am, ready to talk about the things I've been hiding from. Any questions?"

They all stared at me, too shocked to speak.

I turned to Sharon.

"Did Maria tell you about the blast I unleashed?"

"She told me you were a cultivator, yes . . . b-but we tell each other everything. She knows I'd keep it to myself. I'm—"

I held up a hand, forestalling her, then paused for a moment, steeling myself for the question I dreaded the answer to.

"Is Maria part of the cult you've started?"

Whatever blood remained in their faces drained, and I nodded.

"Yes, I know about that, too. I've known for a good while—you haven't really been that subtle in your sneaking around, Snips. No offense." I focused on Sharon again. "Does Maria know? Is she a part of it?"

Sharon, her face pale, shook her head.

"N-no. She doesn't."

I firmed my jaw, pinning her down with my gaze.

"Do you swear? I'm not angry now, but if you lie to me about this, I will never forget it."

She gulped.

"I swear on my life—she doesn't know."

The words lifted a weight from my shoulders, and I closed my eyes. The idea of our time away being some sort of scheme had filled me with dread, and knowing our connection was genuine flooded me with relief.

I let out a long sigh.

"Good."

I looked up at everyone, and when I caught sight of Snips and Claws, I gave them a small smile.

Snips had her head dipped as she blew bubbles of remorse. Claws's eyes welled with tears, and her body trembled, one arm slung around Snips in a side hug.

"I'm not angry, girls. Please don't be upset."

I knelt, set Cinnamon on the sand, and held my arms out.

"Come here."

At my invitation, they exploded into action, both slamming into my chest. They hissed, chirped, and bubbled with apology, and I hugged them tight, letting their affection wash my worries away.

"It's okay, really. I know you both had good intentions for keeping it a secret."

They both nodded fervently, and I got to my feet, still clutching them.

Barry cleared his throat.

"I . . . I can tell you everything. We had a good reason not to involve you, it's—"

"No," I said, cutting him off. "I don't want to know."

He blinked, his brow furrowing in confusion.

"You . . . you don't?"

"Nope. I don't want the details." I glanced down at Snips. "You kept me in the dark to protect me, right?"

She nodded and pressed her carapace closer to me, blowing bubbles of sorrow.

"If it were just you, Barry, no offense, but I'd find it suspect. With Snips and Claws's involvement—and their willingness to participate—I know your intentions are good. All I want to know is, what's the purpose?"

"The purpose?"

"Yeah. What is your goal in doing all this?"

He swallowed.

"The protection of everyone around you, Fischer. Yourself included."

I nodded; it was what I suspected.

"Okay. I won't stop you, then."

His head shot back, as if physically struck by my words.

". . . Really?"

"Nope. But—and this is vital—I want nothing to do with it. If there is a life or death situation, sure, let me know, but otherwise, leave me out of it."

Sharon chewed her lip, made to speak, but stopped.

"You can say whatever you want, Sharon. It's fine."

She swallowed, then spoke.

"What do you want to do?"

I let out a small laugh.

"I want to go fishing with your daughter. I want to spend time with my animal pals and harvest some damn honey from some cute little bees."

"Er . . . bees?" Barry asked.

"Yeah, mate. Bees. I want to live a life filled with laughter, friends, and doing the things that bring me joy. I want to have a party tonight with my friends, celebrate with good food, some moonshine rum my next-door neighbor made, and I want to build silly little things like my new fence. Organizing a damn cult is very, *very* low on the list of activities I want to be taking part in. The less I know about it, the better, as far as I'm concerned."

As I spoke, Sharon's face grew into a smile. Barry remained serious, but his shoulders dipped, losing a hint of the tension they held.

"I know you said you don't want to know, Fischer, but there is something I might need to tell you . . ."

I sighed. "What is it?"

"Remember how I told you Helen's brother got taken away to the capital when they discovered he was a cultivator?"

"You're planning to go get him?" I tossed my head to the side, only needing to think about the prospect for a moment.

"Of course I'll help you, mate."

Barry's eyes opened wide, then he gave me a light laugh.

"Oh, uh . . . no. He's here already."

I blinked, staring at Barry for a long moment.

"You're serious?"

Barry clenched his jaw and nodded.

"I hesitate to tell you this, but it might be necessary. A prince came from Gormona with two collared cultivators while you were away—one of them was Leroy. My brother-in-law has already experienced a rather traumatic few years, and I think he would benefit from spending time with you. I don't want him to need to sneak around, but it's a selfish request on my part. If it'd impose too much on your peaceful life—"

"Not at all, mate. I'd be more than happy to get to know Leroy."

I smiled at him. "Maybe a little fishing is just what he needs to come good. What happened to the other cultivator and the prince, though?"

He glanced at Snips and Claws, then back at me.

"You really want to know?"

"Fair point. Nah, I don't."

I squeezed my girls closer to me, showing my love for them as I looked down.

"I'm sorry you had to do, well . . . whatever you had to do."

They both stared at me, cocking their heads in confusion. Snips, realizing what I was saying, started shaking. I raised an eyebrow, but then I realized what was happening—she was laughing. Claws joined in, covering her mouth with one paw as they giggled.

My brow furrowed in understanding.

"You *enjoyed* it? Great, I'm raising maniacs."

Barry cleared his throat.

"Anything that occurred was done in self-defense. I swear this on my son's life."

"Woah, Barry, no need for that, mate. I was just kidding. I know they're not murder machines, and I trust their judgment."

I let out a deep sigh, a weight having been lifted from my soul.

"I do need one thing from you, Barry."

"Anything. Just tell me, and I'll do it."

"The field of sugarcane . . . I need you to secure it. I don't wish to know your plans with it, and I don't need you to destroy it, but I want no more awakened creatures popping up out of nowhere."

Cinnamon had hopped closer to me after I put her on the sand, and she sat beside my foot, her body lowered to the ground.

"I am happy about Cinnamon, though, if I'm being honest."

Sharon smiled.

"Maria will be ecstatic if she ever finds out."

I beamed. "Oh, I'm gonna tell her right away."

Sharon grimaced. "Are you sure that's a good idea, Fischer?"

"Huh? Why wouldn't it be a good idea?"

Realization struck me, and I barked a laugh. "She didn't tell you about meeting the gang, did she?"

Now it was Sharon's turn to be confused, and she squinted, trying to understand. "The gang? Who is the gang?"

I smiled, casting my gaze around at my animal pals.

"I introduced her to Claws, Snips, Pistachio, and even Rocky yesterday."

Sharon's mouth dropped open. "She didn't tell me that."

"Rocky?" Barry asked.

"Yeah, mate. Remember that deviant rock crab that enjoyed being thrown out to sea by Snips? He awakened somehow—his name is Rocky."

At her subordinate's name, Snips blew a small stream of frustrated bubbles, causing me to laugh.

"Unfortunately, Rocky is just as atypical after ascending, but he's not a bad bloke—er, *crab.*"

"Right . . ." Barry said, scratching his chin. "Rocky . . ."

"Hey! You cut that out this second."

"Er—cut what out, Fischer?"

"Formulating plans! No planning, scheming, or organization of shenanigans in my presence!"

"Oh. Right." He winced. "Sorry."

A silence stretched between all of us, and I realized I had nothing more to say.

"Let's pretend this conversation never happened, yeah?"

Sharon and Barry both nodded, and the former spoke.

"So . . . what do we do now?"

I grinned. "Thanks for asking! I'm gonna go get Maria a coffee and croissant, with which I plan to bribe her into coming fishing with me today. You're welcome to join if you'd like."

She smiled at me. "From hearing Maria speak about it, I don't think you'll need to bribe her."

I shrugged, returning the smile. "It never hurts to be prepared."

* * *

The sun was not yet fully risen when I knocked on the door softly. It opened immediately, and Roger peeked his head out, his scowl softening when he saw Sharon with me.

"Hello again, mate!" I held out my tray. "I brought you guys some coffee and breakfast!"

He looked at me, the tray in my arms, at Sharon, then back at me. No words came from him, and I was just feeling the need to say something when he sighed.

"Do you want to come in, Fischer?"

"Sure! I'll come in for a moment, but I've got things to be about today."

He nodded, swinging the door open as Sharon walked in. She rested a hand on his back, and I noticed the immediate, calming effect it had on his posture. I followed, and the warmth of a lit stove greeted me, banishing the cold from outside.

Maria exited her room, her eyes closed and mouth wide in a yawn. Her shoulders were hunched, and she scratched her ribcage, exposing the lower section of her stomach. Her hair was messy, tangled on one side in a chaotic nest.

"Did I hear someone say coffee?" she asked, opening half-lidded eyes as her yawn finished.

She caught sight of my smirk and froze on the spot. Then, in a rather graceful movement considering her previous actions, she spun on her heel and entered her room, slamming the door shut.

Roger made a confused face, and Sharon smirked at me.

"Perhaps we should have warned her you were here."

Half a minute later, she reappeared, bright-eyed and smooth-haired as she smiled at me.

"Good morning, Fischer!"

"Morning! I brought you some coffee and croissants."

She nodded. "Thank you."

"What happened to your pajamas, by the way? They looked comfy."

Maria missed a step and had to catch herself on the wall.

She gave me a flat look. "They *are* comfy, thank you very much."

"Sorry," I said, laughing. "I couldn't help myself. Here—I brought you croissants and coffee in apology."

"Apology not accepted." She snatched a croissant. "You owe me one."

She emphasized the statement with a chomp of the pastry, her eyes narrowed on me.

"Well, I actually came here to invite you fishing, but if you're too upset at me to join, I'll totally understand."

The moment I'd mentioned fishing, she paused, then chewed the mouthful like her life depended on it. She swallowed, taking a deep drink of coffee as she thumped her chest.

"Maria," Sharon said, shaking her head. "I swear . . ."

Her daughter drank more coffee, trying to get the food down, so Sharon turned her eyes on Roger.

"This is your fault. She takes after you."

Roger was still glaring at me, but he simply nodded at the accusation.

"If you say so, dear."

"*Fishing?*" Maria demanded, her mouth finally empty. "On the beach?"

"That's right. I know not everyone wants some heretical food, but I thought I could catch something for those that do—I know at least Barry will join me."

"Me too! I want more fish!"

A low noise came from Roger's throat, but before he said anything that would get him in trouble with Sharon, he strode to the front door, threw it open, and closed it behind him.

Smart man, I thought.

Sharon gave me a kind smile. "Don't mind him—you know what he's like with anything . . . well, heretical."

"Yeah, no kidding, but you don't have to apologize. I understand his convictions, even if they're objectively wrong."

She snorted a laugh and turned to Maria.

"I like this one—we should keep him around."

Maria's face brightened. "I think I just might."

My face went hot, and by the smirk growing on Sharon's face, I knew I had to be blushing.

"All right, let's get going then, shall we?"

I spun, facing away as I strode for the door.

Maria giggled. "Bye, Mom! I'll see you later!"

"Have fun, you two," she called after us, humor clear in her voice.

Following their departure, Sharon stood in her kitchen, eyes distant and unseeing.

Fischer told her about the creatures . . . and it didn't scare her away . . .

She knew Maria was strong-willed, but to see her readily accept a man that had ascendant creatures . . . it was, frankly, unbelievable—even to her own mother.

The front door opened, and Roger reentered, a frown settled firmly on his face.

Sharon beamed at him. "Hello, dear."

"Don't 'hello, dear,' me, Sharon. What in Hades's deepest circle is going on?"

Sharon gave him a sad smile, but walked over to him, setting her hands on his shoulders.

"Do you trust me, Roger?"

"Of course I do," he replied, his face still scrunched.

"Well, you'll just have to trust me on this one, dear. I told you I'd be doing some odd things, and that you were better off not knowing for now."

He crossed his arms in front of her, and she let out a light laugh, making his scowl only deepen.

"I'm sorry, my love," she said. "You're just so cute when you're flustered."

She wrapped her arms around his neck and pulled herself in for a kiss. Roger kept his lips pressed in a firm line, but as she continued raining down smooches, he gave in.

He uncrossed his arms, and hugged her tight, returning her affection.

"I love you," Sharon said.

"I love you, too."

She pulled back, petting him on the chest.

"I have to go do something, but when I get back, I'll start making that lamb stew you love so much, okay?"

Roger sighed.

"Yes, dear."

CHAPTER EIGHTY-NINE

THE CHURCH

Ruby sat behind the counter of her shop, struggling to keep her eyes open as she repaired the stitching in a shirt. She and Steven had spoken with Brad and Greg early into the morning, and following their conversation, she lay awake until the sun peeked through her drawn curtains.

Steven got some sleep, at least, but the old grouch was non-functional on six hours of sleep, let alone two.

"Good morning, Ruby."

She lazily glanced up, drawn from her introspection.

"Hey, Sharon." She covered her mouth as she yawned. "What can I do for you?"

"I need to speak to you and Steven for a bit. Do you think you could follow me?"

Ruby, even in her sleep-deprived state, cocked her head in confusion.

"What about?"

"It's about Fischer."

A spike of adrenaline shattered Ruby's fatigue, and she stood up straight.

"What about him?"

"I think it needs to be spoken of in private. Would you come with me? There are others waiting for us."

"Steven!" Ruby called.

"Yes?" his lethargic voice responded from the other room.

"Get out here, you big grump. We have places to be."

As Ruby stepped into the woodworking shed, some of her building anxiety fled.

Was it Brad and Greg that organized this?

After she and Steven entered, the door closed behind them. She spun just in time to see Barry engage the deadbolt, stopping anyone else from entering.

"What's going on?" she asked, looking around the room.

She caught sight of Brad and Greg, and when she saw the confused looks on their faces, her anxiety bloomed once more.

"Thank you for coming," Barry said. "Sharon and I wanted to talk to you four."

"You said you wanted to speak about Fischer," Brad said. He cleared his throat. "What about, may I ask?"

Barry nodded. "I'll cut straight to the point. We know you suspect Fischer of being a cultivator."

Everyone present at the meeting last night glanced at each other, and Ruby saw her shock mirrored on their faces.

"And how do you know that, Barry?" Greg asked. The woodworker's gaze didn't hold fear; it held fury. "Have you been spying on us?"

"Yes. Well, I haven't personally, and it was the entire village being watched, not just you, but I guess that's beside the point."

Barry took a deep breath and gave them a kind smile.

"You're half correct. Fischer *is* a cultivator, but not *just* a cultivator."

Greg firmed his jaw. "Explain."

"I will, but first, I need you to promise you won't scream."

Greg slipped a chisel from his belt and held it to his side.

"And why would we scream, Barry?"

Barry held up both hands, showing empty palms in a placating gesture.

"Only because it's shocking, Greg. You won't be hurt."

Greg snorted. "What could startle us enough to scream? We're grown men and women, Barry. You just told us Fischer was a cultivator, and we all held our composure, did we not?"

Barry raised an eyebrow but nodded in acceptance.

"Fair enough. Look up, then."

They did—someone screamed.

At the rather feminine scream that tore from Brad, Barry struggled not to laugh. He had to admit it was understandable; Greg was directly beneath Pistachio, only half a meter from the Leviathan crustacean's head. Pistachio sat on the loft above, and he raised one giant claw in greeting.

As planned, Claws and Snips dropped from the rafters. The former landing in Barry's arms, the latter landing in Sharon's.

"This," Barry said, "is Corporal Claws. That's Sergeant Snips, and the awakened lobster waving at you is Private Pistachio."

Corporal Claws chirped, nodding her greeting. Barry scratched her head, and she leaned into it, purring with joy.

Sergeant Snips's blew a steam of happy bubbles, waving one claw at the four strangers. All of them leaned back, and Ruby sat back on a stool. A long silence stretched as they stared around the room, horror clear on their faces.

Ruby spoke first.

"What . . . what's going on, Barry?"

He smiled at her. "Fischer is a cultivator, and these are creatures he has caused to ascend. They are all friendly, reliable, and serve him directly."

A silence washed over the crowd, and seeing they were too shocked to speak, Barry continued.

"I said Fischer isn't *just* a cultivator, right? Do any of you know what a traveler is?"

Steven gulped. "A traveler . . . like from the stories?"

Barry grinned.

"You've heard of them? Good, that makes it easier to explain. For anyone that doesn't know, a traveler is someone from another world."

Brad blinked rapidly, leaning back against a bench.

"You're saying Fischer is from another world?"

"That's impossible," Greg said. "You really expect us to believe such madness?"

Barry nodded.

"I get it—you're understandably confused but let me explain. Travelers were said to be a relatively common occurrence before the gods fled, but given they left so long ago, the world has forgotten about them. I only knew of their existence because of bedtime stories my mother told me, and until I met Fischer, I assumed it was just that—a tale for adolescents. Now, though, I believe it to be true. Fischer *is* a traveler."

Greg started shaking his head, but then his eyes shot to the creatures, and it stilled.

"That would explain his odd manner of speaking . . ." Steven said, his eyebrows knitted. "But, if it's true, how did he get here? If they haven't existed since the gods departed, why has he shown up now?"

Barry shrugged.

"No clue. Travelers are said to be chosen for their ability to change the world around them. I have no idea what changing the world around them means, but I feel like the three creatures before you are a prime example."

On cue, they hissed, chirped, bubbled, and waved, once more announcing the irrefutable proof of their existence.

"Not only that," Barry said. "But he's impacted humans, too. You all heard of Sharon's miraculous recovery, right?"

They nodded, all their eyes wide.

"I thought that was because of the medicine you made," Ruby said.

"That's half true; I made medicine using sugarcane Fischer grew. It caused Sharon to awaken and become a cultivator, which healed her illness."

Greg dropped the chisel from his hand, its metal clatter the only sound in the building.

Barry understood their shock, and he gave them a kind smile.

"Would you mind showing them, Sharon?"

Nodding, she picked up a thick piece of lumber and, with a casual movement, snapped it over her knee.

Steven's legs gave out, and he sat on the floor, staring up at the two pieces of wood.

"Why are you telling us this?"

"That's simple! Corporal Claws here has been watching Tropica, keeping an eye out on the citizens. She overheard your conversation last night, and she came and told me."

Greg clenched his jaw, and his nostrils flared.

"What are you going to do to us?" he asked, his voice shaking.

Barry's head rocked back, and after a moment, he let out a laugh.

"You've gotten the wrong idea. That's my fault, sorry. I should have led with this."

He looked at them all, feeling trust for each and every one.

"We want you to join the Church of Fischer."

The sun was just rising over the ocean as we approached. The scene, combined with Maria's presence and the events of the morning, left my chest light, my awareness unburdened. I took a deep breath, and as the cool air passed my nose, an immense sense of gratitude washed over me.

"It's beautiful." Maria said.

I glanced at her. She'd closed her eyes and was basking in the sun's warmth.

"It really is," I said.

I crouched down, snipping the small tackle from the rod's line and tying on the larger hook and sinker I used for beach fishing. After slipping on a chunk of eel, I held out the rod to her.

"Would you do the honors?"

She opened her eyes, her gaze half-lidded after her moment of mindfulness, and she grinned at me.

"I'd love to."

She took it, flicked the reel open and held the line firm to the rod, then turned to me.

"How far do I cast it?"

"As far as you like. Cast as hard as you can—the rod won't break."

She grinned and held the rod over a shoulder, gathering strength. All at once, she flung it forward. The rod flexed with the movement, and as it extended forward, the tip flicked out.

The hook and sinker flew high, arcing over the ocean and landing past the rolling waves with a soft *plop.*

"Nice cast," I said, raising an eyebrow.

She smiled at me. "You would have said that regardless."

"You're right," I said with a laugh. "I would have, but that really was a good cast. Reel the line in so it's tight and wait for the fish to come."

She did so, and we both sat down. I luxuriated in the sand beneath me, the sound of waves softly crashing, and the small gusts of air that whipped past me, tickling my skin.

"I have something to confess, Fischer."

I didn't open my eyes, enjoying the sun's rays too much.

"What is it?"

"Promise you won't get mad?"

I did open my eyes this time, and I shot a look at her. She was apprehensive, her eyes averted.

"I promise I won't get mad."

She paused for a long moment, then spoke in a hushed tone.

"I told my mom about you being a cultivator. I'm sorry, I was just so excited when I got home, and you can trust her with your secret. We tell each other everything, it's—"

"Oh, that's all?" I interrupted, laughing. "No worries."

Her head darted toward me, her eyebrows raised.

"You're really not angry?"

"Yeah, that's all good. I told you because I trust you, and you told her because you can trust her, right? I don't know Sharon that well, but I think I've gauged her enough to know she wouldn't go sharing that information—especially if it came from you."

She stared at me for a long moment.

"You are so *weird.*"

Her tone held no accusation or insult, so I laughed again.

"Yeah, I see that as a feature, though. Who wants to be normal? You're pretty weird yourself."

She giggled, covering her mouth with a hand.

"I guess I am, considering I'm happily fishing next to a cultivator right now."

I went to say something else, but the rod jerked in the corner of my eye. Maria's body tensed; she'd felt the bite. She got to her feet, moving the rod so the line didn't jerk. The tip bounced again as the fish had another taste.

I didn't instruct her; I trusted her with striking when the time was right. Maria's eyes focused on the rod, and she held the shaft with a firm grip. It jerked one more time, and then the fish struck. Maria pulled the rod up immediately to set the hook, and the battle began.

She made an excited noise, and my soul sang in response, feeling second-hand excitement for what she was experiencing.

"O-oh!" she said. "It's big!"

The rod was bent almost in half, and as the fish tried to swim away, the rod swayed and pulled with shakes of its head. It tried to swim away, but she kept it in place, winding to bring it closer to the shore.

It swam to the left, to the right, then back to the left, but with each passing second, Maria brought it closer and closer. I squinted at the fight, suspecting it might be a new species—I'd not seen a fish move the way it had.

As it got close to the shore, it took one last desperate run, but Maria brought it up short. I saw a flash of silver in a wave, and my eyes went wide—it *was* big!

With Maria's efforts, and the sturdiness of the rod, she dragged it up onto the beach with one last pull. I dashed down to grab it, and after confirming its mouth held no teeth, I held it up for her to see. As I did so, my eyes were drawn into the new species of fish.

Mature Sea Bass

Rare

With a mild and sweet flavor, this fish is a prized saltwater fish of the Kallis Realm. It is said to bring luck to anyone who catches and eats this rare creature.

"Woah! It's *huge!*" Maria said. "Should we eat it?"

"We absolutely should! This should be enough for everyone that wants a taste of fish tonight."

With a single movement, I dispatched the fish, taking a moment to thank it.

I looked up at Maria. "Do you want to cook it? I have spices I think would pair perfectly with it."

Her eyes sparkled, and she nodded fervently, then her eyebrows narrowed on my torso.

"Fischer."

"Yes, Maria?"

"What is that squirming around your belly?"

"Oh, this?" I pointed to my shirt, where something was shifting to get comfortable.

At my words, the bunny climbed up and poked her head from my shirt. Her ears stood at attention as she peered at Maria, her intelligent eyes glistening.

Maria's mouth dropped open.

I shrugged, feigning nonchalance. "You remember Cinnamon, right?"

CHAPTER NINETY

CAPTIVE

Trent, the crown prince of Gormona who was currently imprisoned under false pretenses, hit his wooden cup on the metal bars of his door. All he had was a candle to see by, and as the door's peephole slid open, the bright light of day flooded through. He squinted against the assault before a familiar set of eyes appeared, blocking the sun's radiance.

"Why, good morning, *prince*," Leroy said, spitting the last word. "What can I do for you?"

"Heeeelp!" Trent hollered at the top of his lungs. "Help me! I'm a prince and I've been captured!"

Leroy sighed, reached behind him, then splashed something through the opening.

It slammed into Trent's face, and he recoiled back, holding his comely features.

"What have you done to me? My beautiful face—what foul attack is this?"

"It's water, you idiot. Screaming for help won't help you—we've insulated your room with mulch."

Trent glared at his abuser.

"Why did you assault me then?"

"Because your voice is annoying, and you looked a little thirsty. Now, did you need anything, or was that pitiful attempt at escape all you had for me?"

Trent stood, puffing his chest out. "I demand that you release me. If you let me go now, I'll put in a good word to my father, the *king*."

Leroy gave him a flat look.

"After what you did, you think we'd release you?"

"I did nothing wrong!"

"You tried to enslave my sister," Leroy replied, his face going dark.

Trent waved a hand, dismissing the accusation. "I would have released her after a while. It was only to punish you for your insolence, and I wouldn't be allowed to keep a non-cultivator collared after we got back to the capital."

Leroy's expression turned thoughtful. "You can remove collars?"

"Of course—if one is smart, handsome, and resourceful enough, it's easy."

"So there's a key?"

Trent tried to keep his face neutral, but his eyebrow twitched.

"Yes, fine, there's a key, okay? Now let me out—my crimes are tenuous, and should you leave me in here, my father will have you executed for this. Your only chance of survival is letting me out."

"I'm not letting you out. Anything else?"

Trent thought for a moment, then nodded.

"I'm bored and hungry. It's too dark in here, and I have to go to the bathroom."

"Why don't you play a little counting game, then? See how high you can count—if you make it past twenty, I'll even give you an extra croissant."

Trent sniffed. "I didn't eat my last one. I need proper food—prince food! Not this peasant drivel."

Leroy shook his head. "If you knew what they fed us cultivators back in the capital, you'd cry tears of happiness at being given a fresh pastry."

"But there's not even any *jam!* How am I supposed to eat a dry pastry?"

Leroy rubbed his chin.

"Tell you what, Trent—if you keep on giving me information on the capital, I'll organize some jam for you. How does that sound?"

Trent, the mastermind that he was, reveled in his successful negotiations. He would have told the jailer for free, but now he had secured blessed jam. It would be a far cry from the sweet treats he was used to, but any sugar-based foodstuffs were always a cause for celebration.

He gave Leroy a small smile. "Yes, I suppose that can be arranged . . ."

"Good. If that's all you had to say, then I'll be on my way."

"Wait! What about the bathroom? I need to use the bathroom!"

Leroy pointed in the corner.

"I gave you a bucket."

"You cannot be serious." Trent gazed back at what he'd assumed was some sort of peasant drum for entertaining oneself. "That isn't a musical instrument?"

Leroy raised an eyebrow, staring at him for a long moment.

"Go in the bucket, Trent."

The peephole slammed closed, and the soft orange light of his candle blossomed following the disappearance of daylight.

Leroy shook his head as he lifted the bail of sugarcane mulch, placing it back atop the others and covering the peephole.

"Are you sure this is a good idea, Leroy?" Barbara asked. "If you need some space from him after everything that happened . . ."

Leroy went to her, putting his hands on her shoulders.

"I'm fine, my love. I promise. Having someone to monitor is a good task for me to focus on."

She smiled at him, her eyes brimming with kindness.

"If you're sure . . ."

"I am." He pulled her into a hug, squeezing her tight. He still couldn't believe that he was back—free of his collar—and he delighted in Barbara's touch at every moment possible.

As their embrace stretched, Leroy replayed his conversation with the prince, and shook his head with a laugh.

"I don't know what to think about our captive."

Barbara pulled back, smiling at him.

"He's a bit . . . silly, isn't he?"

"Silly? The guy is a full-blown moron."

"You're sure it's not an act?"

"If it's an act, he missed his calling as a mummer." Leroy looked back at the door, imagining the idiot playing his waste bucket as a bongo. "He was just as stupid on our way here, and he had no reason to put on a show then. If anything, I think his idiocy is helping him. He's too daft to work out just how bleak his situation is, and he'd rather negotiate for jam than work out a way to escape—not that there is any."

"Well, I'll trust your judgment. You know him better than I do."

Barbara leaned back into him, hugging him tight.

"I missed you, Leroy."

He pet her hair. "I missed you more than words can explain."

"C-Cinnamon?" Maria blurted, staring at the bunny poking from my shirt.

At her name, Cinnamon leaped from me, sailing toward Maria. She landed in Maria's outstretched arms and raised her head, sniffing Maria's chin.

"Hey!" Maria giggled. "That tickles! What are you doing back here, little one? And why aren't you scared of us?"

"So, you know how Snips, Claws, Pistachio, and Rocky are all on the path to ascension, or whatever it is?"

I let the words hang, and when Maria grasped my meaning, her eyes went wide.

"No way . . ."

Cinnamon pulled her head back, gazed deep into Maria's eyes, and nodded once, her ears flopping with the movement.

Maria made a high-pitched sound as she hugged Cinnamon tight, and the bunny leaned into the embrace, rubbing one cheek against Maria's neck.

"I'm *so* happy! Does that mean she's going to stay with us? Cinnamon, are you going to stay here?"

Again, the bunny nodded. She made a little squeak to accompany it, and even with how fresh her ascension was, I understood the meaning.

Yes.

Maria laughed, the sound loud and musical.

"I'm so, so, so happy! I wanted you to stay with us, but you were a wild animal, so it wasn't right . . . but now!" She held up Cinnamon, beaming at the bunny. "Now you're aware!"

She turned her attention to me.

"Fischer, we need to build her a house. A pen, maybe? I've never owned a bunny—what do bunnies live in? Do you want a house, Cinnamon? Do you want to stay with Fischer?"

Her barrage of questions halted abruptly, and she leaned toward Cinnamon, raising an eyebrow.

"Do you want to stay with me?"

Cinnamon, entirely overwhelmed by the verbal assault, cocked her head to the side, her ears shifting.

"I don't think she understands," I said, laughing. "That was entirely too many questions for her."

Maria frowned. "I thought she was the same as the other animals?"

"It's more of a slow-burn thing. From what I've seen so far, they get more aware as time goes on. Cinnamon here has only been awake since this morning."

"Oh!" She gave the bunny a wincing smile. "Sorry, little one. I didn't mean to overwhelm you."

Cinnamon's head tilted the other way, her ears following suit as she let out a confused squeak.

Maria looked up at me, her eyes sparkling and gaze intense.

"That was the cutest damned thing I've ever seen. I love her."

I barked a laugh. "I couldn't agree more. We can work out all the details in the coming days, but for now, would you be interested in helping me?"

"With what?"

I held up the mature sea bass she'd caught.

"With cooking this, of course!"

"Just in here," I said as we rounded the rocks and my home came into view.

Maria gasped, so I spun toward her.

"Everything okay?"

Her eyebrows were raised high as she stared at the front of my house.

"Oh!" I said. "You haven't seen my house before, have you? Come on in—I'll give you the tour. Let's go to the kitchen first so I don't have to carry this fish with me."

I led her around the back, and her eyes drifted everywhere, awe clear on her face as she took in the back deck. I opened the door and held it open for her.

"After you!"

She moved inside, her eyes darting around to take it all in.

"Fischer . . . how . . . ?"

"It's a long story. Do you mind if we leave it for another day?"

She turned back to look at me, but upon seeing my serious expression, gave me a small smile.

"I can handle a bit of waiting."

"Thank you." I gestured toward the kitchen. "This is my non-functional kitchen, as you can see by the lack of an oven."

"Is . . . is that a tap? Where does it connect?"

"No bloody clue, if I'm being honest." I walked over and turned it on. "It works, though, and the water is fresh and clean."

"Fischer, that is amazing."

"If you think that's good, wait until you see the shower."

"Shower?" Maria's hair fell from behind her ear as she cocked her head to the side, and Cinnamon mimicked the movement, her ears flopping to the right.

"I'll show you in a moment."

I put the sea bass in one sink, then washed my hands with soap in the other.

"All right, if you'll follow me, ladies, I'll show you the single best part of my home."

I led her past my room's open door, and Maria stopped on the spot the moment she saw the bed.

"Fischer, I know you said your family was rich, but this . . ."

Her eyebrows were narrowed, her gaze fixed on the lush bedding.

"Can I touch it?"

"Of course you can!"

"Here," she said, holding Cinnamon out to me.

I raised an eyebrow as I grabbed and cuddled the proffered bunny, but then Maria took off.

She sprinted, launching herself as she reached the bedside. She crashed down into the pillows, the blanket puffing up at the edges with her collision. A great sigh escaped her as she rolled to her back, lounging on my luxurious sleep vessel.

"It's pretty nice, huh?" I asked.

"Nice doesn't even begin to cover it. I'm not tired, but I feel like I could fall asleep right this second."

"Have a nap if you want—there's still plenty of time until we need to have the fish ready for tonight."

"And miss out on whatever this 'shower' thing is? I should think not!" She got up with great effort, but as she was just about to climb from the bed, she let out a sigh and lay back down. "It's just so comfy . . ."

"Here, I'll help you." I held out a hand. "You'll be stuck in there all day otherwise."

Her small hand slipped into mine, and I helped her up from the pillowy tomb.

I led her out and toward the bathroom, but after we passed another bedroom, she stopped, then walked backward to peek inside.

"You're serious?"

"Er—about what?"

"You have another bed! It's a little smaller, but the mattress and covering look the same."

"Oh, right. I have three spare beds, actually. Check the closed doors."

She darted around the room, throwing open the other two doors, letting out an increasingly annoyed groan with each one.

"You cannot be serious! Why do you even have four beds?"

I shrugged. "Just in case I have mates that need to stay the night."

"I know you said the shower was the best feature, but I'm finding that hard to believe."

"Follow me—I'll let you be the judge of it."

I strode down the hallway, gesturing for her to go inside. Her eyebrows knitted as she caught sight of the white-tiled floor and walls, and she peeked around the corner with no small amount of hesitation.

"What . . . what is that?"

"That's a toilet. It's for, uh, doing your business, you know?"

"Oh . . ." She scrunched her nose. "How do you empty it?"

I walked over and flushed. Maria's face morphed from confusion, to shock, then to awe, and I laughed.

"You don't empty it—you press this button, and water washes it away."

"Okay, that's my new favorite feature. Hands down."

"That brings us to the magnum opus of my humble abode—the shower."

I opened the glass screen and turned on the water.

"Oh, wow!" She looked at the falling water, then the toilet, then back at me. "I still think I like the turtlet better."

"It's *toilet,* but that was close. You haven't felt the shower's water yet, though . . ."

As if heralded by my words, the hot water finally came through, and steam started rising from the falling liquid. Maria stared at it, her face going through a series of expressions as comprehension hit her once more.

"No. Way."

"Yes way," I replied, grinning. "Feel it."

She held out a hand under the running water, and a groan escaped her.

"This is really, seriously, *absolutely* not fair. How does it even work?"

"As with most things, I have no clue! I do love it, though."

"Okay, you were right—this is the best feature of your home."

"Glad you agree! You're welcome to come try it out sometime."

She raised an eyebrow at me.

"That was rather forward of you, Fischer . . ."

"I-I meant by yourself," I said in a rush, but when I noticed her smirk, I sighed. "And you call me the big meany . . ."

She covered her mouth with a hand as she laughed at me.

"Come on." She patted me on the shoulder and walked from the bathroom. "Let's get started on the fish. I want to get back and help Mom out with the stew at some point."

"You know," I said, following her, "the fish won't take long to cook. Did you want to go help your mom, then come back later? Fish is best eaten soon after it's cooked."

"How long will it take?"

"If I get a fire prepared, it'll only take an hour for seasoning and cooking it."

She nodded.

"That sounds good! I'll come back in the afternoon, then?"

"Before you go, you should see something."

"Oh? What?"

I walked to my bedroom and pointed at the door to the ensuite.

"You should look in there."

She raised an eyebrow, but strode into the room and opened the door to have a hesitant peek.

"Woah! You have two toilets?"

"Look around the corner."

She disappeared from sight, and a shocked gasp escaped her throat.

"Hygieia's cleanly skin!" Her head popped back around the corner, her eyes wide. "There's another shower back here!"

CHAPTER NINETY-ONE

REVELATION

As I walked through the streets of Tropica, a soft breeze blew between the buildings. My shirt ruffled against my skin, and doubt returned for what must have been the tenth time since leaving home. As with every other time, I shoved them aside; it was time to be honest with myself and have a little faith in those around me.

As soon as Maria left to help her mother cook, I'd set off, spurred on by impulse. My stomach fluttered at the thought of the meeting to come, but I embraced the anxiety—accepted it.

The sun was just starting to climb over the rooftops, and its warmth was a blessed distraction; I leaned into the rays beaming down on me.

When I arrived at the building, I held one hand up to knock on the door and paused, a hint of nervousness making my hand shake. I closed my eyes and firmed my resolve; my knuckles rapped three times, announcing my presence.

The door swung open, and Joel, the leader of the Cult of Carcinization, appeared before me.

"Good—*oh!* Good morning, Fischer!"

"G'day, Joel. How's it going?"

"I'm doing great! How are you?"

"Always a good day here in Tropica, mate."

He threw the door wider, smiling at me.

"I couldn't agree more. Did you want to come in? Jess has just gone to get some coffee and breakfast for us, but we'll be doing a meditation when she gets back."

"I'd love to, but today is gonna be a bit busy for me. I actually came to show you something."

"Oh?" His eyebrows rose. "What did you want to show me?"

"Can you come down to the beach for a bit? It's probably easier to show you than explain."

"Will it take long? I don't want to worry Jess if she finds me gone . . ."

I shook my head. "Won't take long at all. I just wanted to introduce you to someone."

His eyebrows rose, then furrowed.

"Someone?"

"Yeah, mate—you'll just have to trust me on this one. You won't regret it."

* * *

Soft waves were crashing on the shore when we arrived. Foam and bubbles were pushing up onto the shore before slowly receding back, and as I watched the ocean's movement, I felt another weight lift from my shoulders.

"Uh, Fischer . . . ?"

"Yes, Joel?"

"There's no one here."

"Sure there is! Right about . . ." I pointed out at the waves, feeling my target. "There."

Joel squinted, holding his hand up to block the sun's light.

"I don't see . . ."

Joel trailed off as Sergeant Snips, in all her spiked, eyepatch-wearing glory, walked from the surf. She ambled up the sand, taking slow and deliberate steps—just as I'd instructed her.

Joel's look of boredom and annoyance was swiftly replaced by shock, confusion, perhaps a touch of denial, and finally, awe.

"This," I said, gesturing at the mighty Snips, "is who I wanted to introduce you to."

Joel dropped to his knees on the sand as he stared at the approaching crab. He let out a whimper and tears welled in his eyes.

"Carcinus's blessed claw . . ."

He prostrated himself before the powerful crustacean, pressing his forehead into the sand.

"You can get up, mate. She won't hurt you."

Joel's tear-streaked face turned toward me.

"I can get up? Fischer, this is an ascendant creature—no, an ascendant *crab,* the most noble and respectable of all beasts. It would be blasphemy to not show deference to such a deity. Bow with me. Show it deference—quickly."

Joel's words were breathy, and I started to worry that meeting Snips might be too much for him.

I bent to rub the Sergeant on her hard carapace to show him she was friendly. Her eye half closed in delight, and she leaned into my scritches.

"She's certainly deserving of respect, but I wouldn't call Sergeant Snips a deity."

"She? S-Sergeant Snips?" He shot to his feet, his eyes going wild. "You dare presume to name such a magnificent being something so childish? You dare presume its gender?"

"Whoa—easy, Joel. No need to get in a tizzy."

"*A tizzy?*" He poked me in the chest with a finger. "I could see you punished for such blatant disrespect of my faith, you—"

His words cut off as a blur of orange shot past me.

Joel's words died in his throat as something cold, hard, and wet clamped itself around his neck.

He gulped and slowly looked down; the ascendant crab's claw was firmly pressed to either side of his neck.

Hadn't it just been on the other side of Fischer? He thought. *I didn't even see it move, how—*

"Sergeant Snips!" Fischer admonished. "That's taking things too far. You put that claw away right now, missy!"

The deity released her hold on Joel and scuttled back to Fischer, blowing a stream of bubbles from her mouth.

"You need to apologize to Joel, Snips. Not me."

The crab turned toward Joel, dipped her head, and blew more bubbles.

Fischer nodded. "She said she's sorry."

Joel opened his mouth, but no words came out, and he stared slack-jawed at the two before him.

Fischer squatted down so he was eye to eyestalk with the crab, then rubbed the top of her head.

"I know you meant well, Snips, but so did our friend here. He just thinks you're magnificent, is all. He worships crabs and was a little overwhelmed at meeting you."

Sergeant Snips hissed and blew more bubbles; Joel didn't understand what she said, but apparently Fischer did.

"There's a good girl." Fischer patted her head. "Now run along, but feel free to show yourself to Joel from now on, okay? I'm sure he and his friends would love to give you treats and attention."

I smiled as I watched Sergeant Snips scuttle back to the depths. The meeting had gone a little off the rails, but all things considered, it could have gone worse.

"That . . . I don't . . . it's a she?" Joel asked, his voice full of exasperation.

"Yeah, mate."

As Snips disappeared from sight, Joel slowly spun toward me.

"I'm sorry, Fischer. I didn't mean to—"

I laughed and clapped him on the shoulder.

"It's fine, mate. I thought that would be a lot for you. Do you regret coming down to meet her?"

He shook his head vehemently.

"No. Thank you for this, Fischer. I just . . . *wow.*"

I nodded, giving him time to think.

"You can speak to her?" he asked. "You truly understand what she was saying?"

"Yeah, I wasn't taking the piss."

"Piss?" Joel asked. "What is the piss?"

"Sorry. It's just a figure of speech. Where I come from, piss is another word for, er . . . urine."

"Oh, oka—*wait, what?*" He frowned, blinking tears from his eyes. "Why would you take the urine? Whose urine?"

I laughed and waved my hand to dismiss the questions.

"Forget it. All I mean is that I'm not messing with you—Snips and I can understand each other."

"This . . ." Joel trailed off, rubbing his chin. "This is a lot to consider . . ."

We stood there in silence for some time, Joel considering the vast implications of his newfound knowledge, while I considered how nice the wind and sun felt on my skin.

"I must get back to the cult with this knowledge. I assume you know I cannot keep this secret from them, considering our beliefs?"

I nodded. "I do."

"Thank you, Fischer," Joel said, his head swimming. "This was a truly wonderful revelation."

He turned to leave, but the moment his back was turned, a cold, hard, immovable claw clamped down on his shoulder. He slowly turned, not wanting to offend the deity, but the crab, Sergeant Snips, was nowhere to be seen. It was Fischer's hand that had grabbed his shoulder, and Joel saw an approximation of the deity's fierce glare mirrored in Fischer's severe eyes.

"I introduced you to Snips knowing that you'd tell the other members of your cult, but if *anyone* else were to find out, it would put her in danger. That would be a betrayal of every ideal and oath you hold dear, yeah?"

Joel's mouth went dry.

"O-of course, Fischer. I would never . . ."

"Good. I'm not a violent bloke, but if anything untoward were to happen to Sergeant Snips . . . I'm not sure I could remain a pacifist. You get that, right?"

Joel nodded, his throat scratchy as he swallowed.

"I—I understand."

"Good!"

Fischer laughed, and the fierce intensity melted away in the blink of an eye.

"Get going, then—I don't want to keep you from Jess any longer. I'll see ya later."

Joel nodded and gave Fischer a forced smile, trying to keep his steps calm and measured as he strode away.

As soon as his feet left the sand, he started running. His thoughts were a jumbled mess as he tore through the streets of Tropica, and he burst through the Cult of Carcinization's door before slamming it behind him.

"There you are, Joel. Where did you get off to? I was worried your croissant would get cold."

Jess sat at a table, and she looked up from her breakfast, her face growing concerned.

"Joel? What's wrong? You look like you've seen a cultivator."

"I . . . I might have . . ."

"*What?*" Jess shot to her feet. "*Where?*"

Joel leaned against the door, sliding down it to sit on the floor.

"Fischer . . ."

"Fischer saw a cultivator?"

"No . . ."

"You're not making sense, Joel. Here."

She passed him a coffee, and he sipped it, the golden liquid wetting his dry throat.

Then, without skipping a single detail, he recounted his tale. Jess listened intently, her face going through the same range of emotions that Joel had.

As his story wound on, and he got to Fischer's warning, Jess's face went pale.

"Your shoulder—take off your robe."

Joel slid it down, and right where Fischer had grasped him, a red mark remained, outlining the cultivator's hand.

Jess let out a gasp and lowered herself to the floor beside him.

"So, Fischer is a cultivator . . ."

Her eyebrows knitted as she chewed her lip. ". . . And he's strong enough to control awakened beasts? I thought that was only spoken of in legends . . ."

"I guess so . . ."

"Where does that leave us? A creature has awakened in our lifetime, one with the superior form of a crab, but she's subservient to a human . . ."

Jess continued chewing her lip, and Joel gazed at her with distant eyes, his thoughts similarly muddied.

"Hang on a second," she said, her posture stiffening. "What if we've read the situation wrong?"

"Wrong? How?"

"What if she's the mastermind behind the entire meeting . . . ?"

"That . . . *that has to be it!*" Joel leaped at the possibility, unwilling to admit the deity they'd long waited for could be subservient to a mere human. "But . . . what's the purpose behind her subterfuge?"

"What if she's in danger?"

They both stared at each other for a long moment, and Jess was the first to lose her composure. A smile crept onto her face, made all the more hilarious by her trying to hide it behind pressed-together lips and an unconvincing smile.

Joel descended into laughter, and Jess joined him. Their joy rang out until their breaths were labored, and Joel's ribs hurt.

"Ah, I needed that, Jess. Thank you," he said, wiping an eye. "As if a human could be more powerful than an ascendent crab. Seriously, though—why would she try to deceive us?"

"You don't think she could have been trying to contact us, do you?"

Joel's eyebrows shot up.

"What if she heard our prayers? Could our meditations have been what lent her the strength to ascend?"

Their energy was feeding off each other's, and Jess's eyes went manic.

"What else could it be? We move here, and suddenly a crab awakens? We have to be the source. That doesn't answer why she's pretending to serve Fischer, though . . ."

"Okay, all right, don't freak out, Joel," he said to himself. "You need to work this out. Think, Joel—think! What is her purpose in pretending to be Fischer's subordinate?"

He rubbed his temples, focusing his attention there to stimulate thought.

Then, it hit him.

"By Carcinus's calamitous carapace! I've worked it out, Jess!"

"What, Joel?" She shot to her feet. "You worked what out?"

"It's a test! Don't you see?" He stood, gripping her shoulders. "She's trialing us, seeing if we have the requisite intellect to properly serve!"

"Holy frack!" Jess shot to her feet. "We have to contact her as soon as possible to let her know!"

"Holy *what?*"

Jess made a dismissive gesture. "It's just something I heard in town—I don't know what it means, but it's sure catchy—wait, that's not important right now! We need to go find the crab!"

"No—we have to play it cool, Jess. You're thinking as a human—if we make a move too soon, we might appear to be hasty. We need to show her we take the proper time to think things through."

"Ugh. Stupid, Jess. Stupid, stupid, stupid!" She punctuated each 'stupid' with a slap to her forehead.

Joel gave her a kind smile. "It's not your fault. We are of an incomplete form—it's only natural we'd be inferior to a mighty crab."

She took a deep, centering breath, then sighed it out.

"You're right—I'm sorry for the outburst. It's just so frustrating inhabiting this fleshy body sometimes . . ."

"I know what you mean. Mere existence is a constant reminder of our inferiority, but now that we have a deity to serve, we can at least be of use to one of superior form."

"Hang on a second . . ." Jess's brows creased in concentration, then she looked up at him with growing wonder. "If we have a deity to serve, does that mean . . . ?"

"We're a church?" Joel finished with a manic grin. "That's right, Jess."

He stuck out his chest, not hiding his pride.

"From today, we are henceforth known as the Church of Carcinization, and we'll be the first congregation in millennia to raise a god into the pantheon."

CHAPTER NINETY-TWO

FEAST

The wind flowed past me, funneling through my back door via the back deck. I stood in the doorway, my clothes rippling under the assault. I held my arms out, closed my eyes, and basked in the sensation. As the moment of mindfulness stretched on, a profound calm washed over me, deeper than the ocean.

"This one, Fischer?" Maria asked, luring me back to reality.

I glanced over at her through half-closed eyes and she giggled.

"Just so you're aware, you look ridiculous right now."

I still had my arms outstretched, and the breeze billowing through was inflating my shirt as it poured into my sleeves.

"It's called fashion, Maria. I'm told looking like a marshmallow is all the rage among the kids these days."

"Do I even want to know what a marshmallow is?"

"It's a little pillow of sugary bliss."

She raised an eyebrow. "Another thing from your old life?"

I nodded and walked back inside, closing the door and cutting off the wind.

"It's food. I don't know how to make them, but maybe we can try . . . they go well with a babyccino."

"A what?"

"It's a coffee for kids—basically just frothed milk with a bit of choccy powder."

"Choccy?" She shook her head at me. "You know, half the time when you answer a question, I just get more confused."

I laughed. "Yeah, my bad. Forget I said anything. What did you ask before?"

"When you were standing in the doorway like a marshmallow? I asked if this was the one you wanted to use—you said the middle one, right?"

She pointed at the medium-sized tray of the three arrayed on the counter, and I nodded.

"That's the one!"

I got the fish from the sink and set it in the tray, then cast my gaze over the spices arrayed in front of us.

"Are any of these speaking to you?"

"Speaking to me? I thought you'd have an idea."

"I do—I've tried all the ones here, and I'm pretty sure they'll pair well with fish."

Maria hummed and rubbed her chin, stopping when her eyes met a shaker of finely chopped leaves. She sprinkled a liberal amount over the fish, then nodded to herself.

"Perfect."

I knew the herb was similar to sage, and it paired well with fish when I'd used it before.

"What made you choose that one?" I asked.

"The shade of green is pretty."

A laugh escaped my throat. "As good a reason as any, I suppose. It will go well with lemon."

I pointed at another container.

"Add a sprinkle of that, I reckon."

"What is it?" she asked, adding it to the tray.

"No idea—it has a lovely, peppery kick to it, though."

I looked at the fish and cocked my head to the side. "One more pinch."

She obliged, adding the same amount as before.

"Perfect. That should do it, I reckon. A bit of salt and lemon after it cooks, and the fish should be delicious."

"What now?"

I grabbed the larger tray and set it atop the one with the fish inside, making the best moisture seal I could.

"Now, we cook."

"Uh, Fischer?"

"Yeah?" I replied as I bent and put the fish atop the bed of coals.

"What are those sticks for?"

She was looking at the torches I'd spent most of the day making while she was helping her mother cook.

"They are called tiki torches where I'm from. They're for mood lighting."

"Mood lighting? Do you put candles on them?"

"Oh, no. They *are* the candles."

She looked at me, the tiki torches, then back at me.

"Are you all right if we skip the back and forth of me being confused and you just skip straight to explaining how you're gonna use sticks as torches?"

"But your confusion is half the fun."

She rolled her eyes at me.

"Just pretend we already had the conversation, I was sufficiently confused, and you got delight from it like the sadist you are."

"Woah, sadist?" I asked, laughing. "You must have been *really* confused in this hypothetical."

"I was—it was rather embarrassing."

"All right, I guess we can skip straight to the explanation. See the wick extending from the top? That leads to a container of oil I got from Fergus. The oil burns rather than the wick, and as the fuel is burned away, more oil soaks up toward the flame."

"That works?"

"Well, in theory. I only made them today, so they could also just explode. I'd keep my distance."

I winked at her, and she shook her head with a laugh. What I didn't mention was that each torch had transformed when I crafted them, so I doubted they wouldn't work.

I started setting up the table and wooden chairs I'd borrowed from Brad and Greg. The table was only large enough to hold the dishes of food everyone was bringing, so I set out the chairs in a ring around the fire.

Maria stood with her arms crossed, and she chewed her lip in thought.

"What are you thinking?" I asked, placing the last chair.

"I was trying to work out if you were kidding about the torches exploding or not."

The last rays of sunlight were fading over the western mountains when my guests arrived. Sharon and Roger—the former carrying a tray of fresh-baked rolls, the latter wielding a giant pot of stew and an impressive scowl—stepped through the gate first.

Close behind them were Barry, Helen, and Paul. Barry carried a crate of glass bottles, Helen had a tray covered in a tea towel, and their son, Paul, toddled behind carrying a board absolutely covered in bowls, plates, cups, and cutlery.

"Hello, Fischer!" Paul yelled, a wide grin plastered over his face.

"G'day, everyone! You're just in time—the fish will be ready soon."

As expected, Roger's eyebrow twitched, but he said nothing—an impressive amount of restraint on his part, in my opinion.

I got to my feet. "Now that we're all here, I'll set the mood!"

I grabbed a long branch jutting from the fire and raised its still-burning tip. I walked around to the tiki torches staked in the ground and lit them one by one.

"Wow, those are beautiful, Fischer," Sharon said, a few of the flames reflecting in her eyes.

Maria snorted. "Don't praise him yet—he said they might explode."

"Hey! That was between me and you! Besides, I was only joking." I shot Maria a sly wink.

"Fischer . . ." Sharon said. "Did you just wink after saying you were joking?"

"Uhhh, no?"

I turned to Maria and winked again, much less covertly this time.

"Paul," Barry said, "don't go near those torches."

I barked a laugh. "I really was just joking—they won't explode."

I fought down the urge to wink at Maria again, knowing the third time would probably convince them I'd surrounded us with fireballs just waiting to happen.

Everyone set their goods on the table I'd set up, and when Sharon put her pot down, she opened the lid.

"Should we start off with some stew while the fish finishes? I made fresh rolls for dipping."

A smell I'd not experienced since coming to Kallis hit me as steam rose from the lamb stew. Hints of unknown spices joined the scent of lamb, and my mouth immediately started salivating.

"Absolutely," Roger replied, sounding more excited than I'd ever imagined he could.

This stew must be serious business . . .

Paul passed Sharon the bowls and she filled each of them with a ladle of the steaming meal. When she handed me mine, I stared down at it, and my mouth may as well have been a faucet for how much it watered. I waited until everyone had their serving; Roger held no such reservations, and for his crimes, Sharon swatted him with a tea towel.

"What?" he complained through a mouthful of stew. "It's not my fault your cooking is so delicious!"

She rolled her eyes at her husband, but I didn't miss the smile curling her lip.

I stared down at the bowl in my hands; vapor billowed from it, and I breathed in the mingling aromas. The seasoning was even stronger now, and the assorted herbs and spices assaulted me. Large chunks of lamb and vegetables riddled the stew, and as I put a spoon through a hunk of lamb, it split right in two. I raised a spoon to my mouth.

The flavor overwhelmed me, and I let out an involuntary *mmm*. The seasoning tasted even better than it smelled. The chunk of lamb fell apart in my mouth, the meat's fatty juices melding with the rest of the stew.

"Sharon . . ." I said, shattering the silence. "This is unreal."

Roger made an approving noise but didn't stop shoveling food long enough to voice his agreement.

"I don't care how rude it is to ask," Helen said. "Can I have that recipe? I'll give you anything for it—even Barry."

Sharon laughed, the sound reminding me of Maria's.

"I'd be glad to swap it for the recipe of that sweet pie you make. Barry shared some with us a few years ago, and no matter how many times I try to replicate it, I can't get it right."

"It's a deal." Helen laid a hand on Barry's shoulder. "It looks like you can stay, dear."

"If you like that pie," Barry said. "You'll love what Helen made for dessert."

Helen batted her husband's arm. "No ruining the surprise!"

I had another half bowl of the lamb stew before I stood to check on the fish. As I lifted the lid, steam roiled out in a thick cloud, dissipating when the fire's heat hit it.

"Fischer . . ." Helen said. "That smells *amazing*."

Both her and Barry's eyes were fixed on the exposed fish. I could practically see them drooling, and it made my heart sing.

"You'll have to let Maria know—she was the chef today, not me."

"Not at all," Maria said, raising both hands to ward off any praise. "I just followed instructions."

"Not true! You followed your instinct when choosing the seasoning, right?"

She opened her mouth to protest, then closed it, realizing she *had* done that.

"Well, the seasoning could be disgusting for all we know—if it tastes bad . . . sorry."

"As the great Guy Fieri says, 'If you're cooking and not making mistakes, you're not playing outside your safety zone.'"

Maria, seeing my quote as the bait it was, narrowed her eyes.

Barry, however, took it hook, line, and sinker.

"Who is Guy Fieri?"

I grinned. "The mayor of flavortown. I actually met him once—he's a good bloke. That's not important right now, though. Focus, Barry."

I pointed down at the fish. "Who wants to try some?"

Everyone but Roger spoke up, and as I started dishing out the fish, the old farmer helped himself to a third bowl of stew.

The flesh easily parted as I separated it with tongs, and I had to grab each portion carefully so it didn't fall apart.

"Can you all eat butter?" I asked.

There were no protests, so I went to add a scrape of butter to each plate, then remembered I shouldn't be contributing to the meal.

"Would you mind, Maria? I don't want to steal your thunder."

She nodded happily, bouncing up to add the ingredient. As the butter hit the flaky meat, it immediately melted and spread itself over the steaming fish.

With all the plates prepared, I reached into my pocket and withdrew the final ingredient—a lemon.

I was greeted with a chorus of *ooooo's* and *aaaaah's*—okay, maybe not a chorus, but both Paul and Barry were audibly impressed.

"Does everyone want lemon?" I asked.

No one objected, so I sliced up the entire fruit and put one wedge on each plate.

"If you don't mind, would you all set aside the seeds for me?"

Roger raised an eyebrow. "You can't grow lemon from seeds, Fischer," he said around a mouthful of stew.

"Yeah, I know, but I wanna try, uh . . . cooking . . . with them?"

Maria snorted at my attempted subterfuge.

"Do we just squeeze the slice above the fish?" Barry asked. "How much do we add?"

"Try a bit at first. You can always add more."

I squeezed the entire wedge over my fish. The lemon was small, so it was the perfect amount. Maria, having already tried lemon with me, also squeezed every drop from her slice.

Even with a stomach half-filled by lamb stew, my mouth was salivating as the scent of fish, sage, butter, and lemon flowed through my nostrils and down into my lungs, suffusing my entire being.

"Add your own salt to taste," I said, pointing at the small container I'd set out. "Same as the lemon—less might be more."

As everyone stood to add salt, I took in the surrounding faces. It was a new experience for most of them, and everyone's features projected a mix of joy, anticipation, curiosity, and childlike wonder. Even Roger exhibited the same expression, but it had nothing to do with the fish—he was just *really* into lamb stew.

"All right," I said. "Dig in, guys."

As everyone took a bite, I watched their faces intently. I was worried about one opinion in particular, and I kept my gaze firmly pinned on Paul as he took his first tentative bite. His little eyebrows furrowed at first, but as the flavors hit his tongue, they flew up. His eyes darted to his parents.

"You like it?" Helen asked, covering her mouth.

"*Mhmm!*" he replied, nodding his head comically fast as he continued chewing.

I grinned at him, knowing I'd pleased the harshest critic—fish could be an acquired taste, and it was pretty hit or miss with children.

Unable to wait any longer, I picked up a forkful and scooped it into my mouth. The first things that hit my senses were butter and salt. Then, I chewed the meat. It was a mature fish of a bigger species than most, so the fibers were larger. Despite this, the tender flesh melted in my mouth.

As the fish's structure disappeared, the flavors hit me. First came the subtle hints of sage and pepper, but then the butter's fatty richness spread over my mouth, threatening to overwhelm everything else—until the lemon joined the fray.

The citrus cut through the butter's heaviness, and all the tastes became one, dancing across my taste buds as I chewed. I swallowed, and the flavors lingered, continuing their enticing dance.

Realizing I had my eyes closed and hadn't heard a peep from anyone else, I held my breath as I looked around the circle. Then, a chorus really did erupt.

Most simply made noises of delight, but there were a few curses to gods I didn't know sprinkled in. I cast a grin over them all, stopping only when my eyes landed on Maria. Her eyes were closed, her shoulders low, and a serene smile covered her face as she chewed.

"Looks like your choice of seasoning was a winner, Maria—we've well and truly arrived at flavortown."

She peered at me, her eyes half-lidded in delight.

"I don't even know what to say, Fischer. I could eat this forever . . ."

Roger, having polished off what must have been his fourth bowl of stew, darted a suspicious gaze around the campfire.

"It can't be *that* good."

"Try some," Sharon said.

"No, I don't think I—"

Faster than he could respond, she dipped her fork in the juices and put it in his mouth.

His eyebrows narrowed, then just as Paul's had, they shot up.

"I . . . I suppose I could try one bite."

Sharon passed him the fork, and he selected a tiny chunk from her plate. He placed it in his mouth, and I watched his gruff features melt away.

A confused "*mmm*" escaped him, and Maria and I beamed at each other before eating more of our respective plates. Each bite was as pleasant as the last, and before I knew it, there was nothing left.

"Anyone for seconds?"

They all wanted more, and only Roger said nothing.

"Did you want a plate, mate?"

He tensed and relaxed his jaw for a long moment.

"He can have some of mine," Sharon said, saving him from his moral conundrum.

I produced another lemon, sliced it into wedges, and we all enjoyed a second plate. We'd eaten one side of the fish, and as I turned it over, I made a shocked noise.

"Oh, no!" I shook my head and sighed. "I must have made the fire too hot—the bottom is completely burned. Sorry, everyone."

"No need to apologize, Fischer!" Barry said. "I don't know about everyone else, but if I have another bite, I won't have any room for dessert."

I gave him my best wincing smile.

"I'll go get rid of it before the pan is ruined—back in a moment."

As I carried the tray into the dark of night, Maria shot me a knowing smile, and I gave her a wink.

I walked toward my house, and when I rounded the headland's corner, I caught sight of my friends. I dashed over to them and set the tray down.

"Here you go, guys!"

Sergeant Snips, Corporal Claws, Pistachio, and Rocky crept forward, their eyes gleaming as the rising steam called to them.

I pulled a length of sugarcane Barry had slipped me and held it out to Cinnamon; she bounded over and immediately bit into it, plucking it from my open palm.

"All right, gang—enjoy, okay?"

I turned and strode back to the fire, and as I arrived, Helen was slicing into and dishing out a pie. Barry was pouring drinks, combining his rum with a pitcher that held sugarcane juice.

"Did you want some, Fischer?"

"I'll have what everyone else is having, Barry."

Understanding my meaning, he gave me a nod and poured another drink from the same jug.

He brought it over to me with a small plate of dessert that looked like apple pie, but with a hint of purple added.

"The color is what throws me off when I try to replicate this, Helen," Sharon said. "I've tried every fruit possible, but just can't work out what gives it that odd flavor."

Curious, I took a bite.

The pastry was chewy and buttery, and if not for the filling, would have been too much. That filling, though . . . it was sweet and syrupy, filled with chunks of apple, lots of sugar, and something familiar.

I raised my eyebrows and looked at Helen. "It's wild berries, isn't it?"

Helen's eyebrows climbed as she gave me an appraising gaze.

"I guess the secret's out of the bag. The mystery ingredient is wild berries that grow in the forest to the west."

Maria inhaled sharply. "I *knew* I recognized the flavor of those berries!"

Sharon, whose face was spread in a glorious smile after learning of the ingredient that had evaded her for so long, darted a look at her daughter.

"You know the berries, Maria?"

"Yeah! Fischer showed them to me while we were away on our camping trip."

As they spoke about the recipe, I took a sip of the rum. I didn't have high expectations, but they were immediately shattered; it was delicious.

"Damn, Barry—this is seriously good."

He beamed and took a sip, letting out a content sigh afterward.

"I thought so too, but I'm glad you agree."

"It reminds me of something where I'm from, though I suppose that makes sense given it's also a sugarcane rum."

Barry gave me a shocked expression. "You've already tried sugarcane rum?"

"Yeah, it's really popular where I'm from, but is sort of looked down on by people from anywhere else. Personally, though . . ." I took another sip and it made me feel at home. "I love the stuff."

"Well, there's plenty more where that came from." He smirked at me. "I can make your next cup stronger if you like."

With the pie finished, the feast was complete and the drinking began.

CHAPTER NINETY-THREE

THE SUMMONING

I leaned against Barry for support as I tried to stand.

"Barry."

"Aye?"

The world spun, and I grinned at him.

"You're the best, mate."

"No, Fischer," he slurred. "*You're* the best."

"Yes, yes—you're both the best," Maria said, helping us stand upright.

"No," Roger said.

I darted my head toward him, raised an eyebrow, and wobbled a little from the sudden shift in perspective.

"Sharon—" Roger hiccuped. "Sharon's the best."

Sharon, who was also drunk but had stopped before we'd cracked into Barry's private reserve, patted his hand.

"Thank you, dear. I also think you're the best."

Roger's head wobbled as he tried to focus on her.

"I love you so much, you know that?"

She laughed and got to her feet.

"I think it's time we get you home, dear—it's well past midnight."

Roger stood abruptly and immediately fell back into his chair.

"Lots of work to do tomorrow," he mumbled, sounding as if his mouth were full of molasses.

Sharon held out a hand, and he grasped it.

She tried to help him to his feet, but she tottered over and fell atop him. She laughed at herself as she got back to her feet and helped Roger up. He put an arm over her shoulder, and she held him around the waist.

"Fischer. Barry." Roger nodded. "Goodbye."

I threw my hand up, waving at them.

"Thanks again for the food, guys. You were lovely."

I narrowed my eyes at myself—*that wasn't right . . .*

"I mean, the stew was lovely. The best—absolute *tastiest* stew I've ever had. Thank you."

"You're most welcome," Sharon said, smiling at me. "See you all tomorrow."

"Gods above, your stew, Sharon," Roger slurred as they walked away. "If we weren't already married, I'd . . ."

His voice trailed off as they closed the gate behind them, and I heard Sharon giggle from the dark of night.

I spun back toward Maria and Barry—too fast, evidently, as I almost fell over. Maria grasped my shoulder, holding me upright, and I beamed my most charming smile at her.

"You know what, Maria? *You're* the best."

Maria saw Fischer wobble and grabbed him by the shoulder.

"You know what, Maria? *You're* the best."

He smiled at her, his face flushed and one eye closed slightly more than the other. She laughed at just how drunk he was. She wasn't sure if they were all lightweights, or if Barry's second batch of rum was that strong, but once the two men remaining had cracked open that bottle, Barry only had one drink, and Fischer had three, yet here they were, absolutely "plastered" as Fischer kept saying.

Barry, finally registering what Fischer had said, nodded his agreement.

"It's true, Maria. Your whole family—I'm so glad we're neighbors, you know that? I love you all so much."

She petted him on the shoulder. "Love you too, Barry."

"Thank you." He wobbled and turned to look around, confusion clear on his face. "Where's Helen?"

Fischer barked a laugh. "She took Paul to bed ages ago, mate—you're drunk."

"Ohhh, that's right."

Fischer slung an arm around his shoulder. "Barry . . ."

He leaned in, conspiratorial.

"I felt something odd tonight . . ." Fischer tilted sideways, but Barry pulled him back. "Thanks mate, but stop changing the subject. Have you been giving Helen sugarcane juice?"

Barry, with all the agility of an inebriated donkey, slowly spun his head toward Fischer.

"Maybe," he replied, giggling.

"Oh, you *scoundrel!*"

They both laughed, heads going back as they roared their delight.

Maria, not having the first clue what they were talking about, shook her head with a smile.

Barry rubbed his cheeks, his giggles still coming in small bursts.

"Ah, I needed that. I should get going, though. Roger was right—there's a lot of work to do tomorrow."

"Are you all right to get home by yourself?" she asked.

"Me? I'm fine," he slurred, sounding anything but. "I'll see you two tomorrow."

Barry ambled off, swaying chaotically with each step.

"See ya, mate!" Fischer called, entirely too loud, and Barry held a hand above his head, waving goodbye.

"All right, Fischer," Maria said. "Let's get you to bed."

He nodded, hiccuped, then paused.

"We have to do something first."

As I wandered through the dark, I spied my quarry.

"There you are, Snips, you little scamp! Come here and let me love you."

I bent down and hugged her, taking solace in her sturdy carapace.

"Uh, Fischer . . ." Maria said from beside me. "That's a rock."

I squinted as I pulled my head back.

"So it is. Rock crab—rock. What's the difference, really?"

"Well, in this case, the rock won't hug you back."

"I don't know . . . that rock was a pretty good hugger."

I heard a joyous hiss and turned just in time to see Snips walking from beneath my porch.

"Come here, you," I said, holding my arms wide.

I didn't see her move, only felt her body collide with mine, then my back hit the sand. I accepted my sandy fate and held Snips close as I looked up at the starry sky.

"How was the meal, Snips?"

She bubbled her delight and pressed her carapace into me.

Maria's head appeared high above me, obstructing the night sky as she peered down. Her hair hung toward me, and I noticed a strand slip from behind her ear.

"Comfy down there?"

Despite what I knew to be a cool night, I was as warm as freshly baked bread, and the sand felt soft as a cloud.

"I've never felt more comfortable ground."

She let out a soft chuckle, covering her mouth. The moonlight lit her hair from behind, and my heart rose into my throat at her attractive face and easy laughter.

"And," I added. "I've never seen a more beautiful sight."

She rolled her eyes. "You're drunk."

"True," I conceded. "But you're still beautiful."

"Hmmm." She rubbed her chin in feigned thought. "Can I trust him, Snips?"

Snips, missing the intended humor in Maria's question, nodded vigorously and blew a stream of affirmative bubbles.

"There you have it!" I declared. "I'm drunk *and* trustworthy."

"Mostly drunk, though. Come on, let's get you to bed."

I accepted her offered hand, and she pulled me from the sand.

"Is Cinnamon safe?" I asked Snips.

Snips nodded and pointed to the door.

"She's asleep inside?"

She nodded again.

"Thank you, Snips. I don't know what I'd do without you."

Sergeant Snips, who had clung to me as Maria helped me up, rubbed the side of her face against my arm, then leaped to the floor and waved a claw.

"You're off to sleep in the pond?"

Positive bubbles.

"Sleep well, all right? I love you."

She returned my feelings with one last stream of bubbles, waved goodbye to Maria, and disappeared into the dark of night.

"Snips is *the best,*" I said as Maria helped me toward the door.

"She is, isn't she?" Maria agreed, laughing. "Wait there a second."

"Huh?" I asked, not understanding, but then Maria started brushing my back, legs, and head free of sand.

"A bed full of sand wouldn't have been nice to wake up to." She patted me on the back. "All done."

I ambled inside, squinting into the dark.

As Fischer stepped inside, he leaned to the side almost immediately.

"Woah!" Maria said, reaching out and stabilizing him. "Easy there."

Fischer laughed at himself as they walked forward together, and he reached an arm out to grab his doorway, then turned to face her.

"Did you want to stay the night?"

Maria's face went hot, but before she could speak, he continued.

"Er—in one of the other beds, I mean. I'm drunk. You're more than welcome to have a shower and spend the night. Er, have a shower alone, I mean."

Maria felt her face going bright, and Fischer shook his head.

"My words aren't working so good right now. Sorry."

"Thank you, Fischer, but I should get back home. My father will be worried if he wakes and I'm not there—I just wanted to make sure you made it to bed and didn't fall asleep in the ocean."

Fischer beamed. "What would I do without you?"

"You'd wake up with crabs."

"That sounds pinchy," he said as Maria helped him walk to the bed.

As she tried to lower him down to the sheets, Maria let out a grunt.

"What on Kallis are you made of Fischer? You're lean but heavy as stone."

"I grew big and strong from eating so much fish."

He flexed an arm; Maria snorted and patted his chest.

"If you say so."

Fischer let out a sigh as he stretched his arms out, rubbing them over his cool sheets.

"Ahhh, my sweet, sweet bed. I missed you—"

His face grew confused. "What is that?"

He pulled his hand from behind a pillow; it clutched a floppy bunny with sleepy eyes.

"Oh! Sorry, Cinnamon."

He put her back behind the pillows, and the tired rabbit let out a soft squeak in thanks.

"You're welcome . . ." Fischer replied, his voice fading.

Maria bent and pulled up his blankets, and when she brought them up to his face, she paused.

Fischer's eyes were closed, a broad smile stretched over his face.

She stared at him for a long moment, her heart fluttering, then she bent and kissed him on the forehead.

"Goodnight, Fischer," she said, running fingers through his hair.

Fischer didn't respond; he'd already fallen asleep.

Maria walked from the room, gave the sleeping heretic one last glance, then closed the door behind her.

When Maria got home, her mother was waiting for her.

Sharon's face was grim, and Maria's thoughts of Fischer were immediately whisked away.

"Mom? What's wrong?"

Sharon gave her a sad smile. "I need to tell you something, Maria. I probably shouldn't, but as your mother . . . what choice do I have?"

"Mom . . . you're scaring me. What is it?"

Her mother put her head in her hands, clearly conflicted. She stayed in the position for a long moment, and when she looked back up, her jaw was set, her eyes unyielding.

"It's about Fischer. There's something you should know before things between you develop any further . . ."

Some hours later, atop a two-story building in Tropica, Gary, the lone disciple of the Cult of the Leviathan's Tropica branch, let out a tired sigh.

"The sun will be up soon . . ."

Sebastian said nothing, merely growled, so Gary peered at him. Sweat poured from Sebastian's forehead, and his entire body was tense, trembling with the effort.

"Maybe it will work tomorrow." Gary tried, but other than a deepening scowl, there was no response from Sebastian.

Gary sighed again and looked up at the stars above.

"Gary . . ." Sebastian ground out, his voice shaky.

"Yes, master?"

"Can you not feel that, Gary?"

"Erm, feel what, master?"

Sebastian's breaths were heavy, and a handful rang out into the night before he responded.

"We're almost there—something is coming. But . . ."

His speech paused, his lungs working like bellows before continuing.

"I need you to help. *Focus,* Gary. Close your eyes and do your damned *job!*"

The last word came out as a screech, and Gary winced.

I hope that didn't wake anyone up, he thought. *Mrs. Jenkins next door has it hard enough with a young child. An unhinged man screaming in the middle of the—*

"Gary!" Sebastian yelled again. "Focus!"

Jolted from his thoughts, Gary let out a sigh.

Maybe if I try for a bit, he'll let me go to bed . . .

He closed his eyes and tried to send his awareness down into the ground, just as Sebastian had instructed repeatedly. He imagined moving down through the roof, past the ground floor, and deep into the sandy soil that was Tropica's foundation. To Gary's immeasurable surprise, something *was* there.

His eyebrows furrowed as he sensed a power below, something that seemed to reach for him. It was far, *far* away, but his soul subconsciously leaped at the challenge, and before he knew it, he was beckoning it forward.

Sweat sprouted from his forehead, yet he barely felt it. The bulk of his awareness was grasping below, clutching for that which wanted to be freed.

Something else was there beside him, and after a moment of bewilderment, he realized it was Sebastian, similarly calling the power forward.

"Good, Gary," his master ground out through gritted teeth.

At Sebastian's praise, Gary realized his error. He snapped back to his body, his eyes going wide; he'd been *helping!* There really was something coming, something which Sebastian intended to sic on Fischer, and he had been complicit.

Gary focused on the surrounding roof, trying to ignore the power below.

No, not a power, he realized. *A creature . . .*

Now that he was no longer helping, he'd hoped the thing's attention would spiral back down, but his hopes were dashed when he felt it still coming, growing stronger with each passing second.

He focused on Sebastian. The leader's body was drenched in sweat, shaking violently from the effort he exerted.

Gary shot to his feet.

If I attack him, distract him, maybe—

A pulse of energy slammed into him, and he fell to his knees, his vision going fuzzy. As his vision cleared, he watched a grin spread over Sebastian's face. It started small, vaguely content, but grew into something vicious within the space of a breath.

The air between them condensed, and reality itself shattered. A crack tore into existence, oozing black smoke darker than night. A paw the size of Gary's head stepped through, and hopelessness took him as he realized the summoning was a success.

CHAPTER NINETY-FOUR

THE DEFENSE FORCE

I woke from a dreamless sleep and sat upright as something punched me in the stomach. My eyes darted around the room, but I was alone. I brought a hand to my abdomen and felt it for pain—there was none; all that remained was a vague sense of wrongness.

Was I dreaming, but can't remember it?

The needs of my body yelled out, and I shook my head, laughing.

"Guess I just needed to pee."

Something made a questioning squeak from beside me, and I glanced over, seeing Cinnamon's ears alert, her gaze fixed on me in alarm.

"Sorry, little one. Go back to sleep, all right?"

She relaxed as I reached a hand out and stroked her fur. I lifted the blanket, and she hopped under it, immediately curling into a ball.

"Good girl," I said in my most reassuring tone.

I shot from bed and immediately fell over.

"Damn, Barry—what was in that rum?" I asked aloud, my head spinning.

I barely remembered Maria helping me back to bed, but from what I could recall, I was even drunker now.

Using the doorway for support, I lurched from my bedroom and made for my front door.

As I opened it, a cool breeze hit me and I swayed there for a moment, enjoying the sensation.

"What a beautiful night . . ."

A pulse of power slammed into Sergeant Snips, and her eye shot open. Rocky made a hiss from beside her; he'd felt it too.

She dashed from the pond, sitting on the sands as her awareness flooded out, trying to grasp what was happening. Rocky and Pistachio joined her a moment later, and they all looked to the north.

The moment stretched on, and just as her worry was receding, something appeared. Its power was distant, muted, yet undeniably strong. They shared a look, then took off toward it.

* * *

Corporal Claws's head darted around, scanning the surrounding buildings. She'd fallen asleep while watching the two idiots on the roof but woke when something slammed into her. It seemed to come from right beside her, and she peeked her head over the roof, checking for any danger.

She saw the two idiots, one on his knees, the other grinning maniacally. When the air shattered and a leg stepped through the crack, her heart skipped a beat. She'd intended to attack whatever it was, but as she felt its strength, her body froze. She needed backup.

The next second, she launched herself from the building, her legs wreathed in lightning as she shot away.

Barry's eyes flew open as something almost physical punched him in the gut. He sprang up, glancing around the room. Helen let out a gasp beside him as she sat up, her eyes wide.

"What . . . what was that?"

"I'll go see."

His head felt woolen, but most of the rum's effect was gone, no doubt cleared away by his new body. He took a moment to thank himself for not making his drink as strong as Fischer's, and with each step toward his bedroom door, his mind cleared a little more.

As he swung the door open, something vast and unknown appeared to the northeast, coalescing from nowhere, and he took an involuntary breath.

Helen whimpered behind him; she'd felt it too.

"Stay here," he said, then ran toward it.

Gary scrambled back from the creature, trying to get as far from it as possible. Death seemed to ooze from its shadowy form, coalescing as waves of smoke roiled out and surrounded its feet.

Its shoulder was tall as a man and lean muscle covered its entire form. A canine's head sat atop its thick neck, and incisors longer than a dagger extended below desiccated lips. Its tail wasn't a tail—it was a snake. The snake's head moved on its own, its tongue flicking out to taste the air.

Every inch of the creature's body, bar the claws, teeth, and serpentine tail, were blacker than the abyss, seeming to draw any light and good from the world.

The hound let out a low growl as it turned to bare its teeth at Gary, its eyes holding intelligence and an accusation.

It knows, he realized, his dread climbing. *It knows I stopped helping it . . .*

"Blessed hound of Hades!" Sebastian yelled, prostrating himself before the beast. "Thank you for heeding our call!"

Though he screamed at the top of his lungs, the sound seemed muted, as if sucked into the creature's blooming aura of death.

The hound turned to look at Sebastian, and feeling its gaze, the cult leader lifted his head, showing a snarl just as vicious as the monster's.

"I offer a life to you, as the contract demands!"

Sebastian reached into his shirt, withdrew a cardboard cup, and held it out before him.

"The man that drank from this—I offer his life to you!"

Gigantic paws strode forward, not a sound coming from their contact. It bent and sniffed the cup, its grotesque nose twitching. It snarled again, but this time, it held something other than anger—the beast showed joy, exhilaration.

Muscles bulged as the hound crouched. It gathered strength, and faster than Gary's eyes could register, disappeared.

All that remained from the beast was a swirl of inky blackness that slowly fell and pooled on the rooftop. The stones hissed and cracked at the swirling cloud's touch, becoming pitted and worn.

"What . . . what have we done?" Gary heard himself say. It sounded flat to his own ears, empty of emotion.

"What have we done?" Sebastian repeated, his voice riddled with manic glee. "We have won, Gary! Let this be a lesson to anyone standing between us and the great Leviathan! We will stop at nothing."

Gary didn't feel like he'd won; he felt hollow.

Sergeant Snips led the charge across the sand. She saw a spark of blue stream across the sky and knew it to be Corporal Claws.

The otter arced toward Barry's home, and Snips took a moment to approve her judgment; they might need everyone here, considering the power she felt coming from the invader.

Snips held her speed back, making sure Rocky and Pistachio could keep up, and they moved as one toward Tropica.

Something ahead of her caught her attention, so she held a claw up, halting the procession.

Wisps of black smoke rose from the sand, and something humongous stepped through space before them.

The humongous dog had a lithe form, vicious teeth set behind cracked lips, and a snake for a tail; it was an abomination.

They stared at each other for a long moment, and when the beast snarled at them, Fischer's disciples, the defense force, attacked.

Corporal Claws led Barry back toward Tropica through fields of cane, hissing and chirping what she'd seen. Barry, having also felt the creature's arrival, followed without complaint. She felt the beast's power swelling, and she increased her speed as electricity sparked out from her body.

The creature's position shifted, and she skidded to a stop. It appeared to her right, somewhere on the sands between Tropica and her master's home. It had teleported far enough that it would arrive at Fischer if it did so again.

Attack, she chirped at Barry, hoping he would understand.

Then, before Barry had a chance to respond, she rocketed from the sand, lightning empowering her flight as she shot directly through the fields of cane, leaving naught but destruction in her wake.

I leaned one hand on the headland's rock as I ambled my way toward the ocean. My head spun, and I slowly made my way toward the water. I breathed deep of the ocean air, the moisture and salt-laden oxygen grounding me and bringing a sense of great calm. Small waves lapped the shore, and I smiled at the sound.

Man, I thought. *I will never get over living in this little slice of paradise.*

The light of a half-moon lit my way, and I gazed up at the blanket of stars.

Looking up was a mistake; I immediately missed a step and stumbled.

"Oof," I said with a laugh. "That rum got me good."

I focused on my steps as I hobbled over to the ocean and started relieving myself. I took another deep breath, making a satisfied sigh as I exhaled it.

"What a beautiful night . . ."

Water flooded from Snips as she activated her ability. She launched to the side, placed her right claw under the hunched and prepared-for-flight Rocky, then fired him at the hound. She dashed just behind him, her water-powered stride easily matching the airborne crustacean.

As Rocky reached the dog, he slammed both claws closed, and dual explosions ripped out, slamming into the creature's flank and causing Rocky to fly back from the blasts. The hound rocked to the side, just in time for Snips to release the energy stored in her left claw.

The blue-tinted arc shot forward and cut into the dog's side. She'd hoped it would slice right through the thing, but as the energy hit, pitch-black smoke roiled out and caught the attack, taking most of the power away. The arc had left a shallow cut, but shadowy wisps leaked from the wound and formed into flesh and skin once more.

The creature opened its maw and snapped at her. The serpent's head lashed out, glistening fangs descending faster than Snips could react.

Private Pistachio's targeted blast hit the beast. Its head smacked into its own tail, throwing both mouths off course. Its vicious jaws slammed shut on open air, the snake's head hissed, and Snips darted back, making space.

A blur of blue sparked in Snips's peripheral vision, and before Snips could turn her eye, an aggressively chirping Corporal Claws slammed into the creature's side.

Lightning spread from Claws's body into the hound, and it shook as electricity ran through it.

Snips prepared to launch another attack, but more movement caught her eye.

Leroy slid toward them, a green glow surrounding his hands, his feet wrapped in vines that carried him forward. He moved at impressive speed, and when he was twenty meters from the hound, he stopped and slammed his fist into the ground. Thick roots shot up around the still trembling creature, cinching its legs and holding it in place.

"Kill it!" he yelled, holding his fist firmly pressed against the sand.

Snips shot forward, collecting power in both claws. Pistachio cocked back his claw once more, preparing to fire another blast. Rocky scuttled toward it, both clackers held high and ready to blow. Corporal Claws shot off the sand, a toothy grin across her face and lightning sparking from her body. Barry arrived, and he kicked off the sand, flying at the hound with one hand held back, ready to punch out.

Roots held the creature down, lightning flared, claws slammed closed, a punch descended, and Snips witnessed every single attack miss. The hound went transparent, a victorious grin of needle-sharp teeth displayed for all to see. The abilities all met in the center of its form and detonated on one another as the powers clashed in a violent explosion. Barry, Claws, and Rocky, who were closest to the epicenter, all flew back, thrown by the explosive force.

The creature became tangible again and chains of smoke flooded from it, wrapping around them all in the blink of a cultivator-empowered eye. The smoke solidified, and a spear of dread wedged itself deep within Snips—the darker-than-night shackles had encased her, and she couldn't move a limb.

The creature hunched, collected strength in its muscles, and burst forward. Instead of attacking anyone, it simply vanished from existence.

Snips felt it appear elsewhere, and her dread rose higher than a king tide under a full moon.

It was by the headland, near her master's abode, and Snips was held in place.

When I finished relieving myself, I set my hands on my hips, letting out another sigh as I gazed at the hypnotically swaying ocean before me. My swimming vision made the churning water even more intense, and I smiled. It really was a beautiful night.

Something appeared beside me on the rocks, and I squinted, trying to make out what it was.

"Snips? Is that you?"

It crept forward, not making a sound.

Not Snips, I thought. *It's on four legs.*

My vision warped, making the creature appear far bigger than it was.

No way, I thought. *Is that what I think it is?*

I held my breath, unbelieving of what I saw.

With a broad grin, I got low, not wanting to scare it away, then held out a hand for it to sniff.

"*Pss. Pss. Pss.* Here, kitty kitty."

CHAPTER NINETY-FIVE

SUCH POWER

Following the gods' departure, the hellhound had spent what felt like millennia in a sort of stasis.

Over the course of weeks, his awareness had slowly returned as power once more trickled through the world he inhabited.

The hound had hoped the returning power heralded the gods coming home—what else could return the world's equilibrium, if not the gods' return, after all?

Alas, his god hadn't returned—none of them had. Worse, the trickle of power wasn't enough to wake his father, leaving the hellhound alone in the realm of shadow. Given his solitude, it was a welcome occurrence when he was summoned forth to the land of the living.

The relic used was as old as it was restrictive; he was limited in the actions he could take. As much as he would have liked to continue toying with the ascendant children atop the sand, the hound's stay in this realm was limited. Thus, he had left them behind and headed for the one person they contracted him to devour.

He didn't enjoy killing for killing's sake; any contract completed was done in his god's service, and doing so was his goal—his very purpose.

Despite not enjoying death for the sake of it, the hellhound had come to expect a certain level of fear from his targets. Thus, when the mortal didn't show fear, and instead crouched low and beckoned him closer, he became filled with rage.

If the mortal wouldn't show terror, he'd give the man something to fear. He lunged, propelled forward by writhing shadows. He opened his jaw, ready to take a bite from the foolish mortal before him.

"*Pss. Pss. Pss.* Here, kitty kitty," I said, one hand holding my inebriated body steady, the other extended forward, beckoning the black cat toward me. I was filled with notions of having a cute house cat companion, and I'd already begun planning what fish to feed it.

Oooooh, perhaps a feast? I thought. *Cats love fish, right? Maybe I should let it try all the fish!*

Black cats were said to be bad luck, but I wouldn't let a silly superstition stop me from acquiring kitty cuddles.

I hunched my body lower, doing everything I could to entice the cat toward me. With a hand out, hunched over like I was doing one of Joel's crab meditations, and with my drunken booty swaying all over, the tone of the fortuitous encounter shifted. The cat leaped forward, and even in my alcohol-riddled state, I caught the flash of vicious teeth.

"W-woah! Bad kitty!"

Sergeant Snips, first disciple of Fischer, was sending herself into an apoplectic rage. Her entire body was restricted, and all she could do was seethe and wait. If it were only a few limbs stuck, she'd have happily severed them to ensure her master's safety, but the shadowy chains held her entire body.

Her eye roamed around, looking at everyone else on the sands. Claws, Barry, and Rocky were only just starting to stir after being hit by the backlash, while Pistachio and Leroy shared Snips's rage, both males fighting against the chains that bound them.

Snips, left absent choice, tried something drastic. Billowing water poured out of her, and she pushed every drop of her essence out, her core trembling under the effort. She pictured the shifting clouds becoming blades, turning razor sharp like the arcs she shot from her claws.

The blue liquid along the back of her claws responded best, and she focused every ounce of hope on them, watching as the ability flattened, transformed, and started cutting into the chains.

Just . . . a bit . . . more . . .

"W-woah! Bad kitty!"

I fell back, instinctively kicking out with one foot to keep the cat at bay. My foot connected and my vision flashed white as my head struck the rocks. I lay on the rocky shore for a long moment before sitting up as I looked around for the creature, but it was gone.

Wincing, I rubbed my head, not looking forward to the headache I'd probably wake up to.

"Bloody cat," I said aloud. "Hope it comes back . . ."

I staggered home, thinking of how nice and warm my bed was going to feel when I crawled back into it.

With the chain almost completely severed by Snips's ability, a white light exploded from the headland, and she instinctively closed her eye. The massive rock formation blocked the source, but a second later, a *crack* louder than lightning rang out and the earth shook. Then, something flew from the explosion.

An enormous mass, streaming a trail of black shadow and white light that clung to it, shot like a meteor toward Tropica, traveling faster than a mortal eye could see.

Snips, enhanced as she was, saw what it was: the hound. Its twisted limbs and the lifeless expression on its face were clear as day before it disappeared between Tropica's buildings.

Another *crack* rang out through the night, cutting the silence. The chains smothering her vanished, and she shifted her body around, testing her movement. The group arrayed over the sands shared a wide-eyed look.

Sebastian, leader of the Cult of the Leviathan Tropica branch, slayer of Fischer, giggled atop the cult headquarters. His gaze was unwavering, cast out over the vast sands and toward Fischer's domain. His lowly disciple sat on the floor—weeping; he was too feeble to handle Sebastian's might.

Inept as Gary might be, Sebastian didn't want to dispose of him, but if he didn't overcome his weakness soon, Sebastian may not have a choice. Sebastian returned his attention to the sand.

The flashing of elements had ceased, and he hoped that meant the hellhound had left to take Fischer's head.

The first flash of blue had been a surprise, but as a moving ball of lightning had shot around, Sebastian understood: the beast was gathering power, preparing for the battle to come.

"Come witness, disciple," he said, but Gary didn't respond.

Sebastian snarled and grabbed him by the shoulder, hauling him to his feet and slapping him across the face.

"Pay attention, Gary! You need to see the justice we have dispensed!"

Gary, his body moving of its own accord, gripped the side of the roof's low wall and leaned against it for support. His disciple's head drifted down, so Sebastian gripped his chin and lifted it.

Sebastian stared out into the darkness just in time for a brilliant light to explode from the headland. He reeled back, his vision consumed by the blast's afterimage as a distant *crack* cut through the silence.

Despite his temporary blindness, Sebastian roared a laugh.

"He's done, Gary! He's really done! We—"

The building shook and Sebastian fell to his knees as a second louder *crack* tore into existence. This one was accompanied by the sound of stone on stone, falling rubble, shattering glass, and finally, the splash of water. Sebastian's eyes went wide as he recognized what the sounds meant.

"M-my crickets!"

He threw the door open and sprinted downstairs, terrified of what he'd find.

Gary slowly walked down the stairs, not at all looking forward to who he suspected would be down there.

I suppose it's my punishment to see Fischer's body after what I did . . .

Gary felt numb. His tears had robbed his thoughts of their vicious edges, and he walked through the world like a ghost, unfeeling.

Sebastian was at the bottom of the stairs, his body frozen.

"What is it, boss?" Gary asked, his voice sounding flat. He walked to Sebastian, turned, and then he understood.

The southern wall of the first floor had been blown in, completely demolished by what flew through it. The wayward body and the wall's rubble had flown through the room and created a scene of destruction. All but one tank of baby lobsters—er, crickets—had been annihilated.

The body that had demolished the room wasn't Fischer's—it was the hound sent to slaughter him.

Its forelimbs were twisted and broken, its flesh seemed burned, transformed from pitch-black muscle to cracked and pitted charcoal. Black smoke oozed from the creature, and wisps of white clung to the darkness, seeming to wrap around and suffocate them.

A soft noise came from Sebastian as he staggered back, leaning against the wall. He slid to the ground, and the soft noise turned to a low-pitched keening.

"N-No . . ." Sebastian whimpered. "He . . . he couldn't have . . ."

Unlike his master, the sight brought Gary nothing but elation. The lives of countless crickets were nothing before the life of another man, and that Fischer had survived was nothing short of a blessing from above. Even if the man were to come and take their life as punishment, Gary's conscience was clear, his soul clean.

The hound stirred, shakily lifting its head. A tear in space, much weaker than the one before, appeared in the air. Instead of shattering open, its lines crawled into existence, more often than not healing before they could expand as the beast tried to lean into it.

The front door blasted off its hinges, thrown clear across the room and into the back wall.

Gary looked toward it, his mind still numbed from the night's events.

"Boss?" He swallowed, unsure if he was hallucinating. "Is . . . is that an otter?"

A lightning-wreathed otter shot into the room, exposing sharp fangs and an even deadlier disposition. It stopped amidst the carnage and twisted toward the hound, a low growl coming from its throat, then it exploded toward the hound.

Gary could barely see the movement, but just as the otter was about to strike, the wounded hound slipped through its tear in space. Fast as the hound had appeared, it was gone, and the otter slammed into the wall. It clung there, defying gravity as its head shot toward them.

Gary saw murder in those eyes, and he took a deep breath, accepting his fate. He waited a long moment, but the death blow never came, and he opened his eyes again as footfalls entered the building.

The procession that entered the building shattered Gary's numbness, and he blinked, now almost positive he was hallucinating.

There was a large crab wearing an eyepatch and streaming blue water; another crab, looking decidedly upset, its claws raised high; an unknown man, his legs wrapped in thick vines; Barry, his jaw set and eyes hard; and of most significance, a lobster of preposterous scale, its eyes intelligent, its antennae moving to taste the air. On one of the lobster's antennae, just above where the appendage met its head, there was a scar, bulbous and raised.

Gary's jaw dropped open.

* * *

Barry stared at the men with disgust.

"You went too far, Sebastian."

Sebastian, the leader of the local Cult of the Leviathan branch, had eyes for one being in the room—Private Pistachio. He stood and stumbled forward, catching himself on the stairwell's banister.

"A . . . you . . ."

His face was streaked with tears as his mouth moved inaudibly, unable to form words.

He shuffled closer, one hand reaching out for Pistachio. His throat bobbed as he swallowed.

"Are . . . are you ascended, great Leviathan?"

Pistachio nodded a single time, acknowledging the question.

Sebastian's lip quivered, and new tears fell.

"I've waited so long for your arrival . . ."

Sebastian shuffled forward as debris crunched under his feet. Tears streamed down his chin, falling to mix with the dust covering the floor. He took heaving breaths, not bothered by how he must have looked; he cared not for anything but the Leviathan.

His foot caught on a shattered stone, and he stumbled, catching himself on the floor with both hands. Even in falling, his eyes never left the lobster's magnificent form.

"Great Leviathan . . ." His lip shook, and he took a deep breath, holding the sobs at bay. "I've waited so long to—*oof!*"

Something slammed into Sebastian from the back, throwing him to the ground and knocking the air from his lungs.

Barry stared his hatred at the man before him. He wasn't in the least bit swayed or moved by Sebastian's emotional reaction; in his petty resentment, he'd released evil into the world, putting everyone's lives at risk.

When Gary sprinted across the room and shoulder-charged Sebastian out of the way, Barry's eyebrows shot up.

When the disciple kept going, making a beeline for Pistachio, Barry took a step to stop him, but Sergeant Snips held a claw up, halting his movement. She shook her head almost imperceptibly, then blew small, insistent bubbles.

Barry understood their meaning: *watch.*

Unlike Sebastian's blubbering visage, Gary's face held different emotions. He projected relief, awe, and sheer, unadulterated joy toward Private Pistachio.

As Gary approached the lobster and reached an arm down, Barry winced; he half expected Pistachio to bat him aside. Instead, the colossal crustacean dipped his head, acknowledging the cultist.

"Pistachio . . ." Gary said, his voice full of adoration as he got to his knees and put a hand against the lobster's head. "It's really you . . ."

Pistachio's antennae moved chaotically, tapping against Gary's arms and face.

"I thought you were dead," Gary whispered, his eyes closed, a single tear rolling down his cheek. "I'm so glad . . ."

Sebastian wheezed as he climbed back to his feet. Having been forced to catch his breath, he'd had a moment to think about the night's events.

A menagerie of awakened beasts had appeared, along with at least one human cultivator. The situation was dire, but with the appearance of an ascendant lobster, there was a path forward.

He had to rely on the deity—it was larger and of the supreme form, so if he could subordinate it, the creature would no doubt deal with the rest.

Gary, ever the fool, had ruined his inaugural meeting with the great Leviathan; rage coursed through Sebastian's veins, replacing every other emotion.

With measured steps, he strode toward the deity, brushing his robe free of dust and splinters. He had to regain control, so he held his head high, his shoulders back, and his chest out.

He was the leader of this cult, and with the Leviathan's appearance in *his* domain, the cult doctrine was clear: Sebastian was now the leader of the entire Cult of the Leviathan.

No, he thought. *The leader of the* Church *of the Leviathan.*

At his disciple's words that identified the Leviathan as Pistachio—the same lobster he'd spent decades molding—a touch of elation joined Sebastian's fury; it would be even easier to subordinate the deity.

He was keenly aware of the others in the room but ignored them entirely—his eyes were locked on Gary and the Leviathan hidden behind him.

"Dispense with the childish name, disciple," Gary projected with grandiose intonation. "He is no longer Pistachio—this is the great Leviathan of legend, and I won't stand for your insubordination any longer."

All eyes were on him as he stopped in front of the lobster.

Good, he thought. *Let them witness their downfall.*

Rather than prostrate himself before the creature, he held out a hand for the Leviathan to shake.

"It's a pleasure to meet you, great Leviathan. I am Sebastian, the leader of your church."

Time crawled to a stop; the entire room froze as he waited for the creature's action. The Leviathan slowly lifted his claw to meet Sebastian's extended hand. Elation roared through him, but he kept his lips pressed together, his face a mask of indifference.

Everything is going to plan, he thought. *As expected.*

The claw was open, so Sebastian grasped the top pincer.

"I look forward to us working togeth—"

Boom!

* * *

Barry cringed as Pistachio's claw slammed shut. A cannon blast exploded out—Sebastian's body became the cannonball. Faster than a mortal eye could see, his limp form slammed into the back door, shattered it into a million pieces, rocketed over the low wall atop the stone walkway, and soared out over the ocean.

Pistachio had swept Gary aside with his free claw, protecting him from the deadly impact. He scuttled toward the back door, sparing Gary a gentle pat on the head in passing.

Gary's eyes were wide, and a soft, high-pitched sound rang in his ears. He hadn't seen what happened, but with Sebastian's disappearance and the door's obliteration, he knew what must have occurred.

Such power . . .

Pistachio lumbered past him and gave him two taps on the head in what must have been a farewell.

"Pistachio!" he called, and the lobster paused, half-turning to look at him.

"Live a good life, okay?" Gary's voice shook. "I'm sorry for everything . . ."

Pistachio's eyes drifted to the eyepatch-wearing crab, and he blew a small burst of bubbles.

Gary smiled at Pistachio through falling tears as his oldest friend ambled out the back door and over the low wall, then disappeared into the pitch-black sea.

He turned to the crab.

"Please make it quick."

Barry raised an eyebrow.

"Make what quick, Gary?"

The cultist swallowed and put on a brave face, but fear and sadness peeked through, tinging his features.

"I know what needs to happen. I'm sorry, Barry. I tried to stop Sebastian, but I couldn't. Worse, I took part in summoning that . . . *thing.*"

Gary closed his eyes and dipped his head. "I'm ready."

Barry couldn't help but smile at the assumptions. "We already know you tried to stop him, Gary."

Gary's head shot up, his eyebrows furrowing. "You do?"

"We've been listening to your plans for weeks." He pulled something from his back pocket and held it up. "It was you that threw this into the ocean, wasn't it?"

Gary's eyes fixed on the artifact and went wide. Barry nodded.

"Sergeant Snips found it beneath the waves and brought it to me weeks ago. Why did you discard it?"

"I . . . I thought it might make Sebastian give up his crusade against Fischer . . ."

"As we thought. You need not die tonight, Gary. How would you like to join us in—"

"Will I be able to see Pistachio?" Gary interrupted, blinking his tears away. "If I join you, I mean."

"Er—I mean . . . *yes?*"

"All right. I'll join."

"You . . . don't want to know *what* you're joining?"

"Nope. As long as Pistachio is there, I'm in."

"Oh . . . okay."

Sergeant Snips scuttled forward and held a claw out. Gary stared at it in confusion, then reached out hesitantly and shook it.

"It was Sergeant Snips, right? It's, um, nice to meet you?"

Snips bubbled her approval, then Corporal Claws dashed over and gave an insistent chirp, demanding an introduction.

"Gary, that is Corporal Claws—she controls lightning. You've met Sergeant Snips—she controls water." Barry pointed at Rocky. "That's Rocky—he makes things explode."

Rocky lowered his claws, looking almost annoyed at not being about to blast something. He turned and left without so much as a goodbye.

Barry shook his head with a soft laugh as he watched the disgruntled crab go.

What has my life become?

CHAPTER NINETY-SIX

VELVET

Thump. Thump. Thump.

I opened my eyes at my head's audible pounding and let out a soft groan.

"What happened last night?"

My mouth was dry and tasted horrible as I sat up slowly, rubbing my temples. The thumping came again, and I cocked my head as I realized it wasn't my brain trying to escape my skull.

"Fischer!" a feminine voice called. "Are you alive in there?"

Despite my hangover, I smiled at the welcome voice. I stumbled to the door and threw it open.

"Ah, there you are!" Maria beamed a smile and held something out. "Coffee?"

I groaned in delight and accepted the drink.

"I could kiss you, Maria."

She smirked at me.

"You could, but maybe you should brush your teeth first—I caught a whiff of Dad's breath this morning, and I was *not* impressed."

My hungover brain shut down at her saying I could kiss her, but at her comment about Roger, I couldn't help but laugh.

"How's he doing today? I can only remember snippets of last night, but I know for a fact that he was absolutely hammered."

"He's doing much worse than you. That storm last night probably didn't help—I know it woke me up a few times."

"There was a storm?"

She covered her mouth and giggled. "You were probably too drunk to hear the thunder. It was the loudest I'd ever heard—the house even shook a few times."

"Really? I slept all the way through the night, far as I can remember . . ."

"Maybe Dad did too, but he still crawled back to bed after he had breakfast."

"He's taking the morning off? Damn—he must be in rough shape."

"Yeah, no kidding. I can't remember the last time he did so."

I sipped my coffee. The golden liquid washed away the bad taste in my mouth, and I luxuriated in its velvety bitterness.

"Ah. I needed that. Thank you." I gave her a sheepish smile. "Were one of those croissants for me, or . . . ?"

"What makes you think I have pastries?" she asked, her hand still hidden behind her back.

"I could smell that flaky, buttery goodness from a mile away."

She grinned and removed a hand from behind her back, revealing a tray with two pastries.

"I *suppose* you can have one of my croissants."

"What would I do without you?"

I grabbed the smaller one and took a bite. As with the coffee, the flavors were a welcome reprieve, and I let out a content *mmm* as I chewed, my eyes closed in delight.

After another sip of coffee, I smiled at Maria.

"Did you want to go fishing?"

"I did—I wanted to talk to you about something, too . . ."

"Oh? What's that?"

She shook her head. "It can wait. Are you ready to go now?"

"Let me just freshen up and have a quick shower."

"All right—I'll wait out here. The sun feels lovely this morning."

As we walked down to the shore, I couldn't help but agree with Maria—the sun felt *amazing* on my skin. A hot shower had done wonders for my hangover, and I felt vastly improved from when I'd woken. A flitting breeze came from the west, and I closed my eyes, a smile coming to my face unbidden. We traveled in a comfortable silence, both simply happy to be there.

I wasted no time in putting a slice of eel on my line, then passed it to Maria to cast.

"You do it," she said, holding her hands up to stop me.

"You're sure? I'm happy to share."

"Yeah, I'm sure—but I have a condition."

"Oh?"

"I want you to cast it as far as you can."

I raised an eyebrow.

"Like . . . as far as a cultivator can, you mean?"

"Yep. Without breaking the rod, I mean."

I shrugged, held the line back, then flicked the rod forward. It was a fraction of my strength, but the bait and sinker soared high over the waves, arcing through the sky for a good ten seconds before hitting the water's surface with an inaudible splash.

Maria laughed. "Well, that confirms it—you're definitely a cultivator."

"You got me," I said, grinning.

I wound the line taut, and we sat on the sand, both watching the ocean's movement.

"So, what did you want to talk about?" I asked.

She chewed her lip as she stared out at sea.

"Mom told me something . . . well, something unbelievable last night when I got home."

My chest constricted, and my vision went distant. Had she told Maria about the cult after I explicitly asked her not to?

I tensed my jaw and did my best to keep my face calm.

"What did she say?"

"She told me you're from another world."

"Anything else?"

"*Anything else?*" she asked, incredulous. "She told me you're from *another world,* Fischer—what else could there be to say?"

The chains constricting my chest faded away, and I let out a small laugh.

"What did she tell you, exactly?"

"She said you're something called a 'traveler' and that if I wanted to . . ." She trailed off, her face going red, then sighed and continued. "She said if I wanted to get involved with you, I should know what you are."

"A 'traveler,' huh?" I leaned back on one hand and looked up at the sky. "I had no idea they knew . . ."

"It's true, then?"

"Yeah. It's true."

"The continent you said you came from—it was in another world?"

"Yeah, it was. Sorry for misleading you—it's . . . well, it's a lot, you know?"

Her eyebrows knitted, and I guessed she was applying her new knowledge to everything I'd told her while camping.

Her gaze shot up, locking eyes with me. They were sharp, curious, and above all, filled with compassion.

"Would you tell me everything? The whole truth?"

I raised an eyebrow. "Maria, I just confirmed I'm some kind of interplanetary traveler."

She raised one back at me. "Yeah, so?"

"You don't want to . . . I don't know . . . run away or something?"

She snorted. "No, I don't want to run away, you big idiot."

She laid a hand on my shoulder. "I want to know more. Would you tell me?"

Her face was sincere; she really did want to know more. I opened my mouth, and the words started pouring out.

By the time I finished talking, the sun had climbed higher in the sky. I'd been talking for what felt like hours, only stopping to catch the mature sea perch that took the hook halfway through my tale.

The midmorning heat had banished any remnant of the cool night, and I stretched my legs out, enjoying the sun's warmth. Maria put a hand on my back and moved it in comforting circles.

"I'm so sorry, Fischer."

I gave her a wincing smile. "You still don't want to run away?"

"No. I don't."

She leaned her head on my shoulder, and my thoughts stirred. I'd told her everything but the cult Barry was heading and that it was my food causing people to become cultivators. I chewed my cheek, considering what to do. Eventually, I decided to be honest.

"There's more . . ."

I unloaded everything, filling in the details I'd skipped over. Her face went through a series of emotions, but she never spoke, simply listening to my story. When I'd finished, she sat across from me, her legs crossed and chin resting on her hands. She looked up at me, her face serious.

"You're telling me Barry and my mom are cultivators?"

"At least them, yeah. There could be more, but I've asked to not be included—the less I know, the better."

"And they view you as . . . what? A god?"

"A god waiting to happen, I guess?"

Her gaze had strayed elsewhere, but it snapped up to me again.

"I won't lie—I'm a little offended that you thought our time away was part of some conspiracy."

I grimaced. "I'm sorry. Despite their good intentions, my friends were sneaking around behind my back. I was feeling a little betrayed and wasn't thinking straight."

"It's fine. You'll just have to make it up to me . . ."

She stood and stretched, raising both arms high as she let out a soft noise. After the stretch, she rubbed her chin in exaggerated thought and narrowed her eyes as she stared into the far distance.

A loud *hmmm* came from her throat, then she turned to me, her mouth ajar in feigned realization.

"What is it?" I asked.

She smirked. "I just had an idea of how you can make it up to me . . ."

Maria lounged in the sand hugging a rather content Corporal Claws. She ran her small fingers through Claws's belly fur, making the otter coo.

"You are just too cute," she said, giggling at the way Claws grinned up at her.

"Stop—you'll make me blush."

Corporal Claws's head darted toward me, a scowl plastered over her face as she chirped indignantly.

"Yes, yes, I know she was talking about you."

Maria giggled again. "You like being the center of attention, don't you, Claws?"

She chirped her unequivocal agreement, nodding her head as Maria resumed giving her scritches.

I spun back around to check on my pan atop the campfire. The fat was bubbling around the fish's sides, turning the crumbing a delightfully golden hue. I'd removed the fish's fillets, cut them into large chunks, then covered them in a herb, spice, and breadcrumb coating.

The smell of seasoning was already wafting up as the chunks of fish fried—my mouth watered, anticipating the meal.

I flipped one piece of fish with some tongs. The bottom side was perfectly cooked, so I rotated the rest of them. Exposing the undersides to the air made the aromas explode out, and I heard a small nose start sniffing the air incessantly.

I spun with a smile. "You want some too, Claws?"

Her fangs were extended, and she nodded fervently.

I looked back toward the pan as nervous butterflies took flight in my stomach. Rather than let my thoughts wander, I fussed over the fish, using the tongs to bob them down below the bubbling tallow.

Before I knew it, every side of crumbing was golden brown, so I removed a chunk to test. I poked it with my trusty tongs and the flesh was firm; the fish was ready. I removed the fish and put it on a rack sitting atop a breadboard, letting any excess oil fall away.

Staring down at them, the butterflies in my abdomen multiplied, feeling as though they were attempting to escape. I took a deep breath, paused a moment, then spun.

Both ladies sat on the ground, their eyes glued to the food in my hands. With small, measured steps, I went to them, placing the breadboard down on the sands.

Claws, ever impatient, picked one up immediately; the fish was still way too hot, so she juggled it from paw to paw, her eyes wide with regret. The sight made me laugh, and some of the butterflies stopped flapping so vigorously.

Then, I glanced at Maria, and they all took flight once more.

She looked up at me, and I knelt down beside her.

"Are . . . are you sure, Maria?"

"What do you mean?" she replied, a smile on her lips.

"This can't be taken back. If you change your mind, there's no way to—"

She leaned in and planted a soft peck on my lips.

My brain short-circuited and the butterflies dissipated like dust in the wind. I blinked at her as she pulled back, my face flushing.

"Er—thank you . . ."

She giggled and covered her mouth, then leaned forward once more. Grabbing the back of my neck with one hand, she pulled me forward and pressed her lips against mine. They were softer than velvet, warmer and more comforting than the sun's rays. The moment lasted an eternity yet was over too soon.

She pulled away, letting out a shaky breath as she stared into my eyes. Her cheeks were flushed as she smiled at me.

"I'm sure, Fischer. I won't regret it."

She turned to Claws, who'd stopped juggling the fish and stared at us with a slack jaw and wide eyes.

"Do you mind, Claws?" Maria asked, pointing at the cooled food in her paws.

Corporal Claws, my troublesome otter, blinked in response then slowly nodded, holding the golden chunk of fish out.

Maria grabbed it and beamed a grin at me.

Her eyes sparkled as she fixed her attention on the fish, and time slowed for me as she lifted it to her mouth.

She bit down and the fried breadcrumbs made a satisfying *crunch.*

EPILOGUE

In a long-abandoned room high above the capital city of Gormona, several kingdoms' worth of ancient constructs sat dormant.

In times long gone, the acquisition of such treasures had been the driving force behind wars, betrayals, the fall of empires, the desolation of entire continents, and more deaths than a mortal could comprehend without losing their mind.

Despite the wealth they represented, these artifacts sat collecting dust—designated a relic of the past—no longer the wonder they once were. Like so many things, the passage of time had erased the memories of what they had been, and barring a single person with a toe-like face, not one other soul had entered the room in years—even the castle's servants had forgotten of the room's existence, busy as they were tending to the whims of the current royals.

If any beings capable of detecting such things were present, they'd have been surprised at the energy swirling around the room, seeming to cling to and linger on the artifacts. But, of course, such a person was not present—no one was.

Despite this lack of an audience, a construct to the rear of the treasure-turned-junk-pile whirred to life for the first time in millennia. Microscopic cogs, gears, and shafts tried to move, but their teeth were clogged with arcane residue.

It started to power back down, but a secondary construct within stirred, sputtered, then started performing its sole purpose: cleaning. Within minutes, the internals were free of the arcane buildup, and the larger artifact started emitting a soft, continuous buzz as it powered on completely.

As with another construct in the room, a screen blinked to life on the newly reawakened artifact. It silently printed words out, one line at a time.

Running diagnostics . . .
System power at 20% . . .
Launching local relay . . .

The internal components were a blur as they drew in resources, pulling from and redirecting the world's very essence.

One last line printed out on the construct's screen.

Success! Local power boosted to 40%.

Abruptly, three more screens lit up in the abandoned room.

ACKNOWLEDGMENTS

I can't fully express how thankful I am to you for reading this book. Becoming a full-time author has been a dream come true. Without you, I'd still be writing my silly little words, but I wouldn't be doing it for a living. Thank you a thousand times.

Indie publishing lives and dies by the algorithm, so if you have the time and inclination, I'd greatly appreciate if you leave a review or share my work with someone who would enjoy the wholesome chaos. If not, no worries. I still love you.

Last but not least, please give your dog a pat for me.

Thank you.

ABOUT THE AUTHOR

Haylock Jobson is the author of the Heretical Fishing series, originally released on Royal Road. He lives on the beautiful shores of Australia's Gold Coast and spends his days writing in local cafes, drinking what some might refer to as "too much" coffee, and annoying strangers by asking if he can pet their dogs.